Christmas, 1949

To Nora

Because it fits
so well with Vol. I
in the box. Symbolism?

love
Gerald

55 SHORT STORIES
FROM
THE
NEW YORKER

SIMON AND SCHUSTER · NEW YORK

CONTENTS

❖

v

FOREWORD

❖

The stories in this volume, selected from those that have appeared in The New Yorker *during the past ten years, are, the editors believe, representative of the magazine's fiction for that period. Some notable stories are missing. They were set aside (with a sharp sense of fallibility) during the process of trying to achieve balance, in theme and technique, for the collection as a whole. Other absentees belong in classifications such as parody, nonsense, and casual essays that are outside the scope of this book.*

THE ENORMOUS RADIO

❖

John Cheever

J IM AND IRENE WESTCOTT were the kind of people who seem to
strike that satisfactory average of income, endeavor, and respect-
ability that is reached by the statistical reports in college alumni
bulletins. They were the parents of two young children, they had
been married nine years, they lived on the twelfth floor of an apartment house in the East Seventies between Fifth and Madison Ave-
nues, they went to the theatre on an average of 10.3 times a year, and
they hoped someday to live in Westchester. Irene Westcott was a
pleasant, rather plain girl with soft brown hair and a wide, fine
forehead upon which nothing at all had been written, and in the
cold weather she wore a coat of fitch skins dyed to resemble mink.
You could not say that Jim Westcott, at thirty-seven, looked younger
than he was, but you could at least say of him that he seemed to feel
younger. He wore his graying hair cut very short, he dressed in the
kind of clothes his class had worn at Andover, and his manner was
earnest, vehement, and intentionally naïve. The Westcotts differed
from their friends, their classmates, and their neighbors only in an
interest they shared in serious music. They went to a great many
concerts—although they seldom mentioned this to anyone—and they
spent a good deal of time listening to music on the radio.

Their radio was an old instrument, sensitive, unpredictable, and
beyond repair. Neither of them understood the mechanics of radio
—or of any of the other appliances that surrounded them—and when
the instrument faltered, Jim would strike the side of the cabinet
with his hand. This sometimes helped. One Sunday afternoon, in
the middle of a Schubert quartet, the music faded away altogether.
Jim struck the cabinet repeatedly, but there was no response; the
Schubert was lost to them forever. He promised to buy Irene a new
radio, and on Monday when he came home from work he told her
that he had got one. He refused to describe it, and said it would
be a surprise for her when it came.

The radio was delivered at the kitchen door the following after-

1

noon, and with the assistance of her maid and the handyman Irene uncrated it and brought it into the living room. She was struck at once with the physical ugliness of the large gumwood cabinet. Irene was proud of her living room, she had chosen its furnishings and colors as carefully as she chose her clothes, and now it seemed to her that the new radio stood among her intimate possessions like an aggressive intruder. She was confounded by the number of dials and switches on the instrument panel, and she studied them thoroughly before she put the plug into a wall socket and turned the radio on. The dials flooded with a malevolent green light, and in the distance she heard the music of a piano quintet. The quintet was in the distance for only an instant; it bore down upon her with a speed greater than light and filled the apartment with the noise of music amplified so mightily that it knocked a china ornament from a table to the floor. She rushed to the instrument and reduced the volume. The violent forces that were snared in the ugly gumwood cabinet made her uneasy. Her children came home from school then, and she took them to the Park. It was not until later in the afternoon that she was able to return to the radio.

The maid had given the children their suppers and was supervising their baths when Irene turned on the radio, reduced the volume, and sat down to listen to a Mozart quintet that she knew and enjoyed. The music came through clearly. The new instrument had a much purer tone, she thought, than the old one. She decided that tone was most important and that she could conceal the cabinet behind a sofa. But as soon as she had made her peace with the radio, the interference began. A crackling sound like the noise of a burning powder fuse began to accompany the singing of the strings. Beyond the music, there was a rustling that reminded Irene unpleasantly of the sea, and as the quintet progressed, these noises were joined by many others. She tried all the dials and switches but nothing dimmed the interference, and she sat down, disappointed and bewildered, and tried to trace the flight of the melody. The elevator shaft in her building ran beside the living-room wall, and it was the noise of the elevator that gave her a clue to the character of the static. The rattling of the elevator cables and the opening and closing of the elevator doors were reproduced in her loudspeaker, and, realizing that the radio was sensitive to electrical currents of all sorts, she began to discern through the Mozart the ringing of telephone bells, the dialling of phones, and the lamentation of a vacuum cleaner. By listening more carefully, she was able to distinguish doorbells, elevator bells, electric razors, and Waring mixers, whose sounds had been picked up from the apartments that surrounded hers and transmitted through her loudspeaker. The powerful and ugly instrument, with its mistaken sensitivity to discord, was more than she could hope to master, so she turned the thing off and went into the nursery to see her children.

When Jim Westcott came home that night, he went to the radio confidently and worked the controls. He had the same sort of experience Irene had had. A man was speaking on the station Jim had chosen, and his voice swung instantly from the distance into a force so powerful that it shook the apartment. Jim turned the volume control and reduced the voice. Then, a minute or two later, the interference began. The ringing of telephones and doorbells set in, joined by the rasp of the elevator doors and the whir of cooking appliances. The character of the noise had changed since Irene had tried the radio earlier; the last of the electric razors was being unplugged, the vacuum cleaners had all been returned to their closets, and the static reflected that change in pace that overtakes the city after the sun goes down. He fiddled with the knobs but couldn't get rid of the noises, so he turned the radio off and told Irene that in the morning he'd call the people who had sold it to him and give them hell.

The following afternoon, when Irene returned to the apartment from a luncheon date, the maid told her that a man had come and fixed the radio. Irene went into the living room before she took off her hat or her furs and tried the instrument. From the loudspeaker came a recording of the "Missouri Waltz." It reminded her of the thin, scratchy music from an old-fashioned phonograph that she sometimes heard across the lake where she spent her summers. She waited until the waltz had finished, expecting an explanation of the recording, but there was none. The music was followed by silence, and then the plaintive and scratchy record was repeated. She turned the dial and got a satisfactory burst of Caucasian music—the thump of bare feet in the dust and the rattle of coin jewelry—but in the background she could hear the ringing of bells and a confusion of voices. Her children came home from school then, and she turned off the radio and went to the nursery.

When Jim came home that night, he was tired, and he took a bath and changed his clothes. Then he joined Irene in the living room. He had just turned on the radio when the maid announced dinner, so he left it on, and he and Irene went to the table.

Jim was too tired to make even a pretense of sociability, and there was nothing about the dinner to hold Irene's interest, so her attention wandered from the food to the deposits of silver polish on the candlesticks and from there to the music in the other room. She listened for a few moments to a Chopin prelude and then was surprised to hear a man's voice break in. "For Christ's sake, Kathy," he said, "do you always have to play the piano when I get home?" The music stopped abruptly. "It's the only chance I have," a woman said. "I'm at the office all day." "So am I," the man said. He added something obscene about an upright piano, and slammed a door. The passionate and melancholy music began again.

"Did you hear that?" Irene asked.

"What?" Jim was eating his dessert.

"The radio. A man said something while the music was still going on—something dirty."

"It's probably a play."

"I don't think it *is* a play," Irene said.

They left the table and took their coffee into the living room. Irene asked Jim to try another station. He turned the knob. "Have you seen my garters?" a man asked. "Button me up," a woman said. "Have you seen my garters?" the man said again. "Just button me up and I'll find your garters," the woman said. Jim shifted to another station. "I wish you wouldn't leave apple cores in the ashtrays," a man said. "I hate the smell."

"This is strange," Jim said.

"Isn't it?" Irene said.

Jim turned the knob again. " 'On the coast of Coromandel where the early pumpkins blow,' " a woman with a pronounced English accent said, " 'in the middle of the woods lived the Yonghy-Bonghy-Bò. Two old chairs, and half a candle, one old jug without a handle . . .' "

"My God!" Irene cried. "That's the Sweeneys' nurse."

" 'These were all his worldly goods,' " the British voice continued.

"Turn that thing off," Irene said. "Maybe they can hear *us*." Jim switched the radio off. "That was Miss Armstrong, the Sweeneys' nurse," Irene said. "She must be reading to the little girl. They live in 17-B. I've talked with Miss Armstrong in the Park. I know her voice very well. We must be getting other people's apartments."

"That's impossible," Jim said.

"Well, that was the Sweeneys' nurse," Irene said hotly. "I know her voice. I know it very well. I'm wondering if they can hear us."

Jim turned the switch. First from a distance and then nearer, nearer, as if borne on the wind, came the pure accents of the Sweeneys' nurse again: " ' "Lady Jingly! Lady Jingly!" ' " she said, " ' "Sitting where the pumpkins blow, will you come and be my wife," said the Yonghy-Bonghy-Bò . . .' "

Jim went over to the radio and said "Hello" loudly into the speaker.

" ' "I am tired of living singly," ' " the nurse went on, " ' "on this coast so wild and shingly, I'm a-weary of my life; if you'll come and be my wife, quite serene would be my life . . ." ' "

"I guess she can't hear us," Irene said. "Try something else."

Jim turned to another station, and the living room was filled with the uproar of a cocktail party that had overshot its mark. Someone was playing the piano and singing the Whiffenpoof Song, and the voices that surrounded the piano were vehement and happy. "Eat some more sandwiches," a woman shrieked. There were screams of laughter and a dish of some sort crashed to the floor.

"Those must be the Hutchinsons, in 15-B," Irene said. "I knew they were giving a party this afternoon. I saw her in the liquor store. Isn't this too divine? Try something else. See if you can get those people in 18-C."

The Westcotts overheard that evening a monologue on salmon fishing in Canada, a bridge game, running comments on home movies of what had apparently been a fortnight at Sea Island, and a bitter family quarrel about an overdraft at the bank. They turned off their radio at midnight and went to bed, weak with laughter. Sometime in the night, their son began to call for a glass of water and Irene got one and took it to his room. It was very early. All the lights in the neighborhood were extinguished, and from the boy's window she could see the empty street. She went into the living room and tried the radio. There was some faint coughing, a moan, and then a man spoke. "Are you all right, darling?" he asked. "Yes," a woman said wearily. "Yes, I'm all right, I guess," and then she added with great feeling, "But, you know, Charlie, I don't feel like myself any more. Sometimes there are about fifteen or twenty minutes in the week when I feel like myself. I don't like to go to another doctor, because the doctor's bills are so awful already, but I just don't feel like myself, Charlie. I just never feel like myself." They were not young, Irene thought. She guessed from the timbre of their voices that they were middle-aged. The restrained melan-

choly of the dialogue and the draft from the bedroom window made
her shiver, and she went back to bed.

The following morning, Irene cooked breakfast for the family—
the maid didn't come up from her room in the basement until ten
—braided her daughter's hair, and waited at the door until her
children and her husband had been carried away in the elevator.
Then she went into the living room and tried the radio. "I don't
want to go to school," a child screamed. "I hate school. I won't go to
school. I hate school." "You will go to school," an enraged woman
said. "We paid eight hundred dollars to get you into that school
and you'll go if it kills you." The next number on the dial produced
the worn record of the "Missouri Waltz." Irene shifted the control
and invaded the privacy of several breakfast tables. She overheard
demonstrations of indigestion, carnal love, abysmal vanity, faith,
and despair. Irene's life was nearly as simple and sheltered as it
appeared to be, and the forthright and sometimes brutal language
that came from the loudspeaker that morning astonished and
troubled her. She continued to listen until her maid came in. Then
she turned off the radio quickly, since this insight, she realized, was
a furtive one.

Irene had a luncheon date with a friend that day, and she left her
apartment at a little after twelve. There were a number of women in
the elevator when it stopped at her floor. She stared at their handsome and impassive faces, their furs, and the cloth flowers in their
hats. Which one of them had been to Sea Island, she wondered.
Which one had overdrawn her bank account? The elevator stopped
at the tenth floor and a woman with a pair of Skye terriers joined
them. Her hair was rigged high on her head and she wore a mink
cape. She was humming the "Missouri Waltz."

Irene had two Martinis at lunch, and she looked searchingly at
her friend and wondered what her secrets were. They had intended
to go shopping after lunch, but Irene excused herself and went
home. She told the maid that she was not to be disturbed; then she
went into the living room, closed the doors, and switched on the
radio. She heard, in the course of the afternoon, the halting conversation of a woman entertaining her aunt, the hysterical conclusion
of a luncheon party, and a hostess briefing her maid about some
cocktail guests. "Don't give the best Scotch to anyone who hasn't
white hair," the hostess said. "See if you can get rid of that liver paste
before you pass those hot things, and could you lend me five dollars?
I want to tip the elevator man."

As the afternoon waned, the conversations increased in intensity. From where Irene sat, she could see the open sky above Central Park. There were hundreds of clouds in the sky, as though the south wind had broken the winter into pieces and were blowing it north, and on her radio she could hear the arrival of cocktail guests and the return of children and businessmen from their schools and offices. "I found a good-sized diamond on the bathroom floor this morning," a woman said. "It must have fallen out of that bracelet Mrs. Dunston was wearing last night." "We'll sell it," a man said. "Take it down to the jeweller on Madison Avenue and sell it. Mrs. Dunston won't know the difference, and we could use a couple of hundred bucks . . ." " 'Oranges and lemons, say the bells of St. Clement's,' " the Sweeneys' nurse sang. " 'Half-pence and farthings, say the bells of St. Martin's. When will you pay me? say the bells at old Bailey . . .' " "It's not a hat," a woman cried, and at her back roared a cocktail party. "It's not a hat, it's a love affair. That's what Walter Florell said. He said it's not a hat, it's a love affair," and then, in a lower voice, the same woman added, "Talk to somebody, for Christ's sake, honey, talk to somebody. If she catches you standing here not talking to anybody, she'll take us off her invitation list, and I love these parties."

The Westcotts were going out for dinner that night, and when Jim came home, Irene was dressing. She seemed sad and vague, and he brought her a drink. They were dining with friends in the neighborhood, and they walked to where they were going. The sky was broad and filled with light. It was one of those splendid spring evenings that excite memory and desire, and the air that touched their hands and faces felt very soft. A Salvation Army band was on the corner playing "Jesus Is Sweeter." Irene drew on her husband's arm and held him there for a minute, to hear the music. "They're really such nice people, aren't they?" she said. "They have such nice faces. Actually, they're so much nicer than a lot of the people we know." She took a bill from her purse and walked over and dropped it into the tambourine. There was in her face, when she returned to her husband, a look of radiant melancholy that he was not familiar with. And her conduct at the dinner party that night seemed strange to him, too. She interrupted her hostess rudely and stared at the people across the table from her with an intensity for which she would have punished her children.

It was still mild when they walked home from the party, and Irene looked up at the spring stars. " 'How far that little candle throws its

beams,'" she exclaimed. "'So shines a good deed in a naughty
world.'" She waited that night until Jim had fallen asleep, and then
went into the living room and turned on the radio.

Jim came home at about six the next night. Emma, the maid, let
him in, and he had taken off his hat and was taking off his coat when
Irene ran into the hall. Her face was shining with tears and her hair
was disordered. "Go up to 16-C, Jim!" she screamed. "Don't take
off your coat. Go up to 16-C. Mr. Osborn's beating his wife. They've
been quarrelling since four o'clock, and now he's hitting her. Go up
there and stop him."

From the radio in the living room, Jim heard screams, obsceni-
ties, and thuds. "You know you don't have to listen to this sort of
thing," he said. He strode into the living room and turned the
switch. "It's indecent," he said. "It's like looking in windows. You
know you don't have to listen to this sort of thing. You can turn
it off."

"Oh, it's so horrible, it's so dreadful," Irene was sobbing. "I've
been listening all day, and it's so depressing."

"Well, if it's so depressing, why do you listen to it? I bought this
damned radio to give you some pleasure," he said. "I paid a great
deal of money for it. I thought it might make you happy. I wanted
to make you happy."

"Don't, don't, don't, don't quarrel with me," she moaned, and
laid her head on his shoulder. "All the others have been quarrelling
all day. Everybody's been quarrelling. They're all worried about
money. Mrs. Hutchinson's mother is dying of cancer in Florida and
they don't have enough money to send her to the Mayo Clinic. At
least, Mr. Hutchinson says they don't have enough money. And
some woman in this building is having an affair with the superintendent—with that hideous superintendent. It's too disgusting. And
Mrs. Melville has heart trouble and Mr. Hendricks is going to lose
his job in April and Mrs. Hendricks is horrid about the whole thing
and that girl who plays the 'Missouri Waltz' is a whore, a common
whore, and the elevator man has tuberculosis and Mr. Osborn has
been beating Mrs. Osborn." She wailed, she trembled with grief
and checked the stream of tears down her face with the heel of her
palm.

"Well, why do you have to listen?" Jim asked again. "Why do
you have to listen to this stuff if it makes you so miserable?"

"Oh, don't, don't, don't," she cried. "Life is too terrible, too sordid and awful. But we've never been like that, have we, darling?

Have we? I mean we've always been good and decent and loving to one another, haven't we? And we have two children, two beautiful children. Our lives aren't sordid, are they, darling? Are they?" She flung her arms around his neck and drew his face down to hers. "We're happy, aren't we, darling? We are happy, aren't we?"

"Of course we're happy," he said tiredly. He began to surrender his resentment. "Of course we're happy. I'll have that damned radio fixed or taken away tomorrow." He stroked her soft hair. "My poor girl," he said.

"You love me, don't you?" she asked. "And we're not hypercritical or worried about money or dishonest, are we?"

"No, darling," he said.

A man came in the morning and fixed the radio. Irene turned it on cautiously and was happy to hear a California-wine commercial and a recording of Beethoven's Ninth Symphony, including Schiller's "Ode to Joy." She kept the radio on all day and nothing untoward came from the speaker.

A Spanish suite was being played when Jim came home. "Is everything all right?" he asked. His face was pale, she thought. They had some cocktails and went in to dinner to the "Anvil Chorus" from "Il Trovatore." This was followed by Debussy's "La Mer."

"I paid the bill for the radio today," Jim said. "It cost four hundred dollars. I hope you'll get some enjoyment out of it."

"Oh, I'm sure I will," Irene said.

"Four hundred dollars is a good deal more than I can afford," he went on. "I wanted to get something that you'd enjoy. It's the last extravagance we'll be able to indulge in this year. I see that you haven't paid your clothing bills yet. I saw them on your dressing table." He looked directly at her. "Why did you tell me you'd paid them? Why did you lie to me?"

"I just didn't want you to worry, Jim," she said. She drank some water. "I'll be able to pay my bills out of this month's allowance. There were the slipcovers last month, and that party."

"You've got to learn to handle the money I give you a little more intelligently, Irene," he said. "You've got to understand that we won't have as much money this year as we had last. I had a very sobering talk with Mitchell today. No one is buying anything. We're spending all our time promoting new issues, and you know how long that takes. I'm not getting any younger, you know. I'm thirty-seven. My hair will be gray next year. I haven't done as well as I'd hoped to do. And I don't suppose things will get any better."

"Yes, dear," she said.

"We've got to start cutting down," Jim said. "We've got to think
of the children. To be perfectly frank with you, I worry about
money a great deal. I'm not at all sure of the future. No one is. If
anything should happen to me, there's the insurance, but that
wouldn't go very far today. I've worked awfully hard to give you
and the children a comfortable life," he said bitterly. "I don't like
to see all of my energies, all of my youth, wasted in fur coats and
radios and slipcovers and—"

"Please, Jim," she said. "Please. They'll hear us."

"*Who'll* hear us? Emma can't hear us."

"The radio."

"Oh, I'm sick!" he shouted. "I'm sick to death of your apprehen-
siveness. The radio can't hear us. Nobody can hear us. And what if
they can hear us? Who cares?"

Irene got up from the table and went into the living room. Jim
went to the door and shouted at her from there. "Why are you so
Christly all of a sudden? What's turned you overnight into a convent
girl? You stole your mother's jewelry before they probated her will.
You never gave your sister a cent of that money that was intended
for her—not even when she needed it. You made Grace Howland's
life miserable, and where was all your piety and your virtue when
you went to that abortionist? I'll never forget how cool you were.
You packed your bag and went off to have that child murdered as
if you were going to Nassau. If you'd had any reasons, if you'd had
any good reasons—"

Irene stood for a minute before the hideous cabinet, disgraced
and sickened, but she held her hand on the switch before she extinguished the music and the voices, hoping that the instrument
might speak to her kindly, that she might hear the Sweeneys' nurse.
Jim continued to shout at her from the door. The voice on the radio
was suave and noncommittal. "An early-morning railroad disaster
in Tokyo," the loudspeaker said, "killed twenty-nine people. A fire
in a Catholic hospital near Buffalo for the care of blind children was
extinguished early this morning by nuns. The temperature is forty-
seven. The humidity is eighty-nine."

DEFEAT

❖

Kay Boyle

Toward the end of June that year and through July, there was a sort of uncertain pause, an undetermined suspension that might properly be called neither an armistice nor a peace, and it lasted until the men began coming back from where they were. They came at intervals, trickling down from the north in twos or threes, or even one by one, some of them prisoners who had escaped and others merely a part of that individual retreat in which the sole destination was home. They had exchanged their uniforms for something else as they came along—corduroys, or workmen's blue, or whatever people might have given them in secret to get away in—bearded, singularly and shabbily outfitted men getting down from a bus or off a train without so much as a knapsack in their hands and all with the same bewildered, scarcely discrepant story to tell. Once they had reached the precincts of familiarity, they stood there a moment where the vehicle had left them, maybe trying to button the jacket that didn't fit them or set the neck or shoulders right, like men who have been waiting in a courtroom and have finally heard their names called and stand up to take the oath and mount the witness stand. You could see them getting the words ready—revising the very quality of truth—and the look in their eyes, and then someone coming out of the post office or crossing the station square in the heat would recognize them and go toward them with a hand out, and the testimony would begin.

They had found their way back from different places, by different means, some on bicycle, some by bus, some over the mountains on foot, coming home to the Alpes-Maritimes from Rennes, or from Clermont-Ferrand, or from Lyons, or from any part of France, and looking as incongruous to modern defeat as survivors of the Confederate Army might have looked, transplanted to this year and place (with their spurs still on and their soft-brimmed, dust-whitened hats), limping wanly back, half dazed and not yet having managed to get the story of what happened straight. Only, this time, they were the men of that tragically unarmed and undirected force which had been the French Army once but was no longer, returning to what orators might call reconstruction but which they knew could never be the same.

Wherever they came from, they had identical evidence to give: that the German ranks had advanced bareheaded, in short-sleeved summer shirts—young, blond-haired men with their arms linked, row on row, and their trousers immaculately creased, having slept all night in hotel beds and their stomachs full, advancing singing and falling singing before the puny coughing of the French machine guns. That is, the first line of them might fall, and part of the second, possibly, but never more, for just then the French ammunition would suddenly expire and the bright-haired, blond demigods would march on singing across their dead. Then would follow all the glittering display: the rustproof tanks and guns, the chromiumed electric kitchens, the crematoriums. Legends or truth, the stories became indistinguishable in the mouths of the Frenchmen who returned—that the Germans were dressed as if for tennis that summer, with nothing but a tune to carry in their heads, while the French crawled out from under lorries where they'd slept maybe every night for a week, going to meet them like crippled, encumbered miners emerging from the pit of a warfare fifty years interred, with thirty-five kilos of kit and a change of shoes and a tin helmet left over from 1914 breaking them in two as they met the brilliantly nickelled Nazi dawn. They said their superiors were the first to run; they said their ammunition had been sabotaged; they said the ambulances had been transformed into accommodations for the officers' lady friends; they said *"Nous avons été vendus"* or *"On nous a vendu"* over and over, until you could have made a popular song of it—the words and the music of defeat. After their testimony was given, some of them added (not the young but those who had fought before) in grave, part-embittered, part-vainglorious voices, "I'm ashamed to be a Frenchman" or "I'm ashamed of being French today," and then gravely took their places with the others.

There was one man, though, who didn't say any of these things, probably because he had something else on his mind. He was a dark, short, rather gracefully made man, not thirty yet, with hot, handsome eyes and a cleft chin. Even when he came back without his uniform and without the victory, a certain air of responsibility, of authority, remained because he had been the chauffeur of the

mail bus before the war. He didn't sit talking in the *bistro* about
what he had seen and where he had been, but he got the black beard
off his face as quickly as he could, and bought a pair of new shoes,
and went back to work in stubborn-lipped, youthful, almost violent
pride. Except one night he did tell the story; he told it only once,
about two months after he got back, and not to his own people or
the people of the village but, as if by chance, to two commercial
travellers for rival fruit-juice firms who were just beginning to cir-
culate again from town to town in the Unoccupied Zone. They sat
at the Café Central together, the three of them, drinking wine, talking about the anachronism of horse-and-mule-drawn cannon in
Flanders and the beasts running amok under the enemy planes, and
saying how they had all believed that the French line was going to
hold somewhere, that it wasn't going to break.

"At first we thought it would hold at the Oise," one of the travelling men said. "We kept on retreating, saying the new front must
be at the Oise, and believing it too, and then, when we dropped
below the Oise, we kept saying it would hold at the Marne, and believing it, and then we thought it would be the Seine, and even
when we were south of Paris we kept on believing about some kind
of a line holding on the Loire. . . ."

"I still don't know why we stopped retreating," said the other
commercial traveller. He sat looking soberly at his glass. "We can't
talk about the Italians any more. I still don't see why we didn't retreat right down to Senegal. I don't see what stopped us," he said.
Then the quiet-mouthed little bus-driver began telling them about
what had happened to him on the fourteenth of July.

He had been told, he said, that in some of the cities the enemy
hadn't taken or had withdrawn from, processions formed on the
fourteenth and passed through the streets in silence, the flagstaffs
they carried draped with black and their heads bowed. In some of
the villages, the mayor, dressed in mourning, laid a wreath on the
monument to the last war's dead while the peasants kneeled about
him in the square.

"I was in Pontcharra on the fourteenth," said one of the travelling salesmen, "and when the mayor put the wreath down and the
bugle called out like that for the dead, all the peasants uncovered
themselves, but the military didn't even stand at attention."

"By that time none of the privates were saluting their officers in
the street anywhere you went," said the other salesman, but the bus-
driver didn't pay any attention to what they said. He went on telling

them that he'd been taken prisoner near Rennes on the seventeenth of June, and that there he saw the tracts the Boche planes had showered down the week before. The tracts said, "Frenchmen, prepare your coffins! Frenchwomen, get out your ball dresses! We're going to dance the soles off your shoes on the fourteenth of July!" He told the commercial travellers exactly what use they made of the tracts in the public places there. He was more than three weeks in the prison camp, he said, and on the night of the twelfth of July he and a *copain* made their escape. They went in uniform, on borrowed bicycles. They kept to the main road all night, wheeling along as free and unmolested in the dark as two young men cycling home from a dance, with their hearts light, and the stars out over them, and the night air mild. At dawn they took to the side roads, and toward eight o'clock of the new day they saw a house standing alone, a little in advance of the village that lay ahead.

"We'll ask there," the bus-driver had said, and they pushed their cycles in off the road and laid them down behind a tree. The house, they could see then, was the schoolhouse, with a sign for *"Filles"* over one door and for *"Garçons"* over the other. The *copain* said there would be nobody there, but the bus-driver had seen a woman come to the window and look at them, and he walked up to the door.

The desks were empty because of what had happened and the time of year, but the bus-driver said he knew it must have been the schoolmistress who was standing in the middle of the room between the benches, a young woman with fair, wavy hair, eying them fearlessly and even sharply as they came. The bus-driver and his *copain* said good morning, and they saw at once the lengths of three-colored stuff in her hands and the work she had been doing. They looked around them and saw four French flags clustered in each corner of the classroom and great loops of bunting that were draped along three sides of the room. The first thing the bus-driver thought was that she ought to be warned, she ought to be told, and then, when he looked at her face again, he knew she knew as much as or more than they.

"You ought to keep the door locked," he had said, and the schoolmistress looked at him almost in contempt.

"I don't care who comes in," she said, and she went on folding the bunting into the lengths she wanted to cut it to drape across the farthest wall.

"So the village is occupied?" the bus-driver said.

"Yes," she said, but she began cutting the tricolor bunting.

"There's one thing," said the *copain,* looking a little bleakly at the two others. "If you give yourself up, at least you don't get shot."

The schoolmistress had put her scissors down and said to the bus-driver, "You'll have to get rid of your uniforms before there's any chance of you getting through." She glanced around the classroom as though the demands of action had suddenly made it strange to her. "Take them off and put them in the cupboard there," she had said, "and cover yourselves with this stuff while you wait," and she heaped the blue and white and red lengths upon the desks. "In case they might come in," she said. She took her hat and *filet* off the hook as she said, "I'll come back with other clothes for you."

"If there would be any way of getting something to eat," the bus-driver had said, and because he asked this, the tide of courage seemed to rise even higher in her.

"Yes," she said. "I'll bring back food for you."

"And a bottle of *pinard,*" said the *copain,* but he didn't say it very loud.

When she was gone, they took their uniforms off and wrapped the bunting around themselves, doing it for her and modesty's sake, and then they sat down at the first form's desk, swathed to their beards in red, white, and blue. Even if the Boches had walked into the schoolhouse then, there probably wasn't any military regulation made to deal with what they would have found, the bus-driver had said to his *copain*—just two Frenchmen in their underwear sitting quietly inside the colors of their country's flag. But whether he said the other thing to the teacher as soon as she brought the bread and sausage and wine and the scraps of other men's clothing back, he didn't know. Sometimes, when he thought of it afterward, he wasn't quite sure he had ever got the actual words out, but then he remembered the look on her face as she stood by the tree where the bicycles had lain and watched them pedalling toward the village just ahead, and he knew he must have said it. He knew he must have wiped the sausage grease and the wine off his mouth with the back of his hand and said "A country isn't defeated as long as its women aren't" or "until its women are" or "As long as the women of a country aren't defeated, it doesn't matter if its army is"—something like that, perhaps saying it just before they shook hands with her and cycled away.

That was the morning of the thirteenth, and the bus-driver told how they rode all day in the heat, two what-might-have-been-peasants cycling slowly hour after hour across the hushed, summery, sunny land. The war was over for them, for this country the war was over; there was no sound or look of it in the meadows or the trees or grain. The war was finished, but the farmhouse they stopped at that evening would not take them in.

"Have you got your bread tickets with you?" the peasant said, and even the white-haired sows behind his legs eyed them narrowly with greed.

"We're prisoners escaped. We've got a bit of money," the bus-driver said. "We'll pay for our soup, and maybe you'll let us sleep in the loft."

"And when the Boches come in for the milk they'll shoot me and the family for having taken you in!" the peasant said, and the bus-driver stood looking at him bitterly a moment before he began to swear. When he had called the man the names he wanted to, he said, "Look here, we were soldiers—perhaps you haven't got that yet? We haven't been demobilized; we were taken prisoner, we escaped. We were fighting a little war up there."

"If you'd fought it better, the Boches wouldn't have got this far," the peasant said. He said it in cunning and triumph, and then he closed the door.

They slept the night at the next farm (the bus-driver told the commercial travellers), eating soup and bread and drinking red wine in the kitchen, and when they had paid for it they were shown up to the loft. But they were not offered the side on which the hay lay; the farmer was thinking of next winter and he told them they could lie down just as well on the boards. They slept heavily and well, and it was very light when they woke in the morning, and so that day, the day of the fourteenth, they did not get far. By six that night they were only another hundred kilometres on, and then the *copain's* tire went flat. But a little town stood just ahead and they pushed their bicycles toward it through the summer evening, and down its wide, treeless street. They hadn't seen the uniform yet, but they knew the Germans must be there. Even on the square in the heart of town they saw no sign, but still there was that unnatural quiet, that familiar uneasiness on the air, so they pushed their wheels through the open doors of a big garage, past the dry and pad-locked gas pumps, and stood them up against the inside wall. There, in the garage's half-security and semi-dark, they looked around them; twenty or more cars stood one beside the other, halted as if forever because of the lack of fluid to flow through their veins. Overhead the glass panes of the roof were still painted blue; the military and staff cars parked in the shadowy silence still bore their green-and-khaki camouflage. The war was over, everything had stopped, and out beyond the wide-open automobile doorway they saw the dance platform that had been erected in the square, and the dark, leafy branches twined on its upright beams and balustrade, and the idle people standing looking. There were no flags up, only this rather dismal atmosphere of preparation, and it was then the bus-driver and his *copain* had remembered it was the fourteenth.

"It's a national holiday and we haven't had a drink yet," the *copain* said. He stood there in the garage with his hands in the pockets of the trousers that didn't belong to him, staring bleakly out across the square. Even when two German soldiers who were putting electric wiring up in the dance pavilion came into view, his face did not alter. He simply went on saying, "We haven't had the *apéritif* all day."

The bus-driver took a packet of cigarettes out of his jacket pocket and put one savagely on his lip. As he lit it, he looked in hot, bitter virulence out to where the Germans were hanging strings of bulbs among the fresh, dark leaves.

" 'Frenchmen, prepare your coffins!' " he had said, and then he gave a laugh. "They've made only one mistake so far, just one," he said, and as he talked the cigarette jerked up and down in fury on his lip. "They've got the dance floor and the decorations all right, and they've probably got the music, and maybe the refreshments too. So far so good," he said. "But they haven't got the partners. That's what's going to be funny. That's what's going to be really funny."

The bus-driver sat there in the Café Central telling it to the two commercial travellers, perhaps because he had had more to drink than usual, telling them the story, or perhaps because it had been weighing long enough heavy on his heart. He told them about the dinner the garage owner gave him and his *copain:* civet and fried potatoes and salad and four kinds of cheese and armagnac with the coffee. He said they could scarcely get it all down and that then their host opened a bottle of champagne for them. That's the kind of man the garage owner was. And during the dinner or afterward, with the wine inside of him, it seems the bus-driver had said it again. He had

said something about as long as the women of a nation weren't defeated the rest of it didn't matter, and just as he said it the music
struck up in the dance pavilion outside.

The place the garage owner offered them for the night was just
above the garage itself, a sort of storeroom, with three windows overlooking the square. First he repaired the *copain's* tire for him, and
behind him on the wall as he worked they read the newspaper cutting he had pinned up, perhaps in some spirit of derision. It ex-
horted all Frenchmen to accept quietly and without protest the
new regulations concerning the circulation of private and public
vehicles.

"Without protest!" the garage owner had said, taking the dripping red tube out of the basin of water and pinching the leak between his finger and thumb. "I'll have to close the place up, and
they ask me to do it without protest." He stood rubbing sandpaper
gently around where the imperceptible hole in the rubber was.
"We weren't ready for war and yet we declared it just the same," he
said, "and now we've asked for peace and we aren't ready for that,
either." When he had finished with the tire he showed them up the
stairs.

"I'll keep the light off," he said, "in case it might give them the
idea of coming up and having a look," but there was no need for
any light, for the illumination of the dance pavilion in the square
shone in through the windows and lit the rows of storage batteries
and the cases of spare parts and spark plugs. From outside, they
heard the music playing—the exact waltz time and the quick, entirely martial version of swing.

"Somebody ought to tell them they're wasting their time," the
bus-driver had said, jerking one shoulder toward the windows. He
could have burst out laughing at the sight of them, he explained,
some with white gloves on even, waiting out there to the strains of
music for what wasn't going to come.

The garage owner shook out the potato sacks of waste on the floor
and gave them the sacks to lie down on, and then he took one look
out the window at the square and grinned and said good night and
went downstairs. The *copain* was tired and he lay down at once on
the soft rags on the floor and drew a blanket up over him, but the
bus-driver had stood a while at one side of the window, watching
the thing below. A little group of townspeople was standing around
the platform where the variously colored lights hung, and the band
was playing in one corner of the pavilion underneath the leaves. No

one was dancing, but the German soldiers were hanging around in expectation, some standing on the steps of the platform and some leaning on the garnished rails.

"For a little while there wasn't a woman anywhere," the bus-driver told the commercial travellers. "There was this crowd of people from the town, perhaps thirty or forty of them looking on, and maybe some others further back in the dark where you couldn't see them, but that was all," and then he stopped talking.

"And then what happened?" said one of the travelling men after a moment, and the bus-driver sat looking in silence at his glass.

"They had a big, long table spread out with things to eat on it," he said in a minute, and he didn't look up. "They had fruit tarts, it looked like, and sweet chocolate, and bottles of lemonade and beer. They had as much as you wanted of everything," he said. "And perhaps once you got near enough to start eating and drinking, then the other thing just followed naturally afterward—or that's the way I worked it out," he said. "Or maybe, if you've had a dress a long time that you wanted to wear and you hadn't had the chance of putting it on and showing it off because all the men were away—I mean if you were a woman. I worked it out that maybe the time comes when you want to put it on so badly that you put it on just the same whatever's happened, or maybe, if you're one kind of a woman, any kind of a uniform looks all right to you after a certain time. The music was good, it was first class," he said, but he didn't look up. "And here was all this food spread out, and the corks popping off the bottles, and the lads in uniform, great, big fellows, handing out chocolates to all the girls. . . ."

The three of them sat at the table without talking for a while after the bus-driver's voice had ceased, and then one of the travelling men said, "Well, that was just one town."

"Yes, that was just one town," said the bus-driver, and when he picked up his glass to drink, something as crazy as tears was standing in his eyes.

MAN HERE KEEPS GETTING
ARRESTED ALL THE TIME

❖

JOHN McNULTY

GROGAN GOT ARRESTED AGAIN Thursday. Talking in this place on
Third Avenue Friday night, he said he was getting sick and
tired of it. That's about the ninth time he got arrested lately. He
seems to be having a streak.

Grogan, a nice, quiet little man, non-supports his wife. He also
bets on race horses and thinks about them night and day. He's been
non-supporting his wife for eleven years and she's mean about it,
even if Grogan intends no harm. So he gets arrested once in a while
on her account. Mostly, though, he gets arrested in raids on puny
horse rooms around Third, Second Avenue, occasionally Lexington Avenue.

Grogan's a solemn, small, scientific-minded little man, with no
laughs at all written on his dead pan. He comes by being scientific-
minded honestly, because in Ireland his old man was a Latin scholar
just for fun. That's how Grogan got his middle name, which is
Vercingetorix. His whole name is Malachy Vercingetorix Grogan,
but they call him Grogan the Horseplayer. It sounds like a trade,
like bricklaying.

Getting arrested doesn't bother Grogan in his pride or leave any
marks on his character. He manages to remain altogether aloof from
the cops that arrest him. But what gets him sore is he says you miss
your dinner when you get arrested in these raids. They almost always
happen half past four in the afternoon and no Night Court to stick
you in front of until about ten o'clock that night.

"I don't know do they folly me around or what, those plain-
clothes policemen," Grogan said. "But it seems lately no sooner am
I settled down nice and busy in one of these horse rooms than along
about the fifth race at Aqueduct in come the policemen again.

"They're decent enough when they come in on a raid, unless
once in a while somebody in the crowd of horseplayers shows signs

of getting tough. They have to paste them a couple then—not too hard—so everybody else will get the idea what's done is done and make the best of it and they'll know it's a raid. These couple of pastes in the jaw for somebody is what they might call in a show establishing a mood. The policemen establishes a mood that way."

This last arrest, Grogan said, just about broke the back on his camel. He got to brooding about it. Paddy Ferrarty, the night bartender at this saloon, often says about Grogan, "He's Irish and he broods easy."

"It's heartbreaking the way I got to do now," Grogan went on. "They got me half scared of the little horse rooms, and I don't ketch holt of enough money for decent poolrooms. I usually got seven dollars, only, to start with. Consequence is I'm playing with guys makes book in an auto on a corner. They sit in the auto and won't let me or the other horseplayers sit in it, naturally—ain't room enough.

"No, we got to stand in the rain or doorways to look at the *Racing Form*, and walk over to the auto and make bets, or get the results that comes in over the radio. You seen that kind of bookmaking. You can tell this auto, on a different corner around here nearly every day, because it has a sign on the front, 'Remember Pearl Harbor.'

"This last raid—I don't know, it got tiresome. I make out better than the other guys arrested. I'm used to it. Like when they're going to lead you out to the patrol wagon at the curb, nobody wants to be first outside the door and pass through the crowd. A crowd always stands around as close as they can to a patrol wagon, and the cops make a space between 'em, like an aisle outside a church for a wedding.

"But I got over all that bashfulness about going out first and let the crowd gape at you. The hell with them in the crowd. You're not criminals anyway, only horseplayers meaning no harm, only want to win a couple dollars. And what the hell, the cops themselves ain't even mad at you; they got to make a couple raids every week to put in the records.

"And what I found out is you get across the sidewalk first and into the wagon and you get a seat. Why, the last time they had twenty-seven guys jammed in there, standing up, sitting on each other, piled up every which way, miserable. So I'm first across the sidewalk—let them gape—and I got a seat.

"First they took us in this last raid down to the police station on East Thirty-fifth Street. The whole twenty-seven in a big room and certainly a mixed-up bunch. They had guys like me, and wops, and some Long-champs waiters with red braids on their coats would probably get fired because it was five o'clock by then and they ought to be back to work. Three or four horseplayers had helmets on. Steel helmets. These helmet guys work in the slaughterhouse on First Avenyuh. They got to wear helmets because the big sides of beefs run along a conveyor on hooks and without the beefs the bare hooks sometimes hits the guys in the head. Therefore helmets.

"The way you mill around in that police station is an awful waste of time. Just mope there, but a guy sells coffee if you want it. That helps and he makes a handy dollar with all the prisoners dumped in there all the time.

"It's about six o'clock before they took us up to East Sixty-seventh Street, what they call Division Headquarters. They count you before they put you in the wagon and they count you up at East Sixty-seventh Street and they count you before they take you out of there. My God, you get sick of being counted! I hate cops counting me, but they have a slip says twenty-seven guys arrested and they deliver them around from station to station like merchandise. Another thing that's not becomin' at all is that in East Sixty-seventh they put you in cells. No matter who you are, getting put in a cell can make you sad, even if only for horseplaying. There's something about seeing a man walk loose by the door and you can't walk loose but got to look through bars that sinks your heart out if you let it. Only I don't let it. The thing that bothers me is why do they go through all this at all, to say nothing of making you miss your dinner? Why do they keep bothering poor, simple, ordinary horseplayers and turn them loose anyway in the finish, which they always do?

"It seems useless to me. I always thought now for years I love to study horses and bet them when I can because it is one thing you can do by yourself and harms nobody at all. I can be busy with horses, the *Racing Form* or maybe the *Morning Telegraph,* all winter nights and summer nights in Bickford's or in my room and never harm anybody, but they got to keep on arresting us. Getting married causes trouble, drinking causes trouble, working wears a man out, and I see guys all around me dying making successes out of themselves. Why can't they let me harm nobody just studying horses and playing 'em when I can?

"I almost forgot to say just before the raid I bet a horse at Suffolk, two dollars win, with Louie the bookie. But then the raid come, and of course they stopped the radio, gathered up all the *Forms* and all,

and with all the moving from station to station I couldn't find out
how the Suffolk race come out. None of the cops were watching me
especially in the raid, and I snuck an Arlington Park part of the
Form into my sock, folded up, and I had that at East Sixty-seventh
Street. I could study that in the cell, and they run late out there
at Arlington because it's in Chicago. Well, damn if I didn't find a
horse in the last race out there I'd been watching for weeks. He
could win easy, and luck would have it Louie walk by the cell and
stopped there. He must have slipped a cop something and they
broke him out of a cell and let him walk in the corridor back and
forth—more comforting than in a cell. I asked Louie if he would let
me bet the last at Arlington, although by that time the race was
over. I didn't have money, but if the Suffolk horse had win, well, I
could 'if' some money off him. That means if the first horse wins,
you can bet some of the win on another one. It's like a cotingency
basis in the legal world, only it's 'iffing' in horse rooms. 'Honest to
God, don't you know how the race come out at Arlington?' Louie
asked me. 'Nobody told you, did they, in jail here?' I told him honest to God I didn't know. 'O.K.,' he says. 'You're an honest guy,
Grogan. You can have four win on the Arlington horse.' Then he
walked away from the cell. They both win, it later turn out, and so
I beat Louie for sixteen-seventy.

"I was glad I went out first to the wagon when they moved us to
Night Court over on West Fifty-fourth Street. I tell you why.

"It was dark when they moved us, and of course the wagon was
jammed up again. The seat I got was up front, and there's a round
hole in the partition that divides the driver off from us. Well, as we
drove along I could look through that round hole and see all the
corners I knew. It was very interesting, just looking through that
hole and seeing a particular building and figuring out 'This is Lexington and Sixty-fourth' or else 'This is Lex and Fifty-ninth.' The
electric signs are blacked out, but I could read some anyway and
they looked pretty through that hole and made me forget how rotten
it is packed in a patrol wagon getting arrested all the time for doing
no harm.

"Of course, they counted us again at the Night Court, where you
stand around in a detention pen. I felt like saying, 'Stop counting
me. I'm still one guy, the same as I been all my life.' But what's the
use? The less said in a detention pen the better.

"The bailiff got me a little mad. They haul you up in a bunch
before the magistrate, and when it came our turn, the bunch from

our particular raid, what do you suppose the bailiff shouted to the magistrate? Well, he hollered, 'Malachy V. Grogan and twenty-six others!' I asked him, 'What's the idea singlin' me out?' 'Aw, you're here all the time,' he says. I let it go at that.

"They dismissed us, the magistrate did, the way he always does. We get charged with dis. con., they call it, means disorderly conduct, and there's a couple minutes' blather and they turn us loose, ten o'clock or so and no dinner yet. They hold Louie. They got him charged with main. nuis., which is maintaining a nuisance, probably meaning Malachy V. Grogan and twenty-six others. It all seems useless, and I don't know why they got to keep arresting us all, not doing anybody a bit of harm but finding an interesting way to put in all the days and nights.

"Louie give me the sixteen-seventy after we got out. He got bailed in no time. I knew he would because Louie's the kind nobody pends him up very long and so I was waiting in Fifty-fourth when he come out. He bought a *Telegraph* at the stand there at Fiftieth and Broadway and we found out how the races we missed in jail come out."

DOWN IN THE REEDS BY THE RIVER

❖

Victoria Lincoln

WHY ARE WE NEVER prepared, why do all the books and all the wisdom of our friends avail us nothing in the final event? How many deathbed scenes we have read, how many stories of young love, of marital infidelity, of cherished ambition fulfilled or defeated. There is nothing that can happen to us that has not happened again and again, that we have not read over a thousand times, closely, carefully, accurately recorded; before we are fully launched on life, the story of the human heart has been opened for us again and again with all the patience and skill of the human mind. But the event, when it comes, is never anything like the description; it is strange, infinitely strange and new, and we stand helpless before it and realize that the words of another convey nothing, nothing.

And still we cannot believe that personal life is, in its essence, incommunicable. We, too, having lived the moment, are impelled to convey it, to speak the words so honest in intent, so false in the final effect. Now, after so many years, I want to tell you about Mr. deRocca, although it is a queer story—not a story at all, really, only an incident in the life of a young girl—simply to show that it was not what you would have expected. It was not like the books or the whispered, ugly confidence that you remember from your school days; it was quite, quite different. I want to tell you, although I know from the outset that I shall fail, as we all fail.

But now that I come up to it, I hesitate. It should have been evil, frightening, all wrong; of course it should. It should have been the repellent accident that can queer an emotional development for years to come. And still, when it was happening, it was not like that at all.

I was fourteen, a wiry, red-headed, unimaginative little tomboy, fond of sand-lot baseball. My parents were dead, killed in an accident a year before, and I lived with an aunt and uncle in Braeburn

25

Heights, a suburb of a small city in Kansas. Bereft, rudely transplanted from the life I had known—a happy-go-lucky life in the
brown hills of California—I was lonely beyond words. I had grown
up in the careless warmth of love, and for my Aunt Elsa's genuine,
if worried, kindness I could feel nothing but ingratitude. The
house was strange, the neighboring children were strange, with
their neat, pretty bedrooms, their queer talk of dates, and formals,
and going steady. I felt dry and hard and empty inside myself, day
after day. I used to take my bicycle and ride out into the country,
but the country was strange, too, and ugly to my eyes, all flat and
dull.

And then, one day, I found White Creek Row. It was the town's
Hooverville, a row of shanties between the creek and the railroad,
little huts like the playhouse that I had built back in the hills with
the children of our Mexican gardener—a tragic, shocking, sordid
shantytown, as I see it now. But to my enchanted eyes it was romantic and delightful and, more than that, comprehensible, as my
aunt's house in Braeburn Heights was not.

It was in White Creek Row that, unknown to Aunt Elsa, I made
my first real friends in Kansas. The squatters in the row were shy
of me at first, as I was shy of the people in Braeburn Heights. My
decent clothes, my bicycle, made me alien, an object for suspicion
and resentment. And still, somehow or other, I managed to scrape
an acquaintance with Posy Moreno, an acquaintance that grew into
love.

She was a gentle creature with a mop of soft black curls piled
high on her head and a womanliness, at sixteen, that made me feel,
for the first time, glad that I, too, was growing near to womanhood.
She lived in the last shanty in the row with her little brother Manuel, and next door was Mrs. Grimes, her self-appointed duenna.
She was very proud of Mrs. Grimes' watchfulness.

"Me, I'm never chasing with the feller," she used to say, "but
if I was to chase with the feller, Mrs. Grimes she's knock me down,
you bet. She's not let anybody get fresh with Posy Moreno."

"I wouldn't want anyone bossing me like that," I said once. And
Posy, lifting her head in the pride of her womanhood, replied,
"You not need. You just a kid." But as we became better acquainted
she treated me less and less like a kid.

Through our long afternoons on the creek bank, listening to her
conversation, I would sit spellbound, infinitely flattered that she
considered me a girl and not a child, feeling within myself a new

softening, a shy preening, a tremulousness delicious and unfamiliar.

Besides Posy and Manuel, the only other child on the row was Chuck Hansen, who was twelve. I liked him, too, and I used to let him ride my bicycle while Posy and I talked. I could never hear enough about life in the row, and the people who lived in it. They had everything, I used to tell myself, everything that anybody could want, for I was too young to understand the need for security, for dignity. They had everything, and they had got it all free—even a church.

Mrs. Grimes had wanted the church, and Mr. deRocca, who had been a carpenter in Italy, had built it for her, although he was a freethinker and had accompanied every hammer blow, so Posy told me, with a lot of bad talk about religion being made up by rich people to keep poor people quiet.

How I wished I might have been there to see him, sitting on the roof, pounding down the shingles that were made from flattened tin cans, with his delicate, hard little old hands, and shouting all the time, "Opium of the people. You getta pie in a sky when you die!" The church even had a piano, with a good many keys that still sounded, nice and loud, if not true, and Mrs. Grimes played gospel hymns on it by ear.

Mr. deRocca would not go to the prayer meetings. He lived in the best shanty in the row, and in his front yard was a beautiful American flag laid out in bits of broken brick and slate and white stones. I admired it intensely and used to stop before his house, the better to enjoy it, but Posy would shy off and draw me away, throwing up her head with a sort of wild-pony elegance. "Better we're not hanging around here," she would say. "Mr. deRocca, he's liking the girl."

I did not understand. Would anyone so old want a wife as young as Posy, I wondered. It must be that, I decided, when Posy told me that Mrs. Grimes had not let Mr. deRocca help with the building of Posy's shack. I supposed they thought it would not be fair to encourage him. But I saw no reason why the caution should also apply to me. I was charmed by the little I had managed to see of Mr. deRocca. He seemed to be a very clever, very nice old man.

And now I come to my story, and it is hard to tell. It is hard to tell because I should have been so different. Perhaps there were undertones that I have forgotten. That is likely, for the memory has a curiously clear and classic air, quite unlike life as I have since found it—the nymph and the old satyr frozen in attitudes of time-less innocence under the box elders by the creek bank, the sacred grove where liquid Peneus was flowing and all dark Tempe lay. And still, still, I remember it like that. If there was fear, if there was guilt, they came later.

One afternoon, Chuck Hansen met me on the cinder track, look-ing wistful. "I don't guess you'll want to stay today, Connie," he said. "Mrs. Grimes and Posy, they went uptown." He rubbed the handle bars of my bicycle with his hands, hard, as if he were fondling a horse. "Guess you won't have much to stick around for," he said humbly.

How nice he was, I thought, never teasing.

"Well, listen, Chuck," I said. "I'm tired, a little. I'll go down and walk around a while and sit on the creek bank."

His grin made me feel warm and pleasant. I began to saunter along the front of the row. Mr. deRocca was sitting on a packing case by his door, eating an onion. His face, lifted to the sky, wore the blank, peaceful expression of one enjoying the quiet of a village street after a procession has passed, the look of remembering in quietness.

I came along very slowly, watching Mr. deRocca from the corners of my eyes. He wore a plaid flannel shirt, ragged and, of course, un-ironed, but fairly clean, and the neck was unbuttoned. I noticed how the flesh under his chin was firm and didn't hang down in wattles, and the cords in his neck didn't stick out. He looked harder and nicer than other old men.

How old was he, really? About fifty, I should guess now, looking back; maybe a little less. But if I had known it then, it would not have changed my picture of him at all. Fifty to eighty in those days were all of a piece in my mind. Mr. deRocca was an old man. And he was nice. As I came very close, I realized with a sudden throb of excitement that he had been watching me all along, just as I had been watching him. Watching me and waiting for the moment to speak, just as I had been, with him. I turned, pretending to have seen him for the first time. I smiled at him. The white teeth gleamed in the thin, brown face; the elegant, small, brown paw that held the onion described a vast semicircle of greeting. "Hi, kid," he said. "Looka for da Posy? She's a not home."

I did not answer. I had realized, quite abruptly, that it was the sight of him sitting down there below me, fully as much as Chuck's longing hands rubbing the handle bars, that made up my mind for me up there on the embankment, and I turned shy, hoping that he would not guess it.

"I always like to look at that flag, Mr. deRocca," I said.

"Come on in a yard," he said. "Looka good. It's a pretty, hey?"

We stood together, eying the charming sight in a sort of shared pride. He pulled out another packing case from the corner of the house and waved me to it with the flattering charm of a courtier.

"Please to sit," he said. "Scusa." He went in the house for a second and returned, extending his hand with the same grave courtesy. "You like-a onion?"

I looked at it dubiously. Father had disliked salads, saying firmly that hay was for God-damned Frenchmen, and Aunt Elsa's were of the pineapple, cream cheese, and mayonnaise school. Raw onions were new to me, and alarming. But it was so lovely, being treated like a lady, that I could not disappoint him.

I took it and bit into it gingerly. The sharp, pungent, biting juice ran over my tongue, the firm, fleshy layers crunched between my teeth in a stinging, breathtaking ecstasy of delicious pain.

"Oh!" I cried in sincere delight. "It's good!" Then, with the snobbery of the young guest who does not wish his host to think him ignorant of the wines he is offered, I added, "It's one of the best onions I ever ate."

"Sure," he said proudly. "Sure, you bet it's a good, it's a fine. I grow."

I regarded him happily, rejoicing in his kingly acceptance of the compliment, so unlike the mincing, genteel self-depreciation which, of all the mannered compulsions of the Heights, I found most unfamiliar and most dismal.

I went on with my compliments, sincerely, but also eager for the continuing pleasure of his openness. "You have a wonderful house," I said. "The church is wonderful, too. You're a fine carpenter."

His eyes glowed and he swayed his head from side to side, like someone keeping time to music. "You bet I'm a good," he replied. "I'm a learn in a Old Country, worka slow, take-a pain, think for the job, for looka pretty, not think for hurry up, getta money. I'm a good like nobody's business."

"I should think you'd get lots of jobs," I said, "and be rich."

He shrugged. "Bad a time," he said. "Everywhere bad a time. Smart a man everywhere hungry, no work. Someday come a good time." He finished the onion and wiped his thin lips on the backs of his neat little fingers. "Someday, different time, all be good, not graba, graba, be man and man together, not dog and dog. First a big fight, maybe, then all be good."

I remembered something we had studied in social science. I leaned forward, trying to look intelligent and grownup. "You mean a revolution?" I said. "Are you a Communist, Mr. deRocca?"

"Pah!" he replied. "Not!" He spat to one side, to emphasize his attitude. Then, with a flashing, all-embracing smile: "Lots good in de Comunista, lots smart. I read, I like, good. Only alla time boss, boss. Boss so bad like we got here, now. I'm a no like all a time boss. I am Anarchista, me."

"What's that?" I asked.

"Everyone's treat everyone else right. No push around, no boss. People no gotta lot of stuff, graba, graba. No law, no boss, everyone a same. Treata them right, they treata you right. All good."

It sounded lovely.

"What do you call that? Anarchista? I guess I'm Anarchista, too," I said.

He threw both arms wide, embracing me in the universal fellowship. "That's a fine. You smart a kid."

Master and disciple, we sat happily together in the blissful country of utopian anarchy, regarding the flag of America spread out at our feet with absent, gently admiring eyes. Gradually, the conversation took a personal turn.

"You name a Constansia?"

"Constance."

"Pretty name," he said. "Pretty name for pretty girl. Nice when a pretty girl have a pretty name."

No one had told me I was pretty since my mother died. I was grateful to him, but unbelieving. "I have awful red hair," I said.

"Pretty," he said. "Pretty hair, pretty eye, pretty shape. How old?"

"Going on fifteen."

He smiled, as if I could not possibly have been a nicer age, as if it were a peculiar grace and wisdom in me to be going on fifteen.

"Last year, da little kid," he said. "Next year, da woman, look at da fella, think for da fella. Now she not know what she think—that right?"

I was deeply struck with the truth of his words. It was what I had been feeling in my inarticulate way all the time I was sitting with Posy on the creek bank, admiring her womanly young beauty, listening to her sternly virtuous, so very sex-conscious conversation, hoping that she did not still think of me as just a little kid.

I looked earnestly at Mr. deRocca sitting on his packing case, as if I could discover in the glowing, friendly eyes the source of his remarkable understanding. He was old, but I thought suddenly that he was handsome, as handsome as my father had been. His features were so sharp and delicate, his body so fine-boned, the shoulders so narrow, compared with the Mexicans with whom I unconsciously classed him. A fleeting wonder passed through my mind if all Italians were like him, so little and handsome and wise.

He held out his hand toward me, palm up and slightly cupped, almost as if he were coaxing a tame bird with seed. "That right?" he said again, quite soft.

I was surprised at my voice when I answered. It was unfamiliar—low and a little unsteady. "That's right," I said.

He stood up, smiling more than ever. "Come on down a creek bank," he said. "I show you where I gotta good catfish net. Other guy wait to fish, watch, work. Me, I sit and they come."

Thinking back, remembering, I wonder for the first time if he spoke in any conscious analogy. I do not believe that he did.

I followed Mr. deRocca trustfully down the creek bank, under the box-elder trees. At the water's edge, he turned and looked at me, and I saw the changed look in his eyes. It was as if the door had opened and I were looking upon a landscape that was both strange and familiar. I glanced around me, and I saw that the box elders grew thick where we stood, that we were in a place that was private, sheltered from the eyes of the world. Suddenly, I understood everything that Posy had said. I knew what she meant when she said, "He's liking the girl."

"Show me the net," I said nervously.

His eyes smiled at me, reassuring, his voice quieted me. "Pretty soon," he said. "Right down here." But he made no move toward going on. Instead, he put out a lean, brown paw and touched my head. "Pretty," he said. "Pretty hair."

His hand slipped down my back and around my waist, the fingers firm and hard against me, warm through my cotton dress. And again he paused, his eyes still smiling with that same gentle reassurance.

He was old at the game, I see now, and grown wise in method, wise and patient. If he had hurried, if he had let me see his eagerness, I should have been terribly frightened, I should have run away crying. I should have run away full of fear and hate, and the fear and hate would have lived in me a long time.

But he stood, smiling at me, until I was used to his arm, his hand, feeling it not as a sexual advance but as warm, human affection in my body that was aching for human affection, for the demonstrative love on which I had thrived through a warm, loving childhood. He was quiet until I felt my fear dissolve in gratitude for the kindness of his arm, his firm, affectionate hand.

It was easy, then, for him to turn me against him, to hold me firm and close, stroking my hair, firm and close against him, waiting till his accustomed, patient hands should tell him that I was ready for more.

I knew that I must be doing something bad, and still I could not feel that it was bad yet, not yet. And his slowness made me confident that I was free to decide if it was really bad, that he would let me go quickly the minute I thought it had begun to be bad. It still did not seem bad when he kissed me, or when his kissing changed and made me feel all soft and strange inside, or when his hands began to describe all the differences that the year had made in my body, and to tell me silently that they were beauties, richness, a bounty of which to be proud.

Once he made a little motion to draw me down in the thick grass, and I had the sense to be frightened, but he felt it at once and waited, and I waited, too, sure that I would know when I should run away, growing softer and stranger by the moment, forgetting everything outside me. I was wholly lost when I heard Posy's shrill voice calling my name, and heard her pushing through the branches down the creek bank.

Mr. deRocca let me go and dropped to his knees at the water's edge. "Like a this," he said. "I'm a tie right here, da fish swim right in. Some net, hey?"

He looked over his shoulder and saw Posy. She was white and out of breath. "Connie!" she cried. "I don't know where you are. I'm scaring." She snatched at my hand, too relieved, too wrought up, to look at my revealing face. "Come along outa here," she said. Then, remembering her manners, "Hello, Mr. deRocca."

She yanked me back to the row. "You crazy," she scolded me. "What you think, you go down there with deRocca? I'm telling you he's liking the girl."

"You said I was just a kid. That's what you said," I repeated.

"I know," she said. "Well, I'm crazy. Just as soon Chuck he tell me you down here, I'm knowing I'm crazy. You no kid, not for looks.

No more. Was a little while ago, now no more. Mother of God, I'm scaring." She paused, momentarily suspicious. "What you going down in there with deRocca for?"

"He said he was going to show me his catfish net."

"Ha, I bet! You poor kid, you got no sense. What he say? He talk dirty?"

"No," I replied with perfect truth. "He talked just as nice as you and Mrs. Grimes."

"Thanks God," said Posy, over and over again. "Thanks God."

In the unpleasant shock of nearly being caught out, all the new feeling that I had learned—the lovely, soft, flowing, flowering openness—was driven back in me, and the present moment closed above it so completely that the afternoon might have been lived years before, or not at all, by anything I felt in myself. Instead, I was troubled by an unwilling anger against Posy, as if she were making a disproportionate fuss.

Something of this she must have felt, or perhaps she now decided that my unwary innocence had been scolded long enough, for she took my hand, smiling again, as if, for her, too, the incident had suddenly dropped away out of sight.

"Come now," she said. "Is early yet, you don't got to going home, come now down to the house. We don't say nothing from this to Mrs. Grimes."

"No, Posy, no, I've got to get home," I said.

All the way home, I pedalled hard, as if I were very late—so hard that there was no room in me for anything else. Even before I saw the letters lying on the hall rug, where they had fallen from the mail slit in the door, I could tell from the silence that the house was empty. I stood in the sun that poured in at the open doorway, absorbing gratefully the quality of an empty house. I had not realized at all, as I forced myself home, faster and faster, how I would need, once I had got there, to be alone. I shut my eyes and sighed heavily, feeling the silence, the aloneness all through me like a merciful, unexpected blessing.

What had happened that afternoon, what had really happened? It wasn't only that I had let Mr. deRocca kiss me and touch me like that. It was something that had happened in me. There was something in me—and in the world, too—that I had never known was there before, something powerful and lovely, something powerful and new.

I stood there alone in the quiet house, in the sunshine, with my eyes closed. "I wish," I thought slowly, "that Posy hadn't come. I wish . . ."

Suddenly, I knew that I had begun to be bad right there in Mr. deRocca's front yard, before we had ever gone down to the creek. I knew that I had been bad all along, terribly bad. Fear and guilt rose in me like a storm, shaking my body until my teeth chattered and I had to sit on the bottom step of the stairs and lean against the wall to hold myself still.

"If Posy knew," I thought, "if she knew about me, if she knew what I did, I'd die. I should die, I'd die."

Aunt Elsa found me like that when she came in a few minutes later. "Why, Connie!" she cried. "What is it, dear? You're sick."

"I got a chill," I said. "Just right now."

"Let me hang up my coat, dear," she said, "and I'll get you right into bed. Why, you poor baby!"

I let her help me up the stairs. I clung to her motherly warmth all the way, hungry for it, like a child that has been lost and found again. "Oh, Aunt Elsa," I cried. "I'm so glad you're home." And her gentle voice soothed me again and again. "There, dear, there. You're going to be all right. There, poor little girl. Aunt Elsa'll put you to bed. Yes, she will. Of course she will."

In the complex agony of the moment, I was broken wide open. She's real, too, I thought in slow wonder; Aunt Elsa is real, too. She was my mother's sister.

I caught at her light, smooth dress, hiding my face in it. She smelled nice, clean and fresh with a light perfume. I let my head fall against her shoulder, and it was soft and firm, comforting, comforting.

"Oh, Aunt Elsa," I cried, wondering because it was true, because it had not been true before, at all, and now it was wholly true. "Aunt Elsa, I love you."

That is the story, and that is all. When I woke in the morning, the ecstasy and the shame alike were gone. I had shut my mind upon them, as I had learned earlier to shut it upon grief and loss.

Oddly enough—for the defense mechanism seldom works that way—I still liked Mr. deRocca. Apparently, his attempted seduction had been quite impersonal, for, as I used to pass his yard, walking up the row to Posy's house in the warm, dusty August afternoons, he would always wave his little paw at me and say, "Hi ya, kid," amiably, but with no attempt to detain me.

For my own part, I always felt a tingling as I passed him; not enough to be unpleasant—just a sort of shy, quickening self-consciousness. It made me avoid his face as I replied, "Hello, Mr. de-Rocca." My voice, as I spoke, was always a trifle breathless. I told myself that it was funny how I hardly remembered that afternoon by the creek at all. But as I passed his house, I always stood up straight and moved slowly, and tried to look grownup.

A WINTER IN THE COUNTRY

❖

ROBERT M. COATES

O LD MR. SHELTON had been sick for some time before the Harrises heard of it, and at first it seemed there was little they could do to help him. That year the Harrises had decided to spend the winter in the country, and it had turned out to be an even pleasanter experience than they had anticipated. There had been a gradual draining away of people from the summer residences scattered through the valley, a slackening of traffic along the valley roads; trade fell off at the I.G.A. store in the village, where the Harrises did their marketing. By November, the town garage took to closing early; except on Saturdays and Sundays, it was shut by six o'clock and Gus Biddle, its proprietor, spent his evenings at home.

As the frosts struck in and the earth grew hard, everything seemed to settle down; even the Harrises found themselves travelling about less than formerly. To be sure, the snow never quite reached the paralyzing depths they had expected, but from December on there was usually enough of it to make the going difficult, particularly on the rutted dirt road where the Harrises' place lay. Then, too, there was little reason for driving out anyway. Expecting blizzards, the Harrises had made elaborate preparations for them, laying in turnips and potatoes, apples and cider by the barrelful, hams and bacon and cauliflower, and though the great storms failed to materialize, they took a peculiar pleasure out of dining off their own stocked larder, listening contentedly to the wind in the bare maple outside and enjoying their solitude. There were days on end when the only car to come past was the mailman's; the mutter of his old Buick as it came shoving down the road, the sharp slap of the mailbox door, and the sudden roar of his motor, the clack of chains as he got under way again came to be an important event in the chronology of their days.

It was the mailman, Bert Giddings, who told Mr. Harris about the old man's illness. There had been a fall of snow the night before, and Mr. Harris was out shovelling a path to the garage when Bert's car came by. Mr. Harris went out to meet it. "How's the road?" he said. "I've got to go down to the city tomorrow."

"You'll need chains," Bert said. " 'Tain't the snow. But there's spots where there's ice beneath, and when you hit them you lose traction." He was a stout, red-faced man with gray hair and a gray mustache. He handed over the Harrises' *Times* and their packet of letters and put the car in gear. But he didn't let up the clutch immediately. He sat there for a moment, staring out through the windshield at the road ahead. Then he jerked his head back in the direction he had come. "Old man Shelton's in a pretty bad way, I guess," he said.

Mr. Harris expressed his surprise. "Is he?" he said. "I didn't know that." The Sheltons were an elderly couple who lived in a rather ramshackle old place farther up the road, and the Harrises had encountered him three or four times in the course of the summer. Tall and thin and white-haired, he had the quick, forward-stepping, free stride of an Indian; though he had never spoken to them or they to him, they had got into the habit of nodding to each other as they passed. "What's the matter with him?" Mr. Harris asked.

"Can't say. He's just getting old, I guess. And when they're old, it's the winter that gets them." Bert glanced at Mr. Harris. "Doctor's been up two or three times this week, they tell me. He comes in this way."

"I guess I just didn't see him," Mr. Harris said. He felt a little embarrassed. He knew that a true countryman would have noticed the passing of any strange car and would probably have found some way of identifying it, too. Bert was staring out through the windshield again. "Yes, he's pretty bad, I guess," he said again. "And with his wife just about as old as he is . . ." He didn't say anything more, but Mr. Harris felt a slight shock run through him. Partly it was caused by a sudden picture of the little house far up the valley and a realization of how helpless an old man and woman would be there, alone, in the winter; partly it was because he had only just now understood what it was that Bert was driving at. "Well, I'm sorry to hear that," he said, somewhat fumblingly. "I didn't know. I'll have to go up to see him. See what we can do."

"It'll be appreciated," Bert said. He was letting in the clutch as he spoke and his face had reddened a little. "The folks in town'll do what they can. But it's kind of a long ways up from the village. . . .

If you could just look in there once in a while." The car was moving away now. Mr. Harris watched it go, the rear chains flicking up little clods of packed snow against its broad black back as it swayed away down the white road and around the bend.

That afternoon he went up to see the Sheltons. He walked, because he wasn't sure he'd find room to turn his car at their place, and though it wasn't yet four o'clock when he got there, the sun had already set behind the ridge at the west of the valley; the house, with its sagging porch and its walls almost bare of paint, looked chill and desolate in the deepening shadows. He found the old couple in the kichen, and Mr. Shelton, who was sitting by the stove with his legs wrapped in an old brown blanket, recognized him at once.

"You're the young man that took the Mitchell place, ain't ye?" he said. Illness had thinned his face somewhat and he needed a haircut, and the combination of the long, bony, wasted face and the flare of white hair above it gave him a kind of demoniac look. He looked like a witch, or a magician. His blue eyes glittered and his big-knuckled hands gripped the chair arms tensely, as if he were ready to pounce. Mr. Harris, who had long passed the age when he expected to be called a young man any more, felt a little confused. The old man gave him no time to think. "What ye figure to do with it? Farm it?" he demanded. He had a high, almost angry-sounding voice. In all the time Mr. Harris had spent in the country, Mr. Shelton was the first man he'd encountered who had what people usually referred to as a Yankee twang. But he didn't drawl in the way that Yankees were supposed to do. He spoke rapidly.

"I—well," Mr. Harris said. He had brought a bottle of sherry along with him and he put it down on a table near his chair. "I thought you might enjoy a little of this now and then," he said. The old man glanced at the bottle and nodded, then his eyes came back to Mr. Harris. Mrs. Shelton, a short, plump woman, was peeling some potatoes at the sink. "I guess Mr. Harris wouldn't have much time for farming," she said. "His business is in the city, I take it."

"Yes, that's it," said Mr. Harris. "Or partly it. I do have to go down to the city fairly often. And then, too, I just don't know anything about farming, either." Then a sudden gush of frankness came over him. "But I feel sort of foolish about it, you know. Having all that land and letting it go wild. Seems that something ought to be done with it."

The old man nodded. "Ninety, ninety-five acres. Good land, too."

He put no particular inflection on the words. But Mr. Harris, who really had developed a sense of guilt over his untended fields, could feel himself flushing. The old man didn't seem to notice. He gave a short, dry laugh. "I ought to know, times I've helped work it. That was in old man Mitchell's day. Not the Mitchell you bought from—he's a footless fellow, we're well rid of him—it's his father I'm thinking of. Bald Mitchell, everybody used to call him. I'd help him with his ploughing and planting, times he needed it, and he'd help with mine. Tobacco was the main crop in them days, and they's one field you got, to the north of the house there, where it runs down to the brook—it was a poor year when he didn't get close to two thousand pounds an acre out of that plot." He pushed himself back in his chair and closed his eyes; it occurred to Mr. Harris that perhaps he was getting tired. "Well, they's many ways of life, and farming is only one of them. Maybe it's just as well you ain't mixed up in it. Can't say as I ever got much out of it, 'cept hard work. Margaret," he said abruptly, "can't ye dig up a corkscrew or something? Seems we might give the visitor a taste of his own wine."

And though Mr. Harris protested that the sherry had been meant for Mr. Shelton, the old man insisted that he have a glass of it before he left.

That was the first of a good many visits the Harrises paid the old man, either singly or together, in the course of the winter. No one seemed to know what was really the matter with him, and when Mr. Harris inquired of the doctor he got little concrete information. The doctor was a fierce-faced old fellow with a bold gray eye and a beard cut vaguely in the "professional" manner of a quarter-century ago, and he wasn't the man the Harrises used when they needed medical attention; there was a younger man in a neighboring village whom they favored, and some slight resentment on this score may have stiffened the doctor's attitude. At any rate, he eyed Mr. Harris somewhat challengingly. "Matter?" he cried. "He's old. That's the main thing that's troubling him." He had a resonant voice of considerable carrying power, and since they had met on the pathway in front of the Sheltons' house, Mr. Harris couldn't help glancing up to see if anyone was listening. "He knows," the doctor went on, no less loudly. "He knows, or I wouldn't be talking to you like this. He caught a cold back there in November and he ain't come back from it like he ought to. And his kidneys—but they've always been a trouble to him. He's old, that's the main thing the

matter with him. Wait twenty years, young man, and you'll find out
yourself what it's like to get through a winter." And with that he
stamped away through the snow to his car.

This scant information was of little comfort to the Harrises, and
to Mrs. Harris it was particularly distressing. The old man's cold,
in her mind, was instantly translated into pneumonia, and when
Mr. Harris demurred at so summary an interpretation of the doctor's remarks, she exploded. "Well, if he hasn't got it now, he will
have it, with the drafts and the cold in that old house. And with no
one but that poor old woman to take care of him. No, Fred," she
said, "we've just got to get him out of there. We've got to get him
to a hospital.

"And if we wait too long," she went on, "it'll be too late to move
him. He'll get weaker and weaker. He'll just die there. Why, last
time I was up there my feet were just freezing, with the drafts coming in through the windows or through the floors, or wherever. You
ask him"—she meant, Mr. Harris understood, the doctor—"what's
his name? Kent? Well, next time you see him, you ask him. Ask him
if we can't get the old man out to a hospital, somewhere where he'll
get decent care."

In a sense, Mr. Harris agreed with her, and a few days later he
managed to waylay the doctor on the road. He felt the embarrassment natural to a man who brings up a subject that has already
earned him a rebuff, and though the doctor had lowered the car
window obligingly to talk with him, he kept tapping the accelerator occasionally, so that the motor alternately raced and subsided
in a way that added to Mr. Harris's discomfiture. Perhaps it was
only a nervous habit the doctor had developed, but the recurrent
roar of the motor and the clouds of dense, steamy vapor the ex-
haust sent up in the icy air gave a curious quality of almost fatal ur-
gency to the interview. The doctor, immune in his cushioned interior, Mr. Harris, arguing futilely outside—it was then, Mr. Harris
later realized, that he first understood that the old man might
really die.

The doctor, however, listened carefully. Once he interrupted.
That was when Mr. Harris mentioned the hospital, and at the word
he glanced up quickly. "Try to get him there," he said. "No, young
man," and then, as he saw that he was interrupting, he bent his
head soberly to listen again. "I just wanted to say," Mr. Harris con-
cluded, "well, I wanted to say what expenses there were—we'd be
willing to pay the expenses."

The doctor waited a moment, as if to make sure that Mr. Harris had nothing further to say. "Well, young man, I know how you feel," he said. He tapped the accelerator, then he looked up at Mr. Harris. "I guess I was kind of hasty the other day. Sam Shelton and I have known each other since—well, since long before I took up doctoring, and ever since then it's been me he turned to when he needed attention. I'd been trying to talk some sense into him—at the least enough so he'd stay abed when I told him to. And I wasn't sure I'd succeeded. I guess when I met you I just boiled over. Now, for what you were saying. The hospital."

But despite the doctor's attempt to maintain a judicial attitude, it had been clear from the start that he was against the Harrises' proposal, and what he said later only confirmed it. To move the old man at that time would be dangerous; even in an ambulance he would be too weak for the journey. Moreover, the shock would be something to consider, both moral and physical; country people, the doctor said, didn't feel the same way about hospitals that city folk did. "Take your city man and you tell him he's got to go to the hospital and he'll think nothing of it. But tell that to Sam Shelton there and he'll think it just about means you've given up all hope for him. It's like telling him to get ready to die." It was clear too that the doctor wasn't used to being interrupted, and when Mr. Harris broke in once or twice, his temper grew visibly shorter. In the end something dangerously close to a personal note intervened. "But wouldn't he be warmer, more comfortable?" Mr. Harris was saying, still arguing for hospitalization. "That house—"

"That house!" the doctor retorted. All along, Mr. Harris had sensed an undercurrent of impatience in the doctor's manner, as if he considered the whole thing a piece of citified meddling on the Harrises' part and something he shouldn't be called on to waste time with at all. Now that feeling broke partly from concealment. "That's the house he was born in. He's lived there all his life and I guess if he has his way, he'll die there. It may not be as warm or as tight as some that've been taken over and remodelled out of all semblance. But it's his house. Take that into consideration." The doctor by this time was sitting hard back in his seat, his hands clutching the wheel like a man who holds the reins on a spirited horse, and the motor was roaring. "You can't buy him well!" he cried. "If you could, there's plenty around here that'd be willing to foot the bill. Get that in your mind, young man, and you may be more help to him."

He drove off, leaving Mr. Harris baffled and resentful, and the
fact that a short time later the doctor hailed him on the road in an
obvious attempt to make amends didn't help matters any. Though
the doctor apologized—"I blew up there the other day. I guess I been
worried more than I'd like to confess about Sam"—he did so in what
was to Mr. Harris an offensively breezy and confident manner, as
if his short temper were something quite beyond his own control-
ling, a kind of infirmity which he had only to mention to win
complete forgiveness.

But what is it that makes an old man die in the winter? As soon
as she could, Mrs. Harris dragged her husband off to consult her
own doctor, a young man named Pendleton, about the old man's
predicament. It was not an entirely satisfactory interview; Dr.
Pendleton had a determined urbanity of manner that was, in its
way, almost as disagreeable to Mr. Harris as Dr. Kent's tartness had
been, and what light he cast on their problem was discouraging
rather than helpful. Somewhat to their surprise—Mrs. Harris, in
particular, had been convinced that all this was pure country tradition and therefore nonsense—he too mentioned the winter as
a factor to be reckoned with. "Watch your churchyard," he said.
"Notice how many more burials there'll be in the next month or
two than there were in the summer. It's the dying season, all right."
The reasons, he said, were simple. Old age, in a way, was itself a
kind of disease, and for age there is no cure, only palliatives:
warmth, sunlight, rest, comfort. "It's precisely these things, of
course, that winter takes away from the patient."
Pendleton refused to accept this, however, as an argument for
hospitalization. Instead, he seized the chance to pay tribute to Dr.
Kent. "Kent may seem old-fashioned," he said. "But he's a good
man just the same. And in this case he knows his patient; if he says
the old codger should stay put, he probably has his reasons." Pendleton was a plump, brisk man of a little over thirty, and he was clearly
trying to be helpful; Mr. Harris would have been hard put to it
to explain why he felt himself stiffening when he heard old Mr.
Shelton referred to as a codger. "His name's Shelton," he said.
"Samuel Shelton."
The doctor glanced at him. "Oh, Shelton," he said agreeably.
"No. I don't know him. And as I say, with Kent there, it'd be foolish
for me to attempt a diagnosis. But just to give you an idea of the

general picture—" He glanced at Mr. Harris again, drew a scratch-pad nearer, and scrawled a few lines upon it. "Look," he said. "Here's the heart."

It was the heart, Mr. Harris gathered, that was at the base of most of the troubles of old age—the heart that begins its functioning even before birth and stops only with death, and that meantime must meet and compensate for all the strains the body puts on it, if the body itself is to survive. "And believe me, as time goes on it has plenty to compensate for. Your liver gets a little sluggish, or your kidneys—well, that way you're heading for Bright's disease and uremia, and if you get that far, there's small hope for you. But meanwhile it's the heart that takes up the slack. Or your lungs get congested, and there's your dyspnea, or shortness of breath." With a kind of aseptic cheerfulness that Mr. Harris found somehow chilling, the doctor panted a little, illustrating the symptoms. "And why? It's because the old heart just isn't pumping the blood in and out of the lungs fast enough. But it makes a fine fallow field for pneumonia, if conditions are right. And meantime you've got hypertension, or hardening of the arteries. Well, the time comes when the heart just gets tired of it all. It slows down, it decompensates, as we call it." Outside the consulting room a bell had sounded, indicating that the street door of the doctor's office had opened and a patient was entering the waiting room. The doctor slashed a swift line across the diagram he had been drawing.

"That's your crisis," he said. "And there's little enough anyone can do about it. It's the heart that decides the matter. If it takes up the job again, if it compensates—well, you go on living. If it stops, why, you stop too. I'm afraid I haven't been able to be much help to you," he went on as the Harrises stood up to go. "And I purposely haven't asked for the old man's symptoms. After all, it's Kent's case, and I know the man's in good hands. But you might just tell me: Is he pale? Lips blue? Breathing difficult? The feet and hands cold, maybe puffy a little?" Though Mr. Harris had an odd feeling, as if he were signing old Mr. Shelton's death warrant in doing so, he was forced to admit that the old man was definitely paler and his lips, if not blue, had certainly lost color.

The doctor nodded. "I'll wager it's the heart that Kent is watching, as much as anything else. But don't worry about it," he went on. They were out in the waiting room and he was already turning toward the next visitor, a heavy-featured woman in a long black coat. "The man's in good hands. If anyone can pull him through, our friend can. . . . Good day, Mrs. Bassett. I see you're still around and about. That's encouraging."

Mrs. Harris summed up the feelings of both herself and her husband when, after a period of silence, she remarked midway of the drive home, "I suppose it's all true, what he said. But I wish we hadn't gone."

Though at the time Mr. Harris agreed with her, in the end he was glad he had gone. He had learned what the old man's chief enemy was—the winter—and, as if to dramatize the struggle, as the winter deepened the old man's condition grew steadily graver. That first visit Mr. Harris had found Mr. Shelton in the kitchen, but in a short while the effort of sitting up became too much for him, and since he refused to spend his days in his bedroom upstairs—"Might's well put me in the grave and be done with it as shut me off all alone up there"—a place was found for him in a small room downstairs, off the kitchen.

The room was long and narrow, with only one window, and it had probably been designed for use as a storeroom or perhaps for what, in the days before refrigeration, was called a winter pantry. But with the door to the kitchen left open it was warm enough, and after an old sofa had been moved in—Mr. Harris at one end and Mrs. Shelton straining at the other—and a chair or two, and a table for the bedside, it served well enough as a sickroom. Its one fault was that it was dark. Since it lay at the rear of the house, it was cut off both from the morning sun and from the broad valley view the front rooms afforded, and its one small window was still further shadowed by the slope of the ridge rising steeply behind the house. And the sun sets early in the winter; there were times, coming in in the late afternoon and finding the old man lying, wrapped in his faded brown blanket, motionless and half dozing—there were times when, to Mr. Harris, he looked more like an animal that had crawled into its burrow to die than like anything else.

Perhaps because the room itself was so confining, the old man's thoughts ranged widely. "I been thinkin'," he'd say, directly Mr. Harris appeared, and what followed might be anything, from his opinion of something the doctor had told him the day before to a tale of a coon-hunting excursion he had made forty years before. "And when he reached for his gun the gun went off, and when he hopped back from that he knocked over the cider jug and broke *that*. We come home mighty thirsty from that night's outing. But we brought back four coon. Jed Folsom that was that wasted the cider, and he always was a clumsy feller. Lived down past the Furness place till he burned the house down, bumpin' into a lamp; you can still see the house foundations, 'longside the road. Or you could," he added, looking up at Mr. Harris uncertainly, for by now he was living in such a mixture of the past and the present that at times he became confused. "I ain't been out that end of the valley much lately. Likely it's all tumbled in by now, and overgrown."

As the winter wore on and the days grew darker, the old man's perceptions darkened too; for a while it was as if Mr. Harris, by his presence, only brought to the surface, and then only momentarily, the wild flood of reminiscence that was streaming continuously, incoherently, through the old man's mind. "Look, now!" he would say. "I told ye!" And from his eyes, staring hard and angrily, Mr. Harris would know as he entered the room that he had been cast in the part of some hired hand or farm companion long vanished and perhaps dead years ago. "Let them calves into the meadow and them jumpin'? Round 'em back to the barn, I tell ye! Ah, there's one down now. And still jumpin'." Then his gaze would clear a little. "Young man!" he would say, but still sternly, for though by now he had settled on Mr. Harris's identity, his emotions would still be aroused. "If ye're goin' to raise cattle . . . What ye plannin' to raise 'em for, market or milkin'? You got good enough land for either. But tobacco's your crop; put tobacco down there by the brook. . . . Well, young man," he would say, and by his firmness of tone Mr. Harris would know that this time the old man had fought his way back to the present again. The pale face, almost hatchet-thin now, would light up in a smile. "You know, I been thinkin' . . ."

The old man liked Mr. Harris, but he had a tart humor of his own, and Mr. Harris didn't always escape the scrape of it. On one occasion—it was in the midst of one of those periods of clear, brilliant weather that come so pleasantly in midwinter, and the snows had melted—Mr. Harris had noticed a field of green halfway up the other side of the valley. And if it was green, it was obviously something growing; in his innocence, Mr. Harris applied to it the only term he had heard of that might fit the circumstances. He decided it was winter wheat, and when he got to the Sheltons' he told the old man about it.

As if in response to the sunlight outside, Mr. Shelton had been perkier than usual that day—his health, Mr. Harris had noted, always seemed to follow the weather—and when he heard "winter wheat" he burst out derisively. "Winter wheat!" he cried, and beneath his laughter Mr. Harris sensed something sharper. What had often been tolerance in the old man's attitude toward Mr. Harris's ignorance of country matters had turned close to contempt. "And ye've lived here how long now—three years? And ye still don't know one crop from the other? Wheat, sir, 's a crop that's planted in the fall, but it don't sprout till spring. And it's rare enough here nowadays, anyway. What ye saw there was rye, most likely." He raised himself up and made a drinking gesture. "You know, if you wait long enough, ye get it in a bottle. That's Art Pritchard's land you were lookin' at, and Art's a careful farmer. He'd put in the rye for a cover crop, to hold down the soil and strengthen it. Margaret!" And to make Mr. Harris's humiliation more complete he called in his wife to tell her the story all over again. "Winter wheat!"

But a day or two later fresh snows came and the green field was covered; the old man sank again. Through it all there was little enough the Harrises could do. Mrs. Harris made soups and broths and baked innocuous cakes; Mr. Harris chopped wood and split up kindling and tried in what other ways he could think of to ease Mrs. Shelton's labors, for though she never complained, it was clear that the strain of caring for the old man, added to her worries about him, had taxed her strength nearly to its limits. Since the Sheltons had no phone, the Harrises could relay messages for them to the doctor or to their friends in the village. But even these attentions were conditioned by the Harrises' own routine of life. Mr. Harris had occasional trips to the city to make, weekend guests came and went, there was a scattering of friends, staying on through the winter, who lived near enough to make dinner engagements possible. Driving out on such occasions, the Harrises always took the road past the Sheltons' place. It was the long way round, in a sense, with a mile or two more of dirt road to be covered before they reached the highway. But it gave them a chance to stop, in passing, to say hello to the couple; when they came back home, late at night—late enough so that most of the farms they passed would be still and dark—they would watch for their lights to strike in at the Sheltons'.

There was always a night lamp left burning there. Mr. Harris never quite realized till long afterward how much meaning that dim point of light had taken on for him, and, pocketed away in the darkness, how deeply it symbolized the winter—the power of winter and its relentlessness, its weight and its freezing pressure—and the feeble fierceness of the old man's struggle against it. In the face of such antagonists, the Harrises' efforts seemed small indeed; it was bitter comfort when, just after one such excursion, the minister called— more or less, Mr. Harris gathered, on behalf of the village—to thank them for the help they had rendered the old couple.

A day came, however, or a night, when the Harrises were to be of more service, after all. This was in the darkest part of winter, which is not, though the almanac may say so, at the solstice in December; time lags, and the earth is huge, and the sun must go well past its southernmost trending before the short days can have cast their deepest melancholy and the long nights their most freezing bite. It was midway in February when, one night at about three o'clock, the Harrises were awakened by a pounding at their door. Mr. Harris went down, to find Mrs. Shelton, near collapse, in a coat and a skirt and a pair of men's boots and with a lantern in her hand. "It's Sam," she said weakly. "Sam." For a while she could hardly speak; how she had managed to walk the long mile from her home, in the night, was something that, for the moment, the Harrises could only wonder at.

They brought her into the living room and wrapped her in a blanket; even then she was chattering mostly about Sam: he'd been taken bad, he'd been thrashing about in the bed, he was worse than he'd even been before, he could hardly breathe, and he wanted the doctor. By that time Mrs. Harris was fumbling through the telephone directory; Mr. Harris was getting into a pair of pants and a shirt. He waited till he heard Dr. Kent's voice over the wire. "Get him up in the bed. Let him breathe. Put some pillows behind him," the doctor's voice said. "Make some tea for him, maybe. Make him comfortable." Seizing Mrs. Shelton's lantern, Mr. Harris plunged out into the night. The rest, for him, was turmoil.

Mrs. Shelton, on leaving her house, had jammed a couple of chairs against the sofa, hoping to keep the old man in bed. He had extricated himself, however, and when Mr. Harris arrived he was standing shivering in the kitchen. Oddly, he recognized Mr. Harris. "What you doing here, young man?" he demanded. "Where's Margaret? Where's she gone?" As gently as he could, Mr. Harris got him back in bed, put a kettle on the stove for tea; then, remembering the doctor's other instructions, he ran upstairs to the bedroom for more pillows.

With the pillows propped behind him, the old man felt better. But his breathing was still terribly hard and labored; at times he would writhe and mumble, and then sweat—a sweat that, when Mr. Harris wiped it away, left the skin feeling chill and clammy—would run streaming. Mostly he lay motionless, his eyes bright and set and staring, his whole conscious will bent solely to the effort of drawing in air to the lungs, and expelling it, and drawing in air again. And Mr. Harris couldn't help noticing the symptoms: the pale, blue-tinted lips, the cold hands. "It's the heart," he told himself, and when Dr. Kent arrived, he asked him, "Is it the heart?"

The doctor had been over an hour getting there, for his car had skidded into a drift just beyond the Harrises' and stalled there; he had walked the rest of the way. "Well, Sam!" he cried, as he came striding in. "Always pick the worst time for things, now, don't you? Gettin' a man out of bed on a night like this." The old man nodded and tried to smile, but he couldn't speak; he was in one of his gasping spells. "But we'll soon fix you up," the doctor went on, with a cheeriness that, clumsy as it was, brought a kind of sanity into the situation. He was already measuring out a spoonful of greenish liquid from a bottle in his case. "Take that now. That's tincture of digitalis. It's bitter, but it ought to bring you some comfort." Later, in the kitchen, he answered Mr. Harris's question. "Yes," he said. "It's the heart. Like with all folks his age, more or less."

"Will he live?"

"I hope so," Kent said. "We'll know more by tomorrow, maybe, and more still the day after that." Suddenly he looked hard at Mr. Harris. "You did your best for him, anyway. Now I'll try to do mine."

The doctor's best, in this case, was enough. Slowly, painfully, in the weeks that followed, the old man grew better; like the year that had reached its depth of darkness and now turned upward, he did not die. Almost imperceptibly, the days grew longer, and as the sun rose higher its warmth became more evident. Snowdrifts shrivelled to crusts and the crusts themselves frayed away; crows appeared in numbers, and even a few other birds; the brook, that had been frozen and almost forgotten, made itself heard again. A day came when the wind stayed persistently in the south; that was the thaw, and with it the last of the frost welled up out of the ground, releasing smells that had lain locked there all winter, of manure, and warm earth, and leafage. The old man had been out of bed for some time by now, but he had still been confined to the kitchen; now, walking

up to the Sheltons' one day, Mr. Harris was surprised to find him sitting out on the porch.

"Been indoors long enough," he cried as Mr. Harris came up the
path. "I figured what I needed was sun." There was still a little snow
left here and there in the hollows, but the rest of the ground was
bare; with his white hair glistening and his shoulders wrapped in the
old brown blanket, the old man looked, at the moment, like a piece
of the earth itself. Suddenly he reached out and seized Mr. Harris's
hand. "Look," he said, and he pointed across the valley. "That green
field over there, that's the one ye was talkin' about, ain't it? Well,
that's rye, and it's time ye learned it. Look beyond there, that patch
up there nearer the woods. That's green too. It's lighter, kind of, but
it's green."

At that distance the patch he was speaking of seemed mainly
brown, but there was the faintest possible tinge of green overlaying
it, like a haze or an almost transparent emerald curtain.

Mr. Harris saw it, and said so.

"Well, that's wheat. Art Pritchard always puts in some for his own
use. Just sproutin', and it's pretty too, ain't it?" Gently, affectionately, he gave Mr. Harris's hand a little shake. "I'll make a farmer
out of you yet, young man, now won't I?" he said. Mr. Harris wasn't
at all sure of that outcome, but at the moment he felt happy enough,
and contented, to smile and nod his head.

THE CATBIRD SEAT

❖

JAMES THURBER

M R. MARTIN bought the pack of Camels on Monday night in the
most crowded cigar store on Broadway. It was theatre time
and seven or eight men were buying cigarettes. The clerk didn't
even glance at Mr. Martin, who put the pack in his overcoat pocket
and went out. If any of the staff at F & S had seen him buy the cigarettes, they would have been astonished, for it was generally known
that Mr. Martin did not smoke, and never had. No one saw him.

It was just a week to the day since Mr. Martin had decided to rub
out Mrs. Ulgine Barrows. The term "rub out" pleased him because
it suggested nothing more than the correction of an error—in this
case an error of Mr. Fitweiler. Mr. Martin had spent each night of
the past week working out his plan and examining it. As he walked
home now he went over it again. For the hundredth time he resented
the element of imprecision, the margin of guesswork that entered
into the business. The project as he had worked it out was casual and
bold, the risks were considerable. Something might go wrong anywhere along the line. And therein lay the cunning of his scheme. No
one would ever see in it the cautious, painstaking hand of Erwin
Martin, head of the filing department at F & S, of whom Mr. Fitweiler had once said, "Man is fallible but Martin isn't." No one
would see his hand, that is, unless it were caught in the act.

Sitting in his apartment, drinking a glass of milk, Mr. Martin reviewed his case against Mrs. Ulgine Barrows, as he had every night
for seven nights. He began at the beginning. Her quacking voice and
braying laugh had first profaned the halls of F & S on March 7, 1941
(Mr. Martin had a head for dates). Old Roberts, the personnel chief,
had introduced her as the newly appointed special adviser to the
president of the firm, Mr. Fitweiler. The woman had appalled Mr.
Martin instantly, but he hadn't shown it. He had given her his dry
hand, a look of studious concentration, and a faint smile. "Well,"
she had said, looking at the papers on his desk, "are you lifting the

oxcart out of the ditch?" As Mr. Martin recalled that moment, over his milk, he squirmed slightly. He must keep his mind on her crimes as a special adviser, not on her peccadillos as a personality. This he found difficult to do, in spite of entering an objection and sustaining it. The faults of the woman as a woman kept chattering on in his mind like an unruly witness. She had, for almost two years now, baited him. In the halls, in the elevator, even in his own office, into which she romped now and then like a circus horse, she was constantly shouting these silly questions at him. "Are you lifting the oxcart out of the ditch? Are you tearing up the pea patch? Are you hollering down the rain barrel? Are you scraping around the bottom of the pickle barrel? Are you sitting in the catbird seat?"

It was Joey Hart, one of Mr. Martin's two assistants, who had explained what the gibberish meant. "She must be a Dodger fan," he had said. "Red Barber announces the Dodger games over the radio and he uses those expressions—picked 'em up down South." Joey had gone on to explain one or two. "Tearing up the pea patch" meant going on a rampage; "sitting in the catbird seat" meant sitting pretty, like a batter with three balls and no strikes on him. Mr. Martin dismissed all this with an effort. It had been annoying, it had driven him near to distraction, but he was too solid a man to be moved to murder by anything so childish. It was fortunate, he reflected as he passed on to the important charges against Mrs. Barrows, that he had stood up under it so well. He had maintained always an outward appearance of polite tolerance. "Why, I even believe you like the woman," Miss Paird, his other assistant, had once said to him. He had simply smiled.

A gavel rapped in Mr. Martin's mind and the case proper was resumed. Mrs. Ulgine Barrows stood charged with willful, blatant, and persistent attempts to destroy the efficiency and system of F & S. It was competent, material, and relevant to review her advent and rise to power. Mr. Martin had got the story from Miss Paird, who seemed always able to find things out. According to her, Mrs. Barrows had met Mr. Fitweiler at a party, where she had rescued him from the embraces of a powerfully built drunken man who had mistaken the president of F & S for a famous retired Middle Western football coach. She had led him to a sofa and somehow worked upon him a monstrous magic. The aging gentleman had jumped to the conclusion there and then that this was a woman of singular attainments, equipped to bring out the best in him and in the firm. A week later he had introduced her into F & S as his special adviser. On that day confusion got its foot in the door. After Miss Tyson, Mr. Brundage, and Mr. Bartlett had been fired and Mr. Munson had taken his hat and stalked out, mailing in his resignation later, old Roberts had been emboldened to speak to Mr. Fitweiler. He mentioned that Mr. Munson's department had been "a little disrupted" and hadn't they perhaps better resume the old system there? Mr. Fitweiler had said certainly not. He had the greatest faith in Mrs. Barrows' ideas. "They require a little seasoning, a little seasoning, is all," he had added. Mr. Roberts had given it up. Mr. Martin reviewed in detail all the changes wrought by Mrs. Barrows. She had begun chipping at the cornices of the firm's edifice and now she was swinging at the foundation stones with a pickaxe.

Mr. Martin came now, in his summing up, to the afternoon of Monday, November 2, 1942—just one week ago. On that day, at 3 P.M., Mrs. Barrows had bounced into his office. "Boo!" she had yelled. "Are you scraping around the bottom of the pickle barrel?" Mr. Martin had looked at her from under his green eyeshade, saying nothing. She had begun to wander about the office, taking it in with her great, popping eyes. "Do you really need *all* these filing cabinets?" she had demanded suddenly. Mr. Martin's heart had jumped. "Each of these files," he had said, keeping his voice even, "plays an indispensable part in the system of F & S." She had brayed at him, "Well, don't tear up the pea patch!" and gone to the door. From there she had bawled, "But you sure have got a lot of fine scrap in here!" Mr. Martin could no longer doubt that the finger was on his beloved department. Her pickaxe was on the upswing, poised for the first blow. It had not come yet; he had received no blue memo from the enchanted Mr. Fitweiler bearing nonsensical instructions deriving from the obscene woman. But there was no doubt in Mr. Martin's mind that one would be forthcoming. He must act quickly. Already a precious week had gone by. Mr. Martin stood up in his living room, still holding his milk glass. "Gentlemen of the jury," he said to himself, "I demand the death penalty for this horrible person."

The next day Mr. Martin followed his routine, as usual. He polished his glasses more often and once sharpened an already sharp pencil, but not even Miss Paird noticed. Only once did he catch sight of his victim; she swept past him in the hall with a patronizing "Hi!" At five-thirty he walked home, as usual, and had a glass of milk, as usual. He had never drunk anything stronger in his life—unless you could count ginger ale. The late Sam Schlosser, the S of F & S, had praised Mr. Martin at a staff meeting several years before for his temperate habits. "Our most efficient worker neither drinks nor smokes," he had said. "The results speak for themselves." Mr. Fitweiler had sat by, nodding approval.

Mr. Martin was still thinking about that red-letter day as he walked over to the Schrafft's on Fifth Avenue near Forty-sixth Street. He got there, as he always did, at eight o'clock. He finished his dinner and the financial page of the *Sun* at a quarter to nine, as he always did. It was his custom after dinner to take a walk. This time he walked down Fifth Avenue at a casual pace. His gloved hands felt moist and warm, his forehead cold. He transferred the Camels from his overcoat to a jacket pocket. He wondered, as he did so, if they did not represent an unnecessary note of strain. Mrs. Barrows smoked only Luckies. It was his idea to puff a few puffs on a Camel (after the rubbing-out), stub it out in the ashtray holding her lipstick-stained Luckies, and thus drag a small red herring across the trail. Perhaps it was not a good idea. It would take time. He might even choke, too loudly.

Mr. Martin had never seen the house on West Twelfth Street where Mrs. Barrows lived, but he had a clear enough picture of it. Fortunately, she had bragged to everybody about her ducky firstfloor apartment in the perfectly darling three-story red-brick. There would be no doorman or other attendants; just the tenants of the second and third floors. As he walked along, Mr. Martin realized that he would get there before nine-thirty. He had considered walking north on Fifth Avenue from Schrafft's to a point from which it would take him until ten o'clock to reach the house. At that hour people were less likely to be coming in or going out. But the procedure would have made an awkward loop in the straight thread of his casualness, and he had abandoned it. It was impossible to figure when people would be entering or leaving the house, anyway. There was a great risk at any hour. If he ran into anybody, he would simply have to place the rubbing-out of Ulgine Barrows in the inactive file forever. The same thing would hold true if there were someone in her apartment. In that case he would just say that he had been passing by, recognized her charming house, and thought to drop in.

It was eighteen minutes after nine when Mr. Martin turned into Twelfth Street. A man passed him, and a man and a woman, talking. There was no one within fifty paces when he came to the house, halfway down the block. He was up the steps and in the small vestibule in no time, pressing the bell under the card that said "Mrs. Ulgine Barrows." When the clicking in the lock started, he jumped forward against the door. He got inside fast, closing the door behind him. A bulb in a lantern hung from the hall ceiling on a chain seemed to give a monstrously bright light. There was nobody on the stair, which went up ahead of him along the left wall. A door opened down the hall in the wall on the right. He went toward it swiftly, on tiptoe.

"Well, for God's sake, look who's here!" bawled Mrs. Barrows, and her braying laugh rang out like the report of a shotgun. He rushed past her like a football tackle, bumping her. "Hey, quit shoving!" she said, closing the door behind them. They were in her living room, which seemed to Mr. Martin to be lighted by a hundred lamps. "What's after you?" she said. "You're as jumpy as a goat." He found he was unable to speak. His heart was wheezing in his throat. "I— yes," he finally brought out. She was jabbering and laughing as she started to help him off with his coat. "No, no," he said. "I'll put it here." He took it off and put it on a chair near the door. "Your hat and gloves, too," she said. "You're in a lady's house." He put his hat on top of the coat. Mrs. Barrows seemed larger than he had thought. He kept his gloves on. "I was passing by," he said. "I recognized—is there anyone here?" She laughed louder than ever. "No," she said, "we're all alone. You're as white as a sheet, you funny man. Whatever *has* come over you? I'll mix you a toddy." She started toward a door across the room. "Scotch-and-soda be all right? But say, you don't drink, do you?" She turned and gave him her amused look. Mr. Martin pulled himself together. "Scotch-and-soda will be all right," he heard himself say. He could hear her laughing in the kitchen.

Mr. Martin looked quickly around the living room for the weapon. He had counted on finding one there. There were andirons and a poker and something in a corner that looked like an Indian club. None of them would do. It couldn't be that way. He began to pace around. He came to a desk. On it lay a metal paper knife with an ornate handle. Would it be sharp enough? He reached for it and knocked over a small brass jar. Stamps spilled out of it and it fell to the floor with a clatter. "Hey," Mrs. Barrows yelled from the kitchen, "are you tearing up the pea patch?" Mr. Martin gave a strange laugh. Picking up the knife, he tried its point against his left wrist. It was blunt. It wouldn't do.

When Mrs. Barrows reappeared, carrying two highballs, Mr. Martin, standing there with his gloves on, became acutely conscious of the fantasy he had wrought. Cigarettes in his pocket, a drink prepared for him—it was all too grossly improbable. It was more than that; it was impossible. Somewhere in the back of his mind a vague idea stirred, sprouted. "For heaven's sake, take off those gloves," said

Mrs. Barrows. "I always wear them in the house," said Mr. Martin. The idea began to bloom, strange and wonderful. She put the glasses on a coffee table in front of a sofa and sat on the sofa. "Come over here, you odd little man," she said. Mr. Martin went over and sat beside her. It was difficult getting a cigarette out of the pack of Camels, but he managed it. She held a match for him, laughing. "Well," she said, handing him his drink, "this is perfectly marvellous. You with a drink and a cigarette."

Mr. Martin puffed, not too awkwardly, and took a gulp of the highball. "I drink and smoke all the time," he said. He clinked his glass against hers. "Here's nuts to that old windbag, Fitweiler," he said, and gulped again. The stuff tasted awful, but he made no grimace. "Really, Mr. Martin," she said, her voice and posture changing, "you are insulting our employer." Mrs. Barrows was now all special adviser to the president. "I am preparing a bomb," said Mr. Martin, "which will blow the old goat higher than hell." He had only had a little of the drink, which was not strong. It couldn't be that. "Do you take dope or something?" Mrs. Barrows asked coldly. "Heroin," said Mr. Martin. "I'll be coked to the gills when I bump that old buzzard off." "Mr. Martin!" she shouted, getting to her feet. "That will be all of that. You must go at once." Mr. Martin took another swallow of his drink. He tapped his cigarette out in the ashtray and put the pack of Camels on the coffee table. Then he got up. She stood glaring at him. He walked over and put on his hat and coat. "Not a word about this," he said, and laid an index finger against his lips. All Mrs. Barrows could bring out was "Really!" Mr. Martin put his hand on the doorknob. "I'm sitting in the catbird seat," he said. He stuck his tongue out at her and left. Nobody saw him go.

Mr. Martin got to his apartment, walking, well before eleven. No one saw him go in. He had two glasses of milk after brushing his teeth, and he felt elated. It wasn't tipsiness, because he hadn't been tipsy. Anyway, the walk had worn off all effects of the whiskey. He got in bed and read a magazine for a while. He was asleep before midnight.

Mr. Martin got to the office at eight-thirty the next morning, as usual. At a quarter to nine, Ulgine Barrows, who had never before arrived at work before ten, swept into his office. "I'm reporting to Mr. Fitweiler now!" she shouted. "If he turns you over to the police, it's no more than you deserve!" Mr. Martin gave her a look of shocked surprise. "I beg your pardon?" he said. Mrs. Barrows snorted and bounced out of the room, leaving Miss Paird and Joey Hart staring after her. "What's the matter with that old devil now?" asked Miss Paird. "I have no idea," said Mr. Martin, resuming his work. The other two looked at him and then at each other. Miss Paird got up and went out. She walked slowly past the closed door of Mr. Fitweiler's office. Mrs. Barrows was yelling inside, but she was not braying. Miss Paird could not hear what the woman was saying. She went back to her desk.

Forty-five minutes later, Mrs. Barrows left the president's office and went into her own, shutting the door. It wasn't until half an hour later that Mr. Fitweiler sent for Mr. Martin. The head of the filing department, neat, quiet, attentive, stood in front of the old man's desk. Mr. Fitweiler was pale and nervous. He took his glasses off and twiddled them. He made a small, bruffing sound in his throat. "Martin," he said, "you have been with us more than twenty years." "Twenty-two, sir," said Mr. Martin. "In that time," pursued the president, "your work and your—uh—manner have been exemplary." "I trust so, sir," said Mr. Martin. "I have understood, Martin," said Mr. Fitweiler, "that you have never taken a drink or smoked." "That is correct, sir," said Mr. Martin. "Ah, yes." Mr. Fitweiler polished his glasses. "You may describe what you did after leaving the office yesterday, Martin," he said. Mr. Martin allowed less than a second for his bewildered pause. "Certainly, sir," he said. "I walked home. Then I went to Schrafft's for dinner. Afterward I walked home again. I went to bed early, sir, and read a magazine for a while. I was asleep before eleven." "Ah, yes," said Mr. Fitweiler again. He was silent for a moment, searching for the proper words to say to the head of the filing department. "Mrs. Barrows," he said finally, "Mrs. Barrows has worked hard, Martin, very hard. It grieves me to report that she has suffered a severe breakdown. It has taken the form of a persecution complex accompanied by distressing hallucinations." "I am very sorry, sir," said Mr. Martin. "Mrs. Barrows is under the delusion," continued Mr. Fitweiler, "that you visited her last evening and behaved yourself in an—uh—unseemly manner." He raised his hand to silence Mr. Martin's little pained outcry. "It is the nature of these psychological diseases," Mr. Fitweiler said, "to fix upon the least likely and most innocent party as the—uh—source of persecution. These matters are not for the lay mind to grasp, Martin. I've just had my psychiatrist, Dr. Fitch, on the phone. He would not, of course, commit himself, but he made enough generalizations to substantiate my suspicions. I suggested to Mrs. Barrows, when she had completed her—uh—story to me this morning, that she visit Dr. Fitch, for I suspected a condition at once. She flew, I regret to say, into a rage, and demanded—uh—requested that I call you on the carpet. You may not know, Martin, but Mrs. Barrows had planned a reorganization of your department—subject to my approval, of course, subject to my approval. This brought you, rather than anyone else, to her mind—but again that is a phenomenon for Dr. Fitch and not for us. So, Martin, I am afraid Mrs. Barrows' usefulness here is at an end." "I am dreadfully sorry, sir," said Mr. Martin.

It was at this point that the door to the office blew open with the suddenness of a gas-main explosion and Mrs. Barrows catapulted through it. "Is the little rat denying it?" she screamed. "He can't get away with that!" Mr. Martin got up and moved discreetly to a point beside Mr. Fitweiler's chair. "You drank and smoked at my apartment," she bawled at Mr. Martin, "and you know it! You called Mr. Fitweiler an old windbag and said you were going to blow him up when you got coked to the gills on your heroin!" She stopped yelling to catch her breath and a new glint came into her popping eyes. "If you weren't such a drab, ordinary little man," she said, "I'd think you'd planned it all. Sticking your tongue out, saying you were sitting in the catbird seat, because you thought no one would believe me when I told it! My God, it's really too perfect!" She brayed loudly and hysterically, and the fury was on her again. She glared at Mr. Fitweiler. "Can't you see how he has tricked us, you old fool? Can't you see his little game?" But Mr. Fitweiler had been surreptitiously pressing all the buttons under the top of his desk and employees of F & S began pouring into the room. "Stockton," said Mr. Fitweiler, "you and Fishbein will take Mrs. Barrows to her home. Mrs. Powell, you will go with them." Stockton, who had played a little football in high school, blocked Mrs. Barrows as she made for Mr. Martin. It took him and Fishbein together to force her out of the door into the hall, crowded with stenographers and office boys. She was still screaming imprecations at Mr. Martin, tangled and contradictory imprecations. The hubbub finally died out down the corridor.

"I regret that this has happened," said Mr. Fitweiler. "I shall ask you to dismiss it from your mind, Martin." "Yes, sir," said Mr. Martin, anticipating his chief's "That will be all" by moving to the door. "I will dismiss it." He went out and shut the door, and his step was light and quick in the hall. When he entered his department he had slowed down to his customary gait, and he walked quietly across the room to the W20 file, wearing a look of studious concentration.

LADY WITH A LAMP

❖

SALLY BENSON

Miss Robbins awoke and, glancing at her watch, saw that the time was twenty minutes to seven. She was stiff from sleeping in the big, upholstered chair, and her nurse's cap had slipped to one side of her head. She lifted her short, heavy arms and pinned the cap back in place, and then, throwing aside the blanket she had used to cover her feet, she stood up and yawned. She had turned off the lamp before she went to sleep, and the room looked gray and chilly in the early-morning light. She glanced at the woman who lay on the couch. The couch stood with its back to the two windows of the apartment living room, so the woman's body lay in shadow. Miss Robbins walked over and stood looking down at her. She lay fully dressed, except for one shoe, which had fallen to the floor, and as Miss Robbins watched, her own mouth tightened and set. The woman's dress was pulled up above her knees, and her stockings, which were twisted on her slender legs, were soiled and had runs in them. She slept heavily, her mouth open slightly. Her eyes were swollen from crying.

Miss Robbins bent down and lifted the woman's arm to take her pulse. Her blunt fingers felt the racing, uncertain throb of the heart and she noticed with distaste that the hand was dirty and that one nail was cracked and broken. She dropped the arm and it fell heavily across the woman's breast. The woman did not stir.

Miss Robbins walked over and picked up the blanket from the floor and, going back to the couch, threw it across the woman's legs. Then she began to walk about the room, her arms folded, so that there would be no possible chance of touching anything. There was dust everywhere, even on the leaves of the ivy, curled and dry, on the mantel. A clock in the center of the mantel had stopped, and next to it stood an empty glass that smelled of whiskey, and there were rings on the paint where other glasses had been set. On one corner stood a picture of a little girl, her hair hanging straight to her shoulders, her small mouth fixed in a smile. Miss Robbins stared at the picture a moment and then moved on, but there was not much to be seen in the room; a small bookcase, half-filled with books, was painted a shiny black and lined with Chinese red, and on top of it were a small ivory elephant and a lamp made from a Chinese vase, as though at one time their owner had had some idea of an Oriental motif; there were three tables, stained and charred by cigarettes, and on one of them lay the woman's handbag. Miss Robbins unfolded her arms deliberately, picked it up, and opened it. She took the contents out item by item and put them on the table—a powder compact with a mother-of-pearl cover that did not shut tight, a lipstick holder with no top, some pennies, a stained, flattened pack of cigarettes, a crumpled piece of Kleenex, a key ring with a rabbit's foot and four keys, a folding checkbook, and a soiled red suède wallet.

Miss Robbins opened the checkbook and noted that there was a satisfying balance as of a few days before, but then, there were several stubs that hadn't been filled in. And then she opened the wallet. There were five one-dollar bills in it and a small envelope which enclosed a card. On the outside of the envelope, "Madge" was written. Miss Robbins took out the card and read it. "Been wondering all day if you were taking care of yourself, and bought these flowers hoping you'd feel all right to enjoy them. Love, Bob." She put the card, wallet, and checkbook back into the bag, and then, holding the open mouth of the bag level with the tabletop, she pushed the rest of the things into it and set it back on the table.

Without looking again at the woman who lay on the couch, Miss Robbins walked into the small kitchen and got out the percolator in which she had made herself coffee the night before. She filled it and lighted the stove. On the floor near the sink were two empty whiskey bottles, and she pushed them under the sink with her foot. She opened the breadbox and saw that there was a half loaf of bread in it. The bread was slightly moldy on the underside, and, cutting the mold away, she sliced a piece. She held it to her nose and sniffed at it, and, finding that it still had a faint sour smell, she decided against toasting it. As she put it down on the table, the doorbell sounded with a short, quick ring, and she hurried to answer it. Although she was small and heavy, she moved quickly and silently.

Another nurse stood at the door. "Miss Robbins?" she said. "I'm Miss Gates."

"I was expecting you," Miss Robbins said. "I put some coffee on for us." She nodded toward the door of the room. "She's in there, so we'll just make ourselves comfy in the kitchen."

Miss Gates stepped to the door of the living room and peered in. She was younger than Miss Robbins, and her face was soft and stupid. "She's on the couch," she said.

"It opens out into a bed," Miss Robbins told her. "But I didn't bother last night." She walked into the living room and, picking up a straight chair, carried it into the kitchen. "You take this," she said, "and I'll sit on the stool."

The coffee had started to percolate.

Miss Gates sat down and threw back her coat. "The agency called me last night," she said. "And I didn't want to come at all, but they asked me as a special favor, so I told them I would. Just for today, though. 'You'll have to get somebody else for tomorrow,' I said."

"I just came on last night myself," Miss Robbins said. "Half past twelve when I got here. She got scared and called the agency herself."

"She couldn't have been so bad, then," Miss Gates said hopefully. "I mean, if she called herself."

"I don't know what she was like when she telephoned," Miss Robbins said. "But when I got here . . ."

"What was she doing?" Miss Gates asked with a show of interest.

"Lying on the floor," Miss Robbins said. "Lying on the floor right in front of the door, and the door open so that anybody could walk in."

"Honestly, can you tie that?" Miss Gates said. "They just don't seem to care or have any pride, do they?"

"They do not," Miss Robbins said firmly. "There she lay, and I could just about get the door open wide enough to get in. I could hardly push her aside. She was a dead weight." She took two cups and saucers from the closet and began to wash one of them. "I washed one for myself last night," she explained. "But I'll have to wash one for you. Everything in the place is a sight."

"I'm afraid of them," Miss Gates said. "It's why I didn't want to come."

"Well, I'm not afraid of them," Miss Robbins said. "And I always ask for them. They're no trouble when they're as bad as she is. There's nothing you can do, so I just bring along the *Mirror*, and some nice little sandwiches, and make myself as comfy as I can."

"What made her go and lie on the floor like that, I wonder?" Miss Gates said. "Maybe she fainted."

Miss Robbins laughed. "She hadn't fainted. She was just trying to get the door open and fell down. Oh, she knew what she was doing all right. They always do."

"Oh, dear," Miss Gates said, sighing.

"Now, don't you worry about her," Miss Robbins said. "She won't come to for a long time yet. And by that time her doctor will probably be here. His name's Purdy. She was asking for him last night. She's got his name on a pad by the telephone." She turned off the flame under the percolator and poured the coffee. There was a warm, comforting smell in the dreary little kitchen.

Miss Gates sipped the hot coffee appreciatively. "This is nice," she said.

"I'm not worth a thing till I've had my coffee," Miss Robbins said. "I was going to make toast, but the bread's no good. I always stop on my way home and have breakfast anyway. I usually meet my friend at Schrafft's. She does night duty, too. We have a nice little breakfast and then we go to a morning movie or something."

"Goodness!" Miss Gates said. "Aren't you sleepy?"

"Oh, on these cases you usually have a chance for a good nap," Miss Robbins said confidentially. "When they're as far gone as she was, they usually quiet down. And when they're not that far gone, sometimes they're kind of funny. Especially the men."

Miss Gates gave a ladylike shudder. "I wouldn't have come if it had been a *man*," she said.

"I'm not afraid of them, man or woman," Miss Robbins said. She clenched her fist and bent her arm, and the muscle stood out under her blue-white skin.

"My!" Miss Gates exclaimed. "I wish I had your muscle. I have a weak back. There's nothing the matter with it, it's just weak. I can't lift very well. I hope she won't expect me to lift her."

"*Don't* lift her," Miss Robbins said. "She can manage all right. I wish you could have seen her last night. It would have given you a laugh."

"What did she do?" Miss Gates asked.

"Well," Miss Robbins told her, "there she was on the floor, with her stockings all full of runs. Nylons, too. *I* haven't any nylons."

"I have two pair," Miss Gates said. "I have a pair on now."

Miss Robbins glanced down at her own legs, which looked thick in their gun-metal stockings. "There are other things I'd rather have than nylons," she said. "But if I did have them, I wouldn't wear them full of runs. One of hers is in shreds. And her hair! I'll bet it hasn't been combed in a week."

"Oh, dear," Miss Gates sighed again. "Maybe that'll be my job!"

"I didn't touch it," Miss Robbins said. "If they can hold a glass, they can hold a comb, I say. No, sir! I just got that door open and took off my hat and coat and read my paper. You have to get used to these cases."

"I thought the door was open," Miss Gates said.

"It was," Miss Robbins told her, a little impatiently, "but she was blocking the way. I had to push hard on the door to get her out of the way. She was kind of crying, but you couldn't make any sense out of her, so I thought to myself there's no use trying, and I put my things away and put my sandwiches in the icebox, so they'd stay nice and moist. I always bring my own sandwiches. You never can tell what you'll find to eat. They never eat."

"Hasn't she had anything?" Miss Gates asked.

"How should I know?" Miss Robbins answered. "She was in no shape to eat last night. She couldn't move for a while. She lay there all the time I was reading my paper. 'Don't you want to get up from that floor?' I asked her. But she didn't know what I was talking about. It took me over an hour to read my paper, and she just lay there and rolled around a little."

"Honestly, what some people do!" Miss Gates said.

"About twenty to two, I got hungry," Miss Robbins went on, "so I came out here and made some coffee, and took my sandwiches to the living room and had my little snack. She must have noticed my moving around, because she began to try to get up off the floor. You should have seen her! I watched her the whole time I was eating."

"What did she *do?*" Miss Gates asked.

"Well, she'd get halfway up and fall back. Halfway up and fall back. She must have done it two dozen times. And pretty soon she got herself kind of around on her hands and knees and she started to crawl. And then back she'd go again!"

"Crawl!" Miss Gates exclaimed. "Really, it makes me ashamed to be a woman when you hear things like that."

"Well, you'd have been ashamed to be a woman if you could have seen *her,*" Miss Robbins said. "Crawling along a few inches, and falling over. I think she was putting a lot of it on in the hopes I'd call the doctor. She had sense enough to ask for him all right. Oh, she knew I was here, I can tell you. But why should I wake a man up in the middle of the night for a thing like you, I thought to myself. She didn't look human."

Miss Gates' breath came out in an audible puff. "Just like an animal," she said, her eyes alive with interest.

"Exactly," Miss Robbins said. "Well, she crawled all the way from the door to the couch, and I sat there and I thought to myself, look at you!"

"Imagine that!" Miss Gates said. "Crawling from the door to the couch!"

"And do you know how long it took her?" Miss Robbins asked. "Two hours!"

"Two hours!" Miss Gates breathed.

"Two hours," Miss Robbins repeated. "I timed her." She went over to the sink and rinsed out her coffee cup. "I'll be running along now," she said.

"Well, I want to thank you for making the coffee," Miss Gates said.

"Oh, that's all right," Miss Robbins said. "I wanted a cup myself. And now I'll just get my things. I left them in the other room."

The two nurses walked into the living room. Miss Robbins got her hat and coat and put them on. She looked over at the figure of the woman lying on the couch. "She hasn't moved once since she crawled up there," she said.

Miss Gates opened her eyes wide in alarm, and Miss Robbins, seeing the expression on her face, laughed. "Oh, don't worry. She isn't dead. I took her pulse, and she isn't dead." She shook her head and smiled, as though she were deeply amused. "I ought to know," she said. "*Nothing* ever kills them."

ACT OF FAITH

❖

IRWIN SHAW

"PRESENT IT TO HIM in a pitiful light," Olson was saying as they picked their way through the almost frozen mud toward the orderly-room tent. "Three combat-scarred veterans, who fought their way from Omaha Beach to . . . What was the name of the town we fought our way to?"

"Königstein," Seeger said.

"Königstein." Olson lifted his right foot heavily out of a puddle and stared admiringly at the three pounds of mud clinging to his overshoe. "The backbone of the Army. The noncommissioned officer. We deserve better of our country. Mention our decorations, in passing."

"What decorations should I mention?" Seeger asked. "The Marksman's Medal?"

"Never quite made it," Olson said. "I had a cross-eyed scorer at the butts. Mention the Bronze Star, the Silver Star, the Croix de Guerre with palms, the Unit Citation, the Congressional Medal of Honor."

"I'll mention them all." Seeger grinned. "You don't think the C.O.'ll notice that we haven't won most of them, do you?"

"Gad, sir," Olson said with dignity, "do you think that one Southern military gentleman will dare doubt the word of another Southern military gentleman in the hour of victory?"

"I come from Ohio," Seeger said.

"Welch comes from Kansas," Olson said, coolly staring down a second lieutenant who was passing. The lieutenant made a nervous little jerk with his hand, as though he expected a salute, then kept it rigid, as a slight, superior smile of scorn twisted at the corner of Olson's mouth. The lieutenant dropped his eyes and splashed on through the mud. "You've heard of Kansas," Olson said. "Magnolia-scented Kansas."

"Of course," said Seeger. "I'm no fool."

"Do your duty by your men, Sergeant." Olson stopped to wipe the cold rain off his face and lectured him. "Highest-ranking noncom present took the initiative and saved his comrades, at great personal risk, above and beyond the call of you-know-what, in the best traditions of the American Army."

"I will throw myself in the breach," Seeger said.

"Welch and I can't ask more," said Olson.

They walked heavily through the mud on the streets between the rows of tents. The camp stretched drearily over the Reims plain, with the rain beating on the sagging tents. The division had been there over three weeks, waiting to be shipped home, and all the meagre diversions of the neighborhood had been sampled and exhausted, and there was an air of watchful suspicion and impatience with the military life hanging over the camp now, and there was even reputed to be a staff sergeant in C Company who was laying odds they would not get back to America before July 4th.

"I'm redeployable," Olson sang. "It's so enjoyable." It was a jingle he had composed, to no recognizable melody, in the early days after the victory in Europe, when he had added up his points and found they came to only sixty-three, but he persisted in singing it. He was a short, round boy who had been flunked out of air cadets' school and transferred to the infantry but whose spirits had not been damaged in the process. He had a high, childish voice and a pretty, baby face. He was very good-natured, and had a girl waiting for him at the University of California, where he intended to finish his course at government expense when he got out of the Army, and he was just the type who is killed off early and predictably and sadly in moving pictures about the war, but he had gone through four campaigns and six major battles without a scratch.

Seeger was a large, lanky boy, with a big nose, who had been wounded at St.-Lô but had come back to his outfit in the Siegfried Line quite unchanged. He was cheerful and dependable and he knew his business. He had broken in five or six second lieutenants, who had later been killed or wounded, and the C.O. had tried to get him commissioned in the field, but the war had ended while the paperwork was being fumbled over at headquarters.

They reached the door of the orderly tent and stopped. "Be brave, Sergeant," Olson said. "Welch and I are depending on you."

"O.K.," Seeger said, and went in.

The tent had the dank, Army-canvas smell that had been so much a part of Seeger's life in the past three years. The company clerk was reading an October, 1945, issue of the Buffalo *Courier-Express,* which had just reached him, and Captain Taney, the company C.O., was seated at a sawbuck table which he used as a desk, writing a letter to his wife, his lips pursed with effort. He was a small, fussy man, with sandy hair that was falling out. While the fighting had been going on, he had been lean and tense and his small voice had been cold and full of authority. But now he had relaxed, and a little pot belly was creeping up under his belt and he kept the top button of his trousers open when he could do it without too public loss of dignity. During the war, Seeger had thought of him as a natural soldier—tireless, fanatic about detail, aggressive, severely anxious to kill Germans. But in the last few months, Seeger had seen him relapsing gradually and pleasantly into the small-town hardware merchant he had been before the war, sedentary and a little shy, and, as he had once told Seeger, worried, here in the bleak champagne fields of France, about his daughter, who had just turned twelve and had a tendency to go after the boys and had been caught by her mother kissing a fifteen-year-old neighbor in the hammock after school.

"Hello, Seeger," he said, returning the salute with a mild, offhand gesture. "What's on your mind?"

"Am I disturbing you, sir?"

"Oh, no. Just writing a letter to my wife. You married, Seeger?" He peered at the tall boy standing before him.

"No, sir."

"It's very difficult." Taney sighed, pushing dissatisfiedly at the letter before him. "My wife complains I don't tell her I love her often enough. Been married fifteen years. You'd think she'd know by now." He smiled at Seeger. "I thought you were going to Paris," he said. "I signed the passes yesterday."

"That's what I came to see you about, sir."

"I suppose something's wrong with the passes." Taney spoke resignedly, like a man who has never quite got the hang of Army regulations and has had requisitions, furloughs, and requests for courts-martial returned for correction in a baffling flood.

"No, sir," Seeger said. "The passes're fine. They start tomorrow. Well, it's just—" He looked around at the company clerk, who was on the sports page.

"This confidential?" Taney asked.

"If you don't mind, sir."

"Johnny," Taney said to the clerk, "go stand in the rain someplace."

"Yes, sir," the clerk said, and slowly got up and walked out.

Taney looked shrewdly at Seeger and spoke in a secret whisper. "You pick up anything?" he asked.

Seeger grinned. "No, sir, haven't had my hands on a girl since Strasbourg."

"Ah, that's good." Taney leaned back, relieved, happy that he didn't have to cope with the disapproval of the Medical Corps.

"It's—well," said Seeger, embarrassed, "it's hard to say—but it's money."

Taney shook his head sadly. "I know."

"We haven't been paid for three months, sir, and—"

"Damn it!" Taney stood up and shouted furiously. "I would like to take every bloody, chair-warming old lady in the Finance Department and wring their necks."

The clerk stuck his head into the tent. "Anything wrong? You call for me, sir?"

"No!" Taney shouted. "Get out of here!"

The clerk ducked out.

Taney sat down again. "I suppose," he said, in a more normal voice, "they have their problems. Outfits being broken up, being moved all over the place. But it's rugged."

"It wouldn't be so bad," Seeger said, "but we're going to Paris tomorrow. Olson, Welch, and myself. And you need money in Paris."

"Don't I know it?" Taney wagged his head. "Do you know what I paid for a bottle of champagne on the Place Pigalle in September?" He paused significantly. "I won't tell you. You wouldn't have any respect for me the rest of your life."

Seeger laughed. "Hanging is too good for the guy who thought up the rate of exchange," he said.

"I don't care if I never see another franc as long as I live." Taney waved his letter in the air, although it had been dry for a long time.

There was silence in the tent, and Seeger swallowed a little embarrassedly. "Sir," he said, "the truth is, I've come to borrow some money for Welch, Olson, and myself. We'll pay it back out of the first pay we get, and that can't be too long from now. If you don't want to give it to us, just tell me and I'll understand and get the hell out of here. We don't like to ask, but you might just as well be dead as be in Paris broke."

Taney stopped waving his letter and put it down thoughtfully. He peered at it, wrinkling his brow, looking like an aged bookkeeper in the single, gloomy light that hung in the middle of the tent.

"Just say the word, Captain," Seeger said, "and I'll blow."

"Stay where you are, son," said Taney. He dug in his shirt pocket and took out a worn, sweat-stained wallet. He looked at it for a moment. "Alligator," he said, with automatic, absent pride. "My wife sent it to me when we were in England. Pounds don't fit in it. However . . ." He opened it and took out all the contents. There was a small pile of francs on the table in front of him when he finished. He counted them. "Four hundred francs," he said. "Eight bucks."

"Excuse me," Seeger said humbly. "I shouldn't've asked."

"Delighted," Taney said vigorously. "Absolutely delighted." He started dividing the francs into two piles. "Truth is, Seeger, most of my money goes home in allotments. And the truth is, I lost eleven hundred francs in a poker game three nights ago, and I ought to be ashamed of myself. Here." He shoved one pile toward Seeger. "Two hundred francs."

Seeger looked down at the frayed, meretricious paper, which always seemed to him like stage money anyway. "No, sir," he said. "I can't take it."

"Take it," Taney said. "That's a direct order."

Seeger slowly picked up the money, not looking at Taney. "Sometime, sir," he said, "after we get out, you have to come over to my house, and you and my father and my brother and I'll go on a real drunk."

"I regard that," Taney said gravely, "as a solemn commitment."

They smiled at each other, and Seeger started out.

"Have a drink for me," said Taney, "at the Café de la Paix. A small drink." He was sitting down to tell his wife he loved her when Seeger went out of the tent.

Olson fell into step with Seeger and they walked silently through the mud between the tents.

"Well, *mon vieux?*" Olson said finally.

"Two hundred francs," said Seeger.

Olson groaned. "Two hundred francs! We won't be able to pinch a whore's behind on the Boulevard des Capucines for two hundred francs. That miserable, penny-loving Yankee!"

"He only had four hundred," Seeger said.

"I revise my opinion," said Olson.

They walked disconsolately and heavily back toward their tent.

Olson spoke only once before they got there. "These raincoats," he said, patting his. "Most ingenious invention of the war. Highest saturation point of any modern fabric. Collect more water per square inch, and hold it, than any material known to man. All hail the quartermaster!"

Welch was waiting at the entrance of their tent. He was standing there peering excitedly and shortsightedly out at the rain through his glasses, looking angry and tough, like a big-city hack driver, individual and incorruptible even in the ten-million colored uniform. Every time Seeger came upon Welch unexpectedly, he couldn't help smiling at the belligerent stance, the harsh stare through the steel-rimmed G.I. glasses, which had nothing at all to do with the way Welch really was. "It's a family inheritance," Welch had once explained. "My whole family stands as though we were getting ready to rap a drunk with a beer glass. Even my old lady." Welch had six brothers, all devout, according to Welch, and Seeger from time to time idly pictured them standing in a row, on Sunday mornings in church, seemingly on the verge of general violence, amid the hushed Latin and the Sabbath millinery.

"How much?" Welch asked loudly.

"Don't make us laugh," Olson said, pushing past him into the tent.

"What do you think I could get from the French for my combat jacket?" Seeger said. He went into the tent and lay down on his cot.

Welch followed them in and stood between the two of them. "Boys," he said, "on a man's errand."

"I can just see us now," Olson murmured, lying on his cot with his hands clasped behind his head, "painting Montmartre red. Please bring on the naked dancing girls. Four bucks' worth."

"I am not worried," Welch announced.

"Get out of here." Olson turned over on his stomach.

"I know where we can put our hands on sixty-five bucks." Welch looked triumphantly first at Olson, then at Seeger.

Olson turned over slowly and sat up. "I'll kill you," he said, "if you're kidding."

"While you guys are wasting your time fooling around with the infantry," Welch said, "I used my head. I went into Reems and used my head."

"Rance," Olson said automatically. He had had two years of French in college and he felt, now that the war was over, that he had to introduce his friends to some of his culture.

"I got to talking to a captain in the Air Force," Welch said eagerly. "A little, fat old paddle-footed captain that never got higher off the ground than the second floor of Com Z headquarters, and he told me that what he would admire to do more than anything else is take home a nice shiny German Luger pistol with him to show to the boys back in Pacific Grove, California."

Silence fell on the tent, and Welch and Olson looked at Seeger.

"Sixty-five bucks for a Luger, these days," Olson said, "is a very good figure."

"They've been sellin' for as low as thirty-five," said Welch hesitantly. "I'll bet," he said to Seeger, "you could sell yours now and buy another one back when you got some dough, and make a clear twenty-five on the deal."

Seeger didn't say anything. He had killed the owner of the Luger, an enormous S.S. major, in Coblenz, behind some bales of paper in a warehouse, and the major had fired at Seeger three times with it, once nicking his helmet, before Seeger hit him in the face at twenty feet. Seeger had kept the Luger, a heavy, well-balanced gun, lugging it with him, hiding it at the bottom of his bedroll, oiling it three times a week, avoiding all opportunities of selling it, although he had once been offered a hundred dollars for it and several times eighty and ninety, while the war was still on, before German weapons became a glut on the market.

"Well," said Welch, "there's no hurry. I told the captain I'd see him tonight around eight o'clock in front of the Lion d'Or Hotel. You got five hours to make up your mind. Plenty of time."

"Me," said Olson, after a pause, "I won't say anything."

Seeger looked reflectively at his feet, and the two other men avoided looking at him.

Welch dug in his pocket. "I forgot," he said. "I picked up a letter for you." He handed it to Seeger.

"Thanks," Seeger said. He opened it absently, thinking about the Luger.

"Me," said Olson, "I won't say a bloody word. I'm just going to lie here and think about that nice, fat Air Force captain."

Seeger grinned a little at him and went to the tent opening to read the letter in the light. The letter was from his father, and even from one glance at the handwriting, scrawly and hurried and spotted, so different from his father's usual steady, handsome, professorial script, he knew that something was wrong.

"Dear Norman," it read, "sometime in the future, you must forgive me for writing this letter. But I have been holding this in so long, and there is no one here I can talk to, and because of your brother's condition I must pretend to be cheerful and optimistic all

the time at home, both with him and your mother, who has never
been the same since Leonard was killed. You're the oldest now, and
although I know we've never talked very seriously about anything
before, you have been through a great deal by now, and I imagine
you must have matured considerably, and you've seen so many
different places and people. Norman, I need help. While the war
was on and you were fighting, I kept this to myself. It wouldn't have
been fair to burden you with this. But now the war is over, and I
no longer feel I can stand up under this alone. And you will have to
face it sometime when you get home, if you haven't faced it already,
and perhaps we can help each other by facing it together."

"I'm redeployable. It's so enjoyable," Olson was singing softly,
on his cot. He fell silent after his burst of song.

Seeger blinked his eyes in the gray, wintry, rainy light, and went
on reading his father's letter, on the stiff white stationery with the
university letterhead in polite engraving at the top of each page.

"I've been feeling this coming on for a long time," the letter continued, "but it wasn't until last Sunday morning that something
happened to make me feel it in its full force. I don't know how
much you've guessed about the reason for Jacob's discharge from
the Army. It's true he was pretty badly wounded in the leg at Metz,
but I've asked around, and I know that men with worse wounds
were returned to duty after hospitalization. Jacob got a medical discharge, but I don't think it was for the shrapnel wound in his
thigh. He is suffering now from what I suppose you call combat
fatigue, and he is subject to fits of depression and hallucinations.
Your mother and I thought that as time went by and the war and
the Army receded, he would grow better. Instead, he is growing
worse. Last Sunday morning when I came down into the living
room from upstairs he was crouched in his old uniform, next to the
window, peering out."

"What the hell," Olson was saying. "If we don't get the sixty-five
bucks we can always go to the Louvre. I understand the Mona Lisa
is back."

"I asked Jacob what he was doing," the letter went on. "He didn't
turn around. 'I'm observing,' he said. 'V-1s and V-2s. Buzz bombs
and rockets. They're coming in by the hundred.' I tried to reason
with him and he told me to crouch and save myself from flying glass.
To humor him I got down on the floor beside him and tried to tell
him the war was over, that we were in Ohio, 4,000 miles away from

the nearest spot where bombs had fallen, that America had never been touched. He wouldn't listen. 'These're the new rocket bombs,' he said, 'for the Jews.' "

"Did you ever hear of the Panthéon?" Olson asked loudly.

"No," said Welch.

"It's free."

"I'll go," said Welch.

Seeger shook his head a little and blinked his eyes before he went back to the letter.

"After that," his father went on, "Jacob seemed to forget about the bombs from time to time, but he kept saying that the mobs were coming up the street armed with bazookas and Browning automatic rifles. He mumbled incoherently a good deal of the time and kept walking back and forth saying, 'What's the situation? Do you know what the situation is?' And once he told me he wasn't worried about himself, he was a soldier and he expected to be killed, but he was worried about Mother and myself and Leonard and you. He seemed to forget that Leonard was dead. I tried to calm him and get him back to bed before your mother came down, but he refused and wanted to set out immediately to rejoin his division. It was all terribly disjointed, and at one time he took the ribbon he got for winning the Bronze Star and threw it in the fireplace, then he got down on his hands and knees and picked it out of the ashes and made me pin it on him again, and he kept repeating, 'This is when they are coming for the Jews.' "

"The next war I'm in," said Olson, "they don't get me under the rank of colonel."

It had stopped raining by now, and Seeger folded the unfinished letter and went outside. He walked slowly down to the end of the company street, and, facing out across the empty, soaked French fields, scarred and neglected by various armies, he stopped and opened the letter again.

"I don't know what Jacob went through in the Army," his father wrote, "that has done this to him. He never talks to me about the war and he refuses to go to a psychoanalyst, and from time to time he is his own bouncing, cheerful self, playing handball in the afternoons and going around with a large group of girls. But he has devoured all the concentration-camp reports, and I found him weeping when the newspapers reported that a hundred Jews were killed in Tripoli some time ago.

"The terrible thing is, Norman, that I find myself coming to believe that it is not neurotic for a Jew to behave like this today. Perhaps Jacob is the normal one, and I, going about my business, teaching economics in a quiet classroom, pretending to understand that the world is comprehensible and orderly, am really the mad one. I ask you once more to forgive me for writing you a letter like this, so different from any letter or any conversation I've ever had with you. But it is crowding me, too. I do not see rockets and bombs, but I see other things.

"Wherever you go these days—restaurants, hotels, clubs, trains —you seem to hear talk about the Jews, mean, hateful, murderous talk. Whatever page you turn to in the newspapers, you seem to find an article about Jews being killed somewhere on the face of the globe. And there are large, influential newspapers and well-known columnists who each day are growing more and more outspoken and more popular. The day that Roosevelt died I heard a drunken man yelling outside a bar, 'Finally they got the Jew out of the White House.' And some of the people who heard him merely laughed, and nobody stopped him. And on V-J Day, in celebration, hoodlums in Los Angeles savagely beat a Jewish writer. It's difficult to know what to do, whom to fight, where to look for allies.

"Three months ago, for example, I stopped my Thursday-night poker game, after playing with the same men for over ten years. John Reilly happened to say that the Jews got rich out of the war, and when I demanded an apology, he refused, and when I looked around at the faces of the men who had been my friends for so long, I could see they were not with me. And when I left the house, no one said good night to me. I know the poison was spreading from Germany before the war and during it, but I had not realized it had come so close.

"And in my economics class, I find myself idiotically hedging in my lectures. I discover that I am loath to praise any liberal writer or any liberal act, and find myself somehow annoyed and frightened to see an article of criticism of existing abuses signed by a Jewish name. And I hate to see Jewish names on important committees, and hate to read of Jews fighting for the poor, the oppressed, the cheated and hungry. Somehow, even in a country where my family has lived a hundred years, the enemy has won this subtle victory over me—he has made me disfranchise myself from honest causes by calling them foreign, Communist, using Jewish names connected with them as ammunition against them.

"Most hateful of all, I found myself looking for Jewish names in the casualty lists and secretly being glad when I saw them there, to prove that there, at least, among the dead and wounded, we belonged. Three times, thanks to you and your brothers, I found our name there, and, may God forgive me, at the expense of your blood and your brother's life, through my tears, I felt that same twitch of satisfaction.

"When I read the newspapers and see another story that Jews are still being killed in Poland, or Jews are requesting that they be given back their homes in France or that they be allowed to enter some country where they will not be murdered, I am annoyed with them. I feel that they are boring the rest of the world with their problems, that they are making demands upon the rest of the world by being killed, that they are disturbing everyone by being hungry and asking for the return of their property. If we could all fall in through the crust of the earth and vanish in one hour, with our heroes and poets and prophets and martyrs, perhaps we would be doing the memory of the Jewish race a service.

"This is how I feel today, son. I need some help. You've been to the war, you've fought and killed men, you've seen the people of other countries. Maybe you understand things that I don't understand. Maybe you see some hope somewhere. Help me. Your loving Father."

Seeger folded the letter slowly, not seeing what he was doing, because the tears were burning his eyes. He walked slowly and aimlessly across the dead, sodden grass of the empty field, away from the camp. He tried to wipe away his tears, because, with his eyes full and dark, he kept seeing his father and brother crouched in the old-fashioned living room in Ohio, and hearing his brother, dressed in the old, discarded uniform, saying, "These're the new rocket bombs. For the Jews."

He sighed, looking out over the bleak, wasted land. Now, he thought, now I have to think about it. He felt a slight, unreasonable twinge of anger at his father for presenting him with the necessity of thinking about it. The Army was good about serious problems. While you were fighting, you were too busy and frightened and weary to think about anything, and at other times you were relaxing, putting your brain on a shelf, postponing everything to that impossible time of clarity and beauty after the war. Well, now, here was the impossible, clear, beautiful time, and here was his father, demanding that he think. There are all sorts of Jews, he thought: there are the sort whose every waking moment is ridden by the knowledge of Jewishness; who see signs against the Jew in every smile on a streetcar, every whisper; who see pogroms in every newspaper article, threats in every change of the weather, scorn in every handshake, death behind each closed door. He had not been like that. He was young, he was big and healthy and easygoing, and people of all kinds had liked him all his life, in the Army and out. In America, especially, what was going on in Europe had been remote, unreal, unrelated to him. The chanting, bearded old men burning in the Nazi furnaces, and the dark-eyed women screaming prayers in Polish and Russian and German as they were pushed naked into the gas chambers, had seemed as shadowy and almost as unrelated to him, as he trotted out onto the stadium field for a football game, as they must have been to the men named O'Dwyer and Wickersham and Poole who played in the line beside him.

These tortured people had seemed more related to him in Europe. Again and again, in the towns that had been taken back from the Germans, gaunt, gray-faced men had stopped him humbly, looking searchingly at him, and had asked, peering at his long, lined, grimy face under the anonymous helmet, "Are you a Jew?" Sometimes they asked it in English, sometimes French, sometimes Yiddish. He didn't know French or Yiddish, but he learned to recognize that question. He had never understood exactly why they asked the question, since they never demanded anything of him, rarely even could speak to him. Then, one day in Strasbourg, a little, bent old man and a small, shapeless woman had stopped him and asked, in English, if he was Jewish. "Yes," he'd said, smiling at them. The two old people had smiled widely, like children. "Look," the old man had said to his wife. "A young American soldier. A Jew. And so large and strong." He had touched Seeger's arm reverently with the tips of his fingers, then had touched the Garand Seeger was carrying. "And such a beautiful rifle."

And there, for a moment, although he was not particularly sensitive, Seeger had got an inkling of why he had been stopped and questioned by so many before. Here, to these bent, exhausted old people, ravaged of their families, familiar with flight and death for so many years, was a symbol of continuing life. A large young man in the uniform of the liberator, blood, as they thought, of their blood, but not in hiding, not quivering in fear and helplessness, but striding secure and victorious down the street, armed and capable of inflicting terrible destruction on his enemies.

Seeger had kissed the old lady on the cheek and she had wept, and the old man had scolded her for it while shaking Seeger's hand fervently and thankfully before saying goodbye.

Thinking back on it, he knew that it was silly to pretend that, even before his father's letter, he had been like any other American soldier going through the war. When he had stood over the huge, dead S.S. major with the face blown in by his bullets in the warehouse in Coblenz, and taken the pistol from the dead hand, he had tasted a strange little extra flavor of triumph. How many Jews, he'd thought, has this man killed? How fitting it is that I've killed him. Neither Olson nor Welch, who were like his brothers, would have felt that in picking up the Luger, its barrel still hot from the last shots its owner had fired before dying. And he had resolved that he was going to make sure to take this gun back with him to America, and plug it and keep it on his desk at home, as a kind of vague, half-understood sign to himself that justice had once been done and he had been its instrument.

Maybe, he thought, maybe I'd better take it back with me, but not as a memento. Not plugged, but loaded. America by now was a strange country for him. He had been away a long time and he wasn't sure what was waiting for him when he got home. If the mobs were coming down the street toward his house, he was not going to die singing and praying.

When he had been taking basic training, he'd heard a scrawny, clerkish soldier from Boston talking at the other end of the PX bar, over the watered beer. "The boys at the office," the scratchy voice was saying, "gave me a party before I left. And they told me one thing. 'Charlie,' they said, 'hold onto your bayonet. We're going to be able to use it when you get back. On the Yids.' "

He hadn't said anything then, because he'd felt it was neither possible nor desirable to fight against every random overheard voice raised against the Jews from one end of the world to the other. But again and again, at odd moments, lying on a barracks cot, or stretched out trying to sleep on the floor of a ruined French farmhouse, he had heard that voice, harsh, satisfied, heavy with hate and ignorance, saying above the beery grumble of apprentice soldiers at the bar, "Hold onto your bayonet."

And the other stories. Jews collected stories of hatred and injustice and inklings of doom like a special, lunatic kind of miser. The story of the Navy officer, commander of a small vessel off the Aleutians, who in the officers' wardroom had complained that he hated the Jews because it was the Jews who had demanded that the Germans be beaten first, and the forces in the Pacific had been starved in consequence. And when one of his junior officers, who had just come aboard, had objected and told the commander that he was a Jew, the commander had risen from the table and said, "Mister, the Constitution of the United States says I have to serve in the same Navy with Jews, but it doesn't say I have to eat at the same table with them." In the fogs and the cold, swelling Arctic seas off the Aleutians, in a small boat, subject to sudden, mortal attack at any moment.... And the million other stories. Jews, even the most normal and best adjusted, became living treasuries of them, scraps of malice and bloodthirstiness, clever and confusing and cunningly twisted so that every act by every Jew became suspect and blameworthy and hateful. Seeger had heard the stories and had made an almost conscious effort to forget them. Now, holding his father's letter in his hand, he remembered them all.

He stared unseeingly out in front of him. Maybe, he thought, maybe it would've been better to have been killed in the war, like Leonard. Simpler. Leonard would never have to face a crowd coming for his mother and father. Leonard would not have to listen and collect these hideous, fascinating little stories that made of every Jew a stranger in any town, on any field, on the face of the earth. He had come so close to being killed so many times; it would have been so easy, so neat and final. Seeger shook his head. It was ridiculous to feel like that, and he was ashamed of himself for the weak moment. At the age of twenty-one, death was not an answer.

"Seeger!" It was Olson's voice. He and Welch had sloshed silently up behind Seeger, standing in the open field. "Seeger, *mon vieux,* what're you doing—grazing?"

Seeger turned slowly to them. "I wanted to read my letter," he said.

Olson looked closely at him. They had been together so long, through so many things, that flickers and hints of expression on each other's faces were recognized and acted upon. "Anything wrong?" Olson asked.

"No," said Seeger. "Nothing much."

"Norman," Welch said, his voice young and solemn. "Norman, we've been talking, Olson and me. We decided—you're pretty attached to that Luger, and maybe, if you—well—"

"What he's trying to say," said Olson, "is we withdraw the request. If you want to sell it, O.K. If you don't, don't do it for our sake. Honest."

Seeger looked at them standing there, disreputable and tough and familiar. "I haven't made up my mind yet," he said.

"Anything you decide," Welch said oratorically, "is perfectly all right with us. Perfectly."

The three of them walked aimlessly and silently across the field, away from camp. As they walked, their shoes making a wet, sliding sound in the damp, dead grass, Seeger thought of the time Olson had covered him in the little town outside Cherbourg, when Seeger had been caught, going down the side of a street, by four Germans with a machine gun in the second story of a house on the corner and Olson had had to stand out in the middle of the street with no cover at all for more than a minute, firing continuously, so that Seeger could get away alive. And he thought of the time outside St.-Lô when he had been wounded and had lain in a minefield for three hours and Welch and Captain Taney had come looking for him in the darkness and had found him and picked him up and run for it, all of them expecting to get blown up any second. And he thought of all the drinks they'd had together, and the long marches and the cold winter together, and all the girls they'd gone out with together, and he thought of his father and brother crouching behind the window in Ohio waiting for the rockets and the crowds armed with Browning automatic rifles.

"Say." He stopped and stood facing them. "Say, what do you guys think of the Jews?"

Welch and Olson looked at each other, and Olson glanced down at the letter in Seeger's hand.

"Jews?" Olson said finally. "What're they? Welch, you ever hear of the Jews?"

Welch looked thoughtfully at the gray sky. "No," he said. "But remember, I'm an uneducated fellow."

"Sorry, bud," Olson said, turning to Seeger. "We can't help you. Ask us another question. Maybe we'll do better."

Seeger peered at the faces of his friends. He would have to rely upon them, later on, out of uniform, on their native streets, more than he had ever relied on them on the bullet-swept street and in the dark minefield in France. Welch and Olson stared back at him, troubled, their faces candid and tough and dependable.

"What time," Seeger asked, "did you tell that captain you'd meet him?"

"Eight o'clock," Welch said. "But we don't have to go. If you have any feeling about that gun—"

"We'll meet him," Seeger said. "We can use that sixty-five bucks."

"Listen," Olson said, "I know how much you like that gun, and I'll feel like a heel if you sell it."

"Forget it," Seeger said, starting to walk again. "What could I use it for in America?"

THE BALLET VISITS THE
SPLENDIDE'S MAGICIAN

❖

LUDWIG BEMELMANS

THE MANAGEMENT of the Hotel Splendide, the luxurious establishment where I once worked as a busboy, a waiter, and eventually as an assistant maître d'hôtel in the banquet department, kept
on file the addresses of a number of men who were magicians,
fortune-tellers, or experts with cards. One of these entertainers frequently appeared at the end of the small dinner parties which were
given in the private suites of the Splendide in the boom days, before
the depression put an end to such pastimes and at last brought about
the demise of the Splendide itself. Our entertainers had acclimated
their acts to the elegance of the hotel, and the magicians, for example, instead of conjuring a simple white rabbit from their hats,
cooked therein a soufflé Alaska or brought out a prize puppy with a
rhinestone collar. When young girls were present, the magician
pulled from their noses and out of corsages Cartier clips, bracelets,
and brooches, which were presented to them with the compliments
of the host.

Among the best and most talented of our performers was Professor Maurice Gorylescu, a magician who did some palmistry on the
side. He came to the hotel as often as two or three times a week.
After coffee had been served, he would enter the private dining
room, get people to write any number they wanted to on small bits
of paper, and hold the paper to their foreheads. Then he would guess
the numbers they had written down and add them up. The total
would correspond to a sum he found on a dollar bill in the host's
pocket. He did tricks with cards and coins, and he told people about
the characteristics and the habits of dress and speech of friends long
dead. He even delivered messages from them to the living.

At the end of his séances he would go into some vacant room
nearby, sink into a chair, and sit for a while with his hand over his
eyes. He always looked very tired. After about half an hour he would

80

shake himself, drink a glass of water slowly, then eat something and go home.

Professor Gorylescu earned a good deal of money. His fee for a single performance was a flat hundred dollars, and he sometimes received that much again as a tip from a grateful host. But although he worked all during the season he spent everything he made and often asked for and received his fee in advance. All he earned went to women—to the support of a Rumanian wife in Bucharest, to an American one who lived somewhere in New Jersey, and to what must have been a considerable number of New York girls of all nationalities to whom he sent little gifts and flowers.

When he came to the hotel during the day, he would hang his cane on the doorknob outside the ballroom office, ask me for a cigarette, and after a while steal a look at the book in which the reservations for small dinners were recorded. Very casually, and while talking of other things, he would turn the leaves and say something like "Looks very nice for the next two months," and put the book back. It took only a few seconds, but in this time his trick mind had stored away all the names, addresses, dates, and telephone numbers in the book. He went home with this information, called up the prospective party-givers, and offered his services.

There was a strict rule that no one should be permitted to look at these reservations, certainly not Professor Gorylescu, but I liked him, and when I was on duty in the ballroom office I would pretend not to see him when he peeked in the book. I also gave him left-over *petits fours,* candies, and after-dinner mints, of which he was very fond. He stuffed them into his pockets without bothering to wrap them up. He would wave goodbye with his immense hands, ask me to visit him soon at his home, and suggest that I bring along some *marrons glacés,* pastry, nuts—anything like that—and then he would leave, a stooping, uncouth figure, bigger than our tallest doorman.

Maurice Gorylescu lived on one of the mediocre streets that run between Riverside Drive and West End Avenue. He had a room in one of the small marble mansions that are common in that neighborhood. The rooming house in which Gorylescu lived was outstanding even among the ornate buildings of that district. It was a sort of junior Frankenstein castle, bedecked with small turrets, loggias, and balconies. It faced the sidewalk across a kind of moat—an air shaft for the basement windows—traversed by a granite bridge. The door was hung on heavy iron hinges that reached all the way across.

The character of this house was, moreover, complemented by the woman who rented its rooms, a Mrs. Houlberg. She stood guard much of the time at the window next to the moat, looking out over a sign that read "Vacancies." She always covered three-quarters of her face with her right hand, a long hand that lay diagonally across her face, the palm over her mouth, the nails of the fingers stopping under the right eye. It looked like a mask, and as if she always had a toothache.

Gorylescu lived on the top-floor front and answered to four short rings and one long one of a shrill bell that was in Mrs. Houlberg's entrance hall. Badly worn banisters led up four flights of stairs. From the balcony of his room one could see the time flash on and off in Jersey and the searchlights of a battleship in the Hudson. The room was large and newly painted in a wet, loud red, the shade of the inside of a watermelon. A spotty chartreuse velvet coverlet decorated a studio couch. Facing this was a chair, a piece of furniture such as you see in hotel lobbies or club cars, covered with striped muslin and padded with down.

There was also a Sheraton highboy, which stood near a door that led into an adjoining room which was not his. From the ceiling hung a cheap bazaar lamp with carmine glass panes behind filigree panels. On shelves and on a table were the photographs of many women; in a box, tied together with ribbons in various colors, he kept packets of letters, and in a particular drawer of the highboy was a woman's garter, an old girdle, and various other disorderly trophies.

Gorylescu reclined on the studio bed most of the time when he was at home. He wore a Russian blouse that buttoned under the left ear, and he smoked through a cigarette holder a foot long. One of his eyes was smaller and lower down in his face than the other, and between them rose a retroussé nose, a trumpet of a nose, with cavernous nostrils. Frequently and with great ceremony he sounded it into an immense handkerchief. His cigar-colored skin was spotted as if with a bluish kind of buckshot, and when he was happy he hummed through his nose, mostly the melody of a song whose title was "Tu Sais."

At home he was almost constantly in the company of women. He made the acquaintance of some of them at parties where he had entertained. They brought him gifts, and if they were fat and old, he read their minds and told them things of the past and future. At other times he went looking for girls along Riverside Drive, humming through his nose, and dragging after him a heavy cane whose handle was hooked into his coat pocket.

He went to various other places to find girls. He picked them up at dance halls in Harlem, on the subway, on roller coasters. He easily became acquainted with them anywhere, and they came to his room willingly and took their chances with him. I always thought I might find one of them, dead and naked, behind the Japanese screen, where he kept a rowing machine on which he built himself up. For the space of time that I knew him, love, murder, and that man seemed to be close together and that room the inevitable theatre for it.

The Professor gave me a series of lectures during my visits to his room in which he detailed for me the routines and the mechanisms of his untidy passions. He insisted during these long *études* that the most important piece of strategy was to get the subject to remove her shoes. "Once the shoes are off, the battle is already half won," he would say. "Get a woman to walk around without shoes, without heels—she looks a fool, she feels a fool, she is a fool. Without her shoes, she is lost. Take the soft instep in your hand, caress her ankles, her calf, her knee—the rest is child's play. But remember, first off with the shoes." While he talked, he would scratch his cat, which was part Siamese. The lecture was followed by a display of the collection of photographs he himself had taken, as evidence of the soundness of his theories.

When the Russian Ballet came to town, Professor Gorylescu was not to be had for any parties at the hotel. He went to all the performances, matinées and evenings alike, and he hummed then the music of "Puppenfee," "L'Après-Midi d'un Faune," and the various *divertissements,* and was completely broke. One day he was in a state of the highest elation because he had invited a ballet dancer to tea. He wanted me to come too because she had a friend, who would be an extra girl for me; both of them were exquisite creatures, he assured me, and I was to bring some tea, *marrons glacés, petits fours,* and ladyfingers.

I came early and I brought everything. He darkened the room, lit a brass samovar, laid out some cigarettes, sliced some lemons, hid the rowing machine under the studio couch, and with the Japanese silk screen divided the room into two separate camps. On one side was the couch, on the other the great chair. He buttoned his Russian blouse, blew his nose frequently, and hummed as he walked up and down. He brushed the cat and put away a Spanish costume doll that might have made his couch crowded. He arranged the *petits fours* in saucers, and when the bell rang four times short and one long, he put a Chopin record on his victrola. "Remember about the shoes," he told me over his shoulder, "and always play Chopin for ballet dancers." He quickly surveyed the room once more, turned on the bazaar lamp, and, humming, opened the door—and then stopped humming suddenly. He had invited two of the dancers, but up the stairs came a bouquet of girls, more than a dozen of them.

All at once it was the month of May in the dimmed room. The lovely guests complimented the samovar, the cat, the music, and the view from the balcony, to which they had opened the door, letting much fresh air come in, which intensified the new mood. Gorylescu's voice became metallic with introductions; he ran downstairs to get more glasses for tea and came back breathing heavily. All the girls, without being asked, took their shoes off immediately, explaining that their feet hurt from dancing. They arranged the shoes in an orderly row, as one does on entering a Japanese house or a mosque, then sat down on the floor in a circle. One of them even removed her stockings and put some slices of lemon between her toes. "Ah-h-h," she said.

There started after this a bewildering and alien conversation, a remote, foggy ritual, like a Shinto ceremonial. It consisted of the telling of ballet stories, and seemed to me a high, wild flight into a world closed to the outsider. The stories were told over and over until every detail was correct. In all of these stories appeared Anna Pavlova, who was referred to as "Madame"—what Madame had said, what Madame had done, what she had thought, what she had worn, how she had danced. There was an atmosphere of furious backstage patriotism. The teller of each story swayed and danced with hands, shoulders, and face. Every word was illustrated; for anything mentioned—color, light, time, and person—there was a surprisingly expressive and fitting gesture. The talker was rewarded with applause, with requests for repetition of this or that part again and again, and there swept over the group of girls waves of intimate, fervent emotion.

The Professor served tea on his hands and knees and retired to the shadows of his room. He sat for a while in the great chair like a bird with a wounded wing, and then, with his sagging and cumbersome gait, he wandered around the group of innocents, who sat straight as so many candles, all with their shoes off. The room was alive with young heads and throats and flanks.

The Professor succeeded finally in putting his head into the lap of the tallest, the most racy of the nymphs. She quickly kissed him,

said "Sh-h-h-h, daaaahrling," and then caressed his features, the
terrible nose, the eyebrows, the corrugated temples, and the great
hands, with the professional detachment of a masseuse, while she
related an episode in Cairo during a performance of "Giselle"
when the apparatus that carried Pavlova up out of her grave to
her lover got stuck halfway, and how Madame had cursed and what
she had said after the performance and to whom she had said it.
An indignant fire burned in all the narrowed eyes of the disciples
as she talked.

Suddenly one of them looked at her watch, remembered a re-
hearsal, and the girls got up and remembered us. They all had
Russian names, but all of them were English, as most ballet dancers are; in their best accents, they said their adieus. With individual graces, they arranged their hair, slipped into their shoes,
and thanked Maurice. Each one of them said "Daaaahrling" to us
and to each other. It was Madame Pavlova's form of address and
her pronunciation.

All the girls kissed us, and it was as if we all had grown up
in the same garden, as if they were all our sisters. The Professor
said a few mouthfuls of gallant compliments, and when they were
gone he fished the rowing machine out from under the couch,
without a word, and carried it in back of the Japanese screen. Together, we rearranged the room. The *marrons glacés* and the ladyfingers were all gone, but the cigarettes were still there.

THE MIDDLE DRAWER

❖

HORTENSE CALISHER

THE DRAWER was always kept locked. In a household where the tangled rubbish of existence had collected on surfaces like a scurf, which was forever being cleared away by her mother and the maid, then by her mother, and, finally, hardly at all, it had been a permanent cell—rather like, Hester thought wryly, the gene that is carried over from one generation to the other. Now, holding the small, square, indelibly known key in her hand, she shrank before it, reluctant to perform the blasphemy that the living must inevitably perpetrate on the possessions of the dead. There were no revelations to be expected when she opened the drawer, only the painful reiteration of her mother's personality and the power it had held over her own, which would rise—an emanation, a mist, that she herself had long since shredded away, parted, and escaped.

She repeated to herself, like an incantation, "I am married. I have a child of my own, a home of my own five hundred miles away. I have not even lived in this house—my parents' house—for over seven years." Stepping back, she sat on the bed where her mother had died the week before, slowly, from cancer, where Hester had held the large, long-fingered, competent hand for a whole night, watching the asphyxiating action of the fluid mounting in the lungs until it had extinguished the breath. She sat facing the drawer.

It had taken her all her own lifetime to get to know its full contents, starting from the first glimpses, when she was just able to lean her chin on the side and have her hand pushed away from the packets and japanned boxes, to the last weeks, when she had made a careful show of not noticing while she got out the necessary bankbooks and safe-deposit keys. Many times during her childhood, when she had lain blandly ill herself, elevated to the honor of the parental bed while she suffered from the "auto-intoxication" that must have been 1918's euphemism for plain piggishness, the

drawer had been opened. Then she had been allowed to play with
the two pairs of pearled opera glasses or the long string of graduated white china beads, each with its oval sides flushed like cheeks.
Over these she had sometimes spent the whole afternoon, pencil-
ling two eyes and a pursed mouth on each bead, until she had
achieved an incredible string of minute, doll-like heads that made
even her mother laugh.

Once while Hester was in college, the drawer had been opened
for the replacement of her grandmother's great sunburst pin, which
she had never before seen and which had been in pawn, and dog-
gedly reclaimed over a long period by her mother. And for Hester's
wedding her mother had taken out the delicate diamond chain—
the "lavaliere" of the Gibson-girl era—that had been her father's
wedding gift to her mother, and the ugly, expensive bar pin that
had been his gift to his wife on the birth of her son. Hester had
never before seen either of them, for the fashion of wearing dia-
monds indiscriminately had never been her mother's, who was con-
temptuous of other women's display, although she might spend
minutes in front of the mirror debating a choice between two relatively gimcrack pieces of costume jewelry. Hester had never known
why this was until recently, when the separation of the last few years
had relaxed the tension between her mother and herself—not
enough to prevent explosions when they met but enough for her to
see, obscurely, the long motivations of her mother's life. In the
European sense, family jewelry was Property, and with all her fault-
less English and New World poise, her mother had never exorcised
her European core.

In the back of the middle drawer, there was a small square of
brown-toned photograph that had never escaped into the large, ramshackle portfolio of family pictures kept in the drawer of the old
break-front bookcase, open to any hand. Seated on a bench, Hedwig
Licht, aged two, brows knitted under ragged hair, stared mournfully into the camera with the huge, heavy-lidded eyes that had continued to brood in her face as a woman, the eyes that she had transmitted to Hester, along with the high cheekbones that she had
deplored. Fat, wrinkled stockings were bowed into arcs that almost
met at the high-stretched boots, which did not touch the floor; to
hold up the stockings, strips of calico matching the dumpy little
dress were bound around the knees.

Long ago, Hester, in her teens, staring tenaciously into the drawer
under her mother's impatient glance, had found the little square

and exclaimed over it, and her mother, snatching it away from her, had muttered, "If that isn't Dutchy!" But she had looked at it long and ruefully before she had pushed it back into a corner. Hester had added the picture to the legend of her mother's childhood built up from the bitter little anecdotes that her mother had let drop casually over the years.

She saw the small Hedwig, as clearly as if it had been herself, haunting the stiff rooms of the house in the townlet of Oberelsbach, motherless since birth and almost immediately stepmothered by a woman who had been unloving, if not unkind, and had soon borne the stern, *Haustyrann* father a son. The small figure she saw had no connection with the all-powerful figure of her mother but, rather, seemed akin to the legion of lonely children who were a constant motif in the literature that had been her own drug—the Sara Crewes and Little Dorrits, all those children who inhabited the familar terror-struck dark that crouched under the lash of the adult. She saw Hedwig receiving from her dead mother's mother—the Grand-mother Rosenberg, warm and loving but, alas, too far away to be of help—the beautiful, satin-incrusted bisque doll, and she saw the bad stepmother taking it away from Hedwig and putting it in the draw-ing room, because "it is too beautiful for a child to play with." She saw all this as if it had happened to her and she had never forgotten.

Years later, when this woman, Hester's step-grandmother, had come to the United States in the long train of refugees from Hitler, her mother had urged the grown Hester to visit her, and she had refused, knowing her own childishness but feeling the resentment rise in her as if she were six, saying, "I won't go. She wouldn't let you have your doll." Her mother had smiled at her sadly and had shrugged her shoulders resignedly. "You wouldn't say that if you could see her. She's an old woman. She has no teeth." Looking at her mother, Hester had wondered what her feelings were after forty years, but her mother, private as always in her emotions, had given no sign.

There had been no sign for Hester—never an open demonstra-tion of love or an appeal—until the telephone call of a few months before, when she had heard her mother say quietly, over the dis-tance, "I think you'd better come," and she had turned away from the phone saying bitterly, almost in awe, "If she *asks me* to come, she must be dying!"

Turning the key over in her hand, Hester looked back at the com-posite figure of her mother—that far-off figure of the legendary child, the nearer object of her own dependence, love, and hate—looked at it from behind the safe, dry wall of her own "American" education. We are told, she thought, that people who do not experience love in their earliest years cannot open up; they cannot give it to others; but by the time we have learned this from books or dredged it out of reminiscence, they have long since left upon us their chill, irremediable stain.

If Hester searched in her memory for moments of animal maternal warmth, like those she self-consciously gave her own child (as if her own childhood prodded her from behind), she thought always of the blue-shot twilight of one New York evening, the winter she was eight, when she and her mother were returning from a shopping expedition, gay and united in the shared guilt of being late for supper. In her mind, now, their arrested figures stood like two silhouettes caught in the spotlight of time. They had paused under the brightly agitated bulbs of a movie-theatre marquee, behind them the broad, rose-red sign of a Happiness candy store. Her mother, suddenly leaning down to her, had encircled her with her arm and nuzzled her, saying almost anxiously, "We do have fun together, don't we?" Hester had stared back stolidly, almost suspiciously, into the looming, pleading eyes, but she had rested against the encircling arm, and warmth had trickled through her as from a closed wound reopening.

After this, her mother's part in the years that followed seemed blurred with the recriminations from which Hester had retreated ever farther, always seeking the remote corners of the household—the sofa-fortressed alcoves, the store closet, the servants' bathroom—always bearing her amulet, a book. It seemed to her now, wincing, that the barrier of her mother's dissatisfaction with her had risen imperceptibly, like a coral cliff built inexorably from the slow accretion of carelessly ejaculated criticisms that had grown into solid being in the heavy fullness of time. Meanwhile, her father's uncritical affection, his open caresses, had been steadiness under her feet after the shifting waters of her mother's personality, but he had been away from home on business for long periods, and when at home he, too, was increasingly a target for her mother's deep-burning rage against life. Adored member of a large family that was almost tribal in its affections and unity, he could not cope with this smoldering force and never tried to understand it, but the shield of his adulthood gave him a protection that Hester did not have. He stood on equal ground.

Hester's parents had met at Saratoga, at the races. So dissimilar were their backgrounds that it was improbable that they would ever have met elsewhere than in the somewhat easy social flux of a spa, although their brownstone homes in New York were not many blocks apart, his in the gentility of upper Madison Avenue, hers in the solid, Germanic comfort of Yorkville. By this time, Hedwig had been in America ten years.

All Hester knew of her mother's coming to America was that she had arrived when she was sixteen. Now that she knew how old her mother had been at death, knew the birth date so zealously guarded during a lifetime of evasion and so quickly exposed by the noncommittal nakedness of funeral routine, she realized that her mother must have arrived in 1900. She had come to the home of an aunt, a sister of her own dead mother. What family drama had preceded her coming, whose decision it had been, Hester did not know. Her mother's one reply to a direct question had been a shrugging "There was nothing for me there."

Hester had a vivid picture of her mother's arrival and first years in New York, although this was drawn from only two clues. Her great-aunt, remarking once on Hester's looks in the dispassionate way of near relations, had nodded over Hester's head to her mother. "She is dark, like the father, no? Not like you were." And Hester, with a naïve glance of surprise at her mother's sedate pompadour, had eagerly interposed, "What was she like, Tante?"

"*Ach,* when she came off the boat, *war sie hübsch!*" Tante had said, lapsing into German with unusual warmth, "Such a color! Pink and cream!"

"Yes, a real Bavarian *Mädchen,*" said her mother with a trace of contempt. "Too pink for the fashion here. I guess they thought it wasn't real."

Another time, her mother had said, in one of her rare bursts of anecdote, "When I came, I brought enough linen and underclothing to supply two brides. At the convent school where I was sent, the nuns didn't teach you much besides embroidery, so I had plenty to bring, plenty. They were nice, though. Good, simple women. Kind. I remember I brought four dozen handkerchiefs, beautiful heavy linen that you don't get in America. But they were large, bigger than the size of a man's handkerchief over here, and the first time I unfolded one, everybody laughed, so I threw them away." She had sighed, perhaps for the linen. "And underdrawers! Long red flannel, and I had spent months embroidering them with yards of white eyelet work on the ruffles. I remember Tante's maid came in from the back yard quite angry and refused to hang them on the line any more. She said the other maids, from the houses around, teased her for belonging to a family who would wear things like that.''

Until Hester was in her teens, her mother had always employed young German or Czech girls fresh from "the other side"—Teenies and Josies of long braided hair, broad cotton ankles and queer, blunt shoes, who had clacked deferentially to her mother in German and had gone off to marry their waiter's and baker's apprentices at just about the time they learned to wear silk stockings and "just as soon as you've taught them how to serve a dinner," returning regularly to show off their square, acrid babies. "Greenhorns!" her mother had always called them, a veil of something indefinable about her lips. But in the middle drawer there was a long rope of blond hair, sacrificed, like the handkerchiefs, but not wholly discarded.

There was no passport in the drawer. Perhaps it had been destroyed during the years of the first World War, when her mother, long since a citizen by virtue of her marriage, had felt the contemporary pressure to excise everything Teutonic. "If that nosy Mrs. Cahn asks you when I came over, just say I came over as a child," she had said to Hester. And how easy it had been to nettle her by pretending that one could discern a trace of accent in her speech! Once, when the family had teased her by affecting to hear an echo of "puplic" in her pronunciation of "public," Hester had come upon her, hours after, standing before a mirror, color and nose high, watching herself say, over and over again, "Public! Public!"

Was it this, thought Hester, her straining toward perfection, that made her so intolerant of me, almost as if she were castigating in her child the imperfections that were her own? "Big feet, big hands, like mine," her mother had grumbled. "Why? Why? When every woman in your father's family wears size one! But their nice, large ears—you must have *those!*" And dressing Hester for Sunday school she would withdraw a few feet to look at the finished product, saying slowly, with dreamy cruelty, "I don't know why I let you wear those white gloves. They make your hands look clumsy, just like a policeman's."

It was over books that the rift between Hester and her mother had become complete. To her mother, marrying into a family whose bookish traditions she had never ceased trying to undermine with the sneer of the practical, it was as if the stigmata of that tradition, appearing upon the girl, had forever made them alien to one another.

"Your eyes don't look like a girl's, they look like an old woman's! Reading! Forever reading!" she had stormed, chasing Hester from room to room, flushing her out of doors, and on one remote, terrible afternoon, whipping the book out of Hester's hand, she had leaned over her, glaring, and had torn the book in two.

Hester shivered now, remembering the cold sense of triumph that had welled up in her as she had faced her mother, rejoicing in the enormity of what her mother had done.

Her mother had faltered before her. "Do you want to be a dreamer all your life?" she had muttered.

Hester had been unable to think of anything to say for a moment. Then she had stuttered, "All you think of in life is money!," and had made her grand exit. But huddling miserably in her room afterward she had known even then that it was not as simple as that, that her mother, too, was whipped and driven by some ungovernable dream she could not express, which had left her, like the book, torn in two.

Was it this, perhaps, that had sent her across an ocean, that had impelled her to perfect her dress and manner, and to reject the humdrum suitors of her aunt's circle for a Virginia bachelor twenty-two years older than herself? Had she, perhaps, married him not only for his money and his seasoned male charm but also for his standards and traditions, against which her railings had been a confession of envy and defeat?

So Hester and her mother had continued to pit their implacable difference against each other in a struggle that was complicated out of all reason by their undeniable likeness—each pursuing in her own orbit the warmth that had been denied. Gauche and surly as Hester was in her mother's presence, away from it she had striven successfully for the very falsities of standard that she despised in her mother, and it was her misery that she was forever impelled to earn her mother's approval at the expense of her own. Always, she knew now, there had been the lurking, buried wish that someday she would find the final barb, the homing shaft, that would maim her mother once and for all, as she felt herself to have been maimed.

A few months before, the barb had been placed in her hand. In answer to the telephone call, she had come to visit the family a short time after her mother's sudden operation for cancer of the breast. She had found her father and brother in an anguish of helplessness, fear, and male distaste at the thought of the illness, and her mother a prima donna of fortitude, moving unbowed toward the unspoken idea of her death but with the signs on her face of a pitiful tension that went beyond the disease. She had taken to using separate utensils and to sleeping alone, although the medical opinion that cancer was not transferable by contact was well known to her. It was clear that she was suffering from a horror of what had been done to her and from a fear of the revulsion of others. It was clear to Hester, also, that her father and brother had such a revulsion and had not been wholly successful in concealing it.

One night she and her mother had been together in her mother's bedroom. Hester, in a shabby housegown, stretched out on the bed luxuriously, thinking of how there was always a certain equivocal ease, a letting down of pretense, an illusory return to the irresponsibility of childhood, in the house of one's birth. Her mother, back turned, had been standing unnecessarily long at the bureau, fumbling with the articles upon it. She turned slowly.

"They've been giving me X-ray twice a week," she said, not looking at Hester, "to stop any involvement of the glands."

"Oh," said Hester, carefully smoothing down a wrinkle on the bedspread. "It's very wise to have that done."

Suddenly, her mother had put out her hand in a gesture almost of appeal. Half in a whisper, she asked, "Would you like to see it? No one has seen it since I left the hospital."

"Yes," Hester said, keeping her tone cool, even, full only of polite interest. "I'd like very much to see it." Frozen there on the bed, she had reverted to childhood in reality, remembering, as if they had all been crammed into one slot in time, the thousands of incidents when she had been the one to stand before her mother, vulnerable and bare, helplessly awaiting the cruel exactitude of her displeasure. I know how she feels as if I were standing there myself, thought Hester. How well she taught me to know!

Slowly her mother undid her housegown and bared her breast. She stood there for a long moment, on her face the looming, pleading look of twenty years before, the look it had once shown under the theatre marquee.

Hester half rose from the bed. There was a hurt in her own breast that she did not recognize. She spoke with difficulty.

"Why . . . it's a beautiful job, Mother," she said, distilling the carefully natural tone of her voice. "Neat as can be. I had no idea

... I thought it would be ugly." With a step toward her mother, she
looked, as if casually, at the dreadful neatness of the cicatrix, at
the twisted, foreshortened tendon of the upper arm.

"I can't raise my arm yet," whispered her mother. "They had to
cut deep. . . . Your father won't look at it."

In an eternity of slowness, Hester stretched out her hand. Trembling, she touched a tentative finger to her mother's chest, where the
breast had been. Then, with rising sureness, with infinite delicacy,
she drew her fingertips along the length of scar in a light, affirmative
caress, and they stood eye to eye for an immeasurable second, on
equal ground at last.

In the cold, darkening room, Hester unclenched herself from
remembrance. She was always vulnerable, Hester thought. As we
all are. What she bequeathed me unwittingly, ironically, was fortitude—the fortitude of those who have had to live under the blow.
But pity—that I found for myself.

She knew now that the tangents of her mother and herself would
never have fully met, even if her mother had lived. Holding her
mother's hand through the long night as she retreated over the
border line of narcosis and coma into death, she had felt the giddy
sense of conquering, the heady euphoria of being still alive, which
comes to the watcher in the night. Nevertheless, she had known with
sureness, even then, that she would go on all her life trying to
"show" her mother, in an unsatisfied effort to earn her approval—
and unconditional love.

As a child, she had slapped at her mother once in a frenzy of rebel-
lion, and her mother, in reproof, had told her the tale of the peasant
girl who had struck her mother and had later fallen ill and died
and been buried in the village cemetery. When the mourners came
to tend the mound, they found that the corpse's offending hand had
grown out of the grave. They cut it off and reburied it, but when
they came again in the morning, the hand had grown again. So,
too, thought Hester, even though I might learn—have learned in
some ways—to escape my mother's hand, all my life I will have to
push it down; all my life my mother's hand will grow again out of
the unquiet grave of the past.

It was her own life that was in the middle drawer. She was the
person she was not only because of her mother but because, fifty-
eight years before, in the little town of Oberelsbach, another
woman, whose qualities she would never know, had died too soon.

Death, she thought, absolves equally the bungler, the evildoer, the unloving, and the unloved—but never the living. In the end, the cicatrix that she had, in the smallest of ways, helped her mother to bear had eaten its way in and killed. The living carry, she thought, perhaps not one tangible wound but the burden of the innumerable small cicatrices imposed on us by our beginnings; we carry them with us always, and from these, from this agony, we are not absolved.

She turned the key and opened the drawer.

THE DILEMMA OF CATHERINE FUCHSIAS

❖

RHYS DAVIES

Puffed up by his success as a ship chandler in the port, forty miles away, where he had gone from the village of Banog when the new town was rising to its heyday as the commercial capital of Wales, John Lewis had retired to the old place heavy with gold and fat. With him was the bitter English wife he had married for her money, and he built the pink-washed villa overlooking Banog's pretty trout stream. And later he set up a secret association with an unmarried woman of forty who was usually called Catherine Fuchsias, this affair—she receiving him most Sunday evenings, after chapel, in her outlying cottage—eluding public notice for two years. Until, on one of those evenings, Lewis, who for some weeks had been complaining of a "feeling of fullness," expired on the bed in her arms.

In every village there is a Jezebel or the makings of one, though sometimes these descend virtuous to their graves, because of lack of opportunity or courage, fear of gossip or ostracism. Lewis the Chandler was Catherine Fuchsias' first real lover, so for her to lose him like that not only dreadfully shocked her but, it will be agreed, placed her in a serious dilemma. She was not a born bad lot, and as a girl she had been left in the lurch by a sweetheart, who had gone prospecting to Australia and never fulfilled his promise to call her there. Thereafter, she had kept house for her father, a farm worker, until he followed her mother into the burial ground surrounding Horeb Chapel, which she cleaned for five shillings a week; in addition, she had a job three days a week in the little wool factory a mile beyond Banog. It was in Horeb Chapel, during service, that Lewis had first studied her and admired her egg-brown face, thick haunches, and air of abundant health. Her cottage stood concealed on a bushy slope outside the village, and she had a great liking for fuchsias, which grew wonderfully in the rich lap of the cottage.

When Catherine's paramour died on her bed, she at first refused to believe it, so pertinacious and active was he and so unlike her idea of a man of sixty-four. Nevertheless, she ran howling downstairs. There she madly poked the fire, flung the night cloth over the canary's cage, ran into the kitchen and swilled a plate or two in a bowl, straightened a mat, and tidied her hair. In the mirror, *there* was her face, Miss Catherine Bowen's face, looking no different—a solid, unharmed fact, with its brown speckles.

But a bad shock can work wonders with a person's sensibility. Buried talents can be whisked up into activity, a primitive cunning reign again in its shady empire of old instincts. Such a shock can create—women especially being given to escape into this—a fantasy of bellicose truth, a performance of the imagination that has nothing to do with hypocrisy but is the terrified soul backing away from reality. After a long collapse in a chair, Catherine sprang up and hurried back to the bedroom.

"Well, Mr. Lewis," she said, "better you are after your rest?" She went close to the bed and peered down at the stout, dusky figure lying on the patchwork quilt. "Well, now, I am not liking the look of you at all," she addressed it, half scoldingly. "What have you taken your jacket off for? Hot you were? Dear me, quite bad you look. Best for me to fetch your wife and the doctor. But you mustn't lie there with your coat off, or a cold you will catch." Volubly tut-tutting, she lit a candle and set about the task. Already, in the hour that had elapsed, he had begun to stiffen somewhat. She perspired and groaned, alternately blenching and going red. He was as heavily cumbersome as a big sack of turnips; she was obliged to prop up his back with a small chair wedged against the bedstead. Luckily, he had removed only his jacket. Finally, buttoned up complete, he rested tidy, and she staggered back, sweating. To lay out her father, she had got the assistance of the blacksmith's wife.

For a minute, Catherine stood in contemplation of her work, then ran downstairs to fetch up his hat, umbrella, and hymnbook. She dropped the umbrella beside the bed, placed the hat on the bedside table, and laid the hymnbook on the quilt, as though it had fallen from his hand. And all the time she uttered clamorous remarks of distress at his condition: "Oh, Mr. Lewis, you didn't ought to have taken a walk, unwell like you are. Climbing! Lucky I saw you leaning over my gate. Dropped dead in the road you might have, and stayed there all night and got bitten by the stoats! You rest quiet, now, and I won't be long." At another thought, she placed a glass of water by the bedside. Then, giving her own person a quick lookover, she put on a raincoat and a flowered hat, blew out the candle, and hastened from the cottage. It was past nine o'clock and quite dark, and she never rode her bicycle in the dark.

Half an hour later, she banged at the costly oaken door of the pink villa, calling excitedly, "Mrs. Lewis, Mrs. Lewis, come to your husband!" Milly Jones, the servant, opened the door, and Catherine violently pushed her inside. "Where's Mrs. Lewis? Let me see her, quick!" But Mrs. Lewis was already standing, stiff as a poker, in the hall.

"Catherine Fuchsias it is!" exclaimed Milly Jones, who was a native of Banog.

Catherine seemed to totter. "Come to your husband, Mrs. Lewis. Crying out for you he is! Oh dear, run all the way I have, fast as a hare." She gulped, sat on a chair, and panted, "Put your hat on quick, Mrs. Lewis, and tell Milly Jones to go to Dr. Watkins."

Mrs. Lewis, who had the English reserve, never attended chapel, and also, unlikably, minded her own business, stared hard. "My husband has met with an accident?" she asked, precise and cold.

"Wandering outside my gate I found him just now!" cried Catherine. "Fetching water from my well I was, and saw him swaying about and staring at me, white as cheese. 'Oh, Mr. Lewis,' I said, 'what is the matter with you? Ill you are? Not your way home from chapel is this!' 'Let me rest in your cottage for a minute,' he said to me, 'and give me a glass of water. My heart is jumping like a toad.' So I helped him in, and he began to grunt awful, and I said, 'Best to go and lie down on my poor father's bed, Mr. Lewis, and I will run at once and tell Mrs. Lewis to fetch Dr. Watkins.' . . . Bring the Doctor to him quick, Mrs. Lewis! Frightened me he has, and no one to leave with him, me watering my chrysanthemums and just going to lock up for the night and seeing a man hanging sick over my gate." She panted and dabbed her face.

Milly Jones was already holding a coat for her mistress, who frowned as Catherine went on babbling of the fright she had sustained. Never a talkative person, the Englishwoman only said, abrupt, "Take me to your house. . . . Milly, go for the Doctor and tell him what you've just heard." And she did not say very much as she stalked along beside Catherine, who still poured out a repetitious wealth of words.

Arrived at the dark cottage, the two women started up the stairs.

Catherine bawled comfortingly, "Come, now, Mr. Lewis, here we are! Not long I've been, have I?"

"You ought to have left a light for him," remarked Mrs. Lewis on the landing.

"What if he had tumbled and set the bed on fire!" said Catherine indignantly. In the heavily silent room, she struck a match and lit the candle. "Oh!" she shrieked.

Mrs. Lewis stood staring through her glasses, and then, in a strangely fallen voice, said, "John! John!" Catherine covered her face with her hands and cried in dramatic woe. "Hush, *woman*, hush," said Mrs. Lewis sternly.

Catherine moved her hands from her face and glared. *Woman*, indeed! In her own house! When she had been so kind! But all she said was "Well, Mrs. Lewis, enough it is to upset anyone with a soft heart when a stranger dies in her house. *Why* was he wandering in the lanes all by himself, in his bad state? Poor man, why is it he didn't go home after chapel? Wandering lost outside my gate, like a lonely orphan child!"

Mrs. Lewis, as though she were examining someone applying for a place in her villa kitchen, gave Catherine a long, glimmering look. "Here is the Doctor," she said.

"Yes, indeed!" Catherine exclaimed. "And I am hoping he can take Mr. Lewis away with him in his motor." The glance she directed at the corpse was now changed to hostility. "He is a visitor that has taken advantage of my poor little cottage." And there was a hint of malice in her manner as she swung her hips past Mrs. Lewis, went to the landing, and called down the stairs, "Come up, Dr. Watkins. But behind time you are."

Having verified the death and listened to Catherine's profuse particulars of how she had found him at the gate and strained herself helping him up the stairs, Dr. Watkins, who was of local birth, and a cheerful man, said, "Well, well, only this evening it was I saw him singing full strength in chapel, his chest out like a robin's. Pity he never would be a patient of mine. 'You mind that heart of yours, John Lewis,' I told him once, free of charge, 'and don't you smoke, drink, or sing.' "

"He liked to sing at the top of his voice," agreed Mrs. Lewis. She took up the hymnbook from the quilt and turned quick to Catherine. "Did he take this with him to the bed, ill as he was?"

"No!" Catherine's voice rang. With Dr. Watkins, the familiar local boy, present, she looked even more powerful. "After I had helped him there and he laid a minute and went a better color, I said, 'Now, Mr. Lewis, you read a hymn or two while I run off—strength they will give you.' "

Mrs. Lewis pounced. "But you put the candle out! It must have been getting quite dark by then."

"There"—Catherine pointed a dramatic finger—"is the box of matches, with the glass of water I gave him." She stood aggressive, while Dr. Watkins' ears moved. "Candles can be lit!"

"This," proceeded Mrs. Lewis, her eyes gazing around and resting, in turn, on a petticoat hanging on a peg and the woman's articles on the dressing table, "*this* was your father's room?"

"Yes," Catherine said, defiant. "Where he died and laid till they took him to Horeb. But when the warm weather comes, I move in here from the back. Cooler it is, and the view in summer very pretty. What are you so inquisitive about?" She began to bridle. "Tidy it is here, and no dust! You would like to look under the bed? In the chest?"

Mrs. Lewis turned to the Doctor. "Could you say how long my husband has been dead?"

He made show of moving the corpse's eyelids, pinching a cheek, swinging an arm. "A good two hours or more," he said with downright assurance.

"Then he must have been dead when he walked up those stairs!" said Mrs. Lewis. "It takes only half an hour to reach my house from here." She turned to Catherine. "You said you came running to me soon as you helped him up here to your father's room."

"A law of the land there is!" Catherine screamed. "Slander and malice is this, and jealous spite!" She took on renewed power and, like an actress towering and swelling into rage, looked twice her size. She turned to Dr. Watkins. "See how it is that kind acts are rewarded, and nipped by a serpent is the hand of charity stretched out to lay the dying stranger on a bed! Better if I had let him fall dead outside my gate, like a workhouse tramp, and turned my back on him to water my Michaelmas daisies. Forty years I have lived in Banog, girl and woman, and not a stain small as a farthing on my character." With her two hands, she pushed up her inflated breasts, as though they hurt her. "Take out of my house my poor, dead visitor that can't rise up and tell the holy truth for me," she sang in crescendo. "No husband, father, or brother have I to fight for my name. Take him!"

"Not possible tonight," said Dr. Watkins, bewildered but appreciative of Catherine's tirade. "Late and a Sunday it is, and the undertaker many miles away."

"The lady by there," said Catherine, pointing a quivering finger, "can hire the handcart of Peter the Watercress, if he can't go in your motor."

"I have no intention of allowing my husband to remain in this house tonight," Mrs. Lewis said. The tone in which she pronounced "this house" demolished the abode to an evil shambles.

"Oh! . . . Oh!" wailed Catherine, beginning again, and moving to the bedside. "John Lewis!" she called to the corpse. "John Lewis, rise up and tell the truth! Swim back across Jordan for a short minute and make dumb the bitter tongue that you married! Miss Catherine Bowen, that took you innocent into her little, clean cottage, is calling to you, and—"

Dr. Watkins, who had twice taken up his bag and laid it down again, interfered decisively at last, for he had been called out by Milly Jones just as he was sitting down to some slices of cold duck. "Hush, now," he said to both women, a man and stern. "Hush, now. Show respect for the passed-away. A cart and horse you would like hired?" he asked Mrs. Lewis. "I will drive you to Llewellyn's farm and ask them to oblige you."

"And oblige *me,* too!" Catherine had the last word, swinging her hips out of the room.

Llewellyn the Farmer agreed readily enough to disturb his stallion, light candles in the cart lanterns, and collect two village men to help carry the heavy man down Catherine Fuchsias' stairs. Already, the village itself had been willingly disturbed out of its Sabbath-night quiet, for Milly Jones, after calling at the Doctor's, was not going to deprive her own people of the high news that rich Mr. Lewis had been mysteriously taken ill in Catherine's cottage. So when the farm cart stopped to collect the two men, news of the death was half expected. Everybody was left agog and expectant of the new week's being a full one. What had Mr. Lewis been doing, wandering around Catherine's cottage up there, after chapel? Strange it was. Married men didn't go for walks and airings after chapel.

On Monday morning, before the dew was off Catherine's flowers, her acquaintance Mrs. Morgans, who lived next door to the post office, bustled into the cottage. "Catherine, dear," she exclaimed, peering at her hard, "there's awful, a man dying on your bed!"

"My father's bed," Catherine corrected her. And at once her body began to swell. "Oh, Jinny Morgans, my place in Heaven I have earned. I have strained myself," she moaned, placing her hands around her lower middle, "helping him up my stairs after I found him whining like an old dog outside my gate. A crick I have got in my side, too. So stout he was, and crying to lay down on a bed. I thought he had eaten a toadstool for a mushroom in the dark."

"What was he doing, walking about up here, whatever?" Mrs. Morgans asked.

"Once before, I saw him going by when I was in my garden. He stopped to make compliments about my fuchsias— Oh," Catherine groaned, clasping her stomach, "the strain is cutting me shocking."

"Your fuchsias . . ." egged on Mrs. Morgans.

"Very big they hung this year. And he said to me, 'When I was a boy, I used to come round here to look for tadpoles in the ponds.' . . . Ah!" she groaned again.

"Tadpoles . . ." Mrs. Morgans nodded, still staring fixed and full on her friend, and sitting tense, with every pore open. As is well known, women hearken to words but rely more on the secret information obtained by the sense that has no language.

Catherine, recognizing that an ambassador had arrived, made a sudden dive into the middle of the matter, her hands flying away from her stomach and waving threatening. And again she went twice her size and beat her breast. "That jealous Mrs. Lewis!" she shouted. "She came here and went smelling round the room, nasty as a cat. This and that she hinted, with Dr. Watkins there for witness! A law of slander there is"—she shot a baleful glance at her visitor— "and let one more word be said against my character and I will go off straight to Vaughan Solicitor and get a letter of warning sent."

"Ha!" said Mrs. Morgans, suddenly relaxing her great intentness. "Ha!" Her tone, like her nod, was obscure of meaning, and on the whole she seemed to be reserving judgment.

Indeed, what real proof was there of unhealthy proceedings having been transacted in Catherine's cottage? Mrs. Morgans went back to the village with her report, and that day everybody sat on it in cautious meditation. In Catherine's advantage was the general dislike of proud Mrs. Lewis, but, on the other hand, a Jezebel, for the common good and the protection of men, must not be allowed to flourish unpunished. All day in the post office, in the Glyndwr Arms that evening, and in every cottage and farmhouse, the matter was observed from several loquacious angles.

On Wednesday afternoon, Mr. Maldwyn Davies, B.A., the minister of Horeb, climbed to the cottage and was received by his member and chapel cleaner with a vigorous flurry of welcome. Needlessly dusting a chair, scurrying for a hair cushion, shouting to the canary, which at the minister's entrance began to chirp and swing his perch madly, to be quiet, Catherine fussily settled him before running to put the kettle on. In the kitchen, she remembered her ill condition and returned slowly, clasping herself. "Ah," she moaned, "my pain has come back! Suffering chronic I've been, off and on, since Sunday night. So heavy was poor Mr. Lewis to take up my stairs. But what was I to be doing with a member of Horeb whining outside my gate for a bed? Shut my door on him, as if he was a scamp or a member of the Church of England?"

"Strange," said Mr. Davies, his concertina neck, which could give forth such sweet music in the pulpit, closing down into his collar, "strange that he climbed up here so far, feeling unwell." He stared at the canary as if the bird held the explanation.

"Delirious and lighted up he was!" Catherine cried. "And no wonder. Did he want to go to his cold home after the sermon and singing in chapel? No! Two times and more, I have seen him wandering around here looking full up with thoughts. One time, he stopped at my gate and had praises for my dahlias, for I was watering them. 'Oh, Mr. Lewis,' I said to him, 'what are you doing walking up here?' And he said, 'I am thinking over the grand sermon Mr. Davies gave us just now, and I would climb big mountains if mountains there were!' Angry with myself I am now that I didn't ask him in for a cup of tea, so lonely he was looking. 'Miss Bowen,' he said to me, 'when I was a boy I used to come rabbiting up here.' "

"Your dahlias are prize ones, and the rabbits a pest," remarked Mr. Davies, still meditatively gazing at the canary.

"Oh!" groaned Catherine, placing her hands around her lower middle. "Grumbling I am not, but there's a payment I am having for my kindness last Sunday! . . . Hush!" she bawled, threatening, to the canary. "Hush, or no more seed today!"

Mr. Davies, oddly, seemed unable to say much. Perhaps he, too, was trying to sniff the truth out of the air. But he looked serious. The reputation of two of his flock was in jeopardy—two who had been nourished by his sermons—and it was unfortunate that one of them lay beyond examination. "Your kettle is boiling over," he reminded Catherine, since in her exalted state she seemed beyond hearing such things.

She darted with a shriek into the kitchen, and when she came back, with a loaded tray, which she had no difficulty in carrying, she asked, "When are you burying him?"

"Thursday, two o'clock. It is a public funeral. . . . You will go to it?" he asked delicately.

This time, Catherine replied sharp and rebuking. "What, indeed, *me*? Me that's got to stay at home because of my strain and can only eat custards? Flat on my back in bed I ought to be this minute. Besides," she said, beginning to bridle again, "Mrs. Lewis, the *lady*, is a nasty!" She paused to take a long breath and to hand Mr. Davies a buttered muffin.

"Her people are not our people," he conceded, and pursed his lips.

Fluffing herself up important, and not eating anything herself, Catherine declared, "Soon as I am well, I am off to Vaughan Solicitor, to have advice." Black passion began to scald her voice, and she pointed a trembling finger ceilingward. "Up there she stood, in the room of my respected father, with Dr. Watkins for witness, and her own poor husband not gone cold and his eyes on us shiny as buttons, and her spiteful tongue made remarks. Hints and sarcastic! Nearly dropped dead I did myself! The hand stretched out in charity was bitten by a viper!" She began to swell still more. "Forty years I have lived in Banog, clean as a whistle, and am left an orphan to do battle alone. Swear I would before the King of England and all the judges of the world that Mr. John Lewis was unwell when he went on the bed up there! Swear I would that my inside was strained by his weight. A heathen gypsy would have taken him into her caravan! Comfort I gave him in his last hour. The glass of water by the bed, and a stitch in my side, racing to fetch his wife, that came here stringy and black-natured as a bunch of dry old seaweed and made evil remarks for thanks." She clasped her breasts as if they would explode. "Oh, if justice there is, all the true tongues of Banog must rise against her and drive the bad-speaking stranger away from us over the old bridge. Our honest village is to be made nasty as a sty, is it? No!"

Not for nothing had she sat all these years in close attention to Mr. Davies' famous sermons, which drew persons from remote farms even in winter, and as she rocked on her thick haunches and her voice passed from the throbbing of harps to the roll of drums, Mr. Davies sat at last in admiration, the rare admiration that one artist gives to another.

"There, now," he said, a compassionate and relenting note in his voice. "There, now, take comfort!" And as he pronounced, "There must be no scandal in Banog!," she knew her battle was won.

The minister took a slice of apple tart and ate it, nodding in meditation. A woman fighting to preserve what is believed to be the most priceless treasure of her sex is a woman to be admired and respected. Especially if she is a Banog one. And it was natural that he should be unwilling to accept that two of his members could have forgotten themselves so scandalously. Nevertheless, as Catherine coiled herself down from her exalted, though aching, state and at last sipped a little strong tea, he coughed and remarked, "It is said that nearly every Sunday night for two years or more Mr. Lewis never arrived home from chapel till ten o'clock, and no trace is there of his occupation in these hours. 'A walk,' he used to tell in his home, 'a Sunday-night walk I take to think over the sermon.' That is what the servant Milly Jones has told in Banog, and that in strong doubt was Mrs. Lewis concerning those walks in winter and summer."

"Then a policeman she ought to have set spying behind him!" said Catherine, blowing on a fresh cup of tea with wonderful assurance. "Oh, a shame it is that the dead man can't rise up and speak! Oh, wicked it is that a dead man not buried yet is turned into a goat!" Calm now, and the more powerful for it, she added, "Proofs they must bring out—strict proofs. Let Milly Jones go babbling more, and *two* letters from Vaughan Solicitor I will have sent!"

"Come, now," said Mr. Davies hastily. "Come, now, the name of Banog must not be bandied about outside and talked of in market. Come, now, the matter must be put away. Wind blows and wind goes." He rose, gave a kind nod to the canary, and left.

Mr. Davies would speak the decisive word to silence offensive tongues, Catherine knew. But as a protest she still stayed retreated in the cottage; serve them right in the village that she withhold sight of herself from the inquisitive eyes down there. On Friday morning, the milkman told her that Mr. Lewis had had a tidy-sized funeral the previous day. She was relieved to hear he was safely in the earth, which was the home of forgetfulness and which, in due course, turned even the most disagreeable things sweet. After the milkman had gone, she mixed herself a cake of festival richness, and so victorious did she feel that she decided to put an end to her haughty exile on Sunday evening and go to chapel as usual. Dropping yet another egg in the bowl, she saw herself arriving at the last minute and marching to her pew in the front, with head held high in rescued virtue.

On Saturday morning, the postman, arriving late at her out-of-the-way cottage, threw a letter inside her door. Within a quarter of an hour, agitated of face, she flew from the cottage on her bicycle. The village saw her speeding through without a look from her bent-over head. She shot past the post office, Horeb Chapel, the inn, the row of cottages where the nobodies lived; past the house of Twsswg, the triple-crowned bard, whose lays of local lore deserved to be better known; past the houses of Mr. Davies, B.A., and of Mrs. Williams Flannel, who had spoken on the radio about flannel weaving; past the cottages of Evans the Harpist and of Chicago Jenkins, who had been in jail in that place; and, ringing her bell furious, spun in greased haste over the crossroads where, in easier times, they had hanged men for sheepstealing. She got out onto the main road without molestation.

"Judging by the way her legs were going on that bike, the strain in her inside has repaired quite well," remarked Mrs. Harpist Evans in the post office.

It was nine miles to the market town where Vaughan the Solicitor had his office, which on Saturday closed at midday. Arrived there, Catherine stamped up the stairs, burst into an outer room, and demanded of a ginger youth that Mr. Vaughan attend to her at once. So distraught was she that the youth skedaddled behind a partition of frosted glass. He came back and took her into the privacy, where Mr. Vaughan, who was thin as a wasp and had a black hat on his head, said, "What are you wanting? Closing time it is." Catherine, heaving and choking, threw down the letter on his desk, and after looking at it he said, flat, "Well, you can't have it yet! Not till after probate. You go back home and sit quiet for a few weeks." Accustomed to the hysteria of legatees, and, indeed, of non-legatees, he turned away and put a bunch of keys in his pocket.

Catherine panted and perspired. And, pushing down her breasts, she drew out her voice, such as it was. "Oh, Mr. Vaughan," she whimpered, "it is not the money I want. Come I have to ask you to let this little business be shut up close as a grave." A poor, misused woman in mortal distress, she wiped sweat and tears off her healthy, country-red cheeks.

"What are you meaning?" He whisked about impatient, for at twelve-five, in the bar-parlor of the Blue Boar, he always met the manager of the bank for conference over people's private business.

Catherine hung her head ashamed-looking as she moaned, "A little favorite of Mr. Lewis I was, me always giving him flowers and vegetables and whatnot, free of charge. But bad tongues there are in Banog, and they will move quick if news of this money will go about."

"Well," Mr. Vaughan said, flat again, "too late you are. There is Mrs. Lewis herself knowing about your legacy since Thursday evening, and—"

Catherine burst out, "But *she* will keep quiet, for sure! She won't be wanting it talked that her husband went and left me three hundred pounds—no, indeed! For *I* can say things about her that poor Mr. Lewis told me. It is of Horeb Chapel I am worrying—for you not to tell Mr. Davies, our minister, or anyone else that I have been left this money." She peeped up at him humble.

"Well," he said, even flatter than before and, as was only proper, not sympathetic, "too late you are again. Same time that I wrote to you, I sent a letter to Mr. Davies that the chapel is left money for a new organ and Miss Catherine Bowen, the cleaner, left a legacy, too; the letter is with him this morning. In the codicil dealing with you, Mr. Lewis said it was a legacy because your cleaning wage was so small and you a good worker."

The excuse would have served nice but for that unlucky death on her bed. She groaned aloud. And as she collapsed on the solicitor's hard chair, she cried out in anguish, entreating aid of him in this disaster. Pay him well she would if he preserved her good name— pounds and pounds.

"A miracle I cannot perform," he said.

Truth, when it is important, is not mocked for long, even in a solicitor's office. The legatee went down the stairs with the gait of one whipped sore. She cycled back to her cottage as though using only one leg, and to avoid the village she took a circuitous way, pushing the cycle up stony paths. At the cottage, after sitting in a trance for a while, she walked whimpering to the well among the chrysanthemums, removed the cover, and sat on the edge in a further trance. An hour passed, for her thoughts hung like lead. She went into the dark night of the soul. But she couldn't bring herself to urge her body into the round black hole that pierced the earth so deep.

Then, on the horizon of the dark night, shone a ray of bright light. For the first time since the postman's arrival, the solid, untrimmed fact struck her that three hundred pounds of good money was hers. She could go to Aberystwyth and set up in partnership with her friend Sally Thomas, who, already living there as a cook, wanted to start lodgings for the college students. The legacy—surprising, because Mr. Lewis had always been prudent of pocket, and she had approved of this respect for cash, believing, with him, that the best things in life are free—the legacy would take her into a new life. She rose from the well. And in the cottage, shaking herself finally out of her black dream, she decided that Mr. Lewis had left her the money as a smack at his wife, the nasty one.

No one came to see Catherine. She did not go to chapel on the Sunday. Three days later, she received a letter from Mr. Davies, B.A., inviting her to call at his house. She knew what it meant. The minister had sat with his deacons in special conclave on her matter, and he was going to tell her that she was to be cast out from membership of Horeb. She wrote declining the invitation and said she was soon to leave Banog to live at the seaside in quiet. She wrote to Sally Thomas at the same time. But she had to go down to the post office for stamps.

She entered the shop with, at first, the mien of an heiress. Two women members of Horeb were inside, and Lizzie Postmistress was slicing bacon. Catherine stood waiting at the post-office counter, in the corner. No one greeted her or took notice, but one of the customers slipped out and in a few minutes returned with three more women. All of them turned their backs on Catherine. They talked brisk and loud while Catherine waited, drawn up. Lizzie Postmistress sang, "Fancy Lewis the Chandler leaving money for a new organ for Horeb!"

"The deacons ought to say no to it," declared the wife of Peter the Watercress.

"Yes, indeed." The cobbler's wife nodded. "Every time it is played, members will be reminded."

"Well," said single Jane the Dressmaker, who had a tape measure around her neck, "not the fault of the organ will that be."

They clustered before the bacon-cutting postmistress. On a tin of biscuits, listening complacent, sat a cat. The postmistress stopped slicing, waved her long knife, and cried, "Never would I use such an organ—no, not even with gloves on—and I, for one, won't like singing hymns to it."

"A full members' meeting about *all* the business there ought to

be! Deacons are men. Men go walking to look at dahlias and fuchsias—"

"And drop dead at sight of a prize dahlia," said the cobbler's
wife.

Catherine rapped on the counter and shouted, "Stamps!"

The postmistress craned her head over the others and exclaimed,
"Why, now, there's Catherine Fuchsias! . . . Your inside is better
from the strain?" she inquired. The others turned and stared in
unison.

"Stamps!" said Catherine, who, under the united scrutiny, suddenly took on a meek demeanor.

"Where for?" asked the postmistress, coming over to the post-office
side and snatching up the two letters Catherine had laid on the
counter. "Ho, one to Mr. Davies, B.A., and one to Aberystwyth!"

"I am going to live in Aberystwyth," said Catherine grandly.

"Retiring you are on your means?" asked Jane the Dressmaker.

"Plenty of college professors and well-offs in Aberystwyth!" com-
mented Peter's wife.

"Well," the postmistress said, and frowned, as if in doubt about
her right to sell stamps to such a person. "I don't know, indeed.
What you wasting a stamp on this one for, with Mr. Davies living
just up the road? Too much money you've got?"

"Ten shillings I get for making up a dress, working honest on it for
three days or more," complained unmarried Jane the Dressmaker.
"Never will *I* retire to Aberystwyth and sit on the front winking at
the sea."

"What you going there so quick for?" asked the cobbler's wife,
her eyes travelling sharp from Catherine's face to below and resting
there suspicious.

"Two stamps." The postmistress flung them down grudgingly,
at last, and took up Catherine's coin, as if she were picking up a
rotten mouse by the tail. "Wishing I am you'd buy your stamps
somewhere else."

Catherine, after licking and sticking them, seemed to regain
strength as she walked to the door, remarking haughtily, "There's
wicked jealousy when a person is left money! Jealous you are not in
my shoes, now *and* before."

But, rightly, the postmistress had the last word: "A cousin I have
in Aberystwyth. Wife of a busy minister that is knowing everybody
there. A letter *I* must write to Aberystwyth, too."

THE NIGHTINGALES SING

❖

Elizabeth Parsons

THROUGH THE FOG the car went up the hill, whining in second gear, up the sandy road that ran between the highest and broadest stone walls that Joanna had ever seen. There were no trees at all, only the bright green, cattle-cropped pastures sometimes visible above the walls, and sweet-fern and juniper bushes, all dim in the opaque air and the wan light of a May evening. Phil, driving the creaking station wagon with dexterous recklessness, said to her, "I hope it's the right road. Nothing looks familiar in this fog and I've only been here once before."

"It was nice of him to ask us—me, especially," said Joanna, who was young and shy and grateful for favors.

"Oh, he loves company," Phil said. "I wish we could have got away sooner, to be here to help him unload the horses, though. Still, Chris will be there."

"Is Chris the girl who got thrown today?" Joanna asked, remembering the slight figure in the black coat going down in a spectacular fall with a big bay horse. Phil nodded and brought the car so smartly around a bend that the two tack boxes in the back of it skidded across the floor. Then he stopped, at last on the level, at a five-barred gate that suddenly appeared out of the mist.

"I'll do the gate," Joanna said, and jumped out. It opened easily and she swung it back against the fence and held it while Phil drove through; then the engine stalled, and in the silence she stood for a moment, her head raised, sniffing the damp, clean air. There was no sound—not the sound of a bird, or a lamb, or the running of water over stones, or wind in leaves; there was only a great stillness, and a sense of height and strangeness, and the smell of grass and dried dung. This was the top of the world, this lost hillside, green and bare, ruled across by enormous old walls—the work, so it seemed, of giants. In the air there was a faint movement as of a great wind far away, breathing through the fog. Joanna pulled the gate shut and got in again with Phil, and they drove on along the smooth crest of the hill, the windshield wipers swinging slowly to and fro and Phil's sharp, redheaded profile drawn clearly against the gray background. She was grateful to him for taking her to the horse show that afternoon, but she was timid about the invitation to supper that it had led to. Still, there was no getting out of it now. Phil was the elder brother of a school friend of hers, Carol Watson; he was so old he might as well have been of another generation, and there was about him, still incredibly unmarried at the age of thirty-one, the mysterious aura that bachelor elder brothers always possess. Carol was supposed to have come with them, but she had developed chicken pox the day before. However, Phil had kindly offered to take Joanna just the same, since he had had to ride, and he had kept a fatherly eye on her whenever he could. Then a friend of his named Sandy Sheldon, a breeder of polo ponies, had asked him to stop at his farm for supper on the way home. Phil had asked Joanna if she wanted to go, and she had said yes, knowing that he wanted to.

Being a good child, she had telephoned her family to tell them she would not be home until late, because she was going to Sandy Sheldon's place with Phil.

"*Whose* place?" her mother's faraway voice had asked, doubtfully. "Well, don't be too late, will you, dear. And call me up when you're leaving, won't you. It's a miserable night to be driving."

"I can't call you," Joanna had said. "There's no telephone."

"Couldn't you call up from somewhere after you've left?" the faint voice had said. "You know how Father worries, and Phil's such a fast driver."

"I'll try to." Exasperation had made Joanna's voice stiff. What earthly good was *telephoning?* She hung up the receiver with a bang, showing a temper she would not have dared display in the presence of her parents.

Now suddenly out of the fog great buildings loomed close, and they drove through an open gate into a farmyard with gray wooden barns on two sides of it and stone walls on the other two sides. A few white hens rushed away across the dusty ground, and a gray cat sitting on the pole of a blue dump cart stared coldly at the car as Phil stopped it beside a battered horse van. The instant he stopped, a springer ran barking out of one of the barn doors and a man appeared behind him and came quickly out to them, up to Joanna's side of the car, where he put both hands on the door and bent his head a little to look in at them.

"Sandy, this is Joanna Gibbs," Phil said.

Sandy looked at her without smiling but not at all with unfriend-
liness, only with calm consideration. "Hello, Joanna," he said, and
opened the door for her.

"Hello," she said, and forgot to be shy, for, instead of uttering the
kind of asinine polite remark she was accustomed to hearing from
strangers, he did not treat her as a stranger at all, but said immediately, "You're just in time to help put the horses away. Chris keeled
over the minute we got here and I had to send her to bed, and Jake's
gone after one of the cows that's strayed off." He spoke in a light,
slow, Western voice. He was a small man about Phil's age, with a
flat, freckled face, light brown, intelligent eyes, and faded brown
hair cut short all over his round head. He looked very sturdy and
stocky, walking toward the van beside Phil's thin, New England elegance, and he had a self-confidence that seemed to spring simply
from his own good nature.

"Quite a fog you greet us with," Phil said, taking off his coat and
hanging it on the latch of the open door of the van. Inside, in the
gloom, four long, shining heads were turned toward them, and one
of the horses gave a gentle, anxious whinny.

"Yes, we get them once in a while," said Sandy. "I like 'em."

"So do I," Joanna said.

He turned to her and said, "Look, there's really no need in your
staying out here. Run in the house, where it's warm, and see if the
invalid's all right. You go through that gate." He pointed to a small,
sagging gate in one wall.

"All right, I will," she answered, and she started off across the
yard toward the end gable of a house she could see rising dimly
above some apple trees, the spaniel with her.

"Joanna!" Sandy called after her, just as she reached the gate.

"Yes?" She turned back. The two men were standing by the runway of the van. They both looked at her, seeing a tall young girl in
a blue dress and sweater, with her hair drawn straight back over her
head and tied at the back of her neck in a chignon with a black bow,
and made more beautiful and airy than she actually was by the
watery air.

"Put some wood on the kitchen fire as you go in, will you?" Sandy
shouted to her. "The woodbox is right by the stove."

"All right," she answered again, and she and the spaniel went
through the little gate in the wall.

A path led from the gate under the apple trees, where the grass was cut short and neat, to a door in the ell of the house. The house it-self was big and old and plain, almost square, with a great chimney settled firmly across the ridgepole, and presumably it faced down the hill toward the sea. It was conventional and unimposing, with white-painted trim and covered with gray old shingles. There was a lilac bush by the front door and a bed of unbudded red lilies around one of the apple trees, but except for these there was neither shrub-bery nor flowers. It looked austere and pleasing to Joanna, and she went in through the door in the ell and saw the woodbox beside the black stove. As she poked some pieces of birchwood down into the snapping fire, a girl's voice called from upstairs, "Sandy?"

Joanna put the lid on the stove and went through a tiny hallway into a living room. An enclosed staircase went up out of one corner, and she went to it and called up it, "Sandy's in the barn. Are you all right?"

"Oh, I'm fine," the voice answered, hard and clear. "Just a little shaky when I move around. Come on up."

Immediately at the top of the stairs was a big, square bedroom, papered in a beautiful, faded paper with scrolls and wheat sheaves. On a four-posted bed lay a girl not many years older than Joanna, covered to the chin with a dark patchwork quilt. Her short black hair stood out against the pillow, and her face was colorless and expressionless and at the same time likable and amusing. She did not sit up when Joanna came in; she clasped her hands behind her head and looked at her with blue eyes under lowered black lashes.

"You came with Phil, didn't you?" she asked.

"Yes," Joanna said, moving hesitantly up to the bed and leaning against one of the footposts. "They're putting the horses away and they thought I'd better come in and see how you were."

"Oh, I'm fine," Chris said again. "I'll be O.K. in a few minutes. I lit on my head, I guess, by the way it feels, but I don't remember a thing."

Joanna remembered. It had not seemed possible that that black figure could emerge, apparently from directly underneath the bay horse, and, after sitting a minute on the grass with hanging head, get up and walk grimly away, ignoring the animal that had made such a clumsy error and was being led out by an attendant in a long tan coat.

Joanna also remembered that when people were ill or in pain you brought them weak tea and aspirin and hot-water bottles, and

that they were usually in bed, wishing to suffer behind partly lowered shades, not just lying under a quilt with the fog pressing
against darkening windows. But there was something here that did
not belong in the land of tea and hot-water bottles—a land that, indeed, now seemed on another planet. Joanna made no suggestions
but just stood there, looking with shy politeness around the room. It
was a cold, sparsely furnished place, and it looked very bare to Joanna, most of whose life so far had been spent in comfortable, chintz-
warmed interiors, with carpets that went from wall to wall. In this
room, so obviously untouched for the past hundred years or more,
was only the bed, a tall chest of drawers, a washstand with a gold-
and-white bowl and pitcher, two plain, painted chairs, and a thread-
bare, oval, braided rug beside the bed. There were no curtains or
shades at the four windows, and practically no paint left on the un-
even old floor. There was dust over everything. The fireplace was
black and damp-smelling and filled with ashes and charred paper
that rose high about the feet of the andirons. Joanna could not make
out whether it was a guest room or whose room it was; here and there
were scattered possessions that might have been male or female—a
bootjack, some framed snapshots, a comb, a dirty towel, some socks,
a magazine on the floor. Chris's black coat was lying on a chair, and
her bowler stood on the bureau. It was a blank room, bleak in the
failing light.

Chris watched her from under her half-closed lids, waiting for
her to speak, and presently Joanna said, "That was really an awful
spill you had."

Chris moved her head on the pillow and said, "He's a brute of a
horse. He'll never be fit to ride. I've schooled him for Mrs. Whit-
taker for a year now and ridden him in three shows and I thought
he was pretty well over his troubles." She shrugged and wrapped
herself tighter in the quilt. "She's sunk so much money in him it's
a crime, but he's just a brute and I don't think I can do anything
more with him. Of course, if she wants to go on paying me to ride
him, O.K., and her other horses are tops, so I haven't any kick,
really. You can't have them all perfect."

"What does she bother with him for?" Joanna asked.

"Well, she's cracked, like most horse-show people," Chris said.
"They can't resist being spectacular—exhibitionists, or whatever
they call it. Got to have something startling, and then more startling,
and so on. And I must say this horse is something to see. He's
beautiful." Her somewhat bored little voice died away.

Joanna contemplated all this seriously. It seemed to her an ardu-
ous yet dramatic way of earning one's living; she did not notice
that there was nothing in the least dramatic about the girl on the
bed beside her. Chris, for her part, was speculating more directly
about Joanna, watching her, appreciating her looks, wondering
what she was doing with Phil. Then, because she was not unkind
and sensed that Joanna was at loose ends in the strange house, she
said to her, suddenly leaving the world of horses for the domestic
scene where women cozily collaborate over the comforts of their
men, "Is there a fire in the living room? I was too queasy to notice
when I came in. If there isn't one, why don't you light it, so it'll be
warm when they come in?"

"I'll look," said Joanna. "I didn't notice, either. Can I get you
anything?"

"No, I'll be down pretty soon," Chris said. "I've got to start supper."

Joanna went back down the little stairs. There was no fire in the
living room, but a broken basket beside the fireplace was half full
of logs, and she carefully laid these on the andirons and stuffed in
some twigs and old comics and lit them. In a few minutes the tall
flames sprang up into the black chimney, shiny with creosote. Joanna sat on the floor and looked around the room. It was the same
size as the bedroom above it, but it was comfortable and snug, with
plain gray walls and white woodwork. A fat sofa, covered with dirty,
flowered linen, stood in front of the fire. There were some big wicker
chairs and four little carved Victorian chairs and a round table with
big, bowed legs, covered with a red tablecloth. A high, handsome
secretary stood against the long wall opposite the fire; its veneer was
peeling, and it was filled with tarnished silver cups and ribbon
rosettes. A guitar lay on a chair. There were dog hairs on the sofa,
and the floor was dirty, and outside the windows there was nothing-
ness. Joanna got up to look at the kitchen fire, put more wood on it,
and returned to the living room. Overhead she heard Chris moving
around quietly, and she pictured her walking about the barren,
dusty bedroom, combing her short black hair, tying her necktie, folding up the quilt, looking in the gloom for a lipstick; and suddenly a
dreadful, lonely sadness and longing came over her. The living room
was growing dark, too, and she would have lit the big nickel lamp
standing on the table but she did not know how to, so she sat there
dreaming in the hot, golden firelight. Presently she heard the men's
voices outside, and they came into the kitchen and stopped there to

talk. Joanna heard the stove lids being rattled. Sandy came to the door and, seeing her, said, "Is Chris all right?"

"Yes, I think so," Joanna said. "She said she was, anyway."

"Guess I'll just see," he said, and went running up the stairs. The spaniel came in from the kitchen to be near the fire. Joanna stroked his back. His wavy coat was damp with fog, and he smelled very strongly of dog; he sat down on the hearth facing the fire, raised his muzzle, and closed his eyes and gave a great sigh of comfort. Then all of a sudden he trotted away and went leaping up the stairs to the bedroom, and Joanna could hear his feet overhead.

Phil came in next, his hair sticking to his forehead. He hung his coat on a chair back and said to Joanna, "How do you like it here?"

"It's wonderful," she said earnestly.

"It seems to me a queer place," he said, lifting the white, fluted china shade off the lamp and striking a match. "Very queer—so far off. We're marooned. I don't feel there's any other place anywhere, do you?"

Joanna shook her head and watched him touch the match to the wick and stoop to settle the chimney on its base. When he put on the shade, the soft yellow light caught becomingly on his red head and his narrow face, with the sharp cheekbones and the small, deep-set blue eyes. Joanna had known him for years, but she realized, looking at him in the yellow light, that she knew almost nothing about him. Before this, he had been Carol's elder brother, but here, in the unfamiliar surroundings, he was somebody real. She looked away from his lighted face, surprised and wondering. He took his pipe out of his coat pocket and came to the sofa and sat down with a sigh of comfort exactly like the dog's, sticking his long, thin, booted feet out to the fire, banishing the dark, making the fog retreat.

Sandy came down the stairs and went toward the kitchen, and Phil called after him, "Chris O.K.?"

"Yes," Sandy said, going out.

"She's a little crazy," Phil said. "Too much courage and no sense. But she's young. She'll settle down, maybe."

"Are she and Sandy engaged?" Joanna asked.

"Well, no," said Phil. "Sandy's got a wife. She stays in Texas." He paused to light his pipe, and then he said, "That's where he raises his horses, you know; this place is only sort of a salesroom. But he and Chris know each other pretty well."

This seemed obvious to Joanna, who said, "Yes, I know." Phil smoked in silence.

"Doesn't his wife *ever* come here?" Joanna asked after a moment.

"I don't think so," Phil answered.

They could hear Sandy in the kitchen, whistling, and occasionally rattling pans. They heard the pump squeak as he worked the handle, and the water splashed down into the black iron sink. Then he, too, came in to the fire and said to Joanna, smiling down at her, "Are you comfy, and all?"

"Oh *yes*," she said, and flushed with pleasure. "I love your house," she managed to say.

"I'm glad you do. It's kind of a barn of a place, but fine for the little I'm in it." He walked away, pulled the flowered curtains across the windows, and came back to stand before the fire. He looked very solid, small, and cheerful, with his shirtsleeves rolled up, his collar unbuttoned, and his gay, printed tie loosened. He seemed so snug and kind to Joanna, so somehow sympathetic, that she could have leaned forward and hugged him around the knees. But at the idea of doing any such thing she blushed again, and bent to pat the dog.

Sandy took up the guitar and tuned it. He began playing absent-mindedly, his stubby fingers straying across the strings as he stared into the fire. Chris came down the stairs. Instead of her long black boots she had on a pair of dilapidated Indian moccasins with a few beads remaining on the toes, and between these and the ends of her breeches' legs were gay blue socks. The breeches were fawn-colored, and she had on a fresh white shirt with the sleeves rolled up. Her curly hair, cropped nearly as short as a boy's, was brushed and shining, and her hard, sallow little face was carefully made up and completely blank. Whether she was happy or disturbed, well or ill, Joanna could see no stranger would be able to tell.

"What about supper?" she asked Sandy.

"Calm yourself," he said. "I'm cook tonight. It's all started." He took her hand to draw her down on the sofa, but she moved away and pulled a cushion off a chair and lay down on the floor, her feet toward the fire and her hands folded, like a child's, on her stomach. Phil had gone into the kitchen, and now he came back carrying a lighted lamp; it dipped wildly in his hand as he set it on the round table beside the other one. The room shone in the low, beneficent light. Sandy, leaning his head against the high, carved back of the sofa, humming and strumming, now sang aloud in a light, sweet voice:

> "For I'd rather hear your fiddle
> And the tone of one string,
> Than watch the waters a-gliding,
> Hear the nightingales sing."

The soft strumming went on, and the soft voice, accompanied by Chris's gentle crooning. The fire snapped. Phil handed around some glasses and then went around with a bottle of whiskey he found in the kitchen. He paused at Joanna's glass, smiled at her, and poured her a very small portion.

> "If I ever return,
> It will be in the spring
> To watch the waters a-gliding,
> Hear the nightingales sing."

The old air died on a trailing chord.

"That's a lovely song," Joanna said, and then shrank at her sentimentality.

Sandy said, "Yes, it's nice. My mother used to sing it. She knew an awful lot of old songs." He picked out the last bars again on the guitar. Joanna, sitting beside him on the floor, was swept with warmth and comfort.

"My God, the peas!" Sandy said suddenly, in horror, as a loud sound of hissing came from the kitchen. Throwing the guitar down on the sofa, he rushed to rescue the supper.

Joanna and Chris picked their way toward the privy that adjoined the end of the barn nearer the house. They moved in a little circle of light from the kerosene lantern that Chris carried, the batteries of Sandy's big flashlight having turned out to be dead. They were both very full of food, and sleepy, and just a little tipsy. Chris had taken off her socks and moccasins and Joanna her leather sandals, and the soaking grass was cold to their feet, which had so lately been stretched out to the fire. Joanna had never been in a privy in her life, and when Chris opened the door she was astonished at the four neatly covered holes, two large and—on a lower level—two small. Everything was whitewashed; there were pegs to hang things on, and a very strong smell of disinfectant. A few flies woke up and buzzed. Chris set the lantern down on the path and partly closed the door behind them.

There was something cozy about the privy, and they were in no particular hurry to go back to the house. Chris lit a cigarette, and they sat there comfortably in the semidarkness, and Chris talked. She told Joanna about her two years in college, to which she had been made to go by her family. But Chris's love was horses, not gaining an education, and finally she had left and begun to support herself as a professional rider.

"I'd known Sandy ever since I was little," she said. "I used to hang around him when I was a kid, and he let me ride his horses and everything, and when I left college he got me jobs and sort of looked after me."

"He's a darling, isn't he?" Joanna said dreamily, watching the dim slice of light from the open door, and the mist that drifted past it.

"Well, sometimes he is," Chris said. "And sometimes I wish I'd never seen him."

"Oh, *no!*" cried Joanna. "Why?"

"Because he's got so he takes charge too much of the time—you know?" Chris said. "At first I was so crazy about him I didn't care, but now it's gone on so long I'm beginning to see I'm handicapped, in a way. Or that's what I think, anyway. Everybody just assumes I'm his girl. And he's got a wife, you know, and he won't leave her, ever. And then he's not here a lot of the time. But the worst of all is that he's spoiled me; everybody else seems kind of tame and young. So you see it's a mixed pleasure."

Joanna pondered, a little fuzzily. She was not at all sure what it was that Chris was telling her, but she felt she was being talked to as by one worldly soul to another. Now Chris was saying, "He said that would happen, and I didn't care then. He said, 'I'm too *old* for you, Chris, even if I was single, and this way it's hopeless for you.' But I didn't care. I didn't want anybody or anything else and I just plain chased him. And now I don't want anything else, either. So it *is* hopeless. . . . I hope you don't ever love anybody more than he loves you."

"I've never really been in love," Joanna said bravely.

"Well, you will be," Chris said, lighting a second cigarette. The little white interior and their two young, drowsy faces shone for a second in the flash of the match. "First I thought you were coming here because you were Phil's girl, but I soon saw you weren't."

"Oh, *no!*" cried Joanna again. "He's just the brother of a friend of mine, that's all."

"Yes," said Chris. "He always picks racier types than you."

Racy, thought Joanna. I wish *I* was racy, but I'm too scared.

"I've seen some of his girls, and not one of them was as good-looking as you are," Chris went on. "But they were all very dizzy. He has to have that, I guess—he's so sort of restrained himself, with that family and all. I went to a cocktail party at his house once, and it was terrible. Jeepers!" She began to laugh.

Vulgarity is what he likes, then, said Joanna to herself. Perhaps I like it myself, though I don't know that I know what it is. Perhaps my mother would say Chris and Sandy were vulgar, but they don't seem vulgar to me, though I'm glad Mother isn't here to hear their language and some of Sandy's songs.

She gave it up as Chris said, with a yawn, "We'd better go back."

As they went toward the house, it loomed up above them, twice its size, the kitchen windows throwing low beams of light out into the fog. Still there was no wind. In the heavy night air nothing was real, not even Chris and the lantern and the corner of the great wall near the house. Joanna was disembodied, moving through a dream on her bare, numb feet to a house of no substance.

"Let's walk around to the front," she said. "I love the fog."

"O.K.," said Chris, and they went around the corner and stopped by the lilac bushes to listen to the stillness.

But suddenly the dampness reached their bones, and they shivered and screeched and ran back to the back door, with the bobbing lantern smoking and smelling in Chris's hand.

When they came in, Phil looked at them fondly. "Dear little Joanna," he said. "She's all dripping and watery and vaporous, like Undine. What in God's name have you girls been doing?"

"Oh, talking," said Chris.

"Pull up to the fire," Sandy said. "What did you talk about? Us?"

"Yes, dear," said Chris. "We talked about you every single second."

"Joanna's very subdued," remarked Phil. "Did you talk her into a stupor, or what?"

"Joanna doesn't have to talk if she doesn't want to," said Sandy. "I like a quiet woman, myself."

"Do you, now?" said Phil, laughing at Chris, who made a face at him and sat down beside Sandy and gave him a violent hug.

Joanna, blinking, sat on the floor with her wet feet tucked under her, and listened vaguely to the talk that ran to and fro above her. Her head was swimming, and she felt sleepy and wise in the warm lamplight and with the sound of the banter in which she did not have to join unless she wanted to. Suddenly she heard Phil saying, "You know, Joanna, we've got to start along. It seems to me you made a rash promise to your family that you wouldn't be too late getting home, and it's nearly ten now and we've got thirty miles to go." He yawned, stretched, and bent to knock out his pipe on the side of the fireplace.

"I don't want to go," Joanna said.

"Then stay," said Sandy. "There's plenty of room."

But Phil said, getting up, "No, we've got to go. They'd have the police out if we didn't come soon. Joanna's very carefully raised, you know."

"I *love* Joanna," said Chris, hugging Sandy again until he grunted. "I don't care how carefully she was raised, I love her."

"We all love her," Sandy said. "You haven't got a monopoly on her. Come again and stay longer, will you, Joanna? We love you, and you look so nice here in this horrible old house."

They really do like me, Joanna thought, pulling on her sandals. But not as much as I like them. They have a lot of fun all the time, so it doesn't mean as much to them to find somebody they like. But I'll remember this evening as long as I live.

Sadly she went out with them to the station wagon, following the lantern, and climbed in and sat on the clammy leather seat beside Phil. Calling back, and being called to, they drove away, bumping slowly over the little road, and in a second Chris and Sandy and the lantern were gone in the fog.

Joanna let herself in the front door and turned to wave to Phil, who waved back and drove off down the leafy street, misty in the midnight silence. Inland, the fog was not so bad as it had been near the sea, but the trees dripped with the wetness and the sidewalk shone under the street light. She listened to the faraway, sucking sound of Phil's tires die away; then she sighed and closed the door and moved sleepily into the still house, dropping her key into the brass bowl on the hall table. The house was cool, and dark downstairs except for the hall light, and it smelled of the earth in her mother's little conservatory.

Joanna started up the stairs, slowly unfastening the belt of the old trench coat she had borrowed from Phil. The drive back had been a meaningless interval swinging in the night, with nothing to remember but the glow of the headlights so blanketed by the fog that they had had to creep around the curves and down the hills, peering out until their eyes ached. Soon after they had left the farm, they had stopped in a small town while Joanna telephoned her family. Through the open door of the phone booth she had watched Phil sitting on a spindly stool at the little marble counter next to the shelves full of Westerns, drinking a coke. She had a coke herself and she sipped it as the telephone rang far away in her parents' house, while back of the counter a radio played dance music. And twice after that Phil had pulled off the road, once to light his pipe, and once for Joanna to put on his coat. But now, moving up the shallow, carpeted stairs, she was back in the great, cold, dusty house with the sound of Sandy's guitar and the smell of the oil lamps, and the night, the real night, wide and black and empty, only a step away outside.

Upstairs, there was a light in her own room and one in her mother's dressing room. It was a family custom that when she came in late she should put out her mother's light, so now she went into the small, bright room. With her hand on the light chain, she looked around her, at the chintz-covered chaise longue, the chintz-skirted dressing table with family snapshots, both old and recent, arranged under its glass top, the polished furniture, the long mirror, the agreeable clutter of many years of satisfactory married life. On the walls were more family pictures, covering quite a long period of time—enlargements of picnic photographs, of boats, of a few pets. There was Joanna at the age of twelve on a cow pony in Wyoming; her father and uncle in snow goggles and climbing boots on the lower slopes of Mont Blanc, heaven knows how long ago; her sister and brother-in-law looking very young and carefree with their bicycles outside Salisbury Cathedral sometime in the early thirties, judging by her sister's clothes. In all of them the sun shone, and everyone was happy in the world of the pictures, which was as fresh and good and simple as a May morning. She stared at the familiar little scenes on the walls with love—and with a sympathy for them she had never felt before— and then she put out the light and went back along the hall.

In her own room she kicked off her sandals and dropped Phil's coat on a chair. A drawn window shade moved inward and fell back again in the night breeze that rustled the thick, wet trees close outside. Her pajamas lay on the turned-down bed with its tall, fluted posts. Joanna did not stop to brush her teeth or braid her hair; she was in bed in less than two minutes.

In the darkness she heard the wind rising around Sandy's house, breathing over the open hill, whistling softly in the wet, rusted window screens, stirring in the apple trees. She heard the last burning log in the fireplace tumble apart, and a horse kick at his stall out in the barn. If I'd stayed all night, she thought, in the morning when the fog burned off I'd have known how far you could see from the top of the hill.

For in the morning the hot sun would shine from a mild blue sky, the roofs would steam, the horses would gallop and squeal in the pastures between the great walls, and all the nightingales would rise singing out of the short, tough grass.

THE SECOND TREE FROM
THE CORNER

❖

E. B. W<small>HITE</small>

"E<small>VER HAVE</small> any bizarre thoughts?" asked the doctor.
Mr. Trexler failed to catch the word. "What kind?" he said.
"Bizarre," repeated the doctor, his voice steady. He watched his patient for any slight change of expression, any wince. It seemed to Trexler that the doctor was not only watching him closely but was creeping slowly toward him, like a lizard toward a bug. Trexler shoved his chair back an inch and gathered himself for a reply. He was about to say "Yes" when he realized that if he said yes the next question would be unanswerable. Bizarre thoughts, bizarre thoughts? Ever have any bizarre thoughts? What kind of thoughts *except* bizarre had he had since the age of two?

Trexler felt the time passing, the necessity for an answer. These psychiatrists were busy men, overloaded, not to be kept waiting. The next patient was probably already perched out there in the waiting room, lonely, worried, shifting around on the sofa, his mind stuffed with bizarre thoughts and amorphous fears. Poor bastard, thought Trexler. Out there all alone in that misshapen antechamber, staring at the filing cabinet and wondering whether to tell the doctor about that day on the Madison Avenue bus.

Let's see, bizarre thoughts. Trexler dodged back along the dreadful corridor of the years to see what he could find. He felt the doctor's eyes upon him and knew that time was running out. Don't be so conscientious, he said to himself. If a bizarre thought is indicated here, just reach into the bag and pick anything at all. A man as well supplied with bizarre thoughts as you are should have no difficulty producing one for the record. Trexler darted into the bag, hung for a moment before one of his thoughts, as a hummingbird pauses in the delphinium. No, he said, not that one. He darted to another (the one about the rhesus monkey), paused, considered. No, he said, not that.

Trexler knew he must hurry. He had already used up pretty nearly four seconds since the question had been put. But it was an impossible situation—just one more lousy, impossible situation such as he was always getting himself into. When, he asked himself, are you going to quit maneuvering yourself into a pocket? He made one more effort. This time he stopped at the asylum, only the bars were lucite —fluted, retractable. Not here, he said. Not this one.

He looked straight at the doctor. "No," he said quietly. "I never have any bizarre thoughts."

The doctor sucked in on his pipe, blew a plume of smoke toward the rows of medical books. Trexler's gaze followed the smoke. He managed to make out one of the titles, "The Genito-Urinary System." A bright wave of fear swept cleanly over him, and he winced under the first pain of kidney stones. He remembered when he was a child, the first time he ever entered a doctor's office, sneaking a look at the titles of the books—and the flush of fear, the shirt wet under the arms, the book on t.b., the sudden knowledge that he was in the advanced stages of consumption, the quick vision of the hemorrhage. Trexler sighed wearily. Forty years, he thought, and I still get thrown by the title of a medical book. Forty years and I still can't stay on life's little bucky horse. No wonder I'm sitting here in this dreary joint at the end of this woebegone afternoon, lying about my bizarre thoughts to a doctor who looks, come to think of it, rather tired.

The session dragged on. After about twenty minutes, the doctor rose and knocked his pipe out. Trexler got up, knocked the ashes out of his brain, and waited. The doctor smiled warmly and stuck out his hand. "There's nothing the matter with you—you're just scared. Want to know how I know you're scared?"

"How?" asked Trexler.

"Look at the chair you've been sitting in! See how it has moved back away from my desk? You kept inching away from me while I asked you questions. That means you're scared."

"Does it?" said Trexler, faking a grin. "Yeah, I suppose it does."

They finished shaking hands. Trexler turned and walked out uncertainly along the passage, then into the waiting room and out past the next patient, a ruddy pin-striped man who was seated on the sofa twirling his hat nervously and staring straight ahead at the files. Poor, frightened guy, thought Trexler, he's probably read in the *Times* that one American male out of every two is going to die of heart disease by twelve o'clock next Thursday. It says that in the paper almost every morning. And he's also probably thinking about that day on the Madison Avenue bus.

A week later, Trexler was back in the patient's chair. And for several weeks thereafter he continued to visit the doctor, always toward the end of the afternoon, when the vapors hung thick above the pool of the mind and darkened the whole region of the East Seventies. He felt no better as time went on, and he found it impossible to work. He discovered that the visits were becoming routine and that although the routine was one to which he certainly did not look forward, at least he could accept it with cool resignation, as once, years ago, he had accepted a long spell with a dentist who had settled down to a steady fooling with a couple of dead teeth. The visits, moreover, were now assuming a pattern recognizable to the patient.

Each session would begin with a résumé of symptoms—the dizziness in the streets, the constricting pain in the back of the neck, the apprehensions, the tightness of the scalp, the inability to concentrate, the despondency and the melancholy times, the feeling of pressure and tension, the anger at not being able to work, the anxiety over work not done, the gas on the stomach. Dullest set of neurotic symptoms in the world, Trexler would think, as he obediently trudged back over them for the doctor's benefit. And then, having listened attentively to the recital, the doctor would spring his question: "Have you ever found anything that gives you relief?" And Trexler would answer, "Yes. A drink." And the doctor would nod his head knowingly.

As he became familiar with the pattern Trexler found that he increasingly tended to identify himself with the doctor, transferring himself into the doctor's seat—probably (he thought) some rather slick form of escapism. At any rate, it was nothing new for Trexler to identify himself with other people. Whenever he got into a cab, he instantly became the driver, saw everything from the hackman's angle (and the reaching over with the right hand, the nudging of the flag, the pushing it down, all the way down along the side of the meter), saw everything—traffic, fare, everything—through the eyes of Anthony Rocco, or Isidore Freedman, or Matthew Scott. In a barbershop, Trexler was the barber, his fingers curled around the comb, his hand on the tonic. Perfectly natural, then, that Trexler should soon be occupying the doctor's chair, asking the questions, waiting for the answers. He got quite interested in the doctor, in this way. He liked him, and he found him a not too difficult patient.

It was on the fifth visit, about halfway through, that the doctor turned to Trexler and said, suddenly, "What do you want?" He gave the word "want" special emphasis.

"I d'know," replied Trexler uneasily. "I guess nobody knows the answer to that one."

"Sure they do," replied the doctor.

"Do *you* know what *you* want?" asked Trexler narrowly.

"Certainly," said the doctor. Trexler noticed that at this point the doctor's chair slid slightly backward, away from him. Trexler stifled a small, internal smile. Scared as a rabbit, he said to himself. Look at him scoot!

"What *do* you want?" continued Trexler, pressing his advantage, pressing it hard.

The doctor glided back another inch away from his inquisitor. "I want a wing on the small house I own in Westport. I want more money, and more leisure to do the things I want to do."

Trexler was just about to say, "And what are those things you want to do, Doctor?" when he caught himself. Better not go too far, he mused. Better not lose possession of the ball. And besides, he thought, what the hell goes on here, anyway—me paying fifteen bucks a throw for these séances and then doing the work myself, asking the questions, weighing the answers. So he wants a new wing! There's a fine piece of theatrical gauze for you! A new wing.

Trexler settled down again and resumed the role of patient for the rest of the visit. It ended on a kindly, friendly note. The doctor reassured him that his fears were the cause of his sickness, and that his fears were unsubstantial. They shook hands, smiling.

Trexler walked dizzily through the empty waiting room and the doctor followed along to let him out. It was late; the secretary had shut up shop and gone home. Another day over the dam. "Goodbye," said Trexler. He stepped into the street, turned west toward Madison, and thought of the doctor all alone there, after hours, in that desolate hole—a man who worked longer hours than his secretary. Poor, scared, overworked bastard, thought Trexler. And that new wing!

It was an evening of clearing weather, the Park showing green and desirable in the distance, the last daylight applying a high lacquer to the brick and brownstone walls and giving the street scene a luminous and intoxicating splendor. Trexler meditated, as he walked, on what he wanted. "What do you want?" he heard again. Trexler knew what he wanted, and what, in general, all men wanted; and he was glad, in a way, that it was both inexpressible and unattainable, and that it wasn't a wing. He was satisfied to remember that it was deep, formless, enduring, and impossible of fulfillment, and that it made men sick, and that when you sauntered along Third Avenue and looked through the doorways into the dim saloons, you could sometimes pick out from the unregenerate ranks the ones who had not forgotten, gazing steadily into the bottoms of the glasses on the long chance that they could get another little peek at it. Trexler found himself renewed by the remembrance that what he wanted was at once great and microscopic, and that although it borrowed from the nature of large deeds and of youthful love and of old songs and early intimations, it was not any one of these things, and that it had not been isolated or pinned down, and that a man who attempted to define it in the privacy of a doctor's office would fall flat on his face.

Trexler felt invigorated. Suddenly his sickness seemed health, his dizziness stability. A small tree, rising between him and the light, stood there saturated with the evening, each gilt-edged leaf perfectly drunk with excellence and delicacy. Trexler's spine registered an ever so slight tremor as it picked up this natural disturbance in the lovely scene. "I want the second tree from the corner, just as it stands," he said, answering an imaginary question from an imaginary physician. And he felt a slow pride in realizing that what he wanted none could bestow, and that what he had none could take away. He felt content to be sick, unembarrassed at being afraid; and in the jungle of his fear he glimpsed (as he had so often glimpsed them before) the flashy tail feathers of the bird courage.

Then he thought once again of the doctor, and of his being left there all alone, tired, frightened. (The poor, scared guy, thought Trexler.) Trexler began humming "Moonshine Lullaby," his spirit reacting instantly to the hypodermic of Merman's healthy voice. He crossed Madison, boarded a downtown bus, and rode all the way to Fifty-second Street before he had a thought that could rightly have been called bizarre.

THE PLEASURES OF TRAVEL

❖

WENDELL WILCOX

U NFORTUNATELY, they had got the seat at the front of the car, the seat opposite the one that was built against the wall of the toilet and couldn't be reversed. It was unfortunate, Mrs. Glaum said, because she did like privacy, and when the very plain woman with the two little girls got on and crowded in facing them, she gave her husband a look of despair. However, she managed a few little smiles of chilly courtesy for the newcomers, and while Mr. Glaum helped the woman with her luggage Mrs. Glaum took out her compact and began making her face.

She had made it in the station, but now she made it again. The two children sat tight together, next to their mother, and watched Mrs. Glaum solemnly. When she had finished her face she took out her comb and worked on her hair.

The woman opposite gave her a nervous look. "Be careful with your feet, girls," she admonished.

Mrs. Glaum straightened her skirt. She was wearing dark blue, of course, for travelling, and a neat little eggshell blouse that wouldn't show soil too quickly. By the time she was settled, the train was well under way and the military were already making tentative sorties into the aisles.

"Now," said Mrs. Glaum to her husband, "if you'd just hand me my knitting."

She opened her blue silk bag and took out a few inches of khaki-colored work. Assuming an erect position, she took hold of her work in a masterful way and then proceeded to knit with cramped absorption. Mr. Glaum suspected she would never acquire that fine, steady motion he had observed in genuine knitters.

After a couple of rows, Mrs. Glaum said to the woman, "It must be dreadful, travelling with children at a time like this."

"Well, it's never easy," the woman answered. The children took their steady gaze away from the hands of Mrs. Glaum and turned it upon their mother.

"Oh, I'm sure you wouldn't be travelling unless you had to. I know we wouldn't."

"For some fool reason, their dad's in the Army," the woman said. "I'm taking the kids down to my sister's. Then *I* go back and get a job."

"It does make it hard, but I suppose your husband felt it his duty," Mrs. Glaum said with slight severity.

The woman looked out the window. The older girl was watching her. "I think he *wanted* to get away from us," the woman said. "I think it was just an excuse. He said he was drafted, but I never saw no papers."

Mrs. Glaum glanced at the children and then at her husband. Her looks were as good as words to him; they meant that it was vulgar to confess to strangers and that children should never be allowed to see any rifts in the marriage lute.

"Trouble everywhere these days," Mr. Glaum said. He took a little paper-bound book from his pocket and hurriedly opened it. Though Mrs. Glaum was motionless, he was aware that her secret inward organs of sensitivity were making adjustments to an indelicate situation.

The invisible struggle over, she began in her nicest voice, "I, too, have children and, oh, it does make me so lonesome having to go places without them. We used to have such lovely trips together, all four of us, when Mr. Glaum went to the city on business. We used to take a drawing room. With children it's the only way. If you're just two adults, the chair car or even one of the modern coaches, like this one, is all right, but . . ."

She looked at Mr. Glaum, who was pretending to be intent on his book. When Tom was still a baby in arms, they had once taken a drawing room.

"I didn't even plan to come myself this year. What with the crowds and soldiers and all, it isn't fair, but Mr. Glaum just hates travelling without me. Don't you, dear?"

"What?" said Mr. Glaum, pretending he hadn't heard, for in truth he dreaded going places with her. She was fussy and difficult, always wanting things they couldn't afford.

"I did so hate leaving the children, even though they're really pretty grown up now. Gloria Jean's nearly eighteen, and Tom—that's my baby—is fifteen. But I knew what an ordeal it would be for Mr.

Glaum. He's the real baby in our house. Can't bear being alone. Why, do you know, we've hardly been separated so much as a whole day out of our entire married life?"

"Doesn't he ever get restless?" the woman asked. There was a shade of awe in her voice.

"Not Arthur Glaum. He's a real family man."

"I don't guess Charlie was," the woman said. "I wonder if he ever thinks about being at home these days. I wonder does he ever give us a thought."

"Most men like getting off on their own once in a while, but not Arthur Glaum. Arthur—"

"If you don't mind," Arthur broke in suddenly, "I think I'll go have a drink and let you spread out a bit."

"Run right along," Mrs. Glaum said.

At the end of the car he looked back. His wife had laid aside her knitting and was using her hands to describe with. He had known from the first she was going to come on this trip with him. Someday he did want to go to the city alone. There were places he wanted to go to, lots of things he wanted to see, by himself.

The club car was jammed and Mr. Glaum had already a blind feeling in anticipation of the intoxication upon which he had not as yet embarked. Holding his highball and cigarette, he stood staring blankly out the window. Every day she had pretended she just couldn't come, but he had known she'd change her mind when the time came to make reservations. The landscape was streaming past and he was trying to look at it in a blurred way as if he were already drunk. He felt restless. He wanted to talk. He decided on a gentleman about his own age who was sitting with his head thrown back, staring up at the ceiling.

"Would you care to have a drink with me?" Mr. Glaum asked.

"Why, yes," said the big man, "of course." He was very simple and direct, with a big, red, open face. They began talking of various cities. They seemed to have been to a lot of the same places and they felt pretty much the same way about them. When they finished their first drink and ordered another, a woman who was sitting in the chair next to the big man glanced at them uneasily and got up and left. Mr. Glaum settled comfortably into the vacated chair. The two men talked on.

As he was starting his third drink, Mr. Glaum suddenly said, "Are you married?"

"Used to be," the man said.

"Did you love your wife?"

"Yes," the man said. "Don't you love yours?"

"Oh, yes," Mr. Glaum replied.

"My wife was too expensive for me," the man went on. "She was very beautiful and expensive, but she felt she could do better by herself. Alone."

"That's very interesting," Mr. Glaum said. "I am almost certain that I love Louisa, but I hate being with her."

"I loved being with Annette," the man said. "She wore the swellest things you ever saw. Came to bed every night soaked in perfume. Wore all kinds of fancy negligees. It was an adventure."

"Why did you leave her, then? Why did you let her go away?"

"Like I said. She did better on her own. She kept me broke all the time and even at that I couldn't be sure where a lot of the stuff was coming from."

"My wife wants to be with me every minute," said Mr. Glaum. "I love my wife best when I'm not with her and when I'm not even thinking about her, if you understand what I mean."

"To me my wife is a beautiful memory," the stranger said. Mr. Glaum looked at him. He was a tall man with an incipient stomach. He had strong, hairy hands and red hair that did not begin to cover the top of a splendidly shaped pink head. He didn't look much like a man who would care for memories.

"Excuse me," said Mr. Glaum, "I must go see to my wife."

Louisa, he found, had invited the woman to sit next her. The smaller of the two children was asleep, with her head in her sister's lap. The older girl had her eyes fixed avidly on Mrs. Glaum, who was doing her nails. She was using a very long buffer and working with great delicacy and freedom. It was strange, Mr. Glaum thought, that she couldn't handle her knitting needles better. As he came up, the woman took the sleeping child into her own lap.

"You're a little intoxicated," his wife said, watching the careful way he let himself down onto the seat.

"Only three whiskeys, Louisa."

She gave him a smile that meant everything was all right and went on with her conversation. "My grandmother's house was right up on a bluff overlooking the river. It was such a beautiful place for a little girl to go."

She dropped her hands in her lap and shut her eyes. "I can hardly

remember Grandpa at all. Grandpa owned most of the town. Oh, it
was just a tiny place, of course." She gave forth the kind of laugh
that is called rippling. "Grandma was his darling. He gave her everything. She had the prettiest clothes and the loveliest china. Grandpa
spoiled her dreadfully. But do you know, she never seemed to miss
him after he was gone. She seemed perfectly happy just walking
about her garden."

Mrs. Glaum drew a sigh and put her pretty head on one side in a
pretty way. "It's wonderful," she said, "having had a beautiful childhood."

Mr. Glaum again opened his book. Why had he come back here
when he had been having such a nice time in the club car? All that
stuff about her grandmother and grandfather. Mr. Toomer had
owned a saloon, a mill, and a tugboat which Louisa's expansive memory was even now turning into several river boats. He thought of old
Mrs. Toomer, in a sunbonnet, looking around at her hollyhocks.
Whenever Louisa spoke of them, all these honest, simple objects
seemed to increase in size, number, and majesty.

The past, it seemed, was cheering the other woman too, for now
she was telling Louisa about her father, who had been a driver of
trotting horses and who used to ride her around the race tracks in his
sulky. "We had a little spotty dog named Trixie," she said. "I always
tried to make him ride too. My, how he barked!" She covered her
face with her hands and laughed.

"We certainly do not live the way we used to, do we?" Louisa said.
"Now, our little house . . ."

"I think I'll go back to the club car," Mr. Glaum said. "A
man there was telling me some very interesting things about the
administration."

Mr. Glaum returned to the crowded club car, made directly for
the pantry, and ordered another highball. He drank it down quickly,
then looked around for his friend. The bald-headed man was drinking with a young woman in uniform. The young woman was holding
his hand. Mr. Glaum walked over to join them.

"There's been a lot of talk," the young woman was saying, "about
whether or not we should take off our caps when we drink."

"The important thing," said the bald-headed man, "is not what
you take off when you drink but what you have on to take off when
you lie down. Personally, I should not like removing you from that
blue serge. Now my wife used to wear"—he looked up—"but here's

a friend of mine. My dear friend, I should like you to meet this young person here. She's the new type of woman, to whom gradually, I suppose, we shall all become accustomed."

Mr. Glaum sat down on the arm of her chair. The young woman put her arm around Mr. Glaum's waist.

"Your friend is charming," she said to the bald-headed man. "He has such a delicate waist. I love a man with a delicate waist."

"Did your wife have a tendency to exaggerate her possessions when she was talking to other women?" Mr. Glaum asked.

"Annette never exaggerated anything," the man said. "She couldn't, because whatever it was, she always had it."

"Why do you worry about other women when, after all, I am here?" the young, military-looking woman asked rather sadly.

"Give us time, for God's sake," said the bald-headed man. "Rome wasn't built in a day."

"Maybe the way Louisa talks is my fault," said Mr. Glaum. "Maybe I don't give her enough stuff."

Beyond the window the passing world was filling with shadow as Mr. Glaum verbally weighed the possibility of his own guilt against his wife's flexible avidity. The bald-headed man argued consolingly in favor of Mr. Glaum, and then all at once the young woman began to cry.

"Talk, talk, talk," she said. "I just don't seem to rate with you boys at all. Oh, my God, I'm so tired."

"Soldiers don't cry," said the bald-headed man. "Why don't you be a good girl and go get us some more drinks."

"Just a sec," she said. She wiped her eyes with her handkerchief. "There now, I'm going to try to please." She took their glasses and went off.

"Maybe it's not just Louisa," Mr. Glaum said. He was now really drunk. "Maybe it's all of them. Did you notice that young woman's expression? As if something were biting her under her blouse? It often seems to me Louisa has a little, sharp-toothed animal hidden in her dress that keeps biting her."

The young woman reappeared with the drinks and handed one to each of the men. The bald-headed man looked at her closely.

"Yes, I think I see," he said. "Would you like to hop on my knee, young woman?"

She smiled. He opened his legs and she sat down on one heavy thigh and put an arm about his neck. "Comfortable?" she asked.

"Just leave me room to drink," he answered.

As they talked, the evening slipped up on them. The young woman sat quietly on the big man's knees, regarding them drowsily, her eyes almost closed. The train stopped at a station. They got up and stood by a window, looking out. Rain drizzled down the glass. The lights of the town were blurred and animated.

"Towns, little towns," said the girl in uniform dreamily, as if she were singing a torch song. "They go by, they go by, but all I want is just a little bit of now." She pressed the big man's fingers.

The train started with a jerk. They threw their arms about each other to save themselves from falling and sat down again.

The train gathered speed. They were silent now and Mr. Glaum was thinking of Louisa.

"It's night," said the young woman. She opened her eyes wide in a baby stare. "We're going so fast. Do you feel how fast we're going?" She put her finger in her mouth, holding the tip between her teeth and staring like a child.

Louisa was very present in Mr. Glaum's thoughts. "Excuse me," he said. "I feel I must be going."

He walked back through the now darkened coaches. There was a general stirring in the seats as of birds settling into their nests. Some people were already asleep, but others turned nervously, attempting to adjust themselves. Mr. Glaum tripped and fell over three or four very tiny sailors who were sleeping on facing seats at the end of a car, folded together like little animals in a lair, their heads in each other's laps and their feet everywhere. The odor of alcohol hung over them as the natural stench above animals. They seemed very sweet and harmless.

He picked himself up and went on along through the cars.

The woman with the children was gone. In place of the three lay a young man, sleeping on his side, his knees drawn up. Louisa, too, was asleep. She had made her face again and fixed her hair. Her head was resting against the doily on the seat back and her face was tilted upward. Her hands were folded sweetly in her lap. A thousand tender thoughts passed through Mr. Glaum's heart. She was like a patient being carried to an operating table. She was like a lovely girl laid out for burial. She might very well have been the Lily Maid of Astolat.

Leaning close, he peered into her face. It had relaxed entirely. The little animal must be asleep. There was no pain at the edge of her eyes, none at the corners of her mouth. He watched her face. It was a face he could have watched forever. It was the face he wanted, the face he felt to be her own. Usually it was so busy with this, that, or the other, but at night, in dreams, it had all the things it wanted and didn't have to plan for them or pretend about them.

Louisa, he thought, should die at night. With a face like that, she would get such a good grade in heaven. They would never ask what she had done. They would never even open the book to find out what secret sins had been gnawing her breast, because her face would be testimony of the fact that she had never even been conscious of sin.

CONTENT WITH THE STATION

❖

John Andrew Rice

B UCKLEY'S CASTLE was given its name in the nearby village, not in
malice—the Florida cracker is only mildly malicious—but out of
justice. When Captain Buckley appeared, around 1910, with carefully drawn plans for his house, he had let the carpenters know that
all he wanted of them was their skill, not curiosity. He chose for
his site an isolated stretch of dune and beach. When the house was
completed, he disappeared for a day or so and, on his return, drove
through the village and on to his house without stopping. Assiduous
watchers caught a glimpse of a woman and a boy. After that no one
ever saw the woman. Father and son—the Captain was heard to call
the boy son—came to town once a week to buy supplies. Within a few
years the boy came alone. But the curious could get almost nothing
out of him. The solitary clue was his mention, only once, of Kissimmee, a town in the center of the state, about sixty miles away, where
there was a small colony of English people. That, and the boy's accent, and the father's, told the local inhabitants all they ever knew
about their unneighborly neighbors.

There was something strange about the boy, people said, besides
his silence. Beyond the details of shopping, he seemed to know nothing. The face he turned to them was not, like his father's, forbidding;
it was simply blank.

A few years after I first saw Buckley's Castle and picked up from
village gossip what I have here set down, I was having tea with an
old lady of my acquaintance who lived near Kissimmee. The tea was
good and I offered the highest praise—that it was as good as one got
in England.

"Well," she said, "I learned to make it from the English."

"In England?" I asked.

"No, not exactly," she said, "not in English England; in American
England, which is even more English.' Before I could smile she went
on, "My husband, you know, was an Episcopal clergyman, and, being

137

the nearest thing they could find to the Established Church, acted as spiritual adviser to the English in Kissimmee. He was very High Church and liked to act as father confessor. I, you know, was born a Methodist and I never got used to my husband's religion. Mind you, I'm not saying I'm glad the dear man's gone, but it is a relief not to go on making meaningless noises and motions. But I'm as particular, though, about tea as he was about genuflection, and it's always good. Have another cup. Nobody can make it any better. I'm not talking about the way I serve it. As a matter of fact, I know only one family where it is still served right. I'll take you there sometime. It'll make you homesick for England. You liked it there, didn't you?"

"Yes," I said, "but I wouldn't use the word 'homesick.' I'd just like to see how it feels again. Who is this family? Still in Kissimmee?"

"No," she said. "Moved away years ago, to the coast."

"Not by any chance the Buckleys?" I asked.

"Yes," she said. "What do you know about them?"

"Practically nothing. What do you know?"

"Practically everything," she said.

"Well, then," I said, "you can tell me about them. I've wanted to know for a long time."

"No, I won't tell you about them. I'll do better; I'll let you see for yourself. I've often wondered how acute you are. This will be a good test."

"Is it that difficult?" I asked.

"I don't really know," she said. "That's not the way I got the story. I got it bit by bit out of my husband, and it took me a long time. Anyway, it will be fun to see you try. Shall we make it next Wednesday afternoon?"

On the drive over to the coast, she shut off further questions. "It wouldn't be right for me to reveal to you secrets of the confessional," she said, and laughed. "They were meant for the Lord, you know."

The road that ran along behind the dunes was of corrugated shell and forbidding. As we came in sight of Captain Buckley's house, my guide told me that she was one of the few people who ever went to see the family. We climbed a long stairway that led up from the road, and as we paused midway for my friend to catch her breath, I had a closeup of the house. It told me nothing.

The story began inside the entrance. The hatrack might have come out of Bloomsbury Square, or a rectory I had visited in Norfolk. I had never seen anything like it in America before. The nearest thing

would have been in Back Bay, but there would have been a difference. This was authentic Victorian, pure British Victorian. When
the door opened to the knocker lifted and let fall once, a knocker
polished thin, time suddenly moved back half a century. I took it
all in—the butler, the figurines in one corner of the hall, the hard,
twisted weave of the carpet, the bulge of a desk, the panelled walls,
and the subdued gleam of wax floors.

First to come into focus was the butler. How is one to describe perfection? The angle of the arm that held the door, the inclination of
the head, the stance, the voice that was deliberately not that of a
gentleman but the voice of a calling, the eyes seeing without looking.
I had forgotten that a thing so perfected and so alien could exist. The
American servant is an amateur, superior to his status or else servile.
This man was neither. Nor was his art a thing that could have been
learned. It was as born in the bones as bird flight.

We followed him down the long hall into a room on the left and
found ourselves standing before the family altar, the tea table. Somewhere within the action we must have met our host and hostess, exchanging the words and responses of introduction, but I cannot now
recall having seen them until after I had made my silent obeisance.
Here was perfection again, nothing accented, nothing omitted: silver
rack in which the British cool their toast; plates with silver hoods
that presently, when lifted, were to give off the incense of melted butter, anchovy, and cinnamon; the light shining through cups; and a
Sheffield tray, with bowls, slop jar, two pitchers, and the Madonna—
a great tea cozy, brooding over the pot like a setting hen.

"We 'ave been 'aving some lovely weather, 'aven't we?" our hostess
said, and her secret was out. The genuine cockney is not content
merely to drop an "h"; a hole is left where the "h" should be, a hole
of silence.

Captain Buckley turned to me. "Have you had a chance at any fishing?" he asked, and his "h" was like the rush of wind among the
palms.

She removed the cozy and began to pour. "Will you 'ave milk or
cream?" she asked. No lemon, mind you.

The unseeing butler passed the sugar, two kinds—lump, and white
and yellow the size of grains of rice. These, and even the crumpets,
which one never sees in America, with holes oozing butter, were a
mere obbligato to the scent of the tea. I exclaimed, and my host said,
"Rather good, eh? My father spent many years in India."

That was the only reference he made that day to anything personal. The talk was desultory, but everything else spoke: the fluted paper in the fireplace, the brass coal scuttle on the hearth (this in Florida, where the staple fuel is fat pine), the pull cord of the heavy drapes, and the priestly butler. I was back in England at the opening of a period drawing-room play, but the designer had been so success-ful that I found myself seeing not the play itself, only the perfection of the set. The illusion was confirmed by the conversation, which flowed around, without touching, me.

There was no mystery, really. When at last I saw my host and host-ess clearly, a long-forgotten sentence popped into my mind: "He married the landlady's daughter," Oxford's final obliteration of a man. He had, in the language of their time, married beneath him. That was why they had fled and created their England here. The story, I reflected, was as old as love itself.

Pleased at having so easily found the answer, I picked up that earlier question of my host and we spoke of fishing, which, as every fisherman knows, is not what it used to be. "Twenty-five years ago," he was saying, "the channel bass were so abundant that the surf was red with them," when I noticed the face of my friend turned half toward me and saying, with the wrinkles around her eyes and mouth, "You think you have it, don't you?" Then, as I was about to answer her with a complacent look, I suddenly remembered that the Buck-leys had fled not only from England; they had also left Kissimmee and perched themselves atop this lonely dune. Why had they done that? That was the real question. Why the second flight, and this time to complete insularity?

It was then that I began in earnest my search for a clue. There was none. The Captain and his wife presented to me the same settled look. Here was contentment if I ever saw it. Every tone and gesture spoke of old, accepted habit. Whatever their secret, it was so deeply imbedded in their life that they were no longer aware of it.

That was all I learned, as I sat there drinking tea, and I knew that I would learn nothing more from them. The clock struck six and we rose to go, and said goodbye where we stood. I was to come again any day, they said. The last I saw of them they were standing as still and impassive as the china shepherd and shepherdess that flanked the clock on the mantel beyond. We were led down the long hall by the silent butler. The sudden glare of Florida sand was like a blow.

One must drive fast on a washboard road or else the car will land in the scrub, and the rattle of mine made speech impossible. When at last we struck paving, I slowed down and looked at my friend. She smiled and asked, "Well, what did you see?"

"Not much, I'm afraid. Not enough to make a mystery. At first I thought it was obvious: remittance man, married the housemaid—"

"Cook," she said.

"Well, married the cook and had to leave England, and can't, or thinks he can't, go home—an outcast of empire."

"A pretty phrase," she said, "but that's all. Wasn't the British Empire created by people who for one reason or another had to leave England? And he was an outcast, as you say, only as long as his father was alive."

"He could go back now, anyway," I said. "Maybe not forty years ago, but by now there are enough like him, even supposing that people remembered that he had married the cook. So that's not all."

"No, that isn't all. It was, when they first came to this country, but now his father is dead, and left him plenty of money, and he's an only son."

"Even so," I said, "he couldn't go back to the England he has kept with him here. There isn't any any more."

"No," she said, "I suppose not. But he can't go back to his or any other England."

"Well, it's beyond me. I give up."

"Try again," she said. "It took me a good while to get the whole story out of my husband. You don't expect me to hand it out to you in five minutes, do you? Think."

We were silent while I went back over the last hour and, finding no clue there, sifted once again the village gossip, which I had almost forgotten. Then I remembered something. "Wasn't there a son?"

"There is a son."

"What's become of him?"

"You know as well as I do," she said, and laughed.

"How on earth would I know?"

"By using your eyes," she said.

"By using my eyes? But that's about all I did."

"I know," she said, "but all the same, the answer was there."

"In the house?"

"In the room," she said.

"But all I saw was the furniture and the Captain and his wife and the butler."

"Well?" she said. Then she added quietly, "The butler is their son."

"Good Lord," I said, "how awful!"

"Why awful?"

"Why, for a man to make a butler out of his own son."

"I didn't say that," she said, "and it isn't true. Nobody made him a butler, unless you agree with my husband. He always said it was the judgment of God. I said why not call it a plain case of heredity. But he wouldn't have that. Wanted to blame somebody—just like a preacher."

"I'm sorry," I said, accepting the rebuke. "But you did sort of drop it on me, you know. How did it begin? I mean, what started them on their second flight?"

"Oh, that," she said. "Well, when the son was four or five they discovered that he was a backward child—a little slow mentally, but not dangerous; not yet. It was then they left Kissimmee and cut themselves off from their compatriots, because of him. That's when my husband came in, and eventually I. He, poor man, believed in the efficacy of prayer, and when, after a few years, that obviously had failed, I told him not to be a fool, to tell them to take the child to New York, to the best doctors they could find. They did, and got the same advice from all of them."

"Yes," I said, "but why a butler?"

"That was their advice," she said, "to let the boy be what he wanted to be. While he was a tiny tot, he had a passion for putting things in order, and as he grew older, the only thing that would get him out of a tantrum was to let him straighten up the house and wait on table. Then, while they were in New York, he saw white servants, costume and all—they had only Negroes in Kissimmee— and his 'call came,' as they say in the church."

I was still feeling a little defensive. "But there was no sign of recognition between him and his parents."

"There never is," she said. "As he grew into his calling he grew away from them and now does not know himself as anything except butler, certainly not as son. He will not permit any familiarity. Good servants don't, you know."

We were silent for a while. Then I asked, "They have no friends?"

"None," she said.

"But how did they know you were coming to tea? Don't tell me they have a telephone."

"They didn't need to."

"You mean they have tea like that every day?"

"Every day," she said. "If they didn't, he would get violent. You would also find dinner something special, every day. It's a little hard on his mother. She has to work like a slave at the cooking. They couldn't keep a cook and a secret."

I laughed and said, "Nice case of comic irony. Her husband took her out of the kitchen and her son put her back."

"Yes, but she doesn't mind, really. She wasn't very happy in the parlor. As you see, she hardly had the makings of a lady."

"No, but—"

"No 'buts,' " she said firmly. "What more could you ask? He lives like a gentleman, with two perfect servants, and these for life. I visit them fairly frequently, and unless I bring someone—and I never bring anybody who lives in Florida—he and I have tea alone, the same kind of tea we had today, and afterward I go out into the kitchen and visit with his wife. The son and I never speak. He knows his place and I try to keep mine."

"Yes, but—"

"I know," she said. "It makes you uncomfortable. It would most people, but it doesn't me. There's something in the prayer book I like to remember—I used to quote it to my husband—something about 'make me content with the station in life to which it has pleased God to call me.' They are, and I am content that they should be."

A PERFECT DAY FOR BANANAFISH

❖

J. D. SALINGER

THERE WERE ninety-seven New York advertising men in the hotel, and, the way they were monopolizing the long-distance lines, the girl in 507 had to wait from noon till almost two-thirty to get her call through. She used the time, though. She read an article in a women's pocket-size magazine, called "Sex Is Fun—or Hell." She washed her comb and brush. She took the spot out of the skirt of her beige suit. She moved the button on her Saks blouse. She tweezed out two freshly surfaced hairs in her mole. When the operator finally rang her room, she was sitting on the window seat and had almost finished putting lacquer on the nails of her left hand.

She was a girl who for a ringing phone dropped exactly nothing. She looked as if her phone had been ringing continually ever since she had reached puberty.

With her little lacquer brush, while the phone was ringing, she went over the nail of her little finger, accentuating the line of the moon. She then replaced the cap on the bottle of lacquer and, standing up, passed her left—the wet—hand back and forth through the air. With her dry hand, she picked up a congested ashtray from the window seat and carried it with her over to the night table, on which the phone stood. She sat down on one of the made-up twin beds and—it was the fifth or sixth ring—picked up the phone.

"Hello," she said, keeping the fingers of her left hand outstretched and away from her white silk dressing gown, which was all that she was wearing, except mules—her rings were in the bathroom.

"I have your call to New York now, Mrs. Glass," the operator said.

"Thank you," said the girl, and made room on the night table for the ashtray.

A woman's voice came through. "Muriel? Is that you?"

The girl turned the receiver slightly away from her ear. "Yes, Mother. How are you?" she said.

"I've been worried to death about you. Why haven't you phoned? Are you all right?"

"I tried to get you last night and the night before. The phone here's been—"

"Are you all right, Muriel?"

The girl increased the angle between the receiver and her ear. "I'm fine. I'm hot. This is the hottest day they've had in Florida in—"

"Why haven't you called me? I've been worried to—"

"Mother, darling, don't yell at me. I can hear you beautifully," said the girl. "I called you twice last night. Once just after—"

"I *told* your father you'd probably call last night. But, no, he had to— Are you all right, Muriel? Tell me the truth."

"I'm fine. Stop asking me that, please."

"When did you get there?"

"I don't know. Wednesday morning, early."

"Who drove?"

"He did," said the girl. "And don't get excited. He drove very nicely. I was amazed."

"*He* drove? Muriel, you gave me your word of—"

"Mother," the girl interrupted, "I just told you. He drove *very* nicely. Under fifty the whole way, as a matter of fact."

"Did he try any of that funny business with the trees?"

"I *said* he drove very nicely, Mother. Now, please. I asked him to stay close to the white line, and all, and he knew what I meant, and he did. He was even trying not to look at the trees—you could tell. Did Daddy get the car fixed, incidentally?"

"Not yet. They want four hundred dollars, just to—"

"Mother, Seymour *told* Daddy that he'd pay for it. There's no reason for—"

"Well, we'll see. How did he behave—in the car and all?"

"All right," said the girl.

"Did he keep calling you that awful—"

"No. He has something new now."

"What?"

"Oh, what's the *difference*, Mother?"

"Muriel, I want to *know*. Your father—"

"All right, all right. He calls me Miss Spiritual Tramp of 1948," the girl said, and giggled.

"It isn't funny, Muriel. It isn't funny at all. It's horrible. It's *sad*, actually. When I think how—"

"Mother," the girl interrupted, "listen to me. You remember that book he sent me from Germany? You know—those German poems. What'd I *do* with it? I've been racking my—"

"You have it."

"Are you *sure?*" said the girl.

"Certainly. That is, I have it. It's in Freddy's room. You left it here and I didn't have room for it in the— Why? Does he want it?"

"No. Only, he *asked* me about it, when we were driving down. He wanted to know if I'd read it."

"It was in German!"

"Yes, dear. That doesn't make any difference," said the girl, crossing her legs. "He said that the poems happen to be written by the *only great poet of the century.* He said I should've bought a translation or something. Or *learned the language,* if you please."

"Awful. Awful. It's *sad,* actually, is what it is. Your father said last night—"

"Just a second, Mother," the girl said. She went over to the window seat for her cigarettes, lit one, and returned to her seat on the bed. "Mother?" she said, exhaling smoke.

"Muriel. Now, listen to me."

"I'm listening."

"Your father talked to Dr. Sivetski."

"Oh?" said the girl.

"He told him *ev*erything. At least, he said he did—you know your father. The trees. That business with the window. Those horrible things he said to Granny about her plans for passing away. What he did with all those lovely pictures from Bermuda—*ev*erything."

"Well?" said the girl.

"Well. In the first place, he said it was a perfect *crime* the Army released him from the hospital—my word of honor. He very *defi*nitely told your father there's a chance—a very *great* chance, he said —that Seymour may com*plete*ly lose control of himself. My word of honor."

"There's a psychiatrist here at the hotel," said the girl.

"*Who?* What's his name?"

"I don't know. Rieser or something. He's supposed to be very good."

"Never heard of him."

"Well, he's supposed to be very good, anyway."

"Muriel, don't be fresh, please. We're *very* worried about you.

Your father wanted to wire you *last night* to come home, as a matter of f—"

"I'm not coming home right now, Mother. So relax."

"Muriel. My word of honor. Dr. Sivetski said Seymour may com-*plete*ly lose contr—"

"I just *got* here, Mother. This is the first vacation I've had in years, and I'm not going to just *pack* everything and come home," said the girl. "I couldn't travel now anyway. I'm so sunburned I can hardly move."

"You're badly sunburned? Didn't you use that jar of Bronze I put in your bag? I put it right—"

"I used it. I'm burned anyway."

"That's terrible. Where are you burned?"

"All over, dear, all over."

"That's terrible."

"I'll live."

"Tell me, did you talk to this psychiatrist?"

"Well, sort of," said the girl.

"What'd he say? Where was Seymour when you talked to him?"

"In the Ocean Room, playing the piano. He's played the piano both nights we've been here."

"Well, what'd he say?"

"Oh, nothing much. He spoke to me first. I was sitting next to him at Bingo last night, and he asked me if that wasn't my husband playing the piano in the other room. I said yes, it was, and he asked me if Seymour'd been sick or something. So I said—"

"Why'd he ask that?"

"*I* don't know, Mother. I guess because he's so pale and all," said the girl. "Anyway, after Bingo he and his wife asked me if I wouldn't like to join them for a drink. So I did. His wife was horrible. You remember that awful dinner dress we saw in Bonwit's window? The one you said you'd have to have a tiny, tiny—"

"The green?"

"She had it on. And all hips. She kept asking me if Seymour's re-lated to that Suzanne Glass that has that place on Madison Avenue—the millinery."

"What'd he say, though? The doctor."

"Oh. Well, nothing much, really. I mean we were in the bar and all. It was terribly noisy."

"Yes, but did—did you tell him what he tried to do with Granny's chair?"

"*No*, Mother. I didn't go into details very much," said the girl. "I'll probably get a chance to talk to him again. He's in the bar *all* day long."

"Did he say he thought there was a chance he might get—you know—funny or anything? Do something to you?"

"Not exactly," said the girl. "He had to have more facts, Mother. They have to know about your childhood—all that stuff. I told you, we could hardly talk, it was so noisy in there."

"Well. How's your blue coat?"

"All right. I had some of the padding taken out."

"How *are* the clothes this year?"

"Terrible. But out of this world. You see sequins—everything," said the girl.

"How's your room?"

"All right. *Just* all right, though. We couldn't get the room we had before the war," said the girl. "The people are awful this year. You should see what sits next to us in the dining room. At the next table. They look as if they drove down in a truck."

"Well, it's that way all over. How's your ballerina?"

"It's too long. I *told* you it was too long."

"Muriel, I'm only going to ask you once more—are you really all right?"

"*Yes,* Mother," said the girl. "For the ninetieth time."

"And you don't want to come home?"

"*No*, Mother."

"Your father said last night that he'd be more than willing to pay for it if you'd go away someplace by yourself and think things over. You could take a lovely cruise. We both thought—"

"No, thanks," said the girl, and uncrossed her legs. "Mother, this call is costing a for—"

"When I think of how you waited for that boy *all* through the war—I mean when you think of all those crazy little wives who—"

"Mother," said the girl, "we'd better hang up. Seymour may come in any minute."

"Where is he?"

"On the beach."

"On the beach? By himself? Does he behave himself on the beach?"

"Mother," said the girl, "you talk about him as though he were a raving *maniac*—"

"I said nothing of the kind, Muriel."

"Well, you *sound* that way. I mean all he does is lie there. He won't take his bathrobe off."

"He won't take his bathrobe off? Why not?"

"*I* don't know. I guess because he's so pale."

"My goodness, he *needs* the sun. Can't you make him?"

"You know Seymour," said the girl, and crossed her legs again. "He says he doesn't want a lot of fools looking at his tattoo."

"He doesn't have any tattoo! Did he get one in the Army?"

"No, Mother. No, dear," said the girl, and stood up. "Listen, I'll call you tomorrow, maybe."

"Muriel. Now, listen to me."

"Yes, Mother," said the girl, putting her weight on her right leg.

"Call me the *instant* he does, or *says*, anything at all funny—you know what I mean. Do you hear me?"

"Mother, I'm not afraid of Seymour."

"Muriel, I want you to promise me."

"All right, I promise. Goodbye, Mother," said the girl. "My love to Daddy." She hung up.

"See more glass," said Sybil Carpenter, who was staying at the hotel with her mother. "Did you see more glass?"

"Pussycat, stop saying that. It's driving Mommy absolutely crazy. Hold still, please."

Mrs. Carpenter was putting sun-tan oil on Sybil's shoulders, spreading it down over the delicate, winglike blades of her back. Sybil was sitting insecurely on a huge, inflated beach ball, facing the ocean. She was wearing a canary-yellow two-piece bathing suit, one piece of which she would not actually be needing for another nine or ten years.

"It was really just an ordinary silk handkerchief—you could see when you got up close," said the woman in the beach chair beside Mrs. Carpenter's. "I wish I knew how she tied it. It was really darling."

"It sounds darling," Mrs. Carpenter agreed. "Sybil, *hold still,* pussy."

"Did you see more glass?" said Sybil.

Mrs. Carpenter sighed. "All right," she said. She replaced the cap on the sun-tan-oil bottle. "Now run and play, pussy. Mommy's going up to the hotel and have a Martini with Mrs. Hubbel. I'll bring you the olive."

Set loose, Sybil immediately ran down to the flat part of the beach and began to walk in the direction of Fisherman's Pavilion. Stopping only to sink a foot in a soggy, collapsed castle, she was soon out of the area reserved for guests of the hotel.

She walked for about a quarter of a mile and then suddenly broke into an oblique run up the soft part of the beach. She stopped short when she reached the place where a young man was lying on his back.

"Are you going in the water, see more glass?" she said.

The young man started, his right hand going to the lapels of his terry-cloth robe. He turned over on his stomach, letting a sausaged towel fall away from his eyes, and squinted up at Sybil.

"Hey. Hello, Sybil."

"Are you going in the water?"

"I was waiting for *you*," said the young man. "What's new?"

"What?" said Sybil.

"What's new? What's on the program?"

"My daddy's coming tomorrow on a nairiplane," Sybil said, kicking sand.

"Not in my face, baby," the young man said, putting his hand on Sybil's ankle. "Well, it's about time he got here, your daddy. I've been expecting him hourly. Hourly."

"Where's the lady?" Sybil said.

"The lady?" The young man brushed some sand out of his thin hair. "That's hard to say, Sybil. She may be in any one of a thousand places. At the hairdresser's. Having her hair dyed mink. Or making dolls for poor children, in her room." Lying prone now, he made two fists, set one on top of the other, and rested his chin on the top one. "Ask me something else, Sybil," he said. "That's a fine bathing suit you have on. If there's one thing I like, it's a blue bathing suit."

Sybil stared at him, then looked down at her protruding stomach. "This is a *yellow*," she said. "This is a *yellow*."

"It is? Come a little closer."

Sybil took a step forward.

"You're absolutely right. What a fool I am."

"Are you going in the water?" Sybil said.

"I'm seriously considering it. I'm giving it plenty of thought, Sybil, you'll be glad to know."

Sybil prodded the rubber float that the young man sometimes used as a headrest. "It needs *air*," she said.

"You're right. It needs more air than I'm willing to admit." He took away his fists and let his chin rest on the sand. "Sybil," he said, "you're looking fine. It's good to see you. Tell me about yourself." He reached in front of him and took both of Sybil's ankles in his hands. "I'm Capricorn," he said. "What are you?"

"Sharon Lipschutz said you let her sit on the piano seat with you," Sybil said.

"Sharon Lipschutz said that?"

Sybil nodded vigorously.

He let go of her ankles, drew in his hands, and laid the side of his face on his right forearm. "Well," he said, "you know how those things happen, Sybil. I was sitting there, playing. And you were nowhere in sight. And Sharon Lipschutz came over and sat down next to me. I couldn't push her off, could I?"

"Yes."

"Oh, no. No. I couldn't do that," said the young man. "I'll tell you what I did do, though."

"What?"

"I pretended she was you."

Sybil immediately stooped and began to dig in the sand. "Let's go in the water," she said.

"All right," said the young man. "I think I can work it in."

"Next time, push her off," Sybil said.

"Push who off?"

"Sharon Lipschutz."

"Ah, Sharon Lipschutz," said the young man. "How that name comes up. Mixing memory and desire." He suddenly got to his feet. He looked at the ocean. "Sybil," he said, "I'll tell you what we'll do. We'll see if we can catch a bananafish."

"A what?"

"A bananafish," he said, and undid the belt of his robe. He took off the robe. His shoulders were white and narrow, and his trunks were royal blue. He folded the robe, first lengthwise, then in thirds. He unrolled the towel he had used over his eyes, spread it out on the sand, and then laid the folded robe on top of it. He bent over, picked up the float, and secured it under his right arm. Then, with his left hand, he took Sybil's hand.

The two started to walk down to the ocean.

"I imagine you've seen quite a few bananafish in your day," the young man said.

Sybil shook her head.

"You haven't? Where do you *live*, anyway?"

"I don't know," said Sybil.

"Sure you know. You must know. Sharon Lipschutz knows where *she* lives and *she's* only *three and a half*."

Sybil stopped walking and yanked her hand away from him. She picked up an ordinary beach shell and looked at it with elaborate interest. She threw it down. "Whirly Wood, Connecticut," she said, and resumed walking, stomach foremost.

"Whirly Wood, Connecticut," said the young man. "Is that anywhere near Whirly Wood, Connecticut, by any chance?"

Sybil looked at him. "That's where I *live*," she said impatiently. "I *live* in Whirly Wood, Connecticut." She ran a few steps ahead of him, caught up her left foot in her left hand, and hopped two or three times.

"You have no idea how clear that makes everything," the young man said.

Sybil released her foot. "Did you read 'Little Black Sambo'?" she said.

"It's very funny you ask me that," he said. "It so happens I just finished reading it last night." He reached down and took back Sybil's hand. "What did you think of it?" he asked her.

"Did the tigers run all around that tree?"

"I thought they'd never stop. I never saw so many tigers."

"There were only six," Sybil said.

"*Only* six!" said the young man. "Do you call that *only?*"

"Do you like wax?" Sybil asked.

"Do I like what?" asked the young man.

"Wax."

"Very much. Don't you?"

Sybil nodded. "Do you like olives?" she asked.

"Olives—yes. Olives and wax. I never go anyplace without 'em."

"Do you like Sharon Lipschutz?" Sybil asked.

"Yes. Yes, I do," said the young man. "What I like par*ti*cularly about her is that she never does anything mean to little dogs in the lobby of the hotel. That little toy bull that belongs to that lady from Canada, for instance. You probably won't believe this, but *some* little girls like to poke that little dog with balloon sticks. Sharon doesn't. She's never mean or unkind. That's why I like her so much."

Sybil was silent.

"I like to chew candles," she said finally.

"Who doesn't?" said the young man, getting his feet wet. "Wow! It's cold." He dropped the rubber float on its back. "No, wait just a second, Sybil. Wait'll we get out a little bit."

They waded out till the water was up to Sybil's waist. Then the young man picked her up and laid her down on her stomach on the float.

"Don't you ever wear a bathing cap or anything?" he asked.

"Don't let go," Sybil ordered. "You hold me, now."

"Miss Carpenter. Please. I know my business," the young man said. "You just keep your eyes open for any bananafish. This is a *perfect* day for bananafish."

"I don't see any," Sybil said.

"That's understandable. Their habits are very peculiar. *Very* peculiar." He kept pushing the float. The water was not quite up to his chest. "They lead a very tragic life," he said. "You know what they do, Sybil?"

She shook her head.

"Well, they swim into a hole where there's a lot of bananas. They're very ordinary-looking fish when they swim *in*. But once they get in, they behave like pigs. Why, I've known some bananafish to swim into a banana hole and eat as many as seventy-eight bananas." He edged the float and its passenger a foot closer to the horizon. "Naturally, after that they're so fat they can't get out of the hole again. Can't fit through the door."

"Not too far out," Sybil said. "What happens to them?"

"What happens to who?"

"The bananafish."

"Oh, you mean after they eat so many bananas they can't get out of the banana hole?"

"Yes," said Sybil.

"Well, I hate to tell you, Sybil. They die."

"Why?" asked Sybil.

"Well, they get banana fever. It's a terrible disease."

"Here comes a *wave*," Sybil said nervously.

"We'll ignore it. We'll snub it," said the young man. "Two snobs." He took Sybil's ankles in his hands and pressed down and forward. The float nosed over the top of the wave. The water soaked Sybil's blond hair, but her scream was full of pleasure.

With her hand, when the float was level again, she wiped away a flat, wet band of hair from her eyes, and reported, "I just saw one."

"Saw what, my love?"

"A bananafish."

"My God, no!" said the young man. "Did he have any bananas in his mouth?"

"Yes," said Sybil. "Six."

The young man suddenly picked up one of Sybil's wet feet, which were drooping over the end of the float, and kissed the arch.

"Hey!" said the owner of the foot, turning around.

"Hey, yourself! We're going in now. You had enough?"

"No!"

"Sorry," he said, and pushed the float toward shore until Sybil got off it. He carried it the rest of the way.

"Goodbye," said Sybil, and ran without regret in the direction of the hotel.

The young man put on his robe, closed the lapels tight, and jammed his towel into his pocket. He picked up the slimy wet, cumbersome float and put it under his arm. He plodded alone through the soft, hot sand toward the hotel.

On the sub-main floor of the hotel, which the management directed bathers to use, a woman with zinc salve on her nose got into the elevator with the young man.

"I see you're looking at my feet," he said to her when the car was in motion.

"I beg your pardon?" said the woman.

"I said I see you're looking at my feet."

"I *beg* your pardon. I happened to be looking at the floor," said the woman, and faced the doors of the car.

"If you want to look at my feet, say so," said the young man. "But don't be a God-damned sneak about it."

"Let me out here, please," the woman said quickly to the girl operating the car.

The car doors opened and the woman got off without looking back.

"I have two normal feet and I can't see the slightest God-damned reason why anybody should stare at them," said the young man. "Five, please." He took his room key out of his robe pocket.

He got off at the fifth floor, walked down the hall, and let himself into 507. The room smelled of new calfskin luggage and nail-lacquer remover.

He glanced at the girl lying asleep on one of the twin beds. Then he went over to one of the pieces of luggage, opened it, and from under a pile of shorts and undershirts he took out an Ortgies calibre 7.65 automatic. He released the magazine, looked at it, then reinserted it. He cocked the piece. Then he went over and sat down on the unoccupied twin bed, looked at the girl, aimed the pistol, and fired a bullet through his right temple.

THE PATTERNS OF LOVE

❖

WILLIAM MAXWELL

KATE TALBOT's bantam rooster, awakened by the sudden appearance of the moon from behind a cloud on a white June night, began to crow. There were three bantams—a cock and two hens—and their roost was in a tree just outside the guest-room windows. The guest room was on the first floor and the Talbots' guest that weekend was a young man by the name of Arnold, a rather light sleeper. He got up and closed the windows and went back to bed. In the sealed room he slept, but was awakened at frequent intervals until daylight Saturday morning.

Arnold had been coming to the Talbots' place in Wilton sometime during the spring or early summer for a number of years. His visits were, for the children, one of a thousand seasonal events that could be counted on, less exciting than the appearance of the first robin or the arrival of violets in the marsh at the foot of the Talbots' hill but akin to them. Sometimes Duncan, the Talbots' older boy, who for a long time was under the impression that Arnold came to see *him*, slept in the guest room when Arnold was there. Last year, George, Duncan's younger brother, had been given that privilege. This time, Mrs. Talbot, knowing how talkative the boys were when they awoke in the morning, had left Arnold to himself.

When he came out of his room, Mrs. Talbot and George, the apple of her eye, were still at breakfast. George was six, small and delicate and very blond, not really interested in food at any time, and certainly not now, when there was a guest in the house. He was in his pajamas and a pink quilted bathrobe. He smiled at Arnold with his large and very gentle eyes and said, "Did you miss me?"

"Yes, of course," Arnold said. "I woke up and there was the other bed, flat and empty. Nobody to talk to while I looked at the ceiling. Nobody to watch me shave."

George was very pleased that his absence had been felt. "What is your favorite color?" he asked.

"Red," Arnold said, without having to consider.

"Mine, too," George said, and his face became so illuminated with pleasure at this coincidence that for a moment he looked angelic.

"No matter how much we disagree about other things," Arnold said, "we'll always have that in common, won't we?"

"Yes," George said.

"You'd both better eat your cereal," Mrs. Talbot said.

Arnold looked at her while she was pouring his coffee and wondered if there wasn't something back of her remark—jealousy, perhaps. Mrs. Talbot was a very soft-hearted woman, but for some reason she seemed to be ashamed—or perhaps afraid—to let other people know it. She took refuge continually behind a dry humor. There was probably very little likelihood that George would be as fond of anyone else as he was of his mother, Arnold decided, for many years to come. There was no real reason for her to be jealous.

"Did the bantams keep you awake?" she asked.

Arnold shook his head.

"Something tells me you're lying," Mrs. Talbot said. "John didn't wake up, but he felt his responsibilities as a host even so. He cried 'Oh!' in his sleep every time a bantam crowed. You'll have to put up with them on Kate's account. She loves them more than her life."

Excluded from the conversation of the grownups, George finished his cereal and ate part of a soft-boiled egg. Then he asked to be excused and, with pillows and pads which had been brought in from the garden furniture the night before, he made a train right across the dining-room floor. The cook had to step over it when she brought a fresh pot of coffee, and Mrs. Talbot and Arnold had to do likewise when they went out through the dining-room door to look at the bantams. There were only two—the cock and one hen—walking around under the Japanese cherry tree on the terrace. Kate was leaning out of an upstairs window, watching them fondly.

"Have you made your bed?" Mrs. Talbot asked.

The head withdrew.

"Kate is going to a houseparty," Mrs. Talbot said, looking at the bantams. "A sort of houseparty. She's going to stay all night at Mary Sherman's house and there are going to be some boys and they're going to dance to the victrola."

"How old is she, for heaven's sake?" Arnold asked.

"Thirteen," Mrs. Talbot said. "She had her hair cut yesterday and it's too short. It doesn't look right, so I have to do something about it."

"White of egg?" Arnold asked.

"How did you know that?" Mrs.Talbot asked in surprise.

"I remembered it from the last time," Arnold said. "I remembered it because it sounded so drastic."

"It only works with blonds," Mrs. Talbot said. "Will you be able to entertain yourself for a while?"

"Easily," Arnold said. "I saw 'Anna Karenina' in the library and I think I'll take that and go up to the little house."

"Maybe I'd better come with you," Mrs. Talbot said.

The little house was a one-room studio halfway up the hill, about a hundred feet from the big house, with casement windows on two sides and a Franklin stove. It had been built several years before, after Mrs. Talbot had read "A Room of One's Own," and by now it had a slightly musty odor which included lingering traces of wood smoke.

"Hear the wood thrush?" Arnold asked, as Mrs. Talbot threw open the windows for him. They both listened.

"No," she said. "All birds sound alike to me."

"Listen," he said.

This time there was no mistaking it—the liquid notes up and then down the same scale.

"Oh, that," she said. "Yes, I love that," and went off to wash Kate's hair.

From time to time Arnold raised his head from the book he was reading and heard not only the wood thrush but also Duncan and George, quarrelling in the meadow. George's voice was shrill and unhappy and sounded as if he were on the verge of tears. Both boys appeared at the window eventually and asked for permission to come in. The little house was out of bounds to them. Arnold nodded. Duncan, who was nine, crawled in without much difficulty, but George had to be hoisted. No sooner were they inside than they began to fight over a wooden gun which had been broken and mended and was rightly George's, it seemed, though Duncan had it and refused to give it up. He refused to give it up one moment, and the next moment, after a sudden change of heart, pressed it upon George—*forced* George to take it, actually, for by that time

George was more concerned about the Talbots' dog, who also wanted to come in.

The dog was a Great Dane, very mild but also very enormous. He answered to the name of Satan. Once Satan was admitted to the little house, it became quite full and rather noisy, but John Talbot appeared and sent the dog out and made the children leave Arnold in peace. They left as they had come, by the window. Arnold watched them and was touched by the way Duncan turned and helped George, who was too small to jump. Also by the way George accepted this help. It was as if their hostility had two faces and one of them was the face of love. Cain and Abel, Arnold thought, and the wood thrush. All immortal.

John Talbot lingered outside the little house. Something had been burrowing in the lily-of-the-valley bed, he said, and had also uprooted several lady slippers. Arnold suggested that it might be moles.

"More likely a rat," John Talbot said, and his eyes wandered to a two-foot espaliered pear tree. "That pear tree," he said, "we put in over a year ago."

Mrs. Talbot joined them. She had shampooed not only Kate's hair but her own as well.

"It's still alive," John Talbot said, staring at the pear tree, "but it doesn't put out any leaves."

"I should think it would be a shock to a pear tree to be espaliered," Mrs. Talbot said. "Kate's ready to go."

They all piled into the station wagon and took Kate to her party. Her too-short blond hair looked quite satisfactory after the egg shampoo, and Mrs. Talbot had made a boutonnière out of a pink geranium and some little blue and white flowers for Kate to wear on her coat. She got out of the car with her suitcase and waved at them from the front steps of the house.

"I hope she has a good time," John Talbot said uneasily as he shifted gears. "It's her first dance with boys. It would be terrible if she didn't have any partners." In his eyes there was a vague threat toward the boys who, in their young callowness, might not appreciate his daughter.

"Kate always has a good time," Mrs. Talbot said. "By the way, have you seen both of the bantam hens today?"

"No," John Talbot said.

"One of them is missing," Mrs. Talbot said.

One of the things that impressed Arnold whenever he stayed

with the Talbots was the number and variety of animals they had. Their place was not a farm, after all, but merely a big white brick house in the country, and yet they usually had a dog and a cat, kittens, rabbits, and chickens, all actively involved in the family life. This summer the Talbots weren't able to go in and out by the front door, because a phoebe had built a nest in the porch light. They used the dining-room door instead, and were careful not to leave the porch light on more than a minute or two, lest the eggs be cooked. Arnold came upon some turtle food in his room, and when he asked about it, Mrs. Talbot informed him that there were turtles in the guest room, too. He never came upon the turtles.

The bantams were new this year, and so were the two very small ducklings that at night were put in a paper carton in the sewing room, with an electric-light bulb to keep them warm. In the daytime they hopped in and out of a saucer of milk on the terrace. One of them was called Mr. Rochester because of his distinguished air. The other had no name.

All the while that Mrs. Talbot was making conversation with Arnold, after lunch, she kept her eyes on the dog, who, she explained, was jealous of the ducklings. Once his great head swooped down and he pretended to take a nip at them. A nip would have been enough. Mrs. Talbot spoke to him sharply and he turned his head away in shame.

"They probably smell the way George did when he first came home from the hospital," she said.

"What did George smell like?" Arnold asked.

"Sweetish, actually. Actually awful."

"Was Satan jealous of George when he was a baby?"

"Frightfully," Mrs. Talbot said. "Call Satan!" she shouted to her husband, who was up by the little house. He had found a rat hole near the ravaged lady slippers and was setting a trap. He called the dog, and the dog went bounding off, devotion in every leap.

While Mrs. Talbot was telling Arnold how they found Satan at the baby's crib one night, Duncan, who was playing only a few yards away with George, suddenly, and for no apparent reason, made his younger brother cry. Mrs. Talbot got up and separated them.

"I wouldn't be surprised if it wasn't time for your nap, George," she said, but he was not willing to let go of even a small part of the day. He wiped his tears away with his fist and ran from her. She ran after him, laughing, and caught him at the foot of the terrace.

Duncan wandered off into a solitary world of his own, and Arnold, after yawning twice, got up and went into the house. Stretched out on the bed in his room, with the Venetian blinds closed, he began to compare the life of the Talbots with his own well-ordered but childless and animalless life in town. Everywhere they go, he thought, they leave tracks behind them, like people walking in the snow. Paths crisscrossing, lines that are perpetually meeting: the mother's loving pursuit of her youngest, the man's love for his daughter, the dog's love for the man, the two boys' preoccupation with each other. Wheels and diagrams, Arnold said to himself. The patterns of love.

That night Arnold was much less bothered by the crowing, which came to him dimly, through dreams. When he awoke finally and was fully awake, he was conscious of the silence and the sun shining in his eyes. His watch had stopped and it was later than he thought. The Talbots had finished breakfast and the Sunday *Times* was waiting beside his place at the table. While he was eating, John Talbot came in and sat down for a minute, across the table. He had been out early that morning, he said, and had found a chipmunk in the rat trap and also a nest with three bantam eggs in it. The eggs were cold.

He was usually a very quiet, self-contained man. This was the first time Arnold had ever seen him disturbed about anything. "I don't know how we're going to tell Kate," he said. "She'll be very upset."

Kate came home sooner than they expected her, on the bus. She came up the driveway, lugging her suitcase.

"Did you have a good time?" Mrs. Talbot called to her from the terrace.

"Yes," she said, "I had a beautiful time."

Arnold looked at the two boys, expecting them to blurt out the tragedy as soon as Kate put down her suitcase, but they didn't. It was her father who told her, in such a roundabout way that she didn't seem to understand at all what he was saying. Mrs. Talbot interrupted him with the flat facts; the bantam hen was not on her nest and therefore, in all probability, had been killed, maybe by the rat.

Kate went into the house. The others remained on the terrace. The dog didn't snap at the ducklings, though his mind was on them still, and the two boys didn't quarrel. In spite of the patterns on which they seem so intent, Arnold thought, what happens to one of them happens to all. They are helplessly involved in Kate's loss.

At noon other guests arrived, two families with children. There was a picnic, with hot dogs and bowls of salad, cake, and wine, out under the grape arbor. When the guests departed, toward the end of the afternoon, the family came together again on the terrace. Kate was lying on the ground, on her stomach, with her face resting on her arms, her head practically in the ducklings' saucer of milk. Mrs. Talbot, who had stretched out on the garden chaise longue, discovered suddenly that Mr. Rochester was missing. She sat up in alarm and cried, "Where is he?"

"Down my neck," Kate said.

The duck emerged from her crossed arms. He crawled around them and climbed up on the back of her neck. Kate smiled. The sight of the duck's tiny downy head among her pale ash-blond curls made them all burst out laughing. The cloud that had been hanging over the household evaporated into bright sunshine, and Arnold seized that moment to glance surreptitiously at his watch.

They all went to the train with him, including the dog. At the last moment Mrs. Talbot, out of a sudden perception of his lonely life, tried to give him some radishes, but he refused them. When he stepped out of the car at the station, the boys were arguing and were with difficulty persuaded to say goodbye to him. He watched the station wagon drive away and then stood listening for the sound of the wood thrush. But, of course, in the center of South Norwalk there was no such sound.

THE LOTTERY

❖

SHIRLEY JACKSON

THE MORNING of June 27th was clear and sunny, with the fresh warmth of a full-summer day; the flowers were blossoming pro- fusely and the grass was richly green. The people of the village began to gather in the square, between the post office and the bank, around ten o'clock; in some towns there were so many people that the lottery took two days and had to be started on June 26th, but in this village, where there were only about three hundred people, the whole lottery took only about two hours, so it could begin at ten o'clock in the morning and still be through in time to allow the villagers to get home for noon dinner.

The children assembled first, of course. School was recently over for the summer, and the feeling of liberty sat uneasily on most of them; they tended to gather together quietly for a while before they broke into boisterous play, and their talk was still of the classroom and the teacher, of books and reprimands. Bobby Martin had al- ready stuffed his pockets full of stones, and the other boys soon followed his example, selecting the smoothest and roundest stones; Bobby and Harry Jones and Dickie Delacroix—the villagers pro- nounced this name "Dellacroy"—eventually made a great pile of stones in one corner of the square and guarded it against the raids of the other boys. The girls stood aside, talking among themselves, looking over their shoulders at the boys, and the very small children rolled in the dust or clung to the hands of their older brothers or sisters.

Soon the men began to gather, surveying their own children, speaking of planting and rain, tractors and taxes. They stood to- gether, away from the pile of stones in the corner, and their jokes were quiet and they smiled rather than laughed. The women, wearing faded house dresses and sweaters, came shortly after their menfolk. They greeted one another and exchanged bits of gossip as they went to join their husbands. Soon the women, standing by their husbands, began to call to their children, and the children came reluctantly, having to be called four or five times. Bobby Martin ducked under his mother's grasping hand and ran, laughing, back to the pile of stones. His father spoke up sharply, and Bobby came quickly and took his place between his father and his oldest brother.

The lottery was conducted—as were the square dances, the teen-age club, the Halloween program—by Mr. Summers, who had time and energy to devote to civic activities. He was a round-faced, jovial man and he ran the coal business, and people were sorry for him, because he had no children and his wife was a scold. When he arrived in the square, carrying the black wooden box, there was a murmur of conversation among the villagers, and he waved and called, "Little late today, folks." The postmaster, Mr. Graves, followed him, carrying a three-legged stool, and the stool was put in the center of the square and Mr. Summers set the black box down on it. The villagers kept their distance, leaving a space between themselves and the stool, and when Mr. Summers said, "Some of you fellows want to give me a hand?," there was a hesitation before two men, Mr. Martin and his oldest son, Baxter, came forward to hold the box steady on the stool while Mr. Summers stirred up the papers inside it.

The original paraphernalia for the lottery had been lost long ago, and the black box now resting on the stool had been put into use even before Old Man Warner, the oldest man in town, was born. Mr. Summers spoke frequently to the villagers about making a new box, but no one liked to upset even as much tradition as was represented by the black box. There was a story that the present box had been made with some pieces of the box that had preceded it, the one that had been constructed when the first people settled down to make a village here. Every year, after the lottery, Mr. Summers began talking again about a new box, but every year the subject was allowed to fade off without anything's being done. The black box grew shabbier each year; by now it was no longer completely black but splintered badly along one side to show the original wood color, and in some places faded or stained.

Mr. Martin and his oldest son, Baxter, held the black box securely on the stool until Mr. Summers had stirred the papers thoroughly with his hand. Because so much of the ritual had been forgotten or discarded, Mr. Summers had been successful in having slips of paper substituted for the chips of wood that had been used for generations. Chips of wood, Mr. Summers had argued, had been all very well when the village was tiny, but now that the population was more than three hundred and likely to keep on growing, it was necessary to use something that would fit more easily into the black box. The night before the lottery, Mr. Summers and Mr. Graves made up the slips of paper and put them into the box, and it was then taken to the safe of Mr. Summers' coal company and locked up until Mr. Summers was ready to take it to the square next morning. The rest of the year, the box was put away, sometimes one place, sometimes another; it had spent one year in Mr. Graves' barn and another year underfoot in the post office, and sometimes it was set on a shelf in the Martin grocery and left there.

There was a great deal of fussing to be done before Mr. Summers declared the lottery open. There were the lists to make up—of heads of families, heads of households in each family, members of each household in each family. There was the proper swearing-in of Mr. Summers by the postmaster, as the official of the lottery; at one time, some people remembered, there had been a recital of some sort, performed by the official of the lottery, a perfunctory, tuneless chant that had been rattled off duly each year; some people believed that the official of the lottery used to stand just so when he said or sang it, others believed that he was supposed to walk among the people, but years and years ago this part of the ritual had been allowed to lapse. There had been, also, a ritual salute, which the official of the lottery had had to use in addressing each person who came up to draw from the box, but this also had changed with time, until now it was felt necessary only for the official to speak to each person approaching. Mr. Summers was very good at all this; in his clean white shirt and blue jeans, with one hand resting carelessly on the black box, he seemed very proper and important as he talked interminably to Mr. Graves and the Martins.

Just as Mr. Summers finally left off talking and turned to the assembled villagers, Mrs. Hutchinson came hurriedly along the path to the square, her sweater thrown over her shoulders, and slid into place in the back of the crowd. "Clean forgot what day it was," she said to Mrs. Delacroix, who stood next to her, and they both laughed softly. "Thought my old man was out back stacking wood," Mrs. Hutchinson went on, "and then I looked out the window and the kids was gone, and then I remembered it was the twenty-seventh and came a-running." She dried her hands on her apron, and Mrs.

Delacroix said, "You're in time, though. They're still talking away up there."

Mrs. Hutchinson craned her neck to see through the crowd and found her husband and children standing near the front. She tapped Mrs. Delacroix on the arm as a farewell and began to make her way through the crowd. The people separated good-humoredly to let her through; two or three people said, in voices just loud enough to be heard across the crowd, "Here comes your Mrs., Hutchinson," and "Bill, she made it after all." Mrs. Hutchinson reached her husband, and Mr. Summers, who had been waiting, said cheerfully, "Thought we were going to have to get on without you, Tessie." Mrs. Hutchinson said, grinning, "Wouldn't have me leave m'dishes in the sink, now, would you, Joe?," and soft laughter ran through the crowd as the people stirred back into position after Mrs. Hutchinson's arrival.

"Well, now," Mr. Summers said soberly, "guess we better get started, get this over with, so's we can go back to work. Anybody ain't here?"

"Dunbar," several people said. "Dunbar, Dunbar."

Mr. Summers consulted his list. "Clyde Dunbar," he said. "That's right. He's broke his leg, hasn't he? Who's drawing for him?"

"Me, I guess," a woman said, and Mr. Summers turned to look at her. "Wife draws for her husband," Mr. Summers said. "Don't you have a grown boy to do it for you, Janey?" Although Mr. Summers and everyone else in the village knew the answer perfectly well, it was the business of the official of the lottery to ask such questions formally. Mr. Summers waited with an expression of polite interest while Mrs. Dunbar answered.

"Horace's not but sixteen yet," Mrs. Dunbar said regretfully. "Guess I gotta fill in for the old man this year."

"Right," Mr. Summers said. He made a note on the list he was holding. Then he asked, "Watson boy drawing this year?"

A tall boy in the crowd raised his hand. "Here," he said. "I'm drawing for m'mother and me." He blinked his eyes nervously and ducked his head as several voices in the crowd said things like "Good fellow, Jack," and "Glad to see your mother's got a man to do it."

"Well," Mr. Summers said, "guess that's everyone. Old Man Warner make it?"

"Here," a voice said, and Mr. Summers nodded.

A sudden hush fell on the crowd as Mr. Summers cleared his throat and looked at the list. "All ready?" he called. "Now, I'll read the names—heads of families first—and the men come up and take a paper out of the box. Keep the paper folded in your hand without looking at it until everyone has had a turn. Everything clear?"

The people had done it so many times that they only half listened to the directions; most of them were quiet, wetting their lips, not looking around. Then Mr. Summers raised one hand high and said, "Adams." A man disengaged himself from the crowd and came forward. "Hi, Steve," Mr. Summers said, and Mr. Adams said, "Hi, Joe." They grinned at one another humorlessly and nervously. Then Mr. Adams reached into the black box and took out a folded paper. He held it firmly by one corner as he turned and went hastily back to his place in the crowd, where he stood a little apart from his family, not looking down at his hand.

"Allen," Mr. Summers said. "Anderson. . . . Bentham."

"Seems like there's no time at all between lotteries any more," Mrs. Delacroix said to Mrs. Graves in the back row. "Seems like we got through with the last one only last week."

"Time sure goes fast," Mrs. Graves said.

"Clark. . . . Delacroix."

"There goes my old man," Mrs. Delacroix said. She held her breath while her husband went forward.

"Dunbar," Mr. Summers said, and Mrs. Dunbar went steadily to the box while one of the women said, "Go on, Janey," and another said, "There she goes."

"We're next," Mrs. Graves said. She watched while Mr. Graves came around from the side of the box, greeted Mr. Summers gravely, and selected a slip of paper from the box. By now, all through the crowd there were men holding the small folded papers in their large hands, turning them over and over nervously. Mrs. Dunbar and her two sons stood together, Mrs. Dunbar holding the slip of paper.

"Harburt. . . . Hutchinson."

"Get up there, Bill," Mrs. Hutchinson said, and the people near her laughed.

"Jones."

"They do say," Mr. Adams said to Old Man Warner, who stood next to him, "that over in the north village they're talking of giving up the lottery."

Old Man Warner snorted. "Pack of crazy fools," he said. "Listening to the young folks, nothing's good enough for *them*. Next thing you know, they'll be wanting to go back to living in caves, nobody work any more, live *that* way for a while. Used to be a saying about 'Lottery in June, corn be heavy soon.' First thing you know, we'd all be eating stewed chickweed and acorns. There's *always* been a lottery," he added petulantly. "Bad enough to see young Joe Summers up there joking with everybody."

"Some places have already quit lotteries," Mrs. Adams said.

"Nothing but trouble in *that*," Old Man Warner said stoutly. "Pack of young fools."

"Martin." And Bobby Martin watched his father go forward. "Overdyke. . . . Percy."

"I wish they'd hurry," Mrs. Dunbar said to her older son. "I wish they'd hurry."

"They're almost through," her son said.

"You get ready to run tell Dad," Mrs. Dunbar said.

Mr. Summers called his own name and then stepped forward precisely and selected a slip from the box. Then he called, "Warner."

"Seventy-seventh year I been in the lottery," Old Man Warner said as he went through the crowd. "Seventy-seventh time."

"Watson." The tall boy came awkwardly through the crowd. Someone said, "Don't be nervous, Jack," and Mr. Summers said, "Take your time, son."

"Zanini."

After that, there was a long pause, a breathless pause, until Mr. Summers, holding his slip of paper in the air, said, "All right, fellows." For a minute, no one moved, and then all the slips of paper were opened. Suddenly, all the women began to speak at once, saying, "Who is it?," "Who's got it?," "Is it the Dunbars?," "Is it the Watsons?" Then the voices began to say, "It's Hutchinson. It's Bill," "Bill Hutchinson's got it."

"Go tell your father," Mrs. Dunbar said to her older son.

People began to look around to see the Hutchinsons. Bill Hutchinson was standing quiet, staring down at the paper in his hand. Suddenly, Tessie Hutchinson shouted to Mr. Summers, "You didn't give him time enough to take any paper he wanted. I saw you. It wasn't fair!"

"Be a good sport, Tessie," Mrs. Delacroix called, and Mrs. Graves said, "All of us took the same chance."

"Shut up, Tessie," Bill Hutchinson said.

"Well, everyone," Mr. Summers said, "that was done pretty fast, and now we've got to be hurrying a little more to get done in time."

He consulted his next list. "Bill," he said, "you draw for the Hutchinson family. You got any other households in the Hutchinsons?"

"There's Don and Eva," Mrs. Hutchinson yelled. "Make *them* take their chance!"

"Daughters draw with their husbands' families, Tessie," Mr. Summers said gently. "You know that as well as anyone else."

"It wasn't *fair*," Tessie said.

"I guess not, Joe," Bill Hutchinson said regretfully. "My daughter draws with her husband's family, that's only fair. And I've got no other family except the kids."

"Then, as far as drawing for families is concerned, it's you," Mr. Summers said in explanation, "and as far as drawing for households is concerned, that's you, too. Right?"

"Right," Bill Hutchinson said.

"How many kids, Bill?" Mr. Summers asked formally.

"Three," Bill Hutchinson said. "There's Bill, Jr., and Nancy, and little Dave. And Tessie and me."

"All right, then," Mr. Summers said. "Harry, you got their tickets back?"

Mr. Graves nodded and held up the slips of paper. "Put them in the box, then," Mr. Summers directed. "Take Bill's and put it in."

"I think we ought to start over," Mrs. Hutchinson said, as quietly as she could. "I tell you it wasn't *fair*. You didn't give him time enough to choose. *Every*body saw that."

Mr. Graves had selected the five slips and put them in the box, and he dropped all the papers but those onto the ground, where the breeze caught them and lifted them off.

"Listen, everybody," Mrs. Hutchinson was saying to the people around her.

"Ready, Bill?" Mr. Summers asked, and Bill Hutchinson, with one quick glance around at his wife and children, nodded.

"Remember," Mr. Summers said, "take the slips and keep them folded until each person has taken one. Harry, you help little Dave." Mr. Graves took the hand of the little boy, who came willingly with him up to the box. "Take a paper out of the box, Davy," Mr. Summers said. Davy put his hand into the box and laughed. "Take just *one* paper," Mr. Summers said. "Harry, you hold it for him." Mr. Graves took the child's hand and removed the folded paper from the tight fist and held it while little Dave stood next to him and looked up at him wonderingly.

"Nancy next," Mr. Summers said. Nancy was twelve, and her

school friends breathed heavily as she went forward, switching her skirt, and took a slip daintily from the box. "Bill, Jr.," Mr. Summers said, and Billy, his face red and his feet overlarge, nearly knocked the box over as he got a paper out. "Tessie," Mr. Summers said. She hesitated for a minute, looking around defiantly, and then set her lips and went up to the box. She snatched a paper out and held it behind her.

"Bill," Mr. Summers said, and Bill Hutchinson reached into the box and felt around, bringing his hand out at last with the slip of paper in it.

The crowd was quiet. A girl whispered, "I hope it's not Nancy," and the sound of the whisper reached the edges of the crowd.

"It's not the way it used to be," Old Man Warner said clearly. "People ain't the way they used to be."

"All right," Mr. Summers said. "Open the papers. Harry, you open little Dave's."

Mr. Graves opened the slip of paper and there was a general sigh through the crowd as he held it up and everyone could see that it was blank. Nancy and Bill, Jr., opened theirs at the same time, and both beamed and laughed, turning around to the crowd and holding their slips of paper above their heads.

"Tessie," Mr. Summers said. There was a pause, and then Mr. Summers looked at Bill Hutchinson, and Bill unfolded his paper and showed it. It was blank.

"It's Tessie," Mr. Summers said, and his voice was hushed. "Show us her paper, Bill."

Bill Hutchinson went over to his wife and forced the slip of paper out of her hand. It had a black spot on it, the black spot Mr. Summers had made the night before with the heavy pencil in the coal-company office. Bill Hutchinson held it up, and there was a stir in the crowd.

"All right, folks," Mr. Summers said. "Let's finish quickly."

Although the villagers had forgotten the ritual and lost the original black box, they still remembered to use stones. The pile of stones the boys had made earlier was ready; there were stones on the ground with the blowing scraps of paper that had come out of the box. Mrs. Delacroix selected a stone so large she had to pick it up with both hands and turned to Mrs. Dunbar. "Come on," she said. "Hurry up."

Mrs. Dunbar had small stones in both hands, and she said, gasping for breath, "I can't run at all. You'll have to go ahead and I'll catch up with you."

The children had stones already, and someone gave little **Davy** Hutchinson a few pebbles.

Tessie Hutchinson was in the center of a cleared space by now, and she held her hands out desperately as the villagers moved in on her. "It isn't fair," she said. A stone hit her on the side of the head.

Old Man Warner was saying, "Come on, come on, everyone." Steve Adams was in the front of the crowd of villagers, with Mrs. Graves beside him.

"It isn't fair, it isn't right," Mrs. Hutchinson screamed, and then they were upon her.

YONDER PEASANT, WHO IS HE?

❖

MARY MCCARTHY

WHENEVER WE CHILDREN came to stay at my grandmother's house, we were put to sleep in the sewing room, a bleak, shabby, utilitarian rectangle, more office than bedroom, more attic than office, that played to the hierarchy of chambers the role of a poor relation. It was a room seldom entered by the other members of the family, seldom swept by the maid, a room without pride; the old sewing machine, some cast-off chairs, a shadeless lamp, rolls of wrapping paper, piles of cardboard boxes that might someday come in handy, papers of pins, and remnants of material united with the iron folding cots put out for our use and the bare floor boards to give an impression of intense and ruthless temporality. Thin white spreads, of the kind used in hospitals and charity institutions, and naked blinds at the windows reminded us of our orphaned condition and of the ephemeral character of our visit; there was nothing here to encourage us to consider this our home.

Poor Roy's children, as commiseration damply styled the four of us, could not afford illusions, in the family opinion. Our father had put us beyond the pale by dying suddenly of influenza and taking our young mother with him, a defection that was remarked on with horror and grief commingled, as though our mother had been a pretty secretary with whom he had wantonly absconded into the irresponsible paradise of the hereafter. Our reputation was clouded by this misfortune. There was a prevailing sense, not only in the family but in storekeepers, servants, streetcar conductors, and other satellites of our circle, that my grandfather, a rich man, had behaved with extraordinary munificence in allotting a sum of money for our support and installing us with some disagreeable middle-aged relations in a dingy house two blocks distant from his own. What alternative he had was not mentioned; presumably he could have sent us to an orphan asylum and no one would have thought the worse of him. At any rate, it was felt, even by those

who sympathized with us, that we led a privileged existence, privileged because we had no rights, and the very fact that at the yearly
Halloween or Christmas party given at the home of an uncle we
appeared so dismal, ill clad, and unhealthy, in contrast to our rosy,
exquisite cousins, confirmed the judgment that had been made on
us—clearly, it was a generous impulse that kept us in the family
at all. Thus, the meaner our circumstances, the greater seemed our
grandfather's condescension, a view in which we ourselves shared,
looking softly and shyly on this old man—with his rheumatism, his
pink face and white hair, set off by the rosebuds in his Pierce-
Arrow and in his buttonhole—as the font of goodness and philan-
thropy, and the nickel he occasionally gave us to drop into the
collection plate on Sunday (two cents was our ordinary contribution) filled us not with envy but with simple admiration for his
potency; this indeed was princely, *this* was the way to give. It did
not occur to us to judge him for the disparity of our styles of living.
Whatever bitterness we felt was kept for our actual guardians, who,
we believed, must be embezzling the money set aside for us, since
the standard of comfort achieved in our grandparents' house—the
electric heaters, the gas logs, the lap robes, the shawls wrapped tenderly about the old knees, the white meat of chicken and red meat
of beef, the silver, the white tablecloths, the maids, and the solicit-
ous chauffeur—persuaded us that prunes and rice pudding, peeling paint and patched clothes were *hors concours* with these persons and therefore could not have been willed by them. Wealth,
in our minds, was equivalent to bounty, and poverty but a sign of
penuriousness of spirit.

Yet even if we had been convinced of the honesty of our guardians, we would still have clung to that beneficent image of our
grandfather that the family myth proposed to us. We were too
poor, spiritually speaking, to question his generosity, to ask why
he allowed us to live in oppressed chill and deprivation at a long
arm's length from himself and hooded his genial blue eye with a
bluff, millionairish gray eyebrow whenever the evidence of our
suffering presented itself at his knee. The official answer we knew:
our benefactors were too old to put up with four wild young children; our grandfather was preoccupied with business matters and
with his rheumatism, to which he devoted himself as though to a
pious duty, taking it with him on pilgrimages to Ste. Anne de
Beaupré and Miami, offering it with impartial reverence to the
miracle of the Northern Mother and the Southern sun. This rheu-

matism hallowed my grandfather with the mark of a special vocation; he lived with it in the manner of an artist or a grizzled
Galahad; it set him apart from all of us and even from my grandmother, who, lacking such an affliction, led a relatively unjustified
existence and showed, in relation to us children, a sharper and
more bellicose spirit. She felt, in spite of everything, that she was
open to criticism, and, transposing this feeling with a practiced old
hand, kept peering into our characters for symptoms of ingratitude.

We, as a matter of fact, were grateful to the point of servility.
We made no demands, we had no hopes. We were content if we
were permitted to enjoy the refracted rays of that solar prosperity
and come sometimes in the summer afternoons to sit on the shady
porch or idle through a winter morning on the wicker furniture
of the sun parlor, to stare at the player piano in the music room
and smell the odor of whiskey in the mahogany cabinet in the
library, or to climb about the dark living room examining the
glassed-in paintings in their huge gilt frames, the fruits of European travel: dusky Italian devotional groupings, heavy and lus-
trous as grapes, Neapolitan women carrying baskets to market,
views of Venetian canals, and Tuscan harvest scenes—secular
themes that, to the Irish-American mind, had become tinged with
Catholic feeling by a regional infusion from the Pope. We asked
no more from this house than the pride of being connected with
it, and this was fortunate for us, since my grandmother, a great
adherent of the give-them-an-inch-and-they'll-take-a-yard theory of
hospitality, never, so far as I can remember, offered any caller the
slightest refreshment, regarding her own conversation as suffi-
ciently wholesome and sustaining. An ugly, severe old woman with
a monstrous balcony of a bosom, she officiated over certain set topics in a colorless singsong, like a priest intoning a Mass, topics to
which repetition had lent a senseless solemnity: her audience with
the Holy Father; how my own father had broken with family tradition and voted the Democratic ticket; a visit to Lourdes; the
Sacred Stairs in Rome, bloodstained since the first Good Friday,
which she had climbed on her knees; my crooked little fingers and
how they meant I was a liar; a miracle-working bone; the importance of regular bowel movements; the wickedness of Protestants;
the conversion of my mother to Catholicism; and the assertion that
my Protestant grandmother must certainly dye her hair. The most
trivial reminiscences (my aunt's having hysterics in a haystack)
received from her delivery and from the piety of the context a

strongly monitory flavor; they inspired fear and guilt, and one searched uncomfortably for the moral in them, as in a dark and riddling fable.

Luckily, I am writing a memoir and not a work of fiction, and therefore I do not have to account for my grandmother's unpleasing character and look for the Oedipal fixation or the traumatic experience which would give her that clinical authenticity that is nowadays so desirable in portraiture. I do not know how my grandmother got the way she was; I assume, from family photographs and from the inflexibility of her habits, that she was always the same, and it seems as idle to inquire into her childhood as to ask what was ailing Iago or look for the thumb-sucking prohibition that was responsible for Lady Macbeth. My grandmother's sexual history, bristling with infant mortality in the usual style of her period, was robust and decisive: three tall, handsome sons grew up, and one attentive daughter. Her husband treated her kindly. She had money, many grandchildren, and religion to sustain her. White hair, glasses, soft skin, wrinkles, needlework—all the paraphernalia of motherliness were hers; yet it was a cold, grudging, disputatious old woman who sat all day in her sunroom making tapestries from a pattern, scanning religious periodicals, and setting her iron jaw against any infraction of her ways.

Combativeness was, I suppose, the dominant trait in my grandmother's nature. An aggressive churchgoer, she was quite without Christian feeling; the mercy of the Lord Jesus had never entered her heart. Her piety was an act of war against the Protestant ascendancy. The religious magazines on her table furnished her not with food for meditation but with fresh pretexts for anger; articles attacking birth control, divorce, mixed marriages, Darwin, and secular education were her favorite reading. The teachings of the Church did not interest her, except as they were a rebuke to others; "Honor thy father and thy mother," a commandment she was no longer called upon to practice, was the one most frequently on her lips. The extermination of Protestantism, rather than spiritual perfection, was the boon she prayed for. Her mind was preoccupied with conversion, the capture of a soul for God much diverted her fancy—it made one less Protestant in the world. Foreign missions, with their overtones of good will and social service, appealed to her less strongly; it was not a *harvest* of souls that my grandmother had in mind.

This pugnacity of my grandmother's did not confine itself to sectarian enthusiasm. There was the defense of her furniture and her house against the imagined encroachments of visitors. With her, this was not the gentle and tremulous protectiveness endemic in old ladies, who fear for the safety of their possessions with a truly touching anxiety, inferring the fragility of all things from the brittleness of their old bones and hearing the crash of mortality in the perilous tinkling of a teacup. My grandmother's sentiment was more autocratic: she hated having her chairs sat in or her lawns stepped on or the water turned on in her basins, for no reason at all except pure officiousness; she even grudged the mailman his daily promenade up her sidewalk. Her home was a center of power, and she would not allow it to be derogated by easy or democratic usage. Under her jealous eye, its social properties had atrophied, and it functioned in the family structure simply as a political headquarters. Family conferences were held there, consultations with the doctor and the clergy; refractory children were brought there for a lecture or an interval of thought-taking; wills were read and loans negotiated and emissaries from the Protestant faction on state occasions received. The family had no friends, and entertaining was held to be a foolish and unnecessary courtesy as between blood relations.

Yet on one terrible occasion my grandmother had kept open house. She had accommodated us all during those fatal weeks of the influenza epidemic, when no hospital beds were to be had and people went about with masks or stayed shut up in their houses, and the awful fear of contagion paralyzed all services and made each man an enemy to his neighbor. One by one, we had been carried off the train—four children and two adults, coming from distant Puget Sound to make a new home in Minneapolis. Waving goodbye in the Seattle depot, we had not known that we had brought the flu with us into our drawing rooms, along with the presents and the flowers, but, one after another, we had been struck down as the train proceeded eastward. We children did not understand whether the chattering of our teeth and Mama's lying torpid in the berth were not somehow a part of the trip (until then serious illness, in our minds, had been associated with innovations—it had always brought home a new baby), and we began to suspect that it was all an adventure when we saw our father draw a revolver on the conductor who, in a burst of sanitary precaution, was trying to put us off the train at a small wooden station in the middle of the North Dakota prairie. On the platform at Minneapolis, there were

stretchers, a wheelchair, redcaps, distraught officials, and, beyond
them, in the crowd, my grandfather's rosy face, cigar, and cane,
my grandmother's feathered hat, imparting an air of festivity to this
strange and confused picture, making us children certain that our
illness was the beginning of a delightful holiday.

We awoke to reality in the sewing room several weeks later, to
an atmosphere of castor oil, rectal thermometers, cross nurses, and
efficiency, and though we were shut out from the knowledge of
what had happened so close to us, just out of our hearing—a scandal
of the gravest character, a coming and going of priests and under-
takers and coffins (Mama and Daddy, they assured us, had gone to
get well in the hospital)—we became aware, even as we woke from
our fevers, that everything, including ourselves, was different. We
had shrunk, as it were, and faded, like the flannel pajamas we wore,
which during these few weeks had grown, doubtless from the disinfectant they were washed in, wretchedly thin and shabby. The
behavior of the people around us, abrupt, careless, and preoccupied, apprised us without any ceremony of our diminished importance. Our value had paled, and a new image of ourselves—the
image, if we had guessed it, of the orphan—was already forming in
our minds. We had not known we were spoiled, but now this word,
entering our vocabulary for the first time, served to define the
change for us and to herald the new order. Before we got sick, we
were spoiled; that was what was the matter now, and everything we
could not understand, everything unfamiliar and displeasing, took
on a certain plausibility when related to this fresh concept. We
had not known what it was to have trays dumped summarily on our
beds and no sugar and cream for our cereal, to take medicine in a
gulp because someone could not be bothered to wait for us, to have
our arms jerked into our sleeves and a comb ripped through our
hair, to be bathed impatiently, to be told to sit up or lie down quick
and no nonsense about it, to find our questions unanswered and
and our requests unheeded, to lie for hours alone and wait for the
doctor's visit, but this, so it seemed, was an oversight in our training, and my grandmother and her household applied themselves
with a will to remedying the deficiency.
    Their motives were, no doubt, good; it was time indeed that we
learned that the world was no longer our oyster. The happy life we
had had—the May baskets and the valentines, the picnics in the
yard, and the elaborate snowmen—was a poor preparation, in truth,

for the future that now opened up to us. Our new instructors could hardly be blamed for a certain impatience with our parents, who had been so lacking in foresight. It was to everyone's interest, decidedly, that we should forget the past—the quicker, the better—and a steady disparagement of our habits ("Tea and chocolate, can you imagine, and all those frosted cakes—no wonder poor Tess was always after the doctor"), praise that was rigorously comparative ("You have absolutely no idea of the improvement in these children") flattered the feelings of the speakers and prepared us to accept a loss that was, in any case, irreparable. Like all children, we wished to conform, and the notion that our former ways had been somehow ridiculous and unsuitable made the memory of them falter a little, like a child's recitation to strangers. We no longer demanded our due, and the wish to see our parents insensibly weakened. Soon we ceased to speak of it, and thus, without tears or tantrums, we came to know they were dead.

Why no one, least of all our grandmother, to whose repertory the subject seems so congenial, took the trouble to tell us, it is impossible now to know. It is easy to imagine her "breaking" the news to those of us who were old enough to listen in one of those official interviews in which her nature periodically tumefied, becoming heavy and turgid, like her portentous bosom, like peonies, her favorite flower, or like the dressmaker's dummy, that bombastic image of herself that lent a museumlike solemnity to the humble sewing room and made us tremble in our beds. The mind's ear frames her sentences, but in reality she did not speak, whether from a clumsy sense of delicacy or from a mistaken kindness, it is difficult to guess. Perhaps she feared our tears, which might rain on her like reproaches, since the family policy at the time was predicated on the axiom of our virtual insentience, an assumption that allowed them to proceed with us as if with pieces of furniture. Without explanations or coddling, as soon as they could safely get up, my three brothers were dispatched to the other house; they were much too young to "feel" it, I heard the grownups murmur, and would never know the difference "if Myers and Margaret were careful." In my case, however, a doubt must have been experienced. I was six—old enough to "remember" —and this entitled me, in the family's eyes, to greater consideration, as if this memory of mine were a lawyer who represented me in court. In deference, therefore, to my age and my supposed powers of criticism and comparison, I was kept on for a time, to roam palely about my grandmother's living rooms, a dangling, transitional creature, a frog becoming a tadpole, while my brothers, poor little polyps, were already well embedded in the structure of the new life. I did not wonder what had become of them. I believe I thought they were dead, but their fate did not greatly concern me; my heart had grown numb. I considered myself clever to have guessed the truth about my parents, like a child who proudly discovers that there is no Santa Claus, but I would not speak of that knowledge or even react to it privately, for I wished to have nothing to do with it; I would not coöperate in this loss. Those weeks in my grandmother's house come back to me very obscurely, surrounded by blackness, like a mourning card: the dark well of the staircase, where I seem to have been endlessly loitering, waiting to see Mama when she would come home from the hospital, and then simply loitering with no purpose whatever; the winter-dim first-grade classroom of the strange academy I was sent to; the drab treatment room of the doctor's office, where every Saturday I screamed and begged on a table while electric shocks were sent through me, for what purpose I cannot conjecture. But this preferential treatment could not be accorded me forever; it was time that I found my niche. "There is someone here to see you"—the maid met me one afternoon with this announcement and a smile of superior knowledge. My heart bounded; I felt almost sick (who else, after all, could it be?), and she had to push me forward. But the man and woman surveying me in the sun parlor with my grandmother were strangers, two unprepossessing middle-aged people—a great-aunt and her husband, so it seemed—to whom I was now commanded to give a hand and a smile, for, as my grandmother remarked, Myers and Margaret had come to take me home that very afternoon to live with them, and I must not make a bad impression.

Once the new household was running, our parents' death was officially conceded and sentiment given its due. Concrete references to the lost ones, to their beauty, gaiety, and good manners, were naturally not welcomed by our guardians, who possessed none of these qualities themselves, but the veneration of our parents' *memory* was considered an admirable exercise. Our evening prayers were lengthened to include one for our parents' souls, and we were thought to make a pretty picture, all four of us in our pajamas with feet in them, kneeling in a neat line, our hands clasped before us, reciting the prayer for the dead. "Eternal rest grant unto them, O Lord, and let the perpetual light shine upon

them," our thin little voices cried, but this remembrancing, so
pleasurable to our guardians, was only a chore to us. We connected
it with lights out, washing, all the bedtime coercions, and particularly with the adhesive tape that, to prevent mouth-breathing, was
clapped upon our lips the moment the prayer was finished, sealing
us up for the night, and that was removed, very painfully, with the
help of ether, in the morning. It embarrassed us to be reminded of
our parents by these persons who had superseded them and who
seemed to evoke their wraiths in an almost proprietary manner, as
though death, the great leveller, had brought them within their
province. In the same spirit, we were taken to the cemetery to view
our parents' graves; this, in fact, being free of charge, was a regular
Sunday pastime with us, which we grew to hate as we did all recrea-
tion enforced by our guardians—department-store demonstrations,
band concerts, parades, trips to the Old Soldiers' Home, to the
Botanical Gardens, to Minnehaha Park, where we watched other
children ride on the ponies, to the Zoo, to the water tower—diversions that cost nothing, involved long streetcar trips or endless
walking or waiting, and that had the peculiarly fatigued, dusty,
proletarianized character of American municipal entertainment.
The two mounds that now were our parents associated themselves
in our minds with Civil War cannon balls and monuments to the
doughboy dead; we contemplated them stolidly, waiting for a sensation, but these twin grass beds, with their junior-executive head-
stones, elicited nothing whatever; tired of this interminable staring, we would beg to be allowed to go play in some collateral
mausoleum, where the dead at least were buried in drawers and
offered some stimulus to fancy.

For my grandmother, the recollection of the dead became a mode
of civility that she thought proper to exercise toward us whenever,
for any reason, one of us came to stay at her house. The reason
was almost always the same. We (that is, my brother Kevin or I)
had run away from home. Independently of each other, this oldest
of my brothers and I had evolved an identical project. The purpose
dearest to our hearts was to get ourselves placed in an orphan asylum, for we interpreted the word "asylum" in the old Greek sense
and looked upon a certain red brick building, seen once from a
streetcar near the Mississippi River, as a sanctuary for the helpless
and a refuge from persecution. So, from time to time, when our
lives became too painful, one of us would set forth, determined to
find the red brick building and to press what we imagined was our

legal claim to its shelter and protection. But sometimes we lost our
way, and sometimes our courage, and after spending a day hanging
about the streets peering into strange yards, trying to assess the
kindheartedness of the owner (for we also thought of adoption),
or after a cold night spent hiding in a church confessional box or
behind some statuary in the Art Institute, we would be brought by
the police, by some well-meaning householder, or simply by fear
and hunger, to my grandmother's door. There we would be silently
received, and a family conclave would be summoned. We would
be put to sleep in the sewing room for a night, or sometimes more,
until our feelings had subsided and we could be sent back, grateful,
at any rate, for the promise that no reprisals would be taken and
that the life we had run away from would go on "as if nothing had
happened."

Since we were usually running away to escape some anticipated
punishment, these flights at least gained us something, but in spite
of the taunts of our guardians, who congratulated us bitterly on
our "cleverness," we ourselves could not feel that we came home
in triumph so long as we came home at all. Our failure to run away
successfully put us, so we thought, at the absolute mercy of our
guardians; our last weapon was gone, for it was plain to be seen
that they could always bring us back, however far we travelled, or
that we would bring ourselves back, too soft to stand cold and
hunger, too cowardly to steal or run away from a policeman; we
never understood why they did not take advantage of this situation
to thrash us, as they used to put it, within an inch of our lives.
What intervened to save us, we could not guess—a miracle, perhaps;
we were not acquainted with any *human* motive that would prompt
Omnipotence to desist. We did not suspect that these escapades
brought consternation to the family circle, which had acted, so it
conceived, only in our best interests, and now saw itself in danger
of unmerited obloquy. What would be the Protestant reaction if
something still more dreadful were to happen? Child suicides were
not unknown, and quiet, asthmatic little Kevin had been caught
with matches under the house. The family would not acknowledge
error, but it conceded a certain mismanagement on Myers' and
Margaret's part. Clearly, we might become altogether intractable
if our homecoming on these occasions were not mitigated with
leniency. Consequently, my grandmother kept us in a kind of neutral detention. She declined to be aware of our grievance and offered no words of comfort, but the comforts of her household acted

upon us soothingly, like an automatic mother's hand. We ate and
drank contentedly; with all her harsh views, my grandmother was
a practical woman and would not have thought it worth while to
unsettle her whole schedule, teach her cook to make a lumpy mush
and watery boiled potatoes, and market for turnips and parsnips
and all the other vegetables we hated, in order to approximate the
conditions she considered suitable for our characters. Humble pie
could be costly, especially when cooked to order.

Doubtless she did not guess how delightful these visits seemed to
us once the fear of punishment had abated. Her knowledge of our
own way of living was luxuriously remote. She did not visit our
ménage or inquire into its practices, and though hypersensitive to a
squint or a dental irregularity (for she was liberal indeed with
glasses and braces for the teeth, disfiguring appliances that remained
the sole token of our bourgeois origin and set us off from our paro-
chial-school mates like the caste marks of some primitive tribe),
she appeared not to notice the darns and patches of our clothing,
our raw hands and scarecrow arms, our silence and our elderly
faces. She imagined us as surrounded by certain playthings she
had once bestowed on us—a sandbox, a wooden swing, a wagon, and
a toy fire engine. In my grandmother's consciousness, these objects
remained always in pristine condition; years after the sand had
spilled out of it and the roof had rotted away, she continued to ask
tenderly after our lovely sand pile and to manifest displeasure if we
declined to join in its praises. Like many egoistic people (I have
noticed this trait in myself), she was capable of making a handsome
outlay, but the act affected her so powerfully that her generosity was
still lively in her memory when its practical effects had long vanished. In the case of a brown beaver hat, which she watched me wear
for four years, she was clearly blinded to its matted nap, its shapeless brim, and ragged ribbon by the vision of the price tag it had
worn when new. Yet, however her mind embroidered the bare tapestry of our lives, she could not fail to perceive that we felt, during
these short stays with her, *some* difference between the two establish-
ments, and to take our wonder and pleasure as a compliment to herself.

She smiled on us quite kindly when we exclaimed over the food
and the nice, warm bathrooms, with their rugs and electric heaters.
What funny little creatures, to be so impressed by things that were,
after all, only the ordinary amenities of life! Seeing us content in
her house, her emulative spirit warmed slowly to our admiration;

she compared herself to our guardians, and though for expedient reasons she could not afford to depreciate them ("You children have been very ungrateful for all Myers and Margaret have done for you"), a sense of her own finer magnanimity disposed her subtly in our favor. In the flush of these emotions, a tenderness sprang up between us. She seemed half reluctant to part with whichever of us she had in her custody, almost as if she were experiencing a genuine pang of conscience. "Try and be good," she would advise us when the moment for leave-taking came, "and don't provoke your aunt and uncle. We might have made different arrangements if there had been only one of you to consider." These manifestations of concern, these tacit admissions of our true situation, did not make us, as one might have thought, bitter against our grandparents, for whom ignorance of the facts might have served as a justification, but, on the contrary, filled us with love for them and even a kind of sympathy—our sufferings were less terrible if someone acknowledged their existence, if someone were suffering for us, for whom we, in our turn, could suffer, and thereby absolve of guilt.

During these respites, the recollection of our parents formed a bond between us and our grandmother that deepened our mutual regard. Unlike our guardians or the whispering ladies who sometimes came to call on us, inspired, it seemed, by a pornographic curiosity as to the exact details of our feelings ("Do you suppose they remember their parents?" "Do they ever say anything?"), our grandmother was quite uninterested in arousing an emotion of grief in us. "She doesn't feel it at all," I used to hear her confide to visitors, but contentedly, without censure, as if I had been a spayed cat that, in her superior foresight, she had had "attended to." For my grandmother, the death of my parents had become, in retrospect, an eventful occasion upon which she looked back with pleasure and a certain self-satisfaction. Whenever we stayed with her, we were allowed, as a special treat, to look into the rooms they had died in, for the fact that, as she phrased it, "they died in separate rooms" had for her a significance both romantic and somehow self-gratulatory, as though the separation in death of two who had loved each other in life were beautiful in itself and also reflected credit on the chatelaine of the house, who had been able to furnish two master bedrooms for the greater facility of decease. The housekeeping details of the tragedy, in fact, were to her of paramount interest. "I turned my house into a hospital," she used to say, particularly when visitors were present. "Nurses were as scarce as hen's teeth, and *high*—you can hardly imagine what those girls were charging an hour." The trays and the special cooking, the laundry and the disinfectants recalled themselves fondly to her thoughts, like items on the menu of some long-ago buffet supper, the memory of which recurred to her with a strong, possessive nostalgia.

My parents had, it seemed, by dying on her premises, become in a lively sense her property, and she dispensed them to us now, little by little, with a genuine sense of bounty, just as, later on, when I returned to her a grown-up young lady, she conceded me a diamond lavaliere of my mother's as if this trinket were an inheritance to which she had the prior claim. But her generosity with her memories appeared to us, as children, an act of the greatest indulgence. We begged her for more of these mortuary reminiscences as we might have begged for candy, and since ordinarily we not only had no candy but were permitted no friendships, no movies, and little reading beyond what our teachers prescribed for us, and were kept in quarantine, like carriers of social contagion, among the rhubarb plants of our neglected yard, these memories doled out by our grandmother became our secret treasures; we never spoke of them to each other but hoarded them, each against the rest, in the miserly fastnesses of our hearts. We returned, therefore, from our grandparents' house replenished in all our faculties; these crumbs from the rich man's table were a banquet indeed to us. We did not even mind going back to our guardians, for we now felt superior to them, and besides, as we well knew, we had no choice. It was only by accepting our situation as a just and unalterable arrangement that we could be allowed to transcend it and feel ourselves united to our grandparents in a love that was the more miraculous for breeding no practical results.

In this manner, our household was kept together, and my grandparents were spared the necessity of arriving at a fresh decision about it. Naturally, from time to time a new scandal would break out (for our guardians did not grow kinder in response to being run away from), yet we had come, at bottom, to despair of making any real change in our circumstances, and ran away hopelessly, merely to postpone punishment. And when, after five years, our Protestant grandfather, informed at last of the facts, intervened to save us, his indignation at the family surprised us nearly as much as his action. We thought it only natural that grandparents should know and do nothing, for did not God in the mansions of Heaven look down upon human suffering and allow it to take its course?

THE DECISION

❖

John O'Hara

THE HOME of Francis Townsend could have been taken for the birthplace of a nineteenth-century American poet, one of those little white houses by the side of the road that are regarded by the interested as national shrines. In front of the house there was a mounting block and a hitching post, iron, with the head of a horse holding an iron ring, instead of a bit, in its mouth. These, of course, had not been used in the last thirty years, but use did not govern the removal of many objects about the Townsend place. Things were added, after due consideration, but very little was ever taken away.

The Townsend place was on the outskirts of the seacoast village, out of the zone where the sidewalks were paved. In the fall of the year and in the spring, the sidewalk was liable to be rather muddy, and Francis Townsend several times had considered bricking the path—not that he minded the mud, but out of consideration for the female pedestrians. This project he had dismissed after studying the situation every afternoon for a week. He sat by the window in the front room and came to the conclusion that (a) there were not really many pedestrians during the muddy seasons, since there were few summer people around in spring or fall, and (b) the few natives who did use the sidewalk in front of his place were people who had sense enough to be properly shod in muddy weather. Another and very satisfying discovery that Francis Townsend made was that few people—men, women, or children—came near his house at all. For a long, long time he had entertained the belief that the street outside was a busy thoroughfare, more or less choked with foot and vehicular traffic. "I am really quite alone out here," he remarked to himself. This allowed for the fact that he had made his study of the muddy-sidewalk problem in the afternoon, when traffic was presumably lighter than in the morning, when, for instance, housewives would be doing their shopping. The housewives and others

could not have made *that* much difference; even if the morning
traffic were double that of the afternoon, it still was not considerable.
It was, of course, impossible for Francis Townsend to make his
study in the morning, except Sunday morning, for Francis Townsend's mornings were, in a manner of speaking, spoken for.

Every morning, Francis Townsend would rise at six-thirty, shave
and have his bath, and himself prepare first breakfast, which consisted of two cups of coffee and a doughnut. In the winter he
would have this meal in the kitchen, cheerful with its many windows
and warm because of the huge range. In the summer he would take
the coffee and doughnut to the front room, where it was dark and
cool all day. He would run water into the dirty cup and saucer and
put them in the sink for the further attention of Mrs. Dayton, his
housekeeper, who usually made her appearance at eight-thirty. By
the time she arrived, Francis Townsend would have changed from
his sneakers and khaki pants and cardigan to a more suitable costume—his black suit, high black kid shoes, starched collar, and black
four-in-hand tie. He would smoke a cigarette while he listened to
Mrs. Dayton stirring about in the kitchen, and pretty soon would
come the sound of the knocker and he would go to the front door.
That would be Jerry Bradford, the letter carrier.

"Good morning, Jerry."

"Good morning, Francis. Three letters an-n-nd the New York
paper."

"Three letters and the paper, thank you."

"Fresh this morning. Wind's from the east. Might have a little
rain later in the day."

"Oh, you think *so?*"

"Well, I might be wrong. See you tomorrow, in all likelihood."
Jerry would go away and Francis would stand at the open doorway
until Jerry had passed the Townsend property line. Then sometimes
Francis would look at the brass nameplate, with its smooth patina
and barely distinguishable name: "F. T. Townsend, M.D." The
plate was small, hardly any larger than the plate for a man's calling
card, not a proper physician's shingle at all, but there it was and
had been from the day of his return from medical school.

He would go back to his chair in the front room and wait for Mrs.
Dayton to announce breakfast, which she did in her own way. She
would say, "Morning," as greeting, and nod slowly, indicating that
breakfast was on the table. Francis then would take his paper and
letters to the dining room and partake of second breakfast—oatmeal,

ham and eggs, toast that was toasted over a flame, and a pot of coffee. Mrs. Dayton appeared only once during breakfast, when she brought in the eggs and took away the cereal dishes.

Francis Townsend's mail rarely was worth the pleasure of antici-pation. That did not keep him from anticipating Jerry Bradford's knock on the door or from continuing to hope for some surprise when he slit the envelopes with his butter knife. The reading of his mail did, in fact, give him pleasure, even though it might be no more than an alumni-association plea, a list of candidates for mem-bership in his New York club, or an advertisement from a drug or instrument company. Francis Townsend would read them all, all the way through, propping them against the tall silver saltcellar, and then he would take them with him to the front room, so that Mrs. Dayton could not see them, and there he would toss them in the fire or, in warm weather, put a match to them.

Then, every day but Sunday, Francis Townsend would take his walk. For the first thirty of the last forty years, Francis Townsend had had a companion on his walk. The companion always had been a collie; not always the same collie, but always a collie. But about ten years ago, when the last Dollie (all of Francis Townsend's dogs had been called Dollie) died, Francis Townsend read some-where or heard somewhere that it took too much out of you to have dogs; you no sooner grew to love them, and they you, than they died and you had to start all over again with a new one. This bit of dog lore came at a time when Francis Townsend had just lost a Dollie and was suffering a slight nosebleed. It was not a proper hemorrhage, but it was not exactly reassuring as to Francis Town-send's life expectancy, and he did not want to take on the respon-sibility of another Dollie if Dollie were to be left without anyone to take care of her, any more than he wanted to go through the pain of losing another dog. Therefore, for the last ten years or so, Francis Townsend had taken his walk alone.

Although he would not have known it, Francis Townsend's daily —except Sunday—walk was as much a part of the life of the village as it was of his own life. The older merchants and their older chil-dren and older employees took for granted that around a certain hour every morning Francis Townsend would be along. Harris, the clothing-store man; McFetridge, the hardware-store man; Blanchard, the jeweller; Bradford, brother of Jerry Bradford, who had the Ford-Lincoln-Mercury agency—among others—took for granted that Francis Townsend would be along around a certain

hour every morning. He had to pass their places on his way to the
bank, and when they saw him, they would say, "Hello, Francis,"
and would usually say something about the weather, and Francis
would nod and smile, and, without coming to a full stop, he would
indicate that the comment or the prediction was acceptable to
him.

His first full stop always was the bank. There he would go to Eben
Townsend's desk and Eben would push toward him a filled-in
check. "Morning, Francis," "Good morning, Eben," they would
say, and Francis would put "F. T. Townsend, M.D.," on the check,
and his cousin would give Francis three five-dollar bills. Francis
would thank him and resume his walk.

At his next stop, Francis would sometimes have to wait longer
than at the bank. Eventually, though, the barkeep would come to
wait on Francis. "Hyuh, Francis," he would say, and place a quart
of rye whiskey and a pitcher of water on the bar.

"Hyuh, Jimmy," Francis would say, and pour himself a rye-and-
water. "Well, well, well."

"Ixcuse me, Francis, I got a salesman here," Jimmy might say.
"Be with you in two shakes of a ram's tail."

"That's all right, Jimmy. Take your time. I'll be here for a
while."

This conversational opening, or something very like it, had been
fairly constant for forty years, inasmuch as the barkeep's name always had been Jimmy, since a father and a son had owned the
business, or at least tended bar, during the forty mature years of
Francis Townsend's life. Jimmy the father had discovered long,
long ago that, as he put it, Francis was good for the entire bloody
morning and didn't take offense if you left him a minute to transact
your business. Francis was indeed good for the entire morning. If
it happened to be one of Jimmy's busy days, he would remember to
put four toofers—two-for-a-quarter cigars—on the bar in front of
Francis before he left him, and Francis would smoke them slowly,
holding them in his tiny, even teeth, looking up at the ceiling with
one of them in his mouth, as though William Howard Taft or Harry
Truman had just asked his advice on whom to appoint to the
Court of St. James. Francis never bothered anybody, not even
during the years of two World Wars. He never tried to buy drinks
for the Coast Guard or the Army Air Forces, and he was not a man
whose appearance welcomed invitations on the part of strangers.
Among the villagers—the few who would drink in the morning out

of habit or temporary necessity—none would bother Francis or expect to be bothered by him. Francis had his place at the bar, at the far corner, and it was his so long as he was present. First-generation Jimmy and second-generation Jimmy had seen to that.

Each day, Monday through Saturday, January through December, Francis Townsend would sip his drinks and smoke his cigars until the noon Angelus from St. Joseph's Church. If he happened to be the only customer in the bar, Francis would say to Jimmy, "Ahem. The angel of the Lord declared, if I may say so."

"Correct, Francis."

Francis would take two of the three five-dollar bills from a lower vest pocket, and Jimmy would size up the rye bottle and pick up the money and return the estimated and invariably honest change. The tradition then was for Jimmy to say, "Now the house breaks down and turns Cath'lic."

"A rye, then," would be Francis Townsend's answer, in Francis Townsend's weak attempt at brogue. Whereupon Jimmy would hand Francis Townsend a wrapped bottle of rye and Francis would go home and eat the nice lunch Mrs. Dayton had prepared and take a good nap till time for supper, and after supper, when Mrs. Dayton had gone home, he would sit and read some of the fine books, like "Dombey and Son," the Waverley Novels, Bacon's "Essays"— the fine books in the front room—till it was time to bank the kitchen fire for the next morning and finish off the last of the wrapped bottle of rye.

That was about the way it had been with Francis Townsend from the time he finished medical school. That year, soon after his graduation, his uncle, who had raised him, said to him one day, "What are your plans, France?"

"First, I thought I'd interne at a hospital in Pittsburgh. A great many mines and factories out there and a man can learn a lot. Then, of course, I'll come back here and hang out my shingle. And I have an understanding with a girl in Philadelphia, Uncle. We're not engaged, but—we have an understanding."

His uncle got up and filled his pipe from the humidor on the mantelpiece in the front room. "No, boy," he said. "I'm sorry to say you can't have any of those things. You can never practice medicine, and you can't marry."

"Why, I can do both. I'm accepted at the hospital out in Pittsburgh, and the girl said she'd wait."

"Not when I tell you what I have to tell you. Do you know that both your father and your mother died in an institution? No, of course you don't know. There aren't many people in this village know. Most of the people my age think your father and mother died of consumption, but it wasn't consumption, France. It was mental."

"I see," said Francis. He stood up and filled his own pipe, with his class numerals in silver on the bowl. "Well, then, of course you're right." He took his time lighting up. "I guess there's no way out of that, is there, Uncle?"

"I don't know. I don't know enough about such things, putting to one side that I do know you shouldn't marry or you shouldn't doctor people."

"Oh, I agree with you, Uncle. I agree with you." Francis sat down again, trying to assume the manner of one Deke talking to another Deke in the fraternity house. "I wonder what I ought to do? I don't think I ought to just sit here and wait till I begin to get loony myself. There ought to be some kind of work where I couldn't do anybody any harm."

"You won't have to worry about money. I've fixed that at the bank. Give yourself plenty of time to pick and choose. You'll decide on something."

"Oh, very likely I will," Francis said. "I won't just stay on here in the village." But that, it turned out, was what he did decide to do.

HER BED IS INDIA

❖

CHRISTINE WESTON

MISS WARBURTON became aware of the silence that had fallen on the house and the landscape around her. The echo of her own voice talking to little Bindoo, the tinkling sound of the child's silver ornaments, the cries of jay birds in the oaks below the garden, bees in the wisteria flowers—all the intricate noises of a Himalayan afternoon seemed to fall away and the ensuing pause to enclose Miss Warburton in uncounted, profound, and breathless seconds. Only her eyes moved, glancing from the child at her feet to the play of sunlight on the oak leaves and wisteria, and beyond these to the motionless contour of the hills. Silence is a herald, but of what, Miss Warburton wondered, holding her breath—of what?

Bindoo, in a sari of red gauze, sat contemplating her silver-circled ankles and her brown, henna-tipped toes. The idea of dressing a child in gold-and-crimson gauze at this hour! In the evening, of course, when the costume would be appropriate enough, she ought to be in bed. But, no, Bindoo stayed up late, or fell asleep whenever and wherever the impulse took her. Miss Warburton, making her rounds of the gardens or the house, would come upon the scrap of gauze, and brown, quiescent flesh slumbering under the wisteria or curled among the embroidered flowers on the old *numdahs* in her sitting room.

"Bindoo! Asleep at this hour?" or "Bindoo, isn't it time you were in bed?" she would say to her little boarder. And once, to Bindoo's mother, a handful of years older than her daughter, Miss Warburton had protested with the severity of the childless, "Really, Mrs. Mehta! How can you expect the child to grow up normal when she leads such an irregular life?"

Mrs. Mehta had smiled and shrunk back, nibbling, like a half-tamed deer, the other's gingerly kindness. "Oh, I know, Miss Warburton! I spoil her," she had said.

"Well, you shouldn't. You mustn't."

"Oh, yes, I know. I shouldn't. I mustn't. But I am so wicked. You must remind me. You are so patient, dear Miss Warburton." And with a cry like something heard in the forest, "Bindoo! Why are you not asleep?," punishment fell like a falling leaf.

Hopeless, thought Miss Warburton now, remembering this conversation, and waited for silence to confirm the verdict, but silence resisted the word, the jays resisted it, the mynas and the cicadas; even the Bunnia's cough in his dark cave of a shop below the hill seemed in some subtle fashion to withhold assent. She remembered silence like this falling at unprepared moments into her life, spreading upon it like wax. Odd, when one knew that everywhere there were men, beasts, birds, the uproar of minds. Suppose silence should prove to be the final, ineffable substance—in what sudden eddy within it would she find herself at last?

Miss Warburton closed her eyes and heard, immediately, the tapping of an iron ferrule on stony ground. It came from the bottom of the hill, where the path from the house joined the main road, invisible from the veranda where she sat. When she opened her eyes, the sound ceased, and when she closed them, it recurred. Am I going deaf, she wondered, or blind, or mad? It happens too often. I am becoming all bits and pieces of consciousness, a tangle of uncertainties.

But Bindoo, too, seemed to be listening, and now turned large, inquiring eyes upon Miss Warburton. The child did not speak, but her glance brimmed with words: *Mrs. Cobb is coming up the hill to see you and to say goodbye.*

"Do be quiet, Bindoo!" exclaimed Miss Warburton in sudden frenzy. "Why can't you be quiet?"

The little girl gathered herself into a frightened knot, murmuring among her bangles, "But I never said anything!"

Again there was silence, without even the tapping sound. And suddenly the strange pause turned to murder in Miss Warburton's heart. Her thoughts crept forth, garbed in the fashion of her friend Louisa Cobb. "Oh, yes, my dear," Louisa Cobb had said to her once. "They're sweet when they're children, but they don't *stay* children. Your pretty little Bindoo will grow up and turn into one just like all the others, and she'll breed more of them. They breed and breed! There are too many of them already. They'll swamp us if we don't look out."

If we don't look out, thought Miss Warburton, and stared at Bindoo, crouched on the floor at her feet. Die, said Miss Warburton

silently, die! I want you to die now, at once. Die like a flower, if you
please, or like an insect under my heel! Die before you have eggs,
die before you change, before you bloat, before . . .

"I never said anything," Bindoo repeated.

A voice like Bindoo's floated down the long veranda. "Bindoo!
Bindoo, you are teasing Miss Warburton. Come inside at once."

"It's all right, Mrs. Mehta," said Miss Warburton. "She's not
doing any harm."

"I am sure she is teasing. Poor Miss Warburton! You have no
peace, and you are so good. Bindoo does not at all deserve it.
Bindoo!"

Silence ebbed under the bird cry of Bindoo's mother, and again
came the tapping of the ferrule on the path below. Bindoo rose,
folding her tiny sari over her shoulder, and confronted Miss Warburton with a look before which the woman saw herself slowly
foundering. "Bindoo, I'm sorry. I didn't mean to be cross," she
said.

"I never said anything. It was the walking stick of Mrs. Cobb."

"Bindoo!" A reed screen at the farther end of the veranda
stirred, silk and silver glittered in the gloom beyond it, and Miss
Warburton fancied she smelled perfume. What was it they were
so fond of using? Sandalwood?

"Bindoo!" Then, with a gust of laughter at her own laborious
English, Mrs. Mehta called out, "Shall I ask that Miss Warburton
beat you for your teasing and disobey of me?"

"You'd better run along, dear," said Miss Warburton. You are
so small, she thought. Why, I could kill you easily, easily! You pre-
carious thing, brittle, brittle . . . "Mrs. Cobb and I have a lot to say
to each other. She is going away, you know, to England. This is the
last time I shall see her."

Bindoo's implacable dark eyes studied Miss Warburton. "I never
said anything," she said again. "It was the walking stick of Mrs.
Cobb."

And indeed it *was* Louisa's stick, tapping as she came up the hill.
It had begun its tapping more than a mile away, Miss Warburton
knew, tapping across the veranda and the steps of Snow View (the
Cobb house, now ignominiously known as the Snow View Hotel, for
Louisa, too, had been forced to take paying guests), and across the
gravelled terrace that faced the snows, and down the green path
where all day long the cicadas droned and doves sobbed among the
leaves. Every house in Jherrapani had verandas and a gravelled

terrace, and all of them faced the hills, but not all had a view like
Louisa Cobb's, of the snows that rose in broken ramparts beyond
Nepal. "If I grudge *them* one thing more than anything else," Louisa
had once said of her Indian boarders, "I grudge them the *view*.
They have such a *different* idea of beauty." And she had meant, by
this, that *they* had none.

The tapping was quite close now, and more leisurely, for the
last fifty yards to the gate marked "Warburton Manor, Paying
Guests" were very steep and Louisa Cobb was no longer young.
Well, she won't have to do it again after today, thought Miss War-
burton, and felt time slide from under her, slide with a hollow,
inaudible roar, taking with it the trees, the birds, the hills; taking
Ram Prasad, and the Bunnia, and his cough; taking herself and
Bindoo and the waiting years.

The reed screen before Mrs. Mehta's door was pushed aside and
Bindoo's mother appeared, framed in the white arch that divided
the veranda in halves. Her sari of pale-green silk had slipped from
her head and revealed the painted hairline and small crimson dot
between her brows. Kohl under her eyes enhanced their depth and
brilliance, as it was meant to do, and her arms were encircled, like
Bindoo's, with thin bands of silver and gold.

Miss Warburton stared at the figure under the arch. I am still
here, she thought, because you are there and I can see you. The
earth reshaped itself under her feet with a sensation she sometimes
experienced on awakening from a dream, when everything seemed
pierced with a new, a totally unexpected and swiftly vanishing
beauty.

"Bindoo!" called Mrs. Mehta.

"Run along, my dear," Miss Warburton urged the child. "You
may come back later, when Mrs. Cobb has gone."

The two figures, one crimson, the other green, disappeared behind
the reed screen, and Miss Warburton rose in time to see a faded
khaki topee bobbing above the wisteria. "Louisa! Why did you
walk?" she called down to her friend.

Mrs. Cobb burst like some practical joke from the bushes and
strode across the gravel, crunching it with her hobnailed shoes.
Arrived on the veranda, she tilted her topee back from her streaming forehead and readjusted a wad of cotton wool in her left ear.
"Walk?" she said. "Why shouldn't I walk? I always walk. I'm not
dead yet, Felicity!" She stretched out her arms and the two women
embraced, awkward as puppets. "You know, Felicity, I had to keep

reminding myself that this was the last time I'd be climbing the hill to Warburton Manor. Just fancy, after more than thirty years!"

"Don't, Louisa."

"No use being sentimental, my dear."

"I'm not, but after all you're the one that's going," said Miss Warburton. "*I* have to stay."

"I know. It's awful. Let's sit down, shall we? It *is* a bit warm after all."

"You're going to miss the sun when you get back to that foggy little island, Louisa."

"I expect so. Shall we go to your room or sit here?"

"It's nice here. No, let's go in." Miss Warburton lowered her voice. "They listen to everything. I've never actually caught them, but I have that feeling—you know? As though every door and window had an ear attached to it."

"And a black ear, at that!"

Miss Warburton glanced at Mrs. Mehta's door. "Let's sit in my room, Louisa. It's cooler there."

Miss Warburton's room opened onto the extreme end of the veranda. It was a combined bed and sitting room, for expediency had compelled its owner to turn all the other rooms into apartments for her paying guests. Into her room she had crammed all her belongings, the freight of a lifetime, of several lifetimes, for many of these cherished objects had belonged to her parents. Here were herded chairs and tables, rugs, umbrella stands, boxes, baskets, mirrors, footstools, books unopened for the past ten years, and an array of tinted photographs—photographs of her parents, of her dead brother and sister, and of cousins and friends who might as well be dead for all she knew.

"I do believe you'll commit suttee here someday," remarked Mrs. Cobb jovially, throwing her topee and stick on the foot of the bed and sniffing the dry, mummified air.

"Louisa!"

"My dear, it was only a joke. Now, tell me honestly, how are they behaving?"

"The Mehtas? All right, really. I haven't met Mr. Mehta yet, but he expects to come up from Calcutta later on. He's an industrialist."

"They're all industrialists nowadays, when they're not being saviors of their country." Mrs. Cobb sat down and crossed her legs, baring the darns in her gray cotton stockings. "The people who bought my place are industrialists, too. They call themselves Persians, but I can't tell one from another. Your Mehtas are quite black, aren't they?"

Miss Warburton winced. "Not exactly. You've seen Bindoo. Her mother is nice."

Mrs. Cobb poked the wad of cotton into her ear, frowning. "I wish this damned thing would get well," she said. "I'll be thankful when I can go to a decent doctor. Sanyal is absolutely no use—just another glorified babu, like the rest of them. Whenever I go to him, he tries to engage me in politics. 'This is a great historical moment,' he had the cheek to tell me yesterday. 'The British are quitting India, and now I think that we can all be friends, Mrs. Cobb.' I tell you I felt pretty browned off when I heard that. 'It may be a great historical moment, Dr. Sanyal,' said I, 'but what does history care about you or me?' Great historical moment, indeed! How they love grand phrases. Felicity, have you thought what you'd do if you ever got really ill in this place, with only Sanyal to attend you?"

"I try not to think about such things, Louisa. I've enough on my mind as it is."

"You poor dear! But just wait until the hot weather and you have the house full of Mehtas! Do you realize that there are to be exactly *three* Europeans at Snow View this season? The place is filled with Indians. And I have another bit of news for you. Charles Goodwin has resigned from the Municipal Board. There isn't a single Englishman on it now."

"So I heard." Miss Warburton stroked a pleat in her skirt. "I can remember when there was not a single Indian on the Board, can't you?"

"I can remember when there wasn't a single Indian in Snow View or Warburton Manor! I can remember when you could walk the length of the Mall and the only Indians you met were rickshaw coolies and box wallahs, and they salaamed when they saw you. I can remember when people like the Mehtas and the Guptas and the Mohammed Alis stayed down on the plains where they belonged. I can remember . . ."

They remembered for some minutes, in detailed and specific anguish, twisting the knife of frustration in each other's wounds until tears rose to Miss Warburton's eyes and fell blazing on her hand.

"Louisa, it's over. It's all over. It's gone, Louisa—our time, our life!"

"Bosh, Felicity. Now, do cheer up. I have something really funny to tell you."

Miss Warburton sniffed back her tears and went to the door. The veranda was empty, the long, cane-backed chairs stood vacant in the sun, and from Mrs. Mehta's room there came faintly the music of a phonograph—a drum and *vina* and a man's voice singing in Bengali.

"Oh, let them listen if they want to," said Mrs. Cobb impatiently. "They might as well know what we think of them."

"That's all very well for you, Louisa, but you must remember that the Mehtas are my bread and butter."

"You mean your *chapatti* and *dal!*" Mrs. Cobb said with a laugh. Then, frowning, "Don't tell me you're to have no one but Indians this season?"

Miss Warburton returned slowly to her chair. "I'm not sure. I've had quite a few cancellations. The Youngs wrote that they're not coming. They've got passages to East Africa in May."

"I know. They're going on the same boat as the Carters. You remember the Carters? They always came to me at Snow View. I used to give them the northwest suite."

"And this morning I heard from Miss Monks," continued Miss Warburton. "Her Airedale died, so she has decided to stick it out in Delhi till she goes home."

"That Susan Monks was a regular old maid about her dog! So you're going to be left with the Mehtas, my dear, and the Mukerjees and the Bannerjees and the Ram Ram Sita Rams! Poor Felicity!"

Miss Warburton smoothed the pleats in her skirt. It gave her something to do. She could not bear to sit still, for then it seemed that she became a target for all the eyes, for all the ears, all the tongues in the house and beyond, in all the houses of Jherrapani, the houses that had lost their old remembered names—Verdun, Sunnybank, Inglenook—and had become Madan This and Bhawan That. Most of all, she dreaded the eyes in the photographs in her own room, the eyes of her mother and father, the eyes of her brother and sister. Felicity, Felicity, you mustn't stay on, they seemed to be saying. You're alone, unprotected, old. You mustn't stay, Felicity, when all your friends have gone. This is no longer our country. . . . Do you remember when we were young, Felicity? the eyes of her brother seemed to say. Do you remember Father planting the Gloire de Dijon rose along the wall, and the sound of Mother's keys when she gave out stores to old Hosain, the cook, and scolded him for using too much butter in the pilau? Do you remember chasing the butterflies up and down these slopes, and riding our ponies to the picnic ground on the Chakrata Road? Do you remember when this house was our home, Felicity? When no one ever came who was not a friend? Do you remember Arthur Groves, who almost married you but who was killed in the war—not the last war, Felicity, but the one before? The changes occurred rather unexpectedly, didn't they? They crept up on us, like the leopards who carried away our dogs. . . . First, the money began to go, Miss Warburton said to herself. Then Father died, then Mother, then Cecil, then Missy—Cecil of malaria on his tea plantation in Assam, Missy of enteric when she was just finishing school. . . . But you survived, the eyes of her sister seemed to say. You were always strong as a horse, and wise, too. You held on to Warburton Manor and turned it into a boarding house and so kept a roof over your head. Do you remember a remark Father once made in fun, when he said, "If one stays long enough in India, one is bound to end up by taking paying guests"? But you made a living for yourself, my dear, and you've got to go on making a living, if not out of the Youngs and the Miss Monkses and their Airedales, then out of the Mehtas and the Mukerjees. One has to go on until one quits. . . .

"My dear, you'll *die* when you hear this!" Mrs. Cobb said. The photographs stopped their whispering and turned attentive eyes upon her. "I happened to mention to one of the guests at Snow View—his name is Gupta, and he's one of the plausible kind—that I was shortly going Home to live with my daughter, who was in school there. He seemed very interested and asked whether he might see a portrait of Doreen. I was a bit mystified, naturally, but didn't see any harm in showing him her picture. He examined it very earnestly, and then—my dear, can you believe it?—he suggested that we—he and I—engineer a marriage between my daughter and his son!"

"Louisa, you're joking!"

"I'm not, Felicity, and neither was he, I assure you. He explained that his son was just twenty, very intelligent and handsome, and heir to the family fortunes, which I was made to understand are far from inconsiderable. It seems that Doreen's beauty had quite floored Mr. Gupta, and he could think of nothing more fitting and proper than that she should become his daughter-in-law!"

The two women gazed at each other eloquently.

"What did you say?" asked Miss Warburton.

"Well, I came to my senses at last and told him rather sharply that we didn't do things that way in England."

"And what did *he* say?"

"I didn't give him a chance to say anything. I just took Doreen's picture and went away."

Miss Warburton shook her head. "I never heard such cheek, really."

"Well, you will, my dear, from now on." Mrs. Cobb contemplated the largest darn in her stocking. "They never have understood us, and they never will. But now tell me more about yourself, Felicity. It's the last chance I'll have to talk to you. Are you sure you can get along all right?"

Miss Warburton had an unexpected glimpse of herself in the mirror. How strange she looked, quite unlike her private image of herself! Her own startled eyes questioned her and she addressed herself to them with an air of defiance. "I'm sure everything is going to be all right."

"Poor darling! You're always trying to make the best of things." Mrs. Cobb leaned toward her old friend. "Felicity, why don't you just make up your mind to come Home, like the rest of us?"

"Home?"

"India is no place for us now, Felicity."

"But I was born here. I've never seen England."

"What difference does that make? You're English. You'd be better off there, or in Australia, or Africa. We're all going. In a couple of years, there won't be any of us left."

Miss Warburton was silent, but someone spoke. Who was it? Father? Mother? Missy? Cecil? "Her bed is India!" Where did the phrase come from? Shakespeare, surely. From "Troilus and Cressida." She had read it in school and it was one of the few bits of Shakespeare she could remember, for it had always seemed addressed especially to her. "Her bed is India."

"It's no use, Louisa. I haven't got the money," she said aloud.

"You could sell Warburton, as I sold Snow View."

"It wouldn't bring enough. You talk about Home." She struggled with a queerness in her voice. "I've lived here for fifty years. I don't know anyone in England, or in Australia, or Africa, or anywhere. All I know is India."

"But you could start afresh, like the rest of us. Has it occurred to you that in a few years there may be no one left for you to *talk* to?"

Miss Warburton dragged her gaze from the mirror and looked, instead, toward the open door and the imperturbable hills beyond.

"Do you want to grow old and die out here, Felicity, and be buried in alien soil?" said Mrs. Cobb.

"Alien?" Miss Warburton repeated. To herself she said, If I had married—even though my husband had left me afterward—or if I had had a daughter, or if I'd been pushing and energetic and had made a success out of hotelkeeping, why, then—why, then I might at this moment be packing my trunks and heading toward England.

Mrs. Cobb sighed and grasped the arms of her chair with large, square, veined hands. "Well, Felicity, goodbye is always hateful. I'm going to cut it short."

"Of course, Louisa. I understand." Miss Warburton rose. "I suppose you've sent off your luggage, and everything is arranged?"

Mrs. Cobb stood with her hands thrust into her pockets. "Nothing left to do," she said, "except get myself down to the bus depot this evening."

Miss Warburton made a small, meaningless gesture. Strange feelings stirred within her—not love, not even friendship, for where in this relation had there been space or inspiration for either? For years they had practiced a concealed but pitiless rivalry, with survival their dull achievement, their goal.

I mustn't think such things—what has come over me, Miss Warburton wondered. They used to say that Father built Warburton Manor out of bribes he took from native contractors when he was in the Public Works Department. I know Louisa has hinted this to her guests, with more than a suggestion that a moral flaw might have been handed down to me. And I, on the other hand, have always been able to point out to the curious that Henry Cobb ran away because he couldn't stand Louisa's carping and penurious ways. And yet we've been friends for thirty years. . . . *Friends?*

Mrs. Cobb was putting on her topee and adjusting the leather strap under her chin. She picked up her stick, then seized her friend's hand and squeezed it excruciatingly. Emotion had dried up in her a long time ago, leaving a harsh residuum. She gave her stick a cheery flourish. "This is au revoir, Felicity. Remember, this is only au revoir!"

"Yes, Louisa, dear," Miss Warburton said. "Goodbye, and good luck." . . . Louisa, don't go! Don't leave me, don't, don't!

But Mrs. Cobb did go. Miss Warburton followed her out onto the porch, watched her disappear behind the wisteria, and listened to the brisk tapping of the stick until the sound was eaten up by distance.

She turned to rush back to her room, but recoiled from an emptiness where voices whispered in the corners and eyes as old as dust stared at her without meaning. Had there been a past, and she young and carefree in it? Had there been love, and Arthur Groves, seeing her in a new dress, exclaiming, "Felicity, you look glorious"? Was she living now, or was she a photograph on the mantel, a dry ghost? Unreality descended on her, sounds and voices she had heard all her life became unearthly, the light blinding, the mountains phantoms reaching into an illimitable sky. Oh, alien, alien! A cry burst from her, and far down on the main road Mrs. Cobb heard it and thought someone must have stoned a dog.

Mrs. Mehta pushed aside the screen before her door and came running out, followed by Bindoo. They saw the rigid figure on the veranda and rushed to it and clasped it in their arms. "Poor Miss Warburton!" Mrs. Mehta exclaimed. "What has happened? What has happened to you?"

"She is grieving for her friend," Bindoo said, and burst into tears.

They stroked Miss Warburton's hair, her face, their bangles rang against her ears, she was enveloped in sandalwood and jasmine and clouds of colored gauze.

"You are lonely," murmured Mrs. Mehta, and put her arm around Miss Warburton's shoulder. "You are lonely! I, too. All day, Bindoo and I have no one to talk to except each other. Come, Miss Warburton. I have sent for some tea. Sit with us, dear Miss Warburton."

She felt their tears on her hands; their voices fell about her like the voices of women singing their children to sleep. They encompassed her in their passionate, pitying affection, constructing a sorrow to match her sorrow, to transcend it and drown it in their own.

Half suffocated, Miss Warburton felt the germ of mirth begin to struggle within her. A smile trembled on her mouth, and, seeing it, they smiled, too, tugging at her hands like velvet puppies tugging at a shoe.

"Miss Warburton, dear Miss Warburton!"

She let them lead her, laughing, to their door.

INFLEXIBLE LOGIC

❖

RUSSELL MALONEY

WHEN THE SIX CHIMPANZEES came into his life, Mr. Bainbridge was thirty-eight years old. He was a bachelor and lived comfortably in a remote part of Connecticut, in a large old house with a carriage drive, a conservatory, a tennis court, and a well-selected library. His income was derived from impeccably situated real estate in New York City, and he spent it soberly, in a manner which could give offense to nobody. Once a year, late in April, his tennis court was resurfaced, and after that anybody in the neighborhood was welcome to use it; his monthly statement from Brentano's seldom ran below seventy-five dollars; every third year, in November, he turned in his old Cadillac coupé for a new one; he ordered his cigars, which were mild and rather moderately priced, in shipments of one thousand, from a tobacconist in Havana; because of the international situation he had cancelled arrangements to travel abroad, and after due thought had decided to spend his travelling allowance on wines, which seemed likely to get scarcer and more expensive if the war lasted. On the whole, Mr. Bainbridge's life was deliberately, and not too unsuccessfully, modelled after that of an English country gentleman of the late eighteenth century, a gentleman interested in the arts and in the expansion of science, and so sure of himself that he didn't care if some people thought him eccentric.

Mr. Bainbridge had many friends in New York, and he spent several days of the month in the city, staying at his club and looking around. Sometimes he called up a girl and took her out to a theatre and a night club. Sometimes he and a couple of classmates got a little tight and went to a prizefight. Mr. Bainbridge also looked in now and then at some of the conservative art galleries, and liked occasionally to go to a concert. And he liked cocktail parties, too, because of the fine footling conversation and the extraordinary number of pretty girls who had nothing else to do with the rest of their evening. It was at a New York cocktail party, however, that Mr. Bainbridge kept his preliminary appointment with doom. At one of the parties given by Hobie Packard, the stockbroker, he learned about the theory of the six chimpanzees.

It was almost six-forty. The people who had intended to have one drink and go had already gone, and the people who intended to stay were fortifying themselves with slightly dried canapés and talking animatedly. A group of stage and radio people had coagulated in one corner, near Packard's Capehart, and were wrangling about various methods of cheating the Collector of Internal Revenue. In another corner was a group of stockbrokers, talking about the greatest stockbroker of them all, Gauguin. Little Marcia Lupton was sitting with a young man, saying earnestly, "Do you really want to know what my greatest ambition is? I want to be myself," and Mr. Bainbridge smiled gently, thinking of the time Marcia had said that to him. Then he heard the voice of Bernard Weiss, the critic, saying, "Of course he wrote one good novel. It's not surprising. After all, we know that if six chimpanzees were set to work pounding six typewriters at random, they would, in a million years, write all the books in the British Museum."

Mr. Bainbridge drifted over to Weiss and was introduced to Weiss's companion, a Mr. Noble. "What's this about a million chimpanzees, Weiss?" he asked.

"Six chimpanzees," Mr. Weiss said. "It's an old cliché of the mathematicians. I thought everybody was told about it in school. Law of averages, you know, or maybe it's permutation and combination. The six chimps, just pounding away at the typewriter keys, would be bound to copy out all the books ever written by man. There are only so many possible combinations of letters and numerals, and they'd produce all of them—see? Of course they'd also turn out a mountain of gibberish, but they'd work the books in, too. All the books in the British Museum."

Mr. Bainbridge was delighted; this was the sort of talk he liked to hear when he came to New York. "Well, but look here," he said, just to keep up his part in the foolish conversation, "what if one of the chimpanzees finally did duplicate a book, right down to the last period, but left that off? Would that count?"

"I suppose not. Probably the chimpanzee would get around to doing the book again, and put the period in."

"What nonsense!" Mr. Noble cried.

"It may be nonsense, but Sir James Jeans believes it," Mr. Weiss said, huffily. "Jeans or Lancelot Hogben. I know I ran across it quite recently."

Mr. Bainbridge was impressed. He read quite a bit of popular science, and both Jeans and Hogben were in his library. "Is that so?" he murmured, no longer feeling frivolous. "Wonder if it has ever actually been tried? I mean, has anybody ever put six chimpanzees in a room with six typewriters and a lot of paper?"

Mr. Weiss glanced at Mr. Bainbridge's empty cocktail glass and said drily, "Probably not."

Nine weeks later, on a winter evening, Mr. Bainbridge was sitting in his study with his friend James Mallard, an assistant professor of mathematics at New Haven. He was plainly nervous as he poured himself a drink and said, "Mallard, I've asked you to come here— Brandy? Cigar?—for a particular reason. You remember that I wrote you some time ago, asking your opinion of . . . of a certain mathematical hypothesis or supposition."

"Yes," Professor Mallard said, briskly. "I remember perfectly. About the six chimpanzees and the British Museum. And I told you it was a perfectly sound popularization of a principle known to every schoolboy who had studied the science of probabilities."

"Precisely," Mr. Bainbridge said. "Well, Mallard, I made up my mind . . . It was not difficult for me, because I have, in spite of that fellow in the White House, been able to give something every year to the Museum of Natural History, and they were naturally glad to oblige me. . . . And after all, the only contribution a layman can make to the progress of science is to assist with the drudgery of experiment. . . . In short, I—"

"I suppose you're trying to tell me that you have procured six chimpanzees and set them to work at typewriters in order to see whether they will eventually write all the books in the British Museum. Is that it?"

"Yes, that's it," Mr. Bainbridge said. "What a mind you have, Mallard. Six fine young males, in perfect condition. I had a—I suppose you'd call it a dormitory—built out in back of the stable. The typewriters are in the conservatory. It's light and airy in there, and I moved most of the plants out. Mr. North, the man who owns the circus, very obligingly let me engage one of his best animal men. Really, it was no trouble at all."

Professor Mallard smiled indulgently. "After all, such a thing is not unheard of," he said. "I seem to remember that a man at some university put his graduate students to work flipping coins, to see if heads and tails came up an equal number of times. Of course they did."

Mr. Bainbridge looked at his friend very queerly. "Then you believe that any such principle of the science of probabilities will stand up under an actual test?"

"Certainly."

"You had better see for yourself." Mr. Bainbridge led Professor Mallard downstairs, along a corridor, through a disused music room, and into a large conservatory. The middle of the floor had been cleared of plants and was occupied by a row of six typewriter tables, each one supporting a hooded machine. At the left of each typewriter was a neat stack of yellow copy paper. Empty wastebaskets were under each table. The chairs were the unpadded, spring-backed kind favored by experienced stenographers. A large bunch of ripe bananas was hanging in one corner, and in another stood a Great Bear water-cooler and a rack of Lily cups. Six piles of typescript, each about a foot high, were ranged along the wall on an improvised shelf. Mr. Bainbridge picked up one of the piles, which he could just conveniently lift, and set it on a table before Professor Mallard. "The output to date of Chimpanzee A, known as Bill," he said, simply.

" ' "Oliver Twist," by Charles Dickens,' " Professor Mallard read out. He read the first and second pages of the manuscript, then feverishly leafed through to the end. "You mean to tell me," he said, "that this chimpanzee has written—"

"Word for word and comma for comma," said Mr. Bainbridge. "Young, my butler, and I took turns comparing it with the edition I own. Having finished 'Oliver Twist,' Bill is, as you see, starting the sociological works of Vilfredo Pareto, in Italian. At the rate he has been going, it should keep him busy for the rest of the month."

"And all the chimpanzees"—Professor Mallard was pale, and enunciated with difficulty—"they aren't all—"

"Oh, yes, all writing books which I have every reason to believe are in the British Museum. The prose of John Donne, some Anatole France, Conan Doyle, Galen, the collected plays of Somerset Maugham, Marcel Proust, the memoirs of the late Marie of Rumania, and a monograph by a Dr. Wiley on the marsh grasses of Maine and Massachusetts. I can sum it up for you, Mallard, by telling you that since I started this experiment, four weeks and some days ago, none of the chimpanzees has spoiled a single sheet of paper."

Professor Mallard straightened up, passed his handkerchief across his brow, and took a deep breath. "I apologize for my weakness," he said. "It was simply the sudden shock. No, looking at the thing scientifically—and I hope I am at least as capable of that as the next man —there is nothing marvellous about the situation. These chimpanzees, or a succession of similar teams of chimpanzees, would in a million years write all the books in the British Museum. I told you some time ago that I believed that statement. Why should my belief be altered by the fact that they produced some of the books at the very outset? After all, I should not be very much surprised if I tossed a coin a hundred times and it came up heads every time. I know that if I kept at it long enough, the ratio would reduce itself to an exact fifty per cent. Rest assured, these chimpanzees will begin to compose gibberish quite soon. It is bound to happen. Science tells us so. Meanwhile, I advise you to keep this experiment secret. Uninformed people might create a sensation if they knew."

"I will, indeed," Mr. Bainbridge said. "And I'm very grateful for your rational analysis. It reassures me. And now, before you go, you must hear the new Schnabel records that arrived today."

During the succeeding three months, Professor Mallard got into the habit of telephoning Mr. Bainbridge every Friday afternoon at five-thirty, immediately after leaving his seminar room. The Professor would say, "Well?," and Mr. Bainbridge would reply, "They're still at it, Mallard. Haven't spoiled a sheet of paper yet." If Mr. Bainbridge had to go out on Friday afternoon, he would leave a written message with his butler, who would read it to Professor Mallard: "Mr. Bainbridge says we now have Trevelyan's 'Life of Macaulay,' the Confessions of St. Augustine, 'Vanity Fair,' part of Irving's 'Life of George Washington,' the Book of the Dead, and some speeches delivered in Parliament in opposition to the Corn Laws, sir." Professor Mallard would reply, with a hint of a snarl in his voice, "Tell him to remember what I predicted," and hang up with a clash.

The eleventh Friday that Professor Mallard telephoned, Mr. Bainbridge said, "No change. I have had to store the bulk of the manuscript in the cellar. I would have burned it, except that it probably has some scientific value."

"How dare you talk of scientific value?" the voice from New Haven roared faintly in the receiver. "Scientific value! You—you—chimpanzee!" There were further inarticulate sputterings, and Mr.

Bainbridge hung up with a disturbed expression. "I am afraid Mallard is overtaxing himself," he murmured.

Next day, however, he was pleasantly surprised. He was leafing through a manuscript that had been completed the previous day by Chimpanzee D, Corky. It was the complete diary of Samuel Pepys, and Mr. Bainbridge was chuckling over the naughty passages, which were omitted in his own edition, when Professor Mallard was shown into the room. "I have come to apologize for my outrageous conduct on the telephone yesterday," the Professor said.

"Please don't think of it any more. I know you have many things on your mind," Mr. Bainbridge said. "Would you like a drink?"

"A large whiskey, straight, please," Professor Mallard said. "I got rather cold driving down. No change, I presume?"

"No, none. Chimpanzee F, Dinty, is just finishing John Florio's translation of Montaigne's essays, but there is no other news of interest."

Professor Mallard squared his shoulders and tossed off his drink in one astonishing gulp. "I should like to see them at work," he said. "Would I disturb them, do you think?"

"Not at all. As a matter of fact, I usually look in on them around this time of day. Dinty may have finished his Montaigne by now, and it is always interesting to see them start a new work. I would have thought that they would continue on the same sheet of paper, but they don't, you know. Always a fresh sheet, and the title in capitals."

Professor Mallard, without apology, poured another drink and slugged it down. "Lead on," he said.

It was dusk in the conservatory, and the chimpanzees were typing by the light of student lamps clamped to their desks. The keeper lounged in a corner, eating a banana and reading *Billboard*. "You might as well take an hour or so off," Mr. Bainbridge said. The man left.

Professor Mallard, who had not taken off his overcoat, stood with his hands in his pockets, looking at the busy chimpanzees. "I wonder if you know, Bainbridge, that the science of probabilities takes everything into account," he said, in a queer, tight voice. "It is certainly almost beyond the bounds of credibility that these chimpanzees should write books without a single error, but that abnormality may be corrected by—*these!*" He took his hands from his pockets, and each one held a .38 revolver. "Stand back out of harm's way!" he shouted.

"Mallard! Stop it!" The revolvers barked, first the right hand, then the left, then the right. Two chimpanzees fell, and a third reeled into a corner. Mr. Bainbridge seized his friend's arm and wrested one of the weapons from him.

"Now I am armed, too, Mallard, and I advise you to stop!" he cried. Professor Mallard's answer was to draw a bead on Chimpanzee E and shoot him dead. Mr. Bainbridge made a rush, and Professor Mallard fired at him. Mr. Bainbridge, in his quick death agony, tightened his finger on the trigger of his revolver. It went off, and Professor Mallard went down. On his hands and knees he fired at the two chimpanzees which were still unhurt, and then collapsed.

There was nobody to hear his last words. "The human equation . . . always the enemy of science . . ." he panted. "This time . . . vice versa . . . I, a mere mortal . . . savior of science . . . deserve a Nobel . . ."

When the old butler came running into the conservatory to investigate the noises, his eyes were met by a truly appalling sight. The student lamps were shattered, but a newly risen moon shone in through the conservatory windows on the corpses of the two gentlemen, each clutching a smoking revolver. Five of the chimpanzees were dead. The sixth was Chimpanzee F. His right arm disabled, obviously bleeding to death, he was slumped before his typewriter. Painfully, with his left hand, he took from the machine the completed last page of Florio's Montaigne. Groping for a fresh sheet, he inserted it, and typed with one finger, "UNCLE TOM'S CABIN, by Harriet Beecher Stowe. Chapte . . ." Then he, too, was dead.

THE FALLING LEAVES

❖

FRANCES GRAY PATTON

HARRIET BLAKE was starting out to shop for a suit. She knew exactly what she wanted, and she'd have thought the simplest thing would be to order it from the store in New York where she had bought most of her clothes before she married and came South. But Bob, her husband, was a native Southerner, and he had urged her to try to find a suit at home. He said he didn't want the people down here in South Carolina to think Harriet was snooty, and, besides, the local merchants depended on local trade. He had suggested that she might at least try Lucy Bowen's little shop. Lucy was a sweet girl, he said, and she was showing a lot of spunk; Sam Bowen hadn't a cent beyond his G.I. readjustment allowance, and God alone knew when he would get tired of sitting around in beer joints talking about Guadalcanal. Bob had heard that Lucy wasn't making a great success in business, and he thought her friends all ought to stand behind her. Since Harriet was a sweet girl herself and a very reasonable one, she had promised to go to Lucy's the first thing, even though she was acquainted with the fussy, dirndlish costumes that establishment generally carried. But as she opened her front door and stepped out into the autumn morning—the slow, absent-minded, Southern autumn morning—she wasn't sure whether she could keep her promise or not. She felt suddenly so homesick and discouraged that she thought she was going to collapse.

The street was lined with willow oaks, and although the weather was calm and tepid, the slender, pointed leaves had been dropping for a week now. They came down in quiet, intermittent showers, like rain descending through sunlight from a wandering handkerchief cloud, and they lay where they fell—on sidewalks and lawns and porches and the tops of parked cars. Everybody said there was no use doing anything about them until the last one had fallen. Harriet had admired the Carolina spring, she had sweated cheerfully through the summer, but the placid dejection of this Southern November was something she could not endure. She leaned against the doorjamb, dismayed by her own weakness, and then, like fever mounting to combat infection in the blood, a sense of irritation rallied her. She looked scornfully at the pale-brown, drifted scene and thought grimly that it was like the people who lived here— vague, feckless, and complacent. "Just like the whole damn South," she said to herself.

As she stood there on the doorstep, she could hear Pearlie, her colored maid, making her usual racket in the kitchen—thumping china down on the drainboard, tossing handfuls of silver into the dishpan. Harriet half turned to go back and caution Pearlie not to chip the cups, but she decided against it. You could tell a person something just so many times and then you might as well save your breath. She had gone over the dishwashing routine with Pearlie not five minutes before, as she did every morning. The glasses first, in very hot water, then the silver, piece by piece, then the plates— "scrape them before you wash them." But nothing in life was routine to Pearlie. Her duties seemed to come to her fresh each day, and she received them always with fresh surprise. "You wants me to bresh up the sittin' room *this* mornin'?" she would ask, beaming.

Bob and his friends had told Harriet how lucky she was to have Pearlie, who had been raised in the country and couldn't read or write or, as Pearlie herself put it, "tell time good." She was an old-fashioned Southern darky, they said, without any fancy modern ideas. Every dumb thing she did seemed to please the young women Harriet knew. When Pearlie invited them to "rest" their hats, their faces assumed expressions of pious satisfaction, and when they asked over the telephone whether Mrs. Blake was in and Pearlie replied, "No, Ma'am, she sho' ain't," they reported it later to Harriet with delight. Sometimes they called up when they knew Harriet was out, just to hear Pearlie tell them she was. Harriet alone was not delighted. Pearlie's remarks made good copy for letters to her family in the North, but Harriet considered Pearlie's twenty dollars a week high wages for comic relief.

However, it would have been impossible not to grow fond of Pearlie, she was so sleek and buxom and had a kind of clean, country grace; and besides, Harriet was sorry for all colored people. She thought it was terrible for Pearlie to be so illiterate, and she had borrowed a primer called "Day by Day with Baby Ray" from the little boy across the street and had started teaching her how to read. She had been amazed by the aptness of her pupil and still more amazed when, after four lessons, Pearlie had said she would have to stop, because learning made her nervous-like. Pearlie said she reckoned she would just keep on going to the Holiness meetings and praying to the Lord to cast out her ignorance; she'd heard tell of a woman who had seen the Spirit and had immediately been able to read as good as the preacher. Harriet opened her mouth to argue, but just in time she became aware of a polite, stubborn glaze settling over Pearlie's eyes that warned Harriet that she was being edged into an apostate position.

After that, she had determined to ignore Pearlie's difficulties and to concentrate on those of the ménage. Harriet knew how to train servants, for she had often observed her mother breaking in a new maid; the important thing was not to let yourself be ruffled by failures. If you continued to be explicit and optimistic, your instructions were supposed to take root. Patiently, then, Harriet had explained to Pearlie that vegetables could, and should, be cooked without grease, though she knew that the moment her back was turned, bits of fat back would be slipped into the boiling spinach. ("Just a morsel, to make it fittin' t'eat.") Over and over, she had drilled Pearlie in the correct, impersonal ritual of the telephone, knowing perfectly well that the next time it rang, it would be answered with the same old Southern Charm.

Harriet heard the phone ringing now, and hurried away from the sound, down the steps to the street. In the big yard next door, Mrs. Youngblood was messing around among her flowers. She was a gray, ungainly woman with liver-spotted, trembly hands and a small head that reared itself up from her spreading body in a way that made her look like a turtle; one almost expected to find some date, like 1807, carved with a pocketknife on her back. At first, Harriet had thought her elderly neighbor's name was a wonderful joke, but when she had giggled about it to Bob, he had said, "Why, honey, Youngblood is one of the best names in the state," and looked perturbed, as if his wife's amusement had betrayed a want of social instinct. This morning, Mrs. Youngblood wore for gardening a sagging silk dress; a Queen Mary hat protected her from the autumnal sunlight, and some leaves had settled among its molting feathers. She was pruning bushes in a desultory way. She would pounce upon a twig, snip it off, and stand back, with the air of an art critic, to consider the effect. (As if anything could bring order to that crowded tangle of marigolds and asters and limp roses, Harriet thought.) An aged colored man in a blue serge suit was digging a hole in the ground. Mrs. Youngblood shook her shears at him and he pretended to cringe, and they both laughed. Their laughter, rakish and melancholy, rustled in the listless air.

Harriet imagined what it would be like at home now in White Plains, with the fresh wind, and the sky so blue it hurt your eyes, and everything shipshape for winter. Storm windows would be up, flower beds would be covered, and the odor of burning leaves would linger everywhere. She thought of her mother, dressed in sensible tweeds, moving briskly about her garden, and of how she would keep her porch steps clean of leaves if she had to sweep them twenty times a day. (Only, the leaves would have been gone for weeks now— which was as it should be, Harriet thought with passionate conviction. Leaves had no business falling in November.) And maybe after lunch, she and her mother would drive out into the country to buy apples—big, fine-flavored apples, not the little, worm-eaten, lopsided things you found in these Southern grocery stores—and to look at the Westchester hills with all the color gone and the familiar folds of the earth and the beautiful, calm structure of bare trees visible once again. She smiled bitterly to think how astounded the people down here would be if they guessed that she, a Northerner, was homesick.

The girls had touched on that at the Bridge Club once. Wasn't it strange, they had said—obviously thinking it the most natural thing in the world—wasn't it strange how all the homesick songs were written about the South—"Swanee River," and "Chattanooga Choo-Choo," and "Carolina in the Morning"? Harriet had mentioned "White Christmas," but they had said no, that didn't count; it wasn't supposed to be about any particular section. It just represented the way men in the tropics felt about America. Why, they could remember two or three Christmases when it had snowed down here. Or near Christmas, anyway. And Lucy Bowen, who was proud of her vocabulary, had said the South was a universal symbol of home, the same way Paris was a symbol of gaiety. "Whenever people think of the South," Lucy had said solemnly, "they feel lethargic." Bob had been obliged to laugh when Harriet related the malapropism to him at supper, but nevertheless he had defended Lucy. "It does sound something like nostalgic," he had said. "Our gals don't draw fine distinctions between words. Remember the rhyme 'Alas for the South! Her books have grown fewer, She was never much given to literature'?" Bob had a degree from Harvard Law School and he was a young man of scholarly tastes, but he had quoted the ridiculous couplet affectionately, with something like pride in his voice. Harriet had wanted to smack him.

Bob and Harriet's brother had been officers on the same ship during the war. The two men had come to White Plains for a brief shore leave, and Bob and Harriet had fallen in love almost immediately. When, a year after the war, they'd been married and had come South to live, in the town where Bob was born, Harriet had resolved to make herself agreeable. Since this was to be her home, it was only plain sense to like it. She would be tactful. She would refer to the Civil War (if she had to refer to it at all) as the War Between the States; she wouldn't discuss the race problem; and, above all, she would suppress that inclination toward condescension that came naturally to a New Yorker, even a suburban New Yorker, when in the provinces. She was prepared, of course, to find Southern people quaint, and she was determined to find them charming.

That hadn't been hard to do, because they were all lovely to her. They had given parties for her and asked her to join their clubs, and never a day passed that some of the girls didn't stop by to see if she'd like to go to the movies, or maybe "just ride around and get a dope with lemon." In fact, they were so constant in their attentions that Harriet occasionally wondered if they'd pledged themselves not to leave her alone to brood, as if she were a nervous invalid who had to be protected and encouraged. They told her anybody would think she had been raised right there in the South, and Mrs. Youngblood, who had a nasal sort of "wa-wa" voice, complimented her upon her speech.

"I was afraid Bob's wife would talk like a Yankee and say 'bananer-rr,' " the old lady had confessed, "but I've always noticed that when people speak correctly, you can't tell where they're from. I met a Boston lady on the train once, and she had such a cultivated accent that I took her for a South Carolinian."

Another time, when Harriet was out with a crowd of the girls, she had expressed surprise at finding the banks closed on Confederate Memorial Day, and they had hastened to assure her that it was simply an old custom, and that The War had been over for a long time, and anyway they didn't hold it against her, personally. Lucy Bowen had gone so far as to say that, one way you looked at it, it was a good thing the North had won. Then somebody had begun to talk rapidly about the length of women's skirts, and they had all taken a deep breath.

Harriet, because she was good-natured and sure of herself, had

thought these incidents merely funny, but now, as she walked
through the drizzle of leaves, she recalled them and they made her
mad. They swarmed over her mind as the leaves swarmed before her
eyes. She began to walk faster, and continued with long, impatient
Yankee strides until she came to Lucy's shop.

Lucy's shop was cute. It had a bottle-green door and a metal scrollwork sign that read, "YE SMALL SHOPPE." Lucy, who was considered
artistic, always took great pains with the decoration of her show window. In the summer, she had painted huge butterflies on the glass
and had banked field flowers (which promptly wilted from the heat)
in the corners. Today, she had set a jar of pine boughs in the window
and had sprinkled leaves around it. The effect was definitely sloppy,
Harriet thought severely, but she forgot about it when she saw the
suit in the window. It was just the sort of suit she wanted, nicely
tailored in monotone tweed and unadorned by any fancy touches of
braid or silver buttons. She opened the door.

"Cuckoo!" chimed the cute little bell, and Lucy, who was reclining
on a chaise longue reading "The Manatee," looked up.

"Hey, Hatsie!" she said. Her face glowed with pleasure.

She was really an extraordinarily pretty girl, thought Harriet. If
only she would slick her long hair back and rip the frill off her dress!
And why did she use that silly greeting, "Hey"?

"Hi, Lucy," Harriet said firmly.

"I'm so glad you came in," Lucy said. "This isn't a very interesting
book and I'm just finishing it from a sense of duty, because the author
has such a wonderful command over the English language. I've
learned heaps of new adjectives."

Harriet said it was difficult to find a good novel.

"Pull yourself up a chair, Hatsie," said Lucy. "I'm too comfortable
to move. Want a dope? I've got some back there in the icebox."

"Thanks," said Harriet, "but I haven't time for a coke." She put
a slight emphasis on the last word.

Lucy laughed. "I tried to call them cokes once," she said. "I made
an honest effort, because I knew the manufacturer wanted me to,
but I couldn't do it. They didn't taste natural by that name. Dopes
are what I was weaned on."

"That's a good-looking suit in the window," said Harriet.

"Isn't it!" Lucy said. "It's your size, too. I thought when I unpacked it that it would look like a love on you."

"It's the kind of thing I'm used to," said Harriet.

"Mm-hm," agreed Lucy. "Smart. We Southern girls can't really wear tailored things."

Harriet said she thought they all dressed very well.

"But we're not *smart*," said Lucy. "Dainty, yes. Glamorous, sometimes. But smart, never." Her rosy, cat-shaped face looked smug. "I think we're too feminine," she added with a sigh.

"I'd like to try the suit on," said Harriet.

"It's your type, all right," mused Lucy. "Of course, you might want to dress it up, sort of. With a flower or a rhinestone pin."

God forbid, thought Harriet. "Well," she said aloud, "suppose I try it now."

Lucy hesitated. She looked politely distressed. "But, Hatsie, darling," she drawled, "that suit is in the window."

Harriet looked blank.

"You see," said Lucy, "I took so much trouble with that window this morning! I came down at the crack of dawn and I had to pick up all those leaves and then I stuck my fingers on those old pine needles." She looked tenderly at her thin, soft hands. "I can't mess it up again this soon."

"You mean," Harriet said softly, "that the suit isn't for sale?"

"Of course it's for sale," Lucy said amiably. "You think I'm in business for my health? I'll give you a ring next time I change the window. Look, I've got a sweet little yellow jersey with sequins."

"I don't want a yellow jersey with sequins," said Harriet.

"I'm awful sorry," said Lucy, "but you understand how it is. If I sold things out of the window, I'd never keep anything in it."

Harriet stood looking down at her. Lucy's face was composed and smiling, but a kind of glaze seemed to have spread over it, like frosting on a bun. Why, she reminds me of Pearlie, Harriet thought with a start. That's the way Pearlie looks when she's shutting her mind against me. "You know, Lucy," she said thoughtfully, "*you* are what's wrong with the South."

"Me?" said Lucy.

"You," Harriet said, "and everybody else down here. You're all alike, white and colored. You're all self-satisfied. You make your faults into virtues. You boast of being lazy, you boast of being ignorant, you—"

"Oh, come, now, Hatsie!" Lucy cried. Her eyes were shining and her round bosom beneath the dowdy frill on her dress rose with her excited breathing. "We haven't had your opportunities."

"It has nothing to do with opportunity," said Harriet. Her voice sounded cold and precise. "You won't move. You won't think. You can't even work up the energy to rake up the leaves."

"We cultivate leisure," said Lucy. "We believe life should be an art."

"Oh, sure, the famous Southern Art of Living!" said Harriet acidly. She turned to the door.

"Don't go!" wailed Lucy. She sat up. "This is fascinating!"

"I'm going, never fear," said Harriet. "All you want to do, ever, is talk. It's a regional disease."

Harriet felt fine as she walked home. Far down in her consciousness, there was a qualm, but it wasn't strong enough to disturb her. She thought of a lot more good things she could have said. As she let herself in at her front door, she heard Pearlie at the telephone. "No, Ma'am," Pearlie was saying in a creamy, fatuous voice. "She sho' ain't!"

Harriet waited until she heard the click of the phone being hung up. Then she went menacingly down the hall to Pearlie. "Listen," she said, biting out her words, "how many times have I told you how to answer the phone?"

Pearlie dimpled and allowed one hand to hang limply from the wrist.

"Don't stand there like a kangaroo," snapped Harriet. "Answer me, how many times?"

"I don't rightly remember," said Pearlie. "I don't keep count good."

"But I did tell you, didn't I?" Harriet insisted. "Why don't you do it my way?"

"I forgets," said Pearlie.

"No, Pearlie," said Harriet, "you don't forget. You don't *want* to remember."

"I ain't had your opportunities, Miz Blake," said Pearlie. "I didn't get no schoolin'. In Gatlin County, where I was raised, white folks is mean to colored folks."

"Abraham Lincoln didn't have many opportunities, either," said Harriet in a flash of inspiration. "And he's a man your race might well remember. He walked five miles barefoot to school every day." (Was it Lincoln who had done all that walking, or had he only studied by firelight? It didn't matter.) "I daresay if you'd been willing to do that, you might have learned something, too." She paused for breath. I'm not being fair, she thought—and then she recognized the expression on Pearlie's face. She had seen it on Lucy's. It was an expression of pure enjoyment. "And if they were mean to you in Gatlin County," Harriet continued venomously, "perhaps they had some provocation. Did you ever consider that?"

Pearlie's face seemed to stiffen, but she said nothing. She only gazed at Harriet with a sorrowful, innocent dignity. Harriet was suddenly silent and very unhappy. I *couldn't* have said a thing like that, she thought. What can I do to make it so I never said it? She imagined how her mother would have looked if she had been there, her face shocked, as it always was by violence or injustice. "My dear child!" her mother would have said incredulously.

Harriet and Pearlie stood staring at each other for a minute with the telephone between them on the scalloped, marble-topped table that had been a wedding present from Mrs. Youngblood. The telephone rang. They both drew back. They both leaned forward, hands stretched out hesitantly. It rang again. Pearlie picked it up.

"Seven-seven-two-one-J," she said in a dull, uninflected voice, keeping her eyes on Harriet all the time. "This is Mrs. Blake's maid speaking. Yes, Ma'am, Miss Lucy. I'll ask her to come."

She offered the instrument to Harriet.

"Thank you," said Harriet.

"You're welcome," said Pearlie.

Harriet took the phone and began wearily to beg Lucy's forgiveness, but Lucy wouldn't listen to apologies. She said Harriet had been absolutely right and that her vocabulary was marvellous. She wanted to bring the suit right out for Harriet to try on.

"But I can't let you do that," Harriet said miserably.

It wouldn't be any trouble, Lucy said. She wasn't doing a thing but reading that silly book and she had her little old Ford car parked in front of the shop. As soon as she could put something else in the window, she'd be along. "I'm going to sweep those nasty old leaves out, like you told me," she said, laughing.

"I didn't mean it," Harriet protested. "Not any of it."

"Oh, don't say that!" begged Lucy. "You were so frank and honest and stimulating. I want to discuss your ideas some more. I'm crazy about ideas!"

When Lucy had at last hung up, Harriet went to her bedroom. She dropped her hat on a chair and lay down on her bed without turning back the coverlet or even kicking off her shoes. Everything seemed unnaturally still, the way things seem to a child when his ride on the merry-go-round is just over. She lay there, inert and hopeless, watching the downward drift of leaves outside her window. After a while, and from what seemed far away, she heard the telephone ringing. I'll have to get up and answer it, she thought. For she knew Pearlie would be gone. She would have put on her good street shoes—the high-heeled pumps that cramped her feet—and left forever, without a word. But as the bell sounded again, Harriet heard someone downstairs shuffling slowly, softly, from the kitchen to the hall.

"Aw ri-ght," she heard Pearlie say in a voice like butter. "Yas, Ma'am. She sho' is home. But she's layin' down. She don't feel s' good. This here's homesick weather."

Harriet got up. Laughing to herself in a baffled way, she ran a comb through her hair and put on a little fresh lipstick. Then she noticed that some leaves had blown against the screen and had stuck there. She went briskly to the window and thumped them off, like a teacher rapping the knuckles of a wool-gathering child.

MY DA

❖

FRANK O'CONNOR

STEVIE LEARY is a boy I remember with extraordinary vividness, so I suppose that even from the first there must have been something outstanding in him. The Learys lived next door to us, and Stevie's mother was a great friend of my mother's. Mrs. Leary was a big, buxom woman with a rich, husky voice, and she made her living as a charwoman. In her younger days she had left Ireland and spent a couple of years in America.

"It was love sent me there, Ma'am," she would say to my mother, in a rich, wheezy, humorous voice. "Love was always the ruination of me. If I might have stuck on there, I could have chummed up with some old, sickly geezer of seventy that would think the world of me and leave me his money when he'd die. I was a fine-looking girl in those days. Frankie Leary used to say I was like the picture of the Colleen Bawn."

I often studied the picture of the Colleen Bawn in her kitchen to see could I detect some resemblance between herself and Mrs. Leary, but I failed. The Colleen Bawn was a glorious-looking creature, plump and modest and all aglow, as if she had a lamp inside her.

"Why then indeed," my mother would say loyally, "you're a fine woman to this day, Mrs. Leary."

"Ah, I'm not, Ma'am, I'm not," Mrs. Leary would say with resignation. "I had great feeling, and nothing ages a woman like the feelings. But I was mad in love with Frankie Leary, and lovers can never agree. I had great pride. If he so much as lay a hand on me, I'd fight in a bag tied up."

"Ah, 'tis a wonder you'd put up with it from him," my mother would say. She had strong ideas about the dignity of womanhood.

"Ah, wisha, you would, Ma'am, you would," Mrs. Leary would say with a sigh for my mother's lack of experience. "A man would never love you properly till he'd give you a clout. I could die for that man when he beat me."

Then, with a tear in her eye, she'd take out the snuffbox she kept in her enormous bosom and tell again the sad story of herself and Frankie. Frankie, it seemed, had even greater pride than herself. He had always been too big for his boots. America, he had said, was the only country for a man of spirit. Now, Mrs. Leary had a weakness for the little drop, and several times Frankie had warned her that if she didn't give it up he'd leave her and go to America. One night when she was on a bat, she came home and found that he had been as good as his word. But she had a spirit as great as his own. Leaving Stevie, still a baby, with her mother-in-law, she had followed her husband to America. True, she had never succeeded in finding him. America was a big place, and Frankie Leary wasn't the sort to leave traces. All the same, she'd had the experience, and she never let you forget it. Even Mrs. Delury, whom she mostly worked for, didn't succeed in keeping her in her place. Mrs. Delury owned a shop and had a son in Maynooth going for the priesthood, but Mrs. Leary dismissed both of these sources of pride with a sarcastic "We have a priest in the family and a pump in the yard." As Mrs. Delury said, you couldn't expect better of anyone who had spent years in that horrible country.

Stevie was twelve, the same age I was, with a big, round, almost idiotic face and a rosy complexion, a slovenly, hasty stride that was almost a scamper, and a shrill, scolding, old woman's voice. He was always in a hurry, and when someone called to him and he stopped, it was just as if some invisible hand had tightened the reins on him; he slithered and skidded to a halt with his beaming face over his shoulder. He was never a kid like the rest of us. He took life too seriously. His mother had told him the story of an American millionaire who had made his way up from rags to riches, and Stevie hoped to do the same thing. He collected swill for the Mahoneys, carried messages for the Delurys, and for a penny would do anything for you, from minding the baby to buying the dinner. He had a frightfully crabbed air, and would talk in that high-pitched voice of his about what was the cheapest sort of meat to make soup of. "You should try Reilly's, Ma'am," he would tell my mother. "Reilly's keeps grand stewing beef." My mother thought he wasn't quite right in the head. "Ah, he's a good poor slob," she would say doubtfully when politeness required her to praise him to his mother. Mrs. Leary would sigh and take a pinch of snuff and say, "Ah, he'll never be the man his father was, Ma'am." I more or less knew Stevie's father as the man Stevie would never be.

Occasionally, Mrs. Leary's feelings would get too much for her. We'd be playing some boys' game and Stevie would be sitting on the wall outside their little cottage, looking at us with a smile that was half superciliousness and half envy. A kid coming up the road would say, "Stevie, I seen your old one on a bat again." "Oh, japers!" Stevie would groan. "That woman will be the death of me. Where is she now, Jerry?" "I seen her down by the Cross." "Clancy's or Mooney's?" Stevie would ask, and away he would go. Sometimes I would go along after him and watch him darting into each pub as he passed, the very image of an up-to-date businessman, and shouting to the barmaid, "You didn't see my ma today, Miss O.? . . . You didn't? I'll try Riordan's." Eventually he would discover her in some snug with a couple of cronies. Mrs. Leary was the warm sort of drunkard who attracts hangers-on.

"Ah, come on home now, Ma," Stevie would cry coaxingly.

"Jasus help us!" the cronies would say in pretended admiration. "Isn't he a lovely little boy, God bless him!"

"Ah, he'll never be the man his father was, Ma'am," Mrs. Leary would say, beaming at him regretfully. "There was a man for you, Ma'am! A fine, educated, independent man!"

It might be nightfall before Stevie got her home—a mountain of a woman, who would have stunned him if she'd collapsed on him. He would make her a cup of tea, undress her, and put her to bed. If my mother were by, she would lend a hand and, furious at any woman's making such an exhibition of herself and before a child, she would rate Mrs. Leary soundly.

Sometimes, late at night, we'd hear Stevie crying, "Ah, stay here, Ma, and I'll get it for you!" and his mother roaring, "Gimme the money!" Stevie would groan and steal away to whatever hiding hole he was then keeping his savings in. "That's all I have now," he would say hopefully. "Will tuppence do you?" With the cunning of all drunkards, Mrs. Leary seemed to know to a farthing how much he had. Night after night she shuffled down to Miss O.'s with nothing showing through the hood of the shawl but one sinister, bloodshot eye, and tuppence by tuppence Stevie's capital vanished, till he started life again with all the bounce gone out of him, as poor as any of us who had never heard the life story of an American millionaire.

Then one night Frankie Leary came back from the States. My mother was at Mrs. Leary's when Frankie strolled up the road one summer evening, without even a bag, and stood in the doorway with an impassive air. "Hallo," he said lightly. Mrs. Leary rose from her stool by the fire, gaping at him; then she tottered, and finally she ran and enveloped him in her arms. "Oh, Frankie!" she sobbed. "After all the years!" This apparently wasn't at all the sort of conduct that the independent Frankie approved of. "Here, here," he said roughly. "There's time enough for that later. Now I want something to eat." He pushed her away and looked at Stevie, who was staring at him, enraptured by the touching scene. "Is this the boy?" he asked, and then all at once he smiled pleasantly and held out his hand. "How're ye, Son?" he asked heartily. "Oh, grand, Father," said Stevie, who was equal to any occasion. "Did you have a nice journey?"

Frankie didn't even reply to that. Maybe he hadn't had a nice journey. Unlike the American Stevie had been told of, Frankie came home as poor as he left, and next day he had to go to work on the railway. It seemed America wasn't all it was cracked up to be.

For a week or two, Stevie was in a state of real hysteria over his father's arrival. For the first time he had, like the rest of us, a da of his own, and as our das generally flaked hell out of us, Stevie felt it was up to him to go in fear and trembling of what "my da" might do to him. Of course, it was all showing off, for his da did nothing whatever to him. On the contrary, Frankie was painfully and anxiously correct with him, as though he were trying to make up for any slight he might have inflicted on the boy by his eleven-year absence. He found that Stevie was interested in America and talked to him patiently for hours on end about it while Stevie, in an appalling imitation of some old man he had seen in a pub, sat back in his chair with his hands in his trousers pockets.

Frankie spoke to him one day about keeping his hands in his pockets, and even this mild criticism, delivered in a low, reasonable tone, was enough to make Stevie jump. He tried in other ways to please Frankie. He tried to moderate his intense, fancy-haunted shamble so that he wouldn't have to pull himself up on the rein, to break his voice of its squeak, and to imitate his father.

Stevie trying to be tough like Frankie was one of the funniest of his phases, for undoubtedly Frankie was the man Stevie would never be. He was a lean, leathery sort of man, with a long face, cold eyes, and a fish's mouth. No doubt he had his good points. He made Mrs. Leary give up the daily work and wear a hat and coat instead of the shawl. He made Stevie give up the swill and the messages and learn to read and write, an accomplishment that had apparently been omitted from the education of whatever American millionaire he had been modelling himself on. Frankie had few friends on the road; he was a quiet, self-centered, scornful man. But with his coming the years seemed to drop from Mrs. Leary. I understood at last what she meant when she said that Frankie in their courting days had compared her to the Colleen Bawn. She seemed to become all schoolgirlish and lit up inside, as though, but for modesty, she'd love to take you aside and tell you what Frankie did to her.

You wouldn't believe the change that came over their little cottage. Of course, a couple of times there were scenes when Mrs. Leary came home with the signs of drink on her. They weren't scenes as we understood them. Frankie didn't make smithereens of the house, as my da did when domesticity became too much for him. But for all that, the scenes frightened Stevie. Each time there was one, he burst into tears and begged his father and mother to agree.

And then one night a terrible thing happened. Mrs. Leary came in a bit more expansive than usual. She wasn't drunk, she told my mother afterward—just friendly. Frankie had been reading the evening paper and he looked up.

"Where were you?" he asked.

"Ah, I ran into Lizzie Desmond at the Cross and we started to talk," Mrs. Leary said good-humoredly.

"Then ye started to drink, you mean."

"We had two small ones," said Mrs. Leary with a shrug of her shoulders. "What harm was there in that? Have you the kettle boiling, Stevie?"

"You know better than anyone what harm is in it," Frankie said. "I hope you're not forgetting what it cost you last time?"

"And if it did, wasn't I well able to get along without you? 'Tisn't many would be able for what I did, with my child to bring up, and no one to advise me or help me."

"Whisht now, Ma! Whisht!" Stevie cried in an agony of fear. "You know my da is only speaking for your good."

"Speaking for my good?" she shouted. With great dignity she drew herself up and addressed Frankie. "How dare you? Is that my thanks after all I did for you—crossing the briny ocean after you, you insignificant little gnat!"

"What's that you said?" Frankie asked quietly. Without waiting for an answer, he threw down his paper and went up to her with his fists clenched.

"Gnat!" she repeated scornfully, looking him up and down. "Insignificant little gnat, that wouldn't make a bolt for a back door! How dare you?"

Even before Stevie could guess what he was up to, Frankie had drawn back his fist and given it to her fair in the mouth. He didn't pull his punch, either. Stevie nearly got sick at the sound. Mrs. Leary gave a shriek that was heard in our house, and then went in a heap on the floor. Stevie shrieked, too, and rushed to her assistance. He lifted her head on his knee. Her mouth was bleeding and her eyes were closed.

"Oh, Ma, look at me, look at me!" he bawled distractedly. " 'Tis all right. I'm Stevie, your own little boy."

She opened one red-rimmed eye and looked at him for a moment. Then she closed it carefully, with a moan of pain, as though the sight of him distressed her too much. Stevie looked up at his father, who seemed to be hardly aware of his presence.

"Will I get the priest for her, Da?" asked Stevie. "She's dying."

"Get to bed out of this," Frankie replied in a tone that put the fear of God into Stevie. He crept into bed, leaving his mother still lying on the floor. A little later he heard his father close the bedroom door on himself. His mother still lay there. He was quite certain she was dead until an hour later he heard her pick herself up and make herself a cup of tea. But never before had Stevie allowed his mother to remain like that without assistance. It couldn't have happened except for Frankie. He was afraid of Frankie.

Stevie woke next morning with all the troubles of the world on his young shoulders. Things were desperate in the home. All the light he had on the subject was contained in a sermon he had once heard in which the preacher said children were a great bond between the parents. Stevie felt it was up to him to be a bond. Purposefully cheerful, he gave Frankie his breakfast and took his mother a cup of tea. After that she insisted on getting up and going out. He begged her to stay in bed, and offered to bring the porter to her, but she wouldn't. He knew she was going out to get drunk, and at the same time that she was far more frightened than he was. That was what she meant when she said that lovers could never agree. It was her terrible pride that wouldn't allow her to give in to his father.

In the afternoon, Stevie found her in a pub in town and brought her home. He did everything he could to make her presentable; he made her tea, washed her face, combed her hair, and finally even tried to induce her to hide in our house. At six, Frankie came in, and Stevie bustled around him eagerly and clumsily, laying the table for his supper. In his capacity of bond, he had reverted to type. "You'd like a couple of buttered eggs?" he squeaked. "You would, to be sure. Dwyer's keeps grand eggs."

After supper, Frankie grimly got up and took his cap. "You won't be late, Da?" Stevie asked appealingly. Frankie didn't answer. Stevie went to the door and watched him all the way down the road. Then he returned and sat opposite his mother by the fire.

"Ah," he said, "I don't suppose he'll come back at all."

"Let him go," his mother muttered scornfully. "We did without him before and we can do without him again. Insignificant little gnat!"

"Ah, I dunno," Stevie said. "'Twas nice having him, all the same."

The dusk fell and they sat there, not speaking.

"You ought to see is he at your Uncle John's," Mrs. Leary said suddenly, and Stevie knew the panic was rising again through the drink.

"I'll try," he said, "but I wouldn't have much hope."

His doubts were fully justified. Whatever way Frankie had of losing himself, he had disappeared again.

Little by little the old air of fecklessness and neglect descended on the Learys' cottage. Mrs. Leary, no longer looking like the Colleen Bawn, went back to the shawl and the daily work for the Delurys, and Stevie to the swill and the messages. Everything was exactly as though Frankie had never returned. Yet in one way it wasn't. After a year or two, Stevie started to go to night school. That caused us all considerable amusement. It was the daftest of Stevie's metamorphoses.

But then a really incredible thing happened—Stevie began to study for the priesthood. It seemed that the teacher in the Technical School had spoken to the parish priest, and the parish priest was arranging for Mrs. Leary to have regular work in the presbytery, so that Stevie could attend the seminary. This wasn't a matter for laughter. In a way, it was a public scandal. Of course, it wouldn't be like Mrs. Delury's son who had been to Maynooth; it would only be for the Foreign Mission, but you'd think that even the Foreign Mission would draw the line somewhere. Even my mother, who had great pity for Stevie, was troubled. I was causing her concern enough as it was, for I had lost my faith for the first time. She was an exceedingly pious woman, and I don't think she ever put it in so many words, but I fancy she felt that if the Catholic Church was having to fall back on people like Stevie, there might be some grounds for a young fellow losing his faith. I remember the incredulity with which I spoke to Stevie myself when for the first time I met him on the road in his black suit and black soft hat. I could see he knew about my losing my faith. He might even have tried to help me with it, but, of course, being Stevie, he was in a hurry to get back to his Latin roots.

When he said his first Mass in the parish church, we all turned up, a few—like my mother—from piety, the rest from curiosity. Mrs. Delury, her two sons, and her daughter were there. Mrs. Delury, of course, was boiling at the thought of her charwoman's son being a priest like her own Jeremiah, and she blamed it all on America. Stevie preached on the Good Shepherd, and whether it was just the excitement or the faces of the Delurys all looking up at him from one pew —a sight to daunt the boldest heart—he got mixed up between the ninety-nine and the one. What else could you expect of Stevie? My mother and I went around to the sacristy afterward to get his blessing. (By this time I had got back my faith again and I didn't lose it a second time till two years afterward.) As we knelt, I could hardly keep my face straight, for at every moment I expected Stevie to say, "Wouldn't a few pounds of stewing beef be better, Ma'am?"

When we came out of the church, I saw that the Opposition, headed by Mrs. Delury, was holding an overflow meeting on the road down from the chapel. "Poor Father Stephen got a bit mixed in his sums," said Mrs. Delury in her pleasant way as we passed.

"Ah, the dear knows, wouldn't anyone get excited on an occasion like that?" said my mother, flushed and angry at this insult to the cloth.

"Ah, well," said Mrs. Delury comfortably, "I don't suppose in America they'll know the difference."

"Why?" I asked in surprise. "Is he going to America?"

"So it seems," she replied with a giggle. "I wonder why."

But I knew why, and for days it haunted my mind. I called the night before Stevie went away, and had a cup of tea with Mrs. Leary and him. I cursed myself for not noticing before what a nice, intelligent, sensitive fellow Stevie was. He was nervous and excited by the prospect before him. "Ah, he'll love it," his mother said in her deep, snug, husky voice. " 'Twill be like a new life to him. The dear knows, I might go out to him myself, one of these days."

"How bad 'twould be now to have you keeping house for him!" I said.

"Japers," said Father Stephen shyly, "that'd be grand."

Of course, all three of us knew it was impossible. There are certain luxuries that a young priest must deny himself and one is a mother whose feelings become too much for her. The whole time Stevie was at home, Mrs. Leary was irreproachable, a perfect lady. But next evening, after she had seen him off, a sympathetic policeman brought her home, and my mother put her to bed. "Ah, indeed," my mother kept saying reproachfully, "what would Father Stephen say if he saw you now?" During the night we heard her shouting, but there was no Stevie to say, "Stay here and I'll get it for you, Ma." Stevie at last had become the man his father was, and left us all far away behind him.

THE FOUR FREEDOMS

❖

EDWARD NEWHOUSE

T HE SLENDER TOWER of the villa was shaped like a Turkish
minaret. From the comfortable chairs on the top balcony, Captain Wyatt could, in fact, see a number of Cairo's real mosques in
the distance. But more frequently he settled behind the window that
opened on the Pyramids. Now, at night, the Great Pyramid was barely
visible.

Four staff cars pulled up in the gravel path below and the solemn
M.P. lieutenant checked the identity of all the passengers. He had
been well briefed about the importance of the general he was guard-
ing. Although the party contained several lesser generals whose faces
must have been familiar to him, he took care to examine all the cre-
dentials. There were women in the group.

Wyatt walked down the spiral staircase, his old Natal boots incongruous against the lavish carpet. Just before he got to the second
floor, he met the servant who had instructions to call him when the
party arrived. The man stood aside and bowed slightly as Wyatt
passed. He had apparently been trained to stand with downcast eyes
in the presence of his superiors; all the servants in the villa, and there
were at least a dozen, did that. They looked you in the eye only when
receiving an order. They were all Egyptian and moved about quietly
in their loose liveries and remembered, after being told once, the
amount of sugar you took in your coffee. Their master, also Egyptian, was away in England, but the arrangements he had made for
the entertainment of Wyatt's general could hardly have been more
elaborate.

"Keep your eyes peeled and let me know if you come across Alad-
din's lamp in one of these rooms," the General had said at the end
of the first day.

Wyatt opened an immense inlaid door and went into the General's bedroom. The reading light was on, but the General had gone
to sleep. He had removed only his tie and was lying behind the mosquito net in his suntans. The net had been installed for the General.

It opened and closed by zipper, and Wyatt found this refinement more staggering, somehow, than the heavy gold plate used at dinner or the half acre of greenhouses or the wine cellar whose treasures the General declared to be beyond comparison.

Sleeping, the General looked fifty-eight, though he was ten years younger. Twenty of those years had been spent in the Army Air Forces. His large, dark face was deeply lined, sagging and loose in sleep; his breathing, obstructed and irregular. He groaned as Wyatt said "Sir . . . General" a number of times. Then he sat up.

"Nine o'clock, sir," Wyatt said. "You asked to be waked when those people got here."

"What people?"

"That U.S.O. troupe you missed in Algiers."

"I remember," the General said. "Can you fill me in on them?"

"They made a big hit in town last night. I wasn't there, but General Crane said they were very good. He's downstairs with them now, I think. They've got a comedian and a juggler and a couple of young movie actresses."

"Are they going to put on a show downstairs?"

"If you like. I understood you just wanted to say hello."

"Well, now that you got me wide awake, I'll go down. The juggler might be worth seeing."

Back in the States, one of Wyatt's chores had been to set up showings of current films at the General's home. The picture companies, who often availed themselves of Air Forces equipment, had always been glad to oblige. The General liked horse operas, murder mysteries, and Popeye cartoons, in that order, and usually overruled his wife, who preferred long pictures in which people grew old.

The General opened the mosquito net and put his feet on the floor. "Dan," he said, "did you read that magazine article about me?"

"Yes, sir."

"What'd you think of it?"

"I thought it was a magazine article about a general."

The General picked a uniform out of the closet. "What do you suppose he meant by calling me a 'bloodless expert in the bloody mathematics of air warfare'?"

"He was turning a phrase," Wyatt said.

"He said I was cold and ruthless. He said I had the instincts of a puma closing for the kill. Compared me to Jack Dempsey at Toledo."

"I doubt if he was more than two years old when that fight was held."

"You know him, do you?"

"I've seen him around," Wyatt said.

"Is he still accredited to us?"

"No, sir."

"I don't want him back here," the General said. "I don't give a hoot in hell where the article was cleared, but I want it understood that the son of a bitch stays out of my command. Pass that on." He adjusted his necktie in front of the full-length mirror.

"And this picture he had of me glaring into the camera," he went on. "If I got killed and buried tomorrow and they dug me up next year, I'd look better than that. All you needed to round out the case history of a homicidal maniac was that god-damned photograph. Where in Christ's name did he get this 'cold, ruthless' baloney from, do you suppose?"

"I think he was referring to Shamrock."

Shamrock had been the code word for an operation early in the war. The General had sent some P-40 squadrons to an advance field within easy fighter range of the Italian Air Force, the mission being to damage as much enemy shipping and as many enemy aircraft as possible. The squadrons were eager, target-hungry, and unaware that they were being expended. They sank a few freighters and a troopship and brought down three times their own number of airplanes before the General considered withdrawing them. He decided against it. His trade balance was already much better than even. With replacements coming through, he viewed all further successes as pure gravy. The squadrons sank another ship, brought down some more bombers, and then they were wiped out in a single afternoon. The operation had completely disrupted the forward air echelons of the enemy and prevented supplies and ground troops from being landed in a contested area. It was regarded as the turning point of an important campaign, and the survivors of the group to which the squadron had belonged received a Presidential citation.

"What the hell does this joker know about Shamrock?" the General said. "I bet he was covering ball games when that show was on. Jack Dempsey at Toledo. Just because a sportswriter wants to make a dollar writing about heroes, my seventy-nine-year-old mother buys a magazine off the newsstand only to read that her son is a puma, closing for the kill. Keep him out of my command is all I can say."

The General was dressed. He looked at Wyatt, who had on a newly pressed uniform.

"Mighty sharp," he said. "Mighty sharp, Dan. What are these

actresses called? I can't ever remember names when people are introduced."

"Their studios call them April Starr and Gail Fiske."

"Any relation to Minnie Maddern Fiske, do you suppose?"

"Can't say, sir."

"Well now, that's just the kind of thing an aide ought to know. Sometimes I wonder what I keep you around for."

He's feeling good again, Wyatt thought. "Well now, sir," he ached to say, "you know quite well what you keep me around for. You've been persuaded that I'm a historian of some attainments and you think it would be little short of delicious if I were to write a full-length, discreet biography of you after the war. You think I keep a journal of all your sayings and doings, and you'd like to see them sifted out and done up in a handsome volume at, say, three and a half bucks a throw. All about the boy who stuck with the Air Corps, got kicked around by the foot-army brass hats, took his beating, and emerged as one of the great tacticians of the war. Come right down to it, that wouldn't be so very much further from the truth than most military history, but I believe I'll pass up the chance all the same. I believe I'll just serve my time and get out, sir."

The reflection that a man, any man, whatever his age and station in life, could treat him with affectionate condescension irked Wyatt, and he did not, though he tried to, find solace in the fact that a fairly large number of West Point colonels would have been pleased to change places with him.

The General will be descending the great staircase soon, Wyatt thought, in full consciousness of his role as the most important man in a room filled with rank. He will slap his current favorite, the new young General Jack Crane, on the shoulder and he will play wicked uncle to April Starr and Gail Fiske. If he likes the comedian and the juggler, he will ask them if they have any relatives in the Air Forces or what they thought of the food at some A.T.C. base. With the juggler and the comedian, he'll be Harun-al-Rashid, incognito on the streets of Bagdad, sounding out public opinion. He might confound them by asking how long they thought the war would last and why.

Like most, though by no means all, other soldiers, the General was obsessed by that question. And well he might be, thought Wyatt, still in a bilious strain. He'll never again attain a fraction of the power he wields. A coal miner's son and still drawing only moderate pay, the chief was living as only the wealthiest men in the history of the world had lived. In England he had stopped at the greatest of feudal castles, elsewhere in a series of royal suites, and here among such Byzantine splendors as gold cups on the table and zippers on the mosquito net. He had at his disposal any means of transport or communication known to man. Presents and honors came to him from everywhere. And large formations of bombers went on critical missions, at tree-top level, against targets selected by him.

There was this: As generals went, the chief was good. He had done perhaps as much as any single man to bring the war and his own prosperity to an end. But he was having the time of his life, and deep in his heart, whether he knew it or not, he loved this war. He loved the change of scene and the heightened awareness and he loved being important.

And I'm the one to talk, Wyatt thought, I, who will accompany him as he makes his entry downstairs, knowing deep in *my* heart that all the little buck generals will be nice to me because they think I'm close to him, and how I shall lap it up.

That was about what happened. The General and Wyatt found thirty or more people in the reception room, five of them generals. Jack Crane immediately introduced Wyatt to the two actresses, who were very young and very beautiful, and selected as contrasts, no doubt, being respectively blond and brunette. Crane even mumbled something about Wyatt's being a good man to know, and that made Miss Fiske, who could not have learned much about the relative ranks of Army officers, reasonably attentive. Her manner, indeed, came to verge on the cuddlesome and she whispered into Wyatt's ear that one of the British generals looked like C. Aubrey Smith, the actor. And the servants brought Wyatt a deep-red brandy he had expressed a preference for some days ago. The evening began to shape up agreeably.

At the General's request, the juggler and the comedian went through their routines. Wyatt enjoyed them both. Then the guests formed in loose groups, mostly around the General and the two actresses. Wyatt found himself attracted by Gail Fiske, who, while perhaps less dazzling than the blond Miss Starr, more nearly realized the Elizabethan ideal—"there is no excellent beauty that hath not some strangeness in the proportion." Gail Fiske had a very large mouth, made up to look sullen but usually parted in a gay, unforced smile. She could not have been more than twenty-two, and she was eager and giddy and altogether the belle of the prom.

Unfortunately, General Crane and a wing commander from the

R.A.F. and an Australian colonel stayed in the running throughout. None of them would leave for any longer than it took to fetch her something from the buffet. Wyatt gave up and got himself a small sandwich, too, and wandered out into the large conservatory.

Hidden behind a cluster of leafy vines in the far corner, someone was playing a piano. An odd place for the instrument. Wyatt had never noticed it there. He walked along the marble path to a point where he had a clear view of the player. She was a small girl, in a pale-blue dress, and she had not heard him come over. He sat down on a bamboo bench.

She was playing the "Moonlight Sonata." The too-familiar piece sounded miraculously fresh and lovely. He had the illusion of listening to it for the first time and in the midst of a green and friendly jungle. Wyatt had been warmed by the brandy and excited by Gail Fiske, and now this piano in the jungle stirred him as deeply, perhaps, as music ever had.

When the girl finished playing, she bent down and drew a bottle of champagne from an ice bucket at her feet. She poured herself a drink and sipped it. Then she played some Debussy and two short pieces that Wyatt had never heard. She paused to drink again, and caught sight of him.

"Don't stop," he said.

"I wasn't going to play any more."

She was not pretty. She had a tiny face, enormous eyes, and a sharp, prominent nose. She smiled without parting her lips. They had signed her for this tour, she told Wyatt, ostensibly to act as accompanist for April Starr, who sang, but actually to chaperone the two girls. She talked well, with a Maine accent, and Wyatt liked her a lot. Her name was Ruth Sedgwick.

"As a matter of fact," she said, "I ought to be inside right now, looking after my charges. But they're probably being taken care of well enough. I thought I'd come out here and celebrate my thirty-fourth birthday with this bottle of champagne. Technically, I'm a week late, but they had nothing of interest to drink in Oran."

She may or may not have been a little tight.

Wyatt said, "Won't you play some more?"

"No. I just wanted to fool around with a good piano, for a change."

"You weren't fooling."

"I suppose not."

"You're a concert pianist, aren't you?"

"No," she said. "I'm an accompanist and chaperone. Where I come

from, you've got to lay two thousand dollars on the line to be a con-
cert pianist."

"Where is that?"

"The United States."

"I don't know what you mean," he said.

"Well, if you want to get engagements in the sticks, you must be
able to produce some New York notices. And if you want to get yourself properly launched with a New York concert, you better have two
thousand dollars to put up. I never did. I used to be pretty bitter
about that."

"I should think you'd still be."

"No," Ruth Sedgwick said, "not any more. Not for years now.
Although I must confess, when I first walked through this villa, I
thought there is something very wrong, very bad about wealth
heaped up on such a scale. Who owns this place?"

"Some Egyptian."

"Maybe that makes it worse. Or does it? I don't know. What a
country. A villa like this and then, a few hundred yards away, all the
filth and horror of the world."

"Have you ever walked a few blocks east or west of Fifth Avenue?"

"It's not the same thing," she said. "This morning, on the Mena
Road, our driver almost ran over a little girl lying in the gutter. He
got out to see what was wrong and the child had been sleeping there,
just sleeping. She sat up and one of her eyes was nothing but a running sore. And all she had on was a frayed old gunnysack with a hole
in it. Why am I telling you all this? I know. It's because you liked my
playing so much, or said you did. Champagne, too. I've been sitting
out here for an hour being righteously wrathful and drinking this
excellent champagne. Won't you have some? They seem to have
quantities of it inside. That general, the important one, is stopping
here, I believe."

"I'm his aide."

"Oh. I heard about him in Algiers. He's something of a legend,
isn't he?"

"Yes," Wyatt said.

"But you're not very fond of him, are you?"

"What makes you think that?"

"The way you said yes."

"No, I'm not very fond of him." Wyatt had no wish to lose his job,
but this girl had been talking openly and he fell in with it.

"Why do people think he's so good?" she asked.

"He *is* good. When he needs fifty airplanes to do a job, he demands a hundred, receives forty, and the job gets done. He's a rough customer, no fooling. That part of the legend is pretty well founded."

"But you're not very fond of him, are you?"

"No, not very," Wyatt said. "He likes war. I don't. Though it isn't as simple as that, of course. Still, people in the abstract or people he doesn't know really well are even less important to him than to most of us. That child you saw on the Mena Road would not have affected him any more than the glimpse of a dead rabbit. She was a foreigner, for one thing. And he doesn't like foreigners, whether they're wogs, nips, krauts, frogs, limeys, greasers, or whatever. Americans are all right, just so they don't go around thinking that battleships and carriers are more important than land-based aviation."

"He sounds awful."

"He isn't. I'm sorry if I'm giving you the impression that he's some sort of moral idiot. He has all kinds of very strong loyalties. And he knows as much about the military uses of the airplane as probably any man alive. I don't know where the Air Forces would be without a few dozen like him. I *do* know where we'd all be without the Air Forces."

"Are you going to keep working for him after the war?"

Wyatt laughed. "No," he said. "I don't think I'll work for anybody if I can help it. I don't like to work directly under people. Do you?"

"I don't mind," she said. "I'm enjoying the job I have now. The girls are both fine kids and a lot of fun to be with. If I can only keep them from getting pregnant."

"Is there a likelihood?"

"Not a likelihood, I hope. A possibility, yes. They're both at the age where they neck around a good deal and, needless to say, their opportunities are ample. With all the chichi, they're two really innocent girls and take quite some looking after. We've had only one major mishap. Before we left England, Gail got herself tangled up in a weekend affair with a baby lieutenant and we had a bit of a moral crisis over that. Luckily, he was not a very intelligent or aggressive boy and the thing died a natural death."

"Are you sure it was natural?"

"Oh, yes."

Wyatt remembered Gail Fiske and he felt intensely jealous of the lieutenant in England. He drank a glass of Ruth Sedgwick's champagne.

She ran off a few delicate arpeggios with her left hand. "You mustn't waste sympathy on him," she said. "He took it quite well. It wasn't as though Gail had forsaken him in the Aleutians or somewhere. There are lots of girls in England and I think he'd noticed that."

"And Miss Fiske?"

"Someone will come along and kiss her and make it good. If he hasn't already. I'm not sure she tells me everything. My, this champagne is stronger than I thought. I'm having a highly successful birthday party, after all. You're a great help, Captain."

It occurred to Wyatt that he could, with a little effort, take her upstairs, and he considered it. She was by all odds the brightest and most congenial girl he had met overseas and her hands on the keyboard were delightful to watch.

"We've spent two whole days in Cairo now," she said, "and we haven't been out to see the Pyramids yet. Maybe I'll go tomorrow."

That was a frankly transparent lead, but before Wyatt had a chance to respond, General Crane came out from the reception room.

"There you are," Crane said. "I hope I'm not intruding. Dan, do you happen to know what the four freedoms are? The General asked me and I couldn't think of more than two to save my life. He said you'd know. Freedom of speech, of worship, and what else?"

"From fear and from want," Wyatt said.

"That's right. I couldn't remember those two to save my life. Well, the chief didn't know them himself. Thanks, Dan. That's the old staff work, boy."

He went away as fast as he had come.

"You mean they didn't know?" she asked.

"You look startled."

"Didn't they, really?"

"I guess not," Wyatt said.

"My God."

"Crane has led about twenty missions across Germany, five over Ploeşti, and he walked back from one of them. I don't think he's had much chance to think about any freedoms."

"I wouldn't have believed it," she said.

Why should she be so appalled, Wyatt wondered. Were there people like her, intelligent and obviously well informed, who expected generals to remember details of the Atlantic Charter? Yes, there must be a great many. But how could this girl, so—what's the word?—so disenchanted, how could she presume that freedoms and such had anything to do with the conduct of this or any other war?

And yet, he thought, there was a time when I might have been appalled myself.

From fear and from want. That child on the Mena Road had not grown up under German or Italian or Japanese rule. How many like her were there in India or in Puerto Rico? Did she have it any better than the children of Kiev or of Tripoli? Did she have it any better than a small Jewish girl in Warsaw?

Yes, she had it better than a small Jewish girl in Warsaw. All right, then, she had it better. But don't expect young Crane to think about that. Don't go cluttering up his excellent reflexes with scruples, qualifications. You do that and he'll start thinking of himself as a murderer. And "if once a man indulges himself in murder, very soon he comes to think little of robbing, and from robbing he next comes to drinking and Sabbath breaking, and from that to incivility and procrastination." And you wouldn't want young Crane to procrastinate, would you? Not over Ploeşti, you wouldn't.

Now, you file my copy of the four freedoms away, Miss Sedgwick, he thought, down in the lower right-hand drawer, in the same folder with the Ten Commandments, the Sermon on the Mount, and Gail Fiske's fan-magazine interviews. Thank you.

And one thing more. Don't look at me with those enormous eyes. I didn't start this war. I just happened to get involved in it, like a number of other people, and now I'm doing my job or playing the game or what the hell ever you want to call it. This is no time to start me thinking about little children and large ideas, Ma'am. This is no time to start me thinking about anything at all. Right now my idea is to live through the war and scurry back where I came from. After that, we'll see.

Wyatt did all this heavy thinking in a very few minutes and on two glasses of champagne. Ruth Sedgwick had drunk one more herself. She ran off another arpeggio and this time she missed a note. She was tight enough to sway a little.

What a really nice girl, Wyatt thought, a nice, complicated, intelligent girl, thin in the chest. What enormous, expectant eyes. She was waiting for him to say yes, he would be glad to show her the Pyramids.

Then she stopped waiting and said, "We'd better go in. I ought to be looking after my girls."

They walked back to the reception room. The largest of the groups had formed around the General. April Starr was coming down the stairs and Ruth Sedgwick joined her. Gail Fiske had remained in the same corner of the room, with only the Australian colonel and the wing commander from the R.A.F. now paying court. She still looked beautiful and, in the light of what Ruth Sedgwick had said about the baby lieutenant, a good deal more accessible. Wyatt asked her if she would like to drive out in the morning and see the Pyramids, but she had already promised to go with General Crane.

A VIEW OF EXMOOR

❖

SYLVIA TOWNSEND WARNER

FROM BATH, where Mr. Finch was taking the waters, the Finches travelled by car into Devonshire to attend the wedding of Mrs. Finch's niece, Arminella Blount. This was in 1936, when weddings could be garish. The Finches made a very creditable family contribution—Mrs. Finch in green moire, Cordelia and Clara in their bridesmaids' dresses copied from the Gainsborough portrait of an earlier Arminella Blount in the Character of Flora, Mr. Finch in, as his wife said, his black-and-gray. Arden Finch in an Eton suit would have looked like any normal twelve-year-old boy in an Eton suit if measles had not left him preternaturally thin, pale, and owl-eyed.

All these fine feathers, plus two top hats, an Indian shawl to wrap around Arden in case it turned cold, and a picnic basket in case anyone felt hungry, made the car seem unusually full during the drive to Devonshire. On the return journey it was even fuller, because the Finches were bringing back Arminella's piping bullfinch and the music box that was needed to continue its education, as well as the bridesmaids' bouquets. It was borne in on Mr. Finch that other travellers along the main road were noticing his car and its contents more than they needed to, and this impression was confirmed when the passengers in two successive charabancs cheered and waved. Mr. Finch, the soul of consideration, turned in to a side road to spare his wife and daughters the embarrassment of these public acclamations.

" 'Pember and South Pigworthy,' " Mrs. Finch read aloud from a signpost. "The doctor who took out my tonsils was called Pember. It's so nice to find a name one knows."

Mr. Finch replied that he was taking an alternative way home. After a while, he stopped and looked for his road map, but couldn't find it. He drove on.

"Father," said Cordelia a little later, "we've been through this village before. Don't you think we had better ask?"

"Is *that* all it is?" said Mrs. Finch. "What a relief. I thought I was having one of those mysterious delusions when one half of my brain mislays the other half."

Mr. Finch continued to drive on. Arden, who had discovered that the bars of the bird cage gave out notes of varying pitch when he plucked them, was carrying out a systematic test with a view to being able to play "Rule Britannia." Cordelia and Clara and their mother discussed the wedding.

Suddenly, Mrs. Finch exclaimed, "Oh, Henry! Stop, stop! There's such a beautiful view of Exmoor!"

Ten-foot hedges rose on either side of the lane they were in, the lane went steeply uphill, and Mr. Finch had hoped that he had put any views of Exmoor safely behind him. But with unusual mildness he stopped and backed the car till it was even with a gate. Beyond the gate was a falling meadow, a pillowy middle distance of woodland, and beyond that, pure and cold and unimpassioned, the silhouette of the moor.

"Why not," Mr. Finch said, taking the good the gods provided, "why not stop and picnic?" It occurred to him that once the car was emptied, the road map might come to light.

The Finches sat down in the meadow and ate cucumber sandwiches. Arden wore the Indian shawl; the bullfinch in its cage was brought out of the car to have a little fresh air. Gazing at the view, Mrs. Finch said that looking at Exmoor always reminded her of her Aunt Harriet's inexplicable boots.

"What boots, Mother?" Cordelia asked.

"She saw them on Exmoor," Mrs. Finch said. "She and Uncle Lionel both saw them; they were children at the time. They were picking whortleberries—such a disappointing fruit! All these folk-art fruits are much overrated. And nobody's ever been able to account for them."

"But why should they have to be accounted for?" Clara asked. "Were they sticking out of a bog?"

"They were in a cab."

"Your Aunt Harriet—" Mr. Finch began. For some reason, it angered him to hear of boots being in a cab while he was still in doubt as to whether the map was in the car.

"Of course," Mrs. Finch went on, "in those days cabs were everywhere. But not on Exmoor, where there were no roads. It was a perfectly ordinary cab, one of the kind that open in hot weather. The driver was on the box, and the horse was waving its tail to keep the flies off. They looked as if they had been there quite a long time."

"Days and days?" Arden asked.

"I'm afraid not, dear. Decomposition had not set in. But as if they had been there long enough to get resigned to it. An hour or so."

"But how could Aunt Harriet tell how long—"

"In those days, children were very different—nice and inhibited," Mrs. Finch said. "So Aunt Harriet and Uncle Lionel observed the cab from a distance and walked on. Presently, they saw two figures— a man and a woman. The man was very pale and sulky, and the woman was rating him and crying her eyes out, but the most re- markable thing of all, even more remarkable than the cab, was that the woman wasn't wearing a hat. In those days, no self-respecting woman could stir out without a hat. And on the ground was a pair of boots. While Harriet and Lionel were trying to get a little nearer without seeming inquisitive, the woman snatched up the boots and ran back to the cab. She ran right past the children; she was crying so bitterly she didn't even notice them. She jumped into the cab, threw the boots onto the opposite seat, the driver whipped up his horse, and the cab went bumping and jolting away over the moor. As for the man, he walked off looking like murder. So what do you make of that?"

"Well, I suppose they'd been wading, and then they quarrelled, and she drove away with his boots as a revenge," said Clara.

"He was wearing boots," said Mrs. Finch.

"Perhaps they were eloping," Clara said, "and the boots were part of their luggage that he'd forgotten to pack, like Father, and she changed her mind in time."

"Speed is essential to an elopement, and so is secrecy. To drive over Exmoor in an open cab would be inconsistent with either," said Mr. Finch.

"Perhaps the cab lost its way in a moor mist," contributed Arden. "Listen! I can do almost all the first line of 'Rule Britannia' now."

"But, Clara, why need it be an elopement?" Cordelia asked. "Per- haps she was just a devoted wife who found a note from her hus- band saying he had lost his memory or committed a crime or some- thing and was going out of her life, and she seized up a spare pair of boots, leaped hatless into a cab, and tracked him across Exmoor, to make sure he had a dry pair to change into. And when Harriet and

Lionel saw them, he had just turned on her with a brutal oath."

"If she had been such a devoted wife, she wouldn't have taken the boots away again," Clara said.

"Yes, she would. It was the breaking point," Cordelia said. "Actually, though, I don't believe she was married to him at all. I think it was an assignation and she'd taken her husband's boots with her as a blind."

"Then why did she take them out of the cab?" inquired Clara. "And why didn't she wear a hat, like Mother said? No, Cordelia! I think your theory is artistically all right. It looks the boots straight in the face. But I've got a better one. I think they spent a guilty night together and, being a forgetful man, he put his boots out to be cleaned and in the morning she was hopelessly compromised, so she snatched up the boots and drove after him to give him a piece of her mind."

"Yes, but he was wearing boots already," Cordelia said.

"He would have had several pairs. At that date, a libertine would have had hundreds of boots, wouldn't he, Mother?"

"He might not have taken them with him wherever he went, dear," said Mrs. Finch.

Mr. Finch said, "You have both rushed off on an assumption. Because the lady drove away in the cab, you both assume that she arrived in it. Women always jump to conclusions. Why shouldn't the cab have brought the man? If she was hatless, she might have been an escaped lunatic and the man a keeper from the asylum, who came in search of her."

"Why did he bring a pair of boots?" Cordelia asked.

"Ladies' boots," said Mr. Finch firmly.

"He can't have been much of a lunatic-keeper if he let her get away with his cab," Clara said.

"I did not say he was a lunatic-keeper, Clara," said Mr. Finch. "I was merely trying to point out to you and your sister that in cases like this one must examine the evidence from all sides."

"Perhaps the cabdriver was a lunatic," said Arden. "Perhaps that's why he drove them onto Exmoor. Perhaps they were *his* boots, and the man and the woman were arguing as to which of them was to pay his fare. Perhaps—"

Interrupted by his father and both his sisters, all speaking at once, Arden returned to his rendering of "Rule Britannia." Mrs. Finch removed some crumbs and a few caterpillars from her green moire lap and looked at the view of Exmoor. Suddenly, a glissando passage on the bird cage was broken by a light twang, a flutter of wings, a cry from Arden. The cage door had flipped open and the bullfinch had flown out. Everybody said "Oh!" and grabbed at it. The bullfinch flew to the gate, balanced there, flirted its tail, and flew on into the lane.

It flew in a surprised, incompetent way, making short flights, hurling itself from side to side of the lane. But though Cordelia and Clara leaped after it, trying to catch it in their broad-brimmed hats, and though Arden only just missed it by overbalancing on a bough, thereby falling out of the tree and making his nose bleed, and though Mr. Finch walked after it, holding up the bird cage and crying "Sweet, Sweet, Sweet" in a falsetto voice that trembled with feeling, the bullfinch remained at liberty and, with a little practice, flew better and better.

"Stop, all of you!" said Mrs. Finch, who had been attending to Arden, wiping her bloodstained hands on the grass. "You'll frighten it. Henry, do leave off saying 'Sweet'—you'll only strain yourself. What we need is the music box. If it hears the music box, it will be reminded of its home and remember it's a tame bullfinch. Arden, dear, please keep your shawl on and look for some groundsel, if you aren't too weak from loss of blood."

The music box weighed about fifty pounds. It was contained in an ebony case that looked like a baby's coffin, and at every movement it emitted reproachful chords. On one side, it had a handle; on the other side, the handle had fallen off, and by the time the Finches had got the box out of the car, they were flushed and breathless. His groans mingling with the reproachful chords, Mr. Finch staggered up the lane in pursuit of the bullfinch, with the music box in his arms. Mrs. Finch walked beside him, tenderly entreating him to be careful, for if anything happened to it, it would break Arminella's heart. Blithesome and cumberless, like the bird of the wilderness, the bullfinch flitted on ahead.

"I am not carrying this thing a step further," said Mr. Finch, setting down the music box at the side of the lane. "Since you insist, Elinor, I will sit here and play it. The rest of you can walk on and turn the bird somehow and drive it back till the music reminds it of home."

Clara said, "I expect we shall go on for miles."

Seeing his family vanish around a bend in the lane, Mr. Finch found himself nursing a hope that Clara's expectation might be granted. He was devoted to music boxes. He sat down beside it and read the list of its repertory, which was written in a copperplate hand inside the lid: *Là Ci Darem la Mano; The Harp That Once Through Tara's Halls; The Prayer from "Moïse"; The Copenhagen Waltz.* A very pleasant choice for an interval of repose, well-earned repose, in this leafy seclusion. He ran his finger over the prickled cylinder, he blew away a little dust, he wound the box up. Unfortunately, there were a great many midges, the inherent pest of leafy seclusions. He paused to light a cigar. Then he set off the music box. It chirruped through three and a half tunes and stopped, as music boxes do. Behind him, a voice said somewhat diffidently, "I say. Can I be any help?"

Glancing from the corner of his eye, Mr. Finch saw a young man whose bare ruined legs and rucksack suggested that he was on a walking tour.

"No, thank you," Mr. Finch said. Dismissingly, he rewound the music box and set it going again.

Around the bend of the lane came two replicas, in rather bad condition, of Gainsborough's well-known portrait of Arminella Blount in the Character of Flora, a cadaverous small boy draped in a bloodstained Indian shawl, and a middle-aged lady dressed in the height of fashion who carried a bird cage. Once again, Mr. Finch was forced to admit the fact that the instant his family escaped from his supervision they somehow managed to make themselves conspicuous. Tripping nervously to the strains of "The Copenhagen Waltz," the young man on a walking tour skirted around them and hurried on.

"We've got it!" cried Mrs. Finch, brandishing the bird cage.

"Why the deuce couldn't you *explain* to that young man?" asked Mr. Finch. "Elinor, why couldn't you explain?"

"But why should I?" Mrs. Finch asked. "He looked so hot and careworn, and I expect he only gets a fortnight's holiday all the year through. Why should I spoil it for him? Why shouldn't he have something to look back on in his old age?"

CHILDREN ARE BORED ON SUNDAY

❖

JEAN STAFFORD

THROUGH THE WIDE doorway between two of the painting galleries, Emma saw Alfred Eisenburg standing before "The
Three Miracles of Zenobius," his lean, equine face ashen and sor-
rowing, his gaunt frame looking undernourished, and dressed in a
way that showed he was poorer this year than he had been last.
Emma herself had been hunting for the Botticelli all afternoon,
sidetracked first by a Mantegna she had forgotten, and then by a
follower of Hieronymus Bosch, and distracted, in an English room
as she was passing through, by the hot invective of two ladies who
were lodged (so they bitterly reminded one another) in an outrageous and expensive mare's-nest at a hotel on Madison. Emma
liked Alfred, and once, at a party in some other year, she had flirted
with him slightly for seven or eight minutes. It had been spring, and
even into that modern apartment, wherever it had been, while the
cunning guests, on their guard and highly civilized, learnedly dis-
puted on aesthetic and political subjects, the feeling of spring had
boldly invaded, adding its nameless, sentimental sensations to all
the others of the buffeted heart; one did not know and never had,
even in the devouring raptures of adolescence, whether this was a
feeling of tension or of solution—whether one flew or drowned.

In another year, she would have been pleased to run into Alfred
here in the Metropolitan on a cold Sunday, when the galleries were
thronged with out-of-towners and with people who dutifully did
something self-educating on the day of rest. But this year she was
hiding from just such people as Alfred Eisenburg, and she turned
quickly to go back the way she had come, past the Constables and
Raeburns. As she turned, she came face to face with Salvador Dali,
whose sudden countenance, with its unlikely mustache and its his-
trionic eyes, familiar from the photographs in public places, momentarily stopped her dead, for she did not immediately recognize
him and, still surprised by seeing Eisenburg, took him also to be
someone she knew. She shuddered and then realized that he was

245

merely famous, and she penetrated the heart of a guided tour and proceeded safely through the rooms until she came to the balcony that overlooks the medieval armor, and there she paused, watching two youths of high-school age examine the joints of an equestrian's shell.

She paused because she could not decide what to look at now that she had been denied the Botticelli. She wondered, rather crossly, why Alfred Eisenburg was looking at it and why, indeed, he was here at all. She feared that her afternoon, begun in such a burst of courage, would not be what it might have been; for this second's glimpse of him—who had no bearing on her life—might very well divert her from the pictures, not only because she was reminded of her ignorance of painting by the presence of someone who was (she assumed) versed in it but because her eyesight was now bound to be impaired by memory and conjecture, by the irrelevant mind-portraits of innumerable people who belonged to Eisenburg's milieu. And almost at once, as she had predicted, the air separating her from the schoolboys below was populated with the images of composers, of painters, of writers who pronounced judgments, in their individual argot, on Hindemith, Ernst, Sartre, on Beethoven, Rubens, Baudelaire, on Stalin and Freud and Kierkegaard, on Toynbee, Frazer, Thoreau, Franco, Salazar, Roosevelt, Maimonides, Racine, Wallace, Picasso, Henry Luce, Monsignor Sheen, the Atomic Energy Commission, and the movie industry. And she saw herself moving, shaky with apprehensions and Martinis, and with the belligerence of a child who feels himself laughed at, through the apartments of Alfred Eisenburg's friends, where the shelves were filled with everyone from Aristophanes to Ring Lardner, where the walls were hung with reproductions of Seurat, Titian, Vermeer, and Klee, and where the record cabinets began with Palestrina and ended with Copland.

These cocktail parties were a *modus vivendi* in themselves for which a new philosophy, a new ethic, and a new etiquette had had to be devised. They were neither work nor play, and yet they were not at all beside the point but were, on the contrary, quite indispensable to the spiritual life of the artists who went to them. It was possible for Emma to see these occasions objectively, after these many months of abstention from them, but it was still not possible to understand them, for they were so special a case, and so unlike any parties she had known at home. The gossip was different, for one thing, because it was stylized, creative (integrating the whole of the garrotted, absent friend), and all its details were precise and all its conceits were Jamesian, and all its practitioners sorrowfully saw themselves in the role of Pontius Pilate, that hero of the untoward circumstance. (It has to be done, though we don't want to do it; 'tis a pity she's a whore, when no one writes more intelligent verse than she.) There was, too, the matter of the drinks, which were much worse than those served by anyone else, and much more plentiful. They dispensed with the fripperies of olives in Martinis and cherries in Manhattans (God forbid! They had no sweet teeth), and half the time there was no ice, and when there was, it was as likely as not to be suspect shavings got from a bed for shad at the corner fish store. Other species, so one heard, went off to dinner after cocktail parties certainly no later than half past eight, but no one ever left a party given by an Olympian until ten, at the earliest, and then groups went out together, stalling and squabbling at the door, angrily unable to come to a decision about where to eat, although they seldom ate once they got there but, with the greatest formality imaginable, ordered several rounds of cocktails, as if they had not had a drink in a month of Sundays. But the most surprising thing of all about these parties was that every now and again, in the middle of the urgent, general conversation, this cream of the enlightened was horribly curdled, and an argument would end, quite literally, in a bloody nose or a black eye. Emma was always astounded when this happened and continued to think that these outbursts did not arise out of hatred or jealousy but out of some quite unaccountable quirk, almost a reflex, almost something physical. She never quite believed her eyes—that is, was never altogether convinced that they were really beating one another up. It seemed, rather, that this was only a deliberate and perfectly honest demonstration of what might have happened often if they had not so diligently dedicated themselves to their intellects. Although she had seen them do it, she did not and could not believe that city people clipped each other's jaws, for, to Emma, urban equalled urbane, and ichor ran in these Augustans' veins.

As she looked down now from her balcony at the atrocious iron clothes below, it occurred to her that Alfred Eisenburg had been just such a first-generation metropolitan boy as these two who half knelt in lithe and eager attitudes to study the glittering splints of a knight's skirt. It was a kind of childhood she could not imagine and from the thought of which she turned away in secret, shameful pity. She had been really stunned when she first came to New York to find that almost no one she met had gluttonously read Dickens, as she had, beginning at the age of ten, and because she was only twenty when she arrived in the city and unacquainted with the varieties of cultural experience, she had acquired the idea, which she was never able to shake entirely loose, that these New York natives had been deprived of this and many other innocent pleasures because they had lived in apartments and not in two- or three-story houses. (In the early years in New York, she had known someone who had not heard a cat purr until he was twenty-five and went to a houseparty on Fire Island.) They had played hide-and-seek dodging behind ash cans instead of lilac bushes and in and out of the entries of apartment houses instead of up alleys densely lined with hollyhocks. But who was she to patronize and pity them? Her own childhood, rich as it seemed to her on reflection, had not equipped her to read, or to see, or to listen, as theirs had done; she envied them and despised them at the same time, and at the same time she feared and admired them. As their attitude implicitly accused her, before she beat her retreat, she never looked for meanings, she never saw the literary-historical symbolism of the cocktail party but went on, despite all testimony to the contrary, believing it to be an occasion for getting drunk. She never listened, their manner delicately explained, and when she talked she was always lamentably off key; often and often she had been stared at and had been told, "It's not the same thing at all."

Emma shuddered, scrutinizing this nature of hers, which they all had scorned, as if it were some harmless but sickening reptile. Noticing how cold the marble railing was under her hands, she felt that her self-blame was surely justified; she came to the Metropolitan Museum not to attend to the masterpieces but to remember cocktail parties where she had drunk too much and had seen Alfred Eisenburg, and to watch schoolboys, and to make experience out of the accidental contact of the palms of her hands with a cold bit of marble. What was there to do? One thing, anyhow, was clear and that was that today's excursion into the world had been premature; her solitude must continue for a while, and perhaps it would never end. If the sight of someone so peripheral, so uninvolving as Alfred Eisenburg could scare her so badly, what would a cocktail party do? She almost fainted at the thought of it, she almost fell headlong, and the boys, abandoning the coat of mail, dizzied her by their progress toward an emblazoned tabard.

In so many words, she wasn't fit to be seen. Although she was no longer mutilated, she was still unkempt; her pretensions needed brushing; her ambiguities needed to be cleaned; her evasions would have to be completely overhauled before she could face again the terrifying learning of someone like Alfred Eisenburg, a learning whose components cohered into a central personality that was called "intellectual." She imagined that even the boys down there had opinions on everything political and artistic and metaphysical and scientific, and because she remained, in spite of all her opportunities, as green as grass, she was certain they had got their head start because they had grown up in apartments, where there was nothing else to do but educate themselves. This being an intellectual was not the same thing as dilettantism; it was a calling in itself. Emma, for example, did not even know whether Eisenburg was a painter, a writer, a composer, a sculptor, or something entirely different. When, seeing him with the composers, she had thought he was one of them; when, the next time she met him, at a studio party, she decided he must be a painter; and when, on subsequent occasions, everything had pointed toward his being a writer, she had relied altogether on circumstantial evidence and not on anything he had said or done. There was no reason to suppose that he had not looked upon her as the same sort of variable and it made their anonymity to one another complete. Without the testimony of an impartial third person, neither she nor Eisenburg would ever know the other's actual trade. But his specialty did not matter, for his larger designation was that of "the intellectual," just as the man who confines his talents to the nose and throat is still a doctor. It was, in the light of this, all the more extraordinary that they had had that lightning-paced flirtation at a party.

Extraordinary, because Emma could not look upon herself as an intellectual. Her private antonym of this noun was "rube," and to her regret—the regret that had caused her finally to disappear from Alfred's group—she was not even a bona-fide rube. In her store clothes, so to speak, she was often taken for an intellectual, for she had, poor girl, gone to college and had never been quite the same since. She would not dare, for instance, go up to Eisenburg now and say that what she most liked in the Botticelli were the human and compassionate eyes of the centurions' horses, which reminded her of the eyes of her own Great-Uncle Graham, whom she had adored as a child. Nor would she admit that she was delighted with a Crivelli Madonna because the peaches in the background looked exactly like marzipan, or that Goya's little red boy inspired in her only the pressing desire to go out immediately in search of a plump cat to stroke. While she knew that feelings like these were not really punishable, she had not perfected the art of tossing them off; she was no flirt. She was a bounty jumper in the war between Great-Uncle Graham's farm and New York City, and liable to court-martial on one side and death on the other. Neither staunchly primitive nor confidently *au courant,* she rarely knew where she was at. And this was her Achilles' heel: her identity was always mistaken, and she was thought to be an intellectual who, however, had not made the grade. It was no use now to cry that she was not, that she was a simon-pure rube; not a soul would believe her. She knew, deeply and with horror, that she was thought merely stupid.

It was possible to be highly successful as a rube among the Olympians, and she had seen it done. Someone calling himself Nahum Mothersill had done it brilliantly, but she often wondered whether his name had not helped him, and, in fact, she had sometimes wondered whether that had been his real name. If she had been called, let us say, Hyacinth Derryberry, she believed she might have been able, as Mothersill had been, to ask who Ezra Pound was. (This struck her suddenly as a very important point; it was endearing, really, not to know who Pound was, but it was only embarrassing to know who he was but not to have read the "Cantos.") How different it would have been if education had not meddled with her rustic nature! Her education had never dissuaded her from her convictions, but certainly it had ruined the looks of her mind—painted the poor thing up until it looked like a mean, hypocritical, promiscuous malcontent, a craven and apologetic fancy woman. Thus she continued secretly to believe (but *never* to confess) that the apple Eve had eaten tasted exactly like those she had eaten when she was a child visiting on her Great-Uncle Graham's farm, and that Newton's observation was no news in spite of all the hue and cry. Half the apples she had eaten had fallen out of the tree, whose branches she had shaken for this very purpose, and the Apple Experience included both the descent of the fruit and the consumption of it, and Eve and Newton and Emma understood one another perfectly in this particular of reality.

Emma started. The Metropolitan boys, who, however bright they were, would be boys, now caused some steely article of dress to clank, and she instantly quit the balcony, as if this unseemly noise would

attract the crowd's attention and bring everyone, including Eisenburg, to see what had happened. She scuttered like a quarry through
the sightseers until she found an empty seat in front of Rembrandt's famous frump, "The Noble Slav"—it was this kind of
thing, this fundamental apathy to most of Rembrandt, that made
life in New York such hell for Emma—and there, upon the plum
velours, she realized with surprise that Alfred Eisenburg's had been
the last familiar face she had seen before she had closed the door of
her tomb.

In September, it had been her custom to spend several hours of
each day walking in a straight line, stopping only for traffic lights
and outlaw taxicabs, in the hope that she would be tired enough
to sleep at night. At five o'clock—and gradually it became more
often four o'clock and then half past three—she would go into a
bar, where, while she drank, she seemed to be reading the information offered by the *Sun* on "Where to Dine." Actually she had ceased
to dine long since; every few days, with effort, she inserted thin
wafers of food into her repelled mouth, flushing the frightful stuff
down with enormous drafts of magical, purifying, fulfilling apple-
jack diluted with tepid water from the tap. One weighty day, under
a sky that grimly withheld the rain, as if to punish the whole city,
she had started out from Ninetieth Street and had kept going
down Madison and was thinking, as she passed the chancery of St.
Patrick's, that it must be nearly time and that she needed only to
turn east on Fiftieth Street to the New Weston, where the bar was
cool, and dark to an almost absurd degree. And then she was hailed.
She turned quickly, looking in all directions until she saw Eisenburg approaching, removing a gray pellet of gum from his mouth
as he came. They were both remarkably shy and, at the time, she had
thought they were so because this was the first time they had met
since their brief and blameless flirtation. (How curious it was that
she could scrape off the accretions of the months that had followed
and could remember how she had felt on that spring night—as trembling, as expectant, as altogether young as if they had sat together
underneath a blooming apple tree.) But now, knowing that her
own embarrassment had come from something else, she thought
that perhaps his had, too, and she connected his awkwardness on
that September day with a report she had had, embedded in a bulle-
tin on everyone, from her sole communicant, since her retreat, with
the Olympian world. This informant had run into Alfred at a party
and had said that he was having a very bad time of it with a divorce,

with poverty, with a tempest that had carried off his job, and, at last, with a psychoanalyst, whose fees he could not possibly afford. Perhaps the nightmare had been well under way when they had met beside the chancery. Without alcohol and without the company of other people, they had had to be shy or their suffering would have shown in all its humiliating dishabille. Would it be true still if they should inescapably meet this afternoon in an Early Flemish room?

Suddenly, on this common level, in this state of social displacement, Emma wished to hunt for Alfred and urgently tell him that she hoped it had not been as bad for him as it had been for her. But naturally she was not so naïve, and she got up and went purposefully to look at two Holbeins. They pleased her, as Holbeins always did. The damage, though, was done, and she did not really see the pictures; Eisenburg's hypothetical suffering and her own real suffering blurred the clean lines and muddied the lucid colors. Between herself and the canvases swam the months of spreading, cancerous distrust, of anger that made her seasick, of grief that shook her like an influenza chill, of the physical afflictions by which the poor victimized spirit sought vainly to wreck the arrogantly healthy flesh.

Even that one glance at his face, seen from a distance through the lowing crowd, told her, now that she had repeated it to her mind's eye, that his cheeks were drawn and his skin was gray (no soap and water can ever clean away the grimy look of the sick at heart) and his stance was tired. She wanted them to go together to some hopelessly disreputable bar and to console one another in the most maudlin fashion over a lengthy succession of powerful drinks of whiskey, to compare their illnesses, to marry their invalid souls for these few hours of painful communion, and to babble with rapture that they were at last, for a little while, no longer alone. Only thus, as sick people, could they marry. In any other terms, it would be a mésalliance, doomed to divorce from the start, for rubes and intellectuals must stick to their own class. If only it could take place— this honeymoon of the cripples, this nuptial consummation of the abandoned—while drinking the delicious amber whiskey in a joint with a juke box, a stout barkeep, and a handful of tottering derelicts; if it could take place, would it be possible to prevent him from marring it all by talking of secondary matters? That is, of art and neurosis, art and politics, art and science, art and religion? Could he lay off the fashions of the day and leave his learning in his private entrepôt? Could he, that is, see the apple fall and not run madly to break the news to Newton and ask him what on earth it was all about? Could he, for her sake (for the sake of this pathetic rube all but weeping for her own pathos in the Metropolitan Museum), forget the whole dispute and, believing his eyes for a change, admit that the earth was flat?

It was useless for her now to try to see the paintings. She went, full of intentions, to the Van Eyck diptych and looked for a long time at the souls in Hell, kept there by the implacable, impartial, and genderless angel who stood upon its closing mouth. She looked, in renewed astonishment, at Jo Davidson's pink, wrinkled, embalmed head of Jules Bache, which sat, a trinket on a fluted pedestal, before a Flemish tapestry. But she was really conscious of nothing but her desire to leave the Museum in the company of Alfred Eisenburg, her cousin-german in the territory of despair.

So she had to give up, two hours before the closing time, although she had meant to stay until the end, and she made her way to the central stairs, which she descended slowly, in disappointment, enviously observing the people who were going up, carrying collapsible canvas stools on which they would sit, losing themselves in their contemplation of the pictures. Salvador Dali passed her, going quickly down. At the telephone booths, she hesitated, so sharply lonely that she almost looked for her address book, and she did take out a nickel, but she put it back and pressed forlornly forward against the incoming tide. Suddenly, at the storm doors, she heard a whistle and she turned sharply, knowing that it would be Eisenburg, as, of course, it was, and he wore an incongruous smile upon his long, El Greco face. He took her hand and gravely asked her where she had been all this year and how she happened to be here, of all places, of all days. Emma replied distractedly, looking at his seedy clothes, his shaggy hair, the green cast of his white skin, his deep black eyes, in which all the feelings were dishevelled, tattered, and held together only by the merest faith that change *had* to come. His hand was warm and her own seemed to cling to it and all their mutual necessity seemed centered here in their clasped hands. And there was no doubt about it; he had heard of her collapse and he saw in her face that she had heard of his. Their recognition of each other was instantaneous and absolute, for they cunningly saw that they were children and that, if they wished, they were free for the rest of this winter Sunday to play together, quite naked, quite innocent. "What a day it is! What a place!" said Alfred Eisenburg. "Can I buy you a drink, Emma? Have you time?"

She did not accept at once; she guardedly inquired where they

could go from here, for it was an unlikely neighborhood for the
sort of place she wanted. But they were *en rapport,* and he, wanting
to avoid the grownups as much as she, said they would go across to
Lexington. He needed a drink after an afternoon like this—didn't
she? Oh, Lord, yes, she did, and she did not question what he meant
by "an afternoon like this" but said that she would be delighted to
go, even though they would have to walk on eggs all the way from
the Museum to the place where the bottle was, the peace pipe on
Lexington. Actually, there was nothing to fear; even if they had
heard catcalls, or if someone had hooted at them, "Intellectual
loves Rubel," they would have been impervious, for the heart
carved in the bark of the apple tree would contain the names Emma
and Alfred, and there were no perquisites to such a conjugation. To
her own heart, which was shaped exactly like a valentine, there
came a winglike palpitation, a delicate exigency, and all the fragrance of all the flowery springtime love affairs that ever were
seemed waiting for them in the whiskey bottle. To mingle their
pain, their handshake had promised them, was to produce a separate entity, like a child that could shift for itself, and they scrambled
hastily toward this profound and pastoral experience.

MR. SKIDMORE'S GIFT

❖

OLIVER LA FARGE

AT THE AGE of forty-five, Mr. Skidmore was a middling good architectural draftsman beginning to realize that the great dreams of his early days would never come true. He was a bachelor. He earned sixty dollars a week for a large, noisy firm specializing in very modern design, which he disliked. Shortly after his forty-fifth birthday he was walking toward the subway on Morningside Heights, on his way home from a party, and thinking rather drably about his future, for the party had been only pretty good and he was tired. Crossing a street, he was all but run down by an automobile. Afterward he wasn't sure it didn't hit him, although he had no bruise to show for it. He remembered seeing the thing swing round the corner, his frantic leap, and a curious sensation which he described to himself later as sliding feet first through the fourth dimension, though he didn't know just what he meant by that.

He wound up on the curb, feeling extraordinarily weak and shaken considering how common such escapes are in New York. His immediate need for a drink was emphasized by the bar which faced him, but at the same time he dreaded the subway ride, including the shuttle, which must follow. He took out his money—one dollar and no change. It seemed a case of no drink or no taxi, and he knew there wasn't any liquor at the moment in his apartment.

He rubbed at the dollar bill with his fingers in the faint hope that it might turn out to be two. Not two months before he had found forty cents in a trouser pocket, but such windfalls were rare. Then, suddenly, for no reason, he was perfectly sure that he had two bills in his hand, and he rubbed again, and so there were.

It was delightful, pennies from heaven, the feeling of pure velvet. He had himself two good highballs and rode home in style, his shock and upset almost forgotten. Arriving at his walkup apart-

ment, which had been picked with an architect's eye for good pro-
portions and never adequately furnished, he was cocky. We all
expect the bad breaks in this world; the unreasonable good, the
little, unimportant bit of luck, restores a longed-for balance. Standing in his living room with his hat on the back of his head, he fished
out his remaining quarter and looked at it.

"I'll double this, too," he said.

And he did.

For a moment he was almost sick. He stared at the paired quarters in his hand. Two bits, four bits. Holy Moses, what was this?
He tried again. Then he had four quarters. He sat down.

They were identical, all George Washington 1932's, all worn in
the same way. They seemed perfectly good. He studied them a long
time while fear and excitement blended.

It was characteristic of Mr. Skidmore that he kept a dollar bill
in his bureau drawer against emergencies and had not spent it long
since. He got it out and it, too, he doubled. Then he knew that
what he needed was drinks, so he went around to the neighborhood
saloon.

There were only a few men at the bar at that hour. Standing at
one corner by himself, he ordered, and paid for, a Scotch-and-soda.
Then, without thinking, he doubled it. The act got no attention
at the time, but when he was halfway through the second, the bartender asked if he had had two. Mr. Skidmore said casually that
yes, he had. The man seemed seriously puzzled. It dawned on Mr.
Skidmore that doubling was a faculty to be used with great dis-
cretion.

He was a temperate man, but this occasion was so extraordinary
that he ordered and paid for several more drinks before he returned
to his rooms. He didn't really believe it, it couldn't be, it would
disappear shortly, but while it lasted he must make use of it. His
eye lit on his one comfortable armchair. Rather tentatively, he
doubled that. When he had arranged the two, the whole business
began to take on reality. A frenzy of doubling came over him. He
had to hold himself in check and at the same time he was terrified
lest this marvellous gift fade away before he made sufficient use
of it. Exhaustion finally drove him to his bed, which by this time
was one of twins.

In the morning, the various duplicates had not evaporated. He
found himself anxious to get out of this place and back to the ordi-

nary, but when it came to putting a nickel in the subway turnstile, thrift conquered and he doubled the nickel. Beating the subway out of a free ride touched a deep chord within him, and he was filled with confidence.

At the office, toiling over the severely functional decoration of a modernistic shoe store, which he considered painfully bleak, his thoughts were occupied with the implications of his gift. The possibilities were tremendous. But then he thought of the frenzy that had seized him the night before and of his mistake in doubling his drink publicly at the bar. He had got away with that and in his rooms he had held himself within reason, but there must be caution and planning, the technique must be fully mastered.

He began with his finances. Time and again, when he approached the counter of his local bank, he had half expected the cashier to remind him of the miserable condition of his balance and to chide him for extravagance. He decided to clear that up for good. He cashed the whole of his weekly pay check and, going home, quickly ran the sixty dollars up to four hundred and eighty. After a few days had elapsed he deposited most of this, keeping only a few nest-egg tens, which could produce as needed. There was, in fact, no need for him ever to cash a check again, but he decided it would be less conspicuous if he made withdrawals from time to time, while allowing his account to grow into a reserve which would be handy if his gift ran out on him.

His other actions were similarly cautious. His friends, of whom he had a fair number, noted that old Skids seemed to be doing better than formerly. They were mildly amused by his fondness for pairs and sets of things. They saw nothing odd, and it occurred to no one to wonder that his supply of liquor never ran out in the course of an evening.

Even so, he made some slips. Wanting to double his bookcase, for lack of care he doubled all the books in it and had to send in a hurry for a second-hand dealer. He did not quibble over the low price offered, specifying only that it be paid in clean bills. He was unwilling to be responsible for the enormous increase of germs that would go with doubling the dirty ones first offered him.

One hot night when he wanted to serve juleps, he tried to double the supply of ice and got two iceboxes, which made the kitchen rather crowded. He contemplated making another kitchen for it, but his architectural mind was staggered by the effect that that would have on the planning of the rest of the building, so he did nothing about it. The extra equipment seriously disturbed his landlord and was a great source of humor to his friends.

Independent of his salary, he decided he need no longer go on working on an endless succession of flat-fronted, virginal modern stores and offices. He left the big firm for a position under a much less successful architect who was strictly traditional in his design and specialized in the Tudor, which Mr. Skidmore particularly loved. This architect, as a matter of fact, had no great need for another draftsman. Mr. Skidmore offered to work for him very cheap, explaining that he had come into a little money and was doing this mainly for the love of the work. He said that of course if people knew what he was being paid, they would think he was slipping, so he asked the head of the firm to give it out that he was being retained at a much higher figure. His real idea in this request was to account to his friends for his clearly greater prosperity.

Life for Mr. Skidmore began to take on the roominess and satisfaction which he had originally hoped it might have. He liked his work and was valued in his office. He gave money freely to beggars and organ-grinders. He indulged in openhanded hospitality, serving excellent whiskey, good brandy, and sound wine without stint. He took long weekends off. He had plenty of plates, glasses, and flat silver, and he never lacked for electric-light bulbs or fuses.

Only one thing disturbed his tranquillity, a feeling that, after all, the uses he was making of his gift were pretty small potatoes. He saw the suspicion, publicity, the utter ending of quiet, private life that would result from any spectacular action. Little incidents like the creation of the extra icebox showed how easy a serious blunder could be. Yet never before in his life had he been able to do anything remarkable or unique. Exercise of his gift was a pleasure to him, and he longed to tackle something really interesting. A bolder man, he felt, would do greater things.

He toyed with various ideas. He thought how beneficial it would be if all the parks in the city could be doubled, but he saw that the process would probably cause a disastrous earthquake and would certainly result in an inquiry. So it went with other possibilities.

He lingered longest over a new form of an old half-wish. Rather lonely in his way of life up to now, he had often thought that a brother, perhaps even a twin, would be a delightful addition to his life. Brothers could live together more easily than other men, he believed. There would be mutual understanding and tolerance. So now it occurred to him that he might double himself and explain that a long-lost brother had turned up.

There were a lot of things the matter with this idea. If he were doubled, which of the two would then be he? Who would the other one be, or would he be both of them? He doubled a lot of curious objects, such as cigarette butts, an unwashed plate, a wet cloth, and studied the utter identity of the duplicates. There was a certain horror in the thought of doing this to himself, but even the horror only added to the fascination.

It kept returning to his mind, and finally he began pretending, experimentally, that there was an alter ego in his apartment. He held imaginary discussions with a person who thought just as he did and heartily shared his opinions and prejudices. He imagined walking in and saying "Hello, old man" to a Skidmore sitting at ease in the duplicate armchair by the fireplace. He came to know this fellow and more and more to wish for his companionship. Furthermore, he felt that re-creating himself would be a real act of virtuosity, worthy of his power.

One night he had in a particularly cheerful party of friends and did himself somewhat better than usual on whiskey. They left before midnight, and he experienced, as he often did, a feeling of letdown. His living room seemed too big and the silence was oppressive. He thought how fine it would be to have someone with whom to talk over the evening, to have continuing companionship. Lack of nerve, he told himself, was all that held him back.

He poured out a nightcap and idly doubled and redoubled it. The four glasses on the table irritated him. He could do better than that. He downed one, then a second. He made up his mind. Then, thinking carefully, he doubled himself. He was trembling as he did it; his heart pounded. But the most frightening thing was that nothing happened. Nothing at all.

He drank the third nightcap and sat staring at the fire, deeply disturbed. Seeing the one drink remaining, he was about to double it again, but he held back. Perhaps he had broken the rules; perhaps he couldn't do it any longer. He thought he'd better wait a while; he'd better let the whole thing rest. Besides, he'd had enough to drink. He finished that one and went to bed.

He had plenty of money and plenty of supplies, so for a week

he stayed quiet and let his gift lie idle. At the end of the week
he was upset by being apparently cut by one of his best friends.
The man was getting off a bus as he got on. He looked straight at
Mr. Skidmore, who smiled and was about to speak, but his friend
went right on by him with a blank face. Two days later Mr. Skidmore ran into him again, this time on the street, and again his
friend seemed about to cut him.

Mr. Skidmore said, "Hey, Dave!"

The man turned, puzzled, and stared at him for a moment. Then
he said, "Why, it's Skids. I didn't recognize you. How are you?
You look thin."

The man's expression was puzzled, and he said "thin" as if it
were not really what he meant but the best he could think of at
the moment. Mr. Skidmore went home and looked in the mirror.
What he saw was thinness not in the sense of loss of fat but of another kind—an effect of having decreased not in size but in substance. In a strange way he was rather hard to see, although he was
not transparent.

He went on with his usual routine of subway and office the next
day, but it was a nightmare. Whenever he was unable to see himself, he feared lest he might have disappeared, so that he was always
running to a mirror to make sure that he was still visible. His behavior aroused much curiosity among the other draftsmen. When
he got home, where he could set a mirror up against the wall and
watch himself, he realized that he would not leave the house again
until this affliction was ended. He holed up, telephoning for such
food as he needed, paying for it from a dwindling stock of cash,
and encouraging himself with somewhat more than his usual temperate drinking.

Mr. Skidmore continued to diminish. Perhaps what he had attempted was against the rules. In trying to double himself, he had
planned to omit from his double one or two characteristics, including his cowlick, which he disliked. Perhaps he had overlooked
the fact that all human beings are incomplete—fractions, really—
and that in trying to double less than all of himself he had multiplied one fraction by another. In any case, he approached steadily
toward real transparency.

At last he was down to the original nest-egg bottle of Scotch
which he had bought months ago, when his power first became
clear to him. He hesitated to crack it. Sometime this thing had to

be settled, he thought. Either he still could use his gift or he couldn't. It was not improbable that what was ailing him was no more than his failure to give outlet to so great a power. Without special effort, as one performing an act that had become almost mechanical, he willed the bottle to double.

The bottle, the kitchen with its two iceboxes, the whole apartment remained the same. The only change was that in the moment of willing, Mr. Skidmore faded totally away.

A SHORT WAIT BETWEEN TRAINS

❖

ROBERT McLAUGHLIN

THEY CAME into Forrest Junction at eleven-thirty in the morning. Seen from the window of their coach, it wasn't much of a town. First there were the long rows of freight cars on sidings with green-painted locomotives of the Southern Railway nosing strings of them back and forth. Then they went past the sheds of cotton ginners abutting on the tracks. There were small frame houses with weed-choked lawns enclosed by broken picket fences, a block of frame stores with dingy windows and dark interiors, a small brick-and-concrete bank, and beyond that the angled roof and thin smokestacks of a textile mill.

The station was bigger than you would expect; it was of dirty brick and had a rolling, bungalow-type roof adorned with cupolas and a sort of desperate scrollwork. The grime of thousands of trains and fifty years gave it a patina suggesting such great age that it seemed to antedate the town.

Corporal Randolph, a big, sad Negro, said, "Here we is."

Private Brown, his pink-palmed hand closed over a comic book, looked out the window. "How long we here?" he asked.

"Until one o'clock," said Randolph, getting up. "Our train west is at one o'clock."

The two other privates—Butterfield and Jerdon—were taking down their barracks bags from the rack. Other passengers bunched in the aisles—two young colored girls in slacks; a fat, bespectacled mother and her brood, with the big-eyed child in her arms staring fixedly at the soldiers; tall, spare, colored farmers in blue overalls.

As they waited for the line to move, Jerdon said, "Who dat?"

Grinning, Brown answered, "Who dat say 'Who dat?' "

Jerdon replied in a nervous quaver, "Who dat say 'Who dat?' when I say 'Who dat?' "

They both began to laugh and some of the passengers looked at them with half-smiles and uncertain eyes.

Butterfield said, "Even the kid thinks you're nuts."

The child in the fat woman's arms looked at him sharply as he spoke, then her eyes went back to Jerdon and Brown.

"You think I'm nuts, baby?" asked Jerdon. "Is it like the man say?"

The line of passengers began to move.

"That baby don't think I'm nuts," said Jerdon. "That baby is sure a smart baby."

Their coach was up by the engine, and they descended to the platform into a cloud of released steam, with the sharp pant of the engine seemingly at their shoulders.

A motor-driven baggage truck, operated by a colored man wearing an engineer's cap, plowed through them. The three privates, with their bags slung over their shoulders, stood watching the corporal. He was checking through the papers in a large manila envelope marked "War Department, Official Business." It contained their railway tickets and their orders to report to a camp in Arizona.

"Man," said Brown, "you better not lose anything. We don't want to stay in this place."

"This don't look like any town to me, either," said Jerdon.

Butterfield, slim, somewhat lighter in complexion, and a year or two older than the others, looked around him. "Hey," he said, "look what's up there."

The others turned. Down the platform they could see two white soldiers armed with carbines and what appeared to be a group of other white soldiers in fatigues. A crowd was forming around them.

"They're prisoners of war," said Butterfield. "You want to see some Germans, Brown? You say you're going to kill a lot of them; you want to see what they look like?"

Brown said, "That what they are?"

"Sure," said Butterfield. "See what they've got on their backs? 'P.W.' That means 'prisoner of war.'"

The four soldiers moved forward. They stood on the fringe of the crowd, which was mostly white, looking at the Nazi prisoners with wide-eyed curiosity. There were twenty Germans standing in a compact group, acting rather exaggeratedly unconscious of the staring crowd. A small mound of barracks bags was in the center of the group, and the eyes of the prisoners looked above and through the crowd in quick glances at the station, the train, the seedy town beyond. They were very reserved, very quiet, and their silence put a silence on the crowd.

One of the guards spoke to a prisoner in German and the prisoner gave an order to his fellows. They formed up in a rough double column and moved off.

Little boys in the crowd ran off after them and the knot of watchers broke up.

When the four soldiers were alone again, Brown said, "They don't look like much. They don't look no different."

"What did you think they'd look like?" Butterfield asked.

"I don't know," said Brown.

"Man, you just don't know nothing," said Jerdon. "You're just plain ignorant."

"Well, what did *you* think they'd look like?" Butterfield asked Jerdon.

Jerdon shifted his feet and didn't look at Butterfield or answer him directly. "That Brown, he just don't know nothing," he repeated. He and Brown began to laugh; they were always dissolving in laughter at obscure jokes of their own.

A trainman got up on the steps of one of the coaches, moved his arm in a wide arc, the pant of the locomotive changed to a short puffing, and the train jerked forward.

The colored baggageman came trundling back in his empty truck and Corporal Randolph said to him, "They any place we can leave these bags?"

The baggageman halted. "You taking the one o'clock?"

"That's right."

"Dump them on the truck. I'll keep them for you."

Randolph said, "Any place we can eat around here?"

"No, they ain't."

"Where we have to go?"

"They ain't no place," the baggageman said, looking at them as though curious to see how they'd take it.

"Man," said Jerdon, "we're hungry. We got to eat."

"Maybe you get a handout someplace," said the baggageman, "but they sure no place for colored around here."

Butterfield said sourly, "We'll just go to the U.S.O."

"Oh, man, that's rich," Brown said, and he and Jerdon laughed.

"They got a U.S.O. in this here town?" Jerdon asked the baggageman.

"Not for you they ain't," said the baggageman.

"Man, ain't that the truth," replied Jerdon.

Randolph said stubbornly, "We got to get something to eat."

The baggageman said, "You want to walk to Rivertown you get something. That the only place, though."

"Where's Rivertown?" Butterfield asked.

"Take the main road down past the mill. It's about three, four miles."

"Hell, man," said Jerdon, "I'm hungry now. I don't have to walk no four miles to get hungry."

"You stay hungry then," said the baggageman, and went off.

"Well, ain't this just dandy?" said Brown.

The men all looked at Corporal Randolph, who transferred the manila envelope from one hand to the other, his heavy face wearing an expression of indecision.

Butterfield said, "There's a lunchroom in the station. You go tell them they've got to feed us."

Randolph said angrily, "You heard the man. You heard him say there's no place to eat."

"You're in charge of us," Butterfield said. "You've got to find us a place to eat."

"I can't find nothing that ain't there."

"You're just afraid to go talk to them," said Butterfield. "That's all that's the matter with you."

Brown said, "Corporal, you just let Mr. Butterfield handle this. He'll make them give us something to eat." He and Jerdon began to laugh.

"O.K.," said Butterfield. "I'll do it."

Brown and Jerdon looked at Randolph.

"My God," said Butterfield, "you even afraid to come with me while I ask them?"

"You're awful loud-talking—" Randolph began, angrily but defensively.

"You coming with me or not?" Butterfield asked.

"We're coming with you," Randolph said.

The four soldiers went into the colored section of the station and walked through it and into the passage that led to the main entrance. The lunchroom was right next to the white waiting room. The four men moved up to the door, bunching a little as though they were soldiers under fire for the first time.

Butterfield opened the screen door of the lunchroom and they followed him in. There were five or six tables and a lunch counter and, although it was around twelve, only a few diners. A cashier's desk and cigarette counter was by the door, and seated behind it was a gray-haired woman, stout and firm-chinned and wearing glasses.

Butterfield went up to her, rested his hands on the edge of the counter, and then hastily removed them.

She looked up.

Butterfield said quickly, "Is there any place we could get something to eat, Ma'am?"

She looked at him steadily, then her eyes shifted to the others, who were looking elaborately and with desperation at their shoes.

"This all of you?" asked the woman.

"Yes, Ma'am, there's just us four."

"All right," she said. "Go out to the kitchen. They'll feed you."

"Thank you, Ma'am."

Butterfield, trailed by the others, started back toward the kitchen.

"Just a minute," said the woman. "Go out and around to the back."

They turned, bumping each other a little, and went back out the door.

Brown said, when they were outside, "Mr. Butterfield, he sure do it."

"That's right," said Jerdon. "You want to look out, Corporal. That Butterfield, he'll be getting your stripes."

Butterfield and Randolph didn't answer, didn't look at each other.

In the kitchen they found a thin, aged colored man in a white apron and a young, thick-bodied colored girl, who was washing dishes.

"What you want?" asked the cook.

"Something to eat."

"Man, we're hungry," Jerdon told him. "We ain't put nothing inside us since before sunup. Ain't that right, Brown?"

"Since before sunup *yesterday*," said Brown.

"The lady say you come back here?" asked the cook.

"That right."

The cook took their orders and, as he worked, asked them what camp they were from, where they were going, how long they'd been in the Army. He told them about his two sons, who were in the Engineers at Fort Belvoir.

"Labor troops," said Butterfield. "A bunch of ditch diggers and road menders."

The cook stared at him. "What the matter with you, man?"

Butterfield didn't answer. He lit a cigarette and walked to the serving window, looking out at the woman at the cashier's desk.

Brown and Jerdon went over to the girl washing dishes, and Corporal Randolph, his manila envelope under his arm, listened mournfully to the cook.

Suddenly Butterfield threw away his half-smoked cigarette and called to the others, "Come here and look at this."

"What?" said Randolph.

"You come here and see this."

They all came over, the cook, the girl, the three other soldiers. Sitting down at the tables in the lunchroom were the twenty German prisoners. One of their guards was at the door with his carbine slung over his shoulder, the other was talking to the cashier. The other diners were staring at the Nazis in fascination. The prisoners sat relaxed and easy at the tables, lighting cigarettes, drinking water, taking rolls from the baskets on their tables, and munching them unbuttered, their eyes incurious, their attitudes casual.

"God damn! Look at that," said Butterfield. "We don't amount to as much here as the men we're supposed to fight. Look at them, sitting there like kings, and we can't get a scrap to eat in this place without bending our knee and sneaking out to the kitchen like dogs or something."

The cook said severely, "Where you from, boy?"

"He from Trenton, New Jersey," said Brown.

Butterfield stared around at them and saw that only Randolph and the cook even knew what he was talking about and that they were both looking at him with troubled disapproval. Brown and Jerdon and the girl just didn't care. He turned and crossed the kitchen and went out the back door.

The cook said to Randolph, "I'll wrap some sandwiches for him and you give them to him on the train." He shook his head. "All the white folks around here is talking about all the nigger killing they going to do after the war. That boy, he sure to be one of them."

Randolph cracked his big knuckles unhappily. "We all sure to be one of them," he said. "The Lord better have mercy on us all."

PARTY AT THE WILLIAMSONS'

❖

ASTRID PETERS

I T TURNED OUT to be quite a party, but no matter how many people
came up the stairway, Kate, pushing the button and looking
over the railing to see who it was, found she knew them all. She
knew them by their first names, although they were people she never
thought of at all. They were friends of her mother and father, and
they had all been around while she had been growing up. She
couldn't remember not knowing them. They were the people who
had houses next to her family's on the Cape; people who were the
parents of the children she had gone to school with or of the children who went to school with her seven-year-old brother, Joe; people with whom her mother and father would reminisce about gay
times that had happened before she was born or when she had been
too little to know anything about them.

"Hi, Kate!"

Bert and Paul Devries came up the stairs, and instantly Joe appeared in the doorway of his room. The apartment was a duplex in
a brownstone house; the bedrooms were on the lower floor, and
every time Joe heard the doorbell ring, he would get out of bed
and stand half in the hallway, his eyes black and shining in the
sudden light, twisting his bare feet, waiting to be noticed.

Bert was hatless, her gray hair fastened in a casual knot. Even for
a party, she wore a heavy tweed suit, careful not to seem in competi-
tion with women who worried about looking pretty.

"How do you like the new school?" Bert asked Kate. Paul disappeared into the back room to leave their coats.

"Oh, I'm crazy about it," Kate said.

"Barbara's on her vacation, too." Bert leaned over and rubbed the
top of Joe's head. "Hello, honey, you ought to be in bed. Come
over tomorrow," she added to Kate as she started up the stairs to
the living room.

"I'd love to," Kate said, watching Bert's broad, heavy body going up the stairs. She felt that Bert had disposed of her as though she were ten years old again. For a moment, she wished she hadn't come home for Christmas vacation. She was sixteen and she had known ever since she had been back that she was grown up. Until this fall, she had never been away from home, and from the moment she had waked up in her old room again, seeing the familiar pink curtains and the snapshot of Bandy sitting up begging on the beach, and underneath the snapshot, carefully arranged on the bureau, the little Indian dolls she had brought back from the summer in the West, she had felt alone, as though she were no longer a part of her family.

Her getting older had been going on for years, she thought curiously, but she would never have known it if she hadn't gone away. When she had been a child, grownups had just seemed like a different race. Now she knew the real difference was a difference of time, and it was like knowing a terrible secret. Their time was passing; soon it was going to be her time.

Kate turned suddenly and glared at her brother. There was something degrading about his willingness to accept the crumbs of the party. "Will you get back into bed, Joe!" she said. Then she went down the hall into the linen closet, almost pulling the door to on herself, and dug toward the back, where the case of Scotch was stored. "All these people!" she whispered fiercely. "These old people!" She took out the two bottles her father had asked her to get, and stood in the dark for a second before she stepped out, a bottle held in each hand, her face remote and gentle. At the landing, she pressed back against the wall to let Max and Elsie Ganes pass.

"Hello, Kate!"

They greeted her loudly, as though amazed to see her there. Then, suddenly unable to think of anything else to say, they continued up the stairs. Max hesitated and looked over his shoulder with a little wave. "My, what a sight," he said. Kate didn't know whether he was referring to her or to the bottles she was carrying. They were both a little high already, she thought.

Upstairs, the sound of people was everywhere. Someone was playing records in the dining room. "Jada, jada, jada jada jing jing jing" rang through her head, and then, as she went by the living room, she heard her mother say clearly, "But that's been discredited."

Politics, Kate thought. "Don't ask any Trotskyites," her father had said. "They get so intense." And Kate had meant to ask him what the word really stood for. Trotskyite. It didn't sound political; it had a gay sound, like the kind of dance people would do in black leather boots.

In the kitchen, her father, his high, bald forehead shining with perspiration, was making drinks. Helen McLean stood beside him. She was hitting herself on her behind with one hand and with the other she was holding out a tray of ice cubes. "It's like iron," she was protesting. "I've been playing so much tennis that I haven't an ounce of fat on me!"

Kate could tell by her father's face that he had been kidding Helen. She knew the look so well, even when it was just beginning— the funny stiffness around his nose, as though only by looking haughty, only by trying to look like someone else, could he keep from laughing.

"Honestly, Hank. Feel it. It's like iron!" Helen said, and Kate's father, still with one hand gripping the neck of a bottle, reached around and patted her gently. "Like iron," he said gravely, and poured another drink.

"Oh, you're just a stinker," Helen said, and when she laughed, her brown face and big white teeth made such a merry pattern that Kate started to laugh without volition, the way one is won to laugh at something in a movie. Helen, suddenly aware of her, turned around. "Isn't he a stinker, Kate? Am I fat or flabby?"

"You're not fat at all," Kate said warmly. "Why, you're thin. Here's the Scotch, Hank." She leaned against the coolness of the refrigerator and watched him fill the glasses, so many with soda, and then, turning to the sink, so many with water. She wished he would never get through, so they could just stay in the kitchen forever.

He straightened up. "Do you feel like trying a highball, Kate?" he said casually. "I'll make you one if you want it."

"No!" she said, and then, trying to soften her vehemence, "Not now, thanks, Hank. I ate too much dinner. I may take a coke later."

Suddenly she looked right at him and they smiled at each other. She never took a drink, but he had asked her this time because she had been away. For a moment, her love for him welled up inside her as though there was no hope for it.

She turned to Helen. "You do look really wonderful, and you're so brown. May I have one?" She took a cigarette from the pack Helen offered and for a second leaned close to her, getting a light. Then Kate's father picked up the tray of glasses and they followed him out to the hall. "See who needs a drink in the dining room for me, will you, Kate?" he said.

The dining room looked bigger than usual, with the long white table pushed against the wall, and the vase of Christmas greens and magnolia leaves made shadows that stretched out the wall as they went up to the ceiling. "Dearly belovèd," someone sang sweetly, and then hummed with the record. The Poores and the Lavines were talking earnestly in a corner, but everyone else was around the phonograph. Sarah Kellogg was sitting cross-legged on the floor and Paul Devries was on one knee beside her. They were going through a pile of old dance records. " 'Hindustan'—remember that one?" she asked. "And here's 'The Sheik of Araby.' In school, we used to add, 'Without a shirt.' "

Kate took little nervous puffs at her cigarette and then put it out. There were glasses scattered on the table, some half full but deserted among the ashtrays. She picked up as many as she could carry and took them to the kitchen. When she came back, she brought a cloth and wiped the table. Then she emptied the ashtrays and wiped them clean.

In the corner, Ann Poore was talking very fast. She had a long, thin face, with a nose that reached down too far and a chin that came out to a point. Kate thought she was very ugly in a sad, frightened way, but from her neck down she was willowy and always very elegant in the latest fashion. As she talked, the soft tip of her nose quivered and shook like the nose of a mouse. She took little, quick gulps of her drink and talked like a person running for safety. Kate turned away, so as not to feel too sorry for her. She picked up the rest of the glasses, and when she came back from the kitchen, the Poores and the Lavines were gone.

Jack Crawford and some girl were trying to do a Lindy Hop, except that Jack wouldn't really try. He just improvised, twirling the girl around and waving his hands in the air, but the girl danced seriously, with a steady, even beat, accommodating herself to his fooling without ever breaking the rhythm.

"Remember the long, swooping steps and how close one used to dance?" Sarah Kellogg said. She was still sitting on the floor, and when Paul Devries leaned down to help her to her feet, she took his hand. But instead of her jumping up, they both stayed quite still, as though frozen in that position, looking at each other so expressionlessly that Kate wanted to cry out, "Be careful, you'll step on the records." Then suddenly the moment was past and they were up dancing. Looking at Paul's face, Kate was reminded of the way her brother Joe sometimes looked when she helped him get dressed. He would sit very quietly on the edge of his bed watching her, his lips parted, intensely concentrated on the little, mothlike sensations of having his shoes tied. Paul's face had the same look of willful helplessness. When the record came to an end, he and Sarah stayed for a second in the middle of the floor, and again they looked at each other with a strange lack of expression before they dropped their arms to their sides and walked back to the phonograph. Sarah went ahead of him primly, holding herself stiff and straight, as though to make up for all the movement before.

As Kate watched, Phil Burry came up in back of her and put his hand on her arm. "How about a twirl, Miss Katydid?" he asked archly. She shook her head, startled. "Oh, no, thank you," she said clearly, and his hand slid off her arm. She stood uncomfortably beside him without looking at him. She didn't know whether he had meant it as a joke or not. When her father came in the room, she turned to him gratefully.

"Anybody need a drink?" he called out. "How are you fixed, Phil? I think you could do with a little something there." He dropped his arm casually on Kate's shoulders. "Come on in the kitchen and help me, Baby," he said.

Then Jack Crawford came up with a little hopping step, waving an empty glass in one hand and shaking the forefinger of the other. "I'm a jitterbug, I'm a hepcat, I'm a crocodile," he announced, his sparse gray hair standing up in a wispy halo, and he hopped and bounced up the hall after them. Kate looked back. Over his head, Sarah and Paul looked stately as they passed in front of the darkness of the big window. They were dancing again.

The kitchen was full of people all talking at the same time, and Kate stayed out in the hall. One place was the same as any other now. While she had been in the dining room, the party seemed to have grown bigger. The people she saw were all the same, but now they seemed to take up more space. A boyish-looking man talking to Helen McLean kept sliding off the corner of the kitchen table. Every time he had edged himself up on it, he would slowly start sliding until he was standing again. When he threw his head back, Kate could see his face, looking tired and wizened. It was Allen Franklinker, and under the bright light he didn't look boyish at all. "He was a great man," she could hear him say. "I used to tell him that. 'You're a great man, Scott,' I'd say, but of course he wouldn't pay any attention to me." His voice sounded as though he were going to cry.

"It was a swell piece," Helen said soothingly. "It was time somebody wrote a piece about him."

"You think so?" he asked. "You really think so?" He looked at Helen intently and slid off the table again, and this time he caught her arm to steady himself.

Why, he's really drunk, Kate thought. It seemed odd for a poet to be drunk. She looked at her father, but if he thought anything of Allen Franklinker's drunkenness, he gave no sign.

"Kate, dear," her mother called to her, coming up the stairs. "Will you run down and stay with Joe a few minutes? He won't go back to sleep." She waved both hands in the air. "There's just too much noise, I suppose."

"Wait a minute, Libby," Kate said. She reached up, and her mother bowed her head docilely as Kate tucked in a lock of hair that was straying down. Marian Holbrook came up beside them, and Kate's mother, looking a little like a bird, with her head on her chest, said, "Did you get her all right?"

"Yes," Marian said. "They're both sound asleep and Johnny hasn't coughed once." She opened her eyes wide in a look of speculation. "I think—I'm going to have another drink!" The two women smiled at each other almost conspiratorially and her mother called out to the kitchen door, "Two Scotch-and-water!" "Coming up!" Kate heard her father answer as she started down the stairs.

In the hall, she passed the Morrisons with their hats and coats on. "Good night!" they called. "Good night, Kate!" A second after they had disappeared, Mike Levy came up the stairs from the front door. "Hello," he said. He gave a half salute and, dumping his coat over the banister, kept on up the second flight to the party. He must have come in when the Morrisons went out, Kate thought.

The big bed in her parents' room was piled high with coats and hats, a soft mountain of fur and cloth, with an occasional glove looking creamy against the darkness. The bathroom door was open and she could see Sarah Kellogg standing in front of the mirror, putting on lipstick. As Kate passed, Sarah turned and suddenly smiled blindly—as though she didn't really see her at all, Kate thought. She went through the passageway to Joe's room and opened the door, but before she could say his name in the dark, she heard his breathing and tiptoed across the floor, feeling her way through the toys. He was lying with his arms flung over his head, and she took the two trucks that were on top of him and put them on the chair beside his bed. Before she went out, she stood still and listened once more to the sound of his breath, like a little pulse in the room; then she shut the door gently behind her.

The sounds of the party upstairs were all mingling together, and hearing them now, when she was alone in the passageway, made her feel that there was something sad in people talking and laughing, making so much noise, unaware that all the time she could hear them. She went down the passageway to her room, opening the door without putting on the light. Bandy looked like a dark shadow on the blanket she had put on the floor for him. He was getting old and he hated parties; whenever they had one, he was always shut up in her room, because the door to the terrace could be left open without freezing the house.

The room was cold and the air felt wonderful, as though she must have been gasping before. After a moment, it didn't seem dark —not as dark as she would have liked it to be. The light from the night outside was almost like moonlight. When she passed Bandy to go onto the terrace, he didn't raise his head, but he thumped his tail softly on the floor and she could see the water in his bowl gleam.

She was just about to step out on the lumpy crust of snow when she heard someone speak and she moved back from the door. "Oh, darling, oh, darling!" someone mortally wounded said.

At first, it looked like a big, thick person with blurred edges; then Kate saw it was two people with their arms around each other. They looked as if they were in some kind of combat, pressing and burrowing fiercely at each other. Kate felt a physical shock, like being hit in the stomach from inside. She knew at once who it was and she stood there watching, her heart pounding so she could feel it shake her with each beat.

Paul lifted his head for a second. "I love you," he said clearly to the night, and leaned down again. "My dear, my love!" Sarah said quickly, and they broke apart, so there was space between them, and stood looking at each other. Then, with a little groan, they kissed again, but finally this time, and hard, like a blow. Then they turned to go in the door to Kate's parents' room. She heard Sarah say, "Lipstick!" and saw a flutter of white. "No, use mine," Sarah whispered imperatively, and they leaned against the door a moment. Then they were gone.

Kate put her head out the door cautiously. Then she went back and sat on the edge of her bed. Why, they had been in love when they had been upstairs dancing. She tried to remember just exactly the way they had looked, and she thought it was as though she had known it before without knowing she knew. All the time she had watched them dance they had known they loved each other—and they were dancing in front of everybody!

What would they do, she wondered. Would they go upstairs and tell Bert and Mr. Kellogg? Were they telling them now? She looked up at the ceiling. No, she thought, not now, at the party. But for a second she could see the living room filled with people moving in violent confusion. It couldn't be true. She had known Paul and Sarah all her life, and it hadn't been at all like watching people make love in the movies. Paul and Sarah had looked so clumsy, and as though it hurt them, standing out in the cold on the grimy snow, surrounded by the bleak back yards and all the lighted windows.

Suddenly, she remembered looking at Sarah a long time ago. She had wanted to touch Sarah's stomach. Sarah had been very big, and even Kate had known that she was waiting to have twins born. It was queer to think that somebody who had had twins could be in love. And Paul had gray hair.

She sat slumped on the bed, shivering from the cold. She knew her mother must be wondering why she was so long and if Joe was still awake, but she felt, all at once, so stricken with tiredness that it was difficult to make herself move. Before she left the room, she glanced out the door at the terrace again. It looked empty and mysterious, and somehow larger, at night. She thought she could never look at it again without seeing Sarah and Paul holding onto each other as though they would fall if they let go.

Going up the stairs, Kate wondered that the sounds of the party were the same as they had been when she came down. She heard the brittle crash of a glass breaking, and as though it might be some kind of sign, her foot hesitated on the top step and her breath quickened. But the laughter and talk went right on. When she came to the door of the living room she heard another crash and someone said, "My God, that's the second."

Allen Franklinker stood by the fireplace, gazing down at the broken glass at his feet. As she watched, he leaned back against the mantel disdainfully; then his foot reached out searchingly and pawed the pieces into the ashes in back of him. He was going to scorch his clothes if he stood so close to the fire, Kate thought.

She looked around for her mother and saw her on the sofa, and, beside her, sitting on the arm of the sofa, resting one hand lightly on her mother's shoulder, was Sarah Kellogg. The two women were talking and Sarah was swinging one leg idly back and forth, her foot just clearing the floor. Kate could see only her back, but she could see her mother's face smiling, and as she started down the hallway, she heard her mother's soft laugh.

She didn't want to face anyone right now, and she walked past the kitchen, which was full of people, and went down the hall to the dining room. No one was playing the phonograph. Her father was talking to Helen McLean. They were both standing, and Helen had her hat on and her coat dangling from her shoulders. When Kate came up, she kissed her.

"I've had such a lovely time, darling. I just stand here and don't go home," she said. She was just being obstinate, Kate's father told her. The evening was young, and as for going home, she hadn't even finished her drink. Helen looked at the drink in her hand speculatively, then tossed it down with such a flourish that it spilled on her chin, and Kate's father lent her his handkerchief. "See?" Helen said. "I'm drunk. I've got to go home."

But she wasn't at all drunk, Kate thought. She was just joking. The three of them walked down the hall together, Kate on one side and her father on the other, pretending to hold Helen up, and they walked straight into Paul Devries.

"There you are, Hank," he said. "I've been looking for you. We've got to go home. Bert's down getting her coat on." He had come up so suddenly that Kate found she was looking right at him and it was too late to look away. He had no trace of lipstick on his mouth, she noticed. He said good night, touching them all on the hand or the shoulder—little, reassuring gestures of friendliness to take away from the bare good night—and then Kate's mother, seeing them from the living room, came out.

"Good night, Libby," Paul said. He leaned over and kissed her. "You give awfully nice parties." Sarah stood in back of her mother and she, too, said good night. "Good night, Paul," she said, and while she was saying something formal, about getting together soon, Paul suddenly stuck his hand out. They had been looking politely at each other, but now Sarah stared down at his hand as though she were going to cry, and Paul started to pump both their hands up and down violently.

Kate turned quickly to her parents. "Libby—" she began, without knowing what she was going to say.

"Darling," her mother interrupted, "did Joe go to sleep all right?" She was leaning dreamily against her husband. "I forgot. Oh, poor, poor Joe!" she exclaimed, as though, because she had forgotten, Joe was cold and naked out in the snow.

"He was sound asleep before I even got there," Kate said. No one knew, no one saw anything—no one except herself, she thought despairingly. Then Sarah asked the time. "Oh, it *is* late!" she said, and gave an artificial laugh, which stopped abruptly, as though she had heard herself. "It is *not* late," Kate's mother said firmly, and as the rest of them went down the stairs, Kate looked over her shoulder and saw her mother herding Sarah back into the living room.

When Kate and her father had given the last wave over the banister and called good night to Paul and Bert, her father turned to her and grinned. "Around this time," he said softly, "I always wish to hell everybody would go home."

Kate leaned against the wall. "How old is Paul, Daddy?" she asked.

"About my age," he said.

"Your age!" she said, startled.

"Sure, why?"

"Oh, nothing," she said. Her father looked at her alertly. "Why don't you go to bed, Baby? You must be tired."

"No!" she said crossly, but suddenly she knew she couldn't go upstairs again. The thought of the party horrified her, as though it were a scene of wild disorder. "I'm not tired, Daddy." Her head drooped and she felt she couldn't move.

"What's the matter, Kit?" It was the pet name he used to call her when she was little, and she lifted her head and smiled. "You go to bed," he said. "This minute!"

"Yes, Daddy," she said gratefully, and put her face up to be kissed.

"Good night, dear," he said. He rubbed her cheek with the back of his hand and she leaned against it. "Good night, Daddy," she said, and waited till he started her with a little pat down the hall.

Kate got undressed quickly and dropped into bed without washing her face or brushing her teeth, but after the light was out, she sat up in the dark. "Bandy!" she called.

When she was little, she had always refused to go to sleep unless

Bandy slept on her bed, but as she had grown older, the habit had somehow been forgotten. It had been years since she had thought of it. Now, without knowing why, she wanted him to be there. "Bandy," she called again, and after a moment she heard his laborious movements as he got to his feet.

"Here, boy."

She patted the bed. Obediently, he heaved himself up beside her. "Lie down, boy," she whispered, and he turned around and then flopped down heavily. She slid lower under the covers, so she could get her arm around his neck. His fur was deep and silky. After a second she could feel the warmth of his body and she put her head against him.

From upstairs she heard the detached sounds of the party. Why, they're still going on, she thought sleepily.

MONSOON

❖

Jerome Weidman

T HE FIRST TWO DAYS out of Aden, when the passengers complained to one another of the heat, they did it with polite, good-humored smiles. Not to mention the heat at all in the Arabian Sea in August would have been ostentatious, even in those late-summer days in 1939, when the clouds of war were so close that they were almost visible in the burning, mirrored skies, and subjects for conversation were not difficult to find. On the third day, when the thermometer in the bar went up above the hundred mark and stayed there, the smiles disappeared. Nobody mentioned the heat all of that third day. Everybody talked about the monsoon, which, according to Mr. Madgwick, was due to strike the vessel along about the middle of the next day, the fourth out of Aden and a full week, perhaps even eight or nine days, before the Baroda would reach Colombo.

Mr. Madgwick was a small, compact, middle-aged Englishman with a large beard which was shaved around his lips, so his face looked like a fur coat from which a round hole had been gouged, revealing a pink section of skin. He was a rubber broker in Singapore, where he lived with his mother, a tiny, fragile, friendly old lady who was stone-deaf. Her son had taken her to England for a gallstone operation, which had been successful, and now they were on their way back to Malaya.

During the first two days out of Aden, Mr. Madgwick had been just another passenger, more odd-looking than most because of the peculiar gap in his otherwise impressive beard. On the third day, however, when the monsoon replaced the heat as a subject of conversation, Mr. Madgwick became the center of a good deal of attention among those gathered in the bar. He knew a lot about the East. He had lived in the Malay Peninsula for almost thirty years, and he was pleasant and modest while imparting his knowledge to others, especially to the six American passengers, who made no secret of the fact that they had always thought a monsoon was a sudden, violent, and dangerous storm quite capable of breaking a vessel of the Baroda's size in two.

"It isn't that at all," said Mr. Madgwick, with a kind smile. "You're thinking of a typhoon, which is a horse of a different color, as the fellow says." Mr. Madgwick had a precise way of wrapping his pink, almost girlish lips around every word he uttered, pronouncing each one with equal clarity and giving each syllable its proper weight, so he seemed to be bestowing on his listeners, in addition to information, a small, unobtrusive lesson in elocution. "A monsoon is a wind and nothing more, a wind that blows part of the year from one direction and part from the opposite direction. The monsoon we are heading into, for example, blows across the Indian Ocean from the southwest from the latter part of May to the middle of September, and from the northeast from about the middle of October to the middle of December. Coming from the southwest, since this is August, it will strike us thus." He arranged an ashtray and a half-dozen matches in a pattern on the black marble top of his bar table. "Assuming the ashtray is our ship and these matches are the wind—here." He moved the matches across the table until they touched the ashtray. "You see? A slow, steady, monotonous wind, and nothing more. The ship will roll a bit, and I daresay we'll all be jolly uncomfortable for a while, until we get used to it, but you needn't worry, really. I've been in it a dozen times or more and so has my mother, and I know. It won't do any of us a tuppenceworth of harm, as the fellow says."

Toward the end of the third day, when Mr. Madgwick's popularity and his authority had been established, he explained about his beard. His mother's deafness had made it necessary for her to learn how to read lips. She was wonderful at it, he said, and could understand almost anyone, except certain cinema stars who specialized in rapid, lipless patter, but Mr. Madgwick's beard had proved a definite obstacle to their conversation. He hadn't wanted to shave it all off, because he had grown fond of it, so he had compromised by shaving only his mustache and a small area under his lower lip. It looked odd, he knew, but he had become accustomed to it and, he added with a twinkle in his eye, he was afraid he had started something of a fashion in Singapore. He had noticed two Dutch planters with similar beards in a club on Pasir Panjang Road before he left, and he was willing to wager a five-pound note against a sixpenny bit that there would be at least a dozen more like it by the time he got back.

The air of quiet authority in Mr. Madgwick's voice and manner when he spoke of the East had led the other passengers to consult him about an anxiety almost as pressing as the monsoon: the two Chinese who were also travelling first class on the Baroda—should you treat them as social equals or should they be ignored?

If there had been a group of easygoing youngsters among the passengers, the question might not have come up. But there were no young people. Even the six Americans were middle-aged. It was an uncomfortable problem to face, especially in the heat of the Arabian Sea in August, and several of the more reactionary English passengers had announced that they were going to write to the line's head office in London at the first opportunity. It wasn't that they objected to having Chinese on board, but they did think it was a bloody outrage for the company to saddle the white passengers with the problem of how to treat them. Luckily, in this particular case, the two Chinese were sensible and, after Mr. Madgwick's authoritative assurance that it was perfectly all right, the problem had disappeared by the end of the third day out of Aden.

Every morning the two Chinese came up on deck together just as the Lascars were finishing their scrubbing, a full hour before any of the other passengers, including the six energetic Americans, were awake. The two Chinese, wearing expensive flannel slacks, silk sports shirts, and complicated leather sandals, would begin pacing the deck for exercise. They would take two of the large, juicy oranges that the Goanese stewards left for morning walkers in a basket near the companionway leading to the bridge. As they circled the vessel side by side, walking firmly but delicately, as though they were anxious not to disturb the other passengers, still asleep below them, they would peel their oranges, picking the strings fastidiously from each segment, and fling the skin and seeds and strings overboard on the lee side so that the wind, of which there was as yet very little, would not carry the refuse back to the deck.

At first glance they looked alike, but only because they were both Chinese. Actually they were very dissimilar. Mr. Ton was tall and thin, with deep hollows under his high cheekbones, and his eyes, which were devoid of lashes, were mere slits. Mr. Wiu was short and plump. Both had strong, black, shiny hair clipped short at the temples. It was impossible to tell their ages, but they looked young— somewhere around thirty or thirty-five.

By the time they had walked a mile and a half, checking the distance against the sign on the capstan just under the bridge, near the basket of oranges, the other passengers would begin to come up on deck for their constitutionals before breakfast. Mr. Ton and Mr. Wiu would move closer to the wall, so that the white men and women could have the more desirable right of way against the rail. When they passed the two Chinese, they would smile and say good morning, and Mr. Ton and Mr. Wiu, grinning delightedly and showing their strong, white, handsome teeth, would nod their heads and say good morning in reply. The other passengers never stopped to chat and never slowed or quickened their pace to catch up with the two Chinese so they could walk beside them. Mr. Ton and Mr. Wiu always walked alone, clearly by their own choice, the other passengers were able to say with relief.

In the dining room, Mr. Ton and Mr. Wiu sat together at one of the small tables for two against the wall. There were eight of these small tables, but the seven others were unoccupied, mainly because the few wisps of air that were caught by the tin scoops stuck in the portholes above these tables passed right over them and benefited only those people who sat at the large tables in the center of the hot dining room. Mr. Madgwick, who sat with his mother and the six Americans at a center table, assured the other passengers that this was perfectly all right. The Chinese were more accustomed to heat than white people, he said, and besides they preferred to be alone. This was undoubtedly true, people agreed. Mr. Ton and Mr. Wiu obviously had a good time. They ate together, with beautiful table manners, and watched the other diners with small, restrained smiles of pleasure.

After breakfast they sat side by side in deck chairs, reading. They would glance up every now and then from their books to nod politely to a passenger who, in passing them, had nodded first. After tiffin, which the six Americans stopped calling lunch on the second day, Mr. Ton and Mr. Wiu would disappear belowdecks for a nap. At three o'clock they would come up, fresh and clean, looking highly polished in more immaculate slacks and more elaborate sports shirts. They would walk slowly and carefully across the games deck, stopping behind the ping-pong table, the deck-tennis court, or the shuffleboard square to watch a game for several minutes before moving on. Occasionally, when a ball or a quoit went out of bounds, Mr. Wiu would retrieve it quickly and, in response to the short smile or nod or word of thanks from the middle-aged player, both Chinese would smile delightedly and bow with pleasure.

They always entered the bar together and they always took the narrow couch under the thermometer, which seated only two. Everybody in the bar had the feeling that Mr. Ton and Mr. Wiu were not being ostracized and at the same time everybody was relieved of the danger of having consciously to avoid sitting down with them. It was considered a bit of luck that the bar had this piece of furniture.

At night, when there was dancing on the upper deck, the two Chinese would appear together, impeccably dressed in white mess jackets, and stand against the rail, smiling with appreciation as their eyes watched the sedate dancers. They always retired just before the dancing broke up, presumably so that nobody would be embarrassed by the necessity of not including them in the groups that were going off to have a nightcap. All in all, it was very well done, and more than one passenger said, somewhat pompously, perhaps, that Mr. Ton and Mr. Wiu deserved a good deal of credit for the discreet and sensible manner in which they were handling a situation that could very easily have been unpleasant.

In the middle of the fourth day, the monsoon struck the Baroda, as Mr. Madgwick had predicted, and, precisely as he had said, nobody was much the worse for it. The ship rolled a little more, and two of the six Americans didn't eat as much dinner as usual, but that was about all. By morning of the sixth day everybody was accustomed to it.

That afternoon, just before tea, the ship took a deep roll. A marble table in the bar broke loose from its fastenings, slithered across the polished floor, and struck the couch on which the two Chinese were sitting. Mr. Wiu's legs were caught between the table and the couch and one of his ankles was crushed.

Mr. Wiu was terribly embarrassed by the excitement this accident caused. He smiled at the circle of sympathetic passengers, his watery, protruding eyes filling with tears of gratitude and remorse, while the doctor examined him. Finally the doctor straightened up and said it was nothing serious. A simple fracture. The bone had not been completely severed. He would put the ankle into splints and Mr. Wiu would have to remain in bed for the rest of the trip. Nothing to worry about. Mr. Ton smiled and nodded his thanks to the other passengers for their kindness and sympathy to Mr. Wiu as he and the doctor and three stewards carried the helpless, apologetic little man out of the bar and down to his cabin.

Neither Mr. Ton nor Mr. Wiu showed up on deck for the rest of the trip.

The first night after the accident several passengers asked the doctor how the injured Chinese was feeling, and he said irritably that he'd told them once there was nothing seriously wrong with Mr. Wiu's ankle. He had bound it in splints, the Chinese was in bed resting comfortably, and there was Mr. Ton to take care of his wants, which, everybody should have known by this time, were simple and few. Within forty-eight hours everybody had forgotten all about the two Chinese.

On the fourth day after the accident, Mr. Madgwick took two of the Americans, whose names were Gerard and Winter, down to B Deck. He wanted to show them the engine room, which he knew intimately, this being his sixth voyage on the Baroda. They were walking forward, through a section of the vessel that was unoccupied because there were so few passengers on this trip, toward the companionway that led down into the bowels of the ship, when they heard a faint cry. They stopped and stared at one another. The cry was repeated, feeble, croaking.

"It's back this way," Gerard said. "One of these cabins on the right."

The three men turned and retraced their steps. Once more the sound came. The three men stopped, turned again, and ran back to Cabin 709, which they had just passed. Mr. Madgwick twisted the knob and pushed the door open. The three men stopped short in the doorway.

Mr. Wiu was lying partly on his bed and partly on the floor, clutching the side of the bunk and trying weakly to raise himself. Both his legs stuck out straight and stiff behind him. His pajamas and the sheets of his bed were soiled. The odor in the room was dreadful. On a table beside the bunk, Mr. Wiu's water bottle was lying on its side, empty. A fruit basket was on the floor, also empty, in the middle of a small pile of curling orange skins and yellowing apple cores. Beside the bed were the splintered remains of a cup and teapot from a tray that had slipped from the table. Mr. Wiu's lips were parched and cracked, and there were little blobs of dried black saliva in the corners. His tongue, dry and thick and heavily coated, stuck far out of his mouth, as though the effort of calling for help had exhausted his control over it and he lacked the strength to pull it back into his head.

"Holy smoke!" Winter said in astonishment. "The poor guy's dying of thirst!"

They rushed into the room. Mr. Madgwick stripped the soiled, foul-smelling sheets from the bed and flung them into a corner of the cabin. The two Americans lifted Mr. Wiu gently back onto the bed. His legs still stuck out stiffly, like the tines of a carving fork. Mr. Madgwick grabbed the water bottle, filled it from the tap at the other side of the room, and brought it to the bed. He wet Mr. Wiu's lips, poured a few drops on his tongue, and then lifted his head gently into drinking position. The water seemed to help Mr. Wiu at once. He clutched at the bottle, but Mr. Madgwick held it firmly and would allow him only a little at a time.

"It looks like nobody's been near this room since he broke his ankle four days ago," Gerard said excitedly. "Where the hell is that sidekick of his, Mr. Ton?"

Winter stepped out into the corridor. "Mr. Ton!" he called. "Mr. Ton! Hey, Mr. Ton!" There was no answer. Winter came back into the room and bent over Mr. Wiu.

"Where's Mr. Ton?" he asked. The fat little Chinese shook his head weakly.

"These cabins are all unoccupied at this end," said Mr. Madgwick. "The ship is terribly understaffed at this season, and those lazy Goanese will only do so much." He looked down at Mr. Wiu. "Where's your friend? Where's Mr. Ton?" Mr. Wiu's puffy eyelids flicked up and down over his protruding eyes. He licked his lips slowly with his bloated tongue. "He can't talk," said Mr. Madgwick. "One of you chaps run up and fetch the doctor, will you? We'll find Mr. Ton later."

The two Americans hurried out. At the companionway they parted. Gerard went off to find the doctor and Winter went forward to the purser's office and told him what they had discovered.

"We couldn't find Mr. Ton anywhere," Winter said, talking rapidly. "He wasn't in their cabin, and even though I yelled my head off in the corridor, he didn't show up. Nobody showed up. Not even a steward. That part of the ship seems deserted. Do you know where we can find him? Nobody's seen Mr. Ton since four days ago, when Mr. Wiu's ankle was broken."

"You might try his cabin," the purser said.

"I just told you we were in there," Mr. Winter said impatiently. "He wasn't anywhere around. We yelled for him and—oh." Mr. Winter looked at the purser in surprise. "You mean they're not—"

"No, of course not. Mr. Wiu is in 709 on B Deck. And Mr. Ton is in—let me see." The purser flipped the pages of a loose-leaf notebook. "Mr. Ton is in 550 on A Deck."

"Oh, I see," Mr. Winter said. "I thought they were both—we all thought they were—I mean, because of the way they were always together, coming up on deck together and going down together, we all thought—"

He stopped talking, as though he could not find words to express the simple thought that had never occurred to him or to any of the other passengers.

"We'd better take a look at the injured one and then have a go at finding his friend," the purser said briskly. "Come along."

On the way down to B Deck, the purser told Winter that Mr. Ton was a research chemist who had recently completed some work in the States at Johns Hopkins and was now on his way to a post in Shanghai. Mr. Wiu was an insurance agent who had been visiting the central office of his firm in London and was now returning to his own office and home in Hong Kong. When the purser and Winter reached Mr. Wiu's cabin, they found the doctor in the middle of a crowd of excited, puzzled, indignant passengers. The purser pushed his way through to the bed on which Mr. Wiu was lying, his round, fat face creased in a smile of apology for this new disturbance he had created.

"He's all right," the doctor said to the purser. "He can't talk yet, but he will in a short while. I've given him some broth and some water. It's my fault, I suppose," he said, scowling. "I should have looked in on him, but it's been so beastly hot and it seemed such a minor injury. You see what happened." He turned to the passengers, as though he were seeking justification for his neglect. "In addition to his broken ankle, he apparently received a severe blow at the base of the spine when the table flung him against the back of the couch. Must have caused a hemorrhage in the spinal canal. The bleeding brings pressure to bear on the nerves leading to the legs and causes paralysis. Temporary, of course. Lasts several weeks, at most. What's known technically as paraplegia." He seemed to take comfort in the sound of the word. "Very rare, you know. There are no immediate symptoms. It occurs twelve to twenty-four hours after the blow. I never dreamed it might happen in this case. Very rare. Very rare indeed." The passengers nodded and looked at Mr. Wiu on the bed. The doctor turned to the purser. "I had no way of knowing, you see. Besides, I assumed his friend was taking care of him and would let me know if anything was wrong. Damned rotten, deserting his pal like this without letting anybody know. The poor beggar might have been done in if Mr. Madgwick hadn't happened along. Where the devil *is* Ton, anyway? Nobody seems to have seen him since—"

The purser was pushing his way through the crowd to the door. Mr. Madgwick, plucking nervously at his beard, followed. They reached the corridor and hurried up the companionway to A Deck. In front of Cabin 550 they stopped and the purser tapped on the door.

"Yes?" Mr. Ton's voice said. "Come in."

As the purser pushed open the door, Winter and Gerard and perhaps a dozen more excited passengers came hurrying down the corridor and crowded in behind them. Mr. Ton was sitting at his writing table, wearing a silk dressing gown, looking very clean and bright as he ate lunch from a tray and read a book that was propped up against the wall. He folded his napkin neatly, dropped it on the tray, and stood up to face the crowd in the doorway. Before the purser could speak, Mr. Madgwick pushed forward.

"Look here," he said petulantly, tumbling his words out with indiscriminate haste, not at all like a man accustomed to precise diction. "We've just found your friend Mr. Wiu in a terrible state. Nobody's been near him since he broke his ankle. He hasn't had food or water for almost four days. The poor man might have died."

"I am so sorry," Mr. Ton said politely. "That is too bad. But I fail to see how that is my responsibility, which I assume you think it is from the tone of your voice."

The passengers behind Mr. Madgwick gasped.

"You fail to see how— But he's a friend of yours! The two of you are—"

"A friend of mine?" Mr. Ton raised one eyebrow disdainfully. "That stupid, fat, ignorant insurance salesman? I never set eyes on him before I boarded this ship."

For the first time since the Baroda had left Aden, Mr. Madgwick was at a loss. He scratched his beard perplexedly and looked behind him at the purser, at the Americans, at the other passengers. Nobody seemed to know what to do or say. Mr. Madgwick turned back to the Chinese, and his full, red lips parted and closed several times, quickly, as he hunted for words.

"If you don't mind," Mr. Ton said with a small, icy, polite bow of dismissal, "I should very much like to finish my lunch."

SONG AT TWILIGHT

❖

WOLCOTT GIBBS

"HE WAS GETTING along beautifully until he shot that pickerel," said Mrs. Crane.

"He did *what?*" said Mrs. Anderson. They had been discussing a man called Ed Herlicher, whom they had both known several years before—one of those rather mysterious young men who for a little while turn up everywhere in New York, spending a good deal of money and acquiring a certain reputation as either comedians or beaux, and then vanish back into the social underbrush from which they came.

"He shot a pickerel," said Mrs. Crane. "With a double-barrelled shotgun. It was one of those absurd stories, like the things that happen in Evelyn Waugh."

The six other people on the porch of the Cranes' ocean-front cottage looked at her hopefully, but she seemed to be overcome by the murmuring sea and the gentle evening air and leaned back with her eyes closed.

"Wake up, dear," said Mrs. Anderson. "Tell us the rest of it."

"That was all," said Mrs. Crane in an exhausted voice. "He shot this fish and that was the end of him."

"No, it wasn't," said her husband. "Not the way you told it to me before."

"Well, it was terribly silly," she said, reluctantly returning to the mortal world. "This Ed Herlicher got around a lot, you know, and one weekend Jimmy Betts asked him up to his place in the Adirondacks. He had a hunting lodge on a lake, and a lot of them used to go up there to fish and shoot and—oh, whatever people like Jimmy Betts do when they aren't annoying girls or going to football games. Give me a drink, George."

She held out her glass and George Crane filled it from the shaker.

"Where was I?" she asked. "Oh, yes. Jimmy's lodge. Well, they had a lot of childish ideas up there, but I guess the worst was about this fish. It was supposed to be the biggest fish of its kind in that part of the world and they kept seeing it all the time right off the end of Jimmy's dock or somewhere, but it was too smart for them and nobody had been able to catch it. It got to be a legend. You know, the way people go on about that kind of stuff in the *Saturday Evening Post*."

Mrs. Crane seemed about to fade away again, but her husband caught her eye and shook his head.

"All *right*," she said, "but that's really all there was. Ed listened to them practically all one night and then early the next morning, when he must have been still drunk, he went down to the dock and threw some stuff on the water, and when the fish came up, he shot it with one of Jimmy's guns. They couldn't even tell how big it had been, because he blew it right in half. As I said, it was the end of him socially. They hardly talked to him for the rest of the weekend, and when he got back to town, it must have got around '21' and places that he wasn't, well, quite a gentleman, because pretty soon he just disappeared. He may have shot *himself*, for all I know." She yawned and settled further down in her chair. "I told you it was a pretty dull story," she said.

In the silence, George Crane looked around at the cocktail party, which had been going on now for about an hour. It was apparently one of his failures. His wife was clearly in a mood when any social effort seemed to tax her unbearably, and his friends, Mark and Virginia Anderson, who could generally be relied on to keep a conversation in motion, also had a rather limp and unpromising air. The other three were comparative strangers—a Mr. and Mrs. Derleth, whom he had known slightly in town and who had just taken a house a little way down the beach, and a man named Freddy Basker, a Princeton classmate of Mark Anderson's, who was out for the weekend. The Derleths weren't particularly hard to classify. They had usually stayed the year round at New Canaan, but this summer they had come to Fire Island in the hope that the sea might do something for her asthma. Mr. Derleth had complained several times that he missed his golf, and Mrs. Derleth found herself unable to get used to the fact that no considerable trees grew on the island. There was a noble elm on her lawn at New Canaan, much admired by artists, that had once cast its shadow on soldiers of the King. Nothing, however, was precisely clear about Mr. Basker, a hoarse, reddish man around thirty-five, except that he was quite drunk and obviously willing to get a good deal drunker. From time to time, he had filled his glass, without urging from his host, but, except for a low, tuneless humming, that had been the extent of his activity. Mr. Crane was about to give them all up—he had had a good many drinks himself and the role of conscientious host had begun to bore him—when help came from an unexpected source.

"You know, Mrs. Crane's pickerel reminds me of our raccoon, Amy," said Mr. Derleth, chuckling and addressing his wife.

"Oh, yes, tell them about that, Sam," she said. "It was awfully sweet. There was this little brook behind our house in New Canaan and almost every morning . . . No, but you go ahead, dear."

"As my wife has told you," said Mr. Derleth, looking at her with faint disgust, "there's a little brook behind our place—empties into the Sound, finally, I guess—and . . ."

Mr. Basker was sitting beside Mr. Crane, who suddenly found that he could detect a sort of lyric in his guest's humming. "Empties into the *Sound*," hummed Mr. Basker. "You don't say. Into the Sound. Well, my God and my Jesus." Mr. Crane looked at Mr. Basker sharply, but there was no particular expression on his face.

". . . and one winter morning," Mr. Derleth was saying when his host caught up with him again, "on my way out back to get the car, I saw this coon sitting on the bank, hell of a cute little specimen—"

"What sex?" hummed Mr. Basker, but this time he was audible to them all.

"I beg pardon?" said Mr. Derleth politely.

"Unimportant point," said Mr. Basker, waving his hand. "Let it go." He began to hum again.

"Anyway," said Mr. Derleth, "he was sitting there, and what do you suppose he was doing?"

"Well," began Mr. Basker.

Mr. Crane cleared his throat. "What *was* he doing?" he asked hastily.

"He'd broken the ice with his little paws," said Mr. Derleth, "and he was sitting there washing his face. Looked just like my own Timmie. That's our little boy."

"How *cunning*," murmured Mrs. Crane, giving him a bright smile, and Mrs. Anderson also made sounds of sweet approval.

"Yes, sir," said Mr. Derleth, "and after that I'd see him practically every day. I guess he got used to me, because after a while he didn't pay any attention to me at all. He'd just come down and break the ice with his little paws—"

"How thick?" Mr. Basker asked. He was leaning forward and his eyes had a bright, peculiar fixity.

"What?" said Mr. Derleth.

"I said how thick was this ice," repeated Mr. Basker. "Approximately? Couple of inches? A foot? What did he do? Take a rock to it?"

"No," said Mr. Derleth. "It was very thin, of course. He just had to tap it with his paws."

"How cunning," said Mrs. Crane, rather desperately. "How terribly, terribly cunning. But everyone says they're awfully intelligent."

Mr. Basker gave her a tolerant smile. "You keep out of this," he said. "You're just supposed to be the pickerel expert." He turned back to Mr. Derleth. "Then what did he do? After he got finished with washing his face."

"How do you mean?" asked Mr. Derleth, whose geniality was beginning to show signs of strain. "That was all he did. Just washed his face."

"Oh," said Mr. Basker. "Well, it's a damn good story, anyway. You'll never have any occasion to regret *that* story, old man."

"*Well*," said Mrs. Derleth, but apparently Mr. Basker didn't hear her.

"Damn good story," he repeated, and got up and poured himself another drink. He sat down again and for a little while stared out to sea, first with concentration, then suddenly with a look of deep, inward pleasure on his face. "Reminds me of a somewhat similar experience *I* once had with a couple of rats," he said at length. "You want to hear about the experience I once had with this wonderful couple of rats?"

"Sure," said Mr. Crane. "What about these rats?"

"It was when I had an apartment down on Tenth Street," said Mr. Basker. "I wasn't married at the time, though God knows how that happened, because I've been married off and on to various women since I was nineteen. It's a hell of a thing—you start marrying dames and, the first thing you know, you begin marrying them *all*. It's like —like collecting almost any kind of stuff." He stopped and looked doubtfully at Mr. Crane. "Say, listen," he said, "what the hell was I talking about?"

"Rats."

"Rats?" said Mr. Basker, and he frowned with brief perplexity. "Oh, sure. *Rats.* That's right. It was down on Tenth Street. I had this apartment down there and for a long time I kept missing—ah—

tennis balls. Many as two or three a week, sometimes." His rather coppery eyes fell on Mrs. Derleth and he winked at her genially. "I used to ask girls up there now and then," he said, "and for a while I thought they might be taking them. But then I thought, Now what the hell would *they* want with tennis balls? Whatever about these girls, they weren't much for playing tennis. I remember an Agnes used to come up there—*you* remember Agnes, Mark."

"I've *heard* about Agnes, Freddy," said Mr. Anderson. "You better get back to the rats."

"O.K.," said Mr. Basker. "The rats. Let me see. Well, after I decided it wasn't the girls, or even Orpena—"

"Orpena?" said Mrs. Crane.

"Some name like that. Anyway, my cook. She was always taking stuff up to Harlem with her after she got through, but only out of the icebox. Not sporting goods. Well, I was ready to give up until one night I was lying in bed reading when I suddenly heard this noise— kind of a squeak and some scratching—in the corner. I looked around and there, by God, was one of the damnedest rats you ever saw. I figured he came out of the closet, which naturally empties into the bedroom."

Mr. Derleth, looking slightly harassed, went over to the table and mixed himself a highball. Mr. Basker waited politely until he had finished.

"So I just lay there and watched," he said, "and what do you suppose the little son of a bitch did?"

"Listen, Freddy," began Mr. Anderson.

Mr. Basker ignored him. "I forgot to tell you there were a couple of tennis balls lying right there on the rug," he said rapidly. "Well, this rat went right up to one of them and gave it a little shove with his nose. Cutest thing you ever saw."

"How about another drink?" said Mr. Crane hopefully.

"Sure," said Mr. Basker, and held out his glass. It was clear, however, that he had no intention of being diverted. "All right, I thought, this is the bastard that's been stealing my balls, but *how?* That's what I asked myself. *How* is he going to get it out of here? He can't take it in his mouth because it's too damn big and he can't carry it because his little arms are too short and I can't see him getting to work and eating it right there on the rug. *How the hell is that damn rat going to get that ball out of the room?* I asked myself. That was my problem. *How—*"

"He pushed it along with his nose, Freddy," said Mrs. Anderson. "That's easy."

Mr. Basker looked at her blankly and Mr. Crane had a momentary impression that the well had run dry. He was mistaken, for Mr. Basker's face suddenly cleared and he beamed at her delightedly.

"Mm," he said. "Well, I suppose he could have done that, but the point is, he didn't. I'll tell you what he *did* do, because I think it's terribly cute. And I'm sure Mr. and Mrs. Deluxe will back me up."

"Derleth," said Mr. Derleth.

"Derleth. All right, here's what he did, and stop me if you don't think it's terribly cute. He lay down on his side next to one of the balls and he reached out his little paws and took it right in his arms. Then he rolled over until he was lying on his back. Just like a kid with a damn doll. Just like—"

"Drink?" said Mr. Crane. "You better let me get you a fresh drink."

"No," said Mr. Basker. "You wait. Damn good story. Where—oh, yes, there he was on his back with the ball in his little arms." He bent forward and tapped Mr. Derleth on the knee. "*Then* what did he do?" he asked more hoarsely than ever. "Give you any number of guesses. It's hopeless."

"All right. I give up," said Mr. Derleth, who was nothing if not a good sport.

"You'd better," said Mr. Basker, "because he didn't do a damn thing. Not personally. He just lay there on his back and the first thing I knew, *another* rat came sniffing out of the closet. The female, of course. The little girl rat."

"Oh?" said Mrs. Crane.

"Certainly," said Mr. Basker firmly, "and pretty as a picture, too." He closed his eyes as if reviewing the scene, and it was clearly hard on his composure, because he choked and had to wipe his eyes. "And what did *she* do?" he said when he had recovered. "Well, sir, she went right up to this boy rat, the husband, and she grabbed the end of his tail in her teeth and, by God, she pulled him right across the rug, ball and all, and right into the closet." He looked around at the members of his audience and his expression was bland and courteous, that of a man anxious only to instruct and entertain. "Couple of minutes," he said, "they came out after the other ball. Same thing all over again—he rolled over with the ball and she pulled him the hell out of the room. Damn if it wasn't the cutest thing you ever saw."

"Well," said Mrs. Derleth, after a considerable pause, "I guess we'd better get started if we're going to get any dinner. Come on, Sam."

She got up and produced suitable farewells.

"Good night," she said to the Cranes. "It's been so nice. Good night, Mrs. Anderson. Mr. Anderson. I'm so glad to have met you."

Her little nod to Mr. Basker was admirable—containing just the correct mixture of ladylike tolerance and amusement. It was wasted on him, though, because by that time he was clearly lost in some other drunken fancy, humming to himself and tapping on the arm of his chair.

RUN, RUN, RUN, RUN

❖

A. J. LIEBLING

WHEN ALLARDYCE MEECHAM heard that the boys were dead, he felt that he should have flown with them. Meecham was a war correspondent, but he had not yet had a chance to see much of the war. He had come to England in February, 1944, straight from the Hotel Algonquin, where he had had only four or five days to wear his uniform in the lobby, and he did not feel natural wearing it even after a fortnight in London. His nearest approach to action so far had been a visit to an American bomber station in Essex, where he had arranged to go on a bombing mission with a Marauder crew. Now he felt guilty because he had not gone. If he had he would have been dead, too, and that had not been part of his plan, but he felt somehow that this was an ignoble consideration. At the field, a squadron intelligence officer named Kobold had told him the mediums had been having very small losses, an average of one in two hundred sorties. "I wanted to fly one mission and write a story about it, and pretend to myself that I was a big man," Meecham thought self-accusingly, "but if I had expected they would be killed I wouldn't have gone with them." This may or may not have been true. There was no way now of proving it. But Meecham never gave himself the benefit of the doubt because he was afraid that if he did it once he would take advantage of the precedent. "What could you have done, anyway," he asked himself, "if you had known they were going to be killed? Would you have made some excuse and left? Or would you have tried to get them not to go? They would have wanted to know how you could be sure. They would have said you were crazy. They would have gone anyway." But he continued to feel as if he had done something wrong. Meecham had left the airfield because he had tired of hanging about waiting for flying weather. Three days' missions had been washed out and there was no sign it would open up, and he had a date with a British woman officer in London for Friday evening.

This was Sunday. Meecham was standing at the bar of his hotel in Piccadilly, and next to him was Kobold, the intelligence officer he had met at the bomber base. Kobold had come into London on a weekend pass, and he had just told Meecham the bad news. "I wasn't frightened," Meecham thought. "I really wasn't. I told them I was coming back to fly with them next week. They expected to be there. They had flown forty missions. They didn't think the weather would clear off during the weekend. They said I would be a sucker to stay." The weather had cleared on Friday afternoon, after he had left. Saturday morning the bomber crew had been killed. At what precise minute, Meecham wondered, but he felt almost sure he knew. It was March, and dawn came medium late. They would not have been fairly on their way before eight. Over Beauvais, in the north of France, at nine, nine-thirty, maybe. Perhaps at the moment he had picked up the telephone by his bed to order breakfast. "Two teas, sausage and tomato. Darling, do you want sausage and tomato or sausage and mushroom? There's bacon, but it's usually like eating a candle." That must have been the minute. "Two sausage and to-mato, then. And lots of toast. Thank you."

"They had all their bombs aboard," Kobold was saying. He was an oldish lieutenant who felt that he should have been a captain months ago. "One big hell of a cloud of smoke, and then parts of the plane falling out of it. No chutes—no time for them. The other boys brought back wonderful pictures of it. Poor bastards." The in-telligence officer talked loudly, a little truculently, because he wanted a couple of B-17 pilots at the other end of the bar to hear him. The heavy-bomber people sometimes talked as if they had all the losses; the lieutenant wanted to impress this pair. He never flew on operations himself.

Meecham stood just six feet in shoes, but because of his thin, long legs and short, beanlike torso he seemed longer than that when he stood up and shorter than that when he sat down. He had a white face, wide at the cheekbones and covered with faint, rusty blotches, and carroty hair that for the last five years had just failed to cover the top of his head. People seeing him at a bar thought of him as tall and red-headed, but others, who had looked at him seated at a restaurant table, remembered him as bald and middle-sized. His eyelashes were almost white. In New York he was a dramatic critic, but as the war entered its fifth year and all his acquaintances—book reviewers, editorial writers, political columnists, racing handicap-pers and publishers' assistants—became war correspondents and went overseas, he had felt lonely. There must be something in the war that none of these people were fine enough to perceive, he had told his wife, who had a responsible job in the promotion department of a woman's magazine and always referred to herself as a "gal." She had agreed with him. She was a good gal. "Besides," she had said, "I think it would be a professional disadvantage for a dramatic critic after the war not to have been a war correspondent. No one would want to hear you lecture." Meecham had been disappointed that even his own wife misread his motives. But, fighting down this disappointment, he had gone to his managing editor and asked to be sent to Europe. The editor had sent him because he rather thought there would be a lull before the invasion of the Continent. Meecham would spell one of the paper's regular correspondents accredited to the Army, who would come home for a short vacation before the big show began. "But, of course, if it should start suddenly, you'll be there," the editor had said. "Yes, sir," Meecham had said in a voice from which he had tried to exclude excitement. He had felt exalted as he walked over to Abercrombie & Fitch to be measured for his uniform. But, as he now reflected, he had not thought that he really might be killed. "I wanted something for nothing," he thought unmercifully. He was on the point of admiring how hard on himself he could be, and then he remembered that that would constitute self-approval, so he stopped.

Meecham remembered the interior of the Nissen hut he had slept in at the Marauder field. There had been cots and a table and a stove, hooks on the walls to hang clothes on, and even coat hangers, but to him it had been a Spartan place, where he had been more conscious of the war than in his room in London, which contained a good deal of inlaid furniture and a double bed with a yellow damask cover. There were electric-light bulbs in the hut, but they were not shaded, and you had to go outdoors to get to the latrine. There were six cots in the hut. A Marauder carries a complement of three officers and three enlisted men; the hut accommodated the officers of two planes. One set of three had gone to town on pass; men who flew together took their passes at the same time. This gave Meecham his choice of three cots. The boys of the other Marauder crew had just come back from forty-eight hours in London. Meecham found them in the hut when Kobold brought him there in the evening. He had stayed at the officers' club drinking gin and Italian with the C.O. and a couple of non-flying intelligence officers until the bar closed, at ten o'clock. Then Kobold had guided him to the hut. It would have been hard to find in the blackout if he had been alone. Kobold had introduced Meecham to the three crewmates. One of them, a large, hairy, blond young man, was in bed already. He was Captain Barry, the pilot. Barry was smoking a last cigarette before going to sleep. One bare, powerful arm lay outside the blankets as he puffed. A B-26, romantically known as a Marauder, is not an easy plane to fly, and old pilots get big forearms and biceps. Barry reached out a big hand to shake Meecham's. "Make yourself at home," he said. Brownlea, the co-pilot, a wiry young man with a crew haircut, sat at the table with his back to the stove, reading what Meecham observed wonderingly was a book by Robert Briffault, an author Meecham associated vaguely with Granville Hicks and Ouida. "I hope you don't mind loud noises," Brownlea said. "Barry is about to go to sleep. Luckily they have radar here or somebody would have shot him down before this. When he snores he sounds exactly like a four-motor job. He has the Air Force sack medal with so many clusters it looks like a bunch of grapes." "Brownlea is an intellectual," Barry said. "He is a wizard intellectual, they would say in the R.A.F. He is very cheesed with life. He thinks life is a ruddy pantomime. Someday when he is at the controls he will be thinking of an ideology and he will prang the crate. A wizard prang." Elkan, the bombardier-navigator, was sitting on a cot, looking over a set of shiny photographer's prints; he had interrupted the examination only long enough to nod at Meecham when Kobold introduced them. He was a thin young man who in civilian clothes could have been mistaken for a high-school junior. He could not weigh more than a hundred and fifteen pounds and he had a long, pointed nose and large ears. He was still wearing the Class A uniform blouse and pinks in which he had come back from London, and the garrison cap was still on his head. The left breast of his blouse was pretty well loaded with ribbons—even Meecham could recognize the Silver Star, the Distinguished Flying Cross, the Air Medal nutmegged with oak-leaf clusters, the E.T.O. ribbon dotted with stars, and a couple of the innocuous red-and-yellow ones that make good background even though they don't mean anything much.

Kobold went away and Meecham settled down on a cot. "I'm glad to have you here, sir," Brownlea said to Meecham. "Barry and Elkan are good joes, but Elkan is emotional and Barry is inclined to pure escapism. I have been wanting a chance to talk to someone who has really been around a lot."

Meecham was ashamed to tell him that his travels, until this trip, had been limited to a tourist-class vacation in France when he was in college and four trips to the Central City, Colorado, annual dramatic festivals, so he said nothing.

"Don't give Brownlea any encouragement, sir," Elkan said, "or he will read you the first ten chapters of his book."

"I wouldn't think of it," Brownlea said. "Anyway, they're only in a kind of outline form. I really don't know anything about writing. What I want to know is what you think of the Russians."

Meecham considered himself an untrammelled liberal—during the Spanish Civil War he had attended several cocktail parties for the benefit of the Loyalists—but he had heard talk at home about the Fascist mind of the Air Corps, so he was careful in answering. He liked these boys so much already that he didn't want to alarm or antagonize them. He said merely, "I know the Russians are our Allies. I mean, I believe they're sincere, and they're certainly fighting hard."

"Is that all?" Brownlea said. "Why, they're absolutely wonderful. They're the only hope I see for civilization. Surely, sir, you don't think capitalist society can survive all this? Say, have you ever read this man Briffault?"

"Brownie got a brushoff from a society dame at a bottle club in London," Barry said. "She said she was going to spend a penny and she never came back. He's been a militant proletarian ever since."

Meecham said that, of course, the role Russia would be called upon to play in the future should not be underestimated.

"Well, I don't worry much about that," Barry said, "although I still have a card in the typographical union, so it gets my tail out when I read in the *Reader's Digest* that organized labor is to blame for about everything that gets screwed up. I worked my way through the University of California that way, setting type at night on a paper in Oakland. Where the hell does the *Reader's Digest* think I am, and where is the bird who is writing that stuff? Sitting on his can, I bet. But being from the Coast, I mean, I don't think very much about this war. I'd like to be out smacking those Japs around. I haven't got anything too much against the Germans, except Hitler is a son of a bitch."

"I have," Elkan said. "I'm a Jew, and they've been killing millions of Jews who didn't do a goddam thing to them. I hate the bastards. I like to think of what the bombs will do to them when we make our run."

"You see?" Brownlea said. "Pure emotion. Barry and Elkan don't

know anything about the economic bases of imperialism. They reduce everything to personal relationships."

"She said she had to spend a penny," Barry said to nobody in particular. "Brownie offered to lend her a shilling. She gave him a look
that said, 'Anybody that dumb . . .' And the brush."

Elkan said, "To change the subject, which of these pictures do
you like the best?"

"Are they of a broad?" Barry asked.

"No, you wolf—me," Elkan answered severely. "I went down to
see the Tower of London yesterday, and then I walked around and
had some pictures taken at a photographer's. I want to pick out the
best one and have some copies made from it to send home. I want
to send them to my mother and my girl and people like that." Meecham had already learned that Elkan's parents lived in Bayonne,
New Jersey, where his father had a dry-cleaning store. He had gone
two years to Rutgers but hadn't had enough money to continue, and
for a year or so before he enlisted he had helped in the store. He
hadn't as much assurance as some of the bigger, louder boys, who
gave the impression that the whole Air Force came from Texas, but
the fellows in his squadron had a lot of respect for him. Barry,
Brownlea, and Meecham began passing the photographer's proofs
from one to another. Meecham could see that the two pilots were
considering them very seriously. In all but one of the proofs, Elkan
had the visor of his cap pulled well down and was scowling and
puffing out his chest. The photographer had got a good, clear picture
of the ribbons. But the thin, triangular face and the frail, bony neck
still looked like a little boy's. Only one of the proofs showed Elkan
smiling. The wide smile made him look younger and more ingen-
uous than ever, but the picture was the only one of the lot that
wasn't absurd. All three of the consultants agreed it was the best.

"That's the only one that looks like the real Ernie," Barry said.

"That's the one your mother would like to have," said Brownlea.

And Meecham said, "That's the best." He could sense that Ernie
was disappointed and that if he had not been there the little bombardier-navigator might have tried to argue with the others.

But Elkan accepted the reinforced verdict. "Christ," he said
sadly, "I guess I'll never look like a hero." Meecham could see that
he was worrying about his girl back home.

They had talked a while longer and then turned in. Meecham
had felt unexpectedly ashamed because his body looked so white
and old compared to theirs. He was forty-three and the last exercise

he could remember had been a fight with the juvenile of a show he had panned in 1937, but the bartender and the home-and-garden editor had stopped it after the first swing, when the juvenile's pince-nez fell on the floor.

There had been no mission the next morning, on account of the weather. Meecham had got up at seven and gone dutifully to mess, but the boys had chosen to sleep until nearly noon.

"It must be awfully slow for you here, sir," Barry had said the next time Meecham saw him. "I suppose you wanted to go over with us and see some fun."

"It isn't dull at all," Meecham had said, and meant it. "It's very interesting." He had not added, "It's all new to me," because he felt a childish reluctance to let the boys know he was so green. He hadn't really thought of flying a mission on his first visit to the field, either. But Barry looked so competent and unworried that Meecham had found himself saying, "I sure would like to go with you. Do you think the C.O. would let me?"

Barry had grinned and said, "Sure. We've flew lots of correspondents in our ship. It breaks the monotony." And they had shaken hands on it.

Meecham had slept in the hut a second and third night and each had been followed by a day of bad weather. Even in this brief time he had begun to think of himself as a member of the crew of the Typographical Error, the name Barry had given his B-26. He had gone through the preliminary processes of a Marauder mission, which at that time he had thought piquant rather than grim. The squadron intelligence officer had told him what to do if he had to bail out over France. He was to hide his parachute and then take cover and lie still until somebody found him. The French underground people would be pretty sure to find him, the intelligence officer said, and they would smuggle him across France and into a neutral country, although it might take months. The prospect had sounded alluring as the intelligence officer described it, and Meecham had been unable to stop daydreaming about adventures with admiring and sympathetic Frenchwomen. The one thing the officer had not said anything about was what to do if you were dead. So Meecham had not thought about it.

On the third bad morning he had begun to feel bored and had remembered the date with the woman officer in London. There was a train at noon and he had decided to leave by it. When he began packing his bag the boys were still in bed, and when he finished he went around to each cot and shook hands before he started for the jeep that was to take him to the railway station. Meecham could remember Barry's strong grip and Elkan's slender hand and Brownlea grinning and waving his clenched left fist. Brownlea's father, Meecham had learned, was president of a savings bank in Boston.

Remembering, Meecham felt that the date with them was more binding than if they had survived and that he could never be pleased with himself again if he did not fly a mission now. But there was no exhilaration in the thought. He returned to Essex three days later. He found it easy to arrange, at Ninth Air Force Headquarters, for permission to go along on a bombardment. "The story has been done a lot of times before," a public-relations officer warned him. "There's nothing much to it." Meecham explained that he just wanted to see what it was like. He didn't say anything about the crew of the Typographical Error. It seemed to him for a moment, after they had said he could go, that he was doing a causeless thing. It isn't being brave, he told himself, because the mathematical chance of getting hurt is no greater now than it was last week, and then it was very small. Barry and his ship just had bad luck. And there won't be any story in it either. Nobody at the field seemed astonished that he wanted to do it. The boys at the officers' club made him welcome with gin and Italian vermouth, and he was introduced to the officers he was now assigned to fly with. Their ship was named the Roll Me Over, and they were nice boys enough, Meecham thought, but it was like a widower's marriage; he could not get as interested in them as in the dead crew. Schifferdecker, the pilot, was a squat, broad-shouldered boy who had played football at Cornell, where he had taken a course in hotel management. He kept telling Meecham that after the war the British would have to build modern hotels all over England if they expected any Americans ever to come back there. Thurman, the co-pilot, a tall, handsome young man from someplace in Wisconsin, did not have much to say for himself. He had a girl in a show in London, his crewmates said, and he considered every hour he had to spend at the field time wasted. "Missions are the only chance he has to catch up on his sleep," Schifferdecker said. Muldowney, the bombardier-navigator, was a pale, gray-eyed young man who looked like a very youthful Franchot Tone and knew it, and who had played in a dance band in St. Paul before enlisting in the Air Corps. "It's a good deal, having a correspondent along," he told Meecham. "We'll be in a soft spot, right in the center of one of the middle elements, where nothing ever happens. Those flak gunners loose off at the first ships, and then, when the first elements drop their bombs, the gunners run like hell. We'll have a breeze. Same thing for fighters. We haven't been getting much fighter opposition. The Heinies keep most of that in Germany to use against the heavy bombers. But what we have been getting usually lays for the rear element, on the way home, hoping to knock off stragglers. We lost a ship that way yesterday. The boys in the middle have a soft touch." Muldowney had a wide, white grin. "An easy one is always all right with me," he went on. "I've had twenty-eight missions so far, and every easy one means that much better a chance to finish the fifty."

There was no cot for Meecham in the hutment where the Roll Me Overs slept, so he spent the night in a hut in another part of the field, about half a mile from the mess hall. The men in the hut with him were armament and engineering officers. Only two were in bed when Meecham got there. The rest were up most of the night preparing planes for the takeoff. They got in so late that they had just begun to snore when an orderly turned on the lights before dawn next morning. They stayed in bed, the blankets over their heads, while Meecham and the two men who had been in bed early began to dress. Meecham hated to get up early in the morning for any reason at all, and on this particular day he felt worse than usual. He dressed fast, for him, but he was not yet familiar with lace boots, and he had to fumble around in his musette bag to find toothpaste and a towel. Then he felt colicky and went out to look for a latrine. By the time he returned the two other men had gone to the mess hall, and he began to fear that he would lose his way in the dark. The buildings were, of course, blacked out, so he would have no lighted windows to guide him. It would sound like an implausible excuse for missing the raid. He went out of the hut and saw the silhouette of a jeep moving up the road past the hut. There were at least a dozen men on it, some sitting on the hood. He yelled, "Going up to mess?" Someone shouted to him to jump on. Awkwardly he ran along beside the slowly moving jeep, not knowing quite how to get aboard without knocking some other rider off his perch. The jeep stopped and somebody said, "Come along, Pop. You can sit in the back." One of the youngsters in the back seat scrambled out and found a few inches of space on a mudguard, and half a dozen hands grabbed Meecham and hoisted him into the place just vacated. He rode along to the mess hall oblivious of everything except his humiliation. At table he found Schifferdecker and Thurman. Muldowney came along a couple of minutes later, carrying a shiny brown quilted flying suit which he had drawn for Meecham. The breakfast was poor—an omelet badly made of powdered egg and bacon that was all rind and grease. The fruit juice was all gone and the coffee tasted metallic. He wondered if the breakfast was really that bad or if he was frightened. "This is pisspoor chow," Thurman said, and Meecham was reassured. The men in the mess hall straggled out in little groups, crewmates and fellows who knew each other, and climbed into weapons carriers for the ride out to the dispersal building for the briefing. Meecham, of course, rode with the Roll Me Overs.

The briefing reminded him of a lecture in a compulsory course at college. The hall was filled with fellows in flying gear who talked to each other and did not seem too attentive. The intelligence officer stood on a dais at one end of the hall and waved a pointer at various spots on a large map that was projected on a screen behind him. Meecham learned later that all the fliers had been to these particular targets several times and that the lecture had about the same interest for them as an explanation of how to reach New Rochelle. "Our primary target today will be the Montdidier airfield," the officer said. Montdidier sounded familiar and important to Meecham, but he couldn't think why. "There is a battery of six mediums on the approach to the Montdidier field. Six mediums." Somebody whistled. "All of you can go now except the bombardiers. Bombardiers stay a minute after the others leave."

Meecham went out with Schifferdecker and Thurman and three sergeants who had joined them in the briefing hall. The sergeants were the rest of the Roll Me Over's crew—radio-gunner, flight engineer, and tail gunner. They were named Mickiewicz, Klopstock, and Leopardi. Muldowney had to stay to get his detailed bombing map. When he came out they all got into a weapons carrier with perhaps twenty other fliers. The carrier rolled along on the cinder path that circled the field, stopping at each plane to let off the men who were going to fly in it. So Meecham found himself eventually standing under the shadow of the Roll Me Over. It was daylight now, but the sky was still pink with the embers of dawn. In the truck the boys had been singing a song of which Meecham had been able to distinguish only the first line, "How's your love life?" He put on the flying suit over his G.I. pants, his sweater, and his combat jacket. Muldowney was brisk and happy, although cold. He rubbed his gloved hands together furiously and stamped about in his flying

boots. Schifferdecker was serious and conscientious, conferring with
the sergeants. Thurman leaned against the fuselage and Meecham
noticed that he looked sleepy. He wondered if Thurman could have
got down to London on a late train and back in time to fly. Meecham nodded toward the ship and asked Muldowney if it was all
right to get aboard. Muldowney said sure, and went ahead to show
the way. This was a moment Meecham had anticipated with distaste, because he didn't know how to get into a B-26 and had a feeling it might call for some display of acrobacy. It was not so hard as
he had feared. There were two metal stirrups, no higher than
those on an English saddle, and when you got one foot up you
reached up with your hands and caught two metal handles in the
interior of the plane. Then you swung yourself up and in. He
could see that it would be easy to get out when they returned—he
would only have to swing himself out by the handles and drop.
Somehow this was a major satisfaction. Muldowney motioned him
into a compartment behind the nose of the plane. There was no
need to kneel or crawl. "There's a hell of a lot of room in these
things," Muldowney said. "More than in a Fort, for instance. You
just sit over there at the side on that pile of chutes." The others
came aboard one by one. Schifferdecker and Thurman went past
Meecham and into the pilots' compartment, in the nose. The sergeants joined Meecham and Muldowney in the compartment behind the pilots' because Schifferdecker would want their weight up
forward for the takeoff. "This is a place for the navigator to work,"
Muldowney told Meecham, "but there isn't any real navigating to
do when we follow the leader in a big formation like today. Of
course, if we got crippled or had to beat it off by ourselves for any
reason, it would be different. I just wander around the ship when
we get going, sometimes here and sometimes in the bomb bay. We're
carrying frag bombs today, by the way. Thirty one-hundred-pound
frag bombs. We drop them on the runway and dispersal area to take
care of planes and personnel. Sometimes we carry a couple of big
ones, but today frags." The motors were turning over. Other planes
taxied by them on their way to the runway. Then the Roll Me Over
began to roll, too. The motors made such a noise that conversation
became impractical, although it was still possible to understand a
shouted monosyllable. The compartment in which Meecham rode
was comfortable, but there was only a view straight out to either side.
There was nothing to see in either direction except other B-26s. The
plane was swaying and slipping about and he could see Thurman

turn and swear. Schifferdecker was running the ship. The pilots sat
next to each other, in front of identical instrument panels. The
backs of their seats were armor-plated, as a protection against pieces
of flak. Meecham could see there was room for a man to crouch behind them, and he looked forward enviously because there was
more to see from the nose of the plane. Thurman, as if reading his
thoughts, waved to him to come forward, and he did, scrunching
his torso and hams down behind Thurman's seat, while his legs extended over behind Schifferdecker's.

Now the sky was as blue as the Bay of Naples on the wall of a
spaghetti joint, and it was full of B-26s. They flew in "loose fives,"
their favorite formation. Meecham started to count all those in
sight; he made it sixty-seven, including the planes on the Roll Me
Over's wings, but more appeared constantly and he stopped counting. He deduced that the B-26s were just circling while the groups
assembled and that the serious part of the expedition had not begun
yet. Then the course began to seem to him more purposeful. Almost before he was sure of this, Thurman was plucking at his elbow,
waving an arm downward. They were over the coast, heading out
over the Channel, which looked not blue but had, at its English
edge, the color of a puddle of rain water glistening in sunlight. Then
it became lead color. Meecham noticed for the first time that the
motors were saying words. They were saying words, groaning,
rather, "No, no, no, no." He had ridden in planes before but he had
never recognized the words. When they got over the French coast,
he thought, "I should be curious. I haven't seen France in nearly
twenty years." He looked and it seemed quite like England. He
leaned close to Thurman's ear and shouted, "How long to over
target?" Thurman howled back, "Twenty minutes." Meecham went
back to the pile of parachutes in the navigator's cabin and Muldowney appeared, probably from the bomb bay, and seemed to be
saying something about "fighters." Meecham returned to his place
behind the pilots and looked down. He saw a midget plane far
below them. It was a Spitfire, but he did not know it; he could not
tell Allied fighters from Germans. All the attention began to em-
barrass Meecham. He felt that Muldowney was treating him like a
grandfather on a Sunday auto ride. Muldowney reached through
the doorway to the pilots' compartment and tapped Meecham on the
shoulder. He wanted to show him something dead ahead, a series
of specks in the sky. Then Muldowney grinned and started back to
the bomb bay. The specks were not fighters, Meecham saw as the

plane drew up on them, but puffs of black smoke. They multiplied, as he watched, and hung in the air, little black balls of grime. He knew what they were from his sporadic attendance at newsreel theatres. The planes of the forward elements were flying through them now. The flak was at very nearly the right altitude, and Meecham began to hear a new sound over the motors—a sharp "Pak!" like a champagne cork popping and then "S-s-s" like half the wine in the bottle fizzing out. The "Pak!" was the shell bursting, and the fizz was the flight of the fragments. Once Thurman threw up a hand in front of his face and flattened himself against the back of his seat, but nothing happened. Meecham wondered if it had been a close one or if Thurman was just jumpy from too much tomcatting. The co-pilot was waving his hand now and Meecham, following his gesture, could see the bombs falling away from the planes up ahead of them, like chewing-gum nuggets out of a vending machine. Then there were no more puffs in the sky. He felt Muldowney's hand on his shoulder again. The boy had been away only an instant, it seemed. Muldowney was laughing and waving his hands palm upward. Thurman took off his earphones and put them on Meecham, so Meecham could listen to the intercom. Schifferdecker said to Meecham through the intercom, "How'd you like it?" Meecham tried to smile, and for all he knew succeeded. Then Schifferdecker made Thurman take the ship. Meecham understood from that that they were on the way home. He gave Thurman the earphones again. The motors said now, "Run, run, run, run." He said to himself, "I am not making this up, that is what they are saying." He listened again and they were indeed saying, "Run, run," instead of "No, no." Meecham looked at the air-speed indicator and it said "330," which pleased him. Then he went back to Muldowney's compartment and relaxed on the parachutes. Muldowney was grinning and waving his hands and shouting into Meecham's ear, and finally Meecham could understand what he was saying: "I told you that flak would stop as soon as the first planes got their bombs away!" Meecham succeeded in asking whether *he* had got his bombs away and Muldowney joined a thumb and forefinger in a circle to show he had put his bombs right on the bull's-eye. Sergeant Mickiewicz, a bulky blond with a red face, appeared in the compartment and grinned at Meecham. Nothing happened on the way back, but it seemed five times as long as it had going out.

   When they got out of the plane, Schifferdecker started swearing. "The goddam wash nearly made me airsick," he said. "Those goddam cowboys in the ships on our wings must think they're driving taxicabs. Whoever checked them out in a bomber ought to have his head examined. What a ratfest!" He explained that a ratfest was "a rat race, but all bollixed up."

Thurman said, "If they don't keep us too long at the goddam interrogation I can catch the twelve-o'clock train to London."

Muldowney said, "Twenty-nine down and twenty-one to go. I hope they send us a correspondent on every trip! I wonder if any of those leading planes got flak in them."

Meecham felt unreasonably exalted. After all, he told himself reprovingly, he had only escaped from a danger that he had got himself into. And not a great danger, either, he thought. I didn't see one plane shot down. Still, he couldn't help thinking, pretty good for a dramatic critic. He had forgotten Barry and Elkan and Brownlea.

Meecham was still in the midst of his euphoria when he boarded the London train at Chelmsford in midafternoon. He had not been in as much haste to get away as Thurman, and had remained to eat a pretty good lunch of pork chops and canned pineapple at the field. The train was crowded, and although he had a first-class ticket, he had to stand in the corridor outside a compartment filled with American enlisted men who had got on further up the line. When they saw his war-correspondent shoulder flash they tapped on the glass and asked him in. They were all Fortress men who, it appeared, had been on dozens of twelve-hour missions over Germany, from almost all of which they had returned with their ships aflame and three engines out. Meecham was ashamed to tell them he had been only as far as France that morning. By the time the train arrived at Liverpool Street station his exuberance was waning. Coming out into Broad Street, he felt hungry again. He had had what for him was a phenomenally long day. He stopped in at a place called Gow's, a combination fishmonger's and restaurant, and ordered a dozen oysters at the counter. He ordered a second dozen, but the man behind the counter said that the Ministry of Food did not allow them to sell more than eight bob worth to a customer and he had had it. Meecham felt a certain resentment; he had half a mind to tell the man where he had been that morning. That would show him. But perhaps the man had a son in the R.A.F., so he would not be impressed. Or three R.A.F. sons, all killed in the Battle of Britain, so he would be pained by any reference to flying. The thought recalled Barry and Brownlea and Elkan for the first time that day. Meecham wondered why it had seemed essential that, because of them, he go on a mission after they were dead. He paid for his oysters and went out into the street to look for a taxi. He hoped his girl was in town and had no date for the evening. After all, this ought to impress her.

THE JOCKEY

❖

CARSON MCCULLERS

THE JOCKEY came to the doorway of the dining room, then after a moment stepped to one side and stood motionless, with his back to the wall. The room was crowded, as this was the third day of the season and all the hotels in the town were full. In the dining room bouquets of August roses scattered their petals on the white table linen and from the adjoining bar came a warm, drunken wash of voices. The jockey waited with his back to the wall and scrutinized the room with pinched, crêpy eyes. He examined the room until at last his eyes reached a table in a corner diagonally across from him, at which three men were sitting. As he watched, the jockey raised his chin and tilted his head back to one side, his dwarfed body grew rigid, and his hands stiffened so that the fingers curled inward like gray claws. Tense against the wall of the dining room, he watched and waited in this way.

He was wearing a suit of green Chinese silk that evening, tailored precisely and the size of a costume outfit for a child. The shirt was yellow, the tie striped with pastel colors. He had no hat with him and wore his hair brushed down in a stiff, wet bang on his forehead. His face was drawn, ageless, and gray. There were shadowed hollows at his temples and his mouth was set in a wiry smile. After a time he was aware that he had been seen by one of the three men he had been watching. But the jockey did not nod; he only raised his chin still higher and hooked the thumb of his tense hand in the pocket of his coat.

The three men at the corner table were a trainer, a bookie, and a rich man. The trainer was Sylvester—a large, loosely built fellow with a flushed nose and slow blue eyes. The bookie was Simmons. The rich man was the owner of a horse named Seltzer, which the jockey had ridden that afternoon. The three of them drank whiskey with soda, and a white-coated waiter had just brought on the main course of the dinner.

310

It was Sylvester who first saw the jockey. He looked away quickly, put down his whiskey glass, and nervously mashed the tip of his red nose with his thumb. "It's Bitsy Barlow," he said. "Standing over there across the room. Just watching us."

"Oh, the jockey," said the rich man. He was facing the wall and he half turned his head to look behind him. "Ask him over."

"God no," Sylvester said.

"He's crazy," Simmons said. The bookie's voice was flat and without inflection. He had the face of a born gambler, carefully adjusted, the expression a permanent deadlock between fear and greed.

"Well, I wouldn't call him that exactly," said Sylvester. "I've known him a long time. He was O.K. until about six months ago. But if he goes on like this, I can't see him lasting out another year. I just can't."

"It was what happened in Miami," said Simmons.

"What?" asked the rich man.

Sylvester glanced across the room at the jockey and wet the corner of his mouth with his red, fleshy tongue. "A accident. A kid got hurt on the track. Broke a leg and a hip. He was a particular pal of Bitsy's. A Irish kid. Not a bad rider, either."

"That's a pity," said the rich man.

"Yeah. They were particular friends," Sylvester said. "You would always find him up in Bitsy's hotel room. They would be playing rummy or else lying on the floor reading the sports page together."

"Well, those things happen," said the rich man.

Simmons cut into his beefsteak. He held his fork prongs downward on the plate and carefully piled on mushrooms with the blade of his knife. "He's crazy," he repeated. "He gives me the creeps."

All the tables in the dining room were occupied. There was a party at the banquet table in the center, and green-white August moths had found their way in from the night and fluttered about the clear candle flames. Two girls wearing flannel slacks and blazers walked arm in arm across the room into the bar. From the main street outside came the echoes of holiday hysteria.

"They claim that in August Saratoga is the wealthiest town per capita in the world." Sylvester turned to the rich man. "What do you think?"

"I wouldn't know," said the rich man. "It may very well be so."

Daintily, Simmons wiped his greasy mouth with the tip of his forefinger. "How about Hollywood? And Wall Street—"

"Wait," said Sylvester. "He's decided to come over here."

The jockey had left the wall and was approaching the table in the corner. He walked with a prim strut, swinging out his legs in a half-circle with each step, his heels biting smartly into the red velvet carpet on the floor. On the way over he brushed against the elbow of a fat woman in white satin at the banquet table; he stepped back and bowed with dandified courtesy, his eyes quite closed. When he had crossed the room he drew up a chair and sat at a corner of the table, between Sylvester and the rich man, without a nod of greeting or a change in his set, gray face.

"Had dinner?" Sylvester asked.

"Some people might call it that." The jockey's voice was high, bitter, clear.

Sylvester put his knife and fork down carefully on his plate. The rich man shifted his position, turning sidewise in his chair and crossing his legs. He was dressed in twill riding pants, unpolished boots, and a shabby brown jacket—this was his outfit day and night in the racing season, although he was never seen on a horse. Simmons went on with his dinner.

"Like a spot of seltzer water?" asked Sylvester. "Or something like that?"

The jockey didn't answer. He drew a gold cigarette case from his pocket and snapped it open. Inside were a few cigarettes and a tiny gold penknife. He used the knife to cut a cigarette in half. When he had lighted his smoke he held up his hand to a waiter passing by the table. "Kentucky bourbon, please."

"Now, listen, Kid," said Sylvester.

"Don't Kid me."

"Be reasonable. You know you got to behave reasonable."

The jockey drew up the left corner of his mouth in a stiff jeer. His eyes lowered to the food spread out on the table, but instantly he looked up again. Before the rich man was a fish casserole, baked in a cream sauce and garnished with parsley. Sylvester had ordered eggs Benedict. There was asparagus, fresh buttered corn, and a side dish of wet black olives. A plate of French-fried potatoes was in the corner of the table before the jockey. He didn't look at the food again, but kept his pinched eyes on the centerpiece of full-blown lavender roses. "I don't suppose you remember a certain person by the name of Mc-Guire," he said.

"Now, listen," said Sylvester.

The waiter brought the whiskey, and the jockey sat fondling the glass with his small, strong, callused hands. On his wrist was a gold link bracelet that clinked against the table edge. After turning the glass between his palms, the jockey suddenly drank the whiskey neat in two hard swallows. He set down the glass sharply. "No, I don't suppose your memory is that long and extensive," he said.

"Sure enough, Bitsy," said Sylvester. "What makes you act like this? You hear from the kid today?"

"I received a letter," the jockey said. "The certain person we were speaking about was taken out from the cast on Wednesday. One leg is two inches shorter than the other one. That's all."

Sylvester clucked his tongue and shook his head. "I realize how you feel."

"Do you?" The jockey was looking at the dishes on the table. His gaze passed from the fish casserole to the corn, and finally fixed on the plate of fried potatoes. His face tightened and quickly he looked up again. A rose shattered and he picked up one of the petals, bruised it between his thumb and forefinger, and put it in his mouth.

"Well, those things happen," said the rich man.

The trainer and the bookie had finished eating, but there was food left on the serving dishes before their plates. The rich man dipped his buttery fingers in his water glass and wiped them with his napkin.

"Well," said the jockey. "Doesn't somebody want me to pass them something? Or maybe perhaps you desire to reorder. Another hunk of beefsteak, gentlemen, or—"

"Please," said Sylvester. "Be reasonable. Why don't you go on upstairs?"

"Yes, why don't I?" the jockey said.

His prim voice had risen higher and there was about it the sharp whine of hysteria.

"Why don't I go up to my god-damn room and walk around and write some letters and go to bed like a good boy? Why don't I just—" He pushed his chair back and got up. "Oh, foo," he said. "Foo to you. I want a drink."

"All I can say is it's your funeral," said Sylvester. "You know what it does to you. You know well enough."

The jockey crossed the dining room and went into the bar. He ordered a Manhattan, and Sylvester watched him stand with his heels pressed tight together, his body hard as a lead soldier's, holding his little finger out from the cocktail glass and sipping the drink slowly.

"He's crazy," said Simmons. "Like I said."

Sylvester turned to the rich man. "If he eats a lamb chop, you can see the shape of it in his stomach a hour afterward. He can't sweat things out of him any more. He's a hundred and twelve and a half. He's gained three pounds since we left Miami."

"A jockey shouldn't drink," said the rich man.

"The food don't satisfy him like it used to and he can't sweat it out. If he eats a lamb chop, you can watch it tooching out in his stomach and it don't go down."

The jockey finished his Manhattan. He swallowed, crushed the cherry in the bottom of the glass with his thumb, then pushed the glass away from him. The two girls in blazers were standing at his left, their faces turned toward each other, and at the other end of the bar two touts had started an argument about which was the highest mountain in the world. Everyone was with somebody else; there was no other person drinking alone that night. The jockey paid with a brand-new fifty-dollar bill and didn't count the change.

He walked back to the dining room and to the table at which the three men were sitting, but he did not sit down. "No, I wouldn't presume to think your memory is that extensive," he said. He was so small that the edge of the table top reached almost to his belt, and when he gripped the corner with his wiry hands he didn't have to stoop. "No, you're too busy gobbling up dinners in dining rooms. You're too—"

"Honestly," begged Sylvester. "You got to behave reasonable."

"Reasonable! Reasonable!" The jockey's gray face quivered, then set in a mean, frozen grin. He shook the table so that the plates rattled, and for a moment it seemed that he would push it over. But suddenly he stopped. His hand reached out toward the plate nearest to him and deliberately he put a few of the French-fried potatoes in his mouth. He chewed slowly, his upper lip raised, then he turned and spat out the pulpy mouthful on the smooth red carpet which covered the floor. "Libertines," he said, and his voice was thin and broken. He rolled the word in his mouth, as though it had a flavor and a substance that gratified him. "You libertines," he said again, and turned and walked with his rigid swagger out of the dining room.

Sylvester shrugged one of his loose, heavy shoulders. The rich man sopped up some water that had been spilled on the tablecloth, and they didn't speak until the waiter came to clear away.

PIGEONS EN CASSEROLE

❖

BESSIE BREUER

FROM THE FIRST I felt uncomfortable. I thought it was the unpleasant news I must break pleasantly to her, but then I am always so
nervous now. To live in New York, to earn a living from its neurotic,
unstable women—that is work for a Tantalus; for a refugee, a man
who has literally, but literally, nothing but his manners and a little
talent, *petit tout petit,* it is more disgusting than a concentration
camp. There, I think, one's honor sustains one, come what may. But
to be always at bay, like a cunning animal, a little animal, in a jungle
of devouring women—that she could never understand.

I telephoned her—I detest writing letters—to say I would meet the
boy at the Grand Central station and bring him up on the first train
to her in the country. It was his summer holiday.

Her voice over the telephone was so warm, so gay and fresh. "How
kind of you!" she said. "How very wonderful of you!" It was always
like that whenever I called her up, most of the time to say I could not
come up to see her. Sometimes for months on end I was unable to
come, and always she answered in that fresh, happy voice, "Yes, darling, I understand."

When we finally got to her station on one of those villainous local
trains, there she was, running toward us, her face aflame with such
joy that it was, in a way, terrible to see. The boy stood slightly to the
rear of me, as if he were afraid of it, almost.

Yet any mother would stare at a son who left her a little boy and
returned, after eight months, a head taller and the bony structure of
a man's head already changing the baby face. I too had stared when I
first saw him.

"*Mon petit!*" she exclaimed. "*Comme tu as grandi!*" In her excitement at seeing him she had forgotten he had begged her never to
speak anything but English to him, especially in public. People passing us looked around curiously, hearing the foreign sounds, and Kurt
frowned. To remind him of anything that makes him different from

315

an American boy is a great pain to him. When he did not step forward to embrace her, she turned toward me, nonplussed.

It is something to handle an adolescent boy. The primitives do that very well. Take him away from the women and when he returns from the ordeals and the rites he is a man and there's an end to all this oppressive mother love. I took her on one arm and Kurt on the other—a boy has enough to contend with in his own self—and I marched them along fast to the house down at the other end of the village street.

The village had had some charm in the early spring, with its white painted fences and houses and blossoming trees, but that day when we walked up the street there was so much green everywhere, such rank growth, lilac and honeysuckle both past their period of flowering, and the sky partly overcast so there was neither sunlight nor sharp shadow. In the corners of her little yard around the house, the weeds were knee-high. (Having lent us a farmer cottage, you would think my client's generosity would extend to sending a gardener twice a year to keep the weeds down, but no.)

However, once inside the house, it was really most astonishing how pleasant Eugénie had managed to make that shabby little room with bouquets of grasses, wild flowers, and whatnot. She ran and lit the kerosene lamps. Then she turned to us, smiling now, for she could see Kurt's stiffness softening out of his face. As his mother helped him off with his topcoat, he could, without loss of that precious dignity of an adolescent, quite naturally embrace her.

Ah, that was much better. She became her old self. "Go upstairs with the bags," she said. "Although I should send them up, somehow. For you are my guests. Especially this first day you are not to lift a finger," she called after us, again the woman whose endless courage gave one the strength to go on. In all the years there had never been a word of complaint from her, even in that first, that frightful year when we finally reached New York without money, without friends or acquaintances. For months I walked the streets of New York without success, and always she would welcome me back to that miserable little hole of a room in which we all three lived, with such grace of spirit that I could go on.

The only things I really knew were how to run a car and fly an airplane. I answered every advertisement, went to every kind of garage —in New York, Brooklyn, across the river in New Jersey, anywhere. But to no effect. Everywhere gruffness and terror. Naw, naw, naw. Then—ah, God, it is really fantastic, this country—I, an amateur, a patron of artists at home, unable to earn a living at motors, which I knew even in my dreams, I become an interior decorator! And to whom do I owe this belief in me, this beginning of a whole new life, I, a monarchist and a Black of Vienna? To a Jew! The ignominy, the humiliation! Yes, only from Jews in New York, from their organizations, did I get help. A Jew lent me the money. Lent, did I say? Pressed it into my hand, the check for two thousand dollars. "You!" he stuttered. "That you should go begging for work! It must never be!" You see, in his mind was still fresh the memory of that old Vienna he had left as a poor ghetto boy. "A count," he said. "It's simple. You must become a Park Avenue decorator."

For herself, for Kurt, Eugénie would take little of the money. I remember he had only one pair of woollen stockings that first winter, they were so expensive, and when she told how she had washed and darned them, she would say that she was a costly luxury—fifty dollars a month just to keep those stockings in order. Then she would laugh. "Really, I am of no earthly use to you," she would say. "Even Kurt does not need me. He's taken to getting his own breakfast not to disturb me when he knows I have a migraine on, the dear." So she would go on making light of everything so that I might not have her on my conscience, with all that I had to worry about and the great outlay that was necessary in this new profession of mine. The studio rent alone was two hundred dollars, the butler seventy-five. That was before I even started to pay for food and drink for the parties I had to give. As Eugénie herself pointed out, it was a double economy for her and the boy to live in the country while he was young. He could go to the village school, she would need no elaborate wardrobe, and I wasn't—a man alone—under endless social obligations. Had I introduced a wife into such a milieu, it would have been complicated and boring. We could not afford to bore anybody. Since I quite definitely had the social flair of the two and she was the solitary, the *spirituelle*, it seemed the only solution for us. She simply would not take one penny more than that fifty dollars, though how she managed I hardly knew, for although it was only fifty miles from town, I didn't get out there more than twice that whole winter. It was such a cold and lonely house, and bad enough that she should have to live there. I simply could not relax out there, and I needed frightfully to relax, I was so nervous all the time. So it was better to go to someone's place on Long Island and have breakfast brought to one's bed and good food and drinks and no responsibility and feel really refreshed, and unexpectedly make a really valuable connection—

one never knows. Eugénie understood all that, understood that no person must be unexplored, no time must be lost. She seemed never to mind when I saw them so rarely in that first winter.

But one year, two years, and now things were much better. Through an influential client (always a woman; one steps ahead on the breasts of women, so to speak), Kurt received a scholarship at this truly magnificent boarding school.

I saw the way he looked around at his bare bedroom, as if it were a strange place, opening his bag so slowly, as if he regretted to take up this life again. It was, indeed, a pity he must return to this forlorn little house, but even that would not be for long, as he knew. "So brace up," I told him. "Smile and make your mother happy. She has such a little while with you," I said, and going down the stairs with him, I wondered how to break the news of this to Eugénie. It must be managed carefully, I knew.

But how to describe that table? So charming! And done with what? Colored paper napkins, kitchen oilcloth, a pair of scissors, and candles, and whatnot from the ten-cent store. In the center of this delightful array, a casserole, the veritable French *cassoulet,* and inside, glazed with judicious cooking, squabs and tiny vegetables.

"But really, Eugénie!" I exclaimed. "How did you manage that? A *cordon bleu* could do no better! And squabs! Where did you get squabs out here?"

She was very pleased at this tribute. "Then I really did surprise you? I am so happy! You know your friend, that Johnson boy, Kurt? He has a new rifle and was most anxious to use it. So I paid him. Six cents for the BB shots and ten cents to clean them, and a blessing to be rid of the wild pigeons, his mother said. So, you see, I am learning to be an American. Also a *cordon bleu.* Please taste it, Kurt, taste my *chef-d'œuvre.*" She leaned over and joggled his elbow to get him started.

It is not a food a growing boy enjoys—a bite of bird flesh in wine sauce—and in any case neither she nor Kurt got very far with their meal, because, during the small talk of passing this and that, most casually I said we had only this day with her, the Vanderdorn boy having invited Kurt for a summer of travel. She dropped her hands from the table.

"Impossible!" she said to me. "He cannot go!"

Just like that, without preamble or softening or grace. Kurt stopped eating and, like any man, began to shift in his chair and look anywhere rather than at her.

"Please, Eugénie," I begged. "It's most wonderful, really. First they go to the plantation near Charleston, and then the whole family goes to the Rocky Mountains. Kurt will see the whole of America. Marvellous. And such valuable connections for his future. Congratulations are in order. But really, Eugénie."

"No, no, no," she went on monotonously, as if to herself alone. "No, he can't. Kurt must not—he can't." Kurt's eyes grew wide with fear. Nothing in his life had prepared him for this, his mother, who had always been so gracious, now with a face like death. I begged her to be sensible, but she shrugged off my words and leaned toward Kurt.

"Kurt! You won't leave me? You don't want to, do you, Kurt?" Kurt could not meet her eyes, naturally not. The boy had made his first friend, an American, and he was happy at this, his first step, his own, in a strange land.

"I don't care," he mumbled, ashamed of the tension, ashamed to look at his mother.

She could not even read the disappointment in his face, so happy was she for the bare, unwilling words. "You see?" she said to me. "Kurt does not wish to go."

If he could not face his mother, I, his father, must and could. "I'm afraid it's too late for Kurt to change his mind. I accepted for him," I said. "They leave in a few days from the Vanderdorn estate outside of Philadelphia. It is my fault, I know, but I had not the time to consult you, and so I took the responsibility in my own hands."

"No, no. This is my time with Kurt," she began all over again. "You promised it when I allowed you to take him away to school. Don't you remember, Richard? You promised me the summer with him!"

Of course I had promised it. But that was before he went off to school, before he knew any boy his own age. Would she never realize that we were beggars, opportunists, who must seize every advantage as it comes?

"That's all I asked of you—this summer," she went on, her voice rising. "I must, I must have something!"

I really could not understand her. So suddenly had this happened, so completely without cause this hysteria. How could she, his mother, be anything but happy that her son at last had an opportunity and a

friend of his own in this strange land? It is hard enough for him. He
speaks English with an accent and all that. Why burden him further
with father, mother, with love? Women have the greed of spoiled children. They will break the world rather than yield this self-centered
thing they call happiness. The senseless, the insane ego! Even revolution, homelessness, the death of a whole world teaches them nothing! Ah, what a business I went through with her.

"It is only this summer, a few weeks," I said. "Why take it so
seriously?"

"Oh no. I know better," she said, staring away with a terrible sadness in her eyes. "I have lost him. I have lost him forever."

"He is only going away for a few weeks of fun," I said. "You would
not deny that to Kurt, would you? What else is there for him this
summer? Be sensible," I urged her. "You were not brought up to be
a housekeeper. It will be much more comfortable for you not to have
to prepare meals on time for a big, hungry boy. And it will be better
for Kurt. He could not possibly bring a friend here." To all that she
nodded an abstracted agreement, for even she knew that his social
life must never enter this house, with its kitchen filled with old golf
bags, gloves, hats, junk; in summer, flies, soiled dishes always standing about. Kurt must go on with the life he had started so well in
boarding school. I would see ahead and work it out for him. All that
would in any capital of Europe be his by right of birth and family
connection for hundreds of years back must be carefully managed in
America. Eugénie and I had come through the first part—the homelessness, the despair—in agreement and fortitude; now, if only I could
persuade her to be reasonable about Kurt's future!

"Boys need lots of good food," I said. "At regular intervals. You
can't even cook, and why should you?"

"But I am learning," she said, and brightened up. "The squabs—
aren't they delicious?"

"My poor Eugénie," I said. "That is once in a life. But string beans
in the pot without water—remember?" I laughed. "No, no. You are
neither housekeeper nor cook, thank God."

I saw immediately that I had gone too far. Her eyes filled with
tears. She looked across at the remains of the bird on my plate, at the
bird untouched on Kurt's, and hers also barely stabbed at, and then
she turned her head away.

I did not dare look toward Kurt. Too bad that he must see and
hear all this. But what is one to do? That is life. And what could I
say? Sometimes it is easier to say soothing words to a stranger than to

a woman you have been married to so long that certain kinds of sentiment are false, no matter how much you love her. We sat there, all
of us, carefully not looking at each other.

"I am utterly to blame," I said, "and I am sorry. It would be most
embarrassing, because of certain business plans, to withdraw Kurt
now. I cannot, I dare not, afford such whims. After this I swear to you
I will make no more plans without consulting you. After this we will
all be together. Always. Trust me, Eugénie."

"Trust?" At last she looked directly into my eyes. "Trust you?"
she said, with her eyes blazing. "You *boulevardier!*"

It was frightful. In all these years, whatever she knew or guessed, it
had never been acknowledged by word or glance. No matter what
the provocation. Then, suddenly, this! How could she do it to Kurt?
Or to me, for that matter? Sometimes people go away right in front
of you. Their eyes turn inward and go staring within and you cannot
tell what land they are living in or what thoughts make their mouths
twitch in that strange way. When they look out at you again, it is with
the eyes of a stranger, an implacable enemy. So now Eugénie turned
from Kurt to me and back again to Kurt.

It must have been something that happened during that long winter when, for the first time in her life, she had been without Kurt.
Because she had been so humble, really, and willing when he went
away to the school in the fall. She knew it was bad for him to be lying
late in bed reading or mooning and saying "What's there to do?" all
the time, and doing nothing, not even helping her with the dishes.
She saw as clearly as I that it was no good for a boy to be cooped up
with his mother after a certain age. "And after his schooling, Kurt
will marry," she said then, "and I'll be left alone anyhow."

"But you like it, don't you, up here, Eugénie?" I asked her at that
time. "Or would you prefer to come in and stay at the studio, perhaps
for a month?"

"Oh no, not at all," she said. Sometimes, when I think I must be
to blame, I remember that answer. "I should only be in the way," she
said. And that would have been true. I could leave her in the country with a clear conscience, for she had none of the petty lonelinesses
of the immature. Occasionally, when I did run up, I would walk into
the house and find her, broom in hand, reading, lost to everything.
She would come awake with a start when I called out. "There is not
enough time in a day," she would say, and tell me about her reading,
her painting, her long walks. So, naturally, I thought she would be
all right. But perhaps the loneliness of an American village—no cafés,

everyone shut tight to himself, and she an alien—perhaps it was too much even for her.

Yet what could I possibly have done? Introduce her suddenly, a wife, into my social life? To those steel-thin, shiny women? Isn't it enough that *I* must live with them? Something one must keep.

So here we were, Eugénie, Kurt, and I, sitting at a festive table in tragic silence. Quickly, quickly, a diversion, anything to bring a light back into their sad faces. I remembered the photographs of me taken by that millionaire girl Millicent, who wants—ah, they all want, all of them—to be a creative artist. "Here, Eugénie, look," I said as I returned to the table. "Please choose the one you like best." I spilled the large, shiny proofs under her eyes. "It is to illustrate an article about my work."

Kurt's hand stretched out quickly for them. He was of an age, you know, when a boy turns to his father. The way he wound his arm around my chair, leaned over me—it was almost tactless in its neglect of her. She took up the photographs as he dropped them to the table. Slowly she ruffled them.

"It comes clear in a photograph, the first signs of corruption," she said bitterly. "Your mouth, your eyes. Like a movie actor." She stared into my face. "America has done this to you."

The boy caught his breath. No one moved. No one spoke. She stared at her little gala dinner, and sighed. Then she arose, removed the plates, and brought in an apricot tart. At any other time it would have been something to exclaim about. I managed to compliment her on it and urged Kurt to taste it. She, also, urged him to eat. Her voice now was over-quiet, humble, but the boy shook his head. She saw that what Kurt had just witnessed could not be sweetened with an apricot tart.

To run away then, the woman's way; to run away when she is crossed or defeated, like a spoiled child. She excused herself. "It's really been too much of a day for me. Do you mind if I clear the table now?" she asked. "Please, nobody move."

After she went upstairs the boy and I were free. We could look at each other. At first with a feeling of guilt; then our voices rose more certainly. Kurt struck the match for my pipe. Ah, it was good. At last we had conversation, and all the stories of his year at school came out —the friends, real friends, Americans, his so thrilling life at school, his teachers, the young man who took him bird-hunting. Everything that Eugénie must have been waiting to hear he told me now. I knew that she must be hearing his voice—not the exact words, only the happy, assured tones that were rolling up the staircase to her avid ears. Ah, well, it could not be helped, her suffering. He would come back to her when he was more certain of himself. She was too hasty. *Kurt is lost to me forever.* That was nothing to say before a growing boy. That sort of bitter looking into the ultimate future is something one keeps to oneself, out of self-respect, out of respect for the other, out of respect for life.

But there it was. Whatever she had lost for the time being, I had gained a son, a big, fine boy. We went upstairs when he was all talked out, arms around each other, the blood flowing from one to the other, strong and assured. What a moment that is for a father! I hoped she was asleep, that she need not hear, like an outcast, the boy talking to me drowsily while I sat on the edge of his bed. At last, under cover of the darkness, he threw his long, bony arms around my neck and kissed me. "Father, Father," he murmured. "Oh, Father . . ."

When I turned toward Eugénie's bedroom, it was with a feeling of guilt. With her usual tact, however, she had withdrawn to the far side of the bed and turned her back to me, so that I had privacy. Whether she was asleep or awake I could not know, she lay so still.

But for me there was no sleep. The lumpy mattress, the miserable thin sheets, the narrow blanket, the wind roaring like waters in the flood, the whole thing so strange; to be lying in a hard bed in a strange land and all the smells and sounds strange, and even the sky weird and violent and the livid moon bright on my face—no curtains, of course. How could she sleep in such a place? Somehow it had never affected her, judging by the letters she wrote me. I would get a letter almost every day, and many of them would be sent special delivery— that was her one extravagance—although they were about nothing, a bird she saw, or something she read, nothing of importance. And I lay there cold and unsleeping, but not moving nearer her, because— ah, well.

I must have drifted off to sleep despite the cold, for something, a movement, awoke me. She was slipping out of the covers. I lay still and listened to the swishing sound of her in Kurt's room. When she returned and stood over the bed ready to slip into it, her face was so gray and terrible that I sat up and cried out, "What is it? What's happened, Eugénie!"

"Nothing. Sh-h-h. Nothing," she whispered. "I thought Kurt might be uncovered."

Ach, the endless dumb obstinacy of women!

"Eugénie!" I said. Now I was really annoyed. "What in God's

name do you think will happen to him? He's been away from you all winter and look at him, a head taller and strong as an ox! You cannot go around wiping his nose forever!"

No answer.

I said nothing more. Of what use? Her sorrow was really all she had. Kurt would escape today. From now on his life must be healthy, I thought, steeling myself against this woman by my side. I, his father, am responsible to him and to my ancestors for him. About this there can be no sentimentality.

In a little while she arose. I heard the rumble of ashes being shaken out of the kitchen stove, and I must have fallen asleep again, for when Kurt and I got downstairs a delightful breakfast was already prepared. She shared in the conversation at the table and she was her sweet, gracious self again, our departure taken for granted, and after breakfast she helped Kurt with his packing.

He had picked out the few things he wanted to save and all about him in his room lay books he would no longer read, a broken model airplane which had taken a whole winter to build, all the oddments and junk a boy collects whether he has money for toys or not. He was finished with all that childishness now, the chrysalis outgrown, and stepping out to his larger youth. She was being so nice about it, bringing him his gun, everything, and as we sat eating sandwiches and milk at noon, there was an atmosphere of something finished, of farewells made and the air empty and strained, although we were not leaving until the evening train.

"There's the two-forty," said Kurt. It slipped out, showing how anxious he was to be off.

"Of course," Eugénie said quickly. "An hour more or less. Really, why not take it, Richard? Dinner, a movie in New York—it would be so jolly for Kurt."

It was enough to look at Kurt's glowing face to see what pleasure it would give him.

"But are you sure you won't mind?" I asked her.

Now I realize the smile on her face was too extravagant. Only now.

We all walked to the station together. When the train drew in, she stood there, profoundly still. She did not put up a hand to touch Kurt or me. Only that upward-looking, radiant, sweet face. I kissed her, but Kurt was too embarrassed to make the first move of emotion. He stood frozen, and then finally he looked down at her.

I am glad his eyes were full of the love he could not express. His hand just brushed over her arm, but, you know, in such a way—gentle, loving. And still she did not move; only her lips began to flutter when his hand tentatively, softly, brushed along her arm.

As nearly as I can find out what happened, she never went back to the house. Straight from the station she must have started off on one of those long walks of hers. The pond was ten miles away and it had a long, sloping beach. She must have walked straight into it, gloves, cane, and all, as some fishermen found her the next day, fastidious to the end.

As for Kurt, it was good he was with strangers. I went immediately to see him. He was immobile. Not now, I told him. Someday we will both try to understand. Now it is only necessary to know that she wished it so.

No more was said. One must grow, one must experience many things before one can taste the true bitterness of death. To a boy, it is still only a fact. Someday he will need to know, to understand. Then the day of reckoning. Of explanation.

Until then everything is finished. I might as well go on the trip to Idaho. I have never seen a ranch or the West, and it isn't as if they knew her. I shall go to Amelia's at Shinnecock Hills and we are to meet Geoffrey and take the plane at La Guardia Field. After all, why should their plans be spoiled? My relations with them are, in a way, professional, and a man cannot, simply cannot, telephone as late as this and say "I had a wife." That would be most embarrassing. I might even get to do Maggie's new ranch house if I handle her impressively. Kurt is settled for the summer in a way that is most fortunate, and I, of course, shall get through somehow, though I can't stop thinking about it.

What I cannot get over is that I, who am so clever, should not have sensed that something was wrong. I reconstruct the whole day over and over again; I go over that whole visit to see where I might have stopped the thing. But it was like any other day in a country village— nothing happening with the sharp form in people or event that gives such style to city life. Except for that outburst at table, quite natural in any mother. Why didn't she give me a hint? Why didn't she say what was really the matter? On the contrary. Walking toward the station, I asked, "Are you all right?," meaning about Kurt. "Yes, my darling," she answered, her eyes profoundly tender, looking into mine the way they did when we first fell in love. Who, looking into that worn face, could possibly suspect what must have formed already in her mind? "I'll try to run up if you like," I told her, walking along with Kurt on my other arm, so content with my whole family. "No. On no account. No," she said. And then she whispered, "I'm ashamed. I'm ashamed, Richard, of the way I behaved." Then later, apropos of nothing, "Do you think, because you are so clever, you can escape all the consequences?" I looked at her, bewildered, and she said, "Oh, I'm so sorry I said that, Richard. Forgive me for everything." Her face, as the train slipped by, was so sweet and virginal, looking toward us, that I was completely reassured.

And it was immediately after that—think of it!—that she turned and went off on that walk. What is one to think or say about a thing like that? She, who was always so considerate!

A KILLING

❖

ROGER ANGELL

THE YOUNG MAN with steel-rimmed glasses walked into the dark hall of the apartment house and let the door close behind him. In a moment the clicking of the lock release stopped and he heard a door being opened two flights above him. A shrill feminine voice called down, "Who's that?" He stood still and said nothing. "Who's down there?" the voice cried, more insistently. Let her call, he thought. It was what Mr. Penney had said was one of the First Points of Approach. In a walkup you rang an upstairs bell but you didn't go up. No housewife would listen to you if you made her wait while you climbed two or three flights and her expecting God knows who —the iceman, perhaps, or the delicatessen or maybe even a boy friend. A salesman would just make her sore. Silently he put down his big case and listened to his breathing in the hall until he heard the upstairs door close. When his eyes became accustomed to the darkness, he carried his case over to a door on his right. He took off his hat and smoothed down his pale hair. He felt in his right overcoat pocket for the box containing the matched English military hairbrushes ("Our quickest seller and a fine opening line," Mr. Penney had said), but he didn't take it out. You didn't show what you had to sell at the door, but you had it handy. First establish your personality, then your merchandise. He felt for his discharge button on his overcoat lapel and made sure it was right side up. That was his own best First Point of Approach. He bent over and read the smudged typewritten card beside the door: "Foltz." Mrs. Foltz. All set. He pressed the doorbell.

Smiling, not touching the door frame, he waited for almost thirty seconds. He was about to press the bell again when the door was thrown open by a woman. She wore a faded pink housecoat that bulged at the seams, and her plump face was powdered dead white. Her bleached hair was pinned in tight curls against her head. Without curiosity she leaned against the door jamb and looked at him with pale little eyes.

"Mrs. Foltz," he began hastily, "Mrs. Foltz, I trust I'm not disturbing you. I would consider myself an intruder if I were not convinced that I am here to help you. I am here because I know that you, like every American housewife, are interested in the latest and the best in modern accessories to ease work and strain in your home. My concern also is anxious to get your reaction to our line of personal accessories for the entire household. We have hairbrushes for your husband and children as well as the finest in hair and nail brushes for feminine allure." He paused for a moment. The woman hadn't moved or spoken; she was still staring at him dully, or rather at the top of his head. Damn! It was all wrong. He should have mentioned brushes right away. Maybe she was a dummy or something.

"What is it?" she said abruptly. "What have you got?"

"Brushes," he said loudly. "Brushes, Madam." He fingered the box in his pocket and wondered whether he should begin again.

Just then there was a hoarse cry from inside the apartment. "Who's 'at? Who's your pal out there?"

Mrs. Foltz suddenly bent from the waist in a loud giggle of laughter. She straightened up, her hand over her mouth, and giggled louder. "My God!" she gasped. "My good, sweet God!" She turned from the open door and walked back into the apartment. She was still laughing. "It's the brush man," she whispered loudly. "The Fuller Brush man."

"Well, go ahead," the voice inside the apartment said. "Don't just stand there. Ask him in, give 'm a drink. I gotta see a Fuller Brush man. Don't let him stand out there in the cold hall with his brushes. Bring him in here."

Mrs. Foltz came back to the door, dabbing at her eyes with a tiny handkerchief. "C'mon in," she said, still giggling faintly. "Come in and sit down."

The young man picked up his case hastily and followed her into the apartment. This was a break, he thought, after a bad start. All the good sales were made inside; in the hall you didn't have a chance. He put his hat down on a chair inside the door and carried his case into the room. The place was small, and the air was thick with smoke and the smell of whiskey. Although it was still afternoon, the shades on the two windows had been drawn and a bridge lamp in the corner was lit. A woman was sitting on a small, flowered couch between the windows, and before her was a small table crowded with two whiskey bottles, a pitcher of water, an overflowing ashtray, and a huge glass bowl, almost an urn, half filled with potato chips. There were ashes and bits of potato chips on the floor. The woman was sitting carefully erect in one corner of the couch, a glass in her hand. Her wrinkled purple dress was pulled up over her knees and she wore a black velvet hat slightly askew. She looked about forty.

"This is Mrs. Kernochan," said Mrs. Foltz. "We were having a little drink here. Honey, this is the brush man."

"Sit down," said Mrs. Kernochan hoarsely. "Sit down there where I can see you. Take off your coat, Mr. Fuller."

"No, thank you," he said, smiling. He put his case down and sat uncomfortably in a little wooden chair under the bridge lamp. "I'll just keep it on, thanks."

"Lily, give Mr. Fuller a drink," said Mrs. Kernochan, squinting her eyes at him across the room.

"I am," said Mrs. Foltz. She poured some whiskey into a glass. "You like it neat or with water?"

"I don't think—"

"Oh, go ahead, go ahead," Mrs. Kernochan said. "We won't snitch on you, Mr. Fuller."

"All right, then," he said. "A small one with water."

"We haven't got no ice," said Mrs. Foltz. She walked over and handed him his drink. "We just ran out."

"So you're Mr. Fuller," Mrs. Kernochan said. "The original one and only. My God! Imagine you right here in the same room with me. How's business, Mr. Fuller?"

The young man smiled and glanced at Mrs. Foltz. "Well, you see, Madam," he said quickly, "I don't represent the Fuller people. They have their line and we have *ours*. Now, I don't like to knock a competitor, so I'll just say that we think we have about as fine an assortment of merchandise as you can find in the field. Now, if you'll let me show you . . ." He put his drink on the floor and knelt down to open his case.

"The original one and only," repeated Mrs. Kernochan, peering at him.

"Honey, didn't you hear him?" asked Mrs. Foltz as she sat down on the other end of the couch. "He's not Mr. Fuller. He don't even work for them. He's Mr. . . . ."

"Mr. Schumacher," the young man said, from the floor. He had his case open and was arranging brushes on the floor. "Mr. Linwood P. Schumacher." He looked up and smiled at Mrs. Foltz.

"Now, Madam," he began, "here you see our complete line. A brush for every imaginable need. You will notice that they are ornamental as well as useful. The modern plastic bristles are—"

"Prince Hal!" cried Mrs. Kernochan from the couch. "My Prince Hal!" Mr. Schumacher started and almost upset his drink.

"Old Prince Hal," she repeated loudly. "Ah, you were the boy. Always in trouble. Always men on the bases. But how you could bear down! Prince Hal and King Carl! What a pair! You two and Fat Freddie. Those were the days, huh, Hal?"

Mr. Schumacher looked around wildly. For a moment he seemed ready to bolt from the room. Then he saw that Mrs. Foltz was shaking with laughter.

"Ballplayers!" she gasped. "She always talks ballplayers when she gets like this. Ballplayers or babies. Today it's ballpayers. She thinks you're Hal Schumacher now. My God! Prince Hal!" She rocked back and forth on the couch, dabbing at her eyes.

"Hubbell, Schumacher, and Fitzsimmons," Mrs. Kernochan intoned, looking now at her glass. "Fitz on Saturday and you and Carl on the doubleheaders. Those were the days, huh? Remember 1933? Remember 1936, Schumie?"

"I'm afraid there's a misunderstanding," said Mr. Schumacher nervously. Still on his knees, he rummaged in his pocket for a card. "I'm Linwood P. Schumacher. No relation to the ballplayer, I'm afraid." He smiled up at Mrs. Foltz, but she was still laughing too hard to see him. "Prince Hal!" she repeated, almost speechless. "Always in trouble."

"You look different, Hal," said Mrs. Kernochan anxiously. She was squinting across the room at him again. "You look thinner. How's the soupbone, Schumie?"

"Well," he said slowly, "I did lose some weight in the Army, but it's coming back now."

"We've missed you, Hal," Mrs. Kernochan said, nodding her head. She downed her drink and unsteadily set the glass on the table. "We've all missed you. I remember when they said you were washed up. And what happened to the Giants then, Hal? What happened then? Who did they get? I'll tell you who. Mungo, that's who." She almost spat the name out. "Van Lingle Mungo. Just a refugee from Brooklyn."

She was silent, vaguely watching him as he began to put the brushes back in his case. Suddenly she groped on the couch beside her and found a pocketbook. Clutching it, she stood up, showering more pieces of potato chips on the floor.

"I'll take them," she said, looking into her purse. He could see the tears squeezing out of her eyes. "I'll take your dear, sweet brushes, Hal—every last one of them. You don't have to get on your knees, Schumie." She found some wadded bills and held them out to him blindly.

He had risen to his feet and stood in the middle of the room, looking from the money to Mrs. Foltz. Mrs. Foltz had stopped laughing. Now she laboriously stood up and walked over to the weeping Mrs. Kernochan.

"Now, wait a minute, Gloria," she said warningly. "This isn't Hal Schumacher and you know it. Hal Schumacher's up at the Polo Grounds with the Giants right now. And you don't need no brushes. Hal Schumacher isn't selling no brushes."

"Don't you do it!" cried Mrs. Kernochan. "Don't you stop me! Schumie was nothing in your life, Lily Foltz, but he'll always be my Prince Hal. And now look at him, with his brushes, the poor lamb!" She burst into a flood of tears, got up, pushed past Mrs. Foltz, and pressed the money into Mr. Schumacher's hand. "Take it, Hal," she sobbed. "Take it and have that chipped elbow operated on."

Mr. Schumacher looked over her shoulder at Mrs. Foltz. She looked at the weeping woman for a minute, then shrugged and turned back to the couch. "O.K.," she said. "Maybe it'll shut her up."

Hastily, Mr. Schumacher sat down on the chair and pulled out his account book. On the printed slip he checked off the names of the brushes and added the figures up. He looked at the money in his hand and felt in his pocket for change. "There you are," he said, cheerfully. "Exactly twenty-seven fifty for the entire line." Then he ripped the receipt off, carried the case to the couch, and took out the brushes in handfuls. They made quite a pile beside Mrs. Foltz. He handed her the receipt and the change. "I'll just give it to you to hold, Mrs. Foltz," he said, talking fast. "Two dollars and a half makes thirty. And thank *you!*"

"O.K.," said Mrs. Foltz. She stood up and walked out behind him. At the door he stopped and looked back, but Mrs. Kernochan had collapsed onto the little wooden chair and was sobbing quietly.

"I'm sure she'll find it useful," he said to Mrs. Foltz as he put on his hat. "We don't often sell the complete line to one person, but I'm sure she'll be satisfied. Of course, I don't usually sell my samples, but with a big order like this at the end of the day I made an exception, just for your friend. Now with—"

"O.K., O.K.," said Mrs. Foltz quickly. "Just beat it now, Prince Hal, that's a good boy."

He went out and slammed the door behind him.

In the hall he put down his empty case—without the brushes it was very light—and lit a cigarette. Twenty-seven fifty! It was a killing, nothing less. Already he knew that Mr. Penney would mention it at the next sales meeting. Perhaps he might even be called on to give a little talk about it. As he picked up his case and started down the hall, he decided that it wouldn't do to tell about the liquor and the ballplayers. They might not understand. But no matter how you looked at it, it was a killing. "The initial resistance was high," he would say, "but once I got admittance and set up the display . . ." He began to whistle as he opened the outside door.

GOODBYE, MY LOVE

❖

MOLLIE PANTER-DOWNES

ADRIAN'S MOTHER welcomed them as though this were just an ordinary visit, with nothing particular about it. They found her, as they had found her so many times before, working in the big herbaceous border facing the sea, crouching girlishly with a frail little green plant in the palm of one earthy hand. She greeted them abstractedly, pushing back her wispy gray hair with the back of the hand that held the trowel and leaving a smudge. While they talked, Ruth looked at the border, which Adrian had built for his mother on a ledge of the cliff garden, facing it with a paved path beside which the rosemary and the seeded mulleins sprang. Even now, in late autumn, with the sea mist hanging in drops on the spiders' webs that festooned the last red-hot pokers, it was beautiful. Sometimes Ruth wondered if the cold woman, her mother-in-law, didn't express some secret frustration in these savage reds and yellows, these sullen purples, which she caused to gush out of the warm Cornish earth.

Ruth was grateful now for the lack of outward emotion which had so often chilled her. When Mrs. Vyner asked Adrian, as they walked back to the house, "Which day do you go?," she might have been asking about some weekend visit that he was going to make. He said "Wednesday," and she repeated "Wednesday" in a vague voice, her attention wandering to a bough of japonica which the wind had loosened from the wall they were passing. She sat down on the porch to unlace her shocking old gardening boots.

"I suppose you don't know where you're being sent," she said. "I know it has to be very secret nowadays, because of the submarines."

"I think it's Syria," Adrian said. "From the stuff we're taking, I'm pretty certain."

"You can't be sure," Mrs. Vyner said. "There's a Mrs. Mason, who's come to live at the Cross Glens. You know, Adrian, where old

Colonel Fox used to live. Well, Captain Mason went off with a topee and shorts, poor man, and the next thing she heard was that he was sitting up on a fiord in Iceland. It's all done to put the spies on the wrong track. I'll point Mrs. Mason out to you in church tomorrow."

Later, when the Rector came in, he made more of an occasion of it than his wife had. He gave Ruth a heartier kiss than usual. "It's good of you to think of the old people when you've got so little time left," he said. Ruth disliked the phrase "so little time left." Suddenly she was inordinately conscious of time. The house was full of it, ticking between simpering shepherdesses on the mantelpiece, grumbling out of the tall mahogany case in the hall, nervously stuttering against Adrian's wrist. The church clock, just across the rectory garden, struck every quarter. Ruth thought, "Four days, and one of them nearly gone."

After dinner the Rector got out the *Times* atlas and pored over it with Adrian, while Mrs. Vyner sat knitting a sock and talking about the garden and the village. The Rector's broad thumb, tracing the possible course that a convoy would take out into the Atlantic, swooped down upon the Cape. He and Adrian sounded quiet and contented, as though they were plotting a fishing holiday.

Ruth and her mother-in-law sat knitting a little apart, chatting in low voices.

"The black spot has been dreadful on the roses this year," Mrs. Vyner said. "Really dreadful. What do you plan to do after he's gone?"

"I shall get a job," Ruth said. "I thought I might go into one of the services. Shorthand and typing ought to be useful. Anyway, I'm going to do something."

"That's sensible," Mrs. Vyner said. "After all, you'll be perfectly free, won't you? It isn't as though you have any ties."

"No, I've got no ties at all," Ruth said.

When they were undressing in the big, chilly guest room, she said to Adrian, "Somehow, now that you're going, I wish we'd had a child. You know, the Sonnets and all that—'And nothing 'gainst Time's scythe can make defence, Save breed, to brave him when he takes thee hence.'"

"I'm not sorry," Adrian said. "This way I shan't be missing anything. When I get back we'll have the fun of kids together."

"Yes, we will," Ruth said, raising her voice slightly, as though she were talking to someone behind him. "How long do you think the war's going to last?" she asked, picking up her hairbrush.

"Darling! As though it matters a damn what I think. I don't know—maybe another couple of years or so."

"Some people say it will be over next spring."

"Some people talk a hell of a lot of nonsense," he said.

The bed was a big, old-fashioned double, its mattress divided into two gentle troughs where successive generations of guests had lain. Ruth got in and pulled the covers up to her chin. She watched Adrian moving around the room. "They were an awful long time demobilizing people after the last war, weren't they?" she said. "Maybe the firm would make a special application for you, or whatever they do. After all, they'll be terribly anxious to get you back. Mr. Hobday told me himself that he didn't know how they were going to get on without you."

"Oh, they'll manage," Adrian said.

At intervals all through the night, Ruth kept waking up and listening to the sea. She pictured it running up the jagged inlets of the long, cruel coast, along which she and Adrian had often sailed in his little boat. He was asleep, breathing softly and lightly, his face close to her shoulder. She lay thinking this way until it began to get light and the birds started shouting in Mrs. Vyner's wild garden.

They went to church next morning, walking through the gate in the yew hedge into the bleak little churchyard. The congregation that had come to hear the Rector preach was small and badly dressed, for the parish was thinly populated and poor. It was easy, without Mrs. Vyner's whisper, to identify the more prosperous Mrs. Mason, tweedy in a front pew, with a plain little girl on either side. Captain Mason had at least provided her with two defences 'gainst Time's scythe, hideous though they were in their spectacles and with gold bands round their teeth, before he took himself off to his Icelandic fiords. Ruth looked across the aisle at Mrs. Mason, who was cheerfully singing the Te Deum. "I'll get used to it, too," she thought. The only other representative of the local gentry in church was Major Collingwood, who read the lessons in a voice beautifully husky with Irish whiskey and buttonholed Adrian afterward in the porch. "Well, my boy! Just off, I hear," he said. "Going East, I suppose? No, no, don't tell me—mustn't ask, mustn't ask. Well, it looks like a big showdown there this winter. Hitler's going to try and break through. Yes, we've got to be prepared for heavy fighting, heavy fighting."

"The old fool," Ruth thought. She walked away and began reading some of the inscriptions on the crosses of local gray stone at the heads of the few green mounds in the churchyard. Most of the men were fishermen who had been drowned in winter storms along the coast. "John Tregarthen, who lost his life off Black Point, December 10th, 1897," she read. "Samuel Cotter, drowned in the wreck of the Lady May, January 25th, 1902."

Adrian came up and took her arm. "Hungry?" he asked. She shook her head, and he saw that there were tears in her eyes. "Damn that old idiot!" he said. "Darling, it's going to be a quiet winter. What do you bet? We'll be stuck in some bloody desert, eating our heads off with boredom. We're going to be forgotten men, forgotten by Hitler, forgotten by the General Staff, forgotten by—"

"It's all right," she said.

Mrs. Vyner came up, fastening her shabby fur round her long, thin neck, and the three of them walked back into the rectory garden.

Next day, Ruth and Adrian went back to London. That night they went out with friends and had plenty to drink. Ruth was able to sleep that night. The next evening, their last, they dined quietly in the flat. She had cooked the things he liked best, but neither of them had much appetite. At last they gave up trying. The one clock in the flat went on sucking time, like an endless string of macaroni, into its bright, vacant face. Every clock in London seemed to crash out the quarters outside their drawn curtains. When the telephone rang as they sat over their coffee, Adrian got up to answer it as though he were glad of the interruption. It turned out to be a man who used to be in love with Ruth and who had been out of England for some time. Adrian had always disliked him, but he sounded very cordial now. Afterward he said, "I'm glad Mike has turned up again. I want you to go out with him. That's why I said to him just now, 'When I'm gone I'd take it as a personal favor if you'd give Ruth a ring now and then and take her out and give her a good time.'"

"I don't want to go out with Mike," she said.

"Please do," he said. "It will make me feel better to think of you looking pretty, out dancing and enjoying yourself."

The following morning there was plenty to do—breakfast, a taxi, last-minute things. Meeting at some moment in the bustling, efficient nightmare, Adrian said, "I don't suppose I'll be able to wire

you, but I'll give someone a letter to post from the port after we
sail," and Ruth said, "That will be fine." She felt cold and frightened and a little sick, as though this were the morning fixed for a
major operation. She wasn't going to the station, so they said goodbye in the hall, a tiny cupboard built for a man to hang his hat in,
for a woman to read a telephone message in—not for heroic partings.

"Well, take care of yourself," Adrian said. "Don't forget what we
said last night. If the bombings start again, you go down to Cornwall, you go anywhere. Anyway, you get out of here. Promise?
Otherwise I won't be able to keep my mind on this war."

"I promise," Ruth said, smiling. Language was inadequate, after
all. One used the same words for a parting which might be for years,
which might end in death, as one did for an overnight business trip.
She put her arms tightly round him and said, "Goodbye, my love."

"Darling," he said. "I can't begin to tell you—"

"Don't," she said. "Don't."

The door shut, and presently Ruth heard the taxi driving away.
She went back into the living room, sat down, and looked at the
breakfast things. Adrian's cup was still half full of coffee, a cigarette
stubbed out in the wet saucer. The cigarette seemed to have acquired a significance, to be the kind of relic which in another age
would have been put carefully away in a little box with the toenail
parings of a dead man, the hair clippings of a dead woman.

The next two days were bad. Ruth felt that the major operation
had come off but that she still had not come round from the anaes-
thetic. She pottered about the flat, went for a walk, bought some
things she wanted, dropped in at a movie and a concert. Time now
seemed to have receded, to be an enormous empty room which she
must furnish, like any other aimless woman, with celluloid shadows
of other people's happiness, with music that worked one up for
nothing. An hour or so after Adrian left, she put through a call to
Cornwall. "Adrian's gone," she said, and across the bad line, across
a rival conversation between two men who were trying to arrange
a board meeting, she heard her mother-in-law's calm, tired voice
saying, "Yes, it's Wednesday, isn't it? I knew he was going on
Wednesday." As she hung up the receiver, she suddenly remembered a French governess out of her childhood who used to rage,
weeping with anger, "Oh, you British, you British!" Her friends
rang her up with careful, planned kindness. Their stock opening
was "Has he gone? Oh, you poor darling! But aren't you terribly

relieved it's over?" and then they would date her up for a dinner or a theatre. Their manner was caressing but sprightly, as though she were a stretcher case who mustn't be allowed to know that she was suffering from shock. She slept very badly and had terrible dreams, into which the sea always seemed to come. She went to sleep picturing the blacked-out ship creeping out cautiously into the dark sea. The girl who washed her hair had once told her that her brother had been torpedoed off Norway and that he had been rescued, covered with oil from the explosion. In one of Ruth's dreams Adrian was struggling in a sea of oil while Mrs. Vyner, watching from her cliff garden, said, "Yes, it's Wednesday, isn't it? I knew he was going to drown on Wednesday."

On the third day, Ruth woke up feeling different. It was a queer feeling, exhausted but peaceful, as though her temperature had fallen for the first time after days of high fever. The end of something had been reached, the limit of some capacity for suffering. Nothing would be quite as bad again. She thought, "After all, there are thousands of women going through what I'm going through, and they don't make a fuss." She got up and dressed, with particular care, because she planned to go round to one of the women's recruiting stations today and find out about a job. It would be important to make a good impression at the first interview. Afterward she would write a funny letter about it to Adrian, she thought. Although it would probably be months before any mail caught up with him, she would write tonight and tell him not to worry, that she had finished making a fuss and was being sensible, like all the other women in England—like Mrs. Mason, the jolly woman in tweeds singing away at the Te Deum as though there were still something to be thankful about.

She was out all day, and when she put her latchkey in the door she was humming. As she took off her hat, the telephone rang, and she went to it, still humming, and said "Hello?" Adrian's voice said "Darling?" and her knees went weak. She sat down suddenly, while his voice raced on, sounding excited and a bit blurred, as though he had had two or three drinks. "I'm at the station. I'll be right round. Got to the port, but something went wrong. We all waited, then the message came through that it was cancelled. I wasn't allowed to phone you."

"Cancelled?" she said stupidly. "You're not going?"

"Not for another week," he said. "Maybe ten days. God, what

luck! I'm going out to find a taxi. Darling, don't move until I get there."

Ruth heard the click as he hung up, and she hung up slowly, too. For a moment she sat quite still. The clock on the table beside her sounded deafening again, beginning to mark off the ten days at the end of which terror was the red light at the end of the tunnel. Then her face became drawn and, putting her hands over it, she burst into tears.

COLETTE

❖

Vladimir Nabokov

IN THE EARLY YEARS of this century, a travel agency on Nevskiĭ Avenue, in St. Petersburg, displayed a three-foot-long model of an oak-brown international sleeping car. In delicate verisimilitude it completely outranked the painted tin of my clockwork trains. Unfortunately, it was not for sale. One could make out the blue upholstery inside, the embossed-leather lining of the compartment walls, their polished panels, inset mirrors, tulip-shaped reading lamps, and other maddening details. Spacious windows alternated with narrower ones, single or geminate, and some of these were of frosted glass. In a few of the compartments, the beds had been made up.

The then great and glamorous Nord Express (it was never the same after the first World War), consisting solely of such international cars, connected St. Petersburg with Paris. I would say directly with Paris had passengers not been obliged to change from one train to a superficially similar one at the Russo-German frontier (Verzhbolovo-Eydtkuhnen), where the ample and lazy Russian sixty-and-a-half-inch gauge was replaced by the fifty-six-and-a-half-inch standard of Europe and coal succeeded birch logs.

On this train in 1909, the year I now single out, my father shared a compartment with our tutor. My brother and I had one separated from theirs by a washroom. My two very small sisters had been left at home with nurses and aunts. My mother and her maid occupied a compartment adjacent to ours. The odd one of our party, my father's valet, Osip (whom, a decade later, the pedantic Bolsheviks were to shoot, because he appropriated our bicycles instead of turning them over to the nation), had a stranger for companion.

In April of that year, Peary had reached the North Pole. In May, Chaliapin had sung in Paris. In June, bothered by rumors of new and better Zeppelins, the United States War Department had told reporters of plans for an aerial Navy. In July, Blériot had flown from Calais to Dover (with a little additional loop when he lost his bearings). It was late August now. The firs and swamps of north-western Russia sped by, and on the following day gave way to German pine barrens and heather. Wearing a checked travelling cap and gray cotton gloves, my father sat reading a book in his compartment. At a collapsible table, my mother and I played a card game called *durachki*. Although it was still broad daylight, our cards, a glass, and, on a different plane, the locks of a suitcase were reflected in the window. Through forest and field, and in sudden ravines, and among scuttling cottages, those discarnate gamblers kept steadily playing on for steadily sparkling stakes.

"Ne budet-li, ty ved' ustal? [Haven't you had enough? Aren't you tired?]" my mother would ask, and then would be lost in thought as she slowly shuffled the cards. The door of the compartment was open and I could see the corridor window, where the wires—six thin black wires—were doing their best to slant up, to ascend skyward, despite the lightning blows dealt them by one telegraph pole after another, but just as all six, in a triumphant swoop of pathetic elation, were about to reach the top of the window, a particularly vicious blow would bring them down, as low as they had ever been, and they would have to start all over again.

When, on such journeys as these, the train changed its pace to a dignified amble and all but grazed house fronts and shop signs as we passed through Berlin, I used to feel a twofold excitement, which terminal stations could not provide. I saw a capital, with its toylike trams, linden trees, and brick walls, enter the compartment, hobnob with the mirrors, and fill to the brim the windows on the corridor side. This informal contact between train and city was one part of the thrill. The other was putting myself in the place of some passerby who, I imagined, was moved as I would be moved myself to see the long, romantic, auburn cars, with their connecting curtains as black as bat wings and their metal lettering copper-bright in the low sun, unhurriedly negotiate an iron bridge across an everyday thoroughfare and then turn, with all windows suddenly ablaze, around a last block of houses.

There were drawbacks to those optical interpenetrations. The wide-windowed dining car, a vista of chaste bottles of mineral water, mitre-folded napkins, and dummy chocolate bars (whose wrappers—Cailler, Kohler, and so forth—enclosed nothing but wood), would be perceived at first as a cool haven beyond a consecution of reeling blue corridors, but as the meal progressed toward its fatal last course, one would keep catching the car in the act of being recklessly sheathed, lurching waiters and all, in the landscape, while the landscape itself went through a complex system of motion, the daytime moon stubbornly keeping abreast of one's plate, the distant meadows opening fanwise, the near trees sweeping up on invisible swings toward the track, a parallel rail line suddenly committing suicide by anastomosis, a bank of grass rising, rising, rising, until the little witness of mixed velocities was made to disgorge his portion of *omelette aux confitures de fraises.*

It was at night, however, that the Compagnie Internationale des Wagons-Lits et des Grands Express Européens lived up to the magic of its name. From my bed under brother's bunk (Was he asleep? Was he there at all?), in the semi-darkness of our compartment, I watched things, and parts of things, and shadows, and sections of shadows cautiously moving about and getting nowhere. The woodwork gently creaked and crackled. Near the door that led to the toilet, a dim garment on a peg and, higher up, the tassel of the blue, bivalved night light swung rhythmically. It was hard to correlate those halting approaches, that hooded stealth, with the headlong rush of the outside night, which I knew *was* rushing by, spark-streaked, illegible.

I would put myself to sleep by the simple act of identifying myself with the engine driver. A sense of drowsy well-being invaded my veins as soon as I had everything nicely arranged—the carefree passengers enjoying the ride I was giving them, smoking, exchanging knowing smiles, nodding, dozing; the waiters and cooks and train guards (whom I had to place somewhere) merrily drinking beer in the diner; and myself, goggled and begrimed, peering out of the engine cab at the tapering track, at the ruby or emerald point in the black distance. And then, in my sleep, I would see something totally different—a glass marble rolling under a grand piano or a toy engine lying on its side with its wheels still working gamely.

A change in the speed of the train sometimes interrupted the current of my sleep. Slow lights were stalking by; each, in passing, investigated the same chink, and then a luminous compass measured the shadows. Presently, the train stopped with a long-drawn Westinghousian sigh. Something (my brother's spectacles, as it proved next day) fell from above. It was marvellously exciting to move to the foot of one's bed, with part of the bedclothes following, in order to undo cautiously the catch of the window shade, which could be made to slide only halfway up, impeded as it was by the edge of the upper berth.

Like moons around Jupiter, pale moths revolved about a lone lamp. A dismembered newspaper stirred on a bench. Somewhere on the train one could hear muffled voices, somebody's comfortable cough. There was nothing particularly interesting in the portion of station platform before me, and still I could not tear myself away from it until it departed of its own accord.

Next morning, wet fields with misshapen willows along the radius of a ditch or a row of poplars afar, traversed by a horizontal band of milky-white mist, told one that the train was spinning through northern France. In Paris, I had always time to purchase something—say, a little brass *Tour Eiffel,* coated with silver paint —before we boarded the Sud-Express, which, on its way to Madrid, dropped us at La Négresse station of Biarritz, a few miles from the Spanish frontier.

Biarritz still retained its quiddity in those days. Dusty blackberry bushes and weedy *terrains à vendre,* abounding in pretty moths, bordered the road that led to our villa. The Carlton was still being built. Some thirty-six years had to elapse before Brigadier General Samuel McCroskey would occupy the royal suite of the Hotel du Palais, where, in the fifties, that incredibly agile medium, Daniel Home, is said to have been caught stroking with his bare foot (in imitation of a ghost hand) the kind, trustful face of Empress Eugénie. On the promenade near the Casino, an elderly flower girl, with carbon eyebrows and a painted smile, nimbly slipped the plump torus of a carnation into the buttonhole of an intercepted stroller whose left jowl accentuated its royal fold as he glanced down sideways at the coy insertion of the flower.

Along the back line of the *plage,* various seaside chairs and stools supported the parents of straw-hatted children who were playing in front on the sand. I could be seen on my knees trying to set a found comb aflame by means of a magnifying glass. Men sported white trousers that to the eye of today would look as if they had comically shrunk in the washing; ladies wore, that particular season, light coats with silk-faced lapels, hats with big crowns and wide brims, dense embroidered white veils, frill-fronted blouses, frills at their wrists, frills on their parasols. The breeze salted one's lips. At a tremendous pace, a stray golden-orange butterfly came dashing across the palpitating *plage.*

Additional movement and sound were provided by venders hawking *cacahuètes,* sugared violets, pistachio ice cream of a heavenly green, cachou pellets, and huge convex pieces of dry, gritty, waferlike cake that came from a red barrel. With a distinctness that no later superpositions have dimmed, I see that vender stomp along through deep, mealy sand, with the heavy cask on his bent back. When called, he would sling it off his shoulder by a twist of its strap, bang it down on the sand in a Tower of Pisa position, wipe his face with his sleeve, and proceed to manipulate a kind of arrow-and-dial arrangement with numbers on the lid of the cask. The arrow rasped and whirred around. Luck was supposed to fix the size of a *sou's* worth of wafer. The bigger the piece, the more I was sorry for him.

The process of bathing took place on another part of the beach. Attendants, burly Basques in black bathing suits, were there to help ladies and children enjoy the terrors of the surf. Such a *baigneur* would place you with your back to the incoming wave and hold you by the hand as the rising, rotating mass of foamy, dull-green water violently descended upon you from behind, knocking you off your feet with one mighty wallop. After a dozen of these tumbles, the *baigneur,* glistening like a seal, would lead his panting, shivering, moistly snivelling charge landward to where an unforgettable old woman with gray hairs on her chin promptly chose a bathing robe from several hanging on a clothesline. In the security of a little cabin, one would be helped by yet another attendant to peel off one's soggy, sand-heavy bathing suit. It would plop onto the boards, and, still shivering, one would step out of it and trample on its bluish, dissolving stripes. The cabin smelled of pine. The attendant, a hunchback with beaming wrinkles, brought a basin of steaming-hot water, in which one immersed one's feet. From him I learned, and have preserved ever since in a glass cell of my memory, that "butterfly" in the Basque language is *"misericoletea."*

On the browner and wetter part of the *plage,* that part which at low tide yielded the best mud for castles, I found myself digging, one day, side by side with a little French girl called Colette. She would be ten in November, I had been ten in April. Attention was called to a jagged bit of violet mussel shell upon which she had stepped with the bare sole of her narrow, long-toed foot. No, I was not English, I was Russian. Her greenish eyes seemed flecked with the overflow of the freckles that covered her sharp-featured face. She wore what might now be termed a play suit, consisting of a blue

jersey with rolled-up sleeves and blue knitted shorts. I had taken her
at first for a boy and then had been puzzled by the bracelet on
her thin wrist and the corkscrew brown curls dangling from under
her sailor cap.

She spoke in birdlike bursts of rapid twitter, mixing governess
English and Parisian French. Two years before, on the same *plage,*
I had been much attached to the lovely, sun-tanned little daughter
of a Serbian physician, but when I met Colette, I knew at once that
this was the real thing. Colette seemed to me so much stranger than
all my other chance playmates at Biarritz! I somehow acquired the
feeling that she was less happy than I, less loved. A bruise on her
delicate, white-downed forearm gave rise to awful conjectures. "He
pinches as bad as my mummy," she said, speaking of a crab. I evolved
various schemes to save her from her parents, who were *"des bourgeois de Paris,"* as I heard somebody tell my mother with a slight
shrug. I interpreted the disdain in my own fashion, as I knew that
those people had come all the way from Paris in their blue-and-
yellow limousine (a fashionable adventure in those days) but had
drably sent Colette with her dog and governess by an ordinary
coach train, second class. The dog was a female fox terrier with
bells on her collar and a most waggly behind. From sheer exuberance, she would lap up salt water out of Colette's toy pail. I remember the sail, the sunset, and the lighthouse pictured on that pail, but
I cannot recall the dog's name, and that bothers me.

During the two months of our stay at Biarritz, my passion for
Colette all but surpassed my passion for butterflies. Since my parents were not keen to meet hers, I saw her only on the beach, but I
thought of her constantly. If I noticed she had been crying, I felt a
surge of helpless anguish that brought tears to my own eyes. I could
not destroy the mosquitoes that had left their bites on her frail neck,
but I could, and did, have a successful fist fight with a red-haired boy
who had been rude to her. She used to give me warm handfuls of
hard candy. One day, as we were bending together over a starfish,
and Colette's ringlets were tickling my ear, she suddenly turned toward me and kissed me on the cheek. So great was my emotion that
all I could think of saying was "You little monkey!"

I had a gold coin that I assumed would pay for our elopement.
Where did I want to take her? Spain? America? The mountains
above Pau? *"Là-bas, là-bas, dans la montagne,"* as I had heard Car-
men sing some months before at the opera. One strange night, I lay
awake listening to the recurrent thud of the ocean and planning

our flight. The ocean seemed to rise and grope in the darkness and then heavily fall on its face.

Of our actual getaway, I have little to report. My memory retains a glimpse of her obediently putting on rope-soled canvas shoes, on the lee side of a flapping tent, while I stuffed a folding butterfly net into a brown-paper bag. The next glimpse is of our evading pursuit by entering a pitch-dark little *cinéma* near the Casino (which, of course, was absolutely out of bounds). There we sat, holding hands across the dog, which now and then gently jingled in Colette's lap, and were shown a jerky, drizzly, but highly exciting bullfight at St. Sebastián. My final glimpse is of myself being led along the promenade by my tutor. His long legs move with a kind of ominous briskness and I can see the muscles of his grimly set jaw working under the tight skin. My bespectacled brother, aged nine, whom he happens to hold with his other hand, keeps trotting out forward to peer at me with awed curiosity, like a little owl.

Among the trivial souvenirs acquired at Biarritz before leaving, my favorite was not the small bull of black stone and not the sonorous sea shell but something that now seems almost symbolic—a meerschaum penholder with a tiny peephole of crystal in its ornamental part. One held it quite close to one's eye, screwing up the other, and when one had got rid of the shimmer of one's own lashes, a miraculous photographic view of the bay and of the line of cliffs ending in a lighthouse could be seen inside.

And now a delightful thing happens. The process of re-creating that penholder and the microcosm in its eyelet stimulates my memory to a last effort. I try again to recall the name of Colette's dog—and, sure enough, along those remote beaches, over the glossy evening sands of the past, where each footprint slowly fills up with sunset-colored water, here it comes, here it comes, echoing and vibrating: Floss, Floss, Floss!

Colette was back in Paris by the time we stopped there for a day before continuing our homeward journey, and there, in a fawn park under a cold blue sky, I saw her (by arrangement between our mentors, I believe) for the last time. She carried a hoop and a short stick to drive it with, and everything about her was extremely proper and stylish in an autumnal, Parisian, *tenue-de-ville-pour-fillettes* way. She took from her governess and slipped into my brother's hands a farewell present, a box of sugar-coated almonds, meant, I knew, solely for me, and instantly she was off, tap-tapping her glinting hoop through light and shade, around and around a fountain choked with dead leaves, near which I stood. The leaves mingle in my memory with the leather of her shoes and gloves, and there was, I remember, some detail in her attire (perhaps a ribbon on her Scottish cap, or the pattern of her stockings) that reminded me then of the rainbow spiral in a glass marble. I still seem to be holding that wisp of iridescence, not knowing exactly where to fit it in, while she runs with her hoop ever faster around me and finally dissolves among the slender shadows cast on the gravelled path by the interlaced arches of its border.

A CLEAN, QUIET HOUSE

❖

DANIEL FUCHS

ON THE SUBWAY ride home from work, Charlie Coopersmith
normally had his nose buried in the newspaper or else he did a
little daydreaming on the sly and so was just as dead to the world,
but this Saturday afternoon what happened was that a lemon-colored
butterfly suddenly swooped in through a window. The Sea Beach
train had pulled out of the tunnel beyond the Fifty-ninth Street
station and the sunshine was flooding in. The butterfly jerked in
nervous curves over the heads of the passengers, and Charlie, smiling at the sight, twisted his head to watch it. That was how he came
to notice Howard Hayman. It was more than fifteen years since
high-school days, but the two friends recognized each other instantly. They pushed their way through the crowd until they came
together.

"Holy smoke, Howard!" Charlie said. "What do you think of
that? Bunking into you on a subway train."

"With me it happens all the time," Howard said. He patted a very
thick leather-covered book he held under his elbow. "Insurance,"
he said rather sadly. "Industrial policies. I'm all over the city every
day and I constantly run into old friends and creditors." He had a
party to visit in Bensonhurst that afternoon, he explained; that was
why he was on the train.

"Board of Transportation," Charlie said. "Me and Fiorello, you
know. I'm working for the city."

"Well, that's the best thing, the Civil Service. It's safe, it's steady,
although now, of course—these days—who can tell what?"

"Listen," Charlie said. "How's about dropping in at the house for
a moment, since you're in the neighborhood already?"

"I don't know," Howard said. "This party I have to see—"

"Oh, what the hell, they can wait! It's an occasion. You don't run into old friends every day in the year. Listen, I insist. You got to meet the wife and see the kid."

"Kid?" Howard said. "I heard you were married, but I guess I didn't hear about the kid."

"Sure. Three years old, maybe older. Jo-Jo. A real nice kid."

"I know, I know," Howard said. "You daddies and your off-spring." He himself was not married, he explained. "I guess I must be still waiting for my dream girl," he said. "Confidentially, if I had met up with some nice girl in the educational system—high-school teacher or elementary-school, either one—it would have been one, two, three and all over with. The way it always was, see, I've got the old folks to support and I never felt I had the right exactly to undertake additional obligations. Under adverse circumstances marriage can be a load around your neck."

Even after they had left the train and were walking up the street to the stucco one-family house in which Charlie lived, Howard balked a little.

"I don't see the sense in it," he said. "Really. Why put the wife to all the trouble?" But Charlie paid no attention to him.

"What the hell," he said as he unlocked the front door. "She'll be glad to see you."

The house was empty. "Martha! Martha!" Charlie called, but there was no answer. As he dropped his hat and the paper on the end table he noticed that the rooms were spick and span and that Jo-Jo's clothes and toys weren't lying all over. It was nice and quiet, with the sun streaming in, and they could hear organ music, peaceful and solemn, from somebody's radio.

"A nice place," Howard said. "Real nice and cozy."

"Yes," Charlie said. "Let's go into the kitchen and investigate the icebox situation. We can have a little something to eat while we wait for Martha."

"Now listen here, Charlie," Howard said. "After all, I just dropped in for a moment, you know. That was the understanding."

"Sit down, sit down," Charlie said. "Who's boss around here?"

He went to the refrigerator, hoping there would be something decent in it so that he wouldn't be shamed before his friend. When the door swung back he saw the shelves were stuffed full. His mouth opened with surprise. For a moment he squatted there without moving, and then he remembered that today was his wife's turn to entertain her girl friends. There were plates of cold cuts all neatly arranged. There were bowls of shrimp salad, coleslaw, and potato salad, and little dishes of olives and pickles. Lying flat in all the corners were bottles of celery tonic and soda pop.

"Say, is this customary around here?" Howard asked, looking over Charlie's shoulder.

Charlie smiled happily. He brought out two bottles of cream soda and the largest, best-looking plate of cold cuts.

"It's funny," Howard said, watching his friend scatter the bread, the plates, the silver, and the paper napkins. "I mean this kind of reminds me of the days when we were kids. You know, when we did something bad and hung around with a guilty conscience, waiting until our mothers should find out and bawl the hell out of us. Gee, you certainly did your best to get me in Dutch all the time."

"Who, me?" Charlie said. He sat down at the kitchen table and began to make a sandwich.

"You well remember," Howard said. "Don't make believe you don't know. The inventions we always made down in the cellar. Like the time with the crystal sets when radio first came out. Hey, Charlie, remember those old crystal sets?"

"You bet. I was the first kid on the block with a crystal set. I got the hookup out of the *Sun*."

"The boat, too," Howard said, helping himself to the cold cuts. "You remember the boat? That was when you got a notion we had to go sailing in Sheepshead Bay, so we both went to work building a boat. The janitor certainly had plenty of firewood that winter."

"Oh boy, oh boy, oh boy," Charlie said. "Those happy days, those happy dreams, those—those—" He took a bite.

"On the level, Charlie, sometimes I think I still got it in for you in my subconscious for all the trouble you caused me."

"We certainly were a screwy pair of kids," Charlie said.

"You," Howard said. "Not me. Please don't include me in the same category." He took a drink and then began making a sandwich for himself. "I just did what you told me. I was too—" He stopped suddenly.

"What's the matter?" Charlie asked.

"Well, it's a note there," Howard said, picking up a piece of blue paper. It had been propped up against the sugar bowl on the table, but apparently Charlie had knocked it aside when he put the bottles down. "It's for you, I guess. I was reading it unconsciously." He handed it to Charlie.

DARLING:

Out getting manicure—baby with me. Your lunch is in bottom shelf refrigerator. You'll find it. Look!!! It's on left side. Please don't touch party food or upset anything. Darling, please be a good boy today.

1. don't touch party food
2. don't lie down on couch or bed
3. don't mess up house with papers
4. don't spoil anything in general and I'll love you loads.   MARTHA

"It's all right," Charlie said, and put the note behind him on the seat of the chair.

Howard held his sandwich in his hand. "If this stuff is for a party," he said, "maybe we shouldn't be eating it."

"Oh, nuts!" Charlie said. "Forget it, will you? Eat, eat. Don't give it a thought."

"Well, all right," Howard said slowly, and began chewing again.

There was a plane tree in the yard outside and its leaves fluttered and sent patches of light dancing on the wall of the kitchen. Watching them, Charlie felt good. The house this afternoon was nice and restful, and in the yard a bird, some kind of bird, was actually singing. He wiped his mouth and picked up Jo-Jo's flute, which was lying on the window sill. While Howard went on eating, Charlie played on the flute, going up and down the scale.

"Howard," he said suddenly, "it was funny about that butterfly in the subway train. Did you see it?"

"Incongruous, wasn't it? I mean a thing like a butterfly in the subway."

"Wonder where it went," Charlie said. "After I saw you I lost track of it." His fingers worked over the holes of the flute and he played a snatch of a tune.

"Travelling around the city the way I do," Howard said, "it's really curious how many of the old gang I keep running into on the subway; that is, of course, the ones who aren't in the Army. A lot of them went in."

"Well," Charlie said, taking the flute out of his mouth, "we're not so old. Sooner or later we'll all be in, one way or the other."

"Yes, I suppose," Howard said, "but only last month or so I saw Walter Verdrager. Remember Verdrager?"

"Oh, sure," Charlie said. "How is Walter?"

"Married eight years now. No kids, though. He's got some kind of a job downtown, Wall Street district, nothing much. He's getting bald."

"Gee," Charlie said. "I never met even one of the old gang, outside of you today."

"Well, I meet them constantly. Lemberger, Henry Lemberger. Lawyer now. Christmastime I bunked into him. Well, we all know what the law's come to for a living these days. Two or three kids, if I recall rightly, and he's holding onto his hair pretty good, too. You ought to see Harry Rand, though. Every time I see him he's got his part in a new place. It's going quick with him, all right. He's on the bum, real down and out, no kidding. Plays the horses. Drinks, too, I should imagine. Well, why not, the poor guy? Why deprive him of his only consolations?"

Charlie was halfway through "Juanita" on the flute when he stopped. "Listen," he said, "what ever happened to Ernest Fabricant?"

He had to wait until his friend finished swallowing.

"Cue ball," Howard finally said. He wiped his mouth and fingers, made a neat wad of the napkin, and then deposited it primly in the center of his plate. "Fabricant's the worst one yet. Hasn't got a hair on his head. Well, that's the way it is. Time passes. You simply got to expect it and put up with it."

" 'Time ever flowing, Bids us be going, Dear Mother Eastern, Far from view. . . .' " Charlie had forgotten the rest. It was the old high-school song.

"Sometimes it's instructive to look back and reflect," Howard said. "Here we were—happy-go-lucky kids with all kinds of hopes and ambitions and plans and a spark of life in us. What happened to us all? What have we attained in the passage of the years? Not so very much."

"Me, too," Charlie said, scratching his head. "Include me, too. I'm a failure. I guess we're all failures. Well, so what?" He put the tin instrument back into his mouth and began to play "Old Black Joe."

"What's that?" Howard asked. "A flute?"

"Well, technically it's not a flute. It's called a flageolet. It costs ten cents."

"It plays real good. I mean you wouldn't think it was a kid's toy to hear it. It gives out an excellent musical tone."

"Try it, why don't you?" Charlie said. "It's very simple to learn."

"Well," Howard said. He took the flute and blew on it for a moment. "Not bad," he said. "I could get the hang of this in no time."

"Wait a minute," Charlie said. He went upstairs to Jo-Jo's room and came back with another flute and a sheet of paper that had bars of music printed on it. "Try 'London Bridge,' " he said. "It's the easiest one, just up and down, practically." He explained the system of notation on the sheet—the numbers corresponded with the openings in the pipe—and Howard went earnestly to work. The third time he ran right through it.

"We ought to be ashamed," he said.

"Listen," Charlie said, "let's harmonize. The two flutes aren't in quite the same key, but it should work out anyway."

"All right," Howard said. "Let's see."

They pushed their chairs closer together in front of the table and rested the sheet against the two bottles. "One, two, three," Charlie said, and they began. It wasn't bad at all.

"Nuts!" Howard said when they finished. "We're certainly acting like a fine pair of adolescents."

"No," Charlie said. "It worked out swell, I thought. Let's do it again."

"All right," Howard said.

They were off again. The tinny music went out through the quiet of the house. The two men were so engrossed that neither of them heard the front door open.

"I specifically asked you not to get the house untidy," a voice called out from the living room. "I specifically mentioned newspapers."

Howard dropped his flute and jumped to his feet.

"Martha!" Charlie said, raising his voice. "My friend is here, Martha."

"Oh," she said, coming to the kitchen door with Jo-Jo at her side. She looked at the table—the plate of cold cuts, the bottles, the flutes, and the mess they had made. Her lips tightened.

Charlie smiled. "My friend, Mr. Hayman, Martha. Howard, this is the ball and chain."

Howard ducked his head and coughed slightly.

"I'm happy to know you, Mr. Hyman," Martha said.

"Hayman," Charlie said.

"What?"

"Nothing. Hayman. It's not Hyman."

"Hayman," she said. "I'm very sorry."

"Oh, it's all right!" Howard said. "No harm done."

"And that's the kid," Charlie said to him, still smiling. "Little Jo-Jo."

Howard bent down and wagged his fingers in front of the boy's
face. "Hello, little man," he said. Jo-Jo wouldn't answer and hid behind his mother. Howard straightened up. "A nice kid," he said
to her.

"Yes," she said, and pushed at Jo-Jo. "Stop pulling on Mother's
dress. Let it go, don't hang on it. It's not a swing."

They all kept standing. Charlie beamed and beamed, but without knowing what to say next. The pause lengthened.

"Say!" Howard cried suddenly. "I'm late. They'll be furious with
me. The time just slipped my mind."

"Yes," Charlie said to his wife. "Howard had a business appointment. He was waiting for you to come."

"I'm sorry," Martha said. "I was delayed."

"It's all right," Howard said, and went into the living room for
his hat and the fat book. Charlie, Martha, and Jo-Jo all followed
after him. "Well," he said, bundling to the door, "goodbye. Goodbye, Charlie. Must rush. They'll be perfectly furious. Goodbye,
Jo-Jo. Nice to have met you, Mrs. Coopersmith—a pleasure." Then
he hurried out without looking back.

"My God!" Charlie said when the door closed. "We were kidding
around. We were only having a little fun. We weren't doing anything so terrible."

"I like that," Martha said. "It's really quite delicious. He bawls
me out."

"What? Am I bawling you out? I'm just saying—"

"Really!" she said, pointing to the kitchen table. "Really,
Charlie! You're hopeless. After I go to the trouble of leaving you
a note. After I beg you in a nice way specifically what not to do."

"I didn't see the note right away," he said. He went on to explain
how it happened, but Martha wouldn't listen.

"What's the use talking?" she said. "There's no use. You're utterly irresponsible. Jo-Jo's got more sense in his head than you have.
Here, hold him with you," she said, and pushed his hand into Charlie's. She walked toward the kitchen. "Now I have to clean up all
over again."

Charlie sat down and hoisted the boy up to his knee. "Nobody
wants to understand," he said aloud. "Nobody wants to see what
you're driving at and how a person can thoughtlessly make a mistake. No one." The whole afternoon had been spoiled for him.
That nice feeling was gone, and instead all he could think of now
was the office at the Board of Transportation and things connected

with his job. He thought of the subway rides every day to and from Canal Street, of the way he threw paper balls over the desks and horsed around with the other fellows, of how they all watched the clock and waited for Friday to come, because it was the day before Saturday. Ah, it was no good. It was depressing.

"Daddy," Jo-Jo was saying. "Daddy, listen."

"What?"

"Make a balloon," the boy said. "You know. Make a balloon."

"All right," Charlie said, and he blew his cheek out. It was a game they always played together. Jo-Jo brought up his little fist and smartly punched his father's cheek. The air was knocked out all at once, the cheek went flat, and Charlie had arranged his lips in such a way that a kind of honking noise was produced. The performance always entranced Jo-Jo.

"Again!" he said. "Daddy, again!"

"All right," Charlie said, and he patiently puffed his cheek out.

VILLAGE INCIDENT

❖

JAMES A. MAXWELL

CAPTAIN JOHN TEDFORD had several letters in his hand and a package under his arm when he walked into the Tripoli Air Transport Command Intelligence office that he and I shared. He dropped the parcel and a couple of letters on my desk and said, "Why is it every time it's my turn to go for the mail you get freight? And I bet it isn't even food."

I felt the package. "Books," I announced.

"It's not a bad idea of your wife's to send you stuff that'll keep you off the streets at night, but I wish she'd give a little thought to me. I'm tired of eating stewed camel."

Conversation ceased as we read our mail. After I had finished my two letters, I unwrapped the package. My wife had sent me five books I had asked her to get for me. The one on top was a copy of Arthur Koestler's "Dialogue with Death." Tedford came over to look at the titles after he had finished his own mail, and picked up a novel by Farrell. "I'd like to take a look at this when you're finished with it," he said.

"Take it along with you," I said. "I'll be reading some of the others first."

"Can't tonight. I'm going out to the beach after work and I don't want it kicking around in the jeep. Look, why don't you come along? Some of us are going out to the British Officers' and Sisters' Beach for a swim and dinner, and we're going to the movies later in the evening. It's Betty Grable. Come along and help us drool."

I told him I'd go. When I finished work late that afternoon, I left the books on my desk. I had found that if I took new books to my room at the Hotel Del Mahari, the British and American officers who wandered in would carry them off. Often they were never returned, so I didn't leave a book lying around my room until I had read it.

The next morning, I got to the office an hour early, because I had to write my monthly report, which was overdue. As soon as I sat down at my desk, I saw that one of the books, the Koestler, was missing. I was exasperated; reading matter was not easily come by in Tripoli in the spring of 1945.

While I was going through the drawers of the desk in what I knew was a fruitless search, a tall, heavily built man of about fifty walked into the office. He had Jewish features, shaggy dark hair, eyebrows that formed a straight black line across his forehead, and startling blue eyes that seemed incongruous in such a dark man. His double-breasted gray suit was worn but well pressed. Under his arm, he carried a book covered with a jacket made of the wrapping paper I had discarded the day before.

He was surprised to find me there but he wasn't flustered. "I didn't expect you here so early," he said, and smiled pleasantly. His voice was deep and resonant, and he spoke English clearly, though with an accent I couldn't define.

"Apparently not," I said.

He took the brown paper jacket off the Koestler and laid the book solemnly on the desk. "To keep it clean," he said, indicating the paper.

"Very kind of you." I tried to keep my voice chilly.

"I always admire your choice of books," he told me in an uncle-to-nephew manner.

"Then this isn't the first time you've taken them?"

"Since I find myself in this awkward position, it would be better if I confessed the full extent of my crimes," he said. "I'm in charge of the night crew that cleans the offices in this building. Each evening, I have to come in here, and on your desk I've found a number of books that have interested me. Since reading material cannot be obtained by civilians, I haven't been able to resist the temptation of borrowing them. Of course, I always protect them from dirt and injury and always return them the next morning before you enter your office. I've lost a lot of sleep under this arrangement, but I've enjoyed those hours."

"Why didn't you ask me?" I said sternly. "I'd have lent the books to you."

He shrugged. "I didn't know that. And if I had asked you and you had refused, I would have felt bound not to take them. It's only in the matter of books that I allow my conscience to follow such warped reasoning."

In spite of myself, I found that I was smiling at him. Book borrowers who took such excellent care of my property and returned it so promptly were rare. "Did you like this book?" I asked.

"You have made me into a great admirer of Mr. Koestler," he told me. "Several months ago, I borrowed 'Darkness at Noon' from your desk. Though I don't pose as a critic of modern literature, I think it's one of the great novels of our time. This book is good, but it's not so powerful as the other. Of course, it may be that 'Darkness at Noon' is closer to my own experience. I've known a little of the mental confusion the author experienced."

While the man was talking, he casually took a chair next to my desk. I offered him a cigarette and then lit it for him. "You're not a native of Tripolitania?" I said.

He shook his head. "I am a citizen of Europe. My family lived in Poland when I was a little boy, but we were driven out by the pogroms. We went to Italy. I went to school in Milan and later I studied in Paris. When the war came—the first war—I fought with the Italian Army. We were quite as bad that time," he added reflectively.

"When did you come to Tripoli?" I asked.

"About six years ago, when Il Duce and Hitler began to merge philosophies and all non-Jewish Italians became Aryans. I was already suspect—my passport had been taken from me—because of my work as a newspaperman."

I wasn't surprised to find an ex-newspaperman in charge of a cleaning staff in Tripoli. North Africa was full of such situations. In Casablanca I had met a bartender who had formerly been an economics professor and had flown bombers against Franco. In Tunis, there had been a Polish novelist who spent his time denouncing James Joyce when he was not sweeping out A.T.C. planes.

"Did you work for Italian papers?" I asked.

"Only for a little while. Writing news so that it conforms to a party philosophy, any party philosophy, is too difficult for a man of my limited imagination." He laughed softly. "I think Mr. Koestler experienced a similar difficulty. Many popes arose in Europe during the past twenty years, and all of them were infallible. Doubters were not popular." He rose. "You will pardon me, but I must go to see that my people have done a satisfactory job of cleaning the offices."

"Look," I said, "I happen to know that Captain Monroe in Civilian Personnel is looking for people who speak English. Are you interested?"

He shook his head. "Thank you, but no. I have a small farm out-side Sugh el Giumaa, and in my present position I'm free in the daytime. I sleep till noon and have the afternoons for my own work."

"Stop in again, when you want another book," I told him.

"I shall take advantage of your kind offer," he said. After he had gone, I realized that I hadn't asked him his name.

I didn't see the man again for about a week, and then, one morn-ing, shortly after I had arrived at the office, he came in. "My wife and I," he said formally, "would like you to have dinner at our home some evening when you are not engaged."

When I said I'd like to come, he asked if the following Friday would be convenient. "That'll be fine," I said.

His formality disappeared. "You are doing much for my home life and my conscience," he said. "Both my wife and my inner voice have been denouncing me for the liberties I took with your prop-erty. Now I may say to them with complete honesty, 'I am borrow-ing books from a friend.' "

"What time shall I come?"

"About seven o'clock, if that is convenient." He described the location of his home and started to leave, but turned back when I said, "I'm afraid I don't know your name."

"Of course. My name is Max Hoffenstein. I have known yours for a long time, from the sign on your desk." We shook hands and then he left.

I found his house without difficulty the night I went there to dinner. It was located about a half mile from the village of Sugh el Giumaa, on the main road to Tripoli. The place was surrounded by a high wall of earth baked to concrete hardness by the sun and bound by the roots of the cactus plants that grew along the top. The yard was filled with lush green bushes and vivid hibiscus blooms. The house was small, but it had attractive lines and its white plaster walls were brilliant in the late-afternoon sun.

Hoffenstein came out of the door when I brought the jeep to a stop, and walked over to meet me. While we exchanged greetings, two women appeared in the doorway. "Come," he said, "I want you to meet my wife and daughter."

The two women wore identical white dresses that had seen much mending. Mrs. Hoffenstein was in her late thirties; Sylvia, the daughter, was about sixteen, with a fully developed figure. Both had light hair, bleached to a pale yellow by the sun. Their faces were rather flat and plain but their dark tans made them attractive. We were introduced, and each of them gave me a firm, one-movement, European handshake. They were beautifully poised, but I sensed excitement in both of them, as though entertaining guests was a rarity at their home.

We walked into the cool living room, which was shaded by wooden roll shutters that had been lowered almost to the bottoms of the windows, and all of us sat down in comfortable chairs around a low table.

"We have heard much about you," Mrs. Hoffenstein said. "It is kind of you to visit us." She spoke English well but not with the fluency of her husband.

Hoffenstein chuckled. "I have told her just how we came to meet. Please reassure her that you don't now find it necessary to lock up everything in your office."

"My husband is a very foolish man," Mrs. Hoffenstein said. "It is possible he would have lost his position with his nonsense over books." She poured some cool wine for us out of a cut-glass decanter.

"Mamma," Hoffenstein said, "you don't understand. No man who reads Koestler could take such a narrow view of life. Now, if my friend here had been a reader of Nietzsche, I would not have taken the liberty."

We talked on for some time about nothing of importance. The atmosphere was pleasant and relaxed. For understandable reasons, most of the civilians in Tripoli were difficult hosts; they either fawned over American guests to obtain some favor, or were tense lest they say something that might offend. Soap, clothing, almost all necessities except food, and such minor luxuries as cigarettes were hard to get. American and, to a lesser extent, British personnel were the only sources of supply.

Hoffenstein had just finished a story about his troubles with Italian censorship when Sylvia, who had not spoken since our introduction, suddenly burst out with a question. "Do you know Bing Crosby in America?" she asked me, with excitement in her voice.

Her father laughed. "It is part of the spread of American culture. She's heard him often on the wireless and once an American officer gave her a Crosby record for our old phonograph."

Fortunately, I was able to tell her that I had once interviewed Crosby for an Army paper in the United States, when he had entertained the troops at the camp where I was stationed. Her eyes grew wide with envy. "Is he as pretty as he appears in the cinema?" she asked. "I saw him once at the Miramare Theatre in Tripoli."

"He looks about the same," I said, and told her the little I knew about him. I rather expected my account of his large family to dampen her romantic fervor.

It didn't, though. She merely smiled happily and said, "It is good to know he is a man of—stability." She looked at her father for approval of the last word. He nodded his head gravely.

After we had finished our third glass of wine, Hoffenstein suggested that we go out the back door to see his small farm. He had about three acres of well-tended ground, laid out in the usual North African checkerboard manner. Each plot was about eight feet square and surrounded by a mound of earth about six inches high, to conserve rain. He pointed to the white superstructure of his well at the back of his property. "That is one thing we may thank the Italians for—an ample supply of water. All over the colony they erected wells like that."

As we watched, an ox driven by an Arab walked back and forth along a path leading to the well. A rope attached to the animal's harness extended over a pulley suspended between the well's uprights. The other end of the rope was tied to a weighted goatskin bag. As the ox walked toward the well, the bag dropped into the water. As it walked in the opposite direction, it brought the goatskin to the top, where the water spilled down into a trough and was carried by gravity to the various plots of ground.

"As effective today as it was at the time of Moses," Hoffenstein said.

"Who is the Arab?" I asked.

"He's one of three men from the village who help me. I, myself, am a very indifferent farmer. We divide the crops between us."

"How are your relations with the Arabs?"

"Usually quite good," he said. "There are only a few European Jews in the village. Most of them live in Tripoli. Almost all the Jewish families here have lived in Libya for over two thousand years, and the majority of them speak only Arabic. In dress and appearance, it's impossible to tell them from Arabs. So there is little reason for trouble. Sometimes, though, I think I see shadows in our village of what is taking place elsewhere, in Egypt and Palestine, but I can't be certain. Today, most Jews are like children in a dark room. Everything frightens us."

His wife called us to dinner, and we reëntered the house. We had an excellent meal. What particularly pleased me were some long strips of white meat covered with a batter and fried to a light brown. It tasted something like lobster. When I asked what the meat was, all of them began to laugh, the women discreetly behind their hands, Hoffenstein heartily. "I have told my wife," he said, "that Americans are not adventurous in their eating and that to tell you before you had tasted might spoil your appetite. They are octopus tentacles. We buy them when they are very young and the meat is tender." I won his approval by asking for another helping.

After dinner, the women cleared the table, and Hoffenstein and I went into the living room. We each had a glass of a local liqueur and talked of the rapidly darkening political situation in the Middle East. I asked him whether he was active in the Zionist movement.

"Only in a small way," he said. "It is difficult, because I do not attend the synagogue. My wife is not a Jew but a Milanese. Such a combination does not take us into the Jewish life of the community. The European Jews in Tripoli do not like us, because we are not religious. The native Jews in Sugh el Giumaa distrust us because we wear European clothes. In many ways, it is a lonely life."

"But there must be other nonreligious Jews in Tripoli," I said.

"Not so many as you might think. In times of deep trouble, people return with renewed faith to their God. To be a Jew today is not good; to be a nonbelieving Jew is worse. Those who do not share the belief are outcasts even from the persecuted minority." He smiled. "You see the result of reading such a book as Mr. Koestler's. Immediately, I begin to talk like a mediocre philosopher."

He refilled our glasses. "Do you want to live in Palestine?" I asked.

"No, I do not. But I want to see the Zionist movement succeed, because I want two things very badly—a passport and the protection of a national state."

"I have heard others say the same thing," I said.

"All over North Africa, all over Europe, all over the world," Hoffenstein said, "there are Jews who live only because some state or other is either sympathetic or indifferent. They cannot move, because they lack the piece of paper that enables them to cross borders. If they are mistreated or if their property is taken away, there is no consul to whom they can go for protection. Only if we Jews become citizens of a recognized nation can we know any measure of freedom."

"Didn't you have to get some sort of passport to come here?" I asked.

"Our trip here was not official," he said dryly. "My wife, my daughter, and I came here in an open sailing boat. We were ten days on the water. But this colony, under Balbo, was never too inquisitive about such matters. A few lire, wisely distributed, took care of our problems."

"But you should have no trouble establishing your Italian nationality after the war's over," I said.

He shook his head. "I'm not sure we could prove our citizenship. And since all nations will be short of food for many years, none of them are eager to recognize people of doubtful national origin. Besides, even if I should obtain an Italian passport and citizenship, who knows when another leader in Europe may resurrect the Protocols of Zion to divert his people? Communist Jews I have known tell me that Zionism is unjust because it is intensely nationalistic, but who am I to insist on perfection in the world today?"

Mrs. Hoffenstein and Sylvia joined us, and I spent the rest of the evening answering questions about the United States. As I was about to leave, Hoffenstein looked at his daughter and said, "After the war, all the young girls in the world will want to go to America. It is the new Promised Land. All of them go to the cinema and see the beautiful ladies and the handsome gentlemen who wear magnificent clothes and live in palaces. It is better than anything Moses ever promised his people."

I didn't see Hoffenstein and his family for several weeks after the dinner. I was too busy. Toward the end of May, the French sent in tanks and bombers to subdue the food rioters in Algeria. Five days later, fighting broke out in the Levant, and Damascus was shelled by French troops. Life in Tripoli became tense, and for a period it seemed that there would be serious trouble. I was trying to keep our headquarters in Casablanca appraised of the situation.

As news of the disorders came in, the immediate reaction of the Arabs was, of course, against the French. But since there were few Frenchmen in Tripoli and the neighboring communities upon whom the Arabs could avenge themselves, the resentment spread to include all Europeans. Two Italians were stabbed, although not fatally, and a British sergeant was badly beaten up, all within a week. But when there was a flareup of fighting in Palestine, all the local Arab resentment suddenly focussed on the Jews.

There were a few acts of violence, and then the British adminis-
trators made a wise move. They gave unofficial permission to the
Arabs to declare a one-day strike and to stage a mass demonstration
against the French. Several thousand Arabs paraded past the Administration Building in downtown Tripoli, and a delegation of
leaders presented the British brigadier with a formal, written protest. The demonstration seemed to provide the necessary outlet for
Arab feelings, and after it was over comparative calm settled over
Tripolitania.

One evening about a week after the parade, I stopped in to see
Hoffenstein at his home. We drank wine in his living room, and he
was as cordial as before, but he seemed distracted. Several times, he
stopped in the middle of a sentence, looked bewildered, and then
was unable to recall what he had been talking about. When we
talked about the recent trouble, he nervously tugged at his fingers
and made his knuckles crack. I involuntarily looked at his hands
and he smiled with embarrassment. "You must forgive me," he said.
"It is an unfortunate habit when I am not at ease."

"Do you think there will be more trouble here?" I asked.

"I know there will," he replied. "Jews have had much experience with the sort of atmosphere that exists here today. I can almost
taste and feel the hatred in the air. It is very familiar to those of us
who have spent many years in Europe. We react to it as one of your
detector machines reacts to a submarine under the water."

Mrs. Hoffenstein and Sylvia joined us, and he dropped his gloomy
mood immediately. He entertained us for an hour by talking about
a brief period in his career when he had been a theatre critic for a
near-bankrupt newspaper in Vienna. Apparently, it was a part of
her father's life Sylvia hadn't heard about before, and she asked
him dozens of eager questions.

Hoffenstein was in the middle of a story about a feud he had had
with a Viennese producer when suddenly, from the farm in back of
the house, came a cry that was both a roar and a scream. We stared
at each other for a moment, then, as the crying continued, Hoffenstein and I ran to the door. A half moon was shining brightly and
we had little trouble seeing that the farm was empty. The horrible
noise was coming from a shed near the well, and as we hurried toward it, I took my small, fountain-pen flashlight from my pocket.
When we reached the open door of the shed, I turned the beam into
the enclosure. On the earthen floor was the ox, its throat cleanly
cut. A thick stream of blood ran down its breast to the ground. Even

so, the big animal kept on bellowing, and with every bellow, the blood spurted. I looked at Hoffenstein. His face was without expression.

"I'd better drive to the village and get the police," I said.

"Thank you." He turned and we walked out of the shed. "There is nothing we can do for the beast," he said.

He went with me to the jeep, and as I climbed behind the wheel, he said, "You must do a favor for me. You must let me have one of the guns you have confiscated from workers at the field."

"You know I can't do that," I said.

"It could be my wife or daughter next time." He spoke with intensity but without pleading in his voice.

"I'm sorry," I said.

He sighed wearily. "Of course," he said, "it was a stupid request."

"I'll talk to the officer in charge of the police in Sugh el Giumaa and see if he can give you some extra protection," I said.

"You are very kind," he said dully, and began to walk toward the house.

When I reached the police station, I found that a Captain Williamson, whom I knew, was on duty. I told him about the ox, and he dispatched a couple of native policemen and a British sergeant to the Hoffenstein farm. I asked him if there was any way he could increase the patrol in Hoffenstein's neighborhood.

"It's a sticky situation," he said, "and there's not a damned thing I can do about it. We can't station a man to sit on their porch, and nothing else would do any good. What makes it particularly bad is the fact that the Arabs have all kinds of weapons buried out in the sand. When Monty was chasing the Jerries out of here, they gave the Arabs everything they couldn't carry just to give us trouble. Hoffenstein's in a spot, I'll admit. The local people have it in for him, both because he's a European and because he's a Jew. I'll do my best, but he hasn't much chance if they really go after him." I said good night and left.

I saw Hoffenstein at the base several times within the next few weeks, but we had no opportunity to talk. Then he stopped me one morning as I was going to work and told me that he and his wife hoped I would come to see them. Thereafter, I called on them regularly. He never referred to the incident of the ox.

In October, I received orders of transfer to Casablanca. Before I left Tripoli, I spent an evening with Hoffenstein and his family and gave him some books that I thought would interest him. Both his wife and daughter kissed me goodbye when I left. Sylvia instructed me to tell Bing Crosby of her admiration, if I ever saw him again.

After I had been in Casablanca for a short time, I was sent to Cairo on temporary duty. The period I spent in Egypt was not pleasant. There were several student riots against the British policy in Palestine and against the British presence in Egypt. There was a lot of street fighting, and a bomb killed a number of South African soldiers.

On a morning in early November, I started back to Casablanca. My plane stopped at Tripoli for gasoline and some minor repairs, and the pilot notified us passengers that we could do what we liked for two hours. As soon as I walked into the terminal building, I knew something had happened. Ordinarily, there were at least a dozen civilians working there, but that morning there was only one man, an old Arab, who was sweeping the floor.

An American sergeant from the Priorities and Traffic office recognized me and came over to speak to me. "Whatsa matter?" he said. "Don't you know enough to stay out of this town?"

I told him I was on my way west, and then asked where all the civilian workers were.

"Hardly anybody's comin' to work," he told me. "You got out of here at a good time. All hell's been breakin' around here the last couple of days. The wogs went nuts and the whole field's confined."

"What happened?"

"A lot of fightin' and killin'. It started in Tripoli and then as soon as they get that half straightened out it starts all over again in Sugh el Giumaa and Tagiura. Whatta clambake! As I get it, the wogs got sore at the Jews about somethin' in Palestine and decided to beat hell out of 'em here."

I told the sergeant that I wanted to use the telephone, and went over to the booth and called the civilian police in Sugh el Giumaa. Fortunately, Captain Williamson was in his office. "You missed quite a show, old boy," he said after we had exchanged greetings. "As a matter of fact, there's no assurance the matter is closed even now."

"What caused the flareup?"

"All that nonsense in Cairo probably touched it off, but it's been brewing for some time, as you know. We had practically a full-scale war for a while. These bloody Arabs just about wrecked the village with grenades and then they set fire to what was left. Nasty bit of business."

I had to ask the question even though I already felt certain of the answer. "What about Hoffenstein, the civilian who lives outside the village?"

"They got him first thing," Williamson said. "One of the Arabs tossed a German potato-masher grenade through his window while the family was at dinner. Got all of them—the man, the wife, and the daughter. I took some of the lads down there as soon as we'd heard the explosion. We kept the Arabs from burning the house, but the room where they were eating wasn't very pretty." He paused. "Are you still there?"

"I'm still here."

"Oh, by the way, when we went through Hoffenstein's house, I came across a dozen or so books with your name in them. I have them here in my office, if you want me to send one of the lads out to the field with them."

"Keep them," I said.

"Thanks. Damned nice of you. I'll take them over to the mess. You know how hard it is to get reading matter here in Tripoli."

DE MORTUIS . . .

❖

John Collier

D R. Rankin was a large and rawboned man on whom the newest
suit at once appeared outdated, like a suit in a photograph
of twenty years ago. This was due to the squareness and flatness of
his torso, which might have been put together by a manufacturer
of packing cases. His face also had a wooden and a roughly constructed look; his hair was wiglike and resentful of the comb. He
had those huge and clumsy hands which can be an asset to a doctor
in a small upstate town where people still retain a rural relish for
paradox, thinking that the more apelike the paw, the more precise
it can be in the delicate business of a tonsillectomy.

This conclusion was perfectly justified in the case of Dr. Rankin.
For example, on this particular fine morning, though his task
was nothing more ticklish than the cementing over of a large patch
on his cellar floor, he managed those large and clumsy hands with
all the unflurried certainty of one who would never leave a sponge
within or create an unsightly scar without.

The Doctor surveyed his handiwork from all angles. He added
a touch here and a touch there till he had achieved a smoothness
altogether professional. He swept up a few last crumbs of soil and
dropped them into the furnace. He paused before putting away the
pick and shovel he had been using, and found occasion for yet
another artistic sweep of his trowel, which made the new surface
precisely flush with the surrounding floor. At this moment of
supreme concentration the porch door upstairs slammed with the
report of a minor piece of artillery, which, appropriately enough,
caused Dr. Rankin to jump as if he had been shot.

The Doctor lifted a frowning face and an attentive ear. He heard
two pairs of heavy feet clump across the resonant floor of the porch.
He heard the house door opened and the visitors enter the hall,
with which his cellar communicated by a short flight of steps. He
heard whistling and then the voices of Buck and Bud crying, "Doc!
Hi, Doc! They're biting!"

Whether the Doctor was not inclined for fishing that day, or whether, like others of his large and heavy type, he experienced an especially sharp, unsociable reaction on being suddenly startled, or whether he was merely anxious to finish undisturbed the job in hand and proceed to more important duties, he did not respond immediately to the inviting outcry of his friends. Instead, he listened while it ran its natural course, dying down at last into a puzzled and fretful dialogue.

"I guess he's out."

"I'll write a note—say we're at the creek, to come on down."

"We could tell Irene."

"But she's not here, either. You'd think *she'd* be around."

"Ought to be, by the look of the place."

"You said it, Bud. Just look at this table. You could write your name—"

"Sh-h-h! Look!"

Evidently the last speaker had noticed that the cellar door was ajar and that a light was shining below. Next moment the door was pushed wide open and Bud and Buck looked down.

"Why, Doc! There you are!"

"Didn't you hear us yelling?"

The Doctor, not too pleased at what he had overheard, nevertheless smiled his rather wooden smile as his two friends made their way down the steps. "I thought I heard someone," he said.

"We was bawling our heads off," Buck said. "Thought nobody was home. Where's Irene?"

"Visiting," said the Doctor. "She's gone visiting."

"Hey, what goes on?" said Bud. "What are you doing? Burying one of your patients, or what?"

"Oh, there's been water seeping up through the floor," said the Doctor. "I figured it might be some spring opened up or something."

"You don't say!" said Bud, assuming instantly the high ethical standpoint of the realtor. "Gee, Doc, I sold you this property. Don't say I fixed you up with a dump where there's an underground spring."

"There was water," said the Doctor.

"Yes, but, Doc, you can look on that geological map the Kiwanis Club got up. There's not a better section of subsoil in the town."

"Looks like he sold you a pup," said Buck, grinning.

"No," said Bud. "Look. When the Doc came here he was green. You'll admit he was green. The things he didn't know!"

"He bought Ted Webber's jalopy," said Buck.

"He'd have bought the Jessop place if I'd let him," said Bud. "But I wouldn't give him a bum steer."

"Not the poor, simple city slicker from Poughkeepsie," said Buck.

"Some people would have taken him," said Bud. "Maybe some people did. Not me. I recommended this property. He and Irene moved straight in as soon as they was married. I wouldn't have put the Doc on to a dump where there'd be a spring under the foundations."

"Oh, forget it," said the Doctor, embarrassed by this conscientiousness. "I guess it was just the heavy rains."

"By gosh!" Buck said, glancing at the besmeared point of the pickaxe. "You certainly went deep enough. Right down into the clay, huh?"

"That's four feet down, the clay," Bud said.

"Eighteen inches," said the Doctor.

"Four feet," said Bud. "I can show you on the map."

"Come on. No arguments," said Buck. "How's about it, Doc? An hour or two at the creek, eh? They're biting."

"Can't do it, boys," said the Doctor. "I've got to see a patient or two."

"Aw, live and let live, Doc," Bud said. "Give 'em a chance to get better. Are you going to depopulate the whole darn town?"

The Doctor looked down, smiled, and muttered, as he always did when this particular jest was trotted out. "Sorry, boys," he said. "I can't make it."

"Well," said Bud, disappointed, "I suppose we'd better get along. How's Irene?"

"Irene?" said the Doctor. "Never better. She's gone visiting. Albany. Got the eleven-o'clock train."

"Eleven o'clock?" said Buck. "For Albany?"

"Did I say Albany?" said the Doctor. "Watertown, I meant."

"Friends in Watertown?" Buck asked.

"Mrs. Slater," said the Doctor. "Mr. and Mrs. Slater. Lived next door to 'em when she was a kid, Irene said, over on Sycamore Street."

"Slater?" said Bud. "Next door to Irene. No."

"Oh, yes," said the Doctor. "She was telling me all about them last night. She got a letter. Seems this Mrs. Slater looked after her when her mother was in the hospital one time."

"No," said Bud.

"That's what she told me," said the Doctor. "Of course, it was a good many years ago."

"Look, Doc," said Buck. "Bud and I were raised in this town. We've known Irene's folks all our lives. We were in and out of their house all the time. There was never anybody next door called Slater."

"Perhaps," said the Doctor, "she married again, this woman. Perhaps it was a different name."

Bud shook his head.

"What time did Irene go to the station?" Buck asked.

"Oh, about a quarter of an hour ago," said the Doctor.

"You didn't drive her?" said Buck.

"She walked," said the Doctor.

"We came down Main Street," Buck said. "We didn't meet her."

"Maybe she walked across the pasture," said the Doctor.

"That's a tough walk with a suitcase," said Buck.

"She just had a couple of things in a little bag," said the Doctor.

Bud was still shaking his head.

Buck looked at Bud, and then at the pick, at the new, damp cement on the floor. "Jesus Christ!" he said.

"Oh, God, Doc!" Bud said. "A guy like you!"

"What in the name of heaven are you two bloody fools thinking?" asked the Doctor. "What are you trying to say?"

"A spring!" said Bud. "I ought to have known right away it wasn't any spring."

The Doctor looked at his cementwork, at the pick, at the large, worried faces of his two friends. His own face turned livid. "Am I crazy?" he said. "Or are you? You suggest that I've—that Irene—my wife—oh, go on! Get out! Yes, go and get the sheriff. Tell him to come here and start digging. You—get out!"

Bud and Buck looked at each other, shifted their feet, and stood still again.

"Go on," said the Doctor.

"I don't know," said Bud.

"It's not as if he didn't have the provocation," Buck said.

"God knows," Bud said.

"God knows," Buck said. "You know. I know. The whole town knows. But try telling it to a jury."

The Doctor put his hand to his head. "What's that?" he said. "What is it? Now what are you saying? What do you mean?"

"If this ain't being on the spot!" said Buck. "Doc, you can see how it is. It takes some thinking. We've been friends right from the start. Damn good friends."

"But we've got to think," said Bud. "It's serious. Provocation or not, there's a law in the land. There's such a thing as being an accomplice."

"You were talking about provocation," said the Doctor.

"You're right," said Buck. "And you're our friend. And if ever it could be called justified—"

"We've got to fix this somehow," said Bud.

"Justified?" said the Doctor.

"You were bound to get wised up sooner or later," said Buck.

"We could have told you," said Bud. "Only—what the hell?"

"We could," said Buck. "And we nearly did. Five years ago. Before ever you married her. You hadn't been here six months, but we sort of cottoned to you. Thought of giving you a hint. Spoke about it. Remember, Bud?"

Bud nodded. "Funny," he said. "I came right out in the open about that Jessop property. I wouldn't let you buy that, Doc. But getting married, that's something else again. We could have told you."

"We're that much responsible," Buck said.

"I'm fifty," said the Doctor. "I suppose it's pretty old for Irene."

"If you was Johnny Weissmuller at the age of twenty-one, it wouldn't make any difference," said Buck.

"I know a lot of people think she's not exactly a perfect wife," said the Doctor. "Maybe she's not. She's young. She's full of life."

"Oh, skip it!" said Buck sharply, looking at the raw cement. "Skip it, Doc, for God's sake."

The Doctor brushed his hand across his face. "Not everybody wants the same thing," he said. "I'm a sort of dry fellow. I don't open up very easily. Irene—you'd call her gay."

"You said it," said Buck.

"She's no housekeeper," said the Doctor. "I know it. But that's not the only thing a man wants. She's enjoyed herself."

"Yeah," said Buck. "She did."

"That's what I love," said the Doctor. "Because I'm not that way myself. She's not very deep, mentally. All right. Say she's stupid. I don't care. Lazy. No system. Well, I've got plenty of system. She's enjoyed herself. It's beautiful. It's innocent. Like a child."

"Yes. If that was all," Buck said.

"But," said the Doctor, turning his eyes full on him, "you seem to know there was more."

"Everybody knows it," said Buck.

"A decent, straightforward guy comes to a place like this and marries the town floozy," Bud said bitterly. "And nobody'll tell him. Everybody just watches."

"And laughs," said Buck. "You and me, Bud, as well as the rest."

"We told her to watch her step," said Bud. "We warned her."

"Everybody warned her," said Buck. "But people get fed up. When it got to truck-drivers—"

"It was never us, Doc," said Bud, earnestly. "Not after you came along, anyway."

"The town'll be on your side," said Buck.

"That won't mean much when the case comes to trial in the county seat," said Bud.

"Oh!" cried the Doctor, suddenly. "What shall I do? What shall I do?"

"It's up to you, Bud," said Buck. "I can't turn him in."

"Take it easy, Doc," said Bud. "Calm down. Look, Buck. When we came in here the street was empty, wasn't it?"

"I guess so," said Buck. "Anyway, nobody saw us come down cellar."

"And we haven't been down," Bud said, addressing himself forcefully to the Doctor. "Get that, Doc? We shouted upstairs, hung around a minute or two, and cleared out. But we never came down into this cellar."

"I wish you hadn't," the Doctor said heavily.

"All you have to do is say Irene went out for a walk and never came back," said Buck. "Bud and I can swear we saw her headed out of town with a fellow in a tan roadster. Everybody'll believe that, all right. We'll fix it. But later. Now we'd better scram."

"And remember. We was never down here," Bud said. "So long."

Buck and Bud ascended the steps, moving with a rather absurd degree of caution. "You'd better get that . . . that thing covered up," Buck said over his shoulder.

Left alone, the Doctor sat down on an empty box, holding his head with both hands. He was still sitting like this when the porch door slammed again. This time he did not start. He listened. The house door opened and closed. A voice cried, "Yoo-hoo! Yoo-hoo! I'm back."

The Doctor rose slowly to his feet. "I'm down here, Irene!" he called.

The cellar door opened. A young woman stood at the head of the steps. "Can you beat it?" she said. "I missed the damn train."

"Oh!" said the Doctor. "Did you come back across the field?"

"Yes, like a fool," she said. "I could have hitched a ride and caught the train up the line. Only I didn't think. If you'd run me over to the junction, I could still make it."

"Maybe," said the Doctor. "Did you meet anyone coming back?"

"Not a soul," she said. "Aren't you finished with that old job yet?"

"I'm afraid I'll have to take it all up again," said the Doctor. "Come down here, my dear, and I'll show you."

THEN WE'LL SET IT RIGHT

❖

ROBERT GORHAM DAVIS

A GREAT MANY new families had come to Marbury since the war began. The little fireworks plant had been expanded, with government help, to twenty times its former size and was producing ammunition in great quantities. The incoming executives had taken all the vacant winter houses, beautiful old houses, many of them, and the summer places were filled with families of officers at Camp Peters, fifteen miles away.

Young Laurence Purvis had been having a wonderful summer. He had never had so many playmates with such interesting backgrounds. Marbury was his second home; his father, who had grown up and had his first law practice here, still made it his legal residence, although the family spent most of their year in the city.

This Saturday, a hot, still, August day, the Purvises had lunched late so that Mr. Purvis, who had come down from town, could be with them. Laurence had eaten very fast, bending low over his plate and putting in one mouthful before the preceding one had been swallowed. He said he did not want dessert.

"What's the matter with you, Laurence?" his mother asked. "You've bolted your food so, and now no dessert!"

Laurence lifted his chin eagerly. His narrow face and close-cropped, knobby head were the same shade of light brown. Only his large, dark eyes gave contrast and focus to his face. "It's the Powderhouse Point gang. We're expecting an attack. They've got an army too. We've had sentinels posted all morning." He jammed his napkin into his ring and pushed his chair back from the table.

"Can I be excused now?" He began backing toward the door, his eyes on his father's face. On the shoulders of his khaki shirt were stars cut from beer cans.

His father was a large man with smooth, soft skin and a statesman-like jaw, slightly cleft in the middle. He looked at his son. "Excused?" he asked mildly.

375

"Yes. They're waiting for me."

"No doubt. But aren't you forgetting something?" Mr. Purvis said.

"What?" Laurence asked in an alarmed and defensive voice.

"I think you know."

"The dishes," Laurence said grudgingly, and came slowly back to the table. "But just this once. It's our big day."

"You think your mother should do them, then?"

"No, but . . ."

"And the garden this morning. How much time did you put in?"

"But . . ." Laurence's voice trailed off, then he sat down in his chair, sprawling defiantly, watching every bite his parents took.

"Come, boy," said Mr. Purvis in his deep, rich voice. "Is this the way your troops obey orders?"

"No . . . sir," Laurence answered, sitting up straight now.

"I wonder what sort of soldier you are." Mr. Purvis paused, looking thoughtfully at Laurence. Laurence returned the gaze, not letting himself hope, moving a finger up and down one seam of his pants. "Because I'm more interested in the spirit in which it's done than in the work itself, I'm going to make a counter-proposal. I could take over your dishwashing this once—" He held up his hand as Laurence moved eagerly. "This is going to be equally hard. You don't want to just get out of something, do you?"

"No, Dad."

"If things are too easy, you don't feel good about them, do you? Well, you may go now if you will come back promptly at four-thirty and work for one full hour and a half in the garden."

Laurence blinked and looked uneasily up at the clock. It was twenty-five minutes past two.

"Without any reminding. You're on your honor, now. Remember."

"All right, Dad." With a little sigh Laurence grabbed up a belt and cap pistol from the table and rushed out the door.

Mr. Purvis smiled and turned to his wife. "He's O.K.," he said cheerfully. "We just have to deal with things as they come up, get them into the open, not let anything build up inside."

From the road, where Laurence was racing to catch up with two members of his company, came the sounds of shooting produced with tireless mechanical precision by the mouths of small boys.

Mr. Purvis put down his spoon and listened. "Anti-aircraft and Thompsons," he said. "In my day we had nothing to guide us on the sounds. We actually went around shouting 'Bang, bang,' the way it was written in books. Very crude by present standards."

"In a way it's terrible, though," his wife said. "Laury told me how to kill a man in the dark with a knife without making a sound."

Mr. Purvis laughed and pretended to cringe away from her. "You aren't going to try it?" he asked. "But really, puss, it's not terrible at all. Death is a word to them, a theatrical fall to the ground. They have all that destructive energy that they can blow off by pretending to shoot each other. It gets it out of their system."

"The terms he uses!" Mrs. Purvis laughed. "And those books in his room. I can't understand a word of them."

"He really organizes those boys," Mr. Purvis said. "Sixteen kids showing up every day, to take his orders and like it. In my day we just bickered." The sweet dessert, the warm air, and thoughts of the weekend merged tranquilly. He looked down at the table.

"Oh, God," he said. "The dishes."

"Oh, I'll do them. You've had a hard week."

"Do you really mind, puss?" he asked, patting her arm.

Laurence's company was encamped in a rarely used sand pit which made a crater in the side of a high, wooded hill. Except for one opening, where the winding truck road ran onto the floor of the pit, it was enclosed by sand walls rising for forty or fifty feet. It was a perfect place for dugouts and foxholes, although not defensible against an enemy who had gained the rim above. This was protected, however, by machine-gun and mortar emplacements.

As Laurence came along the truck road into the pit, a small boy stepped from behind a barricade and presented arms.

"Any news?" Laurence asked.

"We just sent out another scout. Chuck didn't find out anything," the small boy said.

A larger boy with tin bars on his shoulders came up and saluted. "Order the company to fall in, Captain," Laurence said. "We can't just stand around waiting."

A group of four or five boys stood waiting across the floor of the pit. "No more close-order drill!" one of them shouted insubordinately.

Laurence frowned. "Order the company to fall in," he repeated, ignoring the shout. As the group came toward him he said, "This is different. Wait and see."

When the nine boys not on sentry or scout duty were lined up before Laurence and had quieted down, he took a scrap of newspaper from his pocket and looked at it, frowning. "This is what real training is," he said, and began to read: " 'And this program is no strength-through-joy movement. It's a grim, tough business. Weaklings, morally and physically, can't take it; they're not wanted. At Fort Bragg, the emphasis is on developing aggressiveness. There physical toughening takes place in the course of this program to' " —he stumbled over the word—" 'to inculcate the "killer" instinct. There is none of the emphasis on the niceties of the game or on sportsmanship. In some of the contests I witnessed a number of palpable fouls. "We're interested only in teaching them to go out and win," explained . . .' " Laurence broke off impatiently. "Oh, never mind all that. I'll just tell you what the rest of it says."

He took a deep breath and looked directly at his audience, which had grown restless during his reading. "Why did we have so many casualties in Africa at first? Because the men hadn't learned to keep cover, they exposed themselves. And do you know how they cure that now? By using live bullets in training." This was what he had been working toward, and it got some show of interest from the shifting line of boys. "And that's how we're going to train from now on."

Laurence looked around for a moment at the familiar geography of the pit. Then he faced the ranks. "At the command 'Fall out' go back beyond that bush, and then at the command 'Advance' start crawling straight for where I am now. Remember, keep everything down right flat to the ground. Dick, you get into that foxhole beside me with some round stones about this size"—he leaned over and selected one from the ground—"and keep throwing them just thirty inches above the ground. It has to be thirty inches." He waited until they were in their positions and then gave the commands. "Now then, get down flat and crawl. Make it fast. Keep your guns ready."

Laurence looked on with satisfaction as the line of grunting boys, wooden guns in their right hands, crept toward the foxhole across the sand and through the crab grass, while the boy in the foxhole, about twenty feet from them, threw stones happily. But it didn't work out well. The first stone was too high. The second, a piece of slate, curved down and hit the first crawler on the hand. He jumped up angrily.

"You threw that at me on purpose, Dick!"

"No, I didn't," Dick said.

"Well, you were looking right at me when you threw."

"Back to line, all of you, and keep on!" Laurence shouted. He turned to the thrower. "Don't think about them. Just keep throwing level, thirty inches above the ground."

They began to crawl again, but a stone which just missed a boy's face brought another angry protest. "Hey, that was no thirty inches!"

"Well, what is thirty inches?" Dick yelled. "Let's see you try it."

"All right, I will."

"Stop! As you were," Laurence called. "This has got to be right." He stopped a moment to consider. Then he shook his head. "A gun would be the only thing that would be right. We'd have to have a real gun."

"Nuts. You aren't shooting any old bullets at me," one boy said, shaking his head excitedly. The others were held by the idea, testing themselves in their minds.

"We could fix it so it would be safe," Laurence said.

"You could if you had a gun."

"We can get one," Laurence said impressively. He grinned at Ed Peterson for confirmation. "Hey, Ed?"

Ed frowned. "What?" he asked, as if he did not understand. He was a chunky boy with deep-set eyes and a scar showing through his cropped brown hair.

"You know," Laurence said impatiently. "The thirty-two. You said you could have it any time you wanted."

"Well, not over here I can't."

"Why not? If you can have it any time you want it, why can't you have it when we need it here?"

"Well, that isn't the same," Ed said uneasily.

The others were eager. "Come on, Ed." "Does he let you shoot it?" "Could I shoot it, Ed?"

"No, no one else can shoot it but me."

"All right, you'll be the only one to shoot it," Laurence said, "but hurry up."

"I'd have to ask my father."

"You *said* you didn't have to ask him. Anyway, your tool shed's out of sight of the house."

Ed looked around for support, but none was forthcoming. The wooden guns the boys were playing with had become absurd.

"But I have to go home early," Ed said. "We're going on a picnic out on the point."

"I have to be home early too. That's why we've got to hurry."
Laurence glanced over at the captain's wristwatch. "Look, Ed,
we've got to have this right and you're spoiling everything." He
paused and looked firmly at Ed. "I wonder what kind of soldier you
are," he said slowly.

He waited in silence, until Ed had to give in. "I hadn't ought to,
but I suppose this once," Ed said reluctantly, and began trudging
off.

"Be back in ten minutes and bring plenty of shells," Laurence
said, glancing impatiently at the watch again. The boys were excited
now, and all began talking at once with nervous boastfulness.

When Ed came back with the rifle, he was still uneasy. "My father
came out to go to the garden," he said, "and I dropped it in the high
grass. He didn't see it, but I nearly got caught." He blew out his
breath and shook his head.

"O.K.," Laurence murmured, absorbed in what he was doing. By
much winding of string and wire, he was fastening the barrel to the
top of a box placed at the edge of the foxhole. It was very unsteady,
but they piled sand and rocks on it until it was good and firm.

"You won't be able to see to shoot now," Ed said.

"You're not supposed to. That would spoil it." Laurence was still
making adjustments. He finally got the gun fixed and placed a large
cardboard carton about thirty feet away. When Ed dropped into the
foxhole and tried the gun, with three shots, the bullets plopped
through the cardboard at just about the right distance from the
ground. "There!" Laurence said with satisfaction.

The group quieted as the shots sounded, flat and unechoing within
the enclosure of the sand pit. Then their excitement burst out again.
"Boy, you don't get me in front of that gun." "I'd dig right through
the ground like an old mole."

"I'll show you," Laurence said. "Shoot twice when I call out," he
told Ed, who was out of sight, behind the gun. The others, crawling
under the barrage of rocks, had made a track through the sand. Laurence followed it, hitching forward on his elbows. As he approached
the gun he called out to Ed and then put his face almost into the sand
and kept on advancing. The two shots went well above his head and
barely enlarged the hole in the carton. Laurence jumped up.

"See," he said. "But we can't use so many shots for each one. We
can keep in single file and let him fire sort of unevenly so we won't
know when it's going off. That will teach us to keep down."

He considered the faces of the boys. "Anyone afraid?" he asked. "Those who want to get in line, come forward."

"I want to, too," Ed called from the hole.

"All right. Neil, you know how to shoot it, don't you? Just every once in a while. But wait till we're ready."

The first time the file of boys wriggled forward they were obviously fearful and hesitant, flinching at the sound of the gun and struggling with the desire to raise their heads and see where the bullet struck. But once safely past the line of fire, they leaped up in ecstatic joy and ran around the gun pit to take their places again.

Laurence glanced up and saw that the sentries stationed on the rim above were watching the maneuvers in the pit. "Corporal Higgins," he said, turning to the boy at the head of the file, "go up and remind the sentries that we are expecting an attack. They've got to watch those woods for men coming up the hill. Tell them to turn around and forget we are down here."

After the file of boys had gone toward the foxhole twice, Ed halted abruptly and looked at his watch. "I have to have the gun now," he said. "I have to go home."

"Aw, Ed!" they said. "Once more. Come on, Ed. It only takes a minute."

"All right," he said. "Once more, but fast."

It was when the file of boys had started forward toward the gun for the third time, and some twenty-five shots had been fired, that the expected attack from the Powderhouse Point army came. One of the sentinels saw them in the woods at the foot of the hill and shouted a warning, raising his gun horizontally above his head. Ed, who was first in file and a squad leader, recognized the signal and excitedly started to scramble to his feet. Neil, who was down in the pit, could not see the sentinel. He fired the gun again. Ed collapsed on the ground.

"Stop, Neil, stop!" Laurence shouted. He waited a moment, then got to his knees. There were heavy steps behind him as a man in overalls hurried up. "Who's shooting that gun around here?" he bellowed. It was Joe Tobin, the contractor, who owned the pit. "You know what I've told you." He looked past Laurence and saw Ed lying face down on the ground. Blood was draining into the grass around his head.

"For the love of God in heaven!" Tobin cried out, and went over to kneel by Ed. Laurence leaned down beside him. Tobin lifted the boy by the shoulders and looked at his head. There was not much blood at the wound—it came mostly from his mouth—and Tobin could see where the bullet had entered the head and where it had come out.

Up on the rim the sentinels were engaging the enemy. The Powderhouse Point boys were calling, "You're dead," "I got you." The outnumbered sentinels, retreating, looked down to see why help was not coming. When they noticed the circle around Ed and realized someone was hurt, they began running and sliding down the sides of the pit, their attackers with them.

"He isn't *dead*, is he?" Laurence asked Tobin in a protesting voice.

"Of course he's dead!" Tobin shouted angrily. He looked at the boys who had come down from above. "Go on, get out of here!" he yelled. "What's the matter with you!" Then he groaned and sat down heavily on a rock, staring at Ed and twisting his old felt hat in his hands.

There was a hubbub of questions from the boys who had just come down. "Ed got shot," someone said. "He's dead." They fell silent.

"Shouldn't we *do* something?" Laurence said desperately.

"Of course, of course. We're not going to leave him here." Tobin got up, stopped, and went back to the rock. "I've got to stay here," he said, brushing distractedly at a green fly about his head. "Go on, get somebody, quick. Get an ambulance, get his father. I'll stay here."

Some of the boys still stood looking on, silently, at a little distance, but the rest turned and started off down the rutted road. Tobin called them back in sudden fright. "You kids can't go telling the Petersons!" He looked at Laurence. "You live next door. Your father home?" Laurence nodded. "You tell him, then," Tobin said. "And let him break the news."

Laurence whirled and ran. The other boys broke up into small, straggling groups, walking slowly and talking in soft, excited voices.

Mr. Purvis was sitting on his screened porch, alternately reading *Time* and looking at his garden; Laurence could clear out some of the stuff that was past yielding and pick corn and beans for supper. He saw Laurence coming, running hard. "The warrior returneth," he called to his wife. "Only ten minutes late. If you approach him right he really tries."

Laurence leaped over the low picket fence and came up to the porch. His father said, "I think I'll join you on the job. I was relieved of the dishes by the beneficence of your mother." Laurence came in with his face turned away, panting. From the next house down the road they could hear a man's voice calling. Laurence did not speak. Mr. Purvis frowned. "Look," he said, "remember what..." but Laurence pushed past him toward the hall. His father grabbed him angrily and swung him around. "I said I expected..."

Then he saw that Laurence was sobbing. Mr. Purvis looked down at his son in surprise. "Come, boy," he said softly, "I think we can forget these ten minutes." He tried to distract him, as one would a much younger child. "Listen to Mr. Peterson calling Ed," he said. He smiled. "He sounds like an old cow."

The sobs broke out into sound. Mrs. Purvis rushed from the kitchen, but Mr. Purvis held up his hand to silence her. Through a great many domestic crises, he had learned to take a detached and scientific attitude. It was easier on the nerves and accomplished more. Not the attitude of the judge, for Mr. Purvis was well aware of the remedial weaknesses of the law. The attitude of the doctor, the healer, rather, finding first what was wrong and then compounding the proper remedy.

"Is it something else, then?" he asked in a firm, suggestive, soothing voice. "Tell us about it. You know we'll understand. We deal with these things together, you know. Just tell us."

The sobs became still more violent, the boy's body shuddering in a kind of sickness against the man's.

"Nothing's ever so bad once you've told it," Mr. Purvis said to him, shaking his head a little as he talked. He glanced up at Mrs. Purvis, smiling gently in anticipation of early climax and release. They waited. Through the screen they could see Mr. Peterson set a picnic hamper down on his curbstone and, still calling, start up the road. He had huge, freckled arms and a very small cloth cap set squarely on his head. He made a rather absurd figure. Mr. Purvis looked down once more at his son. "Just get it outside so's we can look at it, Laury," he said confidently, "and then we'll set it right."

THE MYSTERIES OF LIFE IN AN ORDERLY MANNER

❖

JESSAMYN WEST

IT WAS INITIATION night, a candle-lighting ceremony, a big night in the lodge, and through the spring twilight of the California hill town, past the parking meters and the street-corner loungers, the matrons carrying their candles unlit drifted like moths. Not mothlike certainly in their plumpness but varicolored, fluttering, and pleasure-bent.

Emily Cooper (Mrs. W. H. Cooper—William H. Cooper, Inc., Insurance—"See Us B 4 U Burn") sat with her husband in their car, parked at the curb. Across the street from them, and a little way down, was the Vasconi Building, where the initiation was being held. Emily was herself to be initiated that night, but she didn't know the Pocahontas women very well and she was sitting for a time with her husband, gathering up courage from his matter-of-factness and checking the suitability of her dress against what she could see of the evening dresses of the other initiates, passing in the fading light. Only the initiates wore evening dresses (formals, formals, Emily reminded herself to say). The established lodge members, the Pocahontases in good standing, went to their meetings in Indian regalia. Emily watched them go by in the twilight, coats thrown back, because the evening was warm, fringes swaying, beaded headbands gleaming, moccasined feet silent on the sidewalk. Emily was proud to recognize some of them.

"There's Mrs. Asta Bell," she said to her husband. "She's Keeper of the Wampum."

"Keeper of what?" asked Mr. Cooper, himself no lodge man. Emily got into Pocahontas because of her father, Clement McCarthy, a long-time Redman, though not a resident of the state. "Join, join," her father had always urged her, but Emily would not so long as the children were little.

"Wampum," said Emily. "Indian for money. She's treasurer."

Mrs. Edna Purvis went by, black-haired and straight, most Indian-like of all, and Mrs. Wanda Turner, married to the county sheriff, and Zula Throne, married to no one at all, the only unmarried Pocahontas in the lodge. When Emily had remarked on this to some of the other lodge members, she had been told, "Most single girls are too frivolous for lodge work. Can't concentrate on ritual and memorizing, let alone beadwork. Spend their time mooning about, thinking of . . ."

Emily, anxious to appear quick-witted before her sisters-to-be, had suggested in this pause "Men," and her informer had repeated the word, but it had seemed not quite to fill the bill. "Yes and no," she had told Emily. "Yes and no." But Zula Throne was an exception—no mooner, they said, and, though maiden, as brisk in ritual and beadwork as any married lady.

More officers, some of the most important, passed by on the sidewalk. "Look, look," said Emily, whispering, "but not right away. Now, that's the Grand Prophetess."

Mr. Cooper looked. "Couldn't tell her from an ordinary prophetess," he said calmly.

"Oh, she's full of authority," said Emily. "A power in the lodge, believe me."

It was exciting for Emily to sit in the car with her husband, pointing out to him the town's leading ladies. It was a novelty, too, for it was he who had usually known everyone and done the pointing. But they were new in Midvale, the insurance office had been open only a couple of months, and Mr. Cooper's work in opening it had kept him too busy for getting acquainted with the Pocahontas ladies.

"That's Mrs. Pleasant Jones," said Emily. "She's First Scout, and the one with her, the tall one with the red headband, I can't remember her name but I know she's the Second Runner."

Following the Second Runner were the Guards of Tepee and Forest, and Pocahontas, herself—Mrs. Virgila Smiley—with feathers in her headband. Emily knew all three of them and pointed them out as they went by carrying their candles and squares or oblongs of home-baked cake. They passed on foot, by twos and threes, or alighted, singly, from cars driven by their husbands. They were laughing and talking, but their voices were low; an initiation by candlelight was solemn and secret; it was spring, it was almost night.

"They shouldn't have candles, really," Emily explained to her husband.

"No candles?" said Mr. Cooper, who had been watching the Second Runner. "Why not?"

"It's not in the Ritual. But the Grand Prophetess says we're so far off the beaten track here in the hills that we can plead ignorance in case of criticism."

"Why, sure," said Mr. Cooper. "Sure you can. Why not?"

"We shouldn't be hit-or-miss," explained Emily. "The lodge treats of the mysteries of life in an orderly manner."

Mr. Cooper looked at his wife inquiringly.

"That's what I was told," she said. "And the candles aren't part of that order."

"Maybe they're part of the mystery," suggested Mr. Cooper.

Emily supposed that her husband was smiling, but no, he was serious, looking intently into the creamy blooms of the laurel trees that lined the sidewalk, and listening to the birds that were singing on into the night because of the springtime.

"It's the second spring," said Emily.

In California, the first spring is in November. March only echoes it. In November the first spring is brief and sharp after the early rains. Then the grass flares up like fire; dry stream beds, as dead to the eye as old snakeskins, revive, all their bends and shallows filled with the curve of bright water; quail call; mushrooms push their blunt heads through the sodden leaves under the valley oaks; and at the end of the town's short streets, early sunsets and winter barley, alike green, meet. Spring is sharp in November—a slap, a blow, a kiss, soon over, soon forgotten, colder weather to follow. In March it is easy, gentle, nothing to wonder at, it will last a long time. Summer will come, the hills be brown and faded, no one able to say just when the rains stopped or the grass withered.

"Counting November, it's the second spring," said Mr. Cooper.

"I *was* counting November," said Emily, dangling a hand out the car window to test the air. It was still warm, though the sun was down, no color left behind, the sky as drab as a cast-iron skillet. Emily pushed her feet, slim in pointed satin slippers, up the incline of the floor boards until they cleared her full, white marquisette skirt. She reset the white daphne she had pinned in her hair and redampened her handkerchief from the bottle of Hoyt's perfume she had in her purse.

"Do I look all right?" she inquired anxiously of her husband.

"Fine, fine," said he. "Couldn't look better."

"Do I smell too strong of cologne?"

"Look fine, smell fine."

With sudden energy, Emily gathered her coat about her shoulders, grasped her candle, prepared to depart. "I always look fine," she said irritably. "I always look fine and I always smell fine to you. You don't give me any confidence."

Mr. Cooper leaned over, detained her with his hand on her arm. "But you do," he said. "You always do. What do you want me to say? Want me to be a liar?"

"No," said Emily, "but if I knew you were critical, it would give me more confidence."

"Oh, critical!" said Mr. Cooper, surprised. "Why, I'm critical, critical as all getout. That Second Runner, now. She's bandy-legged. I criticized it in her first thing. They'd ought to have given her the wampum job. Something she could do sitting down, not put her to running."

Emily opened the car door, jumped out, and banged it behind her. It was dark enough for the first stars to show, not distinctly, a little blurred in their outlines, as if the moist spring air had caused them to run a bit. The birds were still rustling and chirping in the laurel trees, unwilling for this day to end. Down the street the neon signs said "Eat," said "Drink," said "Short Orders," said "Church of the Open Door." There were no Pocahontases in sight and Emily felt a little strange, on the street after dark in her long white dress. A man paused under the "Drink" sign to look at her before pushing the swinging doors apart. She lingered at the car side.

"Don't joke about serious things," she said fiercely. "It makes me nervous. And I'm already nervous to begin with."

"Don't be nervous," said Mr. Cooper. "I'm critical and you look fine and smell fine and you are going to see the marvels of life in an orderly manner."

"Mysteries," said Emily, *"mysteries,"* and she turned away without so much as a goodbye and started toward the Vasconi Building. But before she had taken two angry steps, Mr. Cooper had caught up with her.

"Mysteries was what I meant," he said contritely, and they walked on together arm in arm, past the birds and the trees and the plate-glass windows and the men going in for a drink. "The mysteries of life in an orderly manner," he said, "was what I fully intended to say."

PORTE-COCHÈRE

❖

PETER TAYLOR

CLIFFORD AND BEN JUNIOR always came for Old Ben's birthday, Clifford from Dallas, Ben Junior from Cincinnati. They usually stayed in Nashville through the following weekend, or came the weekend before and stayed through the birthday. Old Ben, seventy-six and nearly blind—the cataracts had been removed twice since he was seventy—could hear them now on the side porch, their voices louder than the others', Clifford's the loudest and strongest of all, Clifford the real man amongst them. There were certain things Clifford could understand. Clifford was a lawyer and knew some history, knew the difference between Chucky Jack Sevier and Judge John Overton. Old Ben kept listening for Cliff's voice above the others. They were all down on the octagonal side porch, which was beyond the porte-cochère and which, under its red tile roof, looked like a pagoda there on the side lawn. Old Ben was in his study.

His study was above the porte-cochère, or what his wife, in her day, had called the porte-cochère—he and the boys called it the drive-under—but the study was not a part of the second floor; it opened off the landing halfway up the stairs. Outside his south window was the red roof of the porch. He sat by the open window, wearing his dark glasses, his watery old eyes focussed vaguely on the peak of the roof. He had napped a little since dinner but had not removed his suit coat or even unbuttoned his linen vest. During most of the afternoon, he had been awake and had heard his five children talking down there on the porch—Cliff and Ben Junior had arrived only that morning—talking on and on in such loud voices that his good right ear could catch individual words and sometimes whole sentences.

Midday dinner had been a real ordeal for Old Ben. Laura Nell's interminable chatter had been particularly taxing and obnoxious. Afterward, he had hurried to his study for his prescribed nap and spent a good part of the afternoon dreading the expedition to the country club for supper that had been planned for that evening. It was almost time to begin getting ready for that expedition now, and simultaneously with the thought of it and with the movement of his hand toward his watch pocket he became aware that Clifford was taking his leave of the group on the side porch. Ah, yes, at dinnertime Clifford had said he had a letter to write before supper—to his wife. Yet here it was six and he had dawdled away the afternoon palavering with the others down there on the porch. Old Ben could recognize Cliff's leave-taking and the teasing voices of the others, and then he heard Cliff's footsteps on the cement driveway, below the study—a hurried step. He heard Cliff in the side hall and then his footsteps at the bottom of the stairs. In a moment he would go sailing by Old Ben's door, without a thought for anyone but himself. Old Ben's lower lip trembled. Wasn't there some business matter he could take up with Cliff? Or some personal matter? And now Cliff's footsteps on the stairs—heavy footsteps, like his own. Suddenly, though, the footsteps halted, and Clifford went downstairs again. His father heard him go across the hall and into the living room, where the carpet silenced his footsteps; he was getting writing paper from the desk there. Old Ben hastily pulled the cord that closed the draperies across the south window, leaving only the vague light from the east window in the room. No, sir, he would not advertise his presence when Cliff passed on the landing.

With the draperies drawn, the light in the room had a strange quality, because Old Ben rarely closed them before night. For one moment, he felt that his eyes or his glasses were playing him some new trick. Then he dropped his head on the chair back, for the strange quality now seemed strangely familiar, and now no longer strange—only familiar. It was like the light in that cellar where, long ago, he used to go to fetch Mason jars for Aunt Nelson. She would send for him all the way across town to come fetch her Mason jars, and even when he was ten or twelve, she made him whistle the whole time he was down in the cellar, to make certain he didn't drink her wine. Aunt Nelson, dead and gone. Was this something for Clifford's attention? Where Aunt Nelson's house had been, the Trust Company now stood—a near-skyscraper. Her cellar, he supposed, had been in the space now occupied by the basement barbershop—not quite so deep or so large as the shop, its area without boundaries now, suspended in the center of the barbershop, where the ceiling fan revolved. Would this be of interest to Cliff, who would soon ascend the stairs with his own train of thoughts and would presently pass the open door to the study without a word or a glance? And whatever Cliff was thinking about—his law, his golf, or his wife and children—

would be of no real interest to Old Ben. But he longed to have Cliff come and talk to him about whatever he would. Did not Clifford know that the sound of his voice gave his father hope, that his attention gave him comfort? What would old age be without children? Desolation, desolation. But what would old age be with children who chose to ignore the small demands that he would make upon them, that he had ever made upon them? A nameless torment! And with his thoughts Old Ben Brantley's white head rocked on his shoulders and his smoked glasses went so crooked on his nose that he had to frown them back into position.

But now Clifford was hurrying up the stairs again. He was on the landing outside the open study door. It was almost despite himself that Old Ben cleared his throat and said hoarsely, "The news will be on in five minutes, if you want to listen to it." Then, as though he might have sounded too cordial (he would not be reduced to toadying to his own boy), "But if you don't want to, don't say you do." Had Cliff seen his glasses slip down his nose? Cliff, no less than the others, would be capable of laughing at him in his infirmity.

"I wouldn't be likely to, would I, Papa?" Cliff had stopped at the doorway and was stifling a yawn as he spoke, half covering his face with the envelope and the folded sheet of paper. Old Ben nodded his head to indicate that he had heard what Cliff had said, but also, to himself, he was nodding that yes, this was the way he had raised his children to talk to him.

"Just the hourly newscast," Old Ben said indifferently. "But it don't matter."

"Naw, can't make it, Papa. I got to go and write Sue Alice. The stupid woman staying with her while I'm away bores her pretty much." As he spoke, he looked directly into the dark lenses of his father's glasses, and for a brief second he rested his left hand on the doorjamb. His manner was self-possessed and casual, but Old Ben felt that he didn't need good sight to detect his son's ill-concealed haste to be off and away. Cliff had, in fact, turned back to the stairs when Old Ben stopped him with a question, spoken without expression and almost under his breath.

"Why did you come at all? Why did you even bother to come if you weren't going to bring Sue Alice and the grandchildren? Did you think I wanted to see you without them?"

Clifford stopped with one foot on the first step of the second flight. "By God, Papa!" He turned on the ball of the other foot and re-appeared in the doorway. "Ever travel with two small kids?" The motion of his body as he turned back from the steps had been swift and sure, calculated to put him exactly facing his father. "And in hot weather like we're having?"

Despite the undeniable thickness in Clifford's hips and the thin spot on the back of his head, his general appearance was still youthful; about this particular turning on the stairs there had been something decidedly athletic. Imperceptibly, behind the dark glasses, Old Ben lifted his eyebrows in admiration. Clifford was the only boy he had who had ever made any team at the university or done any hunting worth speaking of. For a moment, his eyes rested gently on Cliff's white summer shoes, set wide apart in the doorway. Then, jerking his head up, as though he had just heard Cliff's last words, he began, "Two small *kids?* (Why don't you use the word *brats?* It's more elegant.) I have travelled considerably with five—from here to the mountain and back every summer for fifteen years, from my thirty-first to my forty-sixth year."

"I remember," Cliff said stoically. Then, after a moment, "But now I'm going up to my room and write Sue Alice."

"Then go on up! Who's holding you? Is someone holding you, Clifford?" Old Ben reached for his smoking stand and switched on the radio. It was a big cabinet radio with a dark-mahogany finish, a piece from the late twenties, like all the other furniture in the room, and the mechanism was slow to warm up.

Clifford took several steps toward his father. "Papa, we're due to leave for the club in thirty minutes—less than that now—and I intend to scratch off a note to my wife." He held up the writing paper, as though to prove his intention.

"No concern of mine! No concern of mine! To begin with, I, personally, am not going to the club or anywhere else for supper."

Clifford came even closer. "You may go to the club or not, as you like, Papa. But unless I misunderstand, there is not a servant on the place, and we are all going."

"That is, you are going after you scratch off a note to your wife."

"Papa, Ben Junior and I have each come well over five hundred miles—"

"Not to see me, Clifford."

"Don't be so damned childish, Papa." Cliff was turning away again. Old Ben held his watch in his hand, and he glanced down at it quickly.

"I'm getting childish, am I, Clifford?"

This time, Clifford's turning back was not accomplished in one graceful motion but by a sudden jerking and twisting of his shoulder and leg muscles. Behind the spectacles, Old Ben's eyes narrowed and twitched. His fingers were folded over the face of the watch. Clifford spoke very deliberately. "I didn't say *getting* childish, Papa. When ever in your life have you been anything but that? There's not a senile bone in your brain. It's your children that have got old, and you've stayed young—and not in any good sense, Papa, only in a bad one! You play sly games with us still or you quarrel with us. What the hell do you want of us, Papa? I've thought about it a lot. Why haven't you ever asked for what it is you want? Or are we all blind and it's really obvious? You've never given but one piece of advice to us, and that's to be direct and talk up to you like men—as equals. And we've done that, all right, and listened to your wrangling, but somehow it has never satisfied you! What is it?"

"Go on up to your letter-writing; go write your spouse," Old Ben answered.

The room had been getting dark while they talked. Old Ben slipped his watch back into his vest pocket nervously, then slipped it out again, constantly running his fingers over the gold case, as though it were a piece of money.

"Thanks for your permission, sir." Clifford took a step backward. During his long speech, he had advanced all the way across the room until he was directly in front of his father.

"My permission?" Old Ben said. "Let's not forget one fact, Clifford. No child of mine has ever had to ask my permission to do anything whatsoever he took a mind to do. You have all been free as the air, to come and go in this house—"

Clifford smiled. "Free to come and go, with you perched here on the landing registering every footstep on the stairs and every car that passed underneath. I used to turn off the ignition and coast through the drive-under, and then think how foolish it was, since there was no back stairway. No back stairway in a house this size!" He paused a moment, running his eyes over the furniture and the other familiar objects in the shadowy room. "And how like the old times this was, Papa—your listening in here in the dark when I came up! By God, Papa, I wouldn't have thought when I was growing up that I'd ever come back and fuss with you once I was grown. But here I am, and, Papa—"

Old Ben pushed himself up from the chair. He put his watch in the vest pocket and buttoned his suit coat with an air of satisfaction. "I'm going along to the club for supper," he said, "since there's to be no-un here to serve me." As he spoke, he heard the clock chiming the half hour downstairs. And Ben Junior was shouting to Old Ben and Clifford from the foot of the stairs, "Get a move on up there."

Clifford went out on the landing and called down the steps. "Wait till I change my shirt. I believe Papa's all ready."

"No letter written?" Ben Junior asked.

Clifford was hurrying up the second flight with the blank paper. "Nope, no letter this day of Our Lord."

Old Ben heard Ben Junior say, "What did I tell you?" and heard the others laughing. He stood an instant by his chair without putting on a light. Then he reached out his hand for one of the walking canes in the umbrella stand by the radio. His hand lighting on the carved head of a certain oak stick, he felt the head with trembling fingers and quickly released it, and quickly, in three strides, without the help of any cane, he crossed the room to the south window. For several moments, he stood motionless at the window, his huge, soft hands held tensely at his sides, his long body erect, his almost freakishly large head at a slight angle, while he seemed to peer between the open draperies and through the pane of the upper sash, out into the twilight of the wide, shady park that stretched from his great yellow brick house to the Pike. Old Ben's eyes, behind the smoked lenses, were closed, and he was visualizing the ceiling fan in the barbershop. Presently, opening his eyes, he reflected, almost with a smile, that his aunt's cellar was not the only Nashville cellar that had disappeared. Many a cellar! His father's cellar, round like a dungeon; it had been a cistern in the very earliest days, before Old Ben's time, and when he was a boy, he would go down on a ladder with a lantern, and his father's voice, directing him, would seem to go around and around the brick walls and then come back with a hollow sound, as though the cistern were still half full of water. One time, ah—Old Ben drew back from the window with a grimace—one time he had been so sure there was water below! In fright at the very thought of the water, he had clasped a rung of the ladder tightly with one hand and swung the lantern out, expecting certainly to see the light reflected in the depths below. But the lantern had struck the framework that sup- ported the circular shelves and gone whirling and flaming to the brick floor, which Ben had never before seen. Crashing on the floor, it sent up yellow flames that momentarily lit the old cistern to its very top, and when Ben looked upward, he saw the furious face of his father with the flames casting jagged shadows on the long, black beard and high, white forehead. "Come out of there before you burn out my cellar and my whole damn house to the ground!" He had climbed upward toward his father, wishing the flames might engulf him before he came within reach of those arms. But as his father jerked him up onto the back porch, he saw that the flames had already died out. The whole cellar was pitch-black dark again, and the boy Ben stood with his face against the whitewashed brick wall while his father went to the carriage house to find the old plowline. Presently, he heard his father step up on the porch again. He braced himself for the first blow, but instead there was only the deafening command from his father: "Attention!" Ben whirled about and stood erect, with his chin in the air, his eyes on the ceiling. "Where have you hidden my plowlines?" "I don't know, sir." And then the old man, with his coattails somehow clinging close to his buttocks and thighs, so that his whole powerful form was outlined—his black figure against the white brick and the door—stepped over to the doorway, reached around to the cane stand in the hall, and drew out the oak stick that had his own face carved upon the head. "About face!" he commanded. The boy drew back his toe and turned about, and the old man dealt him three blows across the upper part of his back. Tears had run down young Ben Brantley's cheeks, even streaking down his neck under his open collar and soaking the neckline binding of his woollen underwear, but he had uttered not a sound. When his father went into the house, Ben remained for a long while standing with his face to the wall. At last, he quietly left the porch and walked through the yard beneath the big shade trees, stopping casually to watch a gray squirrel and then to listen to Aunt Sally Ann's soft nigger voice whispering to him out the kitchen window. He did not answer or turn around but walked on to the latticed summerhouse, between the house and the kitchen garden. There he had lain down on a bench, looked back at the house through the latticework, and said to himself that when he got to be a grown man, he would go away to another country, where there were no maple trees and no oak trees, no elms, not even sycamores or poplars; where there were no squirrels and no niggers, no houses that resembled this one; and, most of all, where there were no children and no fathers.

In the hall, now, Old Ben could hear, very faintly, Ben Junior's voice and Laura Nell's and Katie's and Lawrence's. He stepped to the door and looked down the dark flight of steps at his four younger children. They stood in a circle directly beneath the overhead light, which one of them had just switched on. Their faces were all turned upward in the direction of the open doorway where he was standing, yet he knew in reason that they could not see him there. They were talking about him! Through his dark lenses, their figures were indistinct, their faces mere blurs, and it was hard for him to distinguish their lowered voices one from another. But they were talking about him! And from upstairs he could hear Clifford's footsteps. Clifford, with his letter to Sue Alice unwritten, was thinking about him! Never once in his life had he punished or restrained them in any way! He had given them a freedom unknown to children in the land of his childhood, yet from the time they could utter a word they had despised him and denied his right to any affection or gratitude. Suddenly, stepping out onto the landing, he screamed down the stairs to them, "I've a right to some gratitude!"

They were silent and motionless for a moment. Then he could hear them speaking in lowered voices again, and moving slowly toward the stairs. At the same moment he heard Clifford's footsteps in the upstairs hall. Presently, a light went on up there, and he could dimly see Clifford at the head of the stairs. The four children were advancing up the first flight, and Clifford was coming down from upstairs. Old Ben opened his mouth to call to them, "I'm not afraid of you!" But his voice had left him, and in his momentary fright, in his fear that in their wrath his children would do him harm, he suddenly pitied them. He pitied them for all they had suffered at his hands. And while he stood there, afraid, he realized, or perhaps recalled, how he had tortured and plagued them in all the ways that his resentment of their very good fortune had taught him to do. He even remembered the day when it had occurred to him to build his study above the drive-under and off the stairs, so that he could keep tab on them. He had declared that he wanted his house to be as different from his father's house as a house could be, and so it was! And now he stood in the half darkness, afraid that he was a man about to be taken by his children and at the same time pitying them, until one of them, ascending the steps, switched on the light above the landing.

In the sudden brightness, Old Ben felt that his senses had returned to him. Quickly, he stepped back into the study, closed the door, and locked it. As the lock clicked, he heard Clifford say, "Papa!" Then he heard them all talking at once, and while they talked, he stumbled through the dark study to the umbrella stand. He pulled out the stick with his father's face carved on the head, and in the darkness, while he heard his children's voices, he stumbled about the room beating the upholstered chairs with the stick and calling the names of his children under his breath.

THE EVOLUTION OF KNOWLEDGE

❖

Niccolò Tucci

THERE IS SOMETHING wrong with the floors of our apartment in New York. Not even our superintendent can do anything about it, for the cause of the trouble lies beyond his reach; it may, in fact, be traced back to the incongruities of Progress and to the decay of Western Civilization. Also to my two children, especially my son Vieri, who is seven. Every bounce of Vieri's ball on the floor evokes the spirit of Mr. Feinstein and sets into motion a long line of actions and reactions, which end in Mr. Feinstein's pounding on the radiator pipe or on his ceiling right under our feet. The spirit of Mr. Feinstein grows bigger, bigger, bigger, until *everything* is Mr. Feinstein. Vieri, in fact, is the real Sorcerer's Apprentice with that ball—tum ti, tum ti, tatata, tum ti, tum ti . . .

But there was a time when Mr. Feinstein didn't allow his spirit to reach us through his ceiling. He kept his fuming downstairs. That is why I think the story should be told; it is a highly philosophical story, because it proves that knowledge is not static but instead is constantly in the process of evolution.

Three years ago, when Mr. Feinstein pounded on the radiator, we did not care. Then, one day, I met him in the elevator. Though we had never happened to meet before, each of us knew instinctively who the other was, so, man to man, we had one of those bitter exchanges of words, just off the limits of politeness, that are usually accompanied by acceleration of the heartbeat and heavy breathing. Alas, in our case the exchange was also marked by an uncontrollable relapse into our foreign accents. Though this last hampered the free flow of profanity, it was how I learned that Mr. Feinstein came from Saxony, and how he, who has lived in my country, understood that I came from Tuscany. But what we chiefly managed to convey to each other was that "Man must sleep" (his theory) and "Children must jump" (mine). The next time we met, we realized that we were both haters of hate more than of each other, so we tried to solve the prob-

lem by means of diplomatic negotiation. "We exiles," I said, "are always in a state of repressed emotion." He nodded and then explained,
with many apologies, that the floor squeaked terribly even when I
walked on it barefoot, and I explained, with my own apologies, that
I had intended for some time to buy carpets for all the rooms, "but
you know . . ." And he said, "Don't I know! You must not misunderstand me, please. It's not your fault. The floors haven't been repaired
for the last two years, because of the war. So, you see, it's definitely
one of those things that cannot be helped."

I thanked him for the acquittal, and he had an even more encouraging observation for me. Children's noise was also just one of those
things that could not be helped, he said. I said, "You're much too
kind, and, to tell you the truth, my children should learn how to behave." "Oh, no," he said, and I knew that he was growing political
in his thoughts, because his face became quite sombre. "We have all
suffered too much because of this idea of restraint," he said. "I, who
was brought up in the strictest discipline, am now all in favor of the
American system. Children here may do just as they please. They
grow healthier, freer."

I nodded gratefully and, feeling that I must now repay him for his
understanding, began to search my mind for something very bad to
say against my children, something that would even make them appear to be unworthy of this blessed American freedom. But before I
could formulate a reply, he made a demand. "All I ask you to do,"
he said, "is to have the children wear slippers on Saturdays and Sundays until at least ten in the morning, for that's the only time in the
week that I can rest a little."

"This is indeed very little to ask," I said, "and I assure you that it
will be done."

When I entered my apartment and found my family gathered in
plenary session in the kitchen, I announced that I had just had a
pleasant talk with the man downstairs. To my wife, I said, by way of
comment, "A very civilized, kind person, really," and to the children,
by way of injunction, "All he wants from you is that on Saturdays
and Sundays, until after ten in the morning, you walk with your slippers on and don't play ball. Can you imagine anything easier than
that?" They immediately saw the adventure in a program of this
kind; the idea of connecting their slippers with a given period of
time seemed full of mystery and charm. Vieri told me that he would
watch the clock and the very instant the hand touched the first tiny
portion of the figure 10, he would throw his slippers against the ceil-

ing. And Bimba, who is only five, immediately went to her room and came back to the kitchen, where we were sitting, with her slippers and Vieri's, to rehearse the Feast of Liberation.

"No, no!" I shouted, and my wife shouted, "No, no!" But since the slippers were already flying in all directions and landing in the sink, on the gas rings, behind the icebox, and on the breakfast table, I saw that the situation was desperate, and I commanded silence. Then I made an announcement.

"First of all," I said, "when he says ten o'clock, he doesn't mean that at ten sharp we have to start making a lot of noise. Ten o'clock means some time in the middle of the morning. We don't want to impose on his kindness."

"Impose?" Vieri asked. "What does that mean?"

"Now, look," I said. "The idea is this: We don't want to be unkind to this man." And I went on to explain that on Saturday and Sunday mornings we would go to the park if the weather was fine or play quiet games at home if it rained.

In back of our apartment building, above the parkway and the Hudson, there is a wild cliff covered with rocks and trees. This is where all the children of the apartment house play, and in summer or on mild winter days many of the grownups sit there in deck chairs and hate the children while enjoying the view of the boats on the river. My wife sometimes goes to the cliff with the children in the afternoon, and it was there, a few days after our family session, that she first met Mrs. Feinstein. From her, she learned that Mr. Feinstein had been a writer in Germany and that he was now again trying to write, in a new language. He had a quiet office downtown where he worked five days a week, but the shattering experiences of the past in Germany and the difficulty of mastering English had so discouraged him that after a day of writing he could hardly sleep at night, which was why he had to have his rest on Saturdays and Sundays. Mrs. Feinstein also expressed the hope that we would see more of each other and become friends. "You see," said my wife to me later, after recounting all this, "it's really a matter of honor for us to make up for our past sins and show that we are able to bring up our children to be civilized human beings."

"Yes, indeed," I said, "especially as the Feinsteins have asked little enough of us. We won't even try to become real friends with them until after we've given them reason to respect us."

Thus began our ordeal.

The first Saturday morning, both children put on their slippers and climbed on the table in their bedroom to reach for the picture books on the top shelf. I was in my room looking at the paper when I heard the most frightful noise. I rushed into the children's room and saw that all the big books and a box filled with wooden blocks, plus three or four wooden cows, had fallen on the floor. The children were blaming each other for the disaster, and they at once began a battle of shoes, books, and marbles. Needless to say, the reaction from downstairs was none too kind, and we learned later that even though we had gone out for the entire afternoon, Mr. Feinstein had found it impossible to repair the damage done to his sleep that day.

I was lucky enough not to see Mr. Feinstein for a whole week after the incident, but one day my wife met his wife when they were both waiting their turns at the washing machine in the basement. My wife renewed our pledge to keep to the ten-o'clock limit on weekends. This happened on a Friday, so very early the next morning, before the children could wake up, I went into their room and put their slippers in a place where they would be sure to see them. Next to the slippers, I put colored pencils, toys, and other accepted items of pre-breakfast entertainment. Everything went splendidly that one day—so splendidly, in fact, that we often recalled the occasion later and said among ourselves, "Why can't we have another December 17th?" But the fact is that we just didn't; in our family, at least, history does not repeat itself.

A couple of months later, rumors began to reach us from reliable sources, as they say in the papers, to the effect that Mr. Feinstein always spoke of us as "the parents of the two noisy children." Not a friendly word about us. This struck my wife and me painfully, and what disturbed us even more was to learn from one of our neighbors that Mr. Feinstein had received bad news from his family in Europe and was quite depressed.

My wife and I then held a secret meeting to plan a new strategy. It was a Monday morning and we had just got the children off to school.

"I am more worried about ourselves than about Mr. Feinstein," said my wife. "What will become of us in the future when, instead of trying to teach the children not to make noise, we will want to teach them not to wage aggressive wars on their neighbors?"

"The future is not yet," I said, "so don't worry."

The next morning, I stopped in at my children's school and consulted the school psychologist, whom I had come to know and like. He said, "Very simple, my friend. If you want to impress upon your children the notion that Mr. Feinstein is asleep, you must first believe it yourself. It's like the psychology of selling—you can never sell a thing in which you yourself have no faith. And furthermore," he said, "your methods are dictatorial. You can't ask children for exceptional behavior on Saturdays without any previous training. Try to approach Saturday by degrees. Accumulate a capital of habit, act artificially by minor doses, until Saturday comes to them naturally, without a shock."

I thanked him very much for his advice and began that same day to think in terms of Saturday. Mr. Feinstein was away in his office downtown, but I was beginning to prepare a nice silence for him upstairs. It was a wonderful feeling. I almost saw myself as a young bride preparing the first meal for her husband, hours before he comes back from the office. I walked cautiously, even typed cautiously (for I work at home), and when the children returned from school, I said to them, "Let's all work together for a better Saturday."

"Hurrah!" they shouted. "Let's work right away! May we use our shovels?"

"Children!" I whispered in my new velveted, tired voice. "Please, my dear, good, gentle children! Come, let's sit peacefully together and have silent fun!" And while saying this, I caressed their heads and closed my eyes to suggest peace.

I have come to the point at which my critics (among them my wife) accuse me of having brought violence into my advocacy of peace. They may be right; perhaps I am too passionate a character anyway. Well, it was Thursday afternoon and the children were playing in their room while I was writing in the living room. Needless to say, Mr. Feinstein was not at home. Suddenly I heard the sound of hammering. I emerged from the nineteenth century in Rome, in which my work had submerged me, to ask my wife with anguish, "What time is it?" Saturday morning was in my subconscious, so much so that I began to plead with my son to stop hammering. My wife took his side against me; she said he had every right to play with his tool kit. I tried everything, even literature. I said, "If Thursday is here, can Saturday be far behind? Think of that poor man downstairs, who will be asleep in less than two days from now!" Neither Vieri nor my wife was impressed.

That night, I committed my greatest mistake. I went downstairs and asked Mr. Feinstein to help me, and although he said again that those two mornings on the weekend were all he cared for, I insisted so earnestly that he made two more demands: a 1-to-3 P.M. silence on Sundays and a nightly silence after nine. It was a little too much, I felt, but after all I'd asked for it. In fairness to Mr. Feinstein, I must say that he did what he could to help me, pounding his disapproval on the radiator pipe each time we played the victrola or I typed after nine. Since his approval was not shown by any applause but was simply left to our guess, our hopeful guessing, plus those occasional ghostlike rappings on the radiator, seemed to summon up Mr. Feinstein's spirit. The whole family began to flee from it. We withdrew to the kitchen and lived there like fugitives; we talked to our guests in whispers and always told them not to walk too confidently, lest the spirit wake up.

One evening, while we were having guests—Mr. Feinstein was, of course, present in spirit—my wife observed that our lot had not improved much with exile; in Italy the tyrant had been constantly awake over us, here he was asleep under our feet. The joke was such a success that one of our guests, laughing convulsively, drummed on the floor with his heels, and at once—bang, bang—the spirit replied. Before long, the phrase "Mr. Feinstein is asleep" was no longer a phrase; it was a dogma. It was, in fact, the Law. I vaguely recall that this was the period when I could no longer work on my historical research, and while my actions were all devoted to the defense of Mr. Feinstein's sleep, my thoughts centered on hating him. Finally, a friend gave me a key to his apartment, so that I could go there to work in peace. But the fact was that I went there only to be able to hate Mr. Feinstein without interruptions. In the meantime, the children went on making a lot of noise, and they even began taking liberties with Mr. Feinstein such as I would never have dared. One day, my son met him in the elevator. It was the eve of the long Easter holidays, the thought of which was already filling me with dread. Mr. Feinstein said to Vieri, "You are lucky to have such a long vacation." "Yes, I am," answered Vieri with a smile, "but you're not."

At this point, I went to see the school psychologist again. He suggested that I now try the progressive method; namely, teach while playing, in the manner of the modern school. I thanked him for the idea, and the same day I began to make many jokes to the children about Mr. Feinstein, the monster downstairs. I taught them to call him Sleepyhead, and whenever his name was mentioned, we made snoring noises. Then the expression was coined: "As lazy as Mr. Feinstein." This worked pretty well until Mr. Feinstein fell sick and actually had to stay in bed all the time. Vieri had taken up bouncing his ball again, so, to save the day, I at once established a Feinstein Prize for silence.

Unfortunately, one Sunday afternoon not long after, while I was walking through the park with my children, we met a group of friends who were on their way to pay us a visit with their own children, six in all. As it was a beautiful day, we decided to stay outdoors and not go back to our apartment until teatime. When we started on our way home, I noticed that each of my friends' children was armed with a ball and that one of them had iron cleats on his shoes, and I began to warn them of the "monster" that lived under our feet. My children helped me, volunteering the usual epithets and noises, and suddenly, whom did we see passing us but Mr. Feinstein, his face pale and stern. He must have been returning from a Sunday walk in the park and certainly had come up behind us and heard everything. He stared at me and said in a dignified tone that stabbed my heart, "Good afternoon."

I did not sleep that night. One always hates to be caught by an enemy in the act of abusing him behind his back, but what made things worse in my case was that I liked Mr. Feinstein as a person and would have given anything to be forgiven by him. "Horrible!" I thought. "Instead of understanding the delicacy of our motives, he will understand only the indelicacy of our remarks." So, after hours of nightmare, I decided that the only thing to do was face the situation squarely and go to him. But, alas, before I did so bad fortune willed it that I meet him right in front of my door. He wasn't coming to see me, that I knew, but I said, "Mr. Feinstein, I would like to talk to you. Won't you come in?" He hesitated, entered, and sat down without saying a word. Despite my confusion, I immediately noticed that in person he occupied a much smaller portion of the air than did his spirit. I had been unjust. And he looked much kinder than his spirit, too.

"I don't know why you want to see me," he began. "Are you looking for inspiration for more vulgar stunts to teach your children? As a matter of fact," he continued, moving his chair back noisily and preparing to leave, "I don't know what made me accept your offer to come in in the first place."

I was almost speechless, but instinctively said what I now always said to my guests: "Please be careful, we have—" And my finger was pointed toward the floor. He understood, for his face reddened and he said with rage, "Never mind! I'm up here now, not downstairs!"

I blushed and sank back on my chair, then stuttered, "Now, Mr. Feinstein, you, who are a philosopher—"

He interrupted me. "I don't see what that has to do with the fact that you teach your children to insult a man who has done you no harm. If that's the way Italian children are brought up, I can almost believe that Italy needs a Mussolini!"

"Please!" I said. "There is no reason why you should insult me! Listen to me, now. I myself never used bad words against you."

"But you laughed when your children used them. You even encouraged them. I heard what you said in the park. So you can hear me 'snore like a pig,' can you?"

"I? We? No, indeed, I never said so."

"You *did* say so. I heard you!"

"I was only joking."

"Only joking! Respect for your neighbor is a joke to you. I knew it all the time, but for a while I thought that you were merely a little casual, like most Italians. But now I know. Respect for others means nothing to you, and you even take pleasure in persecuting others with your jokes. You are a Fascist!"

"Sir!" I cried. "That you should insult me in my own home! I can prove to you that I have fought Fascism, that I have written dozens of articles denouncing all forms of persecution."

"You may have done so, but my experience with you is just the opposite. You have constantly disregarded my very modest demands, and on top of this you make me out a clown to amuse your children. That, sir, is more than I—"

"Please, please!" I said. "All my friends can be witnesses to the fact that your demands for quiet are the only thing I've taken seriously for the last two years. It is, in fact, *I* who may reproach *you* for making me a nervous wreck. Unintentionally, I admit, but still—"

"I?" said he, growing terribly pale. "I? I have made *you* a nervous wreck? All *my* friends are my witnesses, sir, that all I ever asked of you was a few hours of silence a week. Is *that* what makes you a wreck? You and your children have made *me* a wreck! How on earth can you have the nerve to claim that my asking you for those few hours of silence that I never got has made you a wreck! That is indeed Fascist!"

"Sir," I said, "please listen! I admit you never got your rest, and I'm sorry, but you don't know how many sleepless nights I've spent trying to prepare the rest you never got. And let me tell you also that this all came about because I tried to be kind to you. First, I tried to offer you two hours and a quarter of quiet, then three hours, and soon quiet for you became the ruling principle of our existence. Your sleep, Mr. Feinstein, ruled my life! And how could I persuade the children to obey these rules without pretending that I was taking their part against you? If you are to enjoy the sleep of the just, you must allow me to insult you unjustly. If the children know that you are a good man, they will want you to be so good as to cope with their noise, while if they think that you are a monster, they will respect you to avoid trouble."

"But that *is* Fascism! That is horrible! Couldn't you have told them that I was very sick?"

"I did once, when you were, but it didn't help. Besides, though I'm not superstitious, I hate to talk lightly about sickness. To mention it may tempt the Fates."

He looked at me, bit his lip, then said, "Why didn't you just call me a fool?"

"Who was I to do that?" I said. "And you, sir, why did you always ask with such kindness, and look so pale? That made me act the way I did."

He frowned, looked at me again, and then we both started laughing and my wife came in with a bottle of wine and some wineglasses. The children, too, came running in, and started jumping so hard that this time it was for the protection of the house itself that we had to stop them. "I guess," said Mr. Feinstein now, "this all goes back to the incongruities of Progress."

"Also," I said, "to the decay of Western Civilization."

"Perhaps, too, though only a little, to these darling children here," he said.

"Yes," I said, "or to me, who am silly enough to live in town. Let's drink now and be friends."

So our friendship was sealed, and upon leaving Mr. Feinstein said, "Frankly, I prefer your noise to all that unfair propaganda against me. It's bad enough that the grownups should scare each other with lies. Let's spare these babies if we can."

"This time," I said, "I am *sure* I can keep my promise."

But, alas, this time, too, it was a mistake to make a promise. For now every time I think of my good friend Mr. Feinstein, even late at night, I hope the children will play ball, jump, or do something awful, just to let him know that he has friends upstairs, real friends, and that his name is not being taken in vain. Yet he's so nervous now, so jittery, so sad (and, needless to say, his spirit still sometimes manifests itself by the usual rappings), that I still am afraid to let the children act like children. The result is that I never quite know whether to give rest to his body or to his soul.

CONTINUED HUMID

❖

MARK SCHORER

ALBERT SAMPSON was waiting for a student late one afternoon this summer in his office in Morris House, the white clapboard building which sheltered the Romance Language Department of the New England college in which he taught. He had, for the moment, forgotten the heat outside. His office was on the north side of the building, and in the afternoon a row of old elm trees just outside the windows kept it dark and relatively cool; also, he had come across the yearbook of his class, 1930, while straightening his shelves, and now, sitting behind his desk with his chair tipped back against the sill of the open window, he was looking at his photograph in the book.

He could not see any great difference between his face then and the way he looked now; the face in the photograph was more eager, of course, more open, yet not really different. His hair, perhaps, was thinner now, receding at the temples, but he still wore a crew cut. The eyes looked at him from the picture with the same easy candor with which, he supposed, he still looked out at the world. But when he glanced at the print under the photograph, his gray-green eyes narrowed, and the lines on either side of his mouth, wrinkles formed by a characteristic smile, deepened into fretfulness. "Most Popular Man. . . . Destiny: brilliant critic or novelist." Thirteen years. And he was now an instructor in French at thirty-one hundred a year, without prospects of promotion or of a raise in salary.

The ringing of the telephone on his desk was so startling to him that the book slammed shut and the front legs of his chair came down on the floor with a bang.

It was Sally, his wife. "Albert," she said, "there's a letter for you from the Army Air Forces. Shall I open it and read it to you?"

His breath stopped in his throat. He hesitated. Then he said, "No, I'll come right home," and started to put the instrument down.

"Oh, Albert—"

"Yes?"

"Bring a loaf of whole-wheat bread on your way, and a small melon."

"Yes," he said.

"And stop at Larkin's to see if they've repaired the electric fan. The heat has had the baby howling all afternoon."

"Yes," he said again.

He got up quickly, pulled on the seersucker jacket which hung on the back of a chair, and rushed into the corridor and out of the building. Outside, on the steps, the heavy, damp heat of the August afternoon struck him with the force of a blast. He groaned softly and looked up at the pallid sky; its vast insipidity promised no relief. Sweat broke out all over his body. He pulled a damp, wrinkled handkerchief from the hip pocket of his gray flannel trousers and wiped it across his eyes.

When he looked up he saw Richard Crane running toward him along the path that led to the steps where he had paused. "Sorry I'm late, sir," Crane said, panting. He was sweating, too, and, like Albert, mopping his face. "I wanted to say goodbye."

"Where are you going?"

"Fort Devens, sir. Tomorrow."

"You've been drafted? But I thought you were 4F."

"I was reclassified last month."

"Oh. Well, look, walk along with me."

They went down the path between neatly boxed hedges toward the main quadrangle of the campus.

"When it's over," Crane said, "I want to come back and do some more work with you on Racine, if you'll have me."

"Racine," Albert said speculatively, and then, "Crane, I don't care, you know, if I never hear of Racine again."

The boy looked at him with solemn surprise. "Why—" he said, but Albert interrupted him.

"You see, Crane, I'm going in too."

"Into the Army?"

"I've applied for a commission. Army Air Corps." Albert's voice was elated. "They need instructors. Of course, I may not get it— everyone isn't getting a commission now, the way it was a while back—but even so, in my interview the officer said my chances were good. I'll be teaching straight technical subjects. If I teach, that is."

"But if the commission is *for* teaching—"

"Oh, that. I've been told it doesn't matter much. If they like your

looks, they put you in action. I know men from the last war who
went in this way and then found themselves at the front."

"I see," Crane said quietly.

"And you can see, too, can't you, Crane, what it makes of Racine?
And of all this?" Albert swept his arm out in a semicircle.

They were now in the quadrangle, nearly deserted in the hot,
late afternoon. The Georgian buildings, standing tidily on the
brilliant grass, among the well-kept, symmetrical trees, looked like
enormous dolls' houses.

"All dead, Crane. Pretty and dead."

"What about your book on the Symbolists?"

"I've lost interest. That's why I haven't any future here. They
think I'm lazy. They think I haven't lived up to my promise. But
with this ahead of me, I can tell you what I think, and it's to hell
with them."

The boy's eyes, behind his spectacles, were puzzled and hurt. As
he and Albert emerged from the quadrangle, he said, "Here's where
I turn."

"I'm afraid I talked mostly about myself. Good luck, Crane.
Maybe we'll meet somewhere. And don't worry, Racine will keep."

They shook hands, and Crane, as if he suddenly felt shy, ducked
his head and swung off in the direction of his dormitory. Albert began to whistle and walked rapidly away toward his home.

The Sampsons lived on the second floor of an old house which had
been converted into flats. It was painted an intensely ugly color, a
nearly mustard yellow, and whenever Albert approached the building, he found himself doing so with repugnance. But today he did
not notice. He watched the newsboy swing close to the curb on his
bicycle, throw the evening paper up on the steps, and then wheel
out into the street again. As Albert came closer, he saw Claudia, his
six-year-old daughter, playing aimlessly on the steps with some bits
of gravel she had picked up from the drive. One cheek had a gray
smudge on it and wisps of her brown hair had escaped from her pigtails, which were neat and tight in the mornings but disarrayed by
afternoon. He saw that her hands were grimy. He bent down and
kissed her and, more cheerfully than usual, said, "Hello, darling."
He picked up the newspaper and ran up the steps. Claudia followed
him in.

Albert saw the letter at once on the cluttered telephone table in
the hall, a long white envelope which seemed faintly luminous in
the gloom of the dark corridor. He picked it up and walked into the

living room. The baby, whimpering and nearly naked, was in his play pen in the middle of the room and Sally was working at her desk.

"Hello, darling," Albert said.

"What did the letter say?" Sally asked eagerly.

"I haven't read it yet," he answered. He dropped the newspaper in a chair and kept on walking.

Claudia came in after him, holding a doll. "Daddy, fix my doll's—" she began, but Albert was already in the back hall. He went into the bedroom and closed the door behind him.

In the bedroom he waited, with his back against the door, the letter in one hand. Then he walked over to his bureau, which stood between two windows. He looked at his name on the envelope and he saw how the envelope was shaking. He looked away from it and his glance fell on the unused gifts on his bureau top. Sally and he had agreed, before his birthday a few weeks ago, that he had better be given things which he would need when he "got in." The pigskin toilet case was from Sally, the writing kit of durable imitation leather was from Claudia, the black wallet, small enough to fit in a hip pocket and equipped with transparent flaps for all the identification cards one needed to carry, was from the friends who had been asked to his birthday dinner, and the cellophane money belt, which had cost a dollar and nineteen cents, was, Claudia had insisted, from the baby. Albert looked at these things and abruptly tore off one end of the envelope.

A glance was enough. The phrases leaped out at him: ". . . duly considered . . . so many applicants with a high degree of technical training . . . cannot now consider . . ." He crumpled the letter in his fist, put his arms on the bureau, and laid his head down on them.

When he straightened up, he looked at the gifts again, and presently he opened the top drawer of the bureau, where he kept his neckties and handkerchiefs, and pushed the toilet case, the writing kit, the wallet, and the money belt into it. The crumpled letter he stuffed into his pocket. He walked to the door and stared at it, and at last he went back to the living room. The baby was crying.

Sally looked up from the papers on her desk. "Did you get the fan? Bobby's miserable and I've been too busy all day to take him out."

"I forgot," he said dully, "and I forgot the groceries, too."

"Oh, *Al*bert!"

"Daddy, look," Claudia said. She thrust her damaged doll into his hands and held out its wig to him, a matted, carrot-colored cap of imitation hair. Albert glanced at the curious bald head of the doll.

"Well," Sally said, "one of us will have to go for them. We haven't any bread and we haven't any dessert. But first I want you to look at these."

"What?" Albert asked, and turning to Claudia, he said, "Put Bobby's toys back in his play pen and keep him quiet."

"These bills—"

"Oh, Lord." He dropped the doll into a chair, picked up the newspaper, and glanced at the weather report. " 'Continued humid.' Christ, I'll go crazy," he said. He took off his coat and opened the collar of his shirt. "Isn't there anything we can do about this apartment? It's as damp as a cellar."

"Albert," Sally said, "this is the last liquor bill we can pay. We'll have to cut out drinking entirely, even when we have guests. Everything's become so expensive, and all the talk about easy money and high wages just doesn't fit us. Your salary is just what it was three years ago, but prices—"

"Sally, don't," he said. He was looking at her dress, of blue cotton with a mild little pink flower printed all over it. Then he looked at her bare feet under the desk, and her shoes, lying where she had kicked them off. And finally, he looked at her face, white and tired, without makeup, drawn.

"I mean it, Albert. And that isn't all. I've got to let the cleaning woman go, and I've got to do more of the laundry myself—all but your shirts. We just can't run bills like these any more. I'm at the point where I juggle one against the other, figure out which one can slide or which one I can pay just part of, and it gets worse every month. I won't live that way."

"Is that all right, Daddy?" Claudia asked. She had put the toys back in the pen, and for the moment, while the baby threw them out again, he was quiet. Albert saw that his diaper was wet.

"Thanks," he said to Claudia.

"And now will you fix my doll?" asked Claudia. "There's some glue in your desk."

"Did you hear what I said, Albert?" Sally asked, looking at his face, which seemed listless and dull.

"No," he said.

She stood up angrily, and he noticed how small she was without shoes. "You have a streak of absolute infantilism, you know. Darling, we can't *pretend* we have more money than we've got. We can't drink liquor we can't buy or hire a cleaning woman we can't pay. You just won't *face* anything. But I can't live on fantasy. I've even thought this afternoon of putting the children in one room and renting the other to some student."

"Sally, for God's sake—"

"Oh," she said, surprised, "what did the letter say?"

His face became suddenly alive again. "I was turned down," he said, and then, in a rising voice, he cried, "But don't worry, they'll get me yet. I'll be drafted! This war isn't over by a long shot! Don't you worry!"

She drew in her breath sharply and backed away a step as she saw his eyes, narrowed, and burning at her with a kind of wildness.

THE BABY-AMAH

❖

Emily Hahn

PEOPLE ALWAYS looked a little surprised when they first saw Ah Yuk, the baby-amah I acquired after the surrender of Hong Kong to the Japanese. I can't claim to have hired her, exactly. She just joined my household, on the understanding that she would receive the same compensation that satisfied Ah King, my old cook—that is, food to the extent of three bowls of rice twice a day, plus whatever other nourishment we could manage. Beyond that Ah Yuk had to depend on my good faith. When I had money I paid her a salary, and when I hadn't, I put what I owed her down on record, to be paid off in happier times. She seemed content with this arrangement, and ultimately she didn't lose by it.

The reason people were surprised was that Ah Yuk didn't look at all like an amah. She wasn't an amah by training or history. She was just what she looked like, a professionally pretty lady. In China, that did not mean that Ah Yuk had been a prostitute; she hadn't. She had been a singsong girl. Singsong girls are like chorus girls; some are virtuous and some aren't. Ah Yuk had gone the hard way and had married and become a respectable concubine, with a girl child of her own, now old enough to shift for herself, and two foster sons, children of the No. 1 wife. Mr. Liu, her husband, was never a very vivid figure in my mind. Of him Ah Yuk said only that he had a quick temper but was a good provider, and that when he died, at about the time Hong Kong was occupied by the Japanese, she was really quite sorry. Besides, she was left destitute. Her daughter was safe, she presumed, in Shanghai. Her sons were in business up north. Only she, Ah Yuk, who had grown accustomed to the dignity of position and property, was up against it. She was glad to find a home.

Ah Yuk was thirty-five, but, like most Chinese women, she didn't look her age. She dressed soberly and in good taste. Her hair was drawn smoothly back to a plain, flat knot at the nape of her neck, over her stiff collar. She didn't use makeup. Just the same, people were surprised when they learned she was my baby-amah. There was something triumphantly attractive about her that could not be daunted. She didn't have that bovine expression so many Chinese peasant women have. She laughed eagerly and merrily. She walked in a controlled way. Her slim haunches moved so that you looked at her again. Most amahs don't walk that way. In spite of her quiet clothes and unpainted face, any Chinese man who looked at her said, "She was a singsong girl once."

Ah Yuk need not have been an amah in a town like Hong Kong, full of Japanese officers who were looking around for sympathetic housekeepers. The city resounded with housewives' complaints that one couldn't find women to do housework any more, now that the Japanese Army was there. But she chose to stay with us, perhaps because she was farsighted, perhaps because she really did like children. I was very glad to have her. I much preferred her to the usual withered old amah. She was pretty, and Carola, my year-old daughter, liked that. Ah Yuk could sing Chinese opera, another dead giveaway about her past, and I try to sing Chinese opera myself. The nursery rang with unorthodox sounds after Ah Yuk came to stay with us.

There has never yet been a household in China where there hasn't been trouble sooner or later among the servants or about them. I didn't expect trouble between Ah Yuk and Ah King's family, because they had been the agents for getting her into my employ, and I was right in that. Ah King's womenfolk, who lived with us too, would not look down on anyone for having been a singsong girl; the Chinese don't make that social distinction. But there were my companions to reckon with—Irene and Phyllis, the Eurasian girls whose husbands had been killed in the fighting and who, with their children, lived with me for almost a year after the surrender of Hong Kong. Irene and Phyllis had their own amahs and, of course, that made for trouble. It was only to be expected. Unlike me, Irene and Phyllis *liked* servant trouble. It was part of everyday life's little excitement to them. They had grown up happily squabbling with and shrieking at their servants. Until Ah Yuk appeared, Irene scrapped earnestly with Ah King, accusing the old man of "squeezing" (pinching part of the household supplies) and of starving her amah and Phyllis's. I am sure Ah King did squeeze and I am equally sure he didn't starve the amahs. I defended him on both counts, pointing out to Irene the undeniable fact that the amahs were getting awfully fat. I'd been mixed up in so many of these rows in China that I didn't let them worry me any more. Then, when Ah Yuk came, Irene turned her wrath against the newcomer.

This time the situation was more difficult, because Irene was thoroughly justified and Ah Yuk was quite wrong, and yet I could no more have changed things around in the interests of justice than I could have changed the character of China. Ah Yuk snooted the Eurasian girls. She told their servants haughtily that I was the true mistress of the house. She said, "Your mistresses are half-castes. Pooh. My *tai tai* [mistress] is too good-hearted, keeping them here. She should turn them out and enjoy a little peace and quiet."

Such an attack was exceedingly painful to the supersensitive Irene, and it was unjust besides. The girls shared all the expenses of the house. But Far Eastern servants will always boast and lie and quarrel, and I tried to tell Irene so.

"Ignore it, Reeny," I begged her. "They're only servants. Forget it. Don't get down on the floor and fight with them. You have your own troubles."

Irene stared at me in perplexity. Hong Kong was her town; the Chinese were her people. How could she cut herself off from their quarrels and ignore their boasting? She couldn't, she insisted.

"If it weren't that we're leaving soon," she said, "I'd move out now. But I'm going to Kweilin anyway, and I won't give her that satisfaction."

I was distressed. "I would send Ah Yuk away," I said, "but the next one would be as bad. You know that."

"Oh, I know that," she admitted. "I don't blame *you*."

When they went away into Free China, Irene and Phyllis and their babies and their amahs, only my myrmidons and Carola and I were left, rattling around our battered old house, alone with our feudal, outworn European glory. Ah Yuk was happy. She dressed Carola as she thought a British baby should be dressed—in wonderful and awful combinations of color and always a hat. She sang Carola to sleep with arias from ancient Peiping operas. Once, when she had enough money, she took the baby downtown to a Chinese photographer and had a picture taken of the two of them together, sitting on an iron bench, very upright and stiff and smiling determinedly. She talked the Mandarin dialect as well as Cantonese, and, because I don't speak Cantonese, we all talked Mandarin together, so Carola never heard English at all and I began to dream in Chinese. In spite of my commands, Carola had her meals with the servants, and learned to prefer salt fish and bean curd and rice to Jello and cereal. When this diet gave her a stomach ache, Ah Yuk and Ah King disobeyed me again and dosed her with herb tea, *ch'ut sing ch'a,* the local cure-all.

As time went on, money grew less tight. The wealthy Chinese stopped hoarding their currency and the Japanese began looking around for something in which to invest their new-found wealth. Hong Kong dollars had been declared valueless by the new government, but nobody wanted to hang on to large sums of Japanese yen, either, least of all the Japs themselves, so all of a sudden jewels became very valuable. And I had jewels. Each time I sold one, I got a bigger profit. Gold soared in the market and I had a lot of heavy Chinese golden trinkets. Naturally, I kept very quiet about this, but sixteen months after the surrender I was able to give lots of back salary to the servants and the household enjoyed a modest boom. We ate meat again once in a while, and on New Year's Day we even had a duck. When the weather grew cold, I was able to carry out my duty as a Chinese housewife and give the servant women warm, padded coats and quilts. I even bought Ah Yuk a length of blue flannel for a dress. Prices of cloth were fantastically high, but I didn't care. For a year and a half we had starved and shivered, all but Carola, and for that I was grateful to my family.

With due caution, this prosperity was expressed in the parcels I carried to Charles, Carola's father, every Monday to the military prison camp. We, the women who made up the army of basket bringers every week, were ordered to keep the cost of our offerings within bounds when we supplied our men with food. The Japanese in charge of the camps said that "luxuries" would not be accepted, and sometimes the interpreter who examined the parcels would take out some ostensibly expensive article, argue about it, and turn it back. But the Japs had odd ideas about what was a luxury and what wasn't. I maintained stoutly to them that fats—margarine and lard, after butter disappeared from the colony—were necessary and not luxurious. Charles, I said, should have at least five ounces of fat every week. I got that figure out of a book on diet and I honestly didn't consider it unreasonable. Also, I said, I had bought the margarine weeks before, when it was still comparatively cheap. Besides, Charles shared his parcels with seven friends, and I was really supplying eight people. I must have sounded authoritative, because the officer in charge gave in. My parcels slowly grew bigger and bigger, heavier and heavier, as the weeks went by.

Ah Yuk was useful then as never before. She was strong and vigorous and didn't at all mind going with me once a month and carrying Carola, who was a heavy baby, so that Charles could have a glimpse of her. You could see, even at the distance the prisoners were from us, across a wide street, and even though we didn't dare look hard at them because of the sentries, that Carola always caused a lot of excitement in camp when we came by en route to the prison headquarters. The prisoners would run to the barbed wire to look at a real white infant being carried past. Ah Yuk loved her part in the excitement. She would carry my basket of parcels and I would carry Carola as we went past the camp. The men were on our left side, so I carried the baby on my left shoulder and Ah Yuk strolled behind me, further to the left, so that Carola would crane her neck and reach out, giving her father a really good look at her. The first expedition made the amah enthusiastic.

"Oh, Master is good-looking!" she cried. "*Tai tai,* we should make Carola walk when we go by. That way her father can see how beautiful she is, how wonderful her clothes are, and her nice straight legs. That way also we can walk slower, for the child will give us an excuse."

"We could, if only Carola would walk," I said, "but I've tried it before and the little beast just won't. She seems to know something's in the wind when we reach the camp. She'll walk anywhere else, but not going past that camp."

"I will arrange it," said Ah Yuk, with confidence.

"Be careful," I warned her. I was always abnormally nervous about the Monday-morning walks. We all were. Lena, a Russian, had a baby much younger than Carola, and she thought I was foolhardy to bring my child even once a month, because it was such a troublesome expedition on a hot day. Lena did weaken once, however, because her husband had never seen his baby. We all helped and encouraged her that day. We flocked around her and admired little Peter's eyes and asked if we couldn't hold him, and when we reached the camp, we were all worked up. Lena's being Russian somehow made the whole thing more emotional. As we approached the danger zone, with all our men waiting behind the barbed-wire fence and all the guards looking at us suspiciously from their posts, she gasped and grabbed at my arm. "I feel sick to my stomach," she said.

"I know," I replied. "It always happens. You'll get over it in a minute. Now, walk ahead alone, so we won't get in each other's way."

Ten feet ahead of me, scuffing the dust in the baking road, she made the Monday walk, holding the baby over her left shoulder and facing straight ahead, according to the rules, but her eyes swivelled sideways. At first I couldn't see her husband. I saw Charles, as usual, walking along on his side of the wire, keeping step with me. I saw other men I knew, some of them grinning at me, some surreptitiously waving, though they knew I couldn't reply. The eyes of the guards were fixed on us women.

Just as we reached the end of the fence, I saw Lena's husband. He had been transferred to the "medical center," a collection of huts wired off from the rest of the camp and used for light cases of illness, not bad enough for the hospital. The center was closer to the road than the rest of the huts, and Lena's husband stood there, clearly visible, staring with all his eyes at his blond, wobble-headed son.

As we moved away from the camp, to a point where the guards no longer watched us, I caught up with Lena. She was kissing her baby, burying her face in his white dress and holding him so tightly that his eyes bulged. "Oh, Peter darling, that was so close, so close!" she kept saying. I felt awfully tired. One always did after the walk.

The men were allowed to write one card every month, clearly printed and not exceeding fifty words. Apparently by tacit agreement, they never mentioned the Monday walk, but Lena's husband got around that. "I dreamed about you," he wrote. "You were carrying Peter and he was too heavy for you. Be careful. Don't overwork." And Charles kept cautioning me not to get my feet wet and to avoid chills. We used to laugh at those messages.

Ah Yuk's mind kept working on the problem of getting Carola to walk past the camp. She talked to the baby and told her clearly, with great patience, why she was supposed to walk past the barbed wire. She explained over and over about Daddy, who he was and where he was. Carola, who was then only twenty months, probably didn't get the idea thoroughly, because on her next expedition she still refused to walk. I put her down on the ground a long way before we got to the camp. She walked as far as the first guard, and then she stopped short and said, "Carry me."

Taking a great risk, because it annoyed the guards awfully when we stopped on that road, I argued with her for a while. She began to cry. Then I did something no modern mother should do. I picked her up, put her across my knee, and, in full view of the whole prison camp and a portion of the Japanese Army, I *spanked* Carola. It worked. She walked the rest of the way, holding on to her bottom and crying lustily. Stalking ahead of her, shaking with indignation and nerves, I still could see that the whole camp and a portion of the Japanese Army were laughing.

Next time, Carola walked without any demurral. It was Ah Yuk who misbehaved. I had walked along, not noticing that Carola, childlike, had lagged behind and that Ah Yuk had lingered, too, waiting for her. I thought Carola was all right and my attention was naturally focussed on her father. At a corner of a field, still within sight of the camp, we had to turn off down a road that led to prison headquarters, where the parcels were taken in and inspected. For a hundred yards, before buildings intervened, the prisoners could still watch us and we could still see the prisoners. They were such a long way off, however, that the guards never bothered about supervising this part of the walk. I could just spot Charles here, and it was scarcely worth walking slowly to do it.

That day I reached headquarters, out of sight of the camp at last, took my place in the inevitable queue with basket and filled-in paper form, and waited for my turn to be inspected. I assumed, naturally, that Ah Yuk and Carola were just behind me. I had been chatting with the other women in the line for about five minutes when I heard the hoarse yells of some Japanese soldiers, and I turned around to see three or four sentries running like mad toward the spot on the road from which the camp could be seen. One look and I joined the race. I got there first, too. It was my child who was causing all the uproar—my child, knee-deep in daisies in the field, picking flowers. Standing by, with an innocent, dumb smile on her face, was Ah Yuk. Away over in the camp, every one of the eight hundred prisoners was jostling for a good view of an English baby picking flowers, and it was really an alarming sight. It looked like a mutiny.

I swept up Carola and ran back, the sentries trotting along behind me, bayonets fixed. When we reached prison headquarters, the officer in charge raised hell. He screamed and shouted and scolded Ah Yuk in English. When at last he stopped for breath, Ah Yuk was making her little bow of respect and sorrow for the hundredth time, but still smiling, and I spoke up. "She doesn't speak English,

Major Niimori. It's my baby. I'm terribly sorry. She didn't know any better."

"Oh, well," said Niimori, who was talked out, "let it go."

On the way home I made his speech all over again to Ah Yuk as well as I could, in Chinese. I meant it, too. The Japs were perfectly capable of stopping the Monday walks if they got angry enough.

"I'm sorry, *tai tai*," said Ah Yuk. "But Master got a good look at Carola for one time, anyway."

One day I made the wonderful discovery that in a rickshaw one could get much closer to the fence. The guards could not very well stop all street traffic. They could only make us, when we were walking, keep to the sidewalk on the far side of the street. But motorcars, bicycles, and rickshaws used the street, for it was a main thoroughfare. In a rickshaw I would be half again as close to the barbed wire.

There were certain risks. A guard might spot me and object on general principles to a white woman's riding so near to the prisoners. Also, taking a rickshaw at all was being ostentatious with money, always an unwise thing to do in front of the Japanese. I didn't want them to know I had any money. But I was going away soon—I was being repatriated, and was taking Carola with me—and with every day that passed I grew braver. I even managed to persuade the camp commandant, Colonel Tokunaga, to let me see Charles and say goodbye. That was a miracle and I think we must put it down to Ah Yuk's charm that I succeeded. The Colonel, a big, fat man, had often rolled his eyes at Ah Yuk when she accompanied me to camp. When the interpreter presented my plea to him, he consented, after a long hesitation, on the strict understanding that I was to tell none of the other women. Then he added a careless question, which the interpreter conveyed to me. "Colonel says, what will happen to your servants when you are gone?"

"I don't know," I said. "They'll look for new jobs, I suppose."

"Colonel says," continued the interpreter, absolutely deadpan, "that he needs a housekeeper and he thinks your amah would do."

I bowed like anything, and said I would relay the offer to Ah Yuk.

I did. We talked it over very carefully with Ah King. Ah Yuk had already turned down a couple of similar offers, but those Japanese had been of lower rank, and besides that, as she naïvely said, they were more than forty years old and not at all good-looking. I believe that Ah Yuk was considering the Colonel carefully. He was more than forty and certainly not good-looking, but he *was* a colonel.

Ah King cast the deciding vote. "If last year, I say sure, go ahead," he said. "This year I think already too late. How much longer these Japanese stay here? I tell Ah Yuk better not. More better, though, don't tell Colonel until Missy have see Major. Ah Yuk go Chungking after you and Carola go away, Missy."

So I saw Charles, under heavy chaperonage, and we said goodbye, and I thanked the Colonel deeply and sincerely, with Ah Yuk bowing in the background.

The next Monday walk would be my last one. The whole camp knew it was my last and that the exchange ship would sail on Wednesday. All the women knew it. So did the Japanese officers.

I handed in my parcel, getting by with a very questionable item— a homemade housewife full of needles and thread and hooks and eyes, and even a pair of scissors. Ordinarily, the housewife would certainly have been rejected as a luxury (it was made of bright-green satin, the only cloth I could find for the purpose), and they hated passing tools of any sort, scissors or anything. Today, however, they knew I was going away. They unrolled the housewife, admired the satin, tested the scissors, and let me slip it into Charles's sack. We all bowed. I shook hands with the Colonel, and he ogled Ah Yuk understandingly over my shoulder. He confidently expected her to move into headquarters on Thursday.

We moved off, Carola and Ah Yuk and I, down the road to the rickshaws that were waiting for us according to previous arrangement. We were going to break a most important rule. I was going to go *back* past the camp, though this was not permitted by the guards. Ah Yuk and I turned, and she bowed once more to the officers. The Colonel threw a shadowy kiss to her.

"Is it all fixed?" I asked her as we got into our rickshaws. "Are you sure you can get away?"

"All fixed, *tai tai*. I'll be out before Friday."

The rickshaws rolled off, taking us back along the route of the Monday walk. Carola was with me, Ah Yuk was in the rickshaw behind us.

Charles was waiting. He must have guessed I would take some such risk this last time. He turned and started walking step for step with the coolie, and I broke yet another rule and turned my head and looked straight at him. So did Carola.

Then I found out what Ah Yuk had been doing all through that last week, behind the closed nursery door. She had been rehearsing Carola. We were halfway through our usual Monday route and I

could see Charles as plain as anything, for my rickshaw coolie, following Ah Yuk's shouted instructions from the other rickshaw, ran
in as close as he could get to the curb. We were so close we could
have talked to Charles without shouting. We were so close . . .

Carola had been fidgeting on my knee. Now she jumped up. She
stood up in the rickshaw seat and waved. She waved at a prisoner of
war. People in Hong Kong have been shot for that. Worse still, she
shouted. Loud and clear, her shrill voice sounded through the silent
camp: "Daddy, bye-bye! Daddy, bye-bye!"

We were past the camp. At the corner of the barbed-wire fence,
Charles was being hoisted high up by two friends, so that he could
go on watching us until the last minute. Still Carola waved and
shouted, proudly doing her stuff. "Bye-bye, Daddy! Daddy, bye-
bye!"

Nobody shot at us.

TRUTH AND CONSEQUENCES

❖

BRENDAN GILL

S HE HAD STRAIGHT blond hair and a red mouth, and she was lame.
Every day she played golf and went swimming in the center of a
crowd of boys. Charles, sitting with his mother on the hotel porch,
watched her and nodded while his mother repeated, "Isn't it extraordinary, a girl like that? I wonder what in the world they see in
her." Charles took to walking past the pool during the morning as
the girl and boys lay there side by side, laughing. He listened carefully to her voice. It was low, unhurried, forceful. So, he thought,
was her language. Every other word seemed to him to be "damn,"
"hell," and worse. She spoke of God, to whom Charles was preparing to dedicate his life, as if He were a friend in the next block. "I
swear to God," the girl said. "I must have told you this one, for God's
sake." Charles walked out of range of the jokes that followed. He
was eighteen and he was spending this last vacation with his mother
before entering a seminary. In eight more summers he would be a
priest. The girl's language sent sharp lightnings through him. He
had never seen or heard anyone like her before in his life.

One night after dinner, while his mother was upstairs swallowing a pill, the girl sat down beside him on the hotel porch. Her lips
were smiling, her eyes the color of her blue, open blouse. "We ought
to know each other," she said. "You ought to join the rest of us at
the pool."

"I'm with Mother."

The girl covered his hand with hers. "Well, for God's sake, you're
old enough to swim by yourself, aren't you?"

Charles felt that he ought to explain before it was too late, before
she had said something he could never forget. "I'm going to be a
priest," he said.

The girl kept smiling. "A priest? With a turn-around collar and
everything?"

He nodded.

"So you can't come swimming with the gang?"

"That hasn't anything to do with it. I just thought I ought to tell you. I always do tell people."

"You can still come dancing with us if you want to?"

"Certainly."

"Could you take me to a movie if you wanted to?"

"Yes."

"I never met a boy who was going to be a priest. Could you take me out for a ride tonight if you wanted to?"

He said in relief, "We didn't bring our car."

"Oh, hell, I mean in my car. I mean just for example. I didn't say I'd go with you." She stared at him slowly from head to foot. "It would be funny, with a boy who was going to be a priest."

Fortunately, Charles thought, his mother would be coming downstairs at any moment now. She would make short shrift of the girl. "You oughtn't to keep swearing like that," he said.

He expected her to laugh, but she didn't. She ran her hand up and down the bare brown leg that was shorter than the other. "Like what?" she said.

"Like 'for God's sake.' That's taking the name of the Lord in vain. That's one of the Ten Commandments."

"I'm an awful damn fool," the girl said. "I talk like that to keep people from thinking about my leg. But I didn't know you were going to be a priest."

Charles wanted to get rid of her, but he didn't know how. He stood up and said, "I don't think you ought to worry about things like that. I hadn't even noticed."

She stood up beside him. Her eyes shone in the mountain light. "Oh, damn you, please don't lie to me," she said. "Of course you've noticed. But does it bother you? Does it make you want to stay away from me?"

"No," he said. "Oh, no."

She slipped her hand under his arm. "Thanks for saying that so nice and hard. I haven't asked anybody that in a long time."

Without having willed it, stupidly, Charles found himself walking the length of the porch beside the girl. Her blond hair touched the shoulder of his coat. It was difficult to tell, looking down at her, that she was lame. He bent his head to smell her perfume. "Tell me what you do," he said.

"You mean, bang, just like that, what do I do?"

"Not that you have to tell me."

"But I do. It's just that there aren't any surprises in me. I'm not beautiful or tormented—or not much tormented. I don't do anything. I got out of Walker's and I had a party and now I guess I'll be on the loose like this for a couple of years. Finally somebody may ask me to marry him, and quick like a fish I will. I hope I'll have sense enough for that. And I'll be terribly glad when I've done it. I'll try to let him win most of the arguments we'll have. I'll try to be good about satisfying him, the way all those awful books say, and about having good kids for him, and all that."

Charles felt himself stumbling. She had told him everything about herself. She had told him the truth, which he hadn't wanted. They reached the end of the porch and stood facing the valley between the mountains. Two old men were playing croquet in the gathering darkness, the wooden mallets and balls knocking softly together, the white trousers moving like disembodied spirits across the lawn. Charles and the girl could hear, below them in the kitchen, the clatter of dishes being washed and stacked and the high, tired voices of the waitresses.

"Now talk about you," the girl said. "You think you want to be a priest?"

"Why—yes."

"It isn't just a vow your mother made while she was carrying you?"

Charles laughed, and was surprised at how easily he laughed. "Well," he said, "I guess Mother's always wanted me to be a priest, especially after Dad died. We went abroad then, Mother and I. We spent the summer in Rome. We had an audience with the Pope— the old one, a little man with thick glasses and a big ring. We got so we were going to Mass and even to Communion every day. When we came back to this country I started in at a Catholic school. I liked it. I graduated this year. I'm going down to the seminary in the fall. I guess I'll like that, too."

"But isn't there more to it than that?" the girl said. "I'm not a Catholic—I'm not anything—but don't you have to have some kind of a call, bells ringing, something like that?"

"You mean a vocation. Yes. Well, I guess I have a vocation all right."

"But what is it? How can you be sure?"

Charles gripped the railing of the porch. He had never been able to answer that question. He remembered kneeling beside his mother's bed, month after month, year after year. "Don't you feel

it, darling?" his mother had whispered. "Don't you feel how wonderful it will be? Don't you feel how God wants you?" Charles had
told himself finally that he was able to answer that question. The
next day his mother, dabbing her eyes, had said, "Here's my boy,
Father Duffy. I'm giving him to you." And Father Duffy had said,
"Ah, you're an example to Irish mothers everywhere. Are you sure
you want to come with us, boy?" "Yes, Father, I do," Charles had
said, watching his mother. He had spoken an answer, written an
answer, lived an answer, but he had never believed it. He had been
waiting to believe it. Now he heard himself saying, for the first
time, "No, I can't be sure."

The girl said, "Then you're not going to be a priest. You mustn't
be. Why are you so damned afraid to face the truth?"

Charles saw his mother walking heavily along the porch. He
studied her as if she were a stranger. What an enormous old woman
she was, and how strong she was, and how she had driven him! He
took the girl's hand. It was cool and unmoving. He felt the porch
floor trembling under his mother's approach.

BETWEEN THE DARK AND
THE DAYLIGHT

❖

NANCY HALE

THIS WAS THE BED where Sara had always been put when she was
sick. Not her own bed, narrow and tidy against the wall of her
room, among her own books, her own furniture, so well known to
her that she did not see them any more. This bed was different.
This was the guest-room bed, a double bed with white-painted iron
from head to foot. All her fifteen years she had been put here when
she had a cold, or tonsillitis, or measles. It was higher, and broader,
and softer than her own bed, and being here pulled her back to the
books she had read when she had been sick, or that had been read
to her; to the long, unlabored trains of fantasy that had swung in
her mind like slow, engrossing ocean swells.

Within the enchantment of the bed in the guest room her mind
was released over centuries and into palaces and into the future,
and she could alter her person from small to tall, from quiet to com-
manding. In this bed she had been by turns a queen, a Roman, a
man during the Massacre of St. Bartholomew. Here she had imagined herself grownup and having five children, had given them
names and learned their separate faces and spoken to them and
punished them. She had always dreamed in this bed of new things
and new feelings. She had never reached backward for anything
within her own experience.

She had not been sick in several months, but she had bronchitis
now, and since she had been sick last something had dropped away
from her. She had changed. Without questioning what was happening to her, or even being conscious of it, she had stopped playing in
brooks and running fast in sneakers and wearing her hair in two
pigtails. In these autumn months the girls she played with had
changed too. They bought sodas in the drugstore. They walked
slowly, eternally, along the tarred New England sidewalks, with
their arms around each other's waists. Suddenly they would laugh

together helplessly for a moment; at what, they did not know. They cut their hair and curled it, or brushed it out smooth and tied a hair ribbon around it. They watched themselves pass in the shop windows of the town. And all of it had come like a natural change and occupied her fully.

It was not that she turned her head away from one side and looked toward the other. The old things she had known so many years now stood still without a sound to call her as they used, and until she took sick she did not think of them. But as she lay in the guest-room bed she resented more and more what was happening to her. She had no pleasure in remembering the shop windows, the drugstore, the boys—only a sort of weariness and distaste. She did not want to go that way. It all began when she read the Indian book.

After three days her fever went down and she stopped coughing so much and was allowed to go from the guest room into her own room, in her nightgown and wrapper, and take books out of the shelves and bring them back to bed. The first day she brought a book of Poe's short stories that she loved, and two of the Little Colonel books, and a book about English history, and an old book that she had not read for years, about Indians and wood lore. Her Uncle Lyman had sent it to her one autumn after he had been at their house for a visit. That was when she was eleven.

He belonged to a mountain-climbing club and took long walks in the woods behind their house and she used to go with him. She felt something wonderful in the way he walked without noise along the smooth brown paths, and liked to walk behind, watching him. When it grew dark early in those fall afternoons he would still follow the path without hesitation.

One afternoon when it was cold and frosty and the sun was setting, they came out on a hillside that ran down to the road. There was a clump of birches at the top and he took a knife out of his pocket and showed her how to cut away a strip of birch bark and then to pare its delicate, pale-pink paper from within. That was Indian paper, he said. He took up a rock with big spots of mica and held it up into the shining of the late sun. "If there was someone over on that far hill, I could signal to him with this," he said, "if we were Indians."

What he had said about the Indians filled her mind after he was gone. Through the winter and through the spring she went to the woods. In the winter it was only in the afternoons that she could

go, late, after she got home from school. But when the spring came
there was more time; it didn't get dark so early. She found a pool beside a rock, covered with green slime, and at the edges the ice-cold
water was full of the blobs of transparent jelly that held a million
black spots: frogs' eggs. She took them home with her in a tin lard
pail and put them in a glass bowl, to watch the polliwogs hatch out.
They turned from eggs to tadpoles, to strange creatures with a tail
and two legs. And one morning they jumped out of the bowl and
hopped about the dining-room floor and had to be thrown out in
the garden.

When it was summer she could go all day. She asked for Indian
clothes and was given them for her birthday: a fringed coat and skirt,
and a leather band for her head, with a feather in it. The skirt had
a pocket in the side, where she carried her lunch, done up in waxed
paper. When she was alone, on the long paths that had been there
for a hundred years and led, if you could follow them, to other
states, to other woods and meadows miles away, she was satisfied and
at home. She lived within her own private world—this world with a
pine-needle floor, peopled by the shadow shapes of men who moved
without noise, surmounted by tall plumes. This world was beautiful and intricate and still. The ground pine ran along under the
dead leaves in secret; the shallows of the little ponds were filled
with a minute and busy life, tiny fish and frogs and "rowboats" that
skittered across the slimy surface into the shade. The grouse hid in
the underbrush, and the small animals, the rabbits and the sudden
moles, ran at intervals across the path, into the sunlight and out of it.

When she went home late in the afternoons it was walking out of
one world into another. It required a readjustment of the hearing.
From the minute sounds of the woods to which she was acute all
day, she walked down along the road past the cultivated meadows,
where the sounds were bolder—loud crickets and the long squeal of
the cicada—past the hunting dogs that were penned up behind their
neighbor's house and barked at all passers, past the hired man
putting his tools away in the barn.

Finally there was the house, and she would have supper with her
mother and father. In a cotton dress and socks and sneakers, she
would sit at the round table and talk and eat and watch the sun going down at last through the west window. The door stood open on
the garden and the smell of early-evening grass, the sound of birds,
came in as they finished supper. Much later, when she was going to
bed, she would kneel down on the floor in her room and crane her

head far out of the window to smell the smell that came across the fields, to see through the light summer night the dark, irregular silhouette against the sky; that was the smell and the shape of the woods.

But somehow it had sifted away, melted into the next year of her life, and become like a streak of old color in the long stream of being alive. Now, as she read that book, which had been a Bible to her, everything she had been doing for months seemed dingy and dull and unbeautiful. The Indian book awoke in her the recollection of the woods and being in the woods. For the first time in her life, now in this bed, she thought longingly of something that she had already experienced. She felt her mind entering the woods and inhabiting them again. She had never finished with the woods, she decided. She had left them for no reason, and when she was well again she would go back to them. That was what she wanted. She did not know why she had penetrated that other world, the new, sharp, bright-lit life that she had begun lately, but it was not what she wanted. She did not want to grow up and be with people. It was not suited to her, and she rejected it now, lying free to choose in bed.

She lay with her legs spread comfortably beneath the smooth, cool sheet and stared sightless at the bare yellow-and-white buttonwood branches outside her window. Trays were brought to her and she ate thin soup with lemon in it, and hot buns, and scrambled eggs, and ice cream. The sunshine moved regularly across the floor of the guest room, from beside her bed in the morning to the farthest corner by the window at sunset. Then it disappeared and twilight filled the room. In the house across the road the lights went on for supper and the lights went out for sleep. And there were stars in the black square of her window.

She was in bed six days and at the end of that time she got up. She saw things again vertically and shook herself like a dog and went outside on the side porch, where the November sunshine lay in pale, lemon-colored stripes. The outdoors smelled sharp and sunny, and her muscles came to life and itched to move. She ran down through the garden to the apple tree and climbed it as she had always done for years, up through its round, rough, pinky-gray branches to a crotch high up, where she sat and surveyed the land. The swamp lay beyond, all still and golden. The apple trees round her were not as high as this one, and she could look down into them. Across the fields the white farmhouse let a thin stream of smoke up through its chimney, where it wavered and turned blue and vanished into the chilly blue sky. The air smelled of late autumn; the air smelled of dead leaves; the air was sharp and lively and wishful. Sara sat in the tree and swung her legs and thought about nothing until somebody called her and she looked down. It was her friend Catherine, who lived in the farmhouse. She stood under the tree and squinted her eyes up at Sara.

"Hi!" Sara said.

"You all well?"

"Sure!"

"Let's go for a walk."

"O.K."

She clambered down the tree and they left the orchard and started to walk down the road to the town, along the lumpy sidewalk made of tar and pebbles. The trees beside the road were bare and clean, and the sky was blue, and the cars drove by gaily. In this November day there was a feeling of activity and of happiness, the brisk, anticipatory feeling of winter coming. Sara and Catherine put their arms around each other's waist and strolled, smiling and talking about what had been happening in school, and about boys.

It was exciting to talk about school. Talking about it, Sara smelled the smell of the classroom, of new, freshly sharpened lead pencils. The impetus of living took hold of her and she was eager and ready for it. She looked at Catherine's plaid wool skirt switching beside her own blue one, casting a thin, swaying shadow on the sidewalk. They strolled on into the town. All the plate-glass windows of the stores glittered in the sun and there was a busy air about the town, of things to be done, of putting on storm doors, of settling down to wait for winter. They passed Tracey's newsstand, where the boys stood in a group looking around. Catherine waved and Sara looked over her shoulder.

"Ha ya?" the Tracey boy said.

"Ha ya doing?" Sara said. She and Catherine laughed lightly, meaningfully, and walked on down the street to the drugstore. They went inside and sat at one of the black glass-topped tables with triangular seats. The store smelled of soda and drugs and candy. The soda clerk walked over to their table.

"What are you having?" he asked.

"Chocolate float," Catherine said.

"Chocolate float, too," Sara said.

It was somehow delightful in the drugstore, full of promise and undisclosed things. To sit, elbows on the damp black glass, and watch the solid glass door and the people who went in and out was somehow exciting. Sara looked at the other customers out of the corner of her eyes, wisely, with poise, and drank her drink through a straw without looking down at it.

"Gee, I'm glad you're over that old bronchitis," Catherine said.

"Gee, so am I."

"I thought you'd never be out. You must have been in the house a whole week."

"Pretty near."

"Don't you just *hate* being sick?"

"I certainly do. Just lying there in bed."

"My mother's going to buy me four new dresses for school. She said I could pick them out myself."

"That's keen. My mother says . . ."

Sara went on talking, eagerly, with satisfaction. She was glad to be well and out and doing things. She felt new vistas opening up before her: school, the girls at school, boys, and beyond that unimaginable things, growing up. For an instant her thought trembled alone, apart from what she was saying.

She thought it was nice to be well and going on with living. It was horrid to be sick and just lie and think. Then her mind switched away from that, the inaction of it, and back into the occupying present, and was happy.

THE JUDGMENT OF PARIS

❖

James Reid Parker

ONE SUNDAY, a few weeks ago, my wife and I were guests at a Westchester country club that was holding its annual diving exhibition. Our hosts, who were delayed, had reserved a table for us on the umbrella-shaded terrace next to the pool. While waiting for their arrival, we chatted idly and observed the other spectators.

Two girls at the table to our right were more than pretty; they were almost spectacularly beautiful. Neither of them could have been younger than eighteen or older than twenty. From their conversation, which was completely audible, we learned that the dark-haired one was nicknamed Dessie and that the fair-haired one was nicknamed Snitch. They talked comfortably and colloquially of one thing after another: the junior college they attended, the horrors of mathematics, the relative merits of various skirt lengths, the sincerity of Trygve Lie, the delights of homemade peach ice cream, the technique of aquaplaning, the good manners of West Point cadets, and the effect of a non-acid-forming diet on the pimples of a girl named Elaine Tuttle. It was the cheerful talk of two friends who, apart from the color of their hair, seemed almost exactly alike. They even used the same phrases—"to put it mildly," "in a manner of speaking," "to come right out and be painfully frank," "I venture to say," and so on. They ventured to say that aquaplaning looked like the easiest sport in the world but actually was the hardest; they agreed that trigonometry was loathsome, to put it mildly; and they came right out and were painfully frank about Elaine Tuttle.

Suddenly, they stiffened. They uttered several exclamations of approval, and their eyes glinted with admiration. I glanced in the direction in which they were looking and saw a handsome young man approaching the pool from the clubhouse, nodding and waving his hand to several acquaintances who called to him. He was a cheerful-looking youth, lithe, muscular, and tanned. He wore a fragment of white Lastex, much as his counterpart in a museum

432

might wear a fig leaf, as a casual concession to prudery. This remarkable specimen continued to walk toward us. I turned to look
at Dessie and Snitch again and was amazed to see the change that
had come over them.

Snitch had become a shy, delicate, and fragile thing, and her
blond loveliness, which had been healthy and extrovert, now had
an ethereal quality. Dessie, on the other hand, was radiating the
high-powered vitality of a musical-comedy soubrette. She waggled a
finger in admonition at someone on the other side of the pool and,
in pantomime, pretended to scold prettily. Meanwhile, Snitch grew
more tiny and helpless than ever.

"Hello, Dessie," the young man said as he came up beside their
table. "Hello, Snitch."

"You might as well walk right straight by me, Gorham Chatfield,
because I'm going to cut you dead," Dessie said cordially. "I'm not
even going to bow—not after the way you behaved at the dance last
night. You shunned me as if I were a perfect leper—as if I were *un-
clean* or something."

"Hello, Gorham," Snitch said. She spoke softly and reverently.

"I got involved with Jeannette Kenderdine," the young man said.
"She kept talking to me about this job I might be able to get with
her father's company."

"Well, I certainly hope you get the job, and I hope it's a perfectly wonderful job, Gorham," Snitch said with great tenderness.
"I honestly do."

"I took Jeannette home, and she introduced me to her father,"
Gorham went on. "He was reading a detective story, and he said he
didn't believe there would be a prayer for anybody without a lot of
experience in the business. Then he went right on reading."

"Since you've got to fly through the air with the greatest of ease
this afternoon, hadn't you better sit down and hoard your strength?"
Dessie said vivaciously. She patted the chair beside her, but Gorham chose another, wheeled it around, and straddled it, so as to
face the two girls.

"Gorham, it just about killed me when you didn't win the Father
and Son Tournament yesterday," Snitch said timidly. "It really
did, because I think a father-and-son golf tournament is the nicest
kind of tournament there is, and I think Harold Mortenson and his
father just had sheer luck! I think your father is a perfect lamb, Gorham, and I'll tell you something else. The thing I admired most was
your coördination. I thought your coördination was beautiful. As

a matter of fact"—here Snitch faltered, as if a regard for truth forced her to make a statement that might conceivably offend—"I thought it was perfect."

"Why, thanks," Gorham said.

"How do you suppose he *gets* such beautiful coördination?" Dessie asked in a sprightly tone, addressing the air. "Do you think there's any truth in the rumor that it curls naturally and that he doesn't use anything on it but water and Palmolive soap?"

This elaborate jocosity failed to amuse Gorham, who merely looked puzzled and uneasy. Snitch frowned at Dessie. "I saw the semifinals from beginning to end," she said gently, "and I saw the final from beginning to end, and, in my humble opinion, Gorham could be the Amateur National Champion someday if he thinks it's a worth-while thing to go out for. I mean if he thinks it's worth his time. You probably have some totally different ambition, haven't you, Gorham?"

Gorham smiled. "My only ambition is to start earning a living," he said.

Dessie pretended to confide in Snitch. "Meanwhile, in his last few weeks of carefree leisure he dances, he swims, he plays golf, he aquaplanes, he dives"—here she favored Gorham with a roguish glance that surpassed anything ever achieved by Irene Bordoni in her youth—"and they say he's also pretty good at one or two indoor sports, as well."

Gorham seemed to have no trouble comprehending this. "Oh, they do, do they?" he responded.

"Yes, they do," Dessie said.

Gorham raised his arm as if to strike her. "Any more cracks and I'll mow you down," he said. At this delicious threat, Dessie shivered prettily. The two of them went along in this vein for a minute or two, until it became evident that his attenion was wandering dangerously.

"Gorham, do you suppose I *dare* wear that same blue thing to the club dance next Saturday that I wore last night?" Dessie asked suddenly.

"Sure," he said. "Why shouldn't you wear the same dress if you want to?"

"That is, if I decide to go at *all*," Dessie amended. "I haven't actually decided whether I will or not. A perfectly ghoulish individual murmured something about it, but I deliberately gave a rather vague answer."

Snitch's expression was daintily pensive. "I think that, more and more, people are going to think less and less about clothes," she remarked. "I mean it seems to me that with men trying to earn a living, and with girls learning to budget a lot more than they've been doing, it's going to be the accepted thing for girls to use imagination in altering their clothes and make every penny go a long, long way. I may be wrong, but I think we're all going to be a lot more sensible from now on."

"There's certainly something in that," Gorham said with cautious approval.

"I went to a dance once in an old tablecloth," Dessie said, and she almost choked with laughter. "I made a bet with a Finch girl, and she made a bet with me. She said I couldn't get away with it, but I did. A lot of people said it was the smartest evening dress they'd ever seen, and do you know how much it cost?" Dessie's voice was triumphant. "It cost less than two dollars! To be perfectly fair, I ought to admit that I made it out of a lace tablecloth of Mother's that she couldn't use any more because it had a terrible cigarette burn. I wore it over a white silk slip, and the whole effect was too *bridal* for words, especially with the white camellias I had!"

Gorham nodded. "I bet it was," he said politely and impersonally.

"It looked exactly like a wedding dress that had been made over into an evening dress," Dessie said. "Of course, the truth is, if I had a wedding dress, I'd never let it be made over into anything! I'd keep it absolutely in its own original state. You may not suspect it, but I have a certain small streak of sentiment in me."

"Oh, yeah?" Gorham said lightly. He seemed to assume—mistakenly, I'm afraid—that banter was still in order.

Without losing any of its fragile appeal, Snitch's manner became firmer. "I wouldn't dream of insisting on a big church wedding," she said. "Not with times being what they are. I wouldn't mind a bit being married in a going-away suit. I mean, when I think how hard men have to work to get a start in business these days, I don't think it's fair to the *man* to have a big church wedding. The important thing is for the wife to be ready to *help,* and the sooner she starts helping, the better."

"I don't think a modern marriage has to be solid, unrelieved gloom, necessarily," Dessie said with spirit. This led to a decided return to the Irene Bordoni manner. "When my husband feels like relaxing, I'm going to see to it that he *relaxes.*"

"I bet you will," Gorham said courteously. He studied the high-diving platform. "You'd think they'd start on time, wouldn't you? Mr. Hungerford is supposed to announce the events, and I don't see him anywhere."

"They taught us the funniest thing last year," Snitch said. "We'd been studying weaving—I'm a home-crafts minor—and after we'd done our first piece of cloth with a passing grade, they taught us how to make men's neckties." She leaned over and touched Gorham's bronzed neck with a speculative finger. "Long ones. Like this." Her finger traced the outlines of a necktie on his chest.

Dessie was prepared to fight. "Don't forget what Dr. Lingard said the last day of the euthenics course!" she cried gaily. "She said, 'In trying to—' "

At this point, Gorham leaped to his feet. "There's Mr. Hungerford!" he exclaimed. "And Betty Fraker is with him! Elizabeth Fraker, from Greenwich. Wait till you see us. I mean wait till you see us *together*. There isn't anything Betty can't do! We've got three exhibition dives scheduled—combination diving, that is—besides our individual dives. It certainly was swell of the committee to let her come over and compete and be eligible for trophies."

Elizabeth Fraker came toward us. Although Dessie and Snitch were as truly beautiful as any girls I had ever seen in my life, Elizabeth Fraker was equally impressive. But then, of course, considerably more of her was visible. Her own fragment of white Lastex was larger than Gorham's only by the margin that Westchester ethics require. When she smiled, her teeth were as flawlessly white as her costume, and the contrast with her dark and even tan was dramatic.

"Hello, Go!" Elizabeth Fraker said. Dessie and Snitch exchanged a look. I couldn't help suspecting that this abbreviation of the young man's first name had never occurred to them, and that they admired and envied the ingenuity of the brain that had conceived it.

The young man performed the necessary introductions. "Wait till you see her!" he said joyously, presumably referring to the diving that was to take place. "She's got *everything!*"

Gorham and Miss Fraker soon excused themselves and went to the end of the pool, where a number of other contestants had congregated. The discarded goddesses studied the scene for several moments without making any comment.

Dessie sighed deeply. "To come right out and be painfully frank, the woman has her points," she said. "The way she holds herself, for one thing. And it was smart of her to wear the same color and material."

"She's got everything, all right—including Mr. Gorham Chatfield, Esquire," Snitch said. "All I objected to was that eager look he had when he jumped up. That killed me!"

It occurred to me that Snitch had stopped being small, helpless, and fragile, and that Dessie was no longer a determined soubrette. Now that the gentleman had indicated his preference, they were themselves again.

"Let's see who else is here," Snitch said.

The two girls sipped their Coca-Colas, alertly inspecting the world over the rims of their glasses. Then Dessie put her glass down.

"Nobody worth mentioning in the same *breath*," she said with decision.

MARY MULCAHY

❖

LYING QUITE STILL on her bed, so that the pain in her back was only a warning and not an actuality, Mary Mulcahy considered her problems. There were the matters of her back, of the broken novena, of Kathleen's hundred dollars, and, most difficult to face, of this room. Whatever else she thought about, she was aware always of the room. Even while she lay thus, with her eyes closed, she could see its comforting detail, be aware of the fine light that swept in at the east window, of the huge ailanthus that grew in the next back yard. You might look and look in all that district of Manhattan and not find another room like this one, so convenient, so cheap, so clean and pretty, its own running water in the bright washbasin; a quiet room, in a jutting ell to an old house, that looked out down the long reach of the back yards to trees and to privet bushes; a room into which the morning sun poured like a blessing from the dear Virgin.

Oh, but cheap as it was, it was the wasteful extravagance, surely! All the long summer, four solid months, she could, by living in one of the servants' rooms at the Park Avenue apartment where she worked, save the rent she was now paying. And so, without touching the savings that now mounted so slowly again toward security, she could set aside the money for Kathleen's wedding present. Hadn't she given a hundred dollars to the other nieces when they married? To Rosie and to Agnes? But that was before the bad days, before the savings of a lifetime melted suddenly away. If you had asked her in 1929, she would have said she could stop work in another five years, living secure and content in such a room as this—if another such existed. Sixty years would have been the good age for stopping.

But there could be no stopping now. There was the present for Kathleen, and the savings that were so small, and always a little bit here and a little bit there for the blessed Church. You could not say no to a good man like Father Elliott, or to the sweet Sisters who knocked at your door, their lives in their faces, their smiles the reflection of the light of the Blessed Mother herself. She was lucky indeed to have so good a job, for taking care of the apartment in summer was within her powers and the half-days in winter were not that hard to do that she could not do them a while yet—if her back grew no worse. Last night it was so bad after she came home from the apartment that she had to lie down, as she had today, and, for all that her soul troubled her, she had stayed in her bed and so the novena was broken, and it in its eighth day. Surely Father Elliott would understand and be kind, there would be never a reproach to her, but within herself there was the knowledge that what she had set out to do for the glory of God and for the salvation of her own soul was left but partly done. It was like a warning, a portent. What if Mr. Gore, or indeed him and his wife too, should come to New York while she was like this now? How would she stand to fix their tea and to give them breakfast? Mrs. Gore was a beautiful, sweet woman and Mr. Gore the fine, big, strong man. It was a pleasure to make him comfortable and have things nice for him. They would be kind, they would understand, but wouldn't they say to themselves, "Mary Mulcahy is too old now"? Wouldn't they begin casting about for a young one who would not be ill to fail them?

I keep it clean and lovely, she thought, the lovely apartment, but if I am not there for them when they come, what good is the cleanness of it? It's well that I never married, indeed, for a fine wife I'd have been to the old husband in these the last years of his age.

So she lay on the bed, conscious of the warmth of the room, of its high ceiling, of the light beyond the window, the soft, glowing, eastern light of evening, and she felt the problems grow heavy in her breast. The smallness of the savings weighed and weighed on her, the present for Kathleen was a deadly weight, her back warned her, distantly but clearly, of the weight of her years. And behind it all, behind even the distress of the broken novena, lay the knowledge that if she gave up the room, lived in at the apartment, it would be all solved, all simple, and that once she let this room go, it would not be twenty-four hours before another would have it, and then, as sure as God was in His heaven, it would be gone forever. Weren't there people waiting for it now? Hadn't she waited for three years herself to get it? Hadn't she waited till Ellen Smith had died? Ellen had wanted never to move from it, and only death in the end had moved her. You lived in house after house, room after room—life was a series of rooms in a long series of houses. Surely when a room at last said home to you, you had the good right to cling to it?

It was past six o'clock when she heard the knocking at her door. Something told her that the knocking had been going on for some time and that only now had she become fully conscious of it, and it frightened her.

"Come in," she called out. The door rattled.

"It's locked," said the mild voice of Mrs. Gustafson, her landlady.

It was necessary to rise, then, thought Mary Mulcahy. Slowly she began the process, easing herself up till she sat on the edge of her bed, pushing herself upright from there, one hand on her hip, the other hand clinging to the head of her bed. Her back ached painfully. Her left hand still pressed to her hip, she limped to the door, unlatched it, and opened it.

"It's a telegram," said Mrs. Gustafson. "I'm sorry to get you up."

"A telegram!" cried Mary. "Oh!" She took the yellow envelope from Mrs. Gustafson. "Oh God!" she said.

"I hope it ain't some bad news," Mrs. Gustafson said, patting her silver hair in the dusk of the hallway. "It's maybe nothing at all. Sometimes—"

"Aah," Mary said, "them things! You never know." She opened the envelope and read the message on the yellow slip aloud and slowly: "'ARRIVED UNEXPECTEDLY AND SHALL SPEND THE NIGHT PLEASE BRING KEYS TO SILVER CLOSET.' It's himself. It's Mr. Gore."

"And you yust home to rest!" said Mrs. Gustafson. "It's a shame!"

"No, no," Mary said. "He's a fine man. Sometimes he don't have a chance to send word before he has to come. I must go right around." She turned away.

"Can I help you?"

"Oh, no, I thank you," Mary said.

"You look sick, Miss Mulcahy."

"I'm all right," Mary said. "I'm all right. It's only I have the ache in my back. It's the weather, is all it is. It'll pass. It'll pass. It is nothing at all. I thank you for bringing up the telegram, Mrs. Gustafson."

"That's all right," Mrs. Gustafson said. "Let me know if I can help you. It's a shame when you were home already and lying down." She shut the door softly.

"Home already," Mary repeated as she put on her old black hat. Then she slipped her feet into a rather battered pair of white sneakers and left the room.

It was only six blocks to the apartment, so Mary walked it, as always. The beginning of the journey was worse than the end. She stopped at John O'Meara's and bought oranges and lemons and a pint of cream and a loaf of the Italian bread that Mr. Gore liked so well. Mr. Gore was waiting for her at the apartment when she let herself in at the kitchen entrance.

"Well, Mary," he said. "How are you?"

"Fine, fine," said Mary. "And how is yourself and the family?"

"All blooming," he said. "Sorry to rout you out like this. I'd no time to telegraph, even, till I arrived."

"Aah," she said, "that's all right. That's all right. Will you have some tea now?"

"It's rather late," he said, looking at his watch.

"It'll do you good," she said.

"Well—it would. If it's not too much bother?"

"Not a bit of bother in the world," said Mary. "I'll have it for you in a minyute. In just a minyute."

She bustled back to the kitchen, took off her hat and put on an apron, and made tea and toast. It was swiftly and competently done. She took the tray in to him, shuffling in her sneakers, the shuffling walk she had found was easier these days.

"And how is your niece, Kathleen?" he asked her.

"Fine, fine," said Mary. "She's to be wed in October."

"Indeed?" he said. "So soon? I could have wished she'd stayed on. Mrs. Gore liked her so much. A first-rate girl."

"Aah," said Mary, "them young ones today! They don't know when they're well off. All they think of is the men and the marrying."

"Natural enough," said Mr. Gore.

"To be sure," Mary said. "Natural enough. But there's many a one lives to regret it. She had a lovely place here, with lovely people, and she should have stayed in it. Then you know where you are. Aah, them young girls! They're all alike. What time will you be wanting breakfast, sir?"

"Call me at seven-thirty," he said. "Breakfast at eight. I'm off for home again tomorrow. I'll try to give you warning next time I come up. Leave the key of the silver closet on my dresser, will you? I'll give it back in the morning."

"I will," she said. "I will. Is there anything else now?"

"No," he said. "Good night, Mary. You toddle along home. I'll be out of here in half an hour."

"Good night, sir," she said.

She went to his bedroom then and turned down the bed for him, unpacked his bag, and laid out his toilet things and his pajamas. She drew him a warm bath and checked to be sure there were plenty of clean towels. She was pleased now that she'd put the fine, embroidered sheets on his bed, but it was lucky Mrs. Gore wasn't here too, for there'd only been the one pair home from the wash and on her bed were the plain ones. Then Mary went to the kitchen, made herself some tea, and sat down to wait for him to go. It was a long wait. She sat in a wooden chair instead of the upholstered wicker one, because it was easier to get up from, with her back and all, if he should ring for her.

When he had gone out at last she went to his room and hung up his suit, treed his shoes, and laid his underclothes neatly, ready for the morning. Then she cleaned the bathroom and straightened it up and rinsed out the tub, though that was painful, so painful it was frightening. But she was too busy to be really frightened. Then she collected the tea things and washed them and put ice in the ice carafe. She set out a tray with glasses and whiskey and the carafe in the living room. She emptied his ashtray and plumped the cushions. When everything was done, when the apartment was as neat as a pin, proper and comfortable for his return, she looked around her and felt a sort of panic. Her occupations were over. There was nothing to divert her mind from her troubles now.

I'll stay here, she thought. I'll never get home and back. There's Cook's bed I can lie upon. That's the best.

Here she could lie down, lie down indeed. When she got up again, for all the pain, she would be here, where she had to be. There would be no stairs up, no stairs down, no six blocks to walk. She got a blanket from a bureau drawer and unrolled the mattress on the bed in the little, dark, viewless bedroom. Then she took off her sneakers, lay down on the bed, and pulled the one blanket over her. Lying there, she said her prayers twice through and begged the good God and His lovely Son and the merciful Mother of Christ to forgive her that she hadn't the strength left in her to kneel to Their worship. When she lay still, her back was only a portent of pain.

In the morning, before Mr. Gore had left, Mary Mulcahy came to her decision. She told him merely that she was going to give up her room and sleep at the apartment. "Till you and Madam come back in October," she said.

"That's good," he said. "I should think that much more convenient and economical."

"It is, it is," she said. That was all. There was no use bothering him with your own little problems and him probably bowed down with his great ones. And how could you tell a man in his lovely ten-room apartment what a room in a rooming house might mean to you?

When she had everything clean and in order, she put on her hat and left the apartment. On her way home she went by way of St. Anthony's, entered the church, and, going to the Lady Chapel, she knelt there and said many prayers and many of them over. She prayed the Virgin for strength to continue and for forgiveness of her sins. If she had seen Father Elliott, she would have told him about her back and the novena, but there was no one around but the old sacristan, dusting and dusting. All he did, she thought, was move the blessed dust from one place to another. Then she left and walked home.

When she had packed her two old, battered suitcases, she found Mrs. Gustafson in her kitchen.

"I've got to go," she said. "I've got to give up the room. I must live in till October."

"Oh!" cried Mrs. Gustafson. "Why, Miss Mulcahy, I thought you would be here for *always* now."

"It's a lovely room," Mary said. "A lovely, lovely room. But it's my niece is to be married and so on and so on. And my people come often to the apartment and all."

"Well," said Mrs. Gustafson. "If you must, you must. I hate to have you going, Miss Mulcahy. Till October, you say?"

"Till October," Mary said. "That's the truth. I'll want a room then, if you've a vacancy, Mrs. Gustafson. Here's what I owe you." She held out a small wad of crumpled bills.

Mrs. Gustafson took it and counted it. "That's right," she said, and smiled. "We'll be waiting for you. Goodbye. Good luck."

"Goodbye," Mary said.

She said the same thing in a whisper to her room as she left it. The leavetaking was not prolonged. That would have been sinful, and useless. She picked up the two bags and looked at the room around her and said, in a whisper, "Goodbye." That was all. Then she began the painful descent of the stairs. The pain reassured her now. It was so right to go. She opened the front door and stepped out onto the high stoop. She was just going to close the door behind her when Mrs. Gustafson appeared.

"See," said Mrs. Gustafson awkwardly. "We are not young now. Life ain't all money, money. Isn't it? When you come back to me, when you come back in October, the little room will be for you. So."

"Aah," Mary said. "My room! God will remember you, Mrs. Gustafson. It's a lovely thing, it is. A lovely thing. You put the heart back into me."

"It is nothing," said Mrs. Gustafson. "Till October, when you come home. We will expect you, Miss Mulcahy. So long." She closed the door then, rather abruptly.

Mary picked up the suitcases again and descended the stoop. There were tears in her eyes and she had to stop when she reached the sidewalk, put down the cases, and wipe her eyes. "The kind woman," she said aloud. "The lovely, kind woman."

John O'Meara's delivery boy, Julian, pushing his cart, stopped beside her.

"You off to the apartment, Miss Mulcahy?" he said.

"I am," she said. "I am. Good morning, Julian."

"I'll put your bags in and take them up," he said.

"Aah," she said, "it's out of your way, then."

"No," he said. "Never a bit." He took the two suitcases and put them in his cart and together they began walking toward Park Avenue, he in his thick shoes, lightly, as a young man; she in her white sneakers, shuffling.

"The Lord is my shepherd," said Mary Mulcahy.

THE BUMMERS

❖

John Powell

I LEFT THE BEACH toward the end of a very fine North Carolina
summer afternoon, and as I drove up to the bridge over Middle
Sound, I saw three boys sitting on the railing. For a long time that
end of the bridge has been the bumming place for the beach, and if
you ever see anybody waiting there, you know he is looking for a ride
into Wilmington, so I stopped for them.

"Goin' to town?" two of the boys asked at the same time.

"Sure," I said. "Get in."

"All the way?" the third one asked.

"Sure."

They jumped down off the railing and picked up a big red inner
tube with no air in it and their bathing suits, and hurried over to
the car.

"A Ford," one of the boys said. "Just like yesterday." Two of them
were about twelve and the other was a fat little boy of about nine.
They opened the right-hand door, and the fat boy and another one
got in the back seat and the third sat up front with me.

"The water was pretty good today, wasn't it?" I said, and started
to drive on.

"It was good," the one beside me said. "Good waves."

I lit a cigarette and asked them if they wanted a smoke. "No,
thanks," they all said in turn.

"It shows up to a hundred," the older one in back said, leaning
forward with his chin on my seat and pointing at the speedometer.
"I never seen but a few Fords that could make a hundred."

"Most of them can't," I said. "They're too light."

We passed a big, capsule-shaped aluminum tank in the fenced-off
yard that lies to the right of the road after you cross the bridge.

"What's that thing? What's in there?" the fat boy asked.

"Gas," said the boy beside me.

"Would it blow up?"

"No, Curtis, no," the boy beside me said impatiently. I suspected that Curtis was his brother.

"Fords are good cars," the other boy in back said. "If I had a car it ud be a Ford."

"They're all right," I said.

We crossed the bridge over the inland waterway and took the tight curve at the end of it.

"There's a lot of bad curves on this road between here and town," the older boy in back said.

"The worst one's right up here," I said. "Where you turn away from the Sound."

"Yes, sir," he said politely. He ruminated and then said, "I bet a thousand people been killed on that curve."

"A friend of mine got killed there one time," I said.

"When was that?"

"That was ten years ago now."

"Well, what happened?" Curtis asked. He leaned forward, afraid that here was one more thing nobody would tell him anything specific about. "Were they comin' down to the beach and skidded offa the road?"

"I think they were on their way back up to town," I said. "Coming back from a party. Six or seven of them were killed, and he was one."

"Well, how did they get killed? Did they cut offa the road and get drowned?"

"No," I said. "Just the wreck."

"Don't act so dumb, Curtis," the boy beside me said, probably because he thought I might be annoyed, and Curtis didn't ask any more questions for a while.

We made the worst curve in the road without accident. "That man yesterday was really cuttin' it around here," the older boy in back said. Now our road climbed away from the Sound. I passed a car and then another one. The boys seemed to enjoy being in the faster car, and I enjoyed their enjoyment.

We turned the curve just before you get to the bridge over the creek. As we came onto the bridge, I said, "Another friend of mine got in a wreck here one time. The car broke through the railing and went almost off the bridge. It was hanging down the side of the bridge with only the rear axle holding on."

"Was he killed?" the boy beside me asked.

"No, he got out all right."

"Well, how did he get out?"

"He climbed up the beams," I explained.

"It was lucky the back wheels didn't roll off," the older one in back said. "He'd a been killed sure, then."

"Would he a drowned?" Curtis asked him.

"No, it's shalla down there. I don't know. Maybe he wouldn't a gotten killed," the older boy said.

The boy beside me was still trying to picture my friend climbing up the beams. He wanted the inch-by-inch details, but I didn't have them, so I couldn't help him. What I had said about the beams was only a guess, anyway.

We turned the curve beyond the bridge, and there was a green car at the side of the road, with a jack under the rear axle and no wheel on the left rear side.

"Flat tire," I said. There was nobody around the car.

"An uncle of mine got killed in a wreck last month," the boy beside me said.

"Is that so?" I said.

"He was drivin' an overnight truck?" the boy said, with a rising inflection and a look at me that made his statement half expression of fact, half question. "And my uncle was feelin' kinda sleepy, and he had picked up this soldier? And so he let the soldier drive the truck and tol' him the road, U. S. 17, just to keep on that—"

"Where was it?" I interrupted.

"He was drivin' 17 to Whitevul and when they got up to Leland where that curve is? Where the dead end is? And my uncle was still asleep. The soldier was drivin' and he saw the dead end, and he tried to turn off, but he was goin' too fast and he turned her over and my uncle got killed. The soldier wasn't hurt a little."

"I'd rather drive an overnight truck than an oil truck," the older boy in back said.

"That's right," I said. "A lot of oil-truck drivers get killed. An empty one is more dangerous than a full one."

"I heard that if they jes jolt a little too hard on the road, it jes blows up," he said.

"One time we were drivin' along the road up in the country," the boy beside me said. "And this fella came along hittin' it about ninety-five and he tried to pass us? And he saw he wasn't gonna make it and he turned over and hit a telephone pole and didn't eem get killed."

"I seen some bad wrecks," the older boy in back said. "At Third and Bladen? There was this truck? And she had come in from the country with a load of hay and she was goin' back empty to the country? And when she turned the corner at Third and Bladen, she fell over on another car, and the nigger got mashed in between 'em. There was two niggers ridin' on the runnin' board and one of 'em jumped off, but the uvver one got mashed in between the truck and the car. Cut him right half in two."

We were all quiet for a minute and then the boy beside me said, "I heard of a bad wreck out here at the Winter Park crossin'. There was a bus comin' up from the beach and she stopped over there at the gas station. She stopped to let off this woman, and she was carryin' a three-months-old baby in her arms? And there was these two cars comin' and one of 'em tried to turn offa the road but he couldn't make it? And they jes hit together like this." He put the tips of his forefingers together. "And the woman, they said, threw the baby ten feet and he didn't eem get hurt."

"I heard she threw the baby fifty feet," the older one in back said.

"Well. She threw the baby fifty feet and the woman was all mashed up."

"She got killed?" I asked.

"Yeah, that's right, she got killed. And the doctor came and just looked at her. He knew there wasn't no use doin' anything for her and she'd die in a few hours? And the woman's family came and she was broke up so bad they couldn't recanize her. She had a bracelet on her arm and they said that was the only way they could tell who she was."

I was going to ask if the baby hadn't provided a pretty reliable clue, but it was too sad and moving a story to pick at.

"I was in a bad wreck," the older one in back said. "We skidded offa the road and turned over twice, but nobody got hurt. The car was all tore up."

"I ain't been in any bad wrecks," the boy beside me said. "Jes little ones. One time at my uncle's place in the country, somebody was cuttin' his timber. He was cuttin' some himself but he hadn't cut any pine. And somebody came up to my uncle and tol' him they had seen a truck goin' inta town with pine logs. The bark was off, but you can tell pine. And I tol' 'em I had seen the place they were cuttin' from. And he ast me if I ud show him where it was and I said yes. And my uncle and another man and me were drivin' down the road to where it was cut and the door opened and I jes rolled over and over side the road. I fell out? And rolled side the road." He smiled self-consciously.

"Did you get the people who were cutting your uncle's timber?" I asked, as bad as Curtis.

"Yeah, they got 'em," the boy said, but he wasn't so interested in timber just then as he was in wrecks, and so I never heard the rest of that story. Suddenly he turned around. "Curtis, you got the bathing suits? If you ain't, you jes as well get out and start walkin' back to the beach."

The bathing suits were on the floor of the back seat.

"Some of these fellas that get in wrecks," the older boy in back said. "They think they're too tough to die. It's jes luck."

"Wrecks are funny," I said. "One man turns over and everybody's killed, and another man will do the same thing and nobody gets a scratch."

"And sometimes they'll turn over and the driver'll get hurt bad and everybody else'll be all right," the boy in front said. "I had a cousin, his name was Richard? And he got in a wreck about twelve o'clock one night, and he was drivin' and he was the only one hurt. And the doctor jes walked out on him. He wouldn't eem look at him, and tol' 'em there wasn't no hope for him. Jes gave him up? And Richard jes laid there in the bed and pulled out of it some way. The doctor would come ever' day to see if he was dead and wouldn't do nothin' for him. And Richard jes pulled out of it. And now he's as good as ever."

"I heard about a soldier," the older boy in back said. "I think it was out on the Camp Davis road. And he got in a wreck, and one side of his nose? His brains was runnin' out thu one side of his nose, and they had a glass they were ketchin' 'em in, and ever' day they ud pump 'em back in his head."

"Why didn't they bandage him?" the boy in front said. He was a good, solid boy with plenty of sense. "One time my uncle had a baby and she was sick?" he continued. "And the doctor gave her up. He said there wasn't no hope for her. And my uncle went out in the yard and he was holdin' the baby on a pilla in his arms. And the baby stopped breathin'. My uncle was standing out in the yard holdin' her on a pilla in his arms? And my uncle's mother came out in the yard and she put her mouth on that baby's mouth and blew her breath in the baby. And the baby started breathin'. And the doctor jes gave her up."

"That soldier with his brains running out?" the older one in back said. "They gave *him* up and he pulled out of it."

We were close to Wilmington now and the traffic began to get heavier. We passed a golf course and several drive-in places on the edge of town as the afternoon was ending in a fiery sky over the river.

"My mama tol' me about a girl," the older boy in back said. "Mama said when she was coming along they didn't 'balm people? They buried 'em that day or the next day. And the doctor said this girl was dead, and ever'body in the house thought she was dead. And they were fixin' her, dressin' her and washin' her. And the doctor came in where they were and felt of her pulse? He felt of her pulse and he ast would ever'body please leave the room. Him in there alone with her? And they said yes, they would, and they went out and left the doctor in there with her. And he got a mirra and wiped it off and put it up to her mouth. And you know how a mirra does when you breathe on it? The doctor saw it was like that, and he knew she was still livin'. And he dosed her up so much that when they went back in, there she was sittin' up in the bed. Mama said she lived to be fifty or sixty years old."

"How did Richard get hurt?" Curtis wanted to know.

"Oh, Curtis, you're way behine," the boy in front said.

"Well," Curtis said, "how did Richard get hurt? Did he break his arm?"

"Richard got hurt in a wreck, like I tol' you," the boy in front said.

"I know that," Curtis said. "I ain't studyin' that. What I want to know is, how did he get hurt? Did he break his arm?"

"He got all broke up," the boy in front said, to get the subject out of the way.

"He uz all mashed up," the other one in back explained.

"I was workin' out at Van Huesen's dairy one time," the boy in front said. "And he had another little house back of the big house, but he didn't live in it. He had some niggers workin' for him? A nigger and his wife and three childern lived in it. It had a lot of hay around it laying all around in the yard, and one day the hay caught on fire and the nigger woman and three childern were in the house and burned up before they could get out. Four of 'em burned up before they could put out the fire."

"Do you remember that fire last year?" the older boy in back said. "Out on the Sunset Park road, when the baby got burned up? Didn't the firemen do dirty?"

"They did," I said.

"Why didn't the firemen go to the fire?" Curtis asked vaguely, as though he had known the reason once but had forgotten it.

"The fire was outside the city limits."

After a moment, Curtis said, "Someday the firemen ain't goin' to the fire and the whole town is gonna burn up. All across town— whoom!"

"Where do you boys live in town?" I asked after we had passed through the colored section.

"Over on the other side," the boy in front said.

"Brooklyn," Curtis said.

"Then I'd better let you out at this corner," I said. "I live on this street."

"You ain't goin' no further?" Curtis asked.

"It ain't as long as we walked on the beach," the boy in front said. "Not as far as the end of the beach to the bridge."

"Well, I'll let you out here," I said. I turned in to the curb and stopped.

"Thanks for the ride," they all said, one after another. Curtis picked up the inner tube and the bathing suits, and the three boys got out.

"I certainly appreciate the ride," the one who had been sitting in front said.

"Glad to do it," I said.

They were standing on the grass between the curb and the sidewalk smiling, and I saw that I had picked up the right people and had made some friends.

UNDER GEMINI

❖

ISABEL BOLTON

IT WAS THEIR condition that lay at the heart of the matter. But to be able to explain their state—this double identity—to anyone who had not undergone the unique intimacy and awareness of a similar experience was out of the question. And for them to think that Eustace could comprehend anything so inconceivable was, of course, ridiculous. Naturally, having been born to it, conditioned from the first to the music and vibration of their sameness, it had taught them all they knew of joy and sorrow, pity and love. There was something absolute in this knowledge that whatever they experienced when together came to them through an uncanny communion, each knowing that the other twin (the other self, you might as well say) was undergoing simultaneous response, the same necessity of nerves imposing upon them the same words and actions—what amounted, in short, to practically similar behavior, so that they were hardly able to recognize which of them had done or said this, that, or the other thing. With them, it was always what was taking place in the realm of the spirit that seemed to have significance.

Well, as they used to say, they had their memories of childhood. Nobody could deprive them of those—their common joy in bird and flower and cloud, their running over lawn and meadows, happy in their twin response. Their mistake had been to try to carry over into their adult years their inseparability; that was dangerous—sure to bring disaster. And for them to have come to New York, of all places on earth, determined to stick together, with this queer feeling they had of possessing a single personality and but one soul between them! Here they got in each other's way, stood in each other's light. It couldn't be expected that both of them would get the same breaks. And since Katherine had been the one to find the really enthralling job, she should have gone it on her own. They should never have taken that apartment together (never in the wide world!), trying to fool themselves into a belief that they were two girls, each capable of making her own little conquests—having her own little triumphs.

How delighted they'd been when they had made the neighborhood their own, a neighborhood, too, that was so full of color and
atmosphere, with the views and skyscapes from their windows so en-
trancing—to the north the dome and cross of the big Italian church,
rooftops, tenements, gables, chimneys, clotheslines (wash flapping
in the wind, pigeons flying off the roofs), and to the south the out-
look private and enclosed, the facing rows of red brick houses, with
their back yards and little gardens, and the big ailanthus tree that
almost brushed their windows. An appropriate setting for their artistic temperaments; here, they'd thought, they could express themselves.

Poor Kathy! She had certainly done her level best, bringing down
first one and then another of her new-made friends, wanting desperately to share them with Christene. It hadn't seemed to work,
somehow, but then why should it have worked? It must have been
disconcerting enough for anyone a bit gone on Kathy to come down
to her apartment and find ensconced another girl, who resembled
her in every particular. She and Chris, try as they might to avoid it,
had the most disastrous way of expressing the same opinion at exactly the same moment ("Mozart? Oh, absolutely, he's our favorite!"
"We adore Chekhov." "No, we *don't* like modern art"), never able,
somehow, to say "I" or "me" or "mine" but, instead, always "we"
and "us" and "ours." Why, anyone at all observant must have
noticed, when there was general conversation or when they were
listening to the victrola or the radio, that the same expressions were
recorded on their faces. Then there was that unfortunate habit they
had of jumping up and exclaiming, in practically one breath, "Come
and see our tree of heaven!," and the two of them, presently, at the
window, sharing Kathy's friend between them, and something in
their voices—the slight Southern drawl, maybe, or just their talking
there together—that must have suggested to the poor fellow that
they expected him to make love to both of them at once. It was disconcerting, very much on the queer side. One of the young men had
invented names for them—"Tree of Heaven" and "Mississippi
Blues"—but the trouble was he never knew which name belonged to
which girl. The situation had been impossible, utterly impossible!
Each knew just how the other felt about it. And if Kathy frequently
resented working so hard for both of them without appreciable results, and if Christene tried in vain to suppress her envy of Kathy's
better luck, it shouldn't, even so, have seemed so awful to them. It
was only human.

Had Katherine not felt such concern for Christene, she would
have found life in New York a succession of happy events and day-
dreams. As assistant to an older woman who had set up a successful
agency for writers, she found herself on the fringes of the literary
world. What with writers coming in and out of the office, manuscripts received, manuscripts sent off, rejected or accepted, the whole
big city, under the spell of these excitements, seemed to hold out to
her the most wonderful gifts and possibilities. She loved her work
and came to her office every morning and left it every evening in a
state of the highest exhilaration.

As for poor Chris, her situation was exactly the opposite. She hated
her job and regarded it as so much drudgery that had to be undergone day after day, sitting in that office high up in the Cunard
Building, taking down letters, pencil poised ("Ready, Mr. Furkins,"
"Yes, Mr. Furkins," "Yours of the fifteenth received," etc., etc.), yet
caring not a red cent for invoices or exports or imports and having,
later, to sit for long, backbreaking hours at the typewriter, tran-
scribing the hateful dictation, and not entirely unaware that her
employer's somewhat lecherous eye went frequently a-roaming
over her face, her costume, and her exceedingly pretty figure.

Katherine in love with life and Christene bored and disconso-
late—each could nonetheless be relied upon, at all times and in all
places, to keep in mind the other's condition. And so it happened
that on a certain evening in December, as they were leaving their
offices, at just that magic moment when the city seems to shake and
shine with a sudden incandescent brightness, they experienced—one
of them in midtown, the other at the foot of Wall Street—a crisis of
affection and regret. Katherine, in the highest of spirits, crossed Fifth
Avenue, stopped a moment to have a look at the great central shaft
of light at Rockefeller Plaza, and then, wanting further glimpses of
the wonderful town, hastened up the Avenue and west through
Fifty-third Street, glancing across at the terrific concrete cliffs of
Radio City, wildly exhilarated, thinking of her job, of her good fortune. Why, if she didn't have poor, darling Chris hanging around
her neck, she might make her own terms with this formidable town!
She had the weirdest sensation of flying, rather than walking, over to
Sixth and on down Sixth to Bryant Park, with all those skyscrapers
glittering and glamouring away at her. Finally, boarding a bus, her
spirits fell. She dropped from her giddy heights. She decided that she
hated New York, with all its unnatural excitements, and vowed with
tears in her eyes that if she couldn't procure for Chris as good a time

as she was having herself, she wouldn't give a tinker's damn for anything. And Chris, hurrying to the Battery in the very depths of the
doldrums, presently found herself standing in the shabby little park
amid the little leafless trees, the dwarfed benches, the midget people.
Staring up at the stupendous flights of lighted windows erecting
their bright, incredible cities in the air, she was suddenly over-
whelmed by a great wave of jealousy of Katherine that almost resembled hatred. It rushed at her. She fought it down, realizing all the
while that underneath her temporary anger and envy her love was
strong and indestructible, that it was all she had, that without it she
was a creature with neither heart nor soul.

When they met that night, their mood was one of tenderness and
affection; they didn't want to be out of each other's sight a minute,
and both of them seemed almost on the brink of tears. They decided
not to dine at home but to give themselves a treat, so they went to
their favorite Italian restaurant, where they ordered cocktails and
Chianti and, presently, began to discuss their situation. They wept
a little, laughed a lot, were determined not to be tragic, but they
would, they resolved, *do* something about their plight. No, they
wouldn't separate. They couldn't possibly do that, but they would
make a genuine effort to change their behavior. No more coming out
with the same remarks at the same moment—not, at least, if they
could help it. They'd be different. They would, in the first place, put
an end to the silly, romantic habit they had clung to so long of dressing just alike. They would dress as much unlike as possible. Each
would have a style of her own. Kathy would affect the boyish and
severe; she'd take on a new line of talk as well, and try to be slangy,
modern, sophisticated. As for Chris, she'd remain as they had been
before—feminine, a bit provincial. It would be difficult—they admitted it—but nonetheless they would pay strict attention to acting out
their roles as well as they could. They wouldn't waver.

If they hadn't made those crazy resolutions, what then? That was
the question each girl frequently asked herself. However, the prom-
ises had been made, and, after their fashion, they had tried to put
them into practice. But when, a few weeks after Kathy's stupendous
change of personality, Eustace came into her life, fate began to play
a hand in both their destinies. Kathy had fallen dead in love with
him the instant she'd clapped eyes on him. Why, he had everything
—everything! He was so handsome, in that lovely, not too emphatic
way, so modest and intelligent, and, moreover, she'd heard him discussed before she ever met him and knew about the slender book of

poems he'd published and the novel he was writing, with half the publishers in town aware of it. She hadn't run after him; she'd made no advances; she'd just worshipped from a distance and had hardly been able to believe that he was falling for her. But there had been many signs of it—his asking her out so many times for lunch, and then the day he'd told her, in that charming way he had of giving compliments, as though he were ruminating about them before he offered them, that she had the most remarkable eyes he'd ever seen, perfectly astounding eyes. "You're kidding," she'd said, trying out the new line. Oh, no, he wasn't kidding, he'd assured her; her eyes had haunted him for days. She had locked that remark up in her heart all right, and she used to take it out and say it to herself and lock it up again. She hadn't told Chris a word about him but simply allowed herself to get more and more implicated in the enthralling business of being dead in love, of doting on him. And then when she'd asked him down for dinner that fatal Saturday night, she hadn't prepared Chris for it until that afternoon, when she'd just let it slip out, in the most casual, offhand manner she could muster, that she'd invited a young man she had met to dine with them—a man named Eustace Barr.

Chris guessed Kathy's secret at once. Something about the way she looked, everything about the way she acted, gave her away—the expressions of her face, the excitement of her manner, so nervous and particular. The dinner must be cooked to perfection, the table set just so; then, at the last moment, flushed and exhilarated, she insisted on rushing off to buy flowers to put the final touch to her arrangements.

Eustace arrived earlier than expected. "Oh," Chris said, "you're Eustace. Kathy told me. We didn't think you'd be here yet. Kathy will be back in a minute." The admiration in his face was startling. He made no effort to disguise it. It was just as though he'd exclaimed, "God, what a beautiful girl!" Apparently, it didn't occur to him that she was Kathy's twin. She was a creature entirely unique, staring at him, calling him Eustace.

Then out she came with it: "Don't you want to see our tree of heaven?" And in a few minutes there the two of them were, leaning out the window, looking at the back yards, the small gardens, the ailanthus tree. It was spring. The windows in all the houses across the way were open. Curtains blew in the breeze. Someone was playing the piano very professionally. "Oh!" she cried. "Chopin! That's out favorite nocturne. Listen! Isn't it beautiful?," and she began to hum it in perfect tune, keeping just ahead of the notes that floated over the air. Eustace couldn't restrain himself; something took possession of him. He placed his hand over hers and said, "What wonderful eyes you have—remarkable eyes—the most astounding eyes I've ever seen!" Then he leaned over and kissed her very lightly—oh, very lightly—on the lips. "Why," he said, "you're the loveliest girl I ever saw!" It was all so quickly over, before she could even protest, and that ineffable sweetness began filling her heart, and the nocturne floating across the back yards, the air so soft and filled with spring. Then in came Kathy, her arms filled with spring flowers—tulips and lilacs and apple blossoms.

The treachery of it, Chris thought, the awful treachery of her heart! She knew how Kathy felt. She knew that Kathy was on to everything. But this did not prevent her, all the evening, from feeling little, fiery shocks of pleasure and delight each time she exchanged a glance with Eustace. They were in love with each other. It was electrifying.

Eustace stepped right into Chris's heart. Queer thing, the way he took it all so much for granted, sensed no complications in the situation whatsoever. He seemed to think they weren't so much alike, and loved to declare that he could have told them apart even if their clothes had been identical. Didn't Chris have some tiny freckles on the bridge of her nose? Weren't her dimples deeper than Kathy's when she smiled? In almost no time, he assumed they were engaged and went so far as to persuade his mother (just to make the whole thing an official family affair) to invite both girls for a weekend with her in their country. He didn't have the ghost of an idea, though, what they went through before deciding to accept and come along together.

It wasn't that Kathy really blamed Chris for it. How can the heart, she used so often to ask herself, be blamed for its behavior? But what she couldn't quite forgive, what caused her frequently to lose her self-control and lash out against her sister, was that Eustace could have forgotten all there'd been between them at the start. He acted as though he'd never cared for her, just brushing aside all those luncheons and the lovely things he'd said to her. She did her best to suppress her jealousy, but it would flash out all of a sudden and when she least expected it. Then there would be scenes that caused them anguish and heartbreak. "Remember, Chris!" she'd cry, "I knew him first—I introduced him to you!" "Oh, yes, I know," Chris would retort. "You think he's your Eustace. You knew him first. I took him away from you." "You took him away from me. You simply snatched him and no qualms about it, either!" Kathy would come back at her. Then they'd break down and weep and ask each other's forgiveness. Each girl would assert she didn't really care for Eustace. Chris would want to break with him altogether. Nothing mattered, she'd say, but to keep their love—hers and Kathy's—unimpaired. Then Kathy would kiss her and say it *was* absolutely unimpaired and how foolish Chris was, for, after all, one of them must marry first. If it happened to be Chris, so much the better, since she, Kathy, was completely recovered from her infatuation. She liked Eustace—that was all. However, when it came to accepting Mrs. Barr's invitation, her courage failed her. She insisted that Chris should go without her. Chris immediately trotted out the same old threat; she would break the engagement. "Really, Kathy, let us both break with Eustace. Let's act as though we'd never known him. We'll forget about it altogether."

They'd had it back and forth. But now here they were, sitting beside each other on the train, Kathy dressed in a dark-blue suit, very strict and tailor-made, and a rough blue sailor hat not too becoming to her, and Chris in a light summer dress with a large leghorn hat, looking exceedingly soft and feminine. They talked but little—mostly looked out of the window and spoke of the scenery and how lovely it was to see the country again. They had not been out of the city for many months, and this sense they had of coming all at once into full possession of summer added a queer, uneasy rapture to the distress that filled their hearts. Houses standing deep in shade, elm trees, maples arrayed in full, broad leaves, lawns covered with shadows, vegetable gardens, rambler roses—how lovely to look at them again! Long Island Sound appeared, disappeared. There were creeks and winding estuaries, marshes and meadows. The fields were starred with buttercups and daisies. The tenderness between them was excruciating. They regretted the angry words they'd said to one another. To Chris, the all-embracing realization was that Kathy bore her no bitterness and seemed aware only of the twinship that bound them together. Kathy's heart was filled with the inevitability of their plight. Chris loved Eustace, too. How could it be otherwise? The heart cannot be blamed for its behavior, she kept repeating to herself.

When they left New Haven and approached the end of their journey, their excitement grew upon them. They should not, they felt keenly, have accepted Mrs. Barr's invitation—not, at least, together. But here they were, and this sense they had of sharing the

nearness of the sea, the mild blue afternoon, increased their expectation. Perhaps because they had never lived near the water,
the little creeks and estuaries winding inland from the Sound, the
blue-white sky, the mist blown in from the horizon seemed to open
and invade their hearts. "Won't it be wonderful," said Kathy,
"being in the country—seeing the sea?" "Wonderful," said Chris,
"and summer here already. Think of that!" Both girls thought,
naturally enough, of Eustace. "Soon we'll be there. Soon we'll see
him," they kept saying to themselves. Chris slipped her hand into
her sister's. Kathy returned its gentle pressure. They seemed, somehow, to reassure each other. And when, finally, the conductor
called out Saybrook, they got their bags from the rack and walked
down the aisle with considerable increase of courage, smiling and
peering through the windows of the car.

They stepped off the train. The conductor handed them their
bags. They stood together on the station platform, drinking in the
salt air, the space and freshness of the scene; saw the Connecticut
River widening and flowing to the sea, the great reach of broad
blue estuary, the strong rip of the tides, the waves and whitecaps
in the distance. They had a sense of sudden happiness, as though
they might now be able to share everything. "Oh, look," they cried,
"the sea!"

Eustace was waiting for them in a station wagon, and, along with
him, a young man named Francis Tyler, who was small and made
both girls immediately think of a monkey on a string, all nerves
and little jumps and gestures. He said "Righto" and "I should jolly
well say so." He assisted Kathy into the back seat and climbed in
beside her. She winked at Chris; they knew why he'd been brought
along. They turned sharply seaward and drove for several miles
through woods (stunted oaks and pointed cedars, pines and juni-
pers, the air smelling of resin and sandy soil and fresh, salt breeze),
then suddenly emerged in full view of the sea, very calm and the
color of gray hyacinths. Presently, they were driving along a rocky
shore to a point where there were several pleasant houses near a
strip of beach. In front of one of them, they stopped. Mrs. Barr
came out to greet them. The girls liked her immensely, and her
manner, both cordial and casual. They had the most extraordinary
feeling that each was congratulating the other on having such a
satisfactory mother-in-law.

They all had tea and then they changed into their sports clothes, and presently the girls appeared, as like as two peas, in their white shirts and shorts and tennis shoes. Twice, Eustace mistook them, and on each occasion Chris looked at him with an expression of out-and-out hostility and said defiantly, "We told you so!" At dinner, however, they resumed their separate identities, Chris in a long chiffon dress of horizon blue, with a full skirt and a pretty pleated bodice, and Kathy in a somewhat peculiar dress, of dark-green taffeta, that fitted her tightly and made her look severe and older than Chris.

They dined on the veranda, with candles on the table, which flickered and frequently went out and had to be relighted. It all seemed very romantic—the tide coming in and the waves lapping the pebbles on the beach, the air rifted with honeysuckle and nicotiana, the sea breeze fresh, and, off in the distance, the light on Montauk Point flashing white, flashing white, and, directly across the waters, Fishers Island, strewn and strung with little chains and galaxies of light. The girls were terribly conscious of each other, and their exchange of tenderness and reassurance was unremitting, Kathy trying to say silently to Chris, "I'm so happy for you, dear," and Chris feeling in the depths of her heart that she couldn't possibly go on with it but attempting to say, "I'm so happy. Everything's delightful. Aren't you glad we came?"

After dinner, they separated. Eustace took Chris off in the station wagon, and Kathy remained on the veranda with Francis Tyler, who began at once to flirt with her in a manner she thoroughly deplored. She didn't know how she managed to put up with it—heading off his ardor, stringing him along. Soon after midnight, she pleaded a headache and said she'd have to go to her room. When she got there, she sat on the window seat confronted by the sea and the big, starry sky. Suddenly, she seemed to be dressed in Chris's pretty chiffon frock; she seemed, indeed, to be Chris. Nothing could stop her now from running to Eustace's embrace, for was he not her lover? He was Chris's, he was hers. Swiftly, she ran to him. The words she knew he was whispering to Chris he whispered to her. His lips were on hers. In her secret flesh, she felt the fiery tracks and traceries of her response to his kisses, to his words. "Oh, no! It can't go on like this," she cried in her heart. "We've always shared, but not now—not this, not this!" Sitting there alone, she fought her jealousy and her desire. Presently, she heard Francis Tyler come upstairs, and, almost immediately after, Mrs. Barr came up, put out the lights in the hall, and went to her room.

"When the house is quiet," Kathy said to herself, "when they've gone to sleep, before Chris comes back with Eustace." She waited, repeating the words, which seemed to reverberate within her, like a dirge. Finally, she got up and crept as silently as possible down-stairs. All the lights in the big living room were off, but the door onto the veranda was open. She went out, descended the steps, crossed the garden, and cautiously felt her way down the dunes to the beach. The tide was high, and she walked slowly, close to the dunes, in the direction of the dock, which she could see, standing stark against the sky, some distance down the beach. When she reached the dock, she walked to the end of it and onto the float that was anchored in the water, and then, with some difficulty, climbed the diving platform fastened to the float. It did not seem too terrifying now; she was thankful that she could not swim.

The water lapped and gurgled under the float. The night was serene. She wondered whether she had ever seen so many stars. Yes, yes, she had, she thought, remembering, one summer night, running with Chris across a lawn where there were trees and mist, and stars and fireflies upon the air—simply flying off with Chris, not at all certain whether they were treading earth or sky, or whether they were trying to catch the stars or the fireflies (not even certain whether there was one little girl or two), bowing to Chris, changing places with her, pirouetting so delicately on the air—and, at the same time, remembering also that clear December evening when she'd run alone through Fifty-third Street, over to Sixth Avenue, and down to Bryant Park, looking up at the skyscrapers and all the windows filled with light. The two memories seemed to balance each other perfectly and to give her calm and fortitude in her resolve. "Now," she said to herself. "Now I will do it—now, now."

Suddenly, she heard Chris calling, "Kathy, Kathy!," and she turned and saw Chris on the float, trying to climb up to the diving platform. She leaned down; she helped her up.

"My darling," she whispered.

"Oh, my darling Kathy," whispered Chris.

Solemnly they kissed. And then, without a word, an impulse was upon them that needed no explanation, that could not brook delay. Each took the other's hand. They jumped together into the dark waters crowded with the stars.

THE IMPROVEMENT IN
MR. GAYNOR'S TECHNIQUE

❖

S. N. BEHRMAN

I AWOKE ONE MORNING in my family's flat on Providence Street, in Worcester, with a passionate urge to learn to play the piano. I must have been about twelve or thirteen years old. Later that day, I communicated the news of this burning desire to the extraordinary friend of my youth whom I shall call Willie. Willie, it seemed to me then, could accomplish anything; perhaps he could make me a pianist. In any case, he was the only person in the world to whom I could confide so bizarre an ambition without being thought completely insane. We had, of course, no piano in our tenement, and I certainly had no money for lessons even if we had had one. I might as well have wished to go abroad to study, or to get a motorcycle, or to fly to the moon. The impulse was grotesque, it was aberrational—but it was also imperious. I could not wait.

My friendship with Willie was in itself as bizarre as my wish to learn about music, for Willie was six or seven years older than I, a contemporary of my older brother's. The gap between our ages was millennial, and it was a constant source of derisive wonder to Willie's friends that he bothered with me. How our intimacy started I cannot precisely remember, but once having begun, it persisted well into my maturity and as long as Willie lived. At the start, it was as fantastic to me as it was to everyone else. When we first made friends, Willie was a brilliant student at the Worcester Polytechnic Institute and I was a ninth-grade pupil in the Providence Street School. Nevertheless, Willie would take walks with me and talk to me, and we had jokes together. His friends would ask him what we could possibly have to talk about together, and he would answer, enigmatically, "Many things, many subjects."

I am sure Willie and I did have many interests in common, although I cannot remember now precisely what all of them were at the moment I gave birth to the impulse to master the piano. I know that later, when I had the urge to become a writer, Willie would help me with my short stories, and type them out for me, and we would spend hours together weighing an adjective or a locution. He would mail them to the magazines for me, hopefully, and mourn with me over the rejection slips. Still later, when I was a sophomore at Clark College, Worcester, Willie one day had the inspiration that I must go to Harvard and study playwriting with Professor Baker. Willie managed it. The next autumn, I found myself out of Clark and in Harvard, where Willie often came to visit me. He had graduated from Tech some years earlier and was working as a chemist for the Worcester Water Works. I used to visit him there. He worked in a concrete hut filled with cisterns of varicolored waters, and he would humorously expound to me the complicated treatment that made these waters fit for consumption by the citizens of Worcester.

By this time, of course, the difference in our ages was less noticeable, but when our friendship began, the gap was, by ordinary standards, unbridgeable. Willie was a visitor from another planet, whose orbit for a long time did not coincide with my own. I remember lying in my bed at night when I was seven or eight years old and hearing him and my brother and their friends exchange the day's gossip in the living room. Assuming that I was asleep, they were uninhibited in their confidences, and I used to wonder drowsily how fellows as intelligent and mature as Willie and his friends could spend so much of their time talking about girls. Certainly the subject preëmpted a large part of their conversation. Summers, they would tell what had happened in the heady atmosphere generated by the placid waters of Lake Quinsigamond. I knew the lake very well, of course, and had probably trudged there that very day for a swim in the Municipal Pool, but the conversation of Willie and his friends did not center on natatorial prowess. Rather, it focussed on what had happened during canoe trips with various Providence Street girls—what he had said and what she had said, with minute analyses of conversations, involving mood and approach (though I hadn't any idea what the approach was to), and the abashed confessions of the overprecipitate and the triumphal boasts of those whose timing had been more sensitive. To me, it was all boring and essentially irrelevant, and I wondered how Willie, whom I already worshipped, could have so acute an interest in such trivial seminars.

There was a period when the craze for dancing swept over these

elderly adolescents like a mania. A waltz was then fashionable in
which, at a crucial point, you dipped your knee against your part-
ner's in a kind of violent curtsy. The timing and audacity of this
dip, and its possible emoluments in a larger gambit, the exact scope
of which I could not fathom, were discussed thoroughly, in a way
that was at once tantalizing and irritating. The White City, the
pleasure park on the shores of Lake Quinsigamond, had to me many
fascinating aspects—the chute-the-chutes, the Ferris wheel, the
Oriental exhibit, and so forth—but to these mesmerized youths the
only thing that mattered at the lake was the reaction of girls in
canoes and on the dance floor. There were debates on conflicting
theories. Some said it was more climactic to go canoeing first and
then go to the dance hall; the reverse procedure had equally sincere advocates. It all was a nuisance to me, lying there in the dark
and listening. Once, after recounting an exploit with perhaps too
much vividness, one narrator became suddenly conscious that I
was in the next room. I heard him say to my brother, "Is the kid
asleep?" My brother looked in on me. I remember watching,
through half-shut eyes, his precautionary glance through the door.
Reassured by my brother, the cad went on to narrate his triumph.

To me, my brother and all his friends seemed old, and I used
to reflect that the attainment of so great an age must be in some
way a degenerative process. I recall, for example, that at one period
the group seemed to have gone suddenly demented on the subject
of barbers. My mother used to cut my hair when it needed it, and
I had never been in a barbershop. But these gentlemen had begun
to shave, and before special occasions they used to go to the barbershop in the Hotel Warren for shaves and haircuts. There was even
lordly talk of massages, and the merits of each barber were discussed
ad nauseam. I remember an argument about one barber, named
Toussaint, whose obstinacy was so stylized that he insisted on cutting Willie's hair not according to Willie's ideas but according to
his own. One day, Willie had rebelled and switched to another
chair. His revolt was discussed passionately, in terms of a major in-
surrection. Toussaint had ardent defenders, and tempers rose.
There was a lot of talk, too, about lotions and pomades. The effects
of a too pomaded head on a canoe pillow, and even on a sofa pillow,
when in the company of a girl came in for nice adjudication. It was
all very disillusioning. I didn't mind about my brother and the
rest—they could be as inane or vacuous as they liked—but that
Willie should participate so fanatically in the heated evaluation of

these trivia caused me pain. Finally I had a revelation that set my disturbed mental life in order: When Willie was with me, talking about books or ideas or poetry or going to college, he was his true self; his discussions with his own crowd were merely the diplomatic adjustments necessary to a man of the world involuntarily caught up in a corrupt and busy social whirl. Everything was all right as far as Willie and I were concerned after that.

It is still something of a miracle to me that when I told Willie about my wish to play the piano, he took it in his stride, as if it were the most natural thing in the world. He had an odd habit of grasping at a subject in its most generalized terms, never in its immediate, specific application, and he also had a habit of reading up exhaustively on each of his interests in turn. This idiosyncrasy of Willie's was recognized by his friends and he was often teased about it. One day, my brother, who had just discovered that some people went fishing, suggested that Willie try fishing in Lake Quinsigamond. Willie seized upon the idea at once with great enthusiasm and held forth on the importance of hobbies as a relaxation for busy men. My brother told me long afterward that Willie never actually went fishing—he'd got too tangled up in the *theory* of the sport to have time to practice it. He had gone at once to the Worcester Public Library and got out a quantity of books on rods, lines, fly-casting, bait-fishing, salmon and trout fishing—although there were neither trout nor salmon in Lake Quinsigamond—and devoured them all. So when I made known my ambition to master the piano, Willie became instantly dithyrambic. Within a half hour, we were in the Library, on Elm Street, and presently emerged with two books by James Huneker—the one on Chopin, and "Melomaniacs." (Spurred on by Willie, I eventually read everything by Huneker the Worcester Library had, so that by the time I got to New York some years later I knew all about him. My first visit to Luchow's was inspired by the fact that I had read somewhere that Huneker went there. I asked the headwaiter if my hero was around, allowing him to believe that I was an important figure in Huneker's world, and when I was told that he was not, I went out on Fourteenth Street to Walton's for lunch. I have often wondered what would have happened if Huneker *had* been there.)

In his enthusiasm, Willie imagined me already a virtuoso, walking into a drawing room and captivating the distinguished guests by my art. To play the piano beautifully would be not only a social passport, he said, but also a relaxation for me after the vortex of a fevered day. (Willie was always preparing for a future in which we would both be under mighty strains.) He insisted that a powerful argument could be made for music as the greatest of the arts, and quoted many people who thought so. It was even possible to conjecture that Beethoven was greater than Shakespeare, for whom, Willie knew, I already had a high regard. Did I not know huge portions of "Hamlet" and "Macbeth" by heart, and had he not incited me to repeat them to my brother when the latter asked what the hell Willie was doing hanging around with an embryo like me? Willie was happy that I had had this wonderful idea of learning to play the piano; he rather reproached himself for not having had it for me himself. He did not wish me to decide on the instant whether Beethoven was greater than Shakespeare, he said, but what he did wish was to make it possible for me, after having plumbed both these artists, to decide the question for myself. Pending my ultimate decision, Willie asked for time to give the matter a little thought himself. I permitted him to have it.

Willie's fantasia left me excited but unsatisfied during our preliminary discussions, but I believed in the omnipotence he had demonstrated on many occasions where my affairs were concerned, and presently he came to me with a *fait accompli*. He had engaged for me the use of a room with a piano in it, on Pleasant Street, and I could go there to practice for several hours every afternoon. He had telephoned to Mr. Silas Gaynor, one of the best music teachers in Worcester, and had made arrangements for me to study with him. He took me to the room and showed me the piano, and then escorted me to Mr. Gaynor's studio and introduced me to him. Mr. Gaynor gave me pleasant encouragement, some exercise books, and an appointment at his studio for the following week. On our way home to Providence Street, Willie, rather flushed with pleasure at having, singlehanded, transformed a novice into a virtuoso, congratulated me on having become a musician. I was somewhat appalled and asked Willie about the financial implications of these proceedings. He deprecated the intrusion of the money question into the lustral realm of the fine arts. What were the few pennies involved compared to the mastery of so great an art? I was not to think about the cost; he would take care of that. I was to become a nimble executioner, and he would be amply rewarded by the pride he would feel at my first recital. He brushed away the economic aspect with so high a hand that I withdrew the vulgarism. Willie imposed but one condition on me; no one was to know about my secret studies, least of all my brothers. I solemnly promised.

My career began. I had a permanent patron, which is more than Mozart ever had. I was a freshman in the Classical High School by this time, and it was on the same side of town as my piano. Instead of going straight home every afternoon, as had been my custom, I would tell my mother some lie about having to stay after school and go directly from Classical High to Pleasant Street. It was odd to sit down at a piano in a strange room—the instrument itself, by its very presence, connoted a degree of opulence that was faintly illicit —and to begin fumbling over Mr. Gaynor's scales. I had never before had command of a room away from my parents' flat. But it was easier to command the room than the upright. Also, I was conscious, while I was practicing, that this must be costing Willie a lot of money, and although I attacked the exercises fiercely, every time I muffed a bar, I seemed to hear the ominous tolling of invisible cash registers. I soon saw, too, that my entrance into elegant salons aquiver to hear me perform must be indefinitely delayed. Beethoven seemed farther away now than he had in my first excited talks with Willie. Possibly I was drawing nearer to the Master —at least, so Willie assured me when I confided to him my discouragements—but the speed of my approach was too slow and my progress too halting to give me any reassurance.

There were other difficulties. To keep my secret pact with Willie and the piano involved considerable ingenuity. My brother, after a complaint from my mother, began to ask why I was so late getting home from school every day. There were chores that I was relied on to perform after school, and the conflict between my domestic life and my career began to interrupt the normal flow of existence. My lies multiplied and finally wore so thin that I felt certain I would be exposed in the end. But for a month or so Willie's new plan for me seemed pleasingly dangerous, conspiratorial, and altogether wonderful. The only thing really dreary about it was the drudgery of practicing, which, as countless other young people have discovered, is a process that carries in it the germ of hatred for the art it is meant to further.

I adored Mr. Gaynor, and I shall never forget my first lesson with him, nor, indeed, the eight or ten subsequent ones. He was (and still is, I hope) a fair-complexioned man with light hair parted in the middle, and faintly protuberant, mild blue eyes that peered benevolently at you from behind thick glasses. He had a passion for music. At the first lesson, after I had ravished him with the re-sults of my week's labors, he talked to me about music. His en-thusiasm was as keen as Willie's, but it had greater intimacy. As I found it more delicious to discuss music than to play it, I spurred him on. He told me that every week he went to Boston to hear the concerts in Symphony Hall, which were then under the direction of Dr. Karl Muck. He described the program he had heard the week before and regaled me with anecdotes about the steely Dr. Muck and his Brahmin audiences. He had a strong sense of humor, and he was gently derisive of the pseudo-music lovers who went to Symphony Hall only because it was the correct thing to do in Bos-ton on Friday afternoons or Saturday evenings. But I really wanted to find out about music, and somehow—I don't know how I had the courage—I found myself asking Mr. Gaynor if he would play something for me. I had never been to a concert. I had never heard a professional pianist. The nearest I had come to it was to stand outside Mechanics' Hall on an evening when Paderewski was play-ing inside and watch the crowd go in. Sensually, there was some-thing insubstantial about this experience, and perhaps it was the frustration engendered by it that gave me the courage to ask Mr. Gaynor to play for me. Somewhat to my surprise, Mr. Gaynor re-sponded readily. Perhaps I was the first pupil who had ever made such a request of him. He blushed faintly, but he went at once to the piano (his was a grand), sat before it, and played Schumann's "Aufschwung." I shall never forget it. It was thrilling. It was thrill-ing, but at the same time it made me rather miserable, because I could not help comparing my own performance with his.

My first séance with Mr. Gaynor was a model of our later ones, except that as I became more and more conscious of the immense discrepancy between our respective talents, I began to reduce to a minimum my performances to him and to induce him gradually to increase his performances to me. Also, we used to escape from such dull minutiae as scales and exercises by discussing the larger as-pects of music. As I look back on it, it was not a bad use of our time, since it was unlikely that my secret life in art could continue for long. And I like to think that Mr. Gaynor, too, enjoyed our lessons. They gave him a chance to talk freely about the art he loved, and also to play for me many works that he must have been too tired to run through at night, after his long day at his studio. He was a very popular teacher—"the best in Worcester," it was often said—

and I got the same odd thrill of creative patronage from hearing
him that Willie must have got from hearing me. On the first day,
when he played the "Aufschwung," Mr. Gaynor seemed to me to
play it wonderfully. As he got into his swing during subsequent
lessons, he began to play longer and more complicated works, and
I felt—was it really so or was it merely the wish fulfillment of an
eager patron?—that his technique was improving sensibly. By the
time I left him, I think I may say that he was playing in really masterful style. I had every reason to be proud.

Leave Mr. Gaynor I did. Things began to happen thick and fast.
The incessant questionings at home about my late-afternoon dis-
appearances had given way to an ominous silence. Then, one afternoon, when I was blindly practicing on Pleasant Street, there was
a knock on the door. I rushed to open it, sure that it must be Willie,
who often used to drop into my atelier to tell me, when I was depressed about my work, that Brahms had never been a very good
pianist, either. Gradually, Willie had modified his ambition for
me; he had adjusted himself to the compromise that I need not
become a dazzling virtuoso, and had settled for my evolving merely
into a great composer, a career that while I was stumbling over Mr.
Gaynor's exercise books seemed much the easier of the two. But
the knock on the door was not Willie. It was my brother. He had
followed me to my lair. When Mr. Gaynor told me, at my next lesson, that the opening bars of Beethoven's Fifth symbolized the
knocking of Fate, it was my brother's knock on the door of my secret music room that I heard, and even now, when I hear those
measures played, I hear that knock again.

I told my brother all, and he was much nicer about it than I
could have hoped. He simply explained to me that music might
be all right enough for those who could afford it, but that as I could
not, I should not indulge myself with thoughts above my station.
He caused me considerable pain by pointing out to me that although Willie was better off than we were—as, indeed, who was
not?—he still had to work Saturdays and Sundays and holidays and
evenings in order to put himself through Worcester Tech, and
that to launch me on a musical career involved considerable extra
expense for him. I was overcome suddenly by the enormity of my
own selfishness. Later, I discovered that my lessons had cost Willie
three dollars a week—two dollars for the room and the piano, and

one dollar for Mr. Gaynor. Three dollars a week was no mean sum in Worcester then, and to enjoy the luxury of patronage Willie must have had to make many sacrifices. I also found out later that my brother and Willie had a big fight about this. Willie contended stoutly that three dollars a week was nothing at all compared to the magnificence of the vista opened up by my entry into the music world. Willie lost out. I gave up Pleasant Street.

There followed an odd postlude. I gave up my room and my piano, but I could not bear to give up Mr. Gaynor. I had grown very fond of him. Possibly I felt, obscurely, that a few more weeks with me would give his playing that reserve and polish that so often differentiate the routine pianist from the really exceptional one. Willie encouraged me to continue my sessions with Mr. Gaynor—for a while, at any rate. After all, it was only a dollar a week, and I could manage this one hour without complications at home. I used to report to Willie in detail on my meetings with Mr. Gaynor, and from these reports Willie derived a glow of satisfaction. On one occasion, he telephoned to Mr. Gaynor to find out how I was getting on, and Mr. Gaynor reported that I was extremely musical. There was the problem, of course, since I was no longer able to practice at all, of how to get by the mortifying introductory interval when I played for Mr. Gaynor and into the halcyon one in which he played for me. I managed this for a while by simply repeating exercises that I had already learned and, thus, for a brief spell, I was in the rather gratifying position of the eighteenth-century German princes who had their own virtuosos to console them. I think I may say with confidence that I was the only resident of Providence Street at that time who had a private pianist.

The day came when Mr. Gaynor gave me a fresh exercise book, and then I had to break down and tell him I had no piano. He had never known that I practiced on a rented piano in a rented room; he had, naturally, assumed that, like his other pupils, I had an instrument at home. I did not give my secret away. Instead, I invented the lie that my family had sold our piano, because we were moving out of town. I think there was genuine regret on Mr. Gaynor's part when we said goodbye. I promised that should there be a change in the family plans, in which case we would, of course, repurchase our piano, I would resume his auditions at once. I don't know whether Mr. Gaynor, in the long roster of his pupils, remembers me, but I remember him with affection and with joy.

This, then, was my brief encounter with that tantalizing art in which, more than in any other, I should have loved to become accomplished. But it was not to be. The little I learned on Pleasant Street I have long since forgotten. To this day, music remains a black art to me. I sit before it, but I have no actual notion of it. I do not understand it at all. I cannot read the language in which it is written; I am, and always shall be, an outsider.

BLACK SECRET

❖

MARJORIE KINNAN RAWLINGS

THE SHUTTERS WERE DRAWN in the parlor against the afternoon
sun. June lay heavy on the street outside, but the room was dark
and cool. Hummingbirds droned in the honeysuckle over the window. The fragrance filtered through the shutters. Dickie flattened
his face against the rose-patterned Brussels carpet. It was pleasantly
harsh and faintly dusty. He moved his cheek to the smoothness of
his picture book. The page was smooth and slippery. He lay comfortably, imagining that the painted lion under him was alive and
his friend. He shook his loose, tucked blouse and pretended that
the lion was breathing against him. He wished that it was night,
when the new gas lights would flare from their brass pipes on the
wall, for their yellow flickering made the lion's eyes move and
shine. He lifted his head. The double doors of the parlor were sliding open. He heard his mother speak.

"The garden party was lovely, Mrs. Tipton. But aren't you exhausted?"

Dickie thinned himself to a shadow. If he were quiet, they might
let him stay while they talked. There was an excitement in his
mother's talk in this room with Mrs. Tipton that he heard no other
place and with no other person. The women came into the parlor
and Mammy Dee closed the folding doors after them. His mother
saw him. She had on her flowered organdie with the ruffled flounces.
They touched his ankle as she rustled past him.

She said, "Speak to Mrs. Tipton, Dickie."

He scrambled to his feet and jerked his head and put out his
hand.

Mrs. Tipton said, "Precious. And how is Master Merrill today?"

"I'm reading my book," he said.

She said, "Precious."

He flopped down hurriedly on the rug and began turning the
pages of the book. He sank himself in it, hopefully.

His mother said, "Straight chairs are more comfortable when

it's warm, aren't they? Take this one. . . . Oh, the party was beautiful!"

The room was an empty box waiting to be filled.

"Thank you."

His mother said, "I see you had Lulu Wilson again to help."

His heart beat rapidly. They were beginning. They would forget him.

Mrs. Tipton said, "She's marvellous help for that sort of thing. Of course, no one could have her around steadily. You know—"

"I know."

His mother's voice held the vibration of the secret.

Mrs. Tipton said, "You couldn't have Judge Wimberley knocking at your back door."

His mother said, breathlessly, "Judge Wimberley?"

"He's the latest."

Turning his head casually, Dickie saw Mrs. Tipton lean forward in the cool, straight chair.

She said, "Oh, Mrs. Merrill, it's incredible, isn't it?"

"Mrs. Tipton, not Judge Wimberley!"

"Yes."

The parlor hummed, as though the birds in the honeysuckle had flown inside. He heard the soft sound of the women's bosoms rising and falling.

His mother said, "It seems as though something could be done."

Mrs. Tipton said, "If we sent them away, there'd only be others."

He knew exactly whom she meant. She meant Creecy and Long Tom and Lulu Wilson. They were nigger women, and something about them was different, even from other nigger women. Creecy was a Geechee, short and fat and blacker than the soot in the fireplace. Long Tom was as black, but tall and thin and bony. Lulu Wilson was the color of his mother's coffee when the cream and sugar were in it. She was young and slim and pretty. They were the secret. Not quite all of it, for Judy Lane was a part of it. But Judy had moved away.

Mrs. Tipton said, "I learned enough from Lulu this time to run half the men out of town."

His mother rose from her chair and walked up and down the rug. She said, "Oh, Mrs. Tipton, somehow it doesn't seem right, knowing these things."

Her voice had the sick sound that he hated and that made him weak all over. Yet he wanted to hear.

Mrs. Tipton rose too. The two women stood in the center of the dark coolness, like birds fresh caught in a cage.

Mrs. Tipton said, "Well, I want to know. That's why I have her. Women are blind. Women are stupid. I want to know."

His mother said, "Perhaps she's lying."

Her voice sounded the way it sounded when she had a headache.

"She's not lying. I tell you, Mrs. Merrill, men are beasts."

His mother sat down again, and Mrs. Tipton sat too.

Mrs. Tipton said in a low voice, "Dickie?"

His mother said, "Oh, my dear, he's only seven."

"But little pitchers have big ears."

His mother said, "Dickie, dear, wouldn't you like to go out and play?"

He pretended not to hear her.

"Dickie, dear."

He looked up from the picture book. "Mummy, do lions have long tails?"

His mother smiled at Mrs. Tipton. "You see."

They settled back.

Mrs. Tipton said, "I don't tell all this to everyone."

"I know."

"Some women—I just couldn't. Poor things. And never knowing. Oh, men, Mrs. Merrill! Men . . ."

His mother said, "The rest of us must just thank God for ours."

"If anyone could be sure, Mrs. Merrill."

His mother's voice fluttered like a butterfly.

"You mustn't say such things, Mrs. Tipton. My Richard . . . I thank God every night. I don't know what I've done to deserve such —such devotion. I suppose any woman is fortunate to be truly loved."

Dickie wanted to run and bury his head in the lace and ribbons over her soft breast. He wanted to cry out, "I love you, too." Her breast smelled of the sweet lavender that Mammy Dee raised in the herb garden and dried and laid away in all the dresser drawers.

She said, "Mrs. Tipton—it's no excuse, I know—but do you suppose the wives could be in any way to blame?"

Mrs. Tipton said coldly, "I'm sure Judge Wimberley's wife has always done her duty."

"Oh, not duty!"

His mother's voice was a cry.

Mrs. Tipton said, "I tell you, Mrs. Merrill, men are beasts."

The sun found an opening in the shutters. Dickie turned on his side and watched the dust motes dancing across the bright bar.

His mother said, "Only God can judge. . . . Tell me, do they say the cotton has had enough rain?"

Mrs. Tipton said, "I think so. At the bank, they're making more loans."

"I feel guilty sometimes, Richard being in timber and lumber —things already there, so stable—and the people dependent on their annual crops have so much anxiety."

Mrs. Tipton said, "Your husband's uncle, Mr. Baxter Merrill —I believe he has a fine stand of cotton."

"Oh, dear Uncle Baxter. He always prospers. We were at the plantation last Sunday. Everything was beautiful. We have such a gay time when we go there. We depend on Uncle Baxter to be gay. Dickie adores him."

A chime sounded in the depths of the house.

Mrs. Merrill said, "You'll have cake and sherry with me, won't you, Mrs. Tipton?"

"Thank you, Mrs. Merrill."

"Dickie, dear."

He rose in seeming abstraction and went to her. Now he might sink into her laces and her fragrance. She stroked his hair.

"Dickie, darling, I was to take you to Robert to have your hair cut. Dearest, you're such a big boy, couldn't you go alone?"

His heart was pounding.

"Yes, Mummy."

He longed for the hot sunlight outside the parlor.

"Then have Mammy Dee give you a quarter and go to Robert. Cross the streets very carefully, won't you, lamb?"

"Yes, Mummy. Goodbye."

Mrs. Tipton murmured, "Precious."

He ran from the parlor. Mammy Dee was singing in the kitchen.

"I'm old enough to have my hair cut by myself," he said. "Mummy says you're to give me a quarter."

The vast black woman fumbled in a sugar sack on the wall. "You mind how you cross the railroad tracks."

"I'll be careful."

Dickie tightened his fingers over the coin and ran from the house. He was faint from the secret. It had something to do with black women and white men. It was remote and fascinating and more sickening than too much syrup candy. The lawn grass was green, for it was watered every evening, but beyond it the grass that bordered the town sidewalks was parched and brown. He ran west for three blocks and at the corner by Mrs. Tipton's big house he turned and ran south. He had never crossed the tracks alone before.

He was afraid for a moment that he would not find the barbershop, but the striped pole lifted ahead of him like a lighted lamp. He darted inside the open door and stood an instant, catching his breath. Black Robert rose lazily from a stool, and he was at home again.

Robert said, "I declare, Mastuh Dickie. All by yo'self."

Dickie looked about him. The barbershop lay in its summer stupor. The two chairs stood a little separated, one empty, the far one filled with the shapeless form of a man buried under a white apron. Black Perchy scraped at the face of the chair's occupant. Two other white men sat nearby. They were talking together. Now and then the man in the chair joined in with them, his voice muffled by the lather and the apron. They glanced at Dickie and went on talking.

Black Robert said, "Missy know you come alone?"

Dickie nodded and held out the quarter and Robert laid it on the shelf under the glass case where lotions and tonics glittered in the sunlight.

Robert whispered, "Yo' ma ain't changed yo' haircut, is she?"

Dickie understood that he was to be quiet, so the men talking would not be interrupted.

"She's got company," he whispered in return.

Robert nodded. Dickie climbed into the great chair. The headrest was too high and Robert lowered it for him. He leaned back, feeling mature and important. Robert drew a clean white apron around him and tied it behind his neck. He turned to the case and took out a thin comb and a pair of shining scissors. The comb ran through Dickie's hair, lifting it away from his scalp with the feeling of strong wind. The scissors snipped through his upper hair, then lay suddenly, cool and ticklish, against the back of his neck.

The man in the other chair said, "What's new since I've been here?"

One man said, "What do you think? Nothing."

The other said, "We've got a new bridge over the mill creek. Progress!"

All three laughed together.

One man said, "By God, Beck, you didn't tell him Judy Lane was back in town."

The man in the chair said under his soapsuds, "That good-looking high yellow that married the white man in Chicago?"

"That's the one. Breezed into town in one of those electric broughams, dressed in ostrich feathers long enough to cover her yellow shanks."

"I'll swear. Do you suppose the Chicago guy knows?"

"Probably not."

Robert leaned close to run the scissors around Dickie's right ear.

The man in the chair said, "Strikes me she's right bold, coming back here. Was she raised here?"

"Right here. Her mammy was blacker 'n coal'll ever be. One of our leading lights is her daddy."

"Who's that?"

"Baxter Merrill."

"The cotton man?"

"Baxter Merrill, the cotton man. Cotton's the only white crop he's ever raised."

For a moment Dickie saw the secret lie shadowy, as always, in the distance. Then it rose and swelled. It rushed at him with a great roaring, shouting "Uncle Baxter!" He could not breathe. He clawed at the apron around his neck.

Robert murmured, "I'll fix it, Mastuh Dickie."

The glass case of lotions glittered. The barber's chair heaved up and down. He felt something wet on his mouth and splashing on his hands. He was a big boy and he never cried. He was crying.

Robert moved in front of him and planted his bulk between him and the rest of the barbershop. The round ebony face was furrowed and strained.

He said in a low voice, "Hol' still, Mastuh Dickie."

Dickie lifted his fists and beat them on Robert's chest. He twisted his mouth and blinked his eyelids rapidly. It was no use. A sob tore from him. It ripped flesh with it, somewhere in his chest. Two drops of sweat rolled down Robert's face and sank into the white apron.

Dickie said, "I'm sick."

Suddenly Robert gathered him from the chair and wrapped the white apron around him. The black man carried him in the apron to the door and set him on his feet on the sidewalk.

Robert said, "You go down the street a while, Mastuh Dickie."

He untied the apron from around his neck. "You come back about traintime. The gemmuns'll be gone then, at traintime."

Dickie drew a deep breath against the coming cyclone.

Robert said, "You come back, now, to get finished." The sweat ran down the black face like rain. "You come back. You cain't go home to yo' ma part done. A li'l man got to go home to his ma all done."

Dickie wavered on his feet. Robert reached into a pocket under his barber's smock and pulled out a penny. He put it in Dickie's palm and closed his fingers over it.

"You go down the next block and get you a ice ball. They got ras'br'y an' cherry today. Then you come back at traintime."

Dickie began to run down the street. The cyclone was on him. He sobbed so deeply that his side ached before he had gone half a block. The tears washed down his face and over his blue dimity blouse. He clutched the penny tightly. It was wet and sticky with sweat from the black hand and from his own.

INDEX

❖